Golan!

A novel about Israel's next war

Edward (Eliyahu) Truitt
Jerusalem, Israel
5770 (2010)

Golan!

A novel about Israel's next war

Truitt, Edward, 1953/

pages 490

ISBN 1452862133 soft cover edition
EAN-13 9781452862132

Table of Contents

Author's Introduction

This is a "what if" story. What if, instead of dropping the first crude and dirty nuclear weapon they can make on Israel, Iran held off a few more years and developed – or bought – sophisticated nukes that could burst in the stratosphere and create a powerful electromagnetic pulse. And then, what if the same international pack of scoundrels who attacked Israel in 1973 decided to try again? Only this time, with Israel crippled and blinded by a preemptive strike with these EMP (electromagnetic pulse) weapons?

I started this book in the final weeks of December 2008. And it has been a race against the headlines ever since. Every month or so there is a new pronouncement about Iran's growing nuclear possibilities – and about their capabilities for delivering them. Ever since the end of the tense summer of 2006, the stockpiles of short and medium range rockets and missiles have grown in Lebanon, Syria and Gaza with each new Israeli security briefing.

Sometimes it seemed like reality would outpace my book, which I had set in my imagination about four to five years in the future. For instance, in February 2009, Carolyn Glick, a modern-day prophetess who works for the Jerusalem Post, ran a column quoting a source who detailed the extent of the EMP threat against Israel. Some days it felt like everyone is getting the EMP message – that it would be possible to blast our sophisticated and technology-dependent way of life back to about the beginning of the 20th century. Other days, it felt like nobody was listening to the clear and rational warnings – and that there is little being done to protect our precious people and way of life.

I do sincerely hope, and quietly believe, that Israel is quite a bit more prepared for an electronic warfare strike than this book suggests. Whatever you want to call them, you can't call Israelis dumb. However the civilian population is not prepared nearly enough (and that means me and all my family and friends). And so, there begins my tale, with some artistic license allowed. The actual effects of a massive EMP strike of the magnitude I have described are difficult to predict. Some electronics would work but most wouldn't. And that, I think, makes a very interesting story.

I took a few liberties with Israeli geography in my fiction, including making up some imaginary communities in the Golan – such as Moshav Yiftach and Ramat HaGolan. But I put them right next door to some real ones, such as Yonatan. My apologies to anyone who lives in the many real places overrun or shelled in this book. I hope it does not give you nightmares. Remember, it is a work of applied imagination, and enjoy it as such.

Love to my mother, my faithful reader for more than half a century, who always believed in my gifts as a writer and who has saved almost every scrap of years worth of newspapers, magazines and other works.

Thanks to my beautiful, wise and talented wife, and *aishet chayil*, Paula Leven. Here's to another thirty-two wonderful years together.

I owe much of this book to my daughter, Rachel and her husband, Rabbi Ariel Tal (a graduate of Yeshivat HaGolan), who introduced me to the Golan. Alas, there is no elderly Rabbi Beniyahu at the yeshiva. I made him up, but there are many wise teachers there and young men who make you proud to be Israeli.

Thanks to Aviella Trapido Unterberg and the whole Trapido family for being my most enthusiastic readers as this tale emerged, emailed chapter by chapter.

To my son in the IDF, Abraham, I am so proud of you that words fail me... and as you can see from the next four hundred-odd pages, I know a lot of words.

And thanks to my oldest son, Ben and his wife, Carrie, staunch defenders of Israel on college campuses and the Internet.

But, most of all, to Israel and the Jewish people everywhere. *Am Israel Chai!*

Edward (Eliyahu) Truitt
Jerusalem Elul 5770, August 2010

Map of the Golan Heights

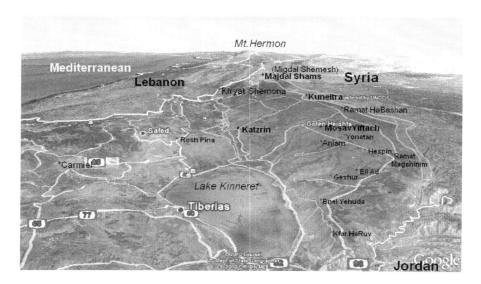

Most of the action in this book takes place in the Golan, shown here in a not-to-scale map. There are two fictitious places – Moshav Yiftach and Ramat HaBashan. The major towns are approximately placed with the help of Google Earth. The spellings of the Hebrew and Arabic place names vary wildly. For instance, Tzfat can be spelled Safed, Tsfat, Zefat, Sfat, Zfat, Safad, Safes, Safet, etc. Imagine, if you will, Nu Yawrk being spelled half a dozen different ways on various official maps and you can begin to see how much fun it is to live in the Middle East.

Moshav Yiftach is named after a military leader and later Judge of the Jewish people in the Book of Judges, chapters 11 and 12. There is a real kibbutz named Kibbutz Yiftah near Kiryat Shemona, which has nothing to do with the one made up for this book.

There is a glossary at the end in case you get stuck and want a definition. Cheers and enjoy the book.

Day One

Mekor Ro'im, (Shepherd's Well) 4 km. from Syria 0345

It was three-twenty a.m. and a hot, dry, end of summer wind blew from the east, sweeping across the high, dry and dusty plains of Syria before rising a few hundred meters to the Golan Heights and cooling only enough to be bearable. Reserve captain David Engel swung his night vision binoculars slowly, deliberately picking out and studying each of the forward positions between his group and the Syrian border. His group of four elderly Mekava II tanks and a single communications humvee were dug in behind earthworks and boulders in a rocky grove of dusty eucalyptus trees. The MKII tanks, older than most of the tankers, were camped near an ancient stone watering trough near a well that was now empty, and by the more recent remains of a pre-'67 Syrian bunker, now quite fallen in. Looking out across the landscape to the east, he could see a network of small bunkers and dugout placements where a 65-ton tank could play hide and seek, moving from one hull-down hiding hole to another to confuse the twice daily satellite photos from a pair of orbiting "communications" satellites launched a few years ago by Syria's Iranian friends.

He could barely pick out six of the eight Merkava III's on the upslope of the next roll of land, 2.5 km. away and just a kilometer from the no-mans-land of minefields that marked the Israel-Syria border. They served as a trip-wire force, slowing any advance just enough to let the artillery and heavy tank brigade behind them go into action with a deadly counter punch. They would probably be overrun in the first ten minutes of any major action if the Syrians came across shooting in anywhere near the numbers that were reported to be massed on the other side of the uneasy frontier. There would be, however, 30-40 tanks less than what started up the hill if his friend in the third tank from the left had anything to say about it.

Captain Yankel Klein had the highest kill rate in every live fire and laser beam exercise ever invented for the Golani Brigade, and he had shot up everything threatening that moved when his unit went into Lebanon in 2006 with a precision that was unerring. Yankel also liked to spell rude things in three-meter high Arabic in the sands of the dry wadis that drained the Golan, just to annoy whoever was looking at the day's satellite Intel on the other side of the border…"assuming they can read," he would add. He dialed up the digital magnification and tried to see if he could make out Klein's unit. He could see the exaggerated white flare of a match and the glow of a lit cigarette – someone in Yankel's group was chain smoking the night away.

The MK III's in Yankel's group were a decade newer than the 1980s version of the tank his platoon was driving. Yankel's MK III packed a 120 mm. cannon, like the top of the line MK IV's; and unlike the 105 mm gun David's "museum piece" was packing, Yankel had 300 more horsepower, modular reactive armor, separate individual canisters for storing ammunition so the rounds wouldn't "cook off" in a chain reaction if one was hit. But tonight, David could afford not to be jealous of his friend's machine. For one thing, Yankel was 2 km closer to the Syrian army than he was, and for another, they were both dinosaurs next to the even more powerful, fourth generation MK IV with its El Op and Elbit Systems advanced fire control and battlefield tactical computers. And, while David did not want to go head-to-head with a main-line, Soviet-built battle tank, he certainly wanted to have his share in any shoot 'em up in the Golan if it was going to happen on his watch, especially with Yankel's platoon on one flank and a battle group of MK IV's behind them.

David strained to remember the details of the latest satellite maps showing the other side of the border, and tried to make sense of the latest intel, radioed in code just before midnight. Almost the entire Syrian 3rd and 4th Divisions facing them across the divide had disappeared from sight into their deep bunkers sometime just after nightfall, leaving only a handful of vehicles above ground. Infrared heat signatures showed them which holes were "hot," but it just didn't make sense. Were they afraid of an imminent Israeli air or missile strike? Were we putting out false rumors just to keep their mobilization off guard? And, what should he think about reports of new, unknown armored units moving up to the front in the last week? Could there really be thousands more Iraqi irregulars and "volunteers" from half a dozen Arab nations as intel suggested? David had never known such Arab unity on the ground before. And, where did they get the heavy armor? But then, seven years of world-wide recession made strange bedfellows in a Middle East filled with advanced armament and poor young men with their heads filled with jihad and virulent strains of Islamic fundamentalism. A job in the army meant a paycheck, and a place in a militia meant arms and a share of smuggled contraband and protection payments from the locals who were not so fortunate.

Somewhere behind him, a rapid-response force of advanced MK IV's and mobile 155 mm. howitzers were roaming the maze of tracks, depots and bunkers that backed up the frontier units. All of them had been on red alert for more than three weeks as Arab rhetoric reached new heights – or should he say, depths – of bellicose pronouncements of death to the Jews and the Zionist Enemy. He had already served his three weeks of *miluim*, compulsory reserve duty, back in March when there was plenty of cause for alarm for any Israeli. Gaza had boiled over yet again, and the Lebanese border was swarming with Hezbollah and missile launchers. Now, in

September, with Rosh Hashanah and Yom Kippur having been spent in a case of national jitters and increasingly dire alerts, Israel was one day before David's favorite holiday of *Sukkot* with no stand-down in sight.

David's unit was just past half of the way down the 75 kilometer-long stretch of Israel known as the Golan that runs from the 2,800-meter Mount Hermon in the north to the heights overlooking the southern tip of the Kinneret (known to the Christian world as the Biblical Sea of Galilee) – a fresh water lake that lies 215 meters below sea level. The Golan is the source of the Jordan River – great in history – but small in size. Among the great rivers of the world, it does not even make it into the top fifty. It rises from the confluence of three springs and streams on the southern and western slopes of Mount Hermon. The largest is *Nahal Dan,* and the other two are *Nahal Senir* and the lovely cascading stream known as Baniyas or *Nahal Hermon.* The pretty, but otherwise unremarkable streams unite about six kilometers south of the Lebanon-Israel border.

David was leaning on a fallen tree trunk near his tank to steady his binoculars. Not far to the south of him, he could see the lopsided, pyramid-shape of a rocky hill called Shomer Tel Parat – which marked a turn in the ruler-straight cease-fire-line that passed for a border between Israel and Syria since 1973. To the north he could see the lights of the Syrian border town of Quneitra – where journalists, the occasional tourist, and UN people could drive from Israel to Damascus in about an hour – but where he and most Israelis had never been and had not been welcome since thrashing the Syrian army in 1948, 1967, 1973 and countless skirmishes in between. The few hundred families that had members scattered on both sides of the border sometimes gathered at opposite fences across the little formal border crossing to shout news of weddings and see and be seen – although nearly universal cell phone ownership on both sides had cut such events to a minimum in David's lifetime.

However it was not family reunions or Druze weddings that worried David, but the increasing probability of another of the cataclysmic upheavals like 1973 when the border suddenly dissolved into a vision of war – with Israel once again forced to defend her very existence.

Some, like Sgt. Baruch Harel, his Sephardic second in command of their little half-platoon of tanks, would say that existence owed itself to the Creator of heaven and earth and the land he promised the Jews, his chosen people. Sgt. Harel had already put up a bamboo and camouflage net sukkah in celebration of the nation's exodus from Egypt 3,600 years ago. But he had not put on the required covering of branches or matting yet, because he fully expected their group to move again in the next 12 – 24 hours. David smiled as he glanced at the makeshift booth behind the tank to his right. Baruch would be relieving him in a little over two hours, with a strong cup of Turkish coffee with a dash of cardamom and more sugar than could possibly dissolve in six ounces of boiling water. Coffee – even Baruch's sweet blast of hyper-caffeinated sludge, would taste real good right now, but he settled for a lukewarm swig from his canteen and resumed his vigil.

Sukkot would begin with the coming evening, and there was no sign of a let up in the red alert that had the Israel Defense Forces (IDF) staying wide awake on their night watches on this relatively lonely stretch of border. Even the Jordanian border was heating up, and the daily exchange of shopping, produce and visitors between Amman and the Israeli side of the Jordan valley had all but stopped. That was bad, very bad. The Syrians might roll out the tanks and buzz their assault helicopters right up to the fences – as they had ten times before the Yom Kippur War of 1973. Syria had rolled out all the hardware for six full-scale military drills this year. And the Egyptians might talk peace while allowing a torrent of arms to flow into Gaza, but the Jordanians were generally anti-Israel in rhetoric without it stopping much of the free trade between them. Even King Abdullah IV was parading in uniform and displaying the military hardware these days. The neighborhood was getting crazy again, crazy like 1973. The whole country had prayed with one ear cocked for the air raid sirens this year. Not even the Egyptians were dumb enough to try a strike on Yom Kippur again. But *Sukkot*? Didn't these people read the Prophets? Obviously not.

David, like most Israelis of his generation, knew his *Tanach* – the books of *Joshua, Judges, Kings, Jeremiah, Isaiah, Amos* and all of the other Prophets very well. He lived and walked in their footsteps, and found that what they prophesized about the Jewish people had come true a thousand-fold over the centuries of human history. It was still unfolding – just look at how the dry, dusty, neglected land had bloomed in the past few hundred years of active Jewish resettlement and 60-some years of statehood. But he knew the reading for *Sukkot* especially well because he had helped his oldest son practice it at least a hundred times. Yosi had his bar mitzvah only a year ago on the Shabbat that fell in the middle of *Sukkot*. It seemed another lifetime ago. He recalled some of the verses, singing the haunting *trop* of the frightening and awesome prophesy of *Ezekiel* about Israel's final war in his mind:

"And you, Son of Man, prophesy against Gog. Say: This is what the Lord your God says to you: 'Behold, I am against you, O Gog, the chief prince of Meshech and Tubal. I will confuse you and drive you on, causing you to leave the distant northern lands, and lead you against the mountains of Israel. And then I smite your bow from your left hand, and your arrows will fall from your right hand. And on the mountains of Israel you will fall, you and all your minions, and all the nations who are with you…'"

So, who was this Gog – chief prince of Meshech and Tubal? He asked himself – reviewing the various sources he had learned with his son. Like any good Jewish question there were at least half a dozen opinions. But the mainstream ones pointed in physical terms to the historic kingdoms to Israel's north – ancient Assyria and the modern day Syria being the most obvious candidates. And the metaphysical interpretations discussed Gog –

the Hebrew word for "roof," and Meshech and Tubal – who were the descendents of Noah responsible for bringing tools and metallurgy into the world. One interpretation was that those who placed their faith in material things and in physical power were the modern day heirs to Gog, Meshech and Tuval. The former states of Soviet Union, the bankrupt heirs to generations of dialectic materialism, that had armed and allied with modern day Syria and Arab powers in the Middle East, came to mind as the modern nations that best fit that description. In either case, the prophets and their commentators were unanimous that trouble was coming from the North. There was hard intelligence in the past few years that Muslim conscripts from the former Soviet republics – Kazakhstan, Turkmenistan, Uzbekistan, Azerbaijan, and even Georgia, Ukraine and Byelorussia, were flocking to the jihadist banner and showing up in places like Lebanon, Syria and Iraq. These days, being a terrorist was just another nine-to-five job for some people. Hamas gunmen strutted in the streets of Gaza City and Jabilya with AK-47s and grenade launchers by day shouting "death to the Jews!" and went home to the wife and nine children to watch themselves on CNN and Al-Jazeera at night. And so these northern conscripts from the steppes of Asia Minor donned the khaki of whatever army paid for lentils, pita and rice, and pawned however many bullets and hand grenades they could steal for better food and goods on the black market.

Given all these developments which had been escalating in recent years in spite of some slight signs of positive economic growth in the Western world, David doubted if he would have any leave over the eight-day *Sukkot – Shemeni Atzertet* holiday to see Anat and the children. He especially missed this time with his oldest son, Avi, who was beginning to blossom into a thoughtful, sweet, interesting and intelligent human being as he emerged from the ranks of children to be someone a father could feel especially proud of--and closer to thanks to their bar mitzvah learning together. Avi now wore his *tefillin* every weekday morning, and had adopted a regular place in the morning *minyan* in a small *Shul* he favored – one of many in their religiously mixed Jerusalem neighborhood.

Then it happened. A sudden flash of light like summer lightning lit up the sky, back-lighting the high cloud cover and giving him a glimpse of the darkened landscape. Almost the same instant, the green light of his night vision binoculars went dark. So did his digital watch though he reflexively pressed it several times to try to mark the time. He fished in his shirt pocket. His cell phone was dead too. Though he had charged it the previous morning, it refused to turn on. Three, four, five, maybe six indistinct flashes ripped the sky apart, far away and yet dominating the whole dome of the night. Soundless, eerie, like the Northern lights he had seen once a long time ago. Then he noticed that the distant glow of lights in the towns across the Syrian border were out. Turning around, he could see only darkness where the string of lights had shown the chain of moshavim in the northern Golan moments earlier. Blackout all over, there was not a light to be seen.

The first shock wave hit him almost subconsciously – like the rolling groundswell of a medium-sized earthquake, and a faint, but powerful feeling of pressure pulsing by, like a ghostly punch to his chest and gut, almost winding him. "I'm going to die," he thought, but he found, almost to his surprise that he could still breathe. And still, no sound for many more seconds, and then came a deep and distant rumble like far away thunder. And with it came diffused shock waves, seemingly from several sides like waves of gravity – a passing heaviness, almost taking his breath away. But he was still breathing, and thinking. How long had passed? Fifteen seconds? Thirty seconds? A minute? What just happened?

All he knew was that this must be the war the whole country had been waiting for. But who started it? And what had just happened overhead in the heavens that was casting his fate at this very moment? No time to wait around for answers. It was time to wake up the unit and get to work.

David strode quickly back to his tank, stooping first to rouse the sleeping bundle of Turkish-coffee-brewing, kamikaze-tank-driving, maniac of a master sergeant, Baruch Harel, who cursed him in what might have been his native Persian from the back streets of Jerusalem with its Iranian exiles. David didn't pause to wonder, he just said "wake up, it's World War Three," and left the muttering master sergeant to chew on those words as he rolled into consciousness.

David banged on the side of the battered MK II and vaulted quickly down the driver's hatch. Digging his flashlight out of a pouch pocket, he was surprised to find that it worked, helping him find the switch for the night lights, the glow plug and the starter, but nothing worked. No instrument lights came on to help him. Nothing came to life under his fingertips as he tried to activate the radios, battlefield information system, fuel pumps, navigational systems, and interior lights. Dead. Nothing.

"EMP. That's got to be what it was," he found himself thinking as he worked through every backup start procedure he could think of. EMP. It was the only thing that made sense – blackouts on the civilian power grid, no radios, no cell phone, no circuit more complicated than a flashlight. David had just stepped from the 21st century into the 19th century in less than a minute. And that told him who must have started it. Whose army, air force and defense forces were the best in the world in high technology? Not Syria, despite all their fancy Russian missile systems and hardware. Not Jordan. Not Lebanon, Iran, Iraq or Egypt. Israel had everything to lose and nothing to gain by playing that nuclear card. Out numbered 20-1 on a good day in their Middle Eastern neighborhood – and this was not a good day in the neighborhood – Israel had to be smarter and faster, as well as miles ahead in technology and tactics to overcome the odds.

EMP.... Now what the heck did that stand for? Electro magnetic something or other. Pulse, that was it, electromagnetic pulse... it must have been. It felt like a huge pulse when the shock waves went through him. "Great, I've been nuked…" he thought grimly. "What a way to start your day." Or, rather, the whole country just got nuked, only with megabursts of nuclear magnetic energy high up in the stratosphere at the edge of space. He wished he could remember what the science guys at IDF reserve officer training had said about fall out. What did they mean by "minimal?" Define "minimal" to a guy standing outside while four or five of the things burst overhead.

Baruch stuck his head in the hatch – "What's the time? My watch and cell phone are dead.… Still under warranty too. Pieces of shit," he muttered. "What's the matter?"

"Everything electrical is dead," David said angrily. "Really, really dead. Like EMP – electromagnetic pulsed dead. We're sitting ducks – get everyone else up, *akshav*! And see if we can get anything else started – try the Humvee and the hand-held radios in the field packs – anything."

He could feel that reality was sinking in as Baruch made the rounds of the four Merks and one Hummer getting everyone moving in ways only a master sergeant could manage. He had gone from dreaming to screaming in less than two minutes, but there was some kind of purpose emerging from the rousing tankers. That reassured him in a small way, but it barely made a dent in the feelings of dread, disgust and anger welling up inside. He pushed the feelings aside as best he could and tried to think about what to do next. He was their leader; he had trained for something like this once a long time ago… several of them had. Now, what the hell were they supposed to do next?

He stashed the dead night vision binocs in a storage net in the driver's compartment and climbed out. Almost instinctively he went towards his bivouac bag and stuffed it in a few swift movements, felt for his helmet and put it on, and took up his M-16 and an extra clip, and tossed the remains of his bivvy gear into his rucksack. He was ready to move, and started barking out orders to his group as he strode back to the tank.

"Drivers--see if you have any charge on the batteries. Communications – try the hand sets. Boris, get under the hood of the hummer and see if there is any way to hot wire it – let's get something running! Everyone, get your rifles and clips and pack up. All tankers meet by *Gimmel* One in ten minutes."

He had found his old fashioned binoculars and run a quick sweep of the eastern horizon by the time his group of 22 reservists and two regulars gathered in the small clearing behind his unit that had been used for meals and meetings. Nothing was moving – no one had managed to get an engine to turn over or found anything working except one spring-wound watch and a few standard-issue flashlights – the halogen and LED wonders didn't light. The watch, which had been his driver's great uncle's time piece in the '67 war in the Sinai, said 3:46. They had been at war for about twenty minutes.

Ilan and Kobi, the other two sharing the midnight-to-four watch with him, had confirmed what he saw: one flash, followed by four or five more lightning-like flashes, followed by some sort of visceral shock waves. Kobi wasn't sure about more than a couple flashes, leading David to suspect he had been almost dozing when the first one came. No one had more than three or four hours sleep in a row for at least a week.

David didn't know what to say except to start talking and let his men know everything he knew and had thought in the last 20 minutes that might help them all stay alive. He went over what he could remember about electromagnetic pulses – how they were high-intensity bursts of energy released in the upper atmosphere by an exploding nuclear weapon – how they created an electrical pulse so strong that it fried every transistor, chip and circuit within about a hundred kilometers. He explained how every centimeter of unshielded wire was turned into an antenna to concentrate the intensity of the pulse. He told how they had once tried to run some training simulations of what would happen to the IDF armored corps if all of a sudden there were no electrical systems, no communications, no controls. How they were all back at the start of the 20th century again in terms of weapons – rifles, grenades, artillery and mortars – with no guidance systems beyond right-left, up and down.

He told them about the intel reports that said the Syrians had gone underground just after nightfall and how that all made sense now. They were hunkering down and protecting themselves in EMP-proof bunkers. No question about who lit off the nukes. But that meant that the bad guys had intact electronics and communications and that we were sitting here blind and dead in the water. Now how the hell were we going to stop the 3rd and 4th armored divisions with a hand full of disabled tanks and no run and shoot technology and no way to stand off and hit them from over the hill?

The good news – if there was any good news left in the world – was that it should be possible to get a diesel engine running after an EMP. Somehow you had to bypass the electronic ignition and all the sophisticated fuel controls. Forget radio and even intercom, it was back to kicking the driver in the helmet (sorry Sasha) – there might be something up and running in a few days if there were any sets and transmitters stored away in metal-protected, EMP-proof vaults underground somewhere. And if they lived long enough to hook up with the command and control center handing them out. Forget electronic navigation, fire control. Probably even moving the turret and aiming the 105 mm main cannon would be a problem because of the switching and servo motors. The 7.62 mm machine guns should work OK and perhaps even the small, 60 mm on-board mortar used mostly for flares and infantry support. That was something.

"Think of this as a set of problems to be solved – we have to find work-arounds for everything we have been used to. We have to remember the old days – think World War II, think Suez 1956. Thinking 1967 is probably too modern. What did our grandfathers do?

"Whenever you figure something out, show everyone. If you have an idea, however crazy, try it out – or ask someone. We have to get up and moving, and figure out how to shoot back. Sunrise is 5:25 and that is probably show time."

For an all-hands meeting of 24 Israelis ranging in age from 19 to 54, there was surprising little cross talk and arguing. The essential information passed quickly. Natan Andreyev, a chemical physics lab tech from the Technion in Haifa filled in a lot of solid information about electromagnetic pulses. Some of it was reassuring – such as that the fallout was fairly low yield, and at such high altitudes would probably be spread on the jet streams around the world within days – diluting its effect certainly, but making Geiger counters around the world count a lot of extra clicks for months to come. Even if they had working hand radio sets, the static would be enormous, making them practically useless.

But the probable effect on all of Israel, with its high tech society and even higher tech military, was devastating. No communications, no radar, no computers, no cell phones, no electricity for probably weeks until thousands of blown transformers and substations could be replaced. They were blown back to the beginning of the last century – along with everyone else in the neighborhood. The Syrians may have bunkered their assault divisions but the effects of four or five EMPs must have blown everything electrical until far beyond Damascus. Their command and control would be working against the static and fallout effects of the blasts too. Natan's best guess was that they had some specialized radio equipment for command units, but that everyone else would be following a pre-set game plan and relying on the simplest possible systems for sighting, fire control and unit communications. And don't expect 35,000 armed Hezbollah proxies in Lebanon to sit on their hands. Their weaponry and tactics were custom made for this kind of fight.

David thanked him both publicly and privately, asking Natan to think through their situation from every angle he could think of. Perhaps they would talk later after they got the vehicles started so he could help him think through their next moves.

"One more thing," he said before dismissing them all to their tasks – "the sun comes up in a little over an hour. I think we can be pretty sure they will be coming at us with the rising sun – so that we can't see a damned thing even with these –" he said, gesturing with his clunky olive drab binoculars. "By 5:25 am we need to be able to move and shoot back.

"Now, as for our communications – once we get moving, commanders will have to stay above hatches to keep in touch – hand signals – fire two quick shots in the air if you have to get someone's attention fast. As for reaching brigade and other units, we're going to have to use runners and couriers. Chaim, drop what you're doing and see if you can get your dirt bike started. I take back every stupid thing I said about bringing toys on *miluim*. Danny, that goes for your mountain bike, G-d bless it. Anton, see if you can get *Alef* Company's attention up there with some flashlight signaling – use Morse code if you have too. Otherwise we'll have to send Danny up there on his bike. Let's go. I want to hear some engines running and turrets turning."

Northern Command, Mount Meron

Brigadier general Anna Tchernikovsky had been up for going on 36 hours when news of the missile launches flashed across the monitors in the underground command center deep under Mount Meron. It was not unexpected – they had been monitoring increased activity in the Iranian desert for weeks. But the Prime Minister and his divided cabinet, with its fragile coalition in the Knesset had been unable to muster the nerve or the political will to do anything about it. And given the beefed up air defenses that had been built up over the past few years of close Russian/Iranian cooperation, striking the hardened silos might have been futile for anything short of a tactical nuke. No one in Israel had the stomach for launching anything bigger than a two-ton, bunker-busting conventional weapon, and that only if the target was guaranteed to stand still for 48 hours while they dithered.

But although the launches were in the Iranian desert, the immediate threat was hunkered down in dozens of deep bunkers just across the Syrian border. And so she and the entire Northern Air Command watched on their radar screens as four wings of F-16s, loaded with 1-and 2-ton bunker busting bombs, lifted slowly from Ramat David air base and headed for their targets. Even the non-religious among them, Anna included, muttered silent prayers as the long-range Arrow III anti-missiles flashed away to meet the missile threat. The Arrow was smarter, faster and now on its third generation of interception technology, but hitting an incoming ICBM was never easy. The next ring of missile defenses waited to acquire any targets getting through the long range interceptors. And everyone, down to the crews of the rapid-fire phalanx cannons around the air bases and high priority installations, swung into action.

There was only five minutes to get word of the launch to ground forces before the aerial fireworks started. In less than five minutes, the F-16s would be crossing the Syrian border. A second wave was already getting ready at the Negev bases, with interceptors standing by to meet any incoming bombers from north or south – Egypt had been moving planes and digging new hardened bunkers in the Sinai for months as well. Even Jordan was being watched for any sign of a take off. Although the IDF did not have much respect for the Jordanian air force, the Royal Jordanian Air Force had plenty of hardware on display, and even they had hardened hangers and had been exceptionally busy for the past year.

But, the life and death question that hung in the over-chilled air of the especially hardened, command center, was – what kind of warheads were hurtling through space? Megatons of nuclear death to wipe Israel off the map, as the Iranian leaders had sworn in the worldwide media for years? Or a tactical strike aimed to take down Israel's command and control system and decimate their air fields so that the 38 divisions massed in Syria, Egypt, Lebanon and Jordan could sweep in to crush Israel's citizen army, with its 6 standing divisions and three reserve divisions called up since mid-summer?

The air conditioning was doing too good a job in spite of the heat of the array of computers and data banks in the pair of 12-meter long steel shipping containers, isolated on insulating short pillars deep within a cavern carved out of the limestone of Mt. Meron. Topside the temperature was still 26°C even at 3:18 am, although the surface gauges showed a steady wind from the east-northeast. The walls of this particular chamber were lined with steel mesh, and only non-conducting optical cables carried information in and out of its electrically isolated, self-contained interior. There was another center like it somewhere near Jerusalem where the Prime Minister and cabinet could convene, and one more near Ramat Hovav, the huge new training base in the Negev for the southern command. Anna shivered in spite of her khaki sweater and glanced around at the half dozen people packed in her trailer, all intent on their screens. Somehow she felt sure that these payloads were packing a nuclear punch. There was something that felt evil and ominous about the blips, the timing, the whole atmosphere of the long tense summer. But how much plutonium did Iran really have? And how had they used it? Intel was divided, but the possible answers were not comforting.

And, what if they went for the EMP option? Everyone had argued for and against that for years, but, except for the three bunkers and a hand full of electrically hardened command mobile units stashed in caves here and there, she knew that they were woefully unprepared. Last fall's electronic warfare drill had showed that, and Anna had fought desperately to have the recommendations of the evaluation committee implemented. But politics existed even in the IDF, especially at the command levels, and everyone's pet project was more precious to them than the theoretical threat of using nuclear warheads in the stratosphere instead of on the ground. At least the Arrows had been funded – that was something everyone could agree on. They silently prayed that the intricate software would do its work as the interceptors streaked aloft.

Seven, eight, no, make that ten.... I see eleven separate trajectories," Kobi said, his voice rising with each number. "We can't possibly hit them all!" Lips were moving in the silence as all eyes watched the eleven blips racing toward the interception point somewhere about 30 km past the Jordan River that divided Israel from the Arab world. Anna forced herself to move her gaze over to the tactical scopes that showed the four flights of F-16s airborne and winging towards their targets across the border. She wondered if the southern command had launched the long range bombers that were one of their scenarios for taking the war back to Iran – hitting their command and control systems hard enough to make a breach for future waves of avenging fighter bombers. If there was a future... she caught herself wondering.

Within a minute the first interceptions were showing scattered pixels of green phosphorescence on the screens – three, four, maybe five separate areas – it was hard to tell – but it was clear in seconds that there were blips still incoming. As they heard the beeps and saw the red LED indicators showing the short range interceptors launching, they saw the whole screen blink and go dark. Theater, tactical, local and long range – all systems restarted, but there was no data for them to display – the radar dishes on top of the mountain were not turning and the forest of antennae seemed to have disappeared. The auxiliary generator power was working, but it was not any use – electronics were blind outside of their metal and rock cocoon. She wondered if the radar dishes were even there at all but then realized that the problem must be electrical, not physical...even their deep bunker would have felt or heard something if the surface had been hit. She picked up a phone to call surface security. It was dead.

In the Air over Northern Israel

Wing commander Chaim Tzippori – Warbird One – was the last of his group of four F-16s to lift off from Ramat David airfield just five flying minutes from Syria and Lebanon. His F-16C felt heavy and sluggish as it heaved a 2000 kg bunker-busting smart bomb off the runway and towed it aloft at full throttle, struggling to gain altitude. To save weight, he carried a quarter load of fuel and only two air-to-air missiles on his wings, two chances against a Syrian air defense system that had grown more aggressive by the week as the summer progressed. He was sure there would be a swarm of MIGs just outside the Israeli air defense range, waiting to pounce on a heavily loaded F-16. He wished their air ops had scrambled some covering fighters rigged for air to air combat. But only the four flights of fighters, all of them toting heavy ordinance, had been cleared for this mission.

The briefing over his cockpit headphones as he ran through an abbreviated flight check was simple – hit the big mystery bunkers they had been training for all summer. He had the GPS coordinates and a recent aerial photo for the hot one that was his target. Fly low and fast, hit the target and blow out of there even faster. His wings carried only two of their best sight-guided air to airs in case a welcoming committee showed up in time. His was the second wing away, but would be the first to hit its targets just south of Quneitra on the stretch of Syria-Israel border marked on his side by a string of post-1967 settlements, and on the Syrian side by one of the most massive buildups of conventional arms ever seen in the Middle East, which had seen plenty.

He leveled off at only 1,200 meters on a flight path that took him just north of the Kinneret – which was below sea level, but not as low as the Dead Sea – to the volcanic plateau that rose to up to 800 meters elevation to the east of the lake. As he saw the warm orange glow of the settlement streetlights come into view to his right, he was watching for the warning lights indicating that Syrian tactical antiaircraft radar had him on their screens. For some reason they were not locking on yet. Wait, there was one, two coming up now…but he was less than a minute from the border, his radar alert display inside his helmet should be alight with amber warning blips by now. Was it luck or was it a trap? No call back signal and barely time for one now. He dipped one wing and jinked to the left, spilling 200 meters of altitude and about 50 knots of airspeed. The wing followed him in picture perfect precision. He had to love these guys – they were the greatest airmen in the world.

The darkened no man's land of the border flashed by almost unseen, and still only two anti-aircraft batteries locking on, both still ahead. He rolled right and began to line up on his approach coordinates, the dark landscape racing by. Towns were right where they had always been on the simulation runs and so was the network of roads, fields and bunkers. He concentrated on the big one a few kilometers ahead, already matching up in his targeting computer. It was nearly half a kilometer long – enough to hide an entire brigade of armor, and deep – estimated at 10 - 20 meters under the surface –however they estimated those things. It was just what his payload was made for. He armed the 2000 kg. of high explosives slung from the belly of his plane and settled in for the release. Still no MIGs, and no missile launches. Was Syria asleep at the switch while Iran launched WWIII? Did not compute. Wait, there were SAMs incoming on the radar screen now. Too late Sammies.

He released the bunker buster to follow its GPS bloodhound nose to the bunker's front door. It was designed to knock once with a small surface detonation, plough its reinforced steel shaft deep, and then let go the big one – guaranteed to open doors up to 20 meters deep in anything but the hardest rock. The jet practically leapt into the air and climbed like a freed falcon once unchained from its engine-straining load. Three, two, one, knock-knock, who's there? IAF. IAF who? The double blast of the bunker buster below him drove the punch line from his mind. Right down the chimney! Warbird 2's blast erupted to his left. Warbird 3 and 4 hit their targets to his right. Together they climbed in a soaring arc, spiraling away to the right in a 180-degree turn that would take them home and away from Syrian missiles and ground fire – which was still mute, except for the two SAMs, now way off target and out of his threat zone, falling harmlessly away. Strange. Very Strange. Were these bunkers big decoys designed to lure Israel into a toothless first strike that would earn them the world's condemnation?

Forget politics, just get home. Home was in sight, peaceful and serene in the night. In spite of war jitters, Israel rocked. He would kick back on his days off and try to shake the tension—wait a minute, what days off you idiot? You just bombed Syria! For a moment it had seemed so much like the simulated scenarios, he had been fooled. A more picture perfect bombing run could not have been imagined.

Just then a greenish white flash split the heavens ahead of him – somewhere between him and Haifa, only much higher in the air – maybe even over the Mediterranean if he could believe his eyes. He was nearly blinded for a split second and then the plane shuddered and his helmet display went out. Frantically he looked for his cockpit display – dark. The flight stick felt dead in his hands, the plane was not responding. The F-16s sensitive "fly-by-wire" system, where electrical wires relay commands, instead of steel cables and linkage controls, had simply turned off. Had he been hit? By what?

The jet, which was basically a huge engine driving a pair of wings, ailerons, tail and rudder, began to yaw to the left – and nothing he could do was stopping it. "MayDay!" he yelled into his helmet mike and he punched the explosive triggers that would blow his seat and canopy clear of the falling wreck.

He must have blacked out for a few seconds, because he was swinging wildly through a dark sky over a now completely dark and unfamiliar landscape. He struggled to get the chute evened out, and was rewarded with a somewhat smoother, but still swift descent. Somewhere to his right he could see the silvery sheen of the waters of the Kinneret – he was somewhere in the Golan…but which side of the border? There were no lights below him and the dark ground was coming up so fast there was barely time to hit and roll. Nasty rocks slammed at his knees, side and shoulder, and he passed out again as the force of the landing drove the air from his lungs, stunning him.

Aboard the USS Sitka SSN 791 Somewhere South of Malta 0510

ComsubGroup Eight was considered a holiday assignment to most of the Los Angeles class subs in the U.S. Navy, and so it had no regular boats assigned to it. Subs rotated through for three-to-six-month tours – not quite long enough to get to know the sub-sea quirks of the Mediterranean, but long enough to have some premium shore leave in the group's adopted home port of Naples. Lately, with the dollar finally gaining in strength against the battered euro, shore leave in Italy meant spending the once-almighty dollar liberally, as only a sailor confined to a 360-foot tube for weeks at a stretch could. It had been two years since a carrier group had been based in the Med. Even cruisers and guided missile frigates were growing scarce in these crowded and highly vulnerable waters since the latest two generations of anti-ship missiles had far outstripped even the most elaborate counter measures. That left the port and the free spending to the submariners. The blue water navy, what was left of it after budget cutting year after year had decommissioned more than half of the large surface ships in the past four years, kept mostly to deep water – standing far off in the Atlantic, Indian and Pacific oceans, with ports of call only where there had been no serious terrorist activity – and such ports were precious few.

Lt. Peter Meier had made the most of his week on shore, hiring a car with the ensign and two pretty Italian girls and motoring off to see the Alps and eat and drink their way across northern Italy. Suddenly the idea of three more weeks lurking under the Mediterranean Sea was not nearly as interesting as learning more Italian and opening a bistro somewhere at the foot of those stupendous Alps. Tia's mother was one hell of a cook – even by Italian standards, and with Peter as wine steward and maitre d', and Tia as the waitress and hostess....Well, it was a pleasant daydream to have for the next twenty days at sea.

But the unusual volume of coded military traffic being picked up from the Navy's listening stations around the Middle East had everyone on extra alert since coming off their shore leave two days ago. There was too much of it in Arabic for the Department of Defense's under-manned Middle East desk to cope with, and so the reprints came through days late, missing vital chunks of information and poorly translated. He hoped that at least someone in Washington or Norfolk had a handle on the situation in real time. As the chief information warfare, communications and intelligence officer, Peter could tune in to just about any channel used by the region's air, sea and land forces and find heavy traffic, as if everyone were having war games at once. Since he spoke a not word of Arabic, and no one else on the ship could manage anything beyond a few phrase book tidbits – like "how much for that camel?" and "where are the restrooms," the chatter was interesting only for its intensity.

Local time in Damascus was 3:20 am, not that it mattered much on a submarine. Peter was not in the least bit sleepy so he flipped through the last few dozen entries of decoded and translated messages distributed by ATLFleetCom Intel. There seemed to be a massive build up of armor in Syria – and of radical militias and irregulars, well armed with short range missiles in Lebanon – both of which were making Israel very nervous. Israel had upgraded to red alert status for the second time this year at about the time he went on shore leave. Apparently they were still maintaining that level of alert because he could see no updates downgrading it.

While Syria appeared to be the new home for half a dozen militias and paramilitary forces with tongue twisting names – with very sinister sounding English translations. Instability in Iraq was the worst it had been at any time since US forces left there four years ago, and that was threatening to lower already curtailed oil production. Even the business-as-usual Gulf emirates were down on production, which had pushed up prices again. Gas was back to the $4.50 a gallon range back home in Detroit, so that filling up the tank took a big chunk out of almost any sized paycheck – those who were lucky enough to have a paycheck. Official unemployment was running at eight percent but that meant that at least three times that many were working for shit wages or part-time pay. Food prices were creeping up again in response to rising oil prices, and that threatened to kill the glimmerings of a recovery that had been brightening the economic forecasts for the past few months – at least for Wall Street.

Asian markets were still deeply depressed, even China and India, despite their growing importance in world markets, were struggling to wring what little prosperity they could out of a deadened world marketplace. There was some hope at least…unless another war in the Middle East blew oil prices through the roof. And that's why Peter concentrated on the tidbits of news buried in the pile of printouts he had saved for his night watch reading matter. When he got tired of the official stuff, he planned to switch over to the latest Tom Clancy thriller and see how it ended.

He had just picked up his novel and started to fall back into the fast-paced plot when an alert from ComsubGroup Eight came over the com channel left open for fleet communications. He acknowledged for SSN 791 and gave his code clearance. It was one of his counterparts in InfoWar/Com. He recalled a pleasant afternoon in a cheap but excellent seaside café with the fellow who knew Naples almost like a native. What was his name, Perelli? Well of course, his great grandparents had come from somewhere near there, he recalled. He listened to SSN 778 sign on, and adjusted his voice scrambler decoder so that everyone sounded at least halfway human.

"SSN 778 and 791, we have a message from SpaceCom. Unidentified missile launch from Iran, 12 mid-range ballistics fired toward Israel. Suspect nuclear payload. Estimate entering Israeli airspace 03:22 GMT+2. Status code red all strategic and tactical forces, acknowledge." Peter glanced at the console clock – 02:21 GMT+1, that was one minute from now. He acknowledged, dazed. It sounded like something off the pages of his geopolitical thriller, but this was not a drill.

"Orders from SubCom – stay deep and prepare for rapid response. FleetCom says…" and then the channel went dead. He checked the status of his antenna towed just below the surface 1,500 feet overhead. No response to the test signal. Had they fouled a fishing net? Sonar showed nothing in the area. Flotsam perhaps.

He told a nearby crewman to go awaken the captain on the double and waited 60 seconds before sounding the code red alert. The captain liked to be half a step ahead in these situations.

Moshav Yiftach 0400

Eli Kaplan got to bed sometime after midnight, so it took a few minutes for him to take in the information that there was some sort of attack going on, that power was out all over the moshav, and that he had better get his gear and head for his station damned fast, because something was about to happen. Definitely not a drill this time, he had never seen Gadi that upset, and even the 50% of the torrent of urgent Hebrew that his awakening brain caught was enough to tell him that this was probably the big one. And Gadi threw in, "and hurry up, damn it!" in his best English for good measure. He unrolled the camouflage fatigue pants from the top of his packed rucksack, stepped into them, and had pulled his olive drab *tallit katan* over his t-shirt and was tugging on a shirt while he started punching the numbers on his gun safe – pausing a moment to remember the last number, because he changed it a couple months ago when he noticed some of the grandkids were in the habit of snooping whenever he retrieved a weapon.

He took out a web belt and holster, buckled it on while he drew out the black 9 mm semiautomatic pistol – checked that the chamber was empty out of habit, and slid home a clip, checking the safety with his thumb as he did so. He stuffed four loaded clips in the left cargo pockets of his fatigues and hoped that and the extra rounds of ammo in his rucksack would see him through. Then he drew out his prize – a long, bolt-action sniper rifle with a 6x power optical scope. In his right hand cargo pockets he loaded another five clips of the long, sharp pointed 7.62 mm magnum rounds that made this rifle deadly at up to 1,500 meters. Slamming the safe and punching a random number out of habit, he reached in the bedside drawer and took out a spare pair of glasses and a pocket *siddur* and buttoned them in his shirt pockets.

Natalie held a pocket flashlight and watched these rituals in silence. She never got used to them, no matter how many times Eli scrambled off to serve the moshav that had been their home these past five years. Somehow in America, 58 year-old Jewish grandfathers did not jump in a pair of camo pants and pick up arms in the middle of the night to go rushing out for hours or even a day or two at a time. They called the police and tried to figure out which end of a Saturday Night Special was which. Or they tried to remember the right delivery to the old Jack Benny joke – "Oh, I thought you said my money or my wife!" that was going to amuse some punk who had no idea who Jack Benny was while he handed over his wallet and watch. Eight years in Israel had not changed her mind about this. She kissed him with a tear in the corner of her eye, and knew he would not like any display of dismay or worry – but he kissed her back more than a running peck – lingering for a long moment. He was worried too. Maybe a little extra worry would make him extra careful? He even put on his helmet before leaving the house. That was a first.

She picked up her well-worn *Tehillim* after she followed him to the door and watched his tall dark figure as it vanished into the night, heading for his rally point on the perimeter of their Golani moshav. Living in Moshav Yiftach, five kilometers from the Syrian border, her *Tehillim* was getting a lot of use lately. She pulled the heavy steel shutter that made their master bedroom into one of the three safe rooms in their hand-built house and lit an oil lamp, slipping the flashlight into her pocket for later. She would only say a few quick psalms and then go next door to see what Tali knew about the alert.

Eli's eyes got used to the darkness quickly as he threaded through his fledgling backyard orchard and stepped toward the dirt track that circled the inside of the moshav fence. He knew that Gadi and the other seven moshavniks who were assigned to the northeast corner would meet him in a sandbagged bunker just outside the fence. The sky was hazy and had an odd, dim glow to it – not the reflected glow of city lights – for the nearest city was either Tiberius, across the lake, or some of the larger villages in Syria less than 10k away. It almost seemed like the smoke of the brush fires that had dimmed the stars a few summers ago after barrages of Katyusha and Grad rockets had rained down on Northern Israel. He shook off the memories. This was not one of Hezbollah's deadly games. There were several divisions of Syrian regulars and perhaps a few more thousand irregulars scraped up from who knows where sitting across the border from Moshav Yiftach and the dozen kibbutzim and moshavim planted in the Golan since 1967. It would take a tank driving at only 20 km an hour about 15 minutes to go from the border fence to the edge of Moshav Yiftach.

Two more figures hurried through the gate and out the path to the bunker after Eli. He was relieved not to be the last one on a night like tonight. Everyone was quieter and less talkative than usual, without the bantering and grousing that generally preceded their checkpoint meeting. Gadi was brief. Something had happened overhead a little before three-thirty. Five or six huge flashes in the sky followed a minute or two later by shock waves – and all the power had gone off. Cell phones were out. The moshav's generators were not started even yet – though someone was on it. No land lines, the radios weren't working, not even side band and the military sets that were supposed to be their backups. Nothing. Someone had been up to the top of the water tower to check all the antennas and had reported that power was off all up and down the Golan and across the lake in Tiberius too. No lights on the Syrian side either.

Gadi said that someone heard some fighters – low and heavy – going east just minutes before the flashes – but they were low and somewhere to the north, and the flashes were high and mostly to the west and south – so they thought the jets were counterattacking. In the meantime there was nothing to do but follow the plans and expect the worst. He hoped everyone had remembered water.

There was little discussion. And though he had a thousand questions racing through his mind, he could not put the words together to ask – but heard most of his questions asked by others: "how do we keep in touch? Who's our relief – and what time should we expect them? Where are the IDF units supposed to be so we don't start shooting friendlies?"

He was relieved to hear that there was supposed to be a company of tanks and several platoons of anti-commando infantry just north of the moshav, and at least half an armored brigade to the south between them and Yonatan. Even better, four trucks towing 155 mm howitzers had bivouacked overnight in the moshav on their way up to Mt. Hermon and were looking to dig in and help cover the armored brigade to their south. That gave the moshav some firepower beyond their motley collection of mortars, light machine guns and aged pair of anti-aircraft guns.

Compared to all that fire power, somehow his bolt action rifle seemed pretty light weight all of a sudden. He shouldered his rucksack with a day's food, three plastic bottles of water, spotter scope and a few hundred rounds of rifle and pistol ammunition and headed off along the foot path that led northeast from the corner of the moshav, climbing towards the low hill that trended east toward the Syrian border.

They walked in single file, with Joshie, the youngest at twenty four, going first, Eli second, and Gadi and Misha bringing up the rear. Joshie, a good-looking, athletic young man, had grown up on Moshav Yiftach in the settlement's second generation of offspring. He had a ready laugh, a quick wit and was very popular among all the moshav's more than three hundred inhabitants, both young and old. His grandparents, now in their eighties and still quite active in the affairs of the moshav, had been among the first settlers in the Golan after the 1967 war reclaimed the land for Israel. His parents, though born near Haifa, had grown up there and spent most of their lives there. Joshie had finished his mandatory three years in the Israeli army and had served one year more rather than enter a stagnant job market. He fully expected to get called up in the reserves any day now. Therefore he was fending off all offers to set him up with a potential bride.

Gadi was short and wiry – somewhere in his late forties, with a swarthy Sephardic look. His parents came to Israel from Syria a generation before statehood. He looked especially dark tonight as he labored under his load. Misha, a burly middle-aged Russian who had immigrated fifteen years ago, had a launching tube for their precious anti-tank bazooka rounds. He and Gadi were loaded with a dozen rounds. Misha was built like a brick – though a brick that bulged a bit at the waistline these days. With mortar rounds weighing three kilos each, they were toting 18 kilos of explosives plus their short-stock, IDF surplus M-16's and regular gear; they were already moving slower along the track. Their job was to try to ambush any tanks or armored vehicles approaching the moshav from the northeast that got through the curtain of mortar fire. Eli's job was to cover them from the end of the ridge. Eli was the oldest of their motley defense squad, and he was the newcomer – he had only been a member of the moshav for five years, but they all made him feel most welcome and appreciated in spite of his pathetic Hebrew.

Passing through the minefield at night was always tense, even though the moshavniks knew the paths by day and night in all weather. It was a warm night with a dry east wind that smelled like parched grass with a hint of smoke like a distant brush fire. Eli was sweating as they reached the path that would take them to the end of the low, rocky hillock that would be their post as the spotters, sniper and anti-tank outer layer of the moshav defense. The moshav's handful of light machine guns were dug in the bunkers just outside the fence commanding fields of fire that overlapped as best they could. And, a row of houses deep inside the moshav, waiting in pits with carefully shielded bunkers of shells, were the four 85 mm and two 120 mm mortars that constituted the maximum firepower allowed by the current government to be held in non-IDF defense groups.

They were lucky to have that much – and the ammunition for them, outside of the sixty rounds allowed "for emergency use," had all been bought on the black market with private money raised by Eli and the handful of American, South African and Canadian *olim* at the moshav. He silently blessed the two New York high rollers and one Canadian millionaire who had met with them last winter in a private meeting after a fund raising dinner for the Yeshiva of the Golan. Each of them had quietly written checks to the half dozen religious moshavim to cover a special purchase of mortar shells, equipment and ammunition that he was sure the government still did not want to know about. Eli privately wished that some of the Peace Now MKs who had run in the last elections could be there with him this morning. They threaded the footpath as it edged along the crumbled rock just below the ridge top. Thank G-d for the artillery passing through, and for their moshav's reputation for taking good care of visiting soldiers.

A streak of light caught his eye, followed by a tremendous BANG! somewhere off to his right. Then, suddenly the sky was alive with flashes and the earth with booms and crashes as more rockets than he could count started falling to earth for miles around them. He was thrown off balance and slammed into the rocky ground on his left knee and shoulder, with his pack pulling him backward as something exploded with a hot flash less than 100 meters to their right. He rose clumsily to his feet, ears ringing and face still feeling the heat as other missiles boomed behind him. He saw the water tower of the moshav lit up as something burst to the left and beyond it – somewhere near the entrance gate – whose houses were there?

Joshie had been knocked down or fell ahead of him, and Eli saw him unsling his weapon and use it for balance as he got up. He turned around to see Gadi and Misha hurrying up the track behind them. "*B'seder*?" he called, his voice sounding odd in his ringing ears. Joshie shrugged and waved him on. They jogged along the crest of the low, broken ridge that trended from west to east, giving a view of the moshav behind and now perhaps 75 meters below them in elevation. Their job was to defend the start of the ridge against anything coming from the east, i.e.; the Syrian border, and try to convince the invaders to keep to the lower ground and off the ridge that could overlook the northern side of their moshav. Somewhere about a quarter kilometer behind them was another group, similarly armed, that faced the north slope, and a third group at the northwest end of ridge to the north of the moshav.

Perhaps another hundred rockets of all sizes and bangs had boomed near and far all around them by the time Eli settled into his rifle pit that had been prepared under a projecting ledge of rock where their ridge petered out into a jumble of boulders to the east. It smelled of fresh earth and the clean scent of basalt that had been baked by the sun all day and was radiating heat into the night. Below him, the moderate slope ended in a natural boulder field that served to discourage tanks and armored trucks from attempting the ridge end on. It would make more sense to swing north and hit the ridge where the second group was placed. Between the second group, some heavy mines and what they hoped would be accurate mortar fire directed from the ridge, the moshavnikim hoped they could hold out until the moshav was either evacuated or reinforced.

Eli was almost used to the flash, crash and bang of the rockets by the time they stopped over an hour later. His watch, an old analog Swiss army watch, was the only one working in their four person group – so he called out the time for his companions in the deeper trench below him. "*Chamesh v'chamisha, netz hachama b'esrim dakot. Ani holech l'hitpallel* - five after five. Sun's up in about twenty minutes, I'm going to pray." He was stiff now from his fall and growing almost cold from lying and crouching under the cave-like ledge that overhung his three firing positions.

He knew the quiet would not last, but until they saw something there was nothing better to do than start morning prayers. He could see that Gadi already had his *siddur* out while Joshie kept watch. Moshav Yiftach was a religious moshav. All of its seventy families agreed to keep *Shabbat* and the laws of the *Torah*. They had two *shuls*, one small one for the Sephardim and the larger synagogue for the Ashkenazim who formed the majority of families. Gadi was one of the Sephardim. His family came from Syria two generations ago, before the State of Israel was declared. Now he was waiting for Syria to come to him.

Already the eastern sky had grown lighter, enough to see the page of his prayer book, though he knew almost all of the morning prayers by heart. He had just finished saying the morning *Shema*, "Hear, Israel, the L-rd your G-d, the Lord is One," when the boom of artillery ahead of him broke the stillness. Soon shells were falling in a curtain of blasts that crept towards their moshav in the predawn twilight. The Syrians were laying down a heavy barrage and they knew right where to shoot. Shells were now falling in and around the moshav, and he prayed that his wife and all his friends and neighbors were safe in their shelters.

Actually, most of his house qualified as a shelter. He had built it more for the earth-sheltered energy savings than for protection against missiles and artillery. Their master bedroom had more than two meters of earth and rock on the northern and eastern sides, thick, natural stone walls with extra insulation, a moisture barrier and a triple reinforced concrete roof, broken only by a deep well skylight on the southern slope. He was sure that Natalie was safe without having to go into one of the underground shelters on each block. He just hoped that someone was with her.

Mekor Ro'im, Shepherds' Well, Four km from the Israel-Syria Border

David was wedged deep on one side of the engine, holding the flashlight for Sasha, who was swearing in Russian, Hebrew and perhaps Bukharian as he tried to wire a bypass around a set of ignition controls that were fried. But the engine compartment did little to dampen the ear-splitting KABOOM! of a missile blowing a crater of earth and rock into the air not far from their grove of trees and making him drop the flashlight. A second and third missile hit a few seconds later – or perhaps they artillery shells – David could not tell with his head and torso jammed the engine compartment He had to see what was coming down. He lunged deeper toward the dropped light, barely grasping it between outstretched finger tips when more blasts went off, only slightly farther away. Dropping the light and then fishing for it again with a desperate dive, he grabbed the now-oily light and started to un-wedge himself. "Here's the light. I gotta go see what's shaking," he yelled at Sasha, who merely swore, reached for the oily light and wedged it upside down under his cap.

"Status!" he yelled as he emerged, still deafened, greasy and kinked from the engine compartment.

"Rockets – probably 122 and bigger," yelled Baruch, who was even more deafened by the explosions. "And I think those are howitzer shells walking their way down the hill towards Yankel's group!"

David turned to see the staggered blasts of shells falling on the hillside two kilometers away. They were grouped closely and looked like they were feeling out the group of tanks dug into the rocky landscape. He watched for a moment, unable to take his eyes off the drama. The sky had lightened a lot since he had been under hatches. His binoculars brought the scene closer, still dim except for the flashes of explosions. Then he saw something odd. One of the tanks had started rolling backwards out of its covering bunker, creeping down the hill. He fixed his binoculars on it. Was it running? How had they done it? Then he saw it nearly jerk to near a full stop, a black cloud of smoke puff from its exhaust, and he heard something that nearly brought tears to his eyes, the throaty, distant roar of a 1,200 horsepower Merkava III tank.

They jump started it – just like Chaim had started his dirt bike, pushing it down a slope and popping the clutch until the engine caught and kept going. Chaim had raced off to link up with Brigade after buzzing up the hill to get the news from Yankel's group. No dirt bikes were allowed in that regular army unit, at least not during a red alert. But how did they pop the clutch with an automatic transmission on a 65 ton tank? David couldn't think of how, but he had just seen it done.

David tried to discern a pattern in the now steady barrage of rockets falling around his position. It seemed almost random, except that perhaps the bulk of the hits were trending away from them, falling mostly behind them now. But the howitzer shells falling two kilometers ahead of them were tightly grouped and were saturating a huge area around where Yankel's group was dug in. As he watched he saw a direct hit, the tank nearly leaping out of its hole and bursting into smoke and flame. No survivors possible there. He forced his mind to remain analytical. Seven left, and his four – and at least they hadn't hit the one that got running. Where was he now? He searched the ridge for him among the shells, falling singly and in one-two's, and even one-two-three spreads of flame.

It was awesome to see what artillery could do; and maddening to realize that they couldn't shoot back. Not yet. Their turrets moved by hydraulics – and for hydraulics, you needed a running engine to build up pressure and maintain it. He almost wanted to jump up on the elongated front of his tank, grasp the stubborn long barrel of the 105 and point it like a big rifle barrel and tell Benny to fire just to lob one over the ridge and make the bad guys duck.

He thought all this while watching the one running tank approach its neighbor from the rear. They were going to chain up and tow the other one out of its pocket and get it started that way. Clever. He prayed the checkerboard of falling shells would keep missing. No, something was burning far to his right – another hit – but maybe survivable. It looked like from the turret on back was intact. The Merkava mounted its engine and most extensive armor to the front. A hit on the front could be survivable, even a hit from a 155 or larger artillery shell. His MK II was re-designed and released while the drawn out Lebanon war was still smoldering in the 1980's. That long and dirty conflict had taught the legendary tank commander General Tal and the Israeli tank designers much about how to keep a tank crew alive. The MK III was better and the IV even better still. Some were used as armored battlefield ambulances.

Two hit, six left, one – soon to be – two running. David tore his attention away from the battle next door to see what was going on with his own group. He could see the dim yellow of the flashlight in his own engine compartment. He walked over to tank *Gimmel* Two. "Any progress?" he had to climb right up to Baruch and shout. Baruch looked grim.

"Yankel managed to roll one down the hill and jump start – we're too level for that here – but if it gives you any ideas, have at it" he yelled. Baruch looked startled, and then almost chagrinned.

"We've got 12 cylinders and a ton of motor that doesn't want to move," he yelled back. "Maybe we can rig a chain hoist to one of the trees."

"Keep at it and try and think of a way to get a gun firing." He jumped down and scrambled through the rocky grove to *Gimmel* Three about 75 meters away. Just as he was reaching the upslope of the tank's earthworks, he heard the grind of a starter behind him. There was a weak sputter and then a roar of a diesel engine coming to life. It sounded ragged – as if odd cylinders kept missing – but it was the sweetest sound in David's forty-two years except for the first cry of his four children – he had been there for each birth, and the oldest was now what? Fourteen? He remembered his first look at that sweet little face. No time to think about them. The pain of tenderness stabbed him like a knife.

A cheer sprang up from around the eucalyptus grove in spite of the booming of rockets – now they were definitely falling behind them. His tank was blowing black smoke, but running. By damn it was running! He was sprinting back to it now. He saw the turret swing right, then back left – the cannon angle up and then down. Sasha was triumphantly banging shut the last engine hatch, the now dead flashlight stuffed in his fireproof coveralls. He was still swearing but cursing for pleasure now as he eased down into the driver's hatch after a grinning gunner wriggled out, exchanging greasy fives. David swung up to his commander's hatch by the right side machine gun, and happy slapped Benyamin, the gunner and the Greg the loader on their helmets as they emerged below him after scrambling in the rear crew door. David climbed out again and jumped down onto the ground by the driver's hatch to help guide Sasha backwards out of the shallow pit of their dug in embankment. "Hold on tight" he shouted at the Benny and Greg, then he motioned to Sasha, who was driving in the heads-out position.

The engine gave a ragged roar, engulfing them in a cloud of half-burned diesel smoke, and the tank gave a tremendous lurch as it jerked into gear. With a tremendous blast of oily smoke and a roar the tank shuddered into motion, shouldered its way over a small embankment and came to rest, still running, while David climbed back aboard. Automatic transmissions must have some electrical components, David thought as he braced himself better for the jolting trip over to the next tank in their group; the shifting was far from smooth. He hung on as the big machine ground its way over a hummock of rocky ground and slammed down again.

He was about to yell to Baruch to get the tow chains ready when he realized that he was already unwinding them from the back of tank *Gimmel* Two. David tried to get a clear look at Yankel's ridge as they clanked through the trees over to the second tank. It was impossible to see as the light-barked tree trunks reeled by, growing ghostly grey in the pre-dawn. Job One was to get his group started.

Boris jogged over from the Humvee and had a consultation with Sasha as they chained up the second tank and prepared to pull start it. Both heads disappeared below for awhile, then both clambered out for a look into the engine compartment with a fresh torch. Meanwhile, David had noted three tanks moving on the far ridge, and perhaps another set of intense flames. Yankel's unit and another were now going up the ridge towards Syria while the other seemed to be busy preparing to tow a fourth. He could see from the rigid point of their cannon that there were no motion stabilizers or run-and-shoot horizon tracking – it bothered his tanker's instinct to see the awkward motions. He knew that was Yankel's tank heading toward the enemy without having to read the *alef* 1 lettered on the back. Only Yankel was that crazy.

He noticed that his own tank was steering roughly as well as running raggedly in the 50 meter trip to the next placement. Almost unconsciously he took in the information, knowing that it was important somehow. How would it be when they got moving? What was their maximum speed now? If they stalled out, would they have to go through a complicated restart again? He would have to get Sasha's opinion on these and more before they left the mostly psychological shelter of the trees.

He forced himself to sweep the whole field that he could see, starting from the right and behind where the rockets still fell – as if there were no running out of them any time soon. There was no way the IDF could afford to spend rockets like that. Every one cost several years' pay of an average Israeli – and the average Syrian made one quarter of what the average Israeli made, even after five years of recession.

To his left, which was northeast, he could see only shells and rockets – no movement yet this side of the border. Although dozens of commandos could be working their way on foot through that broken country – the number of minefields, most of them dating to the 1950s and 60s and laid down by the Syrians themselves, made that a poor bet. Certainly nothing on tracks or wheels was coming from that direction at the moment. There was another huge minefield to the south, which made Yankel's ridge and the valley beyond especially strategic. It looked like the ground assault would be coming from Yankel's direction. Did he have a spotter on top of that ridge? He must have a couple. But of course, their remote controlled aerial drones were out of the question with their high tech electronics. If Yankel had one airborne at the time of the EMP, and he probably did have something feeding him infrared pictures to his upgraded battlefield electronics, it had surely crashed long ago. David's group didn't have those kinds of tech toys. They were lucky to have two shoulder-fired, laser-guided anti-helicopter missiles in the Humvee. They were probably dead weight now, although maybe they could hit something if fired at point blank range like a bazooka.

Boris tugged at his elbow to get his attention away from the far ridge where it seemed that Yankel and his side man had driven up and out of the falling zone of shells and were approaching the crest. "Humvee not going to run – even with tow," Boris yelled in his face. "Too much electric. Everything smoke. Sasha think so too."

David nodded, "Strip it then. Take the 7.62, gas cans, food, ammo, RPGs, anything that might useful and put them in *Gimmel* Four. Disable the rest with a couple grenades when we pull out. Tell Four we'll get to them with a tow in a few minutes. Tell the Humvee team to stand watch for bad guys at the edge of the grove until we get going. Maybe you can rig a bipod for the 7.62." Boris nodded sagely and clambered away. David braced himself as the engine revved to jerk the other tank into motion.

Soon two tanks were smoking and roaring. David's *Gimmel* One went to start tank Four while *Gimmel* Two trundled over to *Gimmel* Three. He shouted down to the driver's head a few feet away – "Sasha, what's the hour?" Sasha looked at his grandfather's watch and flashed a five and then seven fingers. Five o'seven, sunrise was in eighteen minutes. It was much lighter out now as the sun was just below the horizon. The thin, ragged looking clouds high overhead were picking up the pink glow already. It was less than two hours since flashes in the night sky had left him breathless and wondering. It seemed like at least two lifetimes.

David climbed out of his hatch and climbed down to squat by Sasha's driver's hatch for the couple minutes it took to hook up the chains. "If we stall out – can we get started again?" he asked.

"I think so - we have battery power for at least another start, but I'm not sure the alternator is putting out anything much. I don't have any meters working but the cockpit lights dim every time I back off the rpms."

"What's with the steering – and transmission?"

"I'm having control each track separately to steer," Sasha said. "I'm starting to get the hang of it but it's not going to be smooth. Transmission is jerky from neutral to first and reverse – no idea what it will do gearing up or down yet until we get clear."

"Top speed? Best guess?"

"Half maybe 25-30 max on the level – that's assuming we have four speeds working – say 10-20 max if it's first or second only."

David shook his head in wonder. It was like going into a boxing ring with only one hand and one bloody half-closed eye – only it was the first round, not the ninth. He patted Sasha on the shoulder and went off to talk to the gunner and loader, motioning them to join him inside their compartment. He slipped down his commander's hatch into the fire control area just before the engine revved again for the pull.

The three of them braced themselves in the gunner and loader's compartment on either side of the breech of the 105 that dominated the center and front of the space. The loader, Greg, a body builder and something of a surfboard nut in real life, hulked protectively over his canisters of 105 shells – he had a safety canister of four anti-tank rounds ready for instant access.

"OK, tell me what we have and what we don't have," David began as the lurching tank tugged at the inert bulk of its companion, trying to urge kinetic life into its engine.

"Turret – right and left are working but slow. We have to use the hydraulic levers, not the fire control switches. Up and down, same thing but no problem," Benny said. He was a kibbutznik, used to farm equipment. He ran the specialty wines vineyard on a kibbutz in the Galilee and always brought samples when the group got together for their annual training. "Of course, no automated target tracking, no auto level, no horizon tracking, no infrared, no laser range finding. We'll have to practically sight down the bore and guess. Well, not quite that bad, it's all optical now – which means we have to see 'em to shoot 'em."

Greg told him the obvious – that all the auto loading and round selection technology was down, as well as infrared and laser targeting and threat detection systems. It would be all hand work – but he could load almost as fast as any flipping machine any day. It was not so easy to jump back and forth between anti-personnel, armor piercing and smart rounds – but that should be the least of their worries. Besides, the smart rounds just got real dumb after the Iranian light show.

The sudden acceleration and answering roar of another engine joining their out of tune diesel chorus told him that *Gimmel* Four had started successfully. They were mobile at last! He climbed back up to his perch at the starboard hatch. With no radios working he had to wave his three tank commanders over for a fast consultation at the edge of the clearing where they could see at least a 270 degree sweep of the action. What lay behind them was not important at the moment.

A bloody red sun crept above the smoky eastern horizon. It wasn't the blinding blast of light he was used to watching – and training for – on the Golan. Nearly everywhere brush and grass – dry at the end of a particularly dry spring and summer – were burning from the rocket and artillery barrage, which was beginning to ease up. The enemy armor must be moving now. Behind him a few of the trees of their sheltering grove were aflame – he hadn't noticed the hits. The Syrians must not have spotted their little group in their last minute satellite recon that must have identified Yankel's group as prime targets to be pounded. Or perhaps, he thought wryly, it was payback time for all Yankel's insults in Arabic for the satellites. Now that he could look again, he could see that four of the eight were running. Two had gained spots just short of the ridge, and were firing – surrounded in clouds of their own making, and two more were making their way up – moving painfully slowly for anyone used to watching a Merkava muscle its way up the rough and ragged Golan basaltic ridges.

He let his fellow commanders take in the scene for a moment. They needed to fix all the landmarks they could once more before entering the melee where up and down, right and left, north and south made little sense.

"Nothing is flying today – not even them. Think they overdid it on the fireworks?" he yelled at the top of his lungs. Everyone shrugged but looked nervously at the fiery red and orange sky. They were sitting ducks for an attack helicopter and its missiles – but maybe it was too hot in the area to fly yet.

"Three options," he shouted briefly, "go up there and give *Alef* Company a hand, stay and shoot anything topping that ridge, or fall back and regroup with the counterforce near the reservoir."

"Seems like only one option to me," Baruch yelled back, looking towards the two struggling tanks moving through the last scattered shell blasts. The others nodded.

"OK then, follow me. We're going to angle off to the southwest and join them. If I know Yankel, he's going to dip along behind the crest, popping up to shoot a couple rounds at intervals and head west for the moshavim. Keep a good 50 meters between us, and remember the old minefields when we near the top. Stay to my track or anything solid." He waved to Sasha who eased *Gimmel* One out of the clearing and paused a fraction of a second for him to swing aboard. He took a moment to test fire a few rounds from the machine gun, glad to see that something worked smoothly. He heard similar bursts behind him. It looked like they were driving straight into Hell, but at least it felt good to be moving towards the action.

He checked Yankel's progress: two shooting, two still climbing. Yankel was definitely headed west and south with the ridgeline. Turning, David watched the next two tanks swing out of the woods and gather speed behind him. He heard the thump of a grenade as the humvee crew completely disabled their vehicle. *Gimmel* Four waited for them to climb aboard before gunning after the platoon. Four extra bodies and gear fit fairly well in a Merk II – especially since they carried only 50 shells each – an infantry support load, not the maximum 80-90 loads carried for strictly tank-to-tank combat.

For the next fifteen minutes, David's attention was absorbed by picking a slanting route up the long groundswell of the ridge, loosely following a cow path through the rocky meadows and brush. Cows were not smart, but lazy enough to find the easiest way. Forget following a goat path, goats were crazy. Soon he was aware of a new kind of shell falling – the faster, flatter trajectory of tank rounds coming over the ridge top as they approached his imaginary intersection with Yankel. They must be firing at Yankel and missing--or perhaps they had him on radar?

When they cleared a spur of rock, threading the only ground open to them, he saw Yankel's *Alef* One edge up to the ridgeline. It was perhaps 200 meters to his left. He saw it blast a round. There didn't appear to be anyone behind him. Yankel's Merk III jerked around and raced away as two or more rounds flew by the spot he just left. Sasha revved their beast to the max as they ate up the last of the ground between them. He wasn't sure Yankel had noticed them yet – but he could see him yelling to his driver and pointing out a spot for their next jack-in-the-box shot. David whistled for Sasha and pointed out some boulders to the left of Yankel's next hidey hole. He checked to see his next tank, a good three hundred meters behind, and just clearing the spur. He would know what to do.

His mouth was dry as rock dust – and his whistle almost as pathetic, so he gulped a mouthful of water as he ducked down to consult with the gunner. "Almost to the ridge top – we're a hundred meters behind Yankel. Pop up and have a look."

Benny poked his head out of the observation hatch on the other side of the main gun and took his bearings.

"Tank fire is coming at about this angle – low and flat – they must be on the up-slope," David yelled, marking a trajectory with his hand. "So we'll turn the turret on that line. We're going to shoot from the other side of those rocks. Sasha is going to stop and count to seven and the peel off. Take any shot you see – don't get choosy on me."

Benny grinned and clanged the hatch shut. In moments, the turret was swinging left and his perspective with it. David took hold of the machine gun grips and tried to see everywhere at once as they approached the boulders.

In spite of the billowing smoke, noise, dust and roar, it took him barely two seconds to take in the other side of the ridge. Perhaps twenty older-model, Soviet-built tanks were climbing towards them less than half a kilometer distant and blazing away. Behind them he could see scores of vehicles massed and moving along the broad valley between the rolling ridges. Thank G-d, no helicopters or gun ships. Automatically he sprayed an arc of machine gun fire towards the enemy as his tank shuddered to a stop. He counted the seconds, which seemed like forever, as he sprayed bullets like a fire hose at a raging fire. The tank jumped as its cannon fired and spun on its tracks, backing and turning as a round whizzed by. He had no idea if they had hit anything – and he would probably never know.

He felt more than heard the next round bang into the breech as they thundered down the ridge. Yankel had seen them now and waved them toward a slight hollow ahead for a short consult. He was grinning like a maniac and slapped his raised fist twice and then raised four fingers – indicating four kills. How the hell did he keep score in that maelstrom of fire and smoke? He saw *Gimmel* Two run up to the ridgeline and fire a round. *Gimmel* Three was just past the spur and running along a lower angle to meet them. No sign of Four, but they were loaded heavier and started last so he wasn't worried yet. Looking back along the swell of the land, he saw one of Yankel's group laboring along in the shelter of the hill. They appeared to have taken a hit and might be running on a half track on the uphill side. Two smoking ruins farther back told him the rest of the story.

Sasha pulled into the lee of Yankel's tank and David vaulted out and scrambled up for a quick word. Just as he did, he noticed a mortar round flash out of the inboard launch tube. "Good thinking, Benny," he thought as he swung up to Yankel's commander's hatch. Another round lobbed skyward.

"Good to see you. I'm running low on friends up here," Yankel grinned. "Look, we got to high tail it out of here fast – I say we run down to that next gulley. All three of us peek-a-boo and shoot at once. Then we rock and roll on down to the draw north of Moshav Yiftach. That puts a good-sized minefield on either side of us and we can maybe link up with whatever is left of the reaction force."

David nodded. Those were his thoughts almost exactly. "We might pick up some covering fire from the TAP Line batteries," he added.

Yankel gave him a quick clap on the shoulder. Yankel's tank was moving already as David jumped down, motioning Sasha to get going too. He saw *Gimmel* Two and Three fall in behind them, and he tried to convey the plan to them in signs: run – pop up and shoot – run like hell. Now he saw *Gimmel* Four. They had taken a more direct line and were about to link up with Yankel's limping partner. He noted their mortars were in action too. With all the heavy fire power of the main gun, he had almost forgotten the little field-sized mortars built into them. Any return fire could at least slow the enemy advance, or confuse them. A 60 mm round was not going to put much of a dent in a T-72, but it could force them inside, or spray any exposed commanders with deadly shrapnel.

They reached the designated turn and shoot spot quicker than he expected. But he realized now that the landscape was beginning to fall away ahead of him more, and that their ridge was about to peter out into several shallow gullies. He saw one promising line angling to the west that would take them away from the ridge quickly and afford some minimal cover in its twists and turns. *Gimmel* Two and Three had caught up, and the four tank commanders each pointed to a spot where they would take their shots. Incoming rounds were still high and wide but coming every three to five seconds. He called Benny up for a look and then grabbed the machine gun. He hoped Sasha judged the slope correctly for he felt very exposed. He quickly noticed the progress of their two stragglers. They were nearly half a kilometer behind – they must be directly across the rolling ridge from the approaching tanks, who might gain the ridge at any minute now.

"Benny – shoot for anyone closest to the ridge – work from the left!" he yelled down the hatch. As if in answer, the turret swiveled even farther left until it was pointing nearly behind them.

This time the view over the top showed the attacking group plainly – right down the flash of their cannons which seemed to be pointed right at him. He poured machine gun fire at the group closest to the ridge top and heard the answering ping ping ping of bullets on his own armor plated turret. The gun fired and this time he could see a hit on the turret of the tank nearest the ridge two seconds later as they lurched backwards out of sight. Cannons roared on either side of him as Yankel to his right, and Tanks Two and Three from his group fired. Something blazed off the deck armor of Three, scoring a blackened groove before exploding beyond it. More rounds flew directly overhead.

"Sasha – one more – same spot, forward then back!" David yelled at the helmet in the hatch below his turret. "Benny – you hit the turret dead on – now hit the next one to the right from the same spot." He checked the feeder on the machine gun and prepared for another go, praying that no one expected him to appear in the same spot twice. Over his shoulder he could hear Yankel's tank approaching too.

Another desperate blast at the odds, another possible hit. He now saw how Yankel was able to keep score – he was now better at this game by some indefinable edge that made all the difference. This time they scrammed like dinosaur-sized rabbits for the beginning of the gulley. It seemed like the engine was running better – but maybe it was just the downslope. Benny swiveled the turret around so that David could see behind them. He would blaze away at anything that showed itself against the skyline behind them, and so would Benny. He had waved Two and Three ahead of him, and he anxiously watched their two stragglers and the ridgeline.

Four dark shapes emerged from the smoke silhouetted against the orange morning sun. He fired, and *Gimmel* Three fired. Yankel was into the gully already and *Gimmel* Two did not have a clear shot. There was one hit, but machine gun bullets were rattling on their hull again. This time their driver was on the safe side but David was exposed and returning fire for all he was worth, trying to spray the hatches of the nearest tank. The remaining three T-72's fired almost at once, and he saw the back of *Gimmel* Three erupt in smoke and flame. Benny fired again, and then *Gimmel* Two. One more hit – they must have fired at the same target. He poured machine gun fire on the remaining two as he saw three more tanks gain the ridge behind them. Another burst of fire pinged off his turret as the tank gave a sideways lurch and plunged into the beginnings of the gully.

Rocks and brush careened by as they raced for the safety of the next bend. They rounded it to see Yankel's tank sprinting hundreds of meters ahead. Sasha poured on the power and steered straight down the bottom of the gully seeking the fastest line and ignoring logs and smaller rocks. Shells crashed around them, but there was no clear shot for pursuers or pursued for nearly a kilometer as the gulley deepened and twisted its way westward. David clung to his hatchway as best he could and prepared to pepper any sign of pursuers behind them. Somehow he knew that *Gimmel* Four and Yankel's partners were either captured or dead. Escape seemed impossible.

Moshav Yiftach, the Golan Heights 0500

Natalie was still praying when Tali slipped in, with an anxious twelve-year-old daughter and the two littlest ones in tow. She smiled at them and hugged them all, and helped settle the little ones into the big bed she and Eli had left an hour earlier. Tali was her patient, kind-hearted and sweet-faced link to the Hebrew speaking life of the moshav. She understood what Natalie was going through with barely knowing the language for she had spent four unhappy years in Columbus, Ohio as a young mother of young children while her husband did his postdoctoral work in molecular biology. And, though she was more than ten years younger, her wisdom and tutelage on life in a religious moshav in Israel made her seem an older mentor. "Tali will know what's going on," Natalie thought.

Natalie knew enough Hebrew to go shopping, to find her way around, and to make small talk: Where are you from? How many children do you have? How old? Where do they go to school? But for sharing substantial information, getting all the nuances, and making sure she understood and was understood, she knew she would always rely on English. One didn't make aliyah at forty-nine, having had only summer camp and *Talmud Torah* after-school Hebrew, and expect to be fluent. Her youngest daughter, Rivka, and Rivka's four children were chatting away like natives – and that's what counts. Tali understood where Natalie was coming from, and went out of her way to help her improve her *Ivrit*. But Tali was kind enough to switch to English whenever her neighbor had enough of floundering.

Natalie set a teapot on one of the gas burners they kept for such emergencies. "I wish the radio was working. What's the news?"

"That's the problem. There is no news, no radio, no electricity, not even AM on the emergency channel. Nothing. I've never felt so isolated before...Always we had *Galatz* and Radio Israel when we went to the shelters. Tonight there is nothing. I'm not even sure the battery set in the shelter is working – and I know the batteries are fresh."

They exchanged worried looks as they waited for the tea water to boil. Pouring themselves big soothing mugs of herbal tea, they settled into arm chairs at the end of the master bedroom that served as Eli's reading corner and Natalie's spot for knitting and schmoozing with him.

"Ok," Tali began, "you might as well hear this too," she added to Naomi, her oldest, "because you're big enough to worry with the *imas* tonight." Naomi gave a weak smile but looked even graver. She was honored to be included in among the mothers, even if the subject was worry.

"What they're saying is that there has been some sort of nuclear bomb that went off in space – or so far up in the atmosphere it's practically space – and that created a kind of electromagnetic radiation that has knocked out all our power, radio and radar. Everyone says that Syria will attack. The IDF units are already moving into position to counterattack."

Natalie had feared as much. In eight years they had already lived through three "minor" conflicts – if nearly three thousand missiles falling on your homeland in the space of three weeks one summer could be considered minor – but never an all-out war.

"It's too late to evacuate and nowhere to go anyway. The whole country is on the frontline this time," Tali said.

Naomi tucked her feet up and hugged her knees, chin resting on them, worried, but taking in every word. She was scared, but not surprised either.

"Chavi's mom told her that another reserve division was called up, and that their uncle Barak had been called back to his unit for a second time this year – indefinitely," Naomi chimed in. Her English was very good, even though she had left the US at age seven.

Tali continued telling everything she knew about the artillery unit that was digging in behind the community center. She told how all the cars and trucks had stopped working and how they had only managed to start some of the older tractors and the one ancient pickup truck and the caterpillar bulldozer. There was something about anything built after the mid 1970s – too much computerized electronics or something – and that they had all gone haywire. The tractors had towed the cannons while the bulldozer was pushing up earthworks around them. Her other neighbor had told her about the brigade that had moved into the gap between their moshav and the next two moshavim to the south earlier in the afternoon. Everyone was talking about how there were no planes flying either – except for some low flying fighters headed north shortly before the first explosions.

Each of them thought of their husbands going off, puny rifles in hand, into the night to watch and wait for whatever was coming. They spent some time castigating their anti-religious, anti-Jewish, anti-Israel Israeli government. There had been four governments in Natalie's eight years in Israel, each one worst than the last. The next-to-last government had practically disarmed all the settlements – and handed several fully developed communities over to the Palestinians for the sake of a one-sided peace process. The settlements had been demolished and promptly turned into jerry-built slums and tenements that were terrorist-breeding grounds. Some peace.

But their talk drew them inevitably back to the present. "Eli is fifty-eight you know, and he says his night vision is not what it used to be. He doesn't like driving at night much – and he just had his prescription changed last winter," Natalie said.

"Yisrael is no – how you say it in American – spring rooster, either," Tali mused. "He's forty-one next month. Only a few more years of *milluim* for him – but G-d he's going to miss it. His old unit is closer to him than family. It will kill him to have them called out without him being there to tell everyone what they are doing wrong." They laughed together, especially Naomi. "He's probably out there somewhere right now telling the IDF which way to point their cannons."

Their conversation was stopped by the distant boom of rockets beginning to fall. It was a sound they knew too well. They remembered the funerals for the family on the moshav when a mother and three of the couple's five children were killed one night three summers ago when the rockets fell without warning.

"Your house is so much more cozy than the shelter," Tali said, breaking the long silence. "You and Eli were smart to build it into the earth even though everyone was making jokes about your hobbit house."

"Yes, we like being only half underground – although you know we did it mostly for the energy savings," she said, for the north and east sides and most of the roof were earth sheltered, and the south and west faced the winter and afternoon sun. "You know, Eli says he's not some kind of survivalist nut, but how do you explain the extra thousands of liters of water in a holding tank in case the water system is out – not counting the two hundred liters in the *dud shemesh*?" Natalie said. "I don't know, maybe he was a realist after all." She thought about another of his environmentalist toys: the 12-volt solar system Eli had installed for lights and his laptop. "I should see if it's working," she thought. "Eli used to read all those survivalist books and articles, even though he said Y2K was a bunch of hype."

Natalie went to the utility closet in the back hallway and threw some switches. Small, energy efficient reading lamps went on by their bedside and on Eli's desk. "I'll leave only the desk lamp on to save the batteries," she said. There were six automobile batteries wired in the back of the closet along with the gadget that regulated the rooftop panel's charging of the batteries. She knew little about the system, except that Eli was very proud of it, and she was reassured to see a calm amber ready light glowing at the back of the closet.

"Y2K. I remember all that nonsense too," Tali said. "Yisrael was all worried about all the billing and health records being wiped out, and insisted on saving paper copies of everything for at least three years before. It drove me crazy. I think we still have a fireproof file drawer of the stuff somewhere. Yisrael never throws anything away."

They lapsed into silence for a long time, each listening to the boom and crash of rocket fire. Some must be hitting the moshav now; they were so close. Without radio or sirens, how would they know what to do? The whole community could be overrun by Syrian commandos and there they would be, sipping warm mugs of tea and worrying.

What if Eli didn't make it home this time? Natalie reached for her *Tehillim*. Psalm 130 for times of trouble. "From the depths I call to you…" it began. She felt in complete harmony with King David's plea. How many wives and mothers in Israel prayed that psalm tonight? In some quiet place in her heart, she knew Eli was alive – very much alive and doing what he thought right, as he always did. She knew he had been disappointed to make aliyah too late in life to serve in the IDF like his childhood dreams. Now he was out there playing Israeli soldier for real.

Somehow she had never had the same kind of idealistic relationship with Israel. It had been completely abstract to her until their first trip together, when their youngest daughter was learning Hebrew in a kibbutz here and talking about settling permanently. Israel was a name you prayed, a headline in the paper, a picture postcard, or the only place where people throwing rocks was world news. Now it was a real place, full of real people; people she loved more the more she knew them, faults and human foibles and all. She was proud to be an Israeli citizen. It was something she had earned, rather than something she was born with. She knew Eli felt the same way. He had visited once in his youth on some summer program for teenagers that had taken him up and down the country for a few weeks, seeing and doing everything in a whirlwind of motion and activity that only the young can do. But then college, a career, a wife and family had deferred his dream until it seemed too late.

It was funny, but the half dozen English-speaking families in their moshav had all come to Israel at different times in their lives. The Ellmans had come just before the Yom Kippur war as a young couple just after college. The Auerbachs from South Africa came in their thirties. The Levines, both doctors from London, had arrived in their forties, just a little before themselves, and the Lushinskis were new arrivals in their late twenties from New York, now in their second year on the moshav.

But, at age forty-nine and fifty respectively, Natalie and Eli had taken a *cheshbon ha nefesh* – a spiritual accounting – the kind every Jew was supposed to do from the beginning of the month of *Elul* until the end of the holiday of *Sukkot* – but especially on the two days of Rosh Hashanah and on Yom Kippur. They had discussed it at great length and decided that Israel was where they wanted to be for the rest of their lives, living as Jews in their own land, learning to speak their own tongue (not so easy at fifty) and transplanting the seeds of their posterity to the land of their ancestors. Of course, both their mothers thought them crazy, but they knew both their late fathers would have approved deep down, though remonstrating mightily on the surface. There had been discussions almost ten years earlier, about making aliyah after the Gulf War, when their younger passions were stirred, and they wanted desperately to stand together with their people. But their fledgling businesses were just beginning to take off, their children settled happily in a life of schools and friends. Their parents had no intention of flying half way around the world to see grandchildren who were living happily a few blocks away. However, both *zeidies* – may they be remembered for good and for blessing – had been sympathetic about their ideals, but urged caution and deliberation.

And so, nearly ten years later, with much deliberation and a much clearer idea what they were doing, here they were. Eli was now able to conduct much of his communications consulting work over the Internet, with an occasional trip for meetings with clients or trade shows. Ten years ago that would have been nearly impossible. They even had two virtual phone numbers in Chicago, one for their eldest daughter Ruth and various friends to call, and one for Eli's business.

She knew he was very proud to be out there defending his adopted land and moshav, gun in hand, and shoulder to shoulder with the men he admired. These were the men he prayed with every day in the synagogue, the men he learned with two nights a week, and who he danced with at weddings, and sat with at funerals, and ate and drank with on Shabbat and holidays. It wasn't a macho thing. Though he was always quite the outdoorsman for a city boy, Eli was hardly what she called macho. He was more, what should she call it, idealistic. No, fifty-eight year olds had ideals but were not what you would call idealists. Principled, perhaps, although the term did not quite capture it. Moral was a stronger term which people of her morally relativist generation shied away from, but what else could you call it? Eli was a deeply moral person, very principled, thoughtful and decent, and these were the qualities that made her love him these past thirty-three years. And he not only loved Israel, its rocks and hills, sunlight and trees – he felt he belonged here in a profoundly spiritual way that it had taken Natalie many more years to begin feeling.

Somehow all this had become home. She found she could think of nowhere else she would rather be right now either. Her oldest daughter was married and living in Chicago a few miles from where Natalie had grown up and had lived most of her life. Now, she seemed more than half a world away. Natalie found it hard to picture herself anywhere but here. And so, if she had to die for being here – somehow that would be OK.

Northern Command, Mount Meron 0430

General Tchernikovsky was so tired that it took a few seconds for the situation to register. Either Israel had just been leveled in a nuclear holocaust – or all their sensors, radar and antennae had been blinded by a tactical burst and its accompanying mega pulse of electromagnetic radiation. Which was it? She put down the dead phone, glanced around the six shocked faces in the trailer and said, "I have to go topside and see what we have left up there. Everyone replay the last ten minutes of data we have and see what you can figure out."

"I'll go," Kobi volunteered, getting up from his console.

"No, I need you to run the data. I can't think straight until I see what's happening up there," she said. She paused at the door leading out of the trailer into their metal-lined cavern and addressed the room. "Anyone have any instruments working that can tell me if it's radioactive out there?" Everyone looked blank for a few moments, then a young woman spoke up.

"I'm pretty sure there are a couple of Geiger-counters in the emergency supplies stored down here. Let me help you find them," she said, getting up.

The two women exited the trailer, climbed down the concrete steps and went towards the living quarters section of their subterranean command post. Though carved out of limestone, the living quarters had been walled with sheetrock, everyday-looking tile floors and acoustic tile ceilings to look as normal as possible in case the team had to spend days or weeks in isolation. They were well supplied with what comforts the military could provide – and a few touches brought down during various training exercises over the years, such as a guitar, some framed poster-sized prints of pastoral scenes of Israel, and a huge collection of junk food. They rummaged together in some of the supply closets and found a pair of battery operated Geiger counters. They tested the batteries and found them working. The counters registered only the occasional background clicks one would expect to find deep underground with perhaps a trace of radon or other elements that were part of the bedrock.

"You mind if I come with you?" the woman asked, "I can't concentrate either, and there seems to be no radar to watch at the moment." Anna agreed. During their rummage together, she had finally remembered the younger woman's name, Shiri, a casual, pretty and carefree seeming Israeli She was still working her way through a degree in something high tech. Shiri was part of the IDF's elite Talpiot program for scientifically and technically talented students. She would spend an extra few years in military service, but earn her advanced degree and draw a small stipend for her student years, while serving in strategic jobs like this underground command post in the breaks between semesters. Anna had largely ignored her since she was one of the many fresh faces that came and went in her military intelligence and strategic command group, but she found herself glad of the company as they went through the first set of blast-proof doors that led to the long sloping tunnel to the surface.

The pair of guards that should have been manning the cubbyhole of a security booth inside the outer blast door were not there, which was unfortunately not unusual. Being within a secure facility, the base commander did not consider guarding a tunnel from other Jewish soldiers much of a priority. They had not picked up any unusual radiation in the tunnel, which was not protected by the filtered, positive air pressure of the command bunker. They ran their Geiger counters around the seals of the big steel blast door. So far, so good. They turned the big wheel in the center of the door to release the steel rods that secured the edges of the door. When the rods had completely disengaged from their fitted slots, and the door moved a fraction outwards from the released pressure on its seals, they cautiously pointed the Geiger counters at the crack. Taking a deep breath and holding it instinctively, not consciously – they swung the door open and looked out into the predawn darkness with their Geiger counters held in front of them.

A pair of strong flashlights suddenly blinded them and then they heard laughter behind the lights. Their Geiger counters were quiet in their hands. All of a sudden they felt rather silly standing there holding their now superfluous Geiger counters after the lights snapped off,. Anna and Shiri laughed too, with more than a little relief. Israel was not bathed in lethal radiation – at least not at the moment. The two military police who had been assigned to watch the entrance of their bunker explained what little they knew.

"We were outside when the whole sky lit up with the first of the flashes," one explained, "so we closed the blast door but were stupid enough to stay outside. There were four, five, maybe six more – and we felt some kind of a shock wave. That's when all the lights went out – everywhere. We thought of coming back in, but decided we were probably fried anyway. Then you two came out a few minutes later. I'm glad to see that we are not toast after all," he nodded to the Geiger counters.

They stood a few minutes, talking in the warm summer night. Except for the lack of lights, it could be a normal night on Mount Meron. After the artificial cold of their air conditioned bunker, the warm night felt balmy, welcome and embracing. To the south they could see the distant sheen of moonlight on water that shown on the Kinneret. If they had not been at war, she could not imagine a more peaceful and romantic evening scene. Turning to look south and west, she could not see the normal amber urban glare of the city lights. Anna could not see Haifa and the coast behind her over the crest of the mountain top directly, but she had stood there enough nights in all weathers to feel the absence of its amber glow. Although there were not many lights normally showing at night in the mountain top complex which was home to the northern air defense command and various intelligence, communications and strategic command groups, it seemed oddly dark. And, where the lights of Tzfat, Meron, Canaan and the neighboring towns should be, there was only darkness. Not even the headlights of an early morning car or truck appeared on the highway that wrapped through the hamlet of Meron – known mostly for having the tomb of the great sage and kabbalist Rabbi Shimon Bar-Yochai.

Anna told the two young soldiers that they had just tracked a dozen missiles from Iran. Half appeared to have been hit by the Arrow III defense, and the rest seemed to have exploded in the upper atmosphere – causing a catastrophic nuclear electromagnetic pulse, which is what happened to their lights and radios.

Anna sent one of the young men to go check in with the base commander and suggest that he come meet with their group in the electromagnetically protected command center. She told the other to stay by the outer blast door and close it at the first sign of incoming rockets. She and Shiri made their way back down the long tunnel to see what they could do with the information they had. She realized on the way that they probably now had the only working computers in the whole of northern Israel, unless the universities in Haifa or one of the high tech defense industries had an EMP proof room. That was a scary thought.

They got back to the trailer just as the group was coming to the end of their second playback of the final ten minutes of data. Four of the five men were concentrating on the details flashing by on their screens, and one was listening intently on a pair of earphones. Anna waited until they finished, and told them that it was not radioactive topside.

"Let's start fifteen minutes back and replay it with the radar data this time," Kobi suggested. Anna agreed and volunteered to monitor another group of the military radio frequencies. She took another pair of earphones, searched until she found the section of data and channels she wanted, and waited for Kobi to give the signal to start the replays.

For the next fifteen minutes she concentrated on the chatter of urgent commands passing back and forth among various missile defense commands and field units. She heard the Arrow teams getting their incoming coordinates from SatCom, and the various advanced David's Sling, Patriot and Iron Dome intermediate and short range batteries coming on the channel for their targeting information, which she knew was also being flashed digitally to their battlefield tactical computers. Except for the strain in the voices – audible even when scrambled and descrambled – it could have been a drill. She heard confirmation of the first hits of the incoming missiles, launches of the intermediate range counter missiles, and then nothing as their playback ended abruptly. Even though she had just lived through those fifteen minutes already, perhaps an hour ago, she was still shocked and unsettled at the abrupt silence.

Everyone was quiet, exiting their playback programs and checking one more time for any new telemetry from the surface. Anna swiveled around in her typists chair and gestured for everyone to do the same. It was time to compare notes and share their analysis and ideas. The computer jocks reluctantly shifted their seats around to face away from their screens. Data they could handle; face-to-face, well, everyone was more than a little uncomfortable. Anna had to admit she was a bit of a gear head geek herself, but she needed the bigger picture. She asked Kobi to start. He had now replayed the events twice, and as a major and ex reconnaissance pilot in the air force, he was the next highest ranking officer present.

Kobi fiddled with a pen as he talked, but once talking, found he had a lot to say. "Definitely tactical nukes designed for EMP," he said, "which means they were bought from the Ukraine or one of the former Soviet republics. Because Iran could not be nearly that far along, or North Korea either. They were spaced well enough to knock out the whole country – even Eilat. I think there were two over the Negev, at least two over Tel Aviv and the center, and one or two in the Haifa area. I have no idea of megatonnage – except that there was enough to knock us out – and we estimated at least 1.5 mega tons within 30 kilometers was the minimum it would take to shut us down. Five or six going off in sequence like that is not something we ever were able to simulate in the models. But, even figuring a mathematical progression, not something exponential..." He veered off on a highly technical tangent before drawing himself back to the point. "Of course, that's all theoretical – the fact is we're pretty much blind, deaf and dumb at the moment. We're not going to be able to do much here even with working power and the computing equipment we have. No one can hear us out there until they get the emergency radios delivered out to the field commands. Even the hard line to Dimona and MissileCom is out."

Mendel agreed with the chain of events, but thought they should be able to get through to the other two EMP-protected command centers and missile com by radio. He had been trying to raise them on a variety of frequencies after checking to see that the relays to their topside transmitters were indeed operating. "Also, checking AM radio channels, I can hear normal music and civilian broadcasts from Cyprus, Greece and Italy – maybe even Turkey. I couldn't tell – but nothing from Cairo, Damascus, Amman or Baghdad. I'll see if I can pick up the BBC Europe newscast at 0430 here in a few minutes." It had been more than an hour since the EMP. "In the meantime, I'm getting some increasing traffic from the US Navy and Air Force, but it's all too well scrambled to make out."

Anna frowned. Ever since the last time Israel had to go in and clean up the radical scum that had turned the Gaza Strip into a playground for Hamas and even more extreme anti-Israeli groups, the US/Israeli military cooperation had chilled noticeably. And besides, the US Department of Defense no longer had truckloads of money and toys to hand out to its friends ever since withdrawing from Iraq and the start of the worldwide recession. However, she had been to see her counterparts at NORAD and Space Command in Colorado Springs, and met with various NATO command groups in Europe. She knew they would be on the edge of their seats at this very moment trying to figure out what had just happened to Israel.

Avraham went next, interpreting the electronic data he had scanned from the super secure defense data network. He agreed with the launch sequences for the Arrow and Iron Dome missile defenses, noted the scrambling of four flights of F-16s from Ramat David, plus said he had seen coded messages authorizing two flights of interceptors from Negev bases. "But what is really interesting is the traffic on the strategic missile command net. I'm pretty sure I saw launch codes validated and acknowledged there – but I'll have to know something more about their cryptography to know for sure."

Shiri jumped in at this point, "I watched the Negev radar feeds along side ours, and I'm pretty sure I saw outbound tracks from the deep silos. I'll show you," She clicked through a number of screens and command sequences until she isolated one of the feeds from a radar site south of the Rimon crater. The onscreen timer showed 0319 GMT+2. "This is the Midbar Zin site," she said, orienting them to various landmarks superimposed on another layer of the screen. "Now, watch here," she pointed to a blip showing a hard return to the radar beam. They watched as the green smudge moved between sweeps of the beam. It appeared to be accelerating – and Shiri opened up a small box showing supplemental data on altitude and velocity of the object. It appeared to be rising and accelerating quickly.

Anna looked at Kobi and Avraham. "Ballistic missile from CounterStrike-Com?" They nodded in agreement. "Look, there's another one," Anna pointed to a second blip now leaving a trace at another spot swept by the rotating radar beam. They all watched as a third blip appeared, apparently on a completely different trajectory. "If the first two are Iran, the third must be Damascus. It's time to find the latest CounterStrikeCom CD and see what was in the silos."

Anna and Kobi used separate keys to unlock a floor safe under the printer and pulled out a slim, loose-leaf notebook with a large red sticker on the cover, checked the date on the title page, and took one of the data discs out of its protective sleeve and inserted it in a little-used PC that stood alone and isolated from their network. Mendel was twirling dials and listening to two separate earphones. He had a speaker on low playing popular music, waiting for the BBC newscast to come on the air of the commercial station that could have been anywhere in Europe or the Middle East, for it was playing an American oldie "Bye, Bye Miss American Pie." The rest watched impatiently for the computer to boot and find the newly inserted disk. While the various screens and prompts came to life, they heard the beginning of the BBC news. The lead story was about some encouraging movements in the London and Amsterdam stock exchanges the previous day, and a discussion of the strengthening of the pound and the dollar against the euro. Obviously the news had not reached any of their participating news bureaus or stringers yet. Odd, a whole country could disappear off the electronic grid for an hour and nobody noticed…. Or had they?

When the computer was finally reading the CounterStrikeCom CD, and they had skimmed through enough information to select the right sections, they flipped through screens of protocols and counterstrike options until they had centered on the missile groups within radar range of the Midbar Zin station. Shiri played back the radar data until they could see all three launch tracks clearly and froze the screen. Then they consulted the maps and coordinates on the CounterStrikeCom data.

"Silos one and two were targeted with tactical airbursts to take down Iranian command and control electronics. Silo three was fired towards the Syrian strategic command – which is located at the other side of the country as far as possible from Israel. Unless they malfunctioned or were intercepted, Iran and Syria are as blind as we are," Anna announced. "Silo four does not show a launch – and that was aimed at Jordanian air command, while five, six and seven were aimed at Egyptian air defenses and strategic weapons." To make sure, they ran the data from the Sde Boker and Ramat Rav radar sites – and saw nothing else outbound.

Eli found himself thinking about his orchard. Somehow he knew Natalie was safe, and that Rivka and the grandkids were safe in Jerusalem. He had no idea where Rivka's husband, Yoni, was right now. His job in the army was too secret for him to talk much about it, but Eli knew it had a lot to do with advanced electronics and remote surveillance. Those kinds of command sites should be fairly well hardened, although at the moment they were probably quite useless. No, he was wondering if any of the shells and shrapnel had torn through his 40-odd young trees and grapevines – a few dates, almonds figs, pomegranates, and grapevines, the species the Bible mentions in praise of the beauty of the land of Israel, and some oranges, lemons, grapefruit, clementinas, cherries, apples, pears and kiwi fruit. They grew on the sunny south side of their house, all fed by drip irrigation and screened from the north winds that could scour the Golan in winter. The trees turned four years old this past spring. Early that summer, he and their whole family had celebrated their first fruits – *bikkurim*. Ruthie brought her husband and kids to visit from America, and one of the grandmothers, Natalie's mom, had come in spite of the travel warnings. Together they celebrated the end of the four-year wait to harvest the fruits of their trees. They held picnics on their patio, and a *Kiddush* for the whole *Shul*. The trees were now barely more than head high, but nearly all were bearing fruit.

He had never cared for gardening or planting much more than home grown tomatoes in Chicago. Here in Israel, he found digging in the rich, rocky (and in the rainy season, terribly muddy), black soil of the Golan deeply satisfying. More than anything, he wanted to pass this orchard along to the grandchildren, G-d willing.

"And everyone beneath his vine and fig tree, shall live in peace and unafraid, and nation shall not lift up sword against nation, and they shall beat their swords into plowshares, and they shall study war no more." He found himself humming the popular English-Hebrew song he knew to those words from way back in his days as a conservative Jew growing up and going to summer camp in Wisconsin. He vowed he would set up a hammock under the fig tree someday when it was big enough to bear the strain – if he and the fig tree lived so long.

He thought all this while scanning the farthest he could see into the smoke and reddening dawn with his spotter scope. The artillery shells were coming from the east and slightly to the north of their moshav. It made sense. There was a broad series of rolling valleys, perhaps only 100 meters in relief from crest to trough that ran northeast to southwest and would be the natural lines of advance in their rougher part of the Golan. South of them it flattened into almost a plain, but one that broke off and dropped down to the southern end of the Kinneret where the Jordan river began again on its journey to disappear into the Dead Sea miles away down the Jordan valley. He thought he saw something moving – and focused on the spot. The backlighting from the now rising sun made it hard to see, but it looked like a giant bulldozer. It must be sweeping mines for an advance. He signaled to Joshie, Gadi and Misha who were trying out various combinations of hiding places. He gave the sign they had worked out for "enemy in sight," and pointed off to the northeast. Then he realized that they would never be able to see what he could see more than two or three kilometers away with his spotting scope.

He saw them wave back at him – and motion – pointing to the ridge behind him. He was startled, was there a commando patrol sneaking up behind him? But no, their gestures seemed friendly and seemed to be directed at someone joining them. He edged his automatic pistol out of its holster and scrambled to where he could peek behind and above the broken ledge of rock that sheltered him. He could see a team of four regular IDF soldiers lugging gear up to the end of the ridge. He recognized what looked like a pair of surveyor's transits, like the ones he borrowed to lay out his foundations and driveway. He edged, crab-like and stiff out of his burrow and went to greet them. He felt confident since the artillery barrage had concentrated on their moshav and points south and farther west, leaving their ridge almost untouched.

They greeted him briefly and noted where the moshavnik bazooka team was below and nodded with approval. He couldn't remember the Hebrew word for sniper, but mimed aiming a rifle and pointed out his spot under the outcropping. They smiled at his pantomime and told him that they would be spotting for the moshav's mortar teams as well as the artillery. He also pointed out the direction where the distant bulldozer had appeared. They were aware of that too. They busily set up a spotter scope and began measuring off a 100-meter baseline between the two tripod-mounted transit scopes. They jockeyed the tape and end points until satisfied that they were perpendicular enough to the target, and that each had a decent size boulder for cover.

Eli felt guilty watching their industry and returned to his fox holes at the end of the ridge. He took up his spotter scope and began to systematically scan the landscape to the north. His momentary scare about commandos made him extra careful. But his attention was not what it could be – he had been up for what? More than two hours without coffee? He thought longingly of his coffee grinder and selection of gourmet coffee beans at home, one of his morning passions. Alas, no coffee…. Ah, but he did have a couple dark chocolate bars in his rucksack for just such an occasion. He rummaged in the pocket of the pack and devoured one outright – leaving the other for his next caffeine fix after lunch – assuming he lived through lunch time. All of sudden that did not seem like a given fact.

Reenergized by the chocolate, a long drink of water and those thoughts, he returned to scanning the wide swath of land to their north, checking on the progress of the giant dozer and its column of what must be tanks behind it. On his third check, he noticed that shell bursts were beginning to appear around it – the howitzers on the Moshav must have sighted in and found their range. All of a sudden the contest felt a little more equal. He could see black smoke rising from a few points in the confused mass behind the advancing mine sweeper. He had to force himself to return to his methodical sweep. This was no time to be caught by surprise.

His back and forth, up and down sweep had just reached the most prominent ridge far to the north of the Moshav when he noticed movement this side of the ridge. A tank was running along the near side of the ridge – much too far away to make out, just a crawling spec of motion. It must be ten kilometers from him – maybe more. There was a late Bronze Age town site up that way that was at least eight kilometers from the Moshav and the ridge was beyond it, very near the border. He liked to take overseas guests there in his 4-wheel drive pickup for picnics – to show them remains of an ancient synagogue, *mikveh* and an olive press that showed how Jews had lived in these hills for more than 2,500 years. Then he saw a couple more tanks join the lone speck. They were jockeying up to the ridge line and firing. Might they be Israelis? They looked dark and flat like Merkavas, but it was just too far away to tell. He watched, fascinated as they pulled up to the ridge together, then spun and raced down his side of the ridge, disappearing into a wadi that split the ridgeline.

As he tried to spot them again, he noticed movement on the ridge – three or four, more, six, eight, ten, maybe more ant-sized tanks appeared on the ridge – firing after the first group. They too descended towards the wadi and out of his line of sight. The first group must be Israelis! They were out numbered at least four to one. They definitely must have been IDF! He checked the minesweeper's advance and was happy to note it appeared to have been hit too and looked to be ablaze. He scrambled out of his lair and went to tell the artillery spotters his news of the tank force approaching from the north, with a possible four friendlies on the run in front of them. They were cheered by the news and began to relay it to their commander via their blinkered lights. "Glad we had these artifacts packed away in the trucks – never thought we would use them in wartime," one of them told him.

The sun was now well up, but the day seemed dim with all the smoke from cannon fire, bursting shells and burning brush and trees. It suffused the thundering landscape with a reddish haze, suggesting more a smoggy sundown than a fresh sunrise. It was past 6:30 and he returned to his watching. Gadi came up to join him, and to gab with the artillery spotters, leaving Joshie and Misha to lurk in their hiding spot among the boulders. Eli told him about the tank chase over the ridge to the north of them, and showed him where they had disappeared through the spotting scope. He agreed that the ridge was at least 10-12 km away, recalling various landmarks he knew in between. They both hoped the IDF tanks would get away from their pursuers and come and join up with the moshav defense line. They estimated that they might be seeing them within the hour. Although there was a tremendous old mine field between them, there were cleared pathways through it that the IDF must know.

They chatted companionably as they both swept their quadrants of terrain, Gadi with his binoculars, Eli with his spotting scope. They marveled at the absence of aircraft – no jets, no helicopters, not even any UAV's, the unmanned drones that had been buzzing the borders on constant patrol. They figured the EMP had knocked out the Syrian air force unexpectedly, because it made no sense to nuke your own air force if you are going to start a war. Maybe they had been stationed at the far side of the country and were to be flown up for the assault? No, it was less than a half hour's flying time from anywhere in Syria to the Golan. The border had been breached at 5:20 that morning at the latest, so that did not add up. Perhaps though, everyone was working like crazy to put new electronics in the planes and they would be up before the day was out. That was a frightening thought. Attack helicopters and armed MiG fighters in addition to artillery and rockets? They would not stand a chance.

Their attention was drawn back to the main column to the east. Although the huge bulldozer, and another just like it appeared to have been knocked out, there were now smaller units moving forward at the head of the column. These were faster than the big bruiser, and much closer. They were within two kilometers or closer. Eli and Gadi were starting to receive a different kind of fire on their ridge in the past few minutes, possibly tank shells. Someone must have spotted them. Gadi returned to the anti-tank team, sprinting down the slope to the cover of the boulder field.

Eli switched over to his sniper rifle. Two kilometers was extreme range for a 7.62 mm. bullet, but not impossible, and the range was closing every minute. He had sighted in the rifle for 500 meters, so he would be aiming high and guessing at this range. Nevertheless, he would start choosing his targets and open fire when he thought there was even a prayer of hitting something. Eli adjusted his scope and studied the nearest advancing minesweepers. They looked like cut-down, turret-less tanks pushing some sort of roller a few meters in front of their path. He searched for open hatches, commanders or drivers peering out, or for any infantrymen trudging along behind them. They were buttoned up tight. He might try to ping a periscope or antenna, but it seemed futile. He turned his attention to the growing mass of shapes behind them, mostly obscured in the smoke and dust of their passage. Immediately behind the sweepers were huge, ugly-looking, menacing tanks. He now could see them firing every now and then. They too were buttoned up. Nothing much for a sniper to work on. He scanned along the near flanks of the advance – looking for anything.

Then he saw, on a bit of a rise to the left, behind and somewhat clear of the mass of armored vehicles, what looked like a humvee with tiny figures in the turret – and several more on the ground clustered around what? He squinted and waited for a break in the smoke – some sort of tripod. That was it! Artillery spotters, just like the four behind him. He eased a round into the chamber, closed the bolt and began his relaxation routine, evening out his breathing, letting his shoulders and arms loosen and relax into an easy grip. He studied the cluster and chose the figure who appeared behind the scope. He took in an easy breath and let half of it out and then gently squeezed the trigger. The bang and recoil took him almost by surprise, he had done such a good job of relaxing. He shrugged his shoulder loose again and worked the bolt to chamber another round. This time he looked for the one who appeared to be relaying messages from the tripod to the humvee. He caught him moving toward the tripod, waited a moment until he paused, and then squeezed off another round. He automatically worked the bolt to chamber another round and settled in to see if he could hit the man in turret. There was no man in the turret. He swung back to the group at the tripod. Two were clustered around a fallen figure, the others moving towards the vehicle. He aimed at one of the crouching figures, he felt no pity whatsoever. He fired again, and again, and soon the vehicle was moving off to join the mass of the main column, but not before Eli was sure he had landed a round in its broad windshield.

He wiped his brow, wiped his eyes and was surprised to feel a sharp bruise on his right cheekbone. He had been hunched too far over the stock and must have taken a recoil. Eli went back to scanning the edges of the column for anything unprotected in the mass of armor – a window, an antenna, even a tire. He fired at the side window of a halftrack and the windshield too – knowing that a spidery crack of a high powered bullet would be unnerving at the least, and might even make it yield to a future shot.

He fell into the rhythm of shooting, fully absorbed in his work until he had shot all four 10-round clips and had to reload them from the boxes in his pack. He had four boxes of 50 rounds in his pack – and he had just shot 40 rounds in what, ten minutes? Probably less. He told himself to slow down and wait for softer targets. The column was much closer now, under 1,000 meters and beginning to fan out to form a broad front of armor facing the Moshav.

He couldn't tell the difference between the moshav's mortars and the IDF's howitzer shells, except that both were falling among the approaching tanks and scoring hits every few minutes. He prayed that his artillery spotter friends were safe with little but a waist high boulder each to protect them, and that the four howitzers and the moshav's mortar teams, were safe. The mortar teams worked from deep pits dug near the middle of the moshav, screened by houses and trees and camouflage nettings. Each had earthen bunkers for their shells. But still they were vulnerable to the tremendous rain of shells that had been falling on his home for hours now. "Forget your orchard, pray for the people," he told himself.

With his four newly loaded clips he went back to work, slowly, deliberately, cold-bloodedly scanning the approaching army for any weak points, any foot soldiers or exposed bodies. Now he was finding them. Infantry was advancing between the tanks and moving out ahead of the minesweepers. He could hear the staccato ratta tata tata of machine guns on both sides adding to the din. He was sure he caught more than one machine gunner firing from hatchways. No time or reason to keep count. They kept coming. In spite of his deliberation, he worked through his second 40 rounds in even less time. He loaded as fast as he could and concentrated on those closest to his corner of the moshav. He could hear automatic rifles above him now. Perhaps they had reinforced the artillery spotters, or better yet, moved them. A tremendous crash with an immediate Karooooom! stunned him, the blast slamming his head to the earth. Dirt and rock fragments sprayed his head and shoulders. Something big had hit his outcropping of rock. He spat dirt and rock from his mouth, brushed at least a handful of earth out of his beard, straightened his helmet, wiped the dirt out of his eyes and had to pause to clean his glasses. He was now quite deafened to the roar of battle around him. He had to stop shaking before he could check his telescopic sight and start firing again.

Shifting his position away from the blasted section of rock, he resumed his deadly sniping. A few times there was a splatter of rock fragments as bullets hit above his head. He just concentrated harder on his targets. At one point he noticed the flash of a rocket launched below and to his right. Gadi, Misha and Joshie must have fired one of their bazooka rounds. Raising his eyes in the direction of its trail, he was shocked to see a pair of tanks suddenly very close, with their turrets aimed in his direction. He blinked and hugged the earth, clinging to his rifle and praying silently. Two tongues of flame spewed from the menacing barrels and almost at the same moment he felt the earth heave below him, and a tremendous boom above him. Half his overhang caved in, nearly burying his rucksack. Another rocket flashed away below him and burst against the turret of the nearest tank. Almost simultaneously a shell burst in front of it, and another burst right on it. The now burning tank stopped in its tracks while the other swung its turret down and right. Desperate, Eli raised his rifle and fired at the black box he guessed might be a periscope for the driver. He chambered a new round and searched the now-magnified, monstrous looking tank for any chink in its armor. He spotted something else that looked like an optical sight on the turret beside the cannon barrel and fired.

Another spew of flame burst from the tank's cannon and the short snout of a machine gun began to spit fire in his direction. The flash of a third rocket shot away and the machine gun port was engulfed in flame and smoke. Eli saw a topside hatch fly open and he prepared to shoot anyone emerging. They did, and he did, and whoever it was suddenly wasn't. He heard small arms fire rattling all around, and he went back to work shooting advancing figures, stopping their blazing rifles and dropping whoever he could hit. He did not have much practice with moving targets, so those coming directly towards him fared the worst. He was down to his last clip when he realized he needed to crawl into the back of the half-demolished overhang to reach his pack. He fired, inched backwards, and fired again. Bullets dug furrows into the dirt near his leg and he wormed quickly backwards and deeper into the overhang to reach his rucksack.

In spite of the flying bullets and approaching enemy, he couldn't stop himself from taking a long drink from the water bottle he found first before reaching one of his cartridge boxes. He rolled over and fired once again before cradling his rifle while loading an empty clip, keeping low and looking up from moment to moment to make sure no one was charging toward him. He finished loading the clip and emptied what was left of his current magazine in five quick shots. He slapped the fresh clip home and started loading the one he just emptied before firing again. He felt completely alone although he could sense the returning fire above and below him. In this way he reloaded the other three clips, tugged his knapsack to a more reachable spot and sought some better cover.

He continued to search, aim, fire and search like an automaton, nearly senseless of the falling shells. There were mortar shells falling now, he could tell from the incoming whine, as well as tank rounds and the occasional huge artillery burst. But by the time he was reloading his spent clips again, he started to notice that targets were harder to find. The advance was beginning to draw back, beaten off by the spirited fire of the moshav, backed up by whatever IDF units were in the neighborhood. In his next few clips he was picking at stragglers among the blackened and smoking shells of perhaps three or four dozen destroyed tanks and other vehicles that came in a burnt wave to within a few hundred yards of where he fired. Reloading again as he reached his last loaded clip, he drank some more water and dared to peer around the outcropping to search for his companions from the IDF. The top of his ridge was barely recognizable, a jumble of craters and rock that had once been a pastoral outcropping above a rolling, grassy and brushy hillock. He could see perhaps half a dozen riflemen and some sort of larger gun on a bipod where the spotters had been. Their tripods were gone. Good. They were pulled back in time.

He signaled to the nearest soldier who looked at him blankly. Then he noticed that the soldier was crouched beside someone who was not moving. He was shocked to see that death had reached just a few meters away unnoticed by him. Another pair was aiding a prone figure, who, thank G-d, was moving. Two more were still firing in semi-automatic mode – bang-bang, bang. Even in the heat of battle, the IDF was trained to fire in semi-automatic mode to save ammunition. Look, aim, fire, Look aim fire was the IDF mantra. The sad fact was that the whole country had perhaps two or three weeks of ammunition in reserve for an all-out war, and had to pray for re-supply from the US or NATO before that precious stock ran out. Palestinians and their Arab neighbors, on the other hand, loved to fire clip after clip in full automatic mode. You saw that in their training tapes and propaganda videos that saturated the Internet. Poor Palestinians indeed! If the IDF could not afford automatic fire – how could these poor oppressed Palestinians who always paraded with brand new RPG launchers and automatic weapons? "Explain that to me some day you bleeding heart BBC, PLO sympathizers," he muttered as he reloaded from his dwindling supply of bullets.

He slid backwards to his former spot and looked for the moshav team. He couldn't see them anywhere. He forced himself to focus on the retreating column but he found targets were getting even harder to find. They were now more than a kilometer distant and still moving sluggishly away. There was another smattering of burned and burning vehicles littering their retreat. However there were still incoming artillery shells bursting among the homes of the moshav. He could see shells bracketing the retreating army, indicating that more than one piece was still firing on their side. He looked at his watch. Almost 8 a.m. Most mornings he would just be returning from the 7 o'clock *minyan*, or else sitting in the study hall learning a chapter of *Mishnah* with Yisrael if it was a Monday or Thursday. What day was it? Monday? Yes, must be, he had worked yesterday, and the day before that was Shabbat. *Sukkot* starts tonight. He wondered if his frail sections of walls made from light plywood with wood frames bolted together in his side yard had survived the rain of fire – or his fruit trees for that matter. He longed to check in at home and see Natalie, and to be able to call Jerusalem to check up on Rivka and the grandkids. But he must wait until he was either completely out of shells or relieved.

Eli checked his pack and found he was well into his last box of 50 shells. What should he do? He wondered. He couldn't leave his post, but then what could he do with 30-40 rounds left? He could picture the dozen boxes in the ammunition drawer of the safe – locked with a key instead of a combination. He, Natalie and their son-in-law, and the Moshav defense committee had the only keys. Twelve times fifty – another six hundred rounds. At one time he could not imagine shooting that many rounds in a lifetime.

But then he realized with a start, he had never killed a man before. As that overwhelming fact began to sink in, he began to wonder "when did it happen – who was the first?" He remembered clearly the distant figures crouched around the fallen shape of the first man he shot. He felt only a sense of having done his job – no remorse, no lingering doubts.

He knew he had killed in the heat of battle, killed in defense of his friends and his home and family, and had killed without a second thought. Now there was time for thinking. He felt exhausted, physically, emotionally, and deeply tired. Although the day had grown hot, the sun was indistinct and invisible in the smoke and dense haze, as if the air reflected the numbness and weary confusion of his mind as it slid from the sharp awareness into a deep feeling of growing lethargy.

Eli had come of age as the Vietnam war was winding down, and arrived in Israel too old to join the IDF, even as a volunteer. In the weary moments as he waited for the next orders or renewed action, he found himself thinking about the first times he had ever handled a rifle. Eli had learned to shoot in order to hunt deer with a non-Jewish friend in the north woods of Michigan in his younger days. However, the stalking and the camping in the woods appealed more to Eli than watching his well-aimed bullet bring a living, breathing deer to the ground. And since he had started to keep kosher after the first two of their autumn hunts, there was no venison to be had as a reward for this marksmanship. He had given up hunting easily, and only occasionally missed it. He sold the second-hand hunting rifle years ago. It was nothing like the fine, precision instrument he cradled now.

He had never started out to be a sniper. He was really a backup person for one the moshav's two sniper rifles. Nachum and Udi's unit was called up at the beginning of summer, so Eli and another older moshavnik had been assigned the costly rifles. They had been bought with the same hush-hush funds that had supplied the extra mortar shells, and had been smuggled into the country in a chest freezer brought in a cargo container of household furniture. Twelve of the rifles had come in that freezer, he recalled two for each of the six religious moshavim in the Golan, along with some other contraband weapons and equipment.

And so, at fifty-eight, Eli was now a bloodied veteran of one hour and a half, though he had never been a soldier. He had never particularly wanted to be a soldier, though he had to admit that he was fascinated with reading about war – especially Israel's wars.

Eli was not sure how long he lay there, mechanically sweeping the burning landscape with his spotting scope, but seeing nothing alive. How many men had he killed today? He had shot more than two hundred rounds. Many of them at things – turrets, electronics, windows – but how many at men? And how many had hit home? Ten? Perhaps even twenty? Did one out of every ten bullets hit someone? He saw figures stagger, some fall, but how many? It didn't matter. There were more of them, and they would be coming again, perhaps in even greater numbers, determined not to fail. That was one thing he could be sure of.

He saw Gadi and Misha emerge from the boulders far from where he had last seen them. They had Joshie between them, his right leg wrapped in a blood soaked t-shirt. Gadi – who was much shorter – was struggling to keep his grip on the bazooka tube, while Misha had somehow combined two packs into one overflowing lump. Eli crawled out from his half-crumbled shelter and stiffly navigated his way down the slope to meet them. He was stiff all over, and he felt bruises where he had fallen that morning. His knees and back felt a hundred years old, but had backed off to perhaps only seventy or eighty by the time he reached the slow moving trio. He offered to take Gadi's place, or Misha's packs, but Gadi just handed him the launching tube and redoubled his efforts. Joshie looked pale but determined. Misha and Gadi looked plain exhausted. Eli was sure they made a pathetic sight, and sure enough, two young IDF soldiers scrambled down the ridge to take over Joshie. Gadi and Misha let them.

"Joshie was drawing the fire from the second tank so we could get a shot at it," Gadi explained. "He did too good a job of it – but we nailed it. He probably saved all our lives."

"Mine too," Eli said. "That machine gun was spraying all around me – a few more seconds and they would have hit me for sure."

"Looks like someone almost did," Misha said, pointing to a chunk blasted away from Eli's helmet. Eli felt his helmet for the first time, discovering a ragged chunk of its Kevlar reamed out. "I think that must have been flying rock when a shell blew away half my overhang," he said, recalling the stunning crash and falling rock and sand. Gadi told them how Joshie had bandaged himself with his shirt and kept firing until the column retreated out of range. Gadi and Misha had two rockets left out of what they started with – and figured they had hit two tanks and two armored personnel carriers – and that mortar fire from the moshav had finished off two more tanks and half a dozen more armored vehicles that had swung towards them to try to take the ridge. Had the remaining four tanks behind them kept coming instead of breaking off the engagement, there would have been not much left to stop them.

They all rested when they reached a sheltered place a little farther along the ridge, sipped water and compared notes with the half of an IDF platoon that had joined them. The other half had reinforced their companions farther back along the ridge. They had two seriously injured, three lightly wounded, and two dead.

Ten km Northeast of Moshav Yiftach 0500

Yankel's tank was well ahead by the time David's two MK IIs approached where the wadi widened into a broad upland plateau sloping gently away to the west. David recognized it as one of the huge pre-1967 minefields that was off limits for military training, hikers and jeepers alike.

He saw one of the familiar yellow and red signs dangling from a wire fence a few hundred meters ahead of them. Yankel was not stopping though. He drove straight for the fence as shells began to fall around him. Their pursuers must have left some tanks on the high ground above. But at the last minute, the tank slewed to the right and out of the observation hatch he saw a figure tossing smoke grenades and smoke-spewing mortar rounds. Under this limited cover, the tank sped down the fence line.

David knew Yankel well enough to know he had a plan, and that the best he could do was to follow at top speed. He yelled down the hatch for Greg to launch some smoke screen rounds from the mortar. Within seconds he heard the whoosh of a round from behind him. He motioned to Sasha and for *Gimmel* Two to follow Yankel. "Careful to follow his exact track!" he yelled. The helmet in the driver's hatch nodded. He had seen the minefield sign too.

Shells began to fall around them as they roared out from their wadi and sprinted for the fence, launching more smoke and dodging right. Fence posts whirled by, with one just ahead evaporating in a bang and showering them with rock and splinters as they sped by. He was sure they would be hit any moment as they flew down the track – Sasha was getting a good 40 kilometers per hour out of the engine now, but the shells followed relentlessly.

Suddenly he heard and felt something whoosh by in the smoke and dust – a tank round fired from someone on their level. Their turret, which had been facing the ridge above, swung around more to the left and he felt the cannon fire. Benny must have seen something in his bouncing sights. He looked where the wadi opened and saw two T-72s emerge. Their driver and commander were heads up too. He swung his machine gun to give them a burst. As he sprayed short bursts at the enemy, he was slammed backwards against the back of the hatch, nearly losing his footing except for his grip on the machine gun as his tank stopped suddenly. The tank then backed up, nearly colliding with the racing *Gimmel* Two, which dodged around them at the last moment. He could see Baruch pouring machine gun fire behind them as well. His driver looked confused, then recovered and banged the side of his helmet in the universal Israeli sign for crazy driver. David almost laughed, but the bruised ribs hurt too much. His tank then spun left and dived through the fence line. Turning for a moment, he could see they were following two fresh tracks into the minefield.

Benny chanced two more shots as they lurched through the minefield, moving slower in its rocky terrain, and Greg launched a couple more smoke-screen rounds behind them. David saw now that the two pursuing tanks had stopped at the edge of the minefield, joined now by three more, and all five were firing away at his fleeing tanks. Yankel was nowhere to be seen now, but he must not be too far ahead of them. He concentrated on the five now stationary tanks – and fired bursts at their hatches and turrets as best he could, but aim was nearly impossible they were lurching so. He suddenly realized that they were presenting an almost full side profile to the tanks that had stopped head on to the minefield.

In a clearing bit of smoke, for some of their smoke rounds had landed in front of the phalanx of tanks at least partly obscuring their view, he saw one of them erupt into flames. There was no way his two fleeing tanks could have made a hit like that, not without their electronics – Yankel must have found a hiding spot and started firing. Sure enough, about thirty seconds later, another hit registered on a second Syrian tank – blowing the treads away on one side and tilting it crazily. He saw the remaining three move forward to follow down the fence line in pursuit, and another group of five emerge from the wadi, cannons flashing with flame and smoke. David swung his machine gun to concentrate his fire along the now exposed side of the lead tank. The turret below him shook with the blast of a heavy round going outbound.

Their tank slowed abruptly and then pitched steeply down an embankment, slammed into level ground again and spun left. The enemy disappeared from sight, replaced by the banks of a narrow gully. The sides were so close that the turret and gun had to remain facing backwards, there was not enough room to swivel them to either side. *Gimmel* Two came slamming down the same caved-in portion of earthen gully wall behind them. He turned around to face forward. The gully was less than six or seven meters deep, but grass and bushes laced it edges, clinging to whatever dirt they could, not prepared to give into erosion yet. Ahead he could see the back end of Yankel's tank sticking out into the gully where it was overhung by trees. So this was Yankel's hidey hole. Sasha pulled up cautiously close behind Yankel, but saw there was no room to pass and stopped. David quickly signaled *Gimmel* Two to remain stopped where it had entered the gully. Their turret and cannon would be stuck uselessly like his if they tried to enter the narrow gully behind him.

He climbed stiffly out of his hatch and banged on the crew door of Yankel's tank – then, feeling silly, he opened it and climbed in. The loader was just picking up a new round and looked at him with surprise, then relief, and went back to his loading. In the gunner's seat a figure was concentrating on the eyepiece of the optical sight. He could see Yankel's feet and lower half in the commander's hatch. He moved to the rungs and firestep of the observation hatch on the left side of the turret, opened the hatch and emerged to the left of Yankel, whose wiry aggressive form was intent with his binoculars, but acknowledged his presence with a short, rude hand signal that meant "just a second." David took in their position as he waited a few long seconds. He could see why Yankel had picked this spot. It was well screened by brush and overhanging trees. Their cannon barely cleared the ground level ahead of them, its long barrel almost resting in the grassy edge of the gully. Perfect cover.

He saw the first of the three lead tanks edge into the minefield nearly a kilometer away, and then appear to gain confidence and speed as it followed their obvious track ahead. The second one swung in behind, and then the third. The other five tanks, and now a few armored troop carriers as well had drawn themselves up in a semi-circle where they had emerged from the wadi facing the minefield, looking for a target that had just mysteriously disappeared from sight. Higher on the ridge, which they had left before they had disappeared down their wadi, he could see another group of five commanding the heights, while another cluster of tanks and armored vehicles appeared to be pressing their way down the ridge, perhaps to rejoin the main column. He heard the whoosh of the mortar tube and followed the arc of a shell headed toward the five standing tanks. Before it hit, he heard the whoosh of another. A burst of smoke obscured part of the group, then another – and Yankel's 120 mm cannon fired a second later. He saw the last tank to enter the minefield erupt in flames. Damned good shooting!

Two seconds later, he heard the boom of *Gimmel* Two firing, and saw a crippling hit on the first of the three pursuers. The middle tank was now trapped between two crippled tanks in the midst of a minefield. Another mortar round whooshed away to add to their smokescreen. Yankel was being careful not to be seen by the main group while he picked off the middle tank with his second shot. But what about the five on the ridge – had they spotted them? As the smoke cleared away from the cluster of tanks and APCs at the foot of the wadi, he could almost feel their surprise – in the form of their immobility. G-d if he just had a chance to run and shoot like a Merkava should, those five would be cinders in five minutes, and their five APCs with them. Yankel was studying them too, and also taking in the group on the ridge – they were a good three or four kilometers away. They might have missed the whole show, it happened so fast. They were also motionless and presenting tempting targets – but not for optical sights. They would not survive long enough to range in with three or four shots to find the distance and bearing.

"Nice shooting Yankel," David said. Yankel's grin looked more grim than gleeful, and David realized that Yankel had just lost seven out of the eight tanks of his company – and that he, David, was now missing half his platoon of four. He had seen *Gimmel* Three in flames, hit from the rear where it was most vulnerable. Could they have saved the driver? he wondered – but there had been no time. They had to keep running or join their fate. And *Gimmel* Four, with Boris and the Humvee crew was trapped behind, and must be assumed to be dead or captured. The weight of the loss came crashing down on him too. They stood in their respective hatches, watching the enemy and thinking their own thoughts. Finally, Yankel spoke, his voice hoarse and cracked.

"We can stay here until nightfall if you can get your two under better cover. Dudu and I," his voice choked – Lt. Dudu Singer was his number two – probably in the tank his *Gimmel* four had stopped to help, "Dudu and I sat out the Golan VI exercises in this spot, and that was when everyone on the red team had full electronics. We have to kill our motors though."

David suddenly realized that the tank had shuddered to a stop and had been quiet for the past two minutes as he had been absorbed in his thoughts. He realized that he had noticed it at the time but thought nothing of it. Now he thought back to the confused melee of their jump-starting tanks that had begun this day's slaughter, and felt the horror of being trapped again.

As if he read his thoughts, Yankel said, "we may have to walk out if we can't restart. We have only six rounds left anyway. Though my driver has an idea he thinks might work without the tow or slope.

"Sasha figured something out to get us going without help this morning from a stationary start in the dug in spot – he thinks there's at least one more start left. I'll send him over with instructions as soon as we're settled in. Keep an eye out a minute while I look for better cover," he said, and climbed back down and exited the way he came.

Studying the gully more carefully as he walked back, he saw that if they backed up about fifteen meters, they would be in a narrow, deep part of the gully that would be secure if they rolled out the camo netting over the top of the tank and could drag some branches and brush over them. Of course their main gun would still be pointed to the rear and useless. He consulted with Sasha at his hatch, told him the plan and directed him to back up very slowly, being careful not to blow bursts of exhaust skyward. Sasha maneuvered the tank backwards as if parallel parking a compact car and killed the engine. The crew set about covering their machine as David walked down to *Gimmel* Two.

Gimmel Two had already backed gingerly away from the crushed side of the gulley where they had entered and were beyond it in a deeper part of the ravine, looking for a place to park. He walked around and eyed the narrow gully. Perhaps if they dug out a bit of loose dirt on the side they could nestle under a partly overhanging wall. He climbed up and consulted with Baruch – who had been eyeing the very spot. Both of them climbed down and grabbed shovels from the roll of camouflage netting behind the turret. The gunner and loader emerged from the crew hatch, armed with trenching tools and the four of them set to work on the soft dirt, slinging it away and digging just enough for the near side track to embed itself in the soft earth.

The hard work felt good and mindless, and they were done within minutes. Baruch's driver quickly edged the big machine next to the partly overhanging bank. They had judged it closely, and the turret bumped down a rain of loose dirt as it bashed against the side. The driver killed the engine and in the deafening silence, the crew fell to work unfurling the camouflage netting. David walked back to his tank a few dozen meters away, now covered by an increasingly brushy covering net as Sasha, Benny and Greg flung whatever brush and bunches of grass they could wrest from the gully floor on top, being sure to stay out of view of the hill and wadi beyond them. He checked with Sasha to find out the time. It was just after seven in the morning. Their nightmare had been going on since three-thirty – and in the last hour and a half they had lost nine out of twelve tanks. David's group of twenty-four men, four tanks and a humvee was now eight men and two tanks. Yankel had gone from a full platoon of forty men, counting spotters and a communications humvee -- to four men and a tank, with six rounds of ammunition left, hiding in a gully somewhere in the middle of a huge minefield. And there were eleven hours of daylight to go. The war could be over by the time the sun went down.

David told his two crews to set up watches and make some breakfast as soon as they were hidden as well as a tanker's art could hide them. He and Sgt. Harel went to confer with Yankel. They found him heaping branches and brush on his already well-hidden tank. David told Baruch to slither up to the edge of the gully and take in their position while he helped the other crew dress their camouflage netting for a few minutes. He could tell that Yankel was relieved to have something physical to do as he wove branches and stalky head-high grasses into the camo netting. Then he joined Baruch at his observation spot under the thick branches of a tree that grew half in the gully.

Together they watched the two groups of enemy armor. The group at the mouth of the wadi had sought some cover where they could survey the minefield, and two of the armored personnel carriers had gone down to see what happened to the three smoking wrecks of their pursuing tanks. Up on the ridge, it appeared that the other tank group was moving out to join the main column over the ridge. That was a relief. Yankel joined them as they watched the last of the specks disappear over the ridge. Now that it was quiet and their ringing ears had become attuned to the silence, they could hear heavy shelling some kilometers away to their south and behind them. Presumably the other group had gone to join that fight, leaving the five tanks and five APC's to deal with the three Israeli tanks that had disappeared into the landscape. In a normal war, that would be better than even odds for David and Yankel, but this was not a normal war.

After each sweeping a sector to cover 360 degrees around them, they found nothing but the distant cannonade, and they concentrated their view on the two APCs, which had now reached the breach in the fence that turned into their track leading into the minefield. With their field glasses, they could see a commander and a machine gunner in the open hatches studying the terrain and the three smoking wrecks. The first tank was about 400 meters from the lead armored personnel carrier, with the next two smoking hulks another 100 meters or so past it. All three instinctively ducked as they saw the distant field glasses swing their way.

The sun had risen to their right and would not glint off their lenses at this angle; however, a sharp-eyed spotter might be able to see them. Cautiously Baruch, who was well covered in his branches, eased up for a peek, and motioned the all clear. They checked the tank group for movement, and, finding none, zeroed in on the two paused APCs. Both were a clear shot for a tank, even with optical sights, but their engines were shut down, and that meant no hydraulic power to the turrets. Sasha and Yankel's driver were deep in the engine hatch of Yankel's rig, with Yankel's loader passing them things from a tool box.

Even if they were all three running, they could not risk a shot for an APC. The five heavy tanks were their deadliest opponents, and they were drawn up behind partial cover almost two kilometers away. "Any ideas?" David asked, thinking hard about his range of options. Mortars could be spotted, but could be a possibility, though inaccurate. He wished he had the bazooka from the Humvee, but that had been lost with *Gimmel* Four. Machine guns would not stop an APC without giving away their position. They could, perhaps, sneak back along their track and set up an ambush with grenades. He mentioned the ambush on foot as a possibility.

"Let's see what they do first," Yankel said, not taking his eyes off the distant menace. They watched together, forcing themselves to check the clustered tank group at several second intervals, but they remained motionless. One of the APCs edged into the minefield, slowly following the wide tank tracks. At one point it stopped, and they saw four soldiers emerge with automatic rifles and gingerly step around to the front and begin walking ahead, staying inside the tank track. "The callous bastard – better four good men than his precious vehicle!" Yankel said. Baruch swore quietly.

Cautiously the advance men approached the first burned-out tank. One climbed up and peered in the hatch and turned away, obviously sickened by the sight or the smell. They edged around the still-smoldering hulk and the APC idled along until it was behind the smoking tank. The four footmen had nearly reached the second hulk when the APC tried to squeeze around the burning hulk of the first tank. A muffled boom erupted and they saw it thrown end-for-end backwards, landing upside down and in flames. The second APC ran in fast reverse back the way it came. The four infantrymen who had been pushed out of the destroyed APC to walk on point had been saved by their commander's ruthless orders. The four scouts ran back all the way out of the minefield, never leaving the track and never even pausing to look behind them.

They watched them go in silence. "Their own damned mines," Yankel said. "The Soviets made them big and fat back then, and here it is more than fifty years later and they still go boom." By the Syrian's own records and maps captured in '67, they sowed thousands of land mines in all shapes and sizes. This part of the Golan had been thinly populated for hundreds of years before Israeli statehood in 1948, and had perhaps a few thousand permanent inhabitants between then and 1967 when Israel wrested it back at great cost in order to stop the incessant shelling from the heights. The Golan Heights overlooked the Kinneret and the Israeli agricultural settlements and small towns at the foot of the lake. In their nineteen years of occupation, Syria had turned the heights into a maze of minefields, bunkers and military installations. They had also kept up an intermittent and deadly barrage of rockets, mortar and artillery shells on Israel.

There were captured maps of the minefields, but the maps could not be trusted. There had been too much earth movement and settling since then. Yankel explained that he had studied this track over the years and a few of others that crossed the minefields at strategic points, and had noticed the animal trails left by wild goats to make sure before he brought his team to check them out. "We had mine detectors walking point – not like those poor bastards with their rifles. I knew the knowledge might win me the upcoming war games, but I never thought it would save my life," he said. They contemplated their respective memories of Golan VI and other mock battles. David had participated in several as a reservist. Yankel, who was career IDF and almost exactly his age – had been a fiercely competitive player in all of them. The grandson of Irgun freedom fighters who had survived the death camps of Europe to help win Israel's independence in 1948, Yankel Klein was known for his aggressive, no-holds barred approach to tank warfare. Rules were made to be broken by the winners, and only losers complained about rules of engagement in his book.

Together, they watched the four pathetic figures reach the lone APC that had backed up so quickly to the edge of the minefield. After much standing around and waving of arms, they were taken aboard, and the vehicle scooted off to rejoin the armored group in their cluster of positions at the mouth of the wadi.

Baruch harrumphed and spat. "If I know Syrians, they will have those four for breakfast, and then see who is stupid enough to try again if they don't think of something else better." Yankel shrugged and nodded. He was clearly exhausted. The morning was now quite warm, and flies were beginning to buzz them in their pastoral gully. The three commanders talked over their options and agreed that an ambush with grenades and perhaps a dismounted machine gun would be their next option if the APCs probed the incoming track again.

They wondered what the five tanks and the now four APCs were waiting for--besides a coffee break. "What would you do if you were in their treads?" Yankel asked David and Baruch.

David had been wondering the exact same question. "If I was waiting for anything, it would be for mine sweeping equipment. Otherwise I would probably begin to circle the minefield and look for exits. I sure wouldn't just sit there." Baruch agreed, adding that he was still wondering where the helicopters and fighter jets were hiding. Perhaps their opponents were getting on the horn to find out the same thing.

"I wouldn't just sit there either," Yankel said. "Looks like they are piling up some rocks and improving their cover though. Maybe they think that the way we went in is the only way out. They would be wrong, though. Not the first time that's happened."

Yankel sketched a blob-shaped minefield in the dirt in front of them. "We're here," he said stabbing a stick less than a quarter of the way through the blob. "The wadi is here, the ridge runs this way, and over here," he said, setting up some small stones just outside the south side of the blob, "are the settlements along the highway to the south of us. This track keeps going opposite where we came into the ravine – but it's an overhanging wall right now undercut by the stream when it flows in the winter. Its too steep to think of climbing, but the dirt is soft. No way we can dig it out without being seen by our friends over there." He gestured over his shoulder towards the Syrian tanks at the base of the wadi. I followed the track all the way south on foot a couple years ago, and it is do-able, but we'll have to do it at night. Unless you want to go out the way we came in," he added. "Think that over while we all get some rest and get these motors rewired." They each returned to their unit for breakfast and a consult with their crew. They agreed that two from each crew could probably grab some sleep until the next crisis – or two hours, whichever came first.

Tired as he was, David told Greg and Benny to take the first snooze. Sasha was still at work on the engine of *Gimmel* Two. He would interrupt their sleep after he was done, and they could take the next watch while he and Sasha got some shut-eye. David sought out Natan, the chemical physicist, who served as the gunner in *Gimmel* Two, and together they staked out a watch post standing on the turret of the tank jammed under the embankment. They could just get their heads and shoulders above ground level, and they were well hidden with brushy cover. David needed to understand more about electromagnetic pulses, and what had happened to Israel and the IDF.

"So, how much do you think we can get running if we have the afternoon to work on it? David asked.

Natan shook his head. "Not much else, I'm afraid. I took one of the radios apart while everyone was trying to start the engines – parts of the printed circuits are actually melted. Then a little while ago I popped the panels off one of the fire control systems; same thing only worse. It seems that any exposed wiring just acted as an antenna to concentrate the pulse – and wherever it ran into resistance, like resisters, a microchip or capacitators, it just fried them. Basically anything more complicated than a simple switch is toast. You would think that a big steel box like a tank would act as a big Faraday cage and the pulse would flow over and around it. But everything is too interconnected, and there were too many pathways to concentrate the energy. I was surprised that Sasha was able to get a starter to work. The only way I can figure it is that it was isolated by the starter relays, and protected enough deep in the engine compartment surrounded by all this steel that it survived. Same story for the alternator. Good news is that the air conditioning compressor should work. The bad news is that there are no working fans to carry the cool air around unless we can bypass the thermostat and digital controls."

"What about how rough the engines are running--any ideas there?"

"Nothing that I can think of yet. It's basically back to pre-electronic fuel injection days. What we need is a mechanical system, like a good old-fashioned carburetor to be able to enrich and lean out the fuel-air mix on demand. The fuel pumps were protected by being within the fuel tank, and the switches were closed when the pulses hit, so they are working."

David scanned their 150-degree sweep of the perimeter, which overlapped the half-hidden positions of the enemy tank and APC group. No one had joined them. No other traffic appeared on the ridge behind them, and they had not ventured back to the edge of the minefield to probe for the missing Israelis. If they were Jordanians, he knew they would be drinking tea and plotting leisurely. Syrians he was not so sure about. He knew they must be mad as hell to have let three tanks escape in spite of a four to one advantage, and he knew someone's head was on the line – most likely the commander of that group of five heavies. What were they waiting for? He would be laying down mortar fire in a pattern to flush them out if he were the Syrian commander.

"So, what do they appear to have working?" he asked both Natan and himself. Together they went over the evidence they had seen of the Syrian tactics and capabilities. They were up against Soviet-made T-72 tanks, an older model tank by modern standards, similar to their Merkava II in age and weight. The Soviets had sold or given thousands of the T-72s to armies all over the Middle East, and so it was pretty much a known quantity. Fortunately it was fairly slow and had a number of known vulnerabilities. Unfortunately, it packed a heavy punch with a 125 mm. shell. They had also glimpsed some newer T-80s and T-90s in the main group on the ridge. By their bulkier silhouettes, they appeared to be equipped with reactive armor and some of the modern refinements that would make them very tough customers in a fire fight.

The question was what kind of electronics edge did the enemy have since they had sat out the EMP blasts in protected bunkers? Standard equipment meant they at least had working radios – a big plus in working together – and working range finders, laser targeting, automatic leveling and target tracking. They went over the lop-sided fight on the ridge. Yankel had lost his first three tanks to the artillery barrage before the fight even started. But once it began, he lost three tanks out of four in minutes. When they had joined the fight with their few running shots, the incoming rounds had been too close for comfort, fast and quite accurate within a several-second window of presenting themselves as a target, even the first time, when they had appeared unexpectedly.

They debated whether the Syrians had any kind of over-the-horizon radar or tactical tools that had alerted them of their approach on the far side of the ridge. They decided that since Yankel's crippled companion had managed to retread and stay out of harm's way on the lee side of the ridge, and that their *Gimmel* Four had escaped notice until the main force gained the ridge, that they must be working with line-of-sight technologies as well. Of course, anything airborne, such as helicopters or UAV's, would tip that back in the Syrians' favor.

Yankel came by wondering the same thing. He listened and agreed with their assessment. He added a few observations of his own, having dodged their fire all morning and hit five targets himself in the fray. "One thing I do know is that the morning comsat flies over at 10:23 - I don't think I'll write them a love note today," Yankel said bitterly, referring to his well-known pranks of writing rude remarks in the sand for the Arabic intel specialist to see. "And maybe they have a way to download the pix and forward them to the front like we do. That could be what the lazy bastards are waiting for--and means we had better double check our camo nets. It's a few minutes to ten now."

They touched up their camo nets and made sure to scatter some sand and dirt on their dark tank hulls and do things to blur their edges and disguise even their shadows. Sasha, who had one of the two working watches in the group came and joined them, having had a late breakfast and degreased himself as best he could. "Ten twenty-three, everyone smile and say cheese!" he said without humor.

David and Sasha roused the next watch and sacked out in the shade of their tank with a mosquito net to keep the flies off their faces. Sasha was asleep within minutes, emitting a snore loud enough to be heard in Syria. David had just a few moments to be annoyed by Sasha's snores, and his aching rib where he had slammed into the back of the turret, until he too dropped off, dreaming of green fireworks and then darkness.

Moshav Yiftach

Eli, Gadi and the IDF group conferred a while in a sheltered spot on their ridge, and waited out the staggered bursts of a new pair of long range guns ranging in – with the bursts bracketing their ridge before working their way into the Moshav itself and raining more destruction. They decided that Eli, who was six feet tall and the tallest of the soldiers would carry the wounded Joshie between them, and then send back a stretcher for the seriously injured man. He reluctantly handed over the sniper rifle to a young soldier, along with his four clips and promised to return with the rest of the ammunition for it. He watched somewhat jealously as the young soldier hefted the weapon, peered through its scope and quickly got the balance and feel of the long rifle. Eli had gotten rather attached to the piece after all those months of training with it, and after his intense morning's work, he felt very possessive of it.

The two men hoisted Joshie between their shoulders and made their way heavily down the path to the moshav. Once they all dove for the ground as they heard the whistling whine of an incoming mortar round. It burst in the minefield some tens of meters away and no further rounds followed it. However, when they neared the moshav, it seemed like they were approaching a magic curtain of destruction. The perimeter houses were all in shambles of shattered concrete blocks and rubble. The trees, which had grown up since 1967 and were now beautifully mature, looked ragged and torn. Huge shell holes cratered the roads and walkways. The water tower was a mere skeleton. Eli sought out his house in the rubble. It still stood, low and sheltered in its berm of earth and rock. Thank G-d! And even his sukkah on the patio was intact. Though he couldn't see much of his orchard, there was a healthy splash of dusty green where it should be.

They picked their way through the debris towards the Levine's house. Like Eli, the Levines believed in making their bomb shelter an integral part of their house. Their shelter was a full basement, separated from the rest of the house by nearly half a meter of reinforced concrete. He was a pathologist and she was a radiologist – and so they had arranged for their spacious basement shelter to serve as the alternative clinic for the moshav in times of trouble. They even had a surplus X-ray machine set up – with the old-fashioned films processed in the bathtub.

Joshie was still conscious, but appeared both dazed by the destruction to the home where he had been raised for most of his twenty four years, and weak from loss of blood. It felt odd walking in the kitchen door of the Levine's house which had two shell holes in the upstairs roof, but appeared largely intact. In fact, the kitchen appeared perfectly normal, and they experienced an odd contradiction as they stepped from the gray and blasted landscape into the calm and cheery kitchen. They made their way through to the basement stairs and swung the big steel door open. The kitchen side was painted Tzfat blue with a border of red pomegranates and white doves, but the basement side was a business-like painted steel.

They descended the stairs carefully by the light coming from the bottom. Downstairs was a calm buzz of activity. They could see the main room had more than a dozen cots and spare mattresses, each of them holding an injured person. Another had two small children, extensively bandaged and asleep. Dr. Shira Levine, or Dr. Shira to her radiology patients, excused herself from a nearby bedside and came to greet them. She radiated professional calm, confidence and warmth even by the light of the Aladdin kerosene lamps. She took in Joshie's condition in a glance, asked a few short questions about what had happened and when. She helped them maneuver him to a spare bedroom that was being used for initial examinations and treatment. Their downstairs retreat had three bedrooms, one and a half baths, and a kitchenette and well-stocked pantry. And though without power, it had drinking and wash water rigged from five gallon plastic jerry cans, and plenty of light from efficient kerosene lanterns.

They hoisted Joshie onto an actual hospital type examining table – courtesy of the Levine's foresight and generosity – and helped unwrap the field dressing and cut away his pants leg. Then, as Dr. Bernie Levine and an IDF medic came in, Eli and the soldier excused themselves and slipped out of the room.

One of the women who worked in the moshav's health clinic offered them mugs of warm, sweet tea. They gratefully accepted the drinks and went slowly around the room, quietly visiting and catching up on news with their neighbors. The room was about half moshavniks and half soldiers, with injuries ranging from nasty cuts and burns to mangled limbs and bullet wounds. They could tell that there were even more severely wounded in one of the bedrooms, and the third appeared to be a makeshift operating theater, thankfully empty at the moment. Eli saw three unfamiliar faces in the fourth corner with odd looking uniforms as he finished up his tour of friends and soldiers. One, who had a dark Semitic face and the fierce black eyes and eyebrows of a desert-dwelling Arab, appeared to be wearing some sort of insignia. He was deep in a quiet conversation with Yishai, one of the older moshavniks, whose family came from Baghdad in the 1960s and had becoming founding members of Moshav Yiftach after the 1967 war. Eli realized as he approached, that, from the slightly harsher, more guttural sound, they were speaking Arabic. He also noticed that the stranger had his left leg in a fresh cast, and his entire midsection was neatly wrapped in gauze and a clean dressing under his open shirt.

"Meet Major Ibrahim Basrim, one of our unexpected visitors," Yishai said cheerily.

"Salaam," Eli said, which was the extent of his Arabic. Eli shook the major's hand, motioning him not to as he struggled to rise in greeting. To make him more comfortable, Eli sat down next to Yishai and regarded their guest. He noticed that Yishai and the major were drinking small glasses of strong black Turkish coffee together, and the remains of a small meal were sitting nearby.

"It's OK, he speaks English," Yishai reassured him. And, speaking in English, and with the occasional question in Arabic to the major for confirmation or explanation, Yishai briefly told Eli about Major Basrim. He noticed that the less injured of the other two captured soldiers was following at least the Arabic portion of their conversations with his eyes darting back and forth from speaker to speaker, but the other appeared heavily sedated and drifting in and out of sleep.

"As you might be able to tell from his name – the major's family comes from Basri, in Iraq, but his great grandfather moved to Syria late in the last century. That makes him a newcomer there." The major smiled and nodded slightly. "And he is the commander of one of the two companies of Iraqi volunteer commandos who spearheaded the assault on Yiftach with two companies of Syrian armor and mechanized infantry." The major appeared to be following Yishai's version of his story and not contradicting it. "And they were a couple hundred meters from our moshav fence and this close," Yishai held up his thumb and forefinger a few millimeters apart, "to overrunning us when our Syrian friends decided they had lost enough tanks for one day and started to retreat." The major scowled in agreement. Eli could tell he was more furious with his Syrian allies than his Israeli enemy at this point. "Major Basri and his two companions fell bravely and honorably with their face to the enemy and their weapons in hand," Yishai said solemnly, "and it took many bullets and the concussion and shrapnel from a rocket-propelled grenade for him to fall less than 100 meters from our fence. Our medics heard one of his companions calling for help, and we picked all three up in a pause in the shelling."

Eli looked suitably impressed at his enemy's bravery – for he was, he had seen the storm of fire between the moshav and the wave of the Syrian advance from his vantage point on the flanking ridge, and experienced some of the intensity himself. He could not imagine standing up and charging forward on foot through that storm of fire and shells. He offered to refill their coffee cups and excused himself, shaking the major's hand more warmly, and giving a formal nod to his still conscious but silent companion.

Eli delivered the two scalding hot glasses of sweet coffee and turned over in his mind all he had learned in the twenty or thirty minutes he had spent in the Levine's basement. He was surprised, but only a little surprised, to learn that their attackers included Iraqis. He was a regular reader of Debka File – a military intelligence electronic newsletter that had been remarkably accurate – almost prophetic - over many years of Middle Eastern conflict. Eli had read various Internet blogs and snippets of news about the gathering of diverse groups of Arab irregulars under the banner of the Syrian dictator who, well-supplied with petrodollars from Iran and the more radical of the Persian Gulf states, had been forming whole divisions of mercenaries and promising them a liberal share of the glory and plunder from overrunning Israel.

He learned that those moshavniks who had been in the trenches and bunkers on the moshav perimeter had been nearly overwhelmed in a blizzard of fire from the tanks, commandos and armored vehicles that had approached within a hundred meters of the fence – which was largely blown to bits now. If not for the arrival of a full company of IDF infantry – who left their disabled half tracks and walked a dozen kilometers from their counterforce positions – they would have been overrun for sure. The foot soldiers had lugged all the rocket propelled grenades and bazooka rounds they could carry, after stashing the rest beneath a rock outcropping a safe distance from their useless vehicles.

He learned that a team had gone back, accompanied by a pair of mechanics from the moshav with ideas for how to start the half tracks and retrieve their cache. Eli and the soldier who was with him, who had spent several Shabbats on the moshav as a guest, told their news of the fight for the ridge at the northwest corner of the moshav.

Then, feeling the call of duty, they excused themselves, agreeing to carry messages for those they would be likely to meet. Both checked on Joshie's condition one more time (he was sleeping, but would be OK), and went back upstairs. Their next stop was to be Eli's house to pick up the remaining rounds for the sniper rifle, but they were flagged down by an IDF lieutenant on their way and asked – or rather told, somewhat imperatively – to help move a couple crates of mortar rounds to a new position that had been dug next to some better cover. The job entailed scuttling from house to house lugging heavy cases of highly explosive shells while high explosives from distant artillery crashed somewhere in the moshav every fifteen seconds or so. They gestured that they had other urgent business and slipped away quickly after depositing their second case of shells before the lieutenant and his companion could think of any other ideas.

Eli's house was at the extreme northeastern corner of the moshav, one of the last ones built along a new outer drive that looped around the older core of the settlement with its mature trees and gardens. Because they were on the outside edge of the settlement facing the Syrian border, the houses on his street were battered almost beyond recognition, and the haze of dust and smoke gave the street a surreal look. However here and there were untouched reminders of the life he had led there for the past five years. A mailbox, a swing set and teeter-totter, a dog house, whole walls and bits of roof standing here and there. One of the houses had been ripped neatly apart, with the side facing the street peeled away, revealing half-furnished rooms like a derelict doll house.

Eli was surprised to see his simple, cheerily painted plywood sukkah intact, except for some splintered holes in the upper part of the east wall that appeared to have been neatly stitched by machine gun fire. He saw several small craters in his orchard, but his skinny little trees seemed to be mostly standing. He did not take time to identify which was which, although he readily saw that one of the closest craters was where his grapefruit tree had been. Damn, it had been hard to find a ruby red grapefruit seedling in Israel. The metal shutters that protected his patio door were closed, so he went in by way of the kitchen door with his young soldier in tow. The smallest kitchen window, which faced north and was unprotected by the earth, was shattered, but the mess inside had been cleaned up. Except for the shattered window and some plaster damage on the opposite wall, their kitchen looked serene and normal.

He entered the protected part of the house through a fireproof door and saw that there were five soldiers standing around maps spread out on his dining room table, and perhaps half a dozen others resting or asleep in his living room. He was only mildly surprised, and they greeted him absently, absorbed in their conference. His companion identified himself and his unit to the senior of the group, who Eli could now see was a full colonel and looked vaguely familiar.

Before he could say anything more than shalom, Natalie emerged from their master bedroom, and was surprised and overjoyed to see him. He could see a pile of children asleep on their bed through the doorway behind her. She led him to a corner of the living room where she had set up their gas camp stove, for it was not safe to cook in their kitchen with the shells falling. She poured him a cup of real coffee from a big pot and watched as he poured in a dollop of milk. Then they found two unused folding chairs nearby and sat down to drink in each other's presence and share everything that happened since they had parted hours before dawn. Eli was surprised to find out that it was nearly noon. No wonder he was hungry. And the smell of the huge pot of vegetable stew that simmered next to the coffee pot called to him. He got up and helped himself to a bowl while Natalie filled him in on her morning.

Hearing his voice, their twelve-year-old yellow Labrador emerged from her hiding place under their bed in the bedroom and came wagging sheepishly out to greet him. Sheba hated rockets, lightning, fireworks, and anything that went boom. She had made aliyah with them as a vigorous four-year old member of their family, and had adjusted happily to life on the moshav, where a well-behaved dog could roam free and play with any of the children, who, unlike city kids in Israel, were not afraid of dogs. He petted her warm furry head and found it comforting until a shutter-rattling blast nearby drove her scuttling back to her hiding hole.

Meanwhile, Natalie told him about Tali and her children coming over, and then another neighbor and her children. She told how they sat out the bombardment, and felt a few hits on the north side that shook the whole house, but nothing had cracked or broken. The soldiers had showed up about an hour ago. She learned they were part of the brigade to the south, and she had heard through them that the moshav had nearly been overrun and had been saved by the arrival of a company on foot at the last minute.

Eli finished his stew and tanked up on water and coffee, speaking little. When it came his turn to talk, he found himself hard pressed to explain what it was like in his fox hole with his rifle, killing men with a ruthlessness that surprised him. He found himself leaving out many of the details – such as how close the tank round had come that blasted away half his sheltering ledge, or about the machine gun bullets digging into the earth inches from his leg. He told of his relief when Gadi and Misha hit the first tank with their bazooka round, of Joshie's bravery and coolness under fire that helped them hit the second – and how it took a direct hit from their bazooka as well as a lucky mortar round to knock out the tough tank. He told her the story about watching the distant tank battle on the far ridge, and wondering if the outnumbered specks were IDF, and how they had fared after they disappeared from sight. He made a mental note to tell the colonel about his observations before he left.

Together they wondered about their two children. Were Rivka and the grandkids safe in Jerusalem? They had assumed at first that this was a limited war – an attempt by Syria to snatch up the Golan like a smash and grab robbery. But nuclear weapons fired from Iran? An entire army threatening to overrun their country? And what happened to the air force, ours and theirs? Did we strike back with a tactical nuclear punch of our own? Who else was involved? Would the US come to their aid? But, how could they even if they wanted to? Too many questions, not enough answers. And as they talked, the booms went on all around their snug little house. They scarcely paid them any attention, for the shelling had settled down in the past hour to a long range artillery duel, not the intense barrage that heralded an immanent attack.

Technically their living room and dining room were not official "safe" rooms. The south wall was only concrete and field stone, and the earth sheltering tapered off toward the southern edge of the roof. The deep well skylight over their dining room table was not secure from a direct hit, despite its metal grating at the surface level. The grate was designed to keep people from falling into the four foot well of the skylight from their grassy roof rather than keep rockets and mortars out. But it was reinforced with more than twice the normal amount of rebar and wire grid. Eli had gotten a bargain on recycled building supplies and had doubled up there, as well as poured nearly half a meter of steel reinforced, plastic-bonded concrete over his homemade roofing forms. Apparently the commanders around his dining room table felt the same sense of security, for they didn't look up except for the nearest strikes.

Eli realized that he had been away from his comrades on their ridge for more than two hours now. Although they had sent a pair of stretcher bearers directly from the Levine's makeshift hospital, he felt his absence was not fair to his companions. He retrieved the precious 600 rounds from the gun safe and put them in his and his young companion's knapsacks. He realized now that they had spent the morning together without bothering to find out each other's name, so Eli met Kobi, and Kobi met Eli and his wife Natalie and thanked them for their help and hospitality. He had lunched and washed up and rested a bit during their chat.

Eli also introduced himself to the colonel, who was now sipping coffee and talking to only one other officer, a lieutenant who he gathered was from some recon unit that belonged somewhere else, not from the company of de-mechanized infantry that had walked in to join their battle and saved the day – or at least the morning. Colonel Natan Eschol made some kind remarks about Eli's unique home shelter and thanked him for letting him use it for the morning. Eli said he was always glad to help the IDF – and meant it. He urged the colonel to feel free to take advantage of it in any way he saw fit. Eli told him about the extra water supply, and said it could be refilled from a hand pump in the garden if someone carried five gallon jugs up to a filler pipe on the roof. The colonel was relieved to know there was clean water to be had. He asked how many vehicles the moshav had running, and Eli ticked off the caterpillar, three old tractors, two aged bull dozers and one 1960's vintage Dodge power wagon that he knew of. He told him that the power wagon had gone off with soldiers and mechanics to try to start the mechanized company's half tracks. "Oh, and Woody," he added.

The colonel looked puzzled, and became even more so as Eli explained that Woody was his pickup truck. He could tell his Hebrew was going to be put to a real test, but he had explained Woody in elementary-level Hebrew many times before. Woody, he explained, was his wood-burning pickup truck. It was based on some plans that had been printed in the *Mother Earth News* more than 30 years ago for adapting a pickup truck to run on gases produced by burning wood chips – hence the name, Woody. Eli had bought an old Ford 4x4 to help with his do-it-yourself home building about six years ago. Once the home building job was done, the garden in and all the hauling mostly finished, Eli had found himself with a spare pickup truck that drank gas by the gallon. He decided to try something he had always wanted to try – and that was converting the old truck to alternative energy. After all, what good is an aging eco-freak with a solar house and no biofuel-driven truck? With the help of the mechanics who worked on the moshav's agricultural equipment and various friends and most of the students of an engineering class at the local technical college, it had actually worked.

The colonel looked skeptical at first, but he was beginning to follow Eli's broken Hebrew a little better now. The colonel had been admiring the one-of-a-kind house that Eli and his friends had built; so, why not a one-of-a-kind truck too?

At that point in the story, seeing was believing; and so Eli and the colonel, and the young lieutenant who was following the story at this point, went outside to see if Woody was still in one piece. Since it was parked on the other side of their kitchen, Eli had not noticed on his way in. They rounded the corner of the kitchen and Eli was relieved to see that Woody was indeed in one piece. He showed the now fascinated colonel, the lieutenant, and a pair of soldiers who had followed them outside how to fill up the firebox and light it quickly with a propane torch built into the contraption. They almost ignored the bombardment, which was not as intense as it had been earlier. They all watched as the temperature gauges went up, and pressure started to build in the wood-gas collection tank. Once it reached a certain level, you could begin driving and the gas production would be enough to keep going, Eli explained. One burner full of sticks and wood chips could run the truck for a good fifty kilometers – so you had to feed it every hour or so of driving.

"Amazing," the colonel marveled... any chance of borrowing it? We need to link up with the rapid response group of Merkava IV's who are stuck with no power about 15 km from here." The lieutenant was already half in the driver's seat, checking out the controls, which looked normal.

"Woody is at your service and honored to serve his country," Eli said proudly, handing over the key to the lieutenant. He quickly showed him the extra gauges in the cab – told them what they all meant and what to watch for and wished him good luck and good speed. A large shell boomed two houses away, sending fragments of roof tiles spraying in their direction. They watched as the old brown truck disappeared down the cratered street, and ducked back inside.

By now Eli knew he was long overdue at his post, and Kobi was also in a hurry to get out of the house to rejoin his group. The colonel assigned half a dozen soldiers from the chairs and couches to go back with him and relieve the men on Eli's ridge, and so they left, sprinting in ones and twos from the edge of Eli's yard to the first bunker by the blown apart perimeter fence. Two moshavniks volunteered to go with them to relieve Gadi and Misha.

As they threaded their way back through the minefield and up towards the ridge, Eli wondered at the give and take, matter-of-fact flow of communication between civilian and military that could never have been so free even in informal America. They were clearly on the same side of the table, literally and figuratively, and trying to do everything in their power to help their people survive the current threat. And now good old Woody was chugging along in defense of Israel too. Maybe he was getting a bit eccentric in his old age, Eli mused. Ecological, home-made, bomb-shelter houses were one thing, but he had gotten so used to owning a wood burning pickup truck – his eco-tech toy – that he had forgotten all about it in their assessment of what worked and what wouldn't in this post-electronics-as-we-knew-them age.

Peter Meier, the captain and crew of the USS Sitka had spent the past four and a half hours wondering if they were in the middle of World War III because it had taken that long to activate and launch their reserve deep-running communications array. In the meantime, nothing had penetrated to their 1,000-meter depth. There had been no ultra-long-wavelength communications from the deep grid of cables running beneath the ground in a Wisconsin wilderness area. This was the only emergency communications system capable of reaching submarines in the deep ocean. That may have been either good news – or very bad news. All any of them knew was that there had been nuclear warheads launched towards Israel. What had transpired in the intervening four and a half hours could well have changed the world map as they knew it.

However, launching a pod of sophisticated electronics communications equipment from a submarine running more than three thousand feet below the surface was not an easy task, and one they had done only once in the past two years as a drill. Under the supervision of Peter and several electronics and communications technicians, the new pod had been assembled, arranged in a small airlock with more than a mile of half inch steel tow cable that just barely fit the airlock. All connections were triple checked and battened down, and the ship slowed to a near stop as the outer door of the airlock was opened remotely, and the assembly allowed to rise to just below the surface. Rising the thousand meters, the last few hundred meters controlled by a remote controlled winch using telemetry from the pod, had taken nearly an hour. So really, they had made good time – beating their record in the earlier drill by half an hour.

They were relieved to hear ComSubGroup Eight on the second channel they tried, and even more relieved to learn that the war was "just" between Israel, Syria, Iran, Iraq, Lebanon, Jordan and Egypt so far. Tactical nukes only – with half a dozen high altitude strikes in Israel, two in Iran, one in Syria, and perhaps one in the Sinai. Reassuring messages were flying thick and fast between Washington, NATO, the Soviet republics, Saudi Arabia, Turkey and every country they could reach in the region that this conflict was not going to spread.

Their orders were, however, to proceed eastwards to a point about 50 km off the Israel coast – just in case.

General Hajid Al Hassaranah was not happy. Here it was 11 am and he was only two kilometers into Israel. He had planned to be to dipping his toes in the Kinneret by now, having crushed every Israeli settlement and army unit between Quneitra and the southern end of the Kinneret. True they had overrun several northern settlements, smashed through the first lines of Israeli tanks and troops, and thrust a long curving scimitar-shaped swath down the Golan Heights. Within the hour, he expected the final three beleaguered kibbutzim to fall at the south end of his advance, leaving the path clear to descend from the Golan around the south end of the lake – assuming that the roads were intact enough. From there they could join the massive Jordanian offensive in time to help take Tiberius on the far side. The Jordanians to his south had merely rolled across the river at several points, and overrun the poorly protected farming communities at the southern end of the Kinneret. The bulk of them had turned south, taking advantage of easier terrain and, except for stubborn resistance near two IDF bases, were smashing their way down the Jordan Valley towards Beit She'an. There were prosperous towns and easy pickings there.

The first wave of his assault had stalled and ebbed against a stubborn line of settlements – reinforced by somewhat more than a brigade of regular Israeli Defense Forces, and more cursed artillery than he had expected to encounter. He swore sorely about the four companies of long range artillery that were buried in their bunkers – hit by Israeli air force in the first minutes of the war. One of the bombed bunkers had contained 90 assault helicopters that were to have been flown just ahead of the first wave to sweep the terrain before them of any remaining Israeli tanks and mechanized infantry. He had word that some dozen or so of his helicopters might be dug clear with new tunnels and ramps being dug into the undamaged end of one of the bunkers, but it would take two days at least. His information on this was vague, but he knew there was no counting on help from the skies any time soon.

The Israeli tanks, which were supposed to have been knocked out by their ally's secret weapon, appeared to be working – perhaps not well – but running and firing back damned well.

Why had their bunkers been hit at all? How many times had he said it was necessary to leave enough air defenses active to shoot down an Israeli counterstrike? Bah, only two batteries for half the Quneitra sector. That's all the air defense minister could spare. Their anti-aircraft missile batteries had been quickly shuttled into smaller bunkers just before the EMP. But what good was it to bury 90 percent of their air defense system at the very moment it would be needed most? And then roll it out again an hour after the Israeli Air Force ceased to exist? Alas, but there was no arguing with an air defense minister who was the President's first cousin.

Al Hassaranah barked at a lowly captain to fetch him more coffee. He had been up all night and was not bathing in the Kinneret in this rising mid day heat. He was sitting in a black armored staff humvee-type vehicle with bad air conditioning. A few minutes ago he had finally gotten a message by motorcycle courier from the central command. This was not supposed to have happened either. An Israeli missile had killed all their communications with an EMP blast. Apparently this secret weapon was not so secret. And now, their own radios – guaranteed to be free of problems in spite of the electrified stratosphere, were working poorly if at all. His message informed him that the second wave of helicopter gunships, jet fighters and anti-tank gun ships was not going to happen, they were grounded a couple hundred kilometers away from the action. He had little faith in their mechanics or their ability to get flying.

He showed the message to his second in command, who nodded and looked not a bit surprised. "Fine," he said, "tanks and artillery I understand. We use more tanks – and Syrian commandos this time – none of these Iraqi swine who couldn't even charge a pair of machine guns without being cut to ribbons." He rolled out a map on the fold-down table and showed his second what he wanted.

"We have to hit them in daylight," the general told the staffers who were cramped and sweating in the heat. "We don't have enough night vision equipment or communications to risk it at night. Let hit them again at 1700, twenty minutes after prayers. We're going to smash the first two settlements from the north," he squinted at the map, "Yiftach and Yonatan, and break through to their rear – then the rest will crumble like a week-old pita." He spat some coffee grounds on the metal floor.

"Where is that no good scoundrel in charge of the third brigade? I want him to forget those three little tanks he chased and join the assault. In fact, he can go first instead of sitting on his ass like a fat cat watching a mouse hole. Send a message by motorcycle. Either their Israelis are broken down somewhere or they are going to be blown sky high in that mine field. What do three tanks matter? There are seven settlements between us and the Kinneret."

Moshav Yiftach 1200

Without Gadi, Misha and Joshie, Eli was the most experienced of the three moshavniks now making up their outer defenses. The IDF soldier had kindly returned his sniper rifle, although he could see he was eager to try it out in combat. Not a shot had been fired since they left, only heavy artillery shells that boomed back and forth. The moshav had only five bazooka rounds to spare each of their four anti-tank teams. Fortunately, a full platoon of regular army now helped hold their ridge, and they had some advanced rocket propelled grenades that could pierce armor, and a pair of light machine guns. They assigned four young men – barely eighteen years old – to help the moshav bazooka team with screening fire.

A team of scouts had already searched the burned out tanks and APCs in the scorched and shell marked terrain ahead of them. They had looked for anything that could be of value – grenades, weapons, walkie talkies, even unused ammunition. The intensity of the fire and their enemy's slow retreat made pickings very slim. They recovered a few undamaged rifles and one grenade launcher, but only two RPGs that fit it. They had found one radio that crackled with the occasional message in Arabic. They sent the radio down to their command post in the moshav to see if some of their Arabic speakers could glean any useful information – or perhaps get on the channel with confusing directions. The scouts had also found quite a few seriously wounded, and the group had been busy shuttling injured enemy soldiers to a makeshift clinic in another of the moshav's bomb shelters.

Eli was not satisfied with what was left of his cave under the overhanging rock. There had been no aircraft all day, and besides, he had been spotted and nearly killed there this morning. He hunted for a better spot on the top of the ridge near where the artillery spotters had been. The top of the ridge offered a better view to the north and south, as well as the slope to the east that had been the scene of their battle.

He borrowed a trenching tool and improved the fox holes behind one wide, low rock that offered him firing positions to the north and south as well as covering the east slope. News filtered up with every messenger or group coming through. One report said that about half of the half tracks were running now, thanks to the moshav and IDF mechanics. "Half of the half tracks – wouldn't that make them quarter tracks?" Eli quipped. There were smiles and chuckles as various soldiers got the joke. It was rare that Eli could pull off a joke in Hebrew.

Another platoon with artillery spotting equipment came past, heading farther to the east to try to get a better vantage point to direct the three remaining howitzers. He understood from listening to their discussions that one of the big guns and two of its crew had been blown to bits in a direct hit. Only its ammunition and two loaders who were behind a sandbagged wall fetching a shell were spared. "*Baruch Dayan Emet*" Eli said – Blessed is the True Judge – something a Jew says on hearing bad news. He had said it a lot that morning in gathering the news at the Levine's basement hospital. There were more than twenty moshavniks dead in the first assault, and he knew most of them fairly well. Another thirty some IDF soldiers were dead and quite a few of the wounded had been treated in the field, electing to stay at their posts and continue fighting. It was hard to get an accurate count with shells still falling and no phones or radios.

Another platoon moved through on their way to stalk to within shooting range of the enemy. The Syrians and their allies were not going to roll in unopposed this time, but would be harassed the whole distance by snipers, rocket-propelled grenades and machine gun fire.

By the time he was finished with his fox holes to his satisfaction, Eli was hot and thirsty and it was well into the afternoon. The breeze had died down, leaving a baking heat in its place. His pits were deep enough to offer only a smidgeon of shade, but just enough that he could like down and snooze whenever it was not his turn to watch. He had been up since 3:30 that morning and was exhausted. Though full of coffee, he fell asleep easily and slept like the rock next to him.

Gadi shook him awake. Gadi and Misha were back from their relief period in the moshav. As he came to over the cup of coffee that Gadi poured him from a thermos, the two men filled him in on the news. Woody and the lieutenant were back. They had found the rapid response group of eleven tanks and six self-propelled howitzers intact. However only one of the truck-mounted howitzers was able to move under its own power yet – and that was only after nearly half a day of rewiring undertaken by a team of mechanics. The moshav bulldozer and one from the neighboring settlement had been sent out to tow the tanks and artillery in to the half dozen settlements still standing in their section of the Golan.

Thanks to messengers on foot, ancient trucks, motorcycles and mountain bikes, news was beginning to travel along the chain of settlements that were scattered, each of them a few kilometers apart, along the only highway that ran the length of the Golan Heights overlooking the Kinneret. Moshav Yiftach and the next settlement south had borne the brunt of the morning attack. However another large force was now pinning down the southern settlements and was threatening to break through. The southern Golan settlements appeared to be cut off to the north; but no one knew the status of any of the northern Golan communities. The enemy had been recently spotted at the northern end of the Kinneret as well.

As they talked, the shelling of the moshav, which had been intermittent for the last few hours, picked up noticeably. They sought better cover behind Eli's boulder. Since two other moshavniks had the bazooka that they had used in the morning, Misha and Gadi settled in to enlarge Eli's excavations behind the boulder. At least Eli would not be alone this time. In fact, there were quite a few more defenders now than when they made their stand in the early morning fight. There was about an hour and a half to go until sunset when the signals relay team shouted to them that the IDF spotters had indicated that the enemy appeared to be massing for a new strike. Eli, Gadi and Misha decided to *daven* a quick *mincha* in the shelter of their boulder. In deference to the shells falling thicker around the moshav, they prayed the *Amidah* – normally said while standing, sitting in the shelter of the sturdy basaltic boulder.

Eli had given his spotting scope to one of the teams of artillery spotters who had gone forward to engage the enemy, and so he watched for the advance to appear with only his telescopic sight. It was nearly 6 pm before he saw them. The western sky was a fiery red behind him and a setting sun was edging its way towards the horizon. He wondered why the enemy had chosen such a time for their assault, for every tank and vehicle stood out in great detail, and often the setting red sun flashed from their windshields. They must be half blinded driving into the blazing sunset. However, the new assault quickly came into range and Eli started firing as fast as he could with no regard for conserving ammunition from his knapsack of 600 rounds. He had little time for thinking.

The attack came much faster this time – charging ahead in paths already swept of mines, with a double line of tanks smashing their way in the lead. The onrushing tanks pushed aside burnt hulks from the first attack and were soon blasting at the moshav with a rapid fire of shells. A curtain of mortar shells fell, with the bursts edging towards the outer defense line of the moshav. Mortar shells were aimed wide at their ridge too, and the ground shook with their impact and the air was filled with smoke and shrapnel.

However, fire from the moshav was more than twice as thick as in the morning and tanks were being hit nearly every minute. Eli could tell from glimpses in his telescopic sight that a rain of mortar shells was falling immediately behind the enemy advance, cutting up the advancing ground troops something awful. Often he had a commando in his crosshairs, only to see him disappear in a blast of mortar fire. In minutes it was over – the double line of tanks was now a fleeing melee of milling tanks. Eli had the impression that some of them might have been running over their own troops, but it was impossible to tell in the confusion. A ragged cheer went up from the platoon on his ridge, and Eli found himself shouting hoarsely in victory and pounding a beaming Gadi and Misha on the back. A late falling mortar shell hit just down the hill, spraying them with fragments of rock and they tucked their victory dance back under the cover of their boulder until the fiery red sun sank behind the hills on the other side of the Kinneret.

They drank a bottle of water each, parched even though their firefight had lasted less than twenty minutes. The water merely diluted the taste of gunpowder and smoke in their throats. Artillery continued to boom from the moshav, seeking to follow the retreating enemy and to find their long range guns. Part of the platoon on their ridge went out to help the artillery spotters and advance teams. Suddenly worried that the attack had been a diversion, Eli and his companions scanned the growing darkness to the north of them for any sign of a flanking advance – but saw nothing. However, Gadi, who knew the whole area like the proverbial back of his hand, volunteered to lead a trio of IDF scouts through the pathways he knew in the minefields to the north. They soon set out to double check that nothing was likely to surprise them in the nighttime from that direction.

A little while later in the gathering dusk, the two moshavniks and their IDF counterparts came back from their advance positions. The young moshavniks had fired all five bazooka rounds, and the IDF men had launched all but one of their rocket propelled grenades. They were sure of hits on a jeep and two armored personnel carriers – and told of how the IDF men had waited until a tank was at nearly point blank range before popping out of their cover and blasting it and the one behind it within seconds. But two of the soldiers had been badly hit in the resulting fire fight with the commandos following the tanks, and they were carrying them down to the moshav clinic.

Eli remembered the relative calm of the Levine's basement and its already full mattresses and knew it would be chaos there now. Unfortunately, the moshav's other resident doctor, a semi-retired surgeon, was away at the hospital in Haifa when the war broke out.

In the growing quiet of the evening, they could hear calls and crying from the Syrian wounded, and knew that soon armed teams of volunteers with stretchers would be seeking them in the darkness, and praying there were no suicidal jihadists among the wounded preparing to take advantage of Israeli kindness.

The IDF team on the ridge was now down to two riflemen and two spotters, who were watching a blinking light on a distant hill and relaying the signals to the guns in the moshav. As the evening darkness fell around them, artillery fire on both sides was slackening considerably, as if each had tired of their deadly game. Now a round was being fired from the moshav about every three to five minutes, and answering shells from the direction of the blinking light fell only slightly more frequently, but appeared to be bursting outside the moshav as often as in it.

Somewhere in Syria

Chaim Tzippori was dreaming; long, involved, strange dreams that did not make sense. And for a while now, he had been telling himself in his dream that it was time to wake up because things were too confusing and that if he could wake up, then at least he would stop dreaming unsettling images and feelings. And for some minutes his unconscious mind had been puzzling over a sound that was coming nearer, and a strong smell that seemed familiar.

Goats! It was the smell of goats like his uncle's kibbutz where they made goat's cheese near Tzfat. What were goats doing in his dream? But wait, it wasn't a dream any more. He could hear munching nearby, and an occasional low nicker or blaaa aah! of goats busy grazing. The sun was warm and baking him and there was the smell of warm grass and faint wood smoke – no, stronger, perhaps brush burning somewhere. He tried to open his eyes, but the sun was warm and the smell of grass and goat almost soothing, recalling summers of his youth on his uncle's kibbutz, wandering in the Galilean hills.

Goats – and that meant goat herders, and in Israel, that meant a couple Palestinian boys – or Bedouins with rifles... he suddenly thought and then he remembered where he was, or thought he was – somewhere on the Syrian side of the border. The flight, the flash and the crash came back to him in a rush, driving dreams of goats and goat herders from his mind in seconds. He lay still and listened. No sounds but the munching of goats and the buzz of flies by the side of his head. He tentatively opened his eyes a crack and looked out at a hazy, smoky sky obscuring a hot and dry sun that was beating down on him from nearly directly overhead. It must be close to noon! He had bailed out of the cockpit of his out-of-control jet before dawn. And no one had found him yet?

Why? Chaim wondered. If he was on the Syrian side, any farmer, goat herder or village knew that a downed airman meant a great reward. Had no one seen his plane go down in the predawn darkness? Wouldn't there be patrols out scouring the landscape back along his flight path? Commandos in helicopters? An Israeli airman was a prize beyond pearls. Remember Ron Arad, an airman lost near the beginning of the first Lebanon war? Remember how they had ransomed prisoners and favors for years just for a scrap of doubtful information whether he was alive or dead?

Chaim did not want to be the next hostage, held forever and then murdered when his worth as a bargaining chip began to decline over the years. He lay there looking at the sky, not wanting to move his head yet. Come to think of it, his head felt like it had been dropped from an airplane. His left leg was aching and he felt patches of raw skin on his hip and side where he had fallen and the left side of his head was buzzing with flies. He gingerly reached up with his right hand and touched the side of his scalp over his left ear. It was sticky and buzzed with flies, and brought sharp pains with the merest touch.

Goats. He could see two of them now. Dusty, ragged looking creatures that ate steadily at tufts of dried grass and looked at him from time to time, without concern. Where was his flight helmet? What about his pistol? He felt a hard lump against his right leg; he had a pistol at least. And his survival knife? That was strapped to his left calf. He couldn't feel his left calf – or anything below his aching left thigh that felt like one big complaining bruise. What about his left hand? He had obviously landed on his left side – did he remember hitting the ground and rolling? No, only a moonlit glimpse of the Kinneret in the distance, which is how he knew he must still be in Syria – from his perspective on it as he fell through the night sky. Then nothing – until the smell of goats woke him. There must be a buck nearby to smell that strong – though the two does munching the tuft a few meters away might be the source of the musky odor. He flexed the fingers of his left hand – he could feel them at least, but something was wrong with his elbow. Sharp pains shot up and down his arm when he tried to move it slightly.

He groaned involuntarily as he tried to roll onto his right side and move up to his elbow. Pain stabbed his elbow and upper left arm, throbbed in his leg and threatened to overwhelm him with nausea. His head pounded painfully in the attempt. The goats were unimpressed and kept munching. He lay back down and rested a long while. But he was thirsty, and the flies buzzing his wounded head were maddening. He had to do something. Where was his canteen? Chaim went over his flight suit in his mind – he had to concentrate and think it through – somehow his muscle memory felt out of kilter. He could not just automatically reach for it – for he was almost afraid to move again. Left leg, cargo pocket – but just a 750 milliliter flask… there was not much room in a flight suit, and no pilot expected to be on the ground for long – not since the invention of the helicopter. He listened. Nothing was flying anywhere in earshot – which must be what, a ten kilometer radius at least?

He had to pick his head up and lean forward slightly as his hand felt for the familiar water flask. He tugged open the flap with two fingers and fished inside. He could barely grasp the top of the bottle. Carefully he drew it along his leg until he could get a better grasp. He pulled it towards his mouth and bit down on the cap with his teeth, unscrewing it until he could finish the job with his fingers. He spilled some anyway as he maneuvered the sturdy plastic flask to his lips and drank about half of it. Carefully he threaded the cap back on and let the flask rest on his chest, gripping it loosely. The water was warm and tasted like plastic – and a little like goat, but it revived him a bit.

Chaim lay back for a long time – and he must have dozed, for the sun had moved a hand's breadth or two from directly overhead. He did not hear any munching goats now. He listened and heard no voices, no vehicles, no aircraft of any kind. Perhaps a very faint distant thunder? But no, he shook his head slightly, felt a throb of pain and stopped, this was September. The rainy season was at least a month away. He lay still and listened some more. Artillery, definitely artillery – and hard at it from the steady rumble, and far away from the way he had to strain to hear it. Artillery meant war – this was not sniping across the border or lobbing a few nuisance shells. As he lay and listened, it was the full orchestra sound of war – full except for the roar of jets and the chumpa chumpa chumpa of helicopters. Had both air forces been wiped out in strikes and counterstrikes in the first hours of conflict? Or were they busy elsewhere? Too much work to think. He sipped some more water and went back to sleep within minutes of laboriously re-twisting the cap with his right thumb and forefinger.

In a Minefield Northeast of Moshav Yiftach 1455

David Klein woke up hot and thirsty. He threw back the mosquito netting and sat up, blinking in the hot afternoon. The sun was past its zenith, but baking hot and obscured in a smoky hazy sky. David shook his head and reached for his canteen. The water was hot but wet and he drank it all. He sat for a moment and gazed around him as the morning's events tumbled past him in his mind. Sasha was still snoring, but David eased his sleeve up enough to see the time on the driver's great uncle's watch. It was nearly 1500. Someone had let him sleep an extra two hours. Someone in addition to the Syrians, he thought. Why hadn't they attacked? Did they have night vision and infrared and were waiting for nightfall to use their advantage? Did the mine clearing equipment not show up yet? Had they left to circle the minefield?

David got up, stretched, picked up his helmet and went to the water bags hanging by the back hatch of his tank to wash and get some cooler water. He took his time since there appeared to be no current crisis, and even brushed his teeth. He pulled out a couple tins of tuna and some crackers from their pantry shelf inside the tank. He took them topside, exiting through the open observation hatch and joined Greg who was leaning casually against the dirt bank, binoculars around his neck and his coveralls peeled back to a muscle shirt that showed off his bodybuilder's physique.

Greg nodded in the direction of the wadi. "Still there. Nothing has moved, except a dirt bike that came ripping down from over the ridge a little while ago and stopped by the unit in the center. Maybe their radios are out too," he speculated. Greg turned to take a look through a small spotter scope he had set up on a miniature tripod on the grassy edge of the ravine. "Yeah, they're still arguing... have a look."

David took his place at the spotter scope and adjusted the eyepiece slightly. He could see a group of figures standing and gesturing emphatically at a black-clad figure still astride a bike of some sort. Just then the black figure on the bike threw up his arms and tumbled over backwards. A few seconds later the pop, pop, pop of gunfire reached David's ears. Greg looked up and swung his binoculars towards the enemy. "Talk about killing the messenger!" he muttered. "I wonder what news he brought."

David told Greg to go check in with Captain Klein to see if he was awake and give him the tidbit of news if he was – then he could go sack out himself after getting Sasha up. Alone now, David scanned the terrain carefully, first with the binoculars, and then re-checking possible hiding places with the spotter scope. If he were the Syrian commander, he would have some commandos sneaking up along the obvious animal tracks that criss-crossed the old minefield to find the hidden tanks and mark them with smoke grenades before retiring to let the tanks flush them out. But he wasn't the Syrian commander. In fact, he had an uneasy feeling that the he had just watched Syrian commander shoot one of his own messengers in cold blood. First he had seen the bloody deed, and then he had heard it two seconds later.

What were the implications of that? Defying a message from headquarters perhaps. Didn't Syria have working radios either? Wasn't that the whole point of their hiding in massive bunkers and then attacking after a vicious, pre-dawn nuclear strike? David didn't know, he just felt that there was an implacable hatred and a patient, cold-hearted and calculating waiting game going on with this group of tanks and APCs that chilled him in spite of the afternoon heat.

After a while Yankel came by, only somewhat rested, but ready to plot their escape. So David motioned to another of the tankers to cover his watch post and the two of them went for a consultation with Sgt. Baruch Harel, David's second in command, and the senior of the three in age but not in rank. He also spoke Arabic and could second guess the Syrian military mind better than either of them.

Sgt. Harel was awake and his swarthy face was freshly shaved. He had not put his helmet back on yet, and his thinning grey stubble was still wet from his morning wash. He was into his second glass of strong, sweet coffee. He offered them each a steaming, freshly stirred glass, and they settled down beside the open crew hatch of Baruch's *Gimmel* Two, and set their hot glasses down to cool slightly and settle the grounds. Everyone was silent for a few moments as Baruch took tiny sips from his-still too-hot coffee.

Yankel put his glass gingerly to his lips, blew a few moments and took a quick sip – but put the glass down again before it burned his fingers. He lifted his helmet off and set it upside down in the dirt beside him as they sat by the crew door in the welcome shade of the tank in the baking mid-afternoon heat. Yankel ran his fingers through his wavy, ginger hair that managed to be unruly even when barely an inch long. David realized that he had seldom seen Yankel out of his tankers helmet that long and difficult year.

"OK, I've figured out how to create a ramp out of that dirt bank," Yankel said, nodding towards the slightly overhanging, undercut bank opposite where they had all entered the ravine. "We can dig in maybe two rounds near the base until the back end is about flush with the dirt. We set them off with a couple pistol shots or a fuse of some kind. Of course, that's going to make a big boom and wake everyone up and get them firing at us the moment we try to climb out. So we need a diversion – a really good one. I can think of lots of diversions, but not a really, really good one that is going to cover up an explosion that size, even if it is half buried in dirt."

"I've been thinking mortars," David said. "Only not from here – that would give away our position. We need to move their attention at least say half a kilometer away from here... like right back to where we dropped those three tanks." Baruch and Yankel nodded. They had been working out similar ideas.

"Trouble is that the mortar launchers are built into the tanks," Baruch said, "you have ideas for making a launcher? I can't think of a tube big enough that we could spare."

"We don't need a tube and we don't need a whole lot of accuracy. We just need a lot of flash and bang and smoke. I've seen a mortar round launched from a smooth stake stuck in the ground with a piece of wire from a coat hanger as a guide to hold the round. It doesn't go as far without the tube, but it flies."

Yankel had seen a similar trick, and had probably made his own share of crude bombs and missiles in his boyhood, "How do we light them off and be back here in time to scram while they are still going boom? Do we have that much fuse wire? It would take at least five minutes worth," he asked.

"We pour a powder fuse – using the slower burning stuff from an aerial illumination round, nice and thick – no gaps. We cluster the mortar sticks a few meters apart and aim them towards our friends over there." David said.

"OK," Yankel said, "that might work... but I want a little more boom than half a dozen mortar shells, and I don't want to waste any more of ours. So I'm wondering what's left in that tank you hit, Baruch?"

He and Baruch compared notes on the last firefight. They reviewed how Baruch's tank had backed partway up the crumbled bank – just enough to fire when they saw David's turret stuck and Yankel about to fire. Baruch said they had made a clean hit on the front, right below the turret – killing the driver and commander for sure. But in the ensuing smoke and flame, he did not recall seeing secondary explosions from ammunition cooking off. All three agreed that the rearmost two tanks were completely gutted from the resulting fires, but they climbed up on *Gimmel* Two to have a long, hard, expert's second look at the shattered tank nearest them. They studied it in silence for a long time.

"I think you're right," Yankel said at last, "clean hit, maybe a few rounds blew in the turret. But the back end looks almost intact – and no burning except for the turret." Baruch looked satisfied, a rare look on his chronically worried and often critical face. "Now, I want them to think we're coming out that way, and make it look like one of us has just shelled them. In fact, in the dark I want them to think that maybe that hulk is one of us. You see the barrel of their cannon, how it is aimed slightly to the left. I think they must have seen me fire. If we could just push it around another 90 degrees or so, and place a 105 round in it – perhaps there's a way to light off a round from there that will go in the general direction of them."

"That's about three if's in a row," David said, "but a 105 round ought to fit easily inside a 125 mm barrel- perhaps with room for a fuse. We could push, say an anti-personnel round about an arm's length deep with a fuse taped around it, light off the end and have what – say a minute per meter of fuse? Some of the blast is going to be lost in the dead air behind it, but there should be enough left to shove it along. And an anti-personnel is going to give you some scatter and extra boomlets."

"Exactly," Yankel said. He was getting excited by the plan now, and obviously thinking a mile a minute because he almost couldn't talk fast enough to lay out the plans for the three of them as they spilled out of his head.

"Here's the kind of sequence I want. First, a tank round comes whizzing out of the dark over there by our former friends and neighbors. Then mortar fire starts coming at them from along the track so they start thinking they're under attack by tanks and infantry. And then, for the finale, as we have our engines started up and are all pulling out of our hole here, we wire up their remaining ammo and the whole tank blows. They think either we hit a land mine or got hit by their fire, 'cause if it was us, we'd be pouring fire on them within seconds. Come to think of it, we might need a couple mortar rounds after the big boom, just so they don't start thinking they got us and stop shooting."

Baruch shook his head. "No, once an Arab starts shooting in the dark, he doesn't stop until he has run out of ammunition or somebody yells at him to stop….unless he is regular, career army. But one or two more shells wouldn't hurt if you can do it."

"Now, just around sunset when the sun is in their eyes, I want to slip out with the drivers and walk the first half kilometer or so of the track out of here. It's been two years since I was here and I don't want to make any mistakes. Once we're half a kilometer down the track, it bends to the right and we'll have some hill between us and the bad guys. I recall it being much easier running from there. David, you think you can make up about six or eight of those makeshift mortars and have someone take apart a starburst shell or two for the fuses?"

David knew just the person to help him. Benny was a first class pyromaniac. They would have a fireworks display worthy of charging admission, he told them. They cleared up a few more details on the timing, the countermeasures if the diversion failed, which order the tanks would leave – assuming they started. That gave everyone pause. A tank not starting had only happened in the worst winter cold on Mount Hermon, or during the most blinding three day sandstorm in the Sinai, and hardly ever in their lifetimes.

They agreed that David and Benny and the loader from Yankel's tank would creep down the track about two hours after dark – assuming they were not attacked first – and set up the fireworks display. Yankel would borrow Greg as a loader and be standing by to cover them with fire if they were discovered. Baruch would be standing watch and ready to start his tank to pop up and join the fight from the entrance to the gully. It would be two tanks able to fire against five – in the dark with no infrared or laser equipment to help them, but they had faced worse odds that very same morning and survived... so far. David told his crew the plans. He had Sasha scrounge up some wire and some of the tall stakes they used for marking paths through newly cleared minefields. Greg fished out the required explosives from his ammunition archive, now down to under 40 shells. David and Benny set up their fireworks lab spread out on a piece of tarp in a sheltered spot about thirty meters away from the tank, just in case. They saved the antipersonnel shell and its duct-taped fuse for last. They heard the pickets being relieved before they were done and the sun was about a hand's breadth or two above the western horizon – blood red and dim. They could look directly at it and barely have to squint.

Baruch busily rounded up ten out of their twelve men for a *minyan* to say *mincha*, the afternoon prayer. While two kept watch, the ten men stood facing Jerusalem and prayed – most of them from memory, for only three of them carried pocket prayer books, and Baruch had only one spare. Baruch was a Sephardic Jew, so he started with introductory psalms to *mincha* in a somewhat tuneless chant picked up by the three other Sephardim in their assembly – including one of those standing watch. The watchman was a secular Jew from Ashkelon by his generally casually dressed appearance and from what little David knew of him from their reserve training sessions. When they reached the familiar *Ashrei* – where most Ashkenazim begin *Mincha*, David knew the introductory prayer by heart – for it was said three times a day, and joined in – "Happy are those who dwell in your house." Then came the silent *Shemonah Esrei* – the eighteen blessings that were really nineteen because of one added "recently" meaning only 1800 years ago.

He looked down at the small, well-thumbed prayer book Baruch had loaned him and prayed with an intensity he had never felt in synagogue, which might be why he rarely went in recent years except in the past year because of his son's bar mitzvah. He was proud that his son had taken his religious responsibilities seriously, and was learning and going to a regular *minyan* in the year past his bar mitzvah instead of losing interest and eventually his *tefillin*, like many of his 14 and 15-year-old friends.

Every word struck home as if speaking directly to him about his current predicament – "blessed are You – our Lord Most High, King of the Universe, G-d of Abraham, G-d of Isaac, G-d of Jacob….." he felt the deep family connection running from every living Jew back to their forefathers. He knew that generations had stood before G-d saying these same words in times of great distress and worry. *Magen Avraham* – the shield of Abraham, is that what had protected him from all harm that long and bloody morning?

"You are strong, the strength of the universe, Our Lord, bringing life to the dead, abundant in salvation, causing the dew to fall..." he felt part of his burden lifted as he praised the Creator of all and acknowledged that only a truly omnipotent Creator was in complete control of the entire universe – and that nothing happened without His knowledge or will.

"Who nourishes and sustains with loving kindness."

"Who gives life to the dead, upholds the fallen," David felt tears in his eyes and a lump in his throat for the men he had seen fall that day.

"Who heals the sick, straightens the bent and keeps faith with those who sit in the dust, Who is like you…"

Blessing followed blessing – "You are holy, Your Name is holy"

"Blessed are You who gave man knowledge" Knowledge to make war, and to decide not to make war, he thought…

"Bring us back to your Torah, draw us close to Your service…"

"Forgive us…. See our troubles and rescue us….Heal us and we will be healed…Bless us and bless this year…."

"And for the evil ones, let there be no hope…." He felt a surge of righteous anger against the enemies who had attacked Israel so ruthlessly, forcing her people to fight once again for their very survival.

"And the righteous ones and the pure ones and the elders of Israel of your people, the House of Israel…." He thought of the Rabbi in his *Shul* as a youth – so aged and wise and holy in his young eyes. He thought of all the people he had stood with in synagogues and at the Western Wall, praying in a way that no other nation in the world seemed to pray…

"And to Jerusalem Your city return with mercy…" what was happening to Jerusalem… to his wife and his children, to his quiet green neighborhood?

"And the seed of David, Your servant, quickly restore…" David, his namesake. How proud he had been of his name all through his early school years as they read stories about David the warrior, David the wise king.

"Father of mercy, hear our voices…."

Their service was interrupted by the sound of mortar fire. David scrambled for the nearest outlook, but about half the group kept on praying as if nothing were happening outside their ragged circle. "Was it faith or a very bad choice that led them to keep praying?" he wondered as he looked towards the source of the mortars and where they were falling. After watching awhile, it appeared that two small mortars had been set up somewhere behind the dug-in tanks and they were attempting to explode their shells in a pattern designed to flush out any hiding tanks. However, he mentally calculated that they were nearly a kilometer away from their marks and likely to run out of shells before they came anywhere close to their position. Even if they came close, the chance of a direct hit was small, there was just too big an area to cover. He could have finished his prayers. At least the enemy was busy and doing something predictable. That might mean they intended to stay put for a while. *Baruch HaShem!*

Rockets had been falling topside for hours by the time Anna's group received their first radio messages from Jerusalem and Ramat Hovav. In the meantime they had been extremely busy re-establishing their radio reception and transmitting capabilities. However the heavy barrage of rockets threatened their antennae constantly, and several had to be replaced, bypassed or done without as the attacks went on without respite. Large, well-aimed rockets were falling regularly from the direction of Syria, and smaller Katyusha and Grad-type rockets were raining down in abundance, but with not much aim, from nearby Lebanon. A battery of long range artillery stationed on their mountain top was blasting away at the nearby border at a rapid rate. According to the news that filtered down to them over the course of the morning their heavy work may have slowed the incoming rocket fire by a fraction.

They had activated the second electromagnetically shielded trailer in their underground cavern. Since there were no IDF units in radio communication except for those on their mountain and the two other strategic defense bunkers, their job was mostly to listen to the Arabic military traffic on the radio and share any significant tidbits. From what they heard and could verify from more than one source, it appeared that Hezbollah guerillas and bands of irregular armed militias and gangs had swarmed over the northern border of Israel shortly after sunrise, reinforced with captured UN tanks and armored vehicles. UN peacekeepers had caved in to constant ambushes and terrorist assaults earlier that spring and had fled, abandoning most of their equipment to the Hezbollah. They were pretty sure, from the radio traffic, that there were commando and even tank units of the regular Syrian army with them.

The Lebanese borders were so porous that a full division of regular Syrian troops had suddenly popped up from bunkers in Lebanon and had stormed over the hills, taking Kiryat Shemona after some hours of heavy street to street fighting. More guerillas were flowing across the Lebanese border to join the looting behind them. This freelance looting was a source of much radio outrage, with calls for Syrian units to return and supervise the looting. This force was bogged down somewhere near Rosh Pina.

The entire Golan had come under attack from both Syria and Lebanon. The northern-most Syrian assault had broken through at the largely Israeli Arab and Druze town of Migdal Shemesh on the slopes of Mount Hermon – but appeared to have failed to take all of the Israeli-held third of the 2800 meter mountain so far. Leaving a regiment or two to finish capturing the peak, most of the force breaking through at Migdal Shemesh had rolled south along Highway 98, which ran the whole length of the Golan Heights. They overran the small settlements in their path, pushing the better part of a division of Israeli troops in the Golan ahead of their waves.

Deprived of their technology and vehicles, the IDF was forced into a slow retreat, fighting every step of the way The Syria advance had easily crossed the TAP line, a northwest–southeast running pipeline service road that had served to rally the defense of the Golan in 1973. The main Syrian drive seemed for the moment to be stalled near Katzrin, the largest town in the Golan. However, there were unsubstantiated reports of a breakthrough to the north end of the Kinneret.

The second large Syrian army seemed to have jumped the Syria–Israel border along a broad front opposite the line of Israeli settlements that stretched on the uplands to the east of the Kinneret from Keshet in the north, to Ofek in the south where the Syrian border ended and the border with Jordan began. That line of small, tenacious communities appeared to be holding, backed up by regular IDF troops. But they were taking a heavy pounding, and they had their backs to the steep escarpment that plunged from the volcanic rock of the heights to the below-sea-level valley of the lake.

Jordan did not appear to be sitting this war out. Anna's Arab-speaking monitors were picking up much boasting on air that the cluster of agricultural communities at the southern end of the Kinneret, including possibly *Dagenya Alef* and *Bet*, two of the earliest of the Israeli kibbutzim, had fallen to an overwhelming force of Jordanian regulars. This army had split, with most advancing south to sweep the Israeli side of the Jordan Valley. The other force was trying to hammer its way around the southwestern corner of the lake to take the ancient city of Tiberius.

The Jerusalem command post was reporting heavy, indiscriminant rocket fire from Jordan and rumors of a crossing in force at the Allenby bridge near Jericho. There was also street-by-street fighting in the capital. It was especially heavy along the "seam line" between predominantly Arab and Jewish neighborhoods. Well-armed radical groups and regular Palestinian police and Palestinian Authority paramilitary forces were controlling the mostly Arab sectors of the city. It was no secret what was happening right now to the thousands of weapons supplied by the US to prop up the shaky "moderate" Palestinian government. Sporadic fighting was breaking out in mixed neighborhoods and in the walled Old City.

However, all this chaos was not the reason why Jerusalem Command did not get on the air until almost 11 a.m. Some faulty relays had transmitted the effects of the electromagnetic pulse into their inner bunker and fried most of their equipment. They were operating with backup communications put together from undamaged units. Anna also learned that the Prime Minister and Defense Minister had been off visiting Be'er Sheba and Ashkelon respectively, and had not been heard from yet.

News from Ramat Hovav in the Negev was no better. Their installation had been incomplete due to problems with the contractors, budget shortfalls, and the general difficulties of creating such a complex installation. So they were operating with little to work with, especially in the area of long distance radio communications. Their news was equally grim. Egypt had attacked along the perimeter of the Gaza Strip "liberating" thousands of well-armed and bloodthirsty Hamas and other Israel-hating militants. From what they could report, one Egyptian advance was headed towards Ofakim and Be'er Sheva, while the larger thrust was overrunning the battered town of Sederot on its way to try to grab Ashkelon and drive up the coast to Tel Aviv. The Sinai was relatively quiet. Egypt appeared to be ignoring the Negev this war, except for Be'er Sheva. They were aiming to capture cities in Israel's heartland this war, no doubt with dreams of driving all the way to Tel Aviv.

In terms of working technology, there was not much there to stop them, Anna thought bitterly. Why had no one done anything for so many years? She and others in the strategic command had been sounding the alarm for more than a decade.

Her chief concern at the moment was what to do about contacting the Americans and NATO, and who would be in charge of the Israeli side of the high-level communications. Word had reached her a half an hour ago from topside that the commander of forces on Mt. Meron, a major general and his chief aide, a senior brigadier general, had both been killed by a rocket while racing from one installation to another in an open jeep. She was now the most senior officer in charge of the sprawling mountaintop base, with its army and air force units as well as the strategic command. She had quickly delegated a pair of majors to continue coordinating defense of the mountain topside. For the moment there appeared to be no immediate threat there, aside from the rocket fire. Though they were in sight of Lebanon, and although the entire border was aflame with guerilla raids and fighting – it was all small units and there appeared to be nothing large enough afoot in the area that could threaten to do more than shell their mountaintop retreat.

Jerusalem was no help. The center there was staffed by no one higher than a colonel. And he had his hands full between the Minister of Agriculture and the Minister of Transportation, who were fighting over which one was in charge if the Prime Minister, Defense Minister and the rest of cabinet failed to show up. Since it was the day before a major holiday, they were the only cabinet members in Jerusalem.

The senior officer in charge of the Negev strategic command was a brigadier general, but several years her junior in both age and service. He was able to confirm, however, that three tactical nukes had launched as a counterstrike. Two hit western Iran and one hit eastern Syria. Apparently Arab communications were severely disrupted, but not completely down. All the news of the war that was going out to the rest of the world was heavily filtered and colored by Islamist propaganda. The Negev commander also confirmed that at least one air wing had hit its targets just across the Syrian border before the nukes hit, and Anna verified that with their radar data.

And so apart from relaying the basic news of the current situation on the ground, Anna was not sure what else to tell the US European command center she had raised on a secure channel. Apparently all NATO had in the immediate area was a US submarine with Tomahawk cruise missiles standing by somewhere in the Eastern Mediterranean and another just leaving port in Naples. What could she do with 24 or even 48 Tomahawk missiles? Would they be accurate once they entered the electronically confused, still highly charged war zone? And what would she target? She had no satellite intelligence – and the situation on the ground was changing by the minute.

"What can they give me in the way of satellite intel? How much detail can we get over the channels we have working?" she asked Koby. She closed her eyes as he consulted several of his databases on his computer screen. His voice startled her awake when he answered a couple minutes later. She had not slept more than a few minutes at a stretch in more than 40 hours. She desperately needed sleep to keep thinking.

"I think we could download satellite imagery at say, five-meter resolution instead of 1.5 meter. That would give us a couple less orders of magnitude data to receive. If we used one of the standard US image data compression routines, we could download imagery over all of Israel in say, an hour. Maybe an hour and a half max on the secure bandwidth we have open to USCom right now," he told her. He consulted his screens again, popping up a couple new windows and studying them. "They will have a terrain mapping satellite passing over about now, and something that could get us the tactical information, including infrared in about an hour." We can also go back and request one-meter detail in the areas of interest to us."

"OK," Anna said. She got back on her secure radio link with the senior US commander for southern Europe. "Admiral, I'm going to put your IT people on the line with Koby, my information officer. We need the most up-to-the-minute satellite data you can give us – covering all of Israel and say thirty kilometers past the borders. Koby can tell you exactly what we want and he can get on line with your technical people and tell them how to do it quickly. How about you and I get back on the channel in about, say three hours? That will give us time to download what you can give us and take a look at the situation."

The admiral agreed, and soon his technical officer and Koby were deep into the details. Anna excused herself, told the rest of the trailer what to expect, and said she was going to catch some sleep in the crew quarters. She arranged to be woken up in a little over two hours. She spent the next fifteen minutes dazedly eating some cold leftovers from the crew quarters fridge and taking a lukewarm shower before crawling into the nearest bunk and falling instantly asleep.

Although the relative lull in shelling continued, Eli did not make it home until sometime after nine. He stopped first at the bomb shelter beside the community's larger synagogue and *davened maariv*, the evening prayer with his comrades in arms. Then they all checked in with the defense coordinator of the moshav for instructions and their night time and morning assignments. The holiday of *Sukkot* had begun at sundown, which meant slightly longer prayers for the evening. There would normally be a much longer, holiday prayer service in the morning, but Eli doubted that there would be few who might have time to pray. He doubted that the enemy would give them much time for anything if they attacked again. The enemy's unsuccessful attack just before sunset had most of the moshavniks convinced they would not try a night attack. But then, most of them had been convinced that this 16-hour old war was never going to happen – at least not in this desperately lopsided fashion.

There was only one boom of an incoming shell, falling somewhere just to the south of the moshav from the sound of it, in the ten minutes it took Eli to walk from the community center and synagogue shelter to his house. He registered its location with his ears, but did not even turn to look. Amazing how quickly one got used to war when it came. During the prayers, he had heard at least a partial listing of the moshav's dead and wounded. Too many to keep in his mind. Faces and names were blurring in his tired brain.

As he approached his house – seeing first the welcome shadows of his still-mostly standing orchard – he was amazed to smell the unmistakable aroma of a barbeque. Approaching his patio, he could see several soldiers – for they had guns slung over their shoulders in typical IDF fashion – busily grilling an array of meat on the barbeque made out of half a 55-gallon steel drum that he and Natalie used when they were having a major cookout. There was candlelight glowing through the windows of his Sukkah! Admittedly it was well-sheltered next to his sturdy earth-bermed house and only a few steps away from the protection of his living-dining room, but it was fully open to any falling mortar shell!

He met Natalie and Tali coming out of the partially opened steel shutters that protected their patio doors. They were carrying big bowls of salads, and Natalie exchanged a surprised and happy kiss as she passed. Eli found the dining room empty of people. The dining room table was full of plates and bowls of food, more salads, small bowls of fresh hummus with swirls of olive oil and ground spices, rice, some sort of bean dish, and stacks of freshly baked pitas. He quickly washed, but kept his knapsack and rifle slung on one shoulder as he made his way back out to the sukkah.

There were more than two dozen people packed around the two tables in the wooden booth covered with bamboo and palm branches and otherwise open to the smoky night sky. Most of them were soldiers. His neighbor's wife and children were there and a single young woman he recognized as a recent long-term visitor to the moshav. A young soldier got out of his chair next to Natalie and offered Eli his usual seat at the head of the larger two tables. His *kiddush* cup had been rinsed out and was waiting for him, along with half a bottle of Golan Merlot, grown at his moshav and pressed at a winery down the road. He set his pack down behind his chair and stacked his rifle in the corner and stood at his place. He filled the cup brim full, picked up a booklet with the blessings, and said *Kiddush* with his eyes welling with tears – happiness mixed with sorrow. Ever since coming to Israel eight years ago, the greatest joys and the most poignant sadness had always followed each other and mixed together so closely that his tears were often hard to distinguish, one from the other.

First he said the blessing over the wine, then, holding his brimming cup as steady as he could, with wine dripping down his fingers, said the blessing for festival evenings:

"Blessed are You our G-d, King of the universe, Who has chosen us from all peoples, exalted us over every language, and sanctified us with your commandments. You have given us, *HaShem* our God, with love, our appointed festivals for gladness, festivals and times for joy, on this day of the Festival of *Sukkot*, the time of our gladness – a holy meeting, a memorial of the Exodus from Egypt. For You have chosen us and sanctified us above all peoples, and Your holy festivals in gladness and in joy" his voice was cracking at this point, and he continued, "You have granted us our heritage. Blessed are you our G-d, Who sanctifies Israel and the festival seasons."

He sat down, and all two dozen voices in the Sukkah joined him in the final two blessings:

"*Baruch atah Adonai, Elokeinu Melech Ha Olam, Shechianu, v'kimanu, v'higianu, l'ziman ha zeh...* Blessed are You our Lord, Our God, King of the Universe, Who has kept us alive, sustained us and brought us to this season."

"*Baruch atah Adonai, Elokeinu Melech Ha Olam, asher kiddishanu b'mitzvotav, vtzivanu l'eyshev b'sukkah!...*Blessed are you our Lord, Our God, King of the Universe, Who sanctifies us with His commandments and commanded us to dwell in the sukkah."

Then he drank from the cup and poured some into small cups for his wife and the young single woman who had waited for him to return to take part in his blessing. There was not a dry eye in the sukkah despite the flow of conversation and hot steaks, hamburgers, chicken, and sausages from the barbeque. He had joined a meal that had been in progress for more than an hour with new people arriving as others departed to find shelters for sleeping.

Naomi explained, after he had washed his hands again and said the blessing over bread, that their freezer had no power. So she and Tali had decided to serve out almost everything in the freezer tonight and tomorrow night since they had so many guests. He was in complete agreement. Both paused to listen to a distant shell land and for one of the howitzers parked by the remains of the nursery school to respond in kind. Since Eli had a watch in the night ahead, he finished eating and visiting with his guests by eleven pm and sacked out on a spare guest mattress in his bedroom. Their comfortable queen-sized bed was full of an unknown number of small children. Eli usually slept in his sukkah during this holiday – but soldiers were still filtering in from the field, drawn by word of mouth, the smell, or both.

Day Two

Moshav Yiftach 00:15

Natalie awakened Eli for his one am watch duties. She had been washing up the dishes, putting away food and serving the declining trickle of guests. She had just brewed a fresh pot of coffee for the purpose of coaxing Eli back into consciousness. She planned to go to bed after he left, assuming fresh batch of guests did not show up hungry, tired and thirsty.

They had just settled down to wait for Eli's fellow watchmen and have a quiet cup of coffee in the now empty sukkah when they heard the familiar rattle, clank and chug of Woody making its way around the bomb craters that now made up the road to their end of the kibbutz. There had not been a shell falling in the twenty minutes Eli had been awake, a fact that now, in retrospect, he found amazing. It was Colonel Eschol with the lieutenant still at the wheel and a pair of sleeping soldiers sacked out in the bed behind the wood box. The colonel and lieutenant left the soldiers asleep in the back and, seeing the candles lit, came to peek inside the sukkah.

Eli and Natalie welcomed them and offered them a choice of hot coffee, or cold drinks and hot food. "I can throw some more charcoal on the barbeque and grill you up some steaks while you take a shower if you want, there is still a bit of hot water left in the solar. I checked the gauge when I got out ten minutes ago, enough for a couple minutes each" Eli volunteered. The tired officers gratefully accepted and went in the house to shower. Eli set about poking up the embers and adding charcoal. Since it was a holiday, it was permissible under Jewish law to add to an existing flame, or rekindle a light from an already burning candle. With a war going on in his back yard, there were plenty of permissible exceptions available to him if he needed them. It felt good, however, to follow the letter of the law wherever possible – as long as nothing was in danger from the delay.

As it was, he had some good-sized steaks grilling and ready to turn when the colonel emerged, somewhat refreshed. The colonel poured a kiddish cup of wine for himself. He had found no time for a meal that evening and it was still the first night of the festival – albeit a half-over night. The colonel closed his eyes for the blessings, and appeared to doze off for a few minutes between the time he finished the blessing and finished drinking the small cup of wine. He roused and went inside and washed his hands, coming back to the basket of pitas on the table. Col. Eschol took two and said the blessing over bread. Eli and Natalie set out salads and side dishes within his easy reach – encouraged him to help himself, and returned to their quiet conversation, leaving the weary colonel to his own thoughts. Those thoughts seemed heavy and worried when he came in, but lightened somewhat as the food and drink began to work its way into his system.

"I think I've spent most of the *Sukkot* holidays of my life in the field," he said after awhile, "but this is only the third one at war – two were spent in Lebanon in the 80's. But they were nothing like this,"

Eli agreed. The war was now only nineteen hours old, but already felt like an established fact of life.

As he suspected, the grilling steaks soon awakened the bodies in the back of the truck, and they hurried inside to wash as the lieutenant emerged, showered and looking marginally fresher. He also made *Kiddush* for himself, washed for bread and sat down to devour anything on the table within reach, including the steak that was soon served hot from the grill to his plate. The two soldiers joined them, having had lukewarm but most welcome showers. It was still a warm night, perfect shirtsleeve weather if one could ignore the ravages of war outside their candle lit sukkah and, for awhile, they could.

Natalie slipped off to bed shortly before one am. It seemed easier to her to part that way, rather than wait sleepily and anxiously for the last possible moment. There had not been a shell for nearly an hour, and Eli's watch was supposed to stop by and collect him on their way to their posts. She said a sleepy goodbye, one of many goodbyes that day.

The men talked of the war, their homes, and their lives when not fighting wars. Lieutenant Sam Hirsch – for that was the name of the man Eli turned his truck over to earlier that day, was a product development wonk for a high tech Internet services company in real life, but his reserve unit had been called back to active duty in March. His small start-up company, in which he owned a small equity stake, was having to operate with his very limited attention. He was serving as the colonel's go-for and de facto aide de camp, though he belonged to a recon company that was elsewhere. He also filled some sort of public information function because he was one of the few people in the Golan with a working camera. Sam produced a small manual, old-fashioned range finder camera which he kept tucked in a shirt pocket and snapped a picture of Col. Eschol, Eli and the two soldiers as they ate.

Sam had gone off with Woody in the afternoon to contact the stranded rapid response force. He delivered some mechanics and advice, and then he had returned to the moshav to arrange for the bulldozer to tow the disabled tanks into the moshav for re-wiring. Picking up Col. Eschol, they had visited the next three communities to the south and arranged for two more working, early-model bulldozers to come and tow tanks as soon as they were available from other urgent tasks. Col. Eschol, it seemed, was in charge of their sector of the Golan.

As Eli knew, but had forgotten until reminded, Moshav Yiftach had the perfect shelter for repairing a couple of huge 65-ton tanks. For a few years the moshav had experimented with growing exotic varieties of potatoes. To store their crops, they had half buried a large, sturdy, steel Quonset hut and covered it with several feet of earth to achieve the cool, dry, shelter needed for storing potatoes. The experiment ended some years ago without establishing a market for the new product, and the potato barn was now partially used for storing wine from the nearby winery – leaving a large, sheltered space for working on the moshav agricultural machinery. Once the diesel generator was persuaded to start and various quirks with the power converters worked out, it made a fine wartime workshop.

Lt. Hirsch had helped shepherd the first of the disabled Merkava IV tanks fifteen kilometers to the moshav. Then he and the colonel had set off together again shortly after the late afternoon assault had been beaten back from the moshav. They had ranged as far south as the last community still in Israeli hands, checking on the state of defenses, forces and supplies.

The Golan Heights communities were cut off to the south by a massive Jordanian assault that had taken the south end of the Kinneret. It was blasting its way south towards Beit She'an, and had sent another column north to threaten Tiberias.

Eli had already heard that Syrians had broken through to the north of them and were fighting in the streets of Katzrin. Israeli scouts reported that some rogue commando units and irregulars had broken through along the highway to the north of them that led down to the northern shore of the Kinneret, and that some of them had pushed as far south as the narrow strip of shore below the Golan Heights town of Ramot where they had been stopped by shelling from the town.

In other words, their little chain of settlements and the army forces with them were surrounded on three sides by overwhelming enemy forces, and on the fourth side by steep escarpment of the Golan Heights and the lake itself, with its narrow strip of shoreline. The only other road, that reached the lake at Ein Gev, had been bombed so unmercifully that there were now major rock slides blocking it in several places. The heavy shelling that continued at Bnei Yehuda, the largest town at the southern end of the Golan Heights, made any movement in that direction a perilous possibility.

But, the universal problem was that everyone was running out of ammunition. The 155 mm howitzers that had so briskly defended Moshav Yiftach, and their counterparts to the south had shot their way through their own stores, and used up almost all of the shells ferried in from the disabled self-propelled howitzers from the rapid response force. These big guns were being towed in, one-by-one along with the tanks, and they expected to have all in place by morning. However, the sad and unavoidable fact was that there were perhaps twenty rounds left per gun.

The few tanks they had running – older models in the armored brigade to the south of them – were also down to their last dozen shells, if even that many. Machine gun rounds were getting scarce. There was still a fair bit of rifle ammunition for Tavor and M-16 assault rifles, but 5.6 mm bullets did not stop tanks and armored vehicles. There were no more bazooka rounds to be had at Moshav Yiftach and few, if any, rocket-propelled grenades available there or in any of the other communities. One more assault would finish them. It would be hand to hand fighting as tanks overran the settlements, with little left to stop them and little hope of winning.

"There is a huge reserve cache of ammunition in underground bunkers in the mountain just above Tiberias," the lieutenant said as the colonel shook his head sadly. "The question is how to get there. I had been thinking about trying to make a run around the north end of the lake using Woody, but the colonel says there have been commandos breaking though along the highway north of here."

"What about crossing the lake?" Eli asked.

"With what?" the lieutenant asked. "We don't have any boats and we haven't been able to signal across and get an answer with lights. Hell, we don't even know if Tiberias is still ours – our news is several hours old," Lt. Hirsch said bitterly.

"It's only about eight kilometers directly across from Ein Gev," Eli said, "I've paddled across in a kayak half a dozen times. It takes about an hour and a half."

"You have a boat that can get across the lake?" the colonel asked wonderingly. Eli nodded. A true soldier, the colonel had thought about the land only. The lieutenant looked interested.

"It's an inflatable kayak, but a good one – holds two people and weighs less than twenty kilos. I keep it in a duffle bag in the shed. I don't think the shed has been hit."

The colonel was a "show me" sort of guy and the lieutenant a quick thinker always looking for solutions. They followed Eli to the shed with a flashlight. He found the duffle bags with the kayak, foot pump, two-piece paddles, and a pair of life jackets. The lieutenant hefted the kayak bag.

"OK," the colonel said, "now how do we get to the lake in one piece with these? All the roads are closed north and south – and it's what, about ten kilometers from here, with some very steep cliffs and ravines – that's why they made most of it a nature reserve."

"Done that too," Eli said, "there's a dirt road that takes off from Kfar Haruv at the southern end of the Golan Heights. You said you drove there earlier today. A hiking trail goes down the wadi through the Nature Reserve and comes out about a kilometer south of Ein Gev. From the farthest point you can drive to at the top to the lake it's only like about a kilometer and a half. And you could probably pull down some of the posts blocking the trail head and get perhaps a quarter of a kilometer closer before it becomes foot path only. Granted, it's steep, but even an old geezer like me has hiked it. It's one of my favorite get-in-shape hikes. There is perhaps 600 meters elevation gain in a kilometer and a half. Young guys can run down it in about twenty minutes, and back up in about forty."

"We're talking about packing in a lot of ammunition. A 155 round alone weighs fifty kilos," the colonel said skeptically. "Isn't there a jeep road somewhere?"

"The only one is south of there and comes out where the Jordanians broke though," the lieutenant told him. "But we have some possible manpower that we could round up among the   communities. For instance, there are nearly a hundred young men between fifteen and eighteen at the *hesder yeshiva* down in Hespin who are chomping at the bit to help out. We have them digging trenches, running messages on mountain bikes and dirt bikes, hauling water and ammo to the troops. I bet at least half of them are big enough to pack a thirty kilogram tank shell if not a fifty kilo howitzer shell. Two or three round trips each…. That would be 120 rounds right there. And maybe there are civilians in Tiberias that could help."

The colonel thought over the plan, and challenged them with of all the problems it could encounter. What if the Jordanians had launched patrol boats to take Tiberias? What if they had pushed farther north along the shore of the lake to surround the Golan Heights? What if the civil defense forces in Tiberias had launched their own patrols? What were the odds of being shot before they could identify themselves? What if helicopters finally showed up? Could they get across and back while it was still dark? How would they transport all the shells back? Where could they find volunteers in Tiberias to help? Together they worked through the possibilities. Fortunately there were plenty of boats that could normally be found in the resort town of Tiberias. How many of them were in one piece after the shelling and how many of those had an engine that could start and run – these were all open questions.

However they quickly decided it was worth a try and had the potential to get them at least some of the precious ammunition they needed. It would also establish contact across the lake to the rest of Israel, which could be continued with lights and mirrors, and perhaps even radio if they had any working sets over there. They agreed that Eli and Lt. Hirsch would take Woody and two soldiers, and that the colonel and some others would follow them to the trail head in the old Dodge power wagon that was still running. That way everyone would know the way to the trail for sure, with no communications mix ups. The colonel would then go back to the yeshiva and other communities and round up volunteers for a pack train of ammunition carriers. Perhaps there were even horses or mules to be pressed into service. Eli, the lieutenant and the two soldiers would hike down to the lake. Eli and Lt. Hirsch would paddle across, make contact, round up the first load of ammunition and volunteers, and try to be back across the lake before sunrise. The two soldiers would guard their landing spot, and have a flashlight ready to guide them back to the eastern shore. There was no time to spare. Eli needed to be excused from his moshav guard duties in order to go off on their wild early morning expedition. That was quickly arranged. He handed his precious rifle and remaining shells over to Gadi.

Then he left a quick note for Natalie which he knew must sound ridiculous – "Gone to Tiberias in the kayak for help with the IDF – back sometime after sunrise – love you dearly, Eli."

Eli fed Woody's firebox and replenished its wood supply from the shed. They set off, with Eli at the familiar wheel of Woody in a very unfamiliar feeling dark landscape full of potholes and craters. However, he knew the few streets of the moshav well, and most of the larger holes gaped even blacker in the darkness. The night was eerily lit with a smoky haze reflecting back the yellow, red and orange flames of burning brush and the occasional burning building or guttering, blackened truck or halftrack. He drove carefully around the worst of the shell holes and they stopped off at the potato barn workshop for the colonel to leave orders and borrow the moshav's old power wagon.

Eli and the lieutenant went into the workshop with the colonel. There, lit up with an odd collection of lamps – for many light bulbs and light fixtures had blown in the electronic pulse – they saw a dozen men at work re-wiring the ignition and controls of a large, dark Merkava tank that cast huge shadows on the curved ceiling above them. The colonel found one of his senior officers under the tank, quickly relayed their plan, and gave some orders for rearranging their defenses in his absence. It sounded like he had some plans for some pinprick attacks of their own, just to probe the enemy's strength and disposition.

In a short while he was steering Woody around the demolished main gate of the moshav and heading into the darkness down the long narrow road that connected their community to the north-south highway that linked the Golan Heights communities. They were driving without lights and had disconnected the brake and tail lights, and dimmed the dash lights. Sam had dabbed the truck's ugly brown paint with mud and soot to deaden its visibility on one of his earlier errands.

It didn't take long for Eli's eyes to get used to the darkness and begin to see the faint contours of the road and landscape better. Driving at night with no headlights was almost easier for him than driving crowded highways with the oncoming headlights half blinding him, he decided. Maybe the problem was bright lights – not his night vision, he wondered. Even so, they were lucky to hit 20 – 30 km an hour between bomb craters that forced detours. He sensed Sam's impatience with their slow progress.

As they were now on a first-name basis, Eli and Sam were casually sharing details of their lives. Eli shared tidbits about the history of building Woody and the odd reception it garnered every time it went somewhere new.

"If we come out of this war in one piece, I definitely want to build one," the lieutenant said, "It would make a heck of a marketing tool for our company – it would sort of fit the quirky, do-things-differently niche we're trying to create. Besides, I'm tired of making some Arab rich every time I buy a tank of gasoline. Because look how they spend their money," he grumbled, nodding at the light of a distant shell burst.

As they reached the main road and turned south, they could see the occasional burst of shelling much farther to the south, but no action to the north behind them. A few huge shell holes had gouged out the main road near the junction. They had to jockey their way down into some of the craters and gun it back up the other side, a maneuver that would be difficult if not impossible with a load of shells coming back. They would have to plan some time for digging the slopes down a bit on the way back. Sam said the colonel was sure to take note of that and perhaps take care of it on his return trip, for he was really an engineer at heart, although he had spent most of his life in the IDF.

"How long have you worked with Colonel Eschol?" Eli asked.

"Off and on for maybe five years. Most of the time I've been in the reserves, actually. I did my active duty in a reconnaissance unit, and that's where I was supposed to be. I think they are somewhere up along the Lebanese border." Sam answered. "Eschol? He's one heck of a guy. From the stories they tell about him in Lebanon, well, we couldn't be in much better hands as far as hanging on to this little strip of Golan. He's damned good. And as you can probably tell from all the questioning, he's not a bit reckless or cocky like some of the other senior commanders with his kind of reputation. I figure it's his politics that has kept him from making general by now. He tends to say what he thinks, not what he's supposed to think."

They followed the bomb cratered highway south along the backbone of settlements, driving mostly along the cleared right of way on the western side of the highway. They used the raised bed of the highway to their left for shelter from shelling and sniping from the Syrian forces strung out opposite the length of the chain of settlements. They detoured around the large reservoir north of Hespin – for they had heard that the town directly across the highway from the yeshiva community had fallen and was the battleground for fierce fire fights between the forces that were separated only by a highway right of way of perhaps a hundred meters in places.

As they neared the outer fence of Hespin, Eli flashed their parking lights briefly and beeped the horn a few times to alert the defenders they were coming. With no radios, there was no way of telling them in advance. The danger of friendly fire at this point was considerably greater than that of falling shells. Eli could see the dark shapes of the two soldiers riding shotgun in the pickup bed, they were both facing out, had their rifles at the ready and looked ready to dive out at the first sign of trouble. Advancing another slow few hundred meters, Eli flashed the lights again and gave a faint beep, beep, beep with his horn. The lights of the truck behind them flashed too – and he recalled the horn on the old Dodge truck had never worked in the five years he had been on the moshav. That was just one of its many quirks. About half a kilometer ahead a flashlight winked twice in the darkness. Eli drove slowly and steadily about half the distance, then he stopped to let Sam lean out of his window and hail the sentries.

After a guarded exchange of questions, then friendly insults, he nodded for Eli to proceed. Soon they slalomed through large chunks of concrete and debris that blocked the back entrance to the moderate sized community that was home to the region's high school, a large hotel and the Yeshiva of the Golan. It was a high-school-to-army *Hesder yeshiva* for religious students who spent a year and a half in the army in addition to four and a half years in the rabbinic studies program. Hespin was also a *yishuv*, which was less collectively owned and more privately run than Yiftach, which was a moshav that held most of the land and several industries in commonly owned corporations – but not as nearly as communal an enterprise as a kibbutz – like Deganya. Was it really true that Deganya – the quintessential kibbutz and the setting for much of Leon Uris' stirring book *Exodus* – had fallen? Eli couldn't comprehend such an Israel.

The colonel dispatched someone from his group in the old Dodge truck to go and start arranging their ammunition carriers and other volunteers. They spoke briefly to the pickets at the gate and were relieved to hear that there had been no action in the direction of the lake. In fact, a patrol had gone down the path through the nature reserve earlier in the evening and had emerged near Ein Gev to set up an ambush for any commandos that might have broken through at the south end of the lake and keep them from encircling them along the narrow shores. There were plenty of dips and hills on the two lane highway that circled the Kinneret that would make it easy for a small force to keep a larger one at bay until help came.

Eli threaded his way around the *yishuv* – which he heard was even more heavily damaged than Moshav Yiftach only six kilometers away as the crow flew, but more than ten by road. The heaviest fighting here had taken place along the main highway, with Israeli forces dug in to the east of the town, and the town immediately across the highway evacuated, overrun and now a battleground.

They picked up a dirt road that led behind the next three *yishuvim* to the south, Nov and Avnei Eitan and Eli Ad. Fortunately the Syrian advance which had threatened to cut the chain of settlements had stalled in fierce fighting at Eli Ad, where the Golan Heights narrowed to less than two kilometers between the deep canyon and the rugged escarpment that sheered off the southern end of the Golan Heights and another that formed the eastern border with Syria. There was an equally deep canyon or wadi that dissected the thick basaltic mass of the Golan Heights behind Eli Ad and Geshur to the west. In its scenic depths plunged one of the area's few year-round streams, with a series of lovely water falls. In summer, and especially now in September, there was barely a trickle running. They weaved through the nearly deserted *yishuv* that was tensely waiting for the next morning's onslaught with barely enough ammunition to make a stand.

From Eli Ad they were able to follow another series of farm track and dirt roads west of the highway again and make some better time to *Yishuv* HaRuv. Their walking track left from near an empty ticket and information booth, where Nature Reserve rangers collected entrance fees in the summer. The big Dodge was following much closer now as they neared their destination.

When they came to the small parking lot at the trailhead, the soldiers made quick work of knocking down one of the wooden posts that blocked vehicle access to the trail. Putting Woody in its lowest granny gear, Eli guided his old truck carefully down the hiking track, until it prepared to switch back upon itself and plunge steeply. There he pulled on to one of the few halfway level spots and killed the engine. "Chock the wheels," he asked Sam, who relayed the order to the soldiers. The larger, older power wagon was well behind them now, and it stopped when they did. Eli and Lt. Hirsch walked back up the trail to them and held a quick conference at the window.

"This is as far as we can go with four wheels," Eli said. The colonel's driver, a moshavnik he recognized from the field crops group at the moshav, prepared to back up to where he could turn the bigger rig around.

The colonel gave Sam last minute instructions to relay to whoever he found in charge of Tiberias, and quickly prioritized their "shopping list" of shells and supplies. "Tell them we need 155 mm shells first, mortar rounds second, and tank ammo third. But tell them also that if we can restock at least half a dozen Merks, we might be able to do something about that force at the north end of the lake from our side. I think we have four shooting 105 mm, and only two using the regular 120, so keep that in mind. But when we get the eleven Merk IV's up and running, we will need all the 120 ammo they can give us and I think we could definitely break through somewhere."

Eli was shocked to hear that last bit. He had been thinking in terms of defense, of digging in and trying not to be overrun. But apparently the colonel was thinking ahead to when he could take the battle back to the enemy.

Sam took the heavier bag with the rolled up kayak, while Eli took the lighter bag with the paddles, pump and lifejackets – which were bright orange – should they be caught in daylight. He debated leaving them, but if their kayak was shot full of holes, it would make a swim easier – or would it just make them better targets? He decided that they could sit on the life preservers. It would make the seats more comfortable and give the a little more leverage for the long paddle ahead of them. Eight kilometers at a steady four to six kilometers an hour was a stiff, but do-able pace for the inflatable, assuming that they could steer a straight course. Eli could barely see the surface of the lake, which usually glowed with a silver sheen in all but the darkest nights from here at the top of the canyon.

One of the soldiers went ahead of them, his rifle loosely at the ready, while the other fell in behind them. Eli was glad of that, because he could concentrate on where he was feeling ahead with his feet and let them worry about ambushes and lurking patrols. The trail was steep and winding until it finally reached the floor of the stream-cut canyon. Although it was considerably darker at the bottom of the canyon, Eli's eyes were better tuned to the nuances of the darkness, and all four of them were walking along fairly easily now that the trail had leveled somewhat. They appeared to have the dark canyon to themselves. No one talked, except in low, brief exchanges in whispers. Occasionally they all stopped to listen and watch for any signs of movement. The sky overhead had an odd, faint burnt red-orange glow, and the smell of smoke from the many wildfires now burning out of control up and down northern Israel was strong in the warm night. Every now and then they moved through still pockets of cool, earth-smelling air in the depths of the canyon which were refreshing and served to sharpen their senses further.

At two points they had to scramble down iron rungs set into the rock as they bypassed waterfalls. Eli's girls – now both married young women, had always liked these short sections of rock scrambling. He could see now that it would be slow, difficult work trudging up them with a 50 kilogram pack. He figured that about 25kg would be his maximum load with his 58-year-old back and knees. He remembered how stiff he had felt just that morning, well really it was yesterday morning, after a few hours of crawling around in his sniper's nest. That seemed a lifetime away. Now there was just a dark canyon, his three companions, the load on his shoulders, and the need to hurry.

After perhaps fifteen minutes more brisk walking from the last of the waterfalls, the canyon began to open up and the trail zigzagged the final descent to a banana grove at near the level of the lake. Soon they reached the deserted highway that encircled the lake. They stopped to attempt to signal the patrol that had left earlier that evening, who were supposed to be perhaps a kilometer or two to the north where the steep shoulders of the Golan heights crowded the highway down to a narrow strip, with a steep bank on one side dropping to the lake, and an even steeper rocky slope above rising towards the heights above. They chanced a few discreet flashes from their flashlight, and sang a couple bars of some popular Israeli folk tunes. There was no response, so they slipped across the highway one by one and picked their way down the slope to the lake. It was a farther drop than Eli had remembered, and he had forgotten that the trail ended at the highway.

Soon they stood on the rocky shore of the Kinneret. They stood a while, watching and listening. The smoke was heavier down here and appeared to be lying in thick banks like fog along the lake. Normally one could see the other side even by starlight, but tonight the other side of the lake was lost in smoke and darkness. Eli unrolled the kayak, connected the foot pump and let Sam pump up the boat while he assembled the two-piece paddles mostly by feel. The pump seemed abnormally loud as air whooshed into the boat's three main chambers. Their guards moved nervously off to stand some few dozen paces away so as to see and hear better. There was sand in the tight fitting sleeve of the second paddle and he had to wash it out with lake water in order to fit them together. In the dark he had one of the blades at the wrong angle. They needed to be at 90 degrees to each other, and set up just right for a right handed paddler, so he undid them and twisted them right, placing the lower blade between his feet and feeling the upper blade with his hand.

"You're right handed, aren't you?" he asked Sam, who answered affirmatively as he pumped up the third section. Eli finished the paddle and was blowing up one of the seat backs by mouth when he could tell by the sound of the pump the chamber was full enough. He thumped the now taut tubes. "Just right" he said, and screwed in the valve caps, glad that they were permanently attached by retaining loops. He had put the kayak together by moonlight for a few romantic trips on the lake with Natalie, but never tried it in near pitch darkness. He had checked his watch quickly when they had flashed their lights before crossing the highway. It was shortly after two am. It would be three-thirty or later by the time they reached Tiberias.

Eli fitted in the back rests, folded the life vests for seats, and waded out into the slippery rocky shallows of the lake, placing his pack behind the rear seat. He had only his sidearm, and felt somewhat naked without a rifle after only twenty-some hours of wartime. Sam had brought a short-barreled M16 with a folding stock, while their escorts carried the longer barreled version. Eli told him to stash the rifle and his pack behind the front seat to keep them dry, and instructed him to climb in first. He handed him one of the long, double-bladed paddles and told Sam to concentrate on keeping his balance while Eli pushed off. Eli slid the boat, heavy at Sam's end, a few meters into slightly deeper water and stepped in. The trim of the small boat evened out, and they were afloat with a few inches of water under them. The shore at this point was a broad rocky shallows that extended out into the lake for many meters, with willows and cattails thick in places, forcing them to pick their way slowly at first.

"Let me take us out, then you can dig in," Eli said after a few enthusiastic but misguided paddle strokes spun them towards the nearest weeds. He made a few sweeping strokes, corrected their course and threaded evenly out between the clumps of willows and weeds. In a few more even strokes they reached open water.

"You control the paddle with your right hand, letting it rotate freely through your left," Eli explained. "Smooth, even strokes, equal on each side – the guy at the back – that's me – does most of the steering in one of these things." Sam obviously had no experience in a small boat, or with a double-bladed paddle either, and the boat tipped this way and that. There was much splashing as he plied his paddle with much enthusiasm and strength, but little skill.

However, with patience and having had much experience with initiating such newcomers to the art of kayaking, Eli soon had him pulling through the water at a more manageable pace. "You actually get most of the power from pushing with the top hand than pulling with the bottom hand. And the middle of the stroke when it is nearly even with your body is where we get most of the thrust. So save your power for that part of the stroke. Slow and steady. Try to pick up my rhythm and we'll stop bonking our paddles so much."

A few more minutes and they were pulling strongly and evenly and keeping a much straighter course. Eli began to wonder, however, where exactly they were headed. It had been a long while since he had glimpsed the shore behind them, and he could see nothing but ghostly grey, lazily rolling banks of fog and smoke ahead and all around them. He looked overhead to see if he could find a star to keep his orientation, but the sky was overhung with a smoky haze. He did not want to wander to the south where they might be spotted by Jordanians holding the southern end of the lake.

Eli had paddled on the lake at night several times – but always by the light of a moon, or on a crystal clear night with bright starlight and the lights of Tiberias to guide him. Tonight he could not even see where they had been a few minutes before. Their slight, swirling wake disappeared within a few boat lengths behind them as they entered one of the thicker banks of smoky fog. He tried to concentrate on keeping their track arrow straight, but he was not pulling as strongly and evenly as the beginning.

After a while Sam sensed his uneasiness and slowed his pace – "What's wrong?" he asked.

"I have no idea which direction is which any more. I've lost all bearings and can't get a fix on anything solid to steer by," Eli admitted.

"Seems like we've been going pretty straight to me," Sam said, "although we might be pulling a bit to the right."

"Yeah, I want to make sure we don't stray too far south – but for all I know we could have turned straight north and be running up the lake past Tiberias," Eli said. "Hang on, let's drift a couple minutes and see if I can get the feel of the water and see if there's a slight breeze I can use to orient myself."

Sam didn't turn around, but Eli could feel he found that suggestion not very reassuring, and perhaps more than a bit absurd. However he stopped paddling, and they drifted nearly to a stop in the foggy darkness.

Eli studied the sky again, hoping for a glimpse of a star, or the moon – which should be full tonight – for *Sukkot* always started on the 14th of the Jewish lunar month of Tishrei. But the moon, if he could see it, would be setting soon if it hadn't set already. He knew the full moon rose fairly early and set early, and then rose later each night as it waned. Come to think of it, he had not noticed a full moon from his sukkah earlier in the evening. Usually it rose during their first *Sukkot* meal and was always a magnificent sight. Where was it tonight? Was there any part of the fog that glowed brighter? Sam shifted restlessly, but kept quiet. Eli couldn't tell anything from the sky, so he concentrated on the slow rolling, smoky fog around them. His eyes had been burning for some time from all the smoke that had collected at the surface of the lake. The Kinneret, he reminded himself, looked like an alpine lake surrounded by hills, but was actually below sea level. Therefore all the smoke from the fires burning all over the north of Israel were draining down to its basin and collecting.

"Draining," he thought, "is there a flow to these clouds that would be moving down the lake to the outlet? He focused on the bank of fog about to engulf them again, but it appeared to have an almost circular swirl to it.

That left the water as his only remaining clue, for shouting and listening for an echo would tell the nothing useful at this point. The lake was surrounded by hills that would echo back with no preference – one direction for another.

Their kayak was rising and falling gently with a certain rhythm. It was very slight, perhaps a matter of a two or three inch rise and fall, but it was steady. He leaned over to the right and watched the ripple of waves along the hull. The faint swell seemed to be coming from somewhere to the right. He leaned over to the left and Sam shifted uneasily to counterbalance him. Eli stared for a long time, then returned to peering over the right side again.

Sam had enough at this point, "What the hell are you doing?" he asked with a mix of mystification and impatience. "Are we just going to sit here until the sun comes up?"

"I'm reading the water," Eli said simply.

"Is it in English or Hebrew?" Sam inquired.

Eli chuckled, "the creator of the universe speaks to us in many languages – but this one is wind and water. There has been one of our hot summer east winds blowing for several days now. I remember how much water I was drinking on watch at the Moshav. Nothing dries you out like an east wind up here."

Sam agreed, but still professed to be mystified. "So, are you telling me we're lost?"

"Not yet," Eli said.

"But you have no idea where we are."

"Not really."

"That means 'lost' in my book," Sam said. "What's the difference between having no idea where we are and being lost?"

"Having no idea where we are on the lake is one thing, but if I can get a clue about which direction is which, then I will know which way to go," Eli said.

"Still sounds like lost to me," Sam muttered.

"OK," Eli said, "So, assuming that the same wind has been blowing down here, only it generally blows a little more like from the northeast to the southwest across the lake. I'm thinking that these regular swells I'm seeing are running in that direction. So, if I can tell which direction is which, I might not know exactly where we are, but I'll be able to tell which way we need to go."

Sam saw his logic, but needed some coaching and some precarious leaning over the side peering at the water along the side of the kayak to see these swells that Eli was talking about. "Damned if you're not Davy Crockett himself," Sam said, impressed. He had been raised half in America, half in Israel in his early years by Israel-born parents, so he had at least heard of Daniel Boone and Davy Crockett.

Once Eli had oriented himself and got the feel of the subtle waves, he was able to guide them in line with the waves, angling nearly broadside to their faint swells. He reasoned that he would much rather land north of Tiberias than anywhere to the south of it. They resumed paddling, only easier and cutting a much straighter course. Their little kayak had no rudder, but was stiff enough to track fairly well in the calm water. Soon they were gliding along at close to the five or six kilometers an hour that Eli had estimated would be necessary to cross the lake in an hour and a half.

They paddled along for a little under an hour – pausing twice to drink and stretch and make sure their rifle and pistol were still dry. It had grown light enough for Eli to tell the hour from his watch if he held it to the sky, and it looked to be about three-thirty. If they had gone fairly straight and not veered too far off to the north or south, they should be approaching Tiberias by now.

"In the summertime you can smell the falafel and French fries from at least half a kilometer away," Eli said, sniffing the air hopefully. Although with a war and no power, falafel was probably not being cooked in Tiberias at 3:30 in the morning, Still, he hoped to catch some sort of scent of the sleeping city – overflowing dumpsters, maybe a gasoline smell from spilled gas? "Let's try a yell," he suggested.

Sam rested his paddle on the side tubes and cupped his hands for a yell, "*Boker Tov Tiveria*!" he shouted at the top of his powerful lungs. Eli thought he caught a faint echo as if from a building or hillside. "*Boker Tov, Tiveria*," Sam yelled again a minute later, "*Anachnu kol ha Yehudim,*" Good morning Tiberias – we are all Jews!" This time there was a definite echo.

A few moments later a voice challenged from the mist, maybe a few hundred meters away and to their left – "*Mi zeh*? Who's that?"

Sam shouted back his name and unit – and said they were from the Golan.

"*Baruch HaShem*" the voice echoed back.

They paddled towards the sound of the voice and soon saw a pair of figures behind a sand-bagged machine gun on the stone jetty protecting one of the city's boat harbors. Eli knew exactly where he was now. He couldn't have planned it better. They had paddled right up to the largest of the city's harbors, the one where all the larger tourist boats collected, and where he hoped to find something running to ferry their ammunition across the lake. He guided their boat quickly around the jetty and they drew it up to the empty boat ramp. The two guards waved from their machine gun post, and several soldiers came down from a nearby concession stand to greet them – looking curiously at their inflatable kayak. They all pulled it ashore and carried it up to the shelter of their lakefront camp.

Sam quickly ascertained how the city was holding up, and asked how they could get to the IDF storehouses up the mountain in a hurry. One of the soldiers told them to follow him. They set off towards the heart of town with its tourist shops, restaurants and stores. He hailed another soldier by a kiosk, who promptly kicked a motor scooter to life, and motioned Eli and Sam to another one parked at the curb.

Eli hated motorcycles, and especially riding on the back of motorcycles. But he had no choice and climbed on the seat behind Sam. The young lieutenant started up the bike and peeled off after the speeding soldier. Eli felt his stomach lurch and hung on for dear life. Sam was clearly paying him back the kayak lessons as they roared up the streets of Tiberias, climbing up and away from the lakefront. He saw a small crowd clustered in the predawn darkness at the grave of the 12th century sage and scholar, the Rambam – Rabbi Moses ben Maimon – better known to the western world as the philosopher Maimonides.

The little scooter was laboring now with the weight of both full-sized men as it climbed the switch backing road towards the upper city. Eli held on as they swerved and swung around debris and potholes blasted by falling rockets. It was clear that the city had been subjected to a severe bombardment. As the road was beginning to clear the city and head out into open country, their guide ahead of them dived right and down a narrow one-lane road that contoured around the mountain. He beeped to alert sentries at a fence ahead, and the two scooters paused to be quickly scrutinized by a guard at a gate in the tall wire fence topped with razor wire – the Israeli national flower, Eli thought wryly.

They were told they would find the commander of the installation and the civil defense director for the city down in the first bomb shelter by the gate. There were about a dozen tired looking soldiers and a few civilians smoking by the stairs at the entrance to the shelter. The stairs themselves were cluttered with people who had to scoot over to let them by. Israelis have a fine, all-purpose word for the scene that presented itself at the main room at the bottom of the stairs – a *balagan.* The plain, white-painted cement room, about the size of a large classroom, was full of people. Most of them were busy arguing with each other and about half of them jammed around two battered metal desks. The rest were waiting impatiently to jam themselves around one or the other of the two battered metal desk, or else they stood around having loud, animated discussions with those who were also waiting. Two harassed middle-aged men, one in uniform, were dealing with the barrage of questions, complaints and opinions.

Sam shouldered his way to the desk with the man in uniform in less than a minute. Eli could see he was a real pro at the fine Israeli art of butting into lines and followed in his wake as best he could. He was just trying to squeeze by the last two of the dense pack around the desk when they fell silent and he could tell they were now listening to Sam – somehow taking in the news that he had come across the lake from the Golan. That news quickly spread around the room, and the hubbub in the low-ceilinged room changed slightly in pitch. Sam was done with the IDF commander and moving over to the home front coordinator by the time Eli reached the first desk. The man in uniform rose briefly to shake his hand and with him a "*yasher koach* – well done!" before plunging into earnest discussion with the big men Eli had been stuck behind.

Eli arrived at the second desk to hear a rapid give and take appraisal of the chances of getting working trucks, boats and volunteers.

"Finally, someone with a problem I CAN solve," the home front coordinator said with relief. "This one thinks we should evacuate. This one thinks we should give every one a gun and fight in the streets. I've got two hundred who are convinced that praying at Ben-Maimon's *kever* during a rocket attack is the best thing to do. And a hundred and fifty more at the *kever* of Rabbi Meir BalHaNess with the same idea. And now you want to rearm the whole Golan." He stood up and pounded Sam enthusiastically on the shoulder. "People and boats are no problem," he boomed, but the trucks were all busy elsewhere. Sam looked desperate and was about to launch into a more urgent plea when the man stopped him.

"Wait," he said. "Maybe there is a possibility of towing a few pallets of ammunition down the hill with a couple of the propane powered fork lifts that work in the warehouse. Go see Uriel in supply about that – they're his babies and I know they are running. For your boats, see Avram Gross down at the police station by the harbor," Eli and Sam indicated that they knew where that was before he could launch into directions. "And Avram can probably help you round up your people too – or tell you who can. Good luck and get out of here. It's quarter to four already."

They threaded their way back through the crowded room, which was still digesting the news of contact with the Golan, and squeezed their way back up the stairs. Eli was glad to be back in the fresh air, but even more glad to be away from the din. They found Uriel among the soldiers smoking at the entrance to the bomb shelter when they asked how to find him. They told him their story and what they needed as Uriel led them quickly to a pair of sliding metal doors set in a shed-like opening that disappeared into the dark mountain. There were some cubbyhole offices just inside the doors, one of them lit with a candle, another with a small lantern. Uriel called some helpers out from the shadows within them, and they set about finding their 155 mm shells for the first load.

One of Uriel's helpers showed up a few minutes later with a battery powered safari light and one of the propane-powered loaders towing a rubber-tired wagon just as they reached the neatly stacked pallets of the big 155 mm shells. Two pallets of shells took up most of the room the small wagon. Acting just like a kid loose in the candy story, Sam balanced two cases of mortar shells and half a dozen cases of machine gun ammunition before the ordinance warehousemen told him to stop or there would be no way to get it down the mountain in one piece.

"You have wheels? How did you get here?" Uriel asked them.

"We borrowed a scooter from the police station," Eli said.

Uriel put another two cases of machine gun ammunition either side of the driver's seat, and then the two supply men quickly and expertly tied off the load.

"I can only spare the one loader right now if I'm going to pull the rest of your supplies," he said. "So Moshe is going to take this load down to the dock with you and you can get started with finding your boats and people. He might have time to come back and get one more load before you shove off. If I find you some trucks, there will be even more coming down after you. Damn, I wish I had a cell phone!"

Sam thanked him and said that he needed to get on the water and headed back by about 4:30 at the latest – for it would be getting light by five. The sun would be rising by 5:25. They gave Uriel the rest of their wish-list, and hoped he could find more transportation. He wished them luck and strode back into the depths of his warehouse, his flashlight beam swinging among the shadows, to roust out the next load.

Sam and Eli hung on to the loaded wagon as the little forklift towed them to the gate where they collected their motor scooter. They made a strange procession through the gate and down the winding road to the lakeside, but few spared them a second glance. The forklift was actually fairly zippy going downhill. They could tell the driver was having to be careful that the heavy load did not push him over on the steeper sections. They reached the dock almost as fast as they had gotten up the mountain.

Finding Avram Gross was no problem. He had already learned of their mission from the soldiers at the harbor, and had a pair of sturdy older wooden tour boats parked alongside the nearest pier, their engines idling. A growing crowd of volunteers was gathering. They were mostly looking uneasily at the dark, foggy lake and fortifying themselves with coffee and sandwiches. Most of them had brought, or been issued, a large sturdy knapsack or backpack. Since the pallets of shells could not be lowered into the boat, they quickly formed two lines and passed the precious shells carefully from hand to hand, and set them securely between the middle rows of benches in the first tour boat. There were 36 shells to a pallet, and each of the large shells weighed 50 kilos – more than 100 pounds. The cases of mortar shells and machine gun ammunition came next, and were used to better wedge the tall artillery shells so they would not tip.

The captain of the craft was an elderly Druze with a ferocious walrus mustache. He passed a line around the shells for good measure, sized up his load, and said there would be room for eighteen more passengers besides Eli and Sam. Sam chose half a dozen soldiers and a dozen sturdy looking young men, and swung aboard with them.

In the meantime, Eli showed Avram their landing spot on a map of the lake and how to find the beginnings of the trail up to Yishuv Haruv so that he could direct the boatloads to follow. Avram had walked the track himself in his younger days. He would steer the next and subsequent boat loads of supplies and volunteers to their landing. "What I wouldn't give for a cell phone or a radio," he sighed. He promised to look after Eli's kayak. Then he wished them luck.

They were headed back across the lake by 4:40. The predawn sky was lightening almost by the minute. But in a power boat, even a slow one like the tour boat, it would take them perhaps only twenty minutes to get across the route that Eli and Sam had labored across a few hours ago, half lost in the fog. Their skipper had a reliable compass, with a proper binnacle to protect it from magnetic fluctuations. However, the shallows by their landing place were a problem. "No good" he said as Eli showed him on a chart where they had entered the lake. Eli hadn't thought of that in their shallow draft kayak. The skipper jabbed a weathered finger at the chart about half a kilometer north of their landing. The chart showed deeper water right up to shore just inside a point of land. "I can get...maybe ten-twenty meters to shore," he said, "but you walk with bombs." He indicated the direction of shore with a wave of his hand with the cigarette. He chewed one end of his mustache thoughtfully. "Many many year ago we bring picnickers here – before everyone have cars. I anchor with stern and pull up close if no waves." Since they were motoring through a profound calm of fog and smoke, Eli doubted that waves would be a problem.

"Avram says you two pay for boat if she get bomb," the skipper said solemnly.

Eli did a double take, but studied the skipper a moment before replying. He had a feeling the waterman was pulling a bluff somehow. "If we get bombed, we're all fish food," he said back.

The walrus mustache did not crack a smile, but Eli could tell the subject was dealt with. "About two hundred meters to your friends now," the skipper said. Eli had no idea how he could tell, but took his word for it.

Sam let loose a yell into the fog, "Roee, *Matai n'etz*? What time is sunrise?" he yelled into the bank of cloud and smoke.

"Five twenty five, you're too early" came the reply from not far away though neither Eli or Sam could see the shore yet.

"We have to land about half a K north of here," Sam shouted, "Follow us and we'll share our toys with you."

The skipper swung the boat north and, after a couple minutes of slow running, swung it in a broad arc to the left with its bow pointed back out into the lake. They drifted the last part of the swing with the motor in idle. Then he reversed the engine and the propeller cut the water behind them, easing them towards the barely visible shore. Eli hadn't noticed him before, but the skipper had a small, skinny boy help him at the back of the boat. The boy suddenly came to life and started tossing a lead line off the stern to check the depth. He called out a sing-song read out of his line in an accent that Eli could not understand, but he could tell the bottom was rising with the young boy's voice. When he reached a certain pitch, the skipper put the engine in neutral and let the boat drift slowly backwards. He clambered to the bow and prepared to release a small anchor. He let it go with a splash as the boat lost momentum and he paid out its muddy line and then tied it off on a cleat. Taking a long boat pole, he made his way aft and changed places with the boy. Now Eli had a clearer glimpse of the dark shoreline perhaps 20 meters away.

The skipper probed with his pole, and found bottom. He used his pole to check the last of the boat's momentum and straighten it out more perpendicular to the shore. Now he picked up another small anchor, stood astride the low stern counter and swung it back and forth several times, before sending it in a short arc and a solid splash about five meters behind them. He began to pull the boat slowly toward the anchor. Eli noticed that the young boy had scurried to the bow and was easing out the bow anchor line as the skipper took in the stern line. They gently bumped to a stop – and both cleated their lines. It was a very seaman-like job for an old wooden boat in the middle of a small lake well below sea level. Eli decided that the skipper must have some genuine seagoing experience in his past.

The skipper picked up a motley scrap of carpeting from somewhere and plunked it down on the stern counter so that they could walk without damaging his woodwork. He hung a four-rung, hooked swimming ladder over the stern. Sizing up Eli, who at six feet was one of the tallest men present, he motioned him towards the ladder. Since time was of the essence – (his watch now said a few minutes after five, and the sky was lightening overhead) Eli climbed down the ladder and felt with his feet from the bottom rung. He was mid-chest deep in water when he found the bottom firm beneath his feet. Another of the taller men was coming down the ladder, and he stepped to one side to let him pass. The two of them stood on either side of the swimming ladder as the rest of their company came down and, at Sam's direction, formed a double line to the shore, two by two, about a meter apart. The water was cool, but not cold, and there were no waves to deal with beyond the gentle three or four inch swell that had guided Eli across the lake.

The first cases of ammunition were lowered to his outstretched hands before the last of the group had waded ashore and formed their end of the line. He and his partner had only to turn and lower the case before the next pair seized it. As he turned around with perhaps the third shell, he was surprised to see Sam on shore steadying a small camera on a pack and snapping a picture. How in the world did he carry a camera across the lake and back and never mention it, Eli wondered.

Closer to shore, the partners had to take a few steps with their load to reach the next pair. By the time they were ready to start with the heavy 50 kilo artillery shells, Eli's arms were worn out. He had been up all night, paddled across eight kilometers of still water, motor-scootered up and down a small mountain, and now unloaded nearly half a ton of ammunition. His partner was looking tired too and so they traded places with the next pair in the chain, and then moved several more pairs after them until they were slightly less than waist deep and had a much easier time carrying the big shells. Eli shrugged a knot out of his shoulders and stepped forwards to accept next shell. It was mind numbing work, and he kept going like an automaton. Sam had joined the line a couple pairs up the beach, he noticed.

By the time their human chain had unloaded all 72 shells, they heard the buzz of a speedboat out on the lake, and the eastern sky had brightened into what promised to be a cloudy red sunrise. The half dozen soldiers with them, plus Sam and their two escorts from the night's hike, hurried ashore and took up positions behind whatever cover they could find, facing the sound of the approaching boat. Eli's pack had been handed from the boat to the pile of ammunition on shore, so he wearily pulled himself behind some willows and waited. He saw the skipper pull out a long rifle and ready it on the gunwale. The young boy (a grandson or son of his old age perhaps?), crouched next to him, too curious to see to be able to take cover completely.

A boat horn tooted two blasts and a voice called in Hebrew from the fog. "Who ordered a pizza with mushrooms?"

The tension evaporated instantly. Someone called back that he had asked for anchovies and extra cheese. A moment later they saw a small speedboat packing a pair of machine guns and a soldier with a grenade launcher behind them. "Say hello to the Kinneret squadron of the Israeli navy," the driver called cheerily. Your second load is about five minutes behind us."

No one looked more relieved than the Druze skipper, who slipped his rifle out of sight, and fished up his light stern anchor. Poling off from the bank, he idled out a bit, pulled in his bow anchor, and was off at full throttle.

Eli wearily got up and went to retrieve his pack and get a drink. The sun had begun to rise behind the massive escarpment of the Golan Heights, and he could now see the tops of the hills across the lake still shrouded in morning mist and smoke. He figured the Druze with the walrus mustache would just make it back to Tiberias without being spotted. Taking a long drink, Eli studied the low hanging clouds of the sky, reddened with the still-unseen rising sun. No sign of helicopters, spotter planes or jets. Thank G-d.

Eli and slightly more than half of the unloading party were too weary to help the second boat unload, but fortunately it carried its own team of porters and loaders. He found his pocket *siddur* still dry in a pocket of his pack, and said the first part of morning prayers, up to the *Shema Israel*. The rest could wait until later. Home seemed a very long way away at the moment. In normal times, home would be an easy 25 minute drive from here. Would there ever be such a thing as normal again, he wondered?

In the Minefield 19:50

About an hour after complete darkness fell, and perhaps an hour before the full moon was due to rise, David Engel was crawling on his belly along a freshly churned tank track. He wore a pack full of bags of powder from an illumination round, some fuse wire, pliers, hammer and hack saw. It felt just like basic training, only he had been younger then. Nobody did this kind of shit in the real army. But, there he was, snaking along on his knees and elbows, rifle in his hands, trying to get back into the rhythm of it. The burnt out tank that was going to be the stage for their night's theater performance was still a long crawl away. "Live from the Golan, it's the IDF sound and light show. Brought to you by the pyromaniacs in *Gimmel* One and Two," he thought as he crawled along in the rocky earth. He had no cause for complaint though. Benny had volunteered to take the 35 kilo antipersonnel tank shell and the tall stakes for their makeshift mortar launchers. David could tell that it was not only a heavy load, but an awkward one that threatened to topple from one side to the other as they crawled along their parallel tracks. Behind them, Yankel's burly loader, Udi, was grunting along bringing the mortar shells and other paraphernalia for their show. Whenever they paused to have a look, all was quiet at the mouth of the wadi where the five Syrian tanks had been dug in all day watching the minefield like so many sixty-ton cats watching a mouse hole.

After what seemed like forever, but was probably less than 20 minutes, they reached the blackened shadow of the nearest tank they had hit that morning in their desperate escape. It was eerily silent. The moon had not risen yet and the overcast and smoke were so thick, they doubted that it would matter much. But, if the enemy had night vision glasses, or worse, infrared scopes, they would be spotted if they were not careful. It was tempting to try to set up their display on the sheltered side of the tank away from the Syrians. But the tank had been following their safe track through the minefield exactly – and had been stopped dead in its – and their – tracks. David could see the jagged hole torn by Natan's beautifully aimed shell. He shuddered to think of the dead and burnt bodies that must be within the silent hulk that loomed in the night. He forced himself to concentrate on laying out the tools for his part of the exhibition. He knelt in the deep shadow in front of the killed tank and was relieved to slip his pack to the ground.

Act One was to see if they could rearrange the cannon on the blasted tank to face the wadi. Seeing the damage up close, he doubted that the turret would turn at all. Carefully and quietly he and Benny climbed up on the big T-72 and tried to see if they could move the long, thick cannon barrel by hand. He had been in many a T-72 at the tank museum in Latrun, and had trained in refurbished, captured 72's in war games. It was funny how the information came back to him here in the dark on a partly destroyed tank, with no clue who might be watching and about to blow him to bits. It wouldn't budge. That meant one of them needed to go down the hatch into the burnt out turret and see if the manual crank for turning the turret, used more for maintenance than combat, was still working, or if it had been blown off or melted in the inferno. He was almost glad it was pitch black inside, he did not want to see what was down there. The hatch had been blown open and a black hole gaped below him. Taking a deep breath, David edged himself down until he could feel something solid to stand on. Then, keeping his left hand hanging on the hatch rim, he reached out in the darkness for where he knew the steel wheel that turned the turret gear should be. It was a farther reach than he remembered, so he took another breath, held it, and ducked fully inside, bracing himself with what was left of the massive breach of the main gun. His hands found the wheel. It was bent and pitted feeling, but right where it should be. He had to breathe and he knew he was being stupidly superstitious holding his breath. He cautiously let out his breath and took in some air, breathing through his mouth, determined not to smell the burnt death he knew must be within.

Benny was leaning low along the turret near the hatch, prepared to help if needed, and trying hard not to present a silhouette in the darkness. "Find it?" he whispered.

"Yeah," David said, and he turned the wheel as hard as he could to the left. It didn't want to move, but he could feel a fraction of a millimeter of give – as if it might. He tried harder, giving it a series of tugs. Maybe... He got a better grip, moved his body closer and braced one foot against the front of the turret and put his whole body into the effort. It creaked and gave a bit, and then turned a notch. He redoubled his efforts and it began to turn, cog by cog. "Way to go!" Benny whispered from above. David re-braced himself and kept turning the wheel, swearing as he ripped his sleeve and cut his elbow on something jagged. He should have brought Greg along for this chore. As a body builder, Greg could have probably spun the turret 360 degrees if needed. But all they needed was 90 degrees, and David, sweating now and feeling claustrophobic in the cramped darkness, was straining to move it that much. The gear felt ragged and uneven as it turned, and the toothed track it turned against was warped. Finally he could turn it no further. There was something either wedged or broken blocking further progress.

"Just a little more and we'll have a bead on them," Benny whispered.

"That's as far as she goes," David answered, and reached for the remains of the ladder. His hand felt something crumbly and charred instead and he recoiled, disgusted. He stood up, nearly losing his balance, and reached for the dim circle of sky that marked the hatchway. He grabbed it with first one and then both hands and heaved and floundered his way out of the dark hole like the greenest newbie of a tanker. Benny slipped back to the ground and waited for him. The need for silence took hold again now that he was out of that blackened hole of unseen death. He tried to persuade himself it was not a charred body that had met his hand in the darkness, but he could not shake off the image. He had seen too many tanker films. He knew what death must have been like for the gunner and the loader in that blasted turret.

He wiped his hands in loose dirt when he reached the ground. He crouched, breathing the smoky, but clean night air in the shadow of the front tracks. Benny had to shinny out the length of the cannon barrel, which overhung the un-trod ground to the left of the tank and pointed in the general direction of the wadi where the Syrians were waiting and watching. They were obviously not watching closely enough. Udi cautiously handed the big 105 mm shell up to Benny, who hung like a tree sloth from the long barrel. He cradled the big shell on his abdomen, using his chin and an occasional steadying hand to keep it from falling as he inched out to the very end of the barrel. How he managed to keep a grip while stuffing the shell into the end of barrel, David had no idea. After much gasping and grunting, he did it. Once part way in, it became easier to push it until it was almost wholly inside. Then Benny quickly shinnied back, righted himself on the deck of the tank, and scooted back out again. This time he slid along on top of the barrel. Reaching the end, he somehow managed to keep his grip and his balance while he shoved the shell and its fuse at least half an arm's length down the barrel. Benny then slid quickly back to the deck of the tank, paying out his fuse as he came. He snubbed it to a protrusion at the base of the barrel, and hopped down to help David assemble their makeshift mortars.

David had driven in half a dozen tall stakes, angled about 60 – 70 degrees with their tips inclining towards the mouth of the wadi where their enemy sat. Benny helped him slide the mortar shells with their makeshift wire harnesses, down the stakes, and set them in a handful of incendiary powder. Together they dug shallow trenches with their hands, like two kids playing at a beach making roads in the sand – only the dirt and rocks were less cooperative. Perhaps a hand's breadth deep, these would serve as their makeshift fuses. Benny was in his element now. He guided handfuls of the flammable gunpowder into the grooves in the dirt as David poured slowly from the plastic garbage bags they had used. They were crawling on their hands and knees now – feeling that they would have been spotted by now if they were going to be caught, but with the feeling of caution still upon them. Act Two was ready.

Act Three depended on there being some live rounds left in the back of the burned tank. Since it had been almost pitch black inside, and he had been intent only on reaching the wheel to turn the turret, David had no idea if there was anything useable. For this, they knew the must risk a light. Benny had brought a small red flashlight used for reading maps and instruments inside a darkened tank on night maneuvers. As their chief pyro and ammunition expert, it was his turn to venture into the gutted tank. They staked the final mortar round of Act Two as close to the hatch of the tank as they could.

They attached the free end of a fuse wire to a small stake set in the middle of a few handfuls of powder so it would be sure to light right after the last mortar shell fired. Benny took the roll of fuse wire and unwound it as he climbed up on the tank and into the hatch, with some tools in a small pack and his small red map light. The light looked bright to their dark-adjusted eyes when he snapped it on just inside the turret to guide his way. Udi and David looked nervously toward the distant enemy. It appeared that they had a campfire going. Judging from how they had to strain to see any details in its great light, David decided that their dim red light would not be noticed. They could hear muffled clunks and thunks as Benny scrambled around inside the burnt tank. At one point they heard him say "yecch." Then, a few moments later they heard him say "*yofi!* Good!" After that there was much thumping and clanking and scraping around within. Benny must be creating quite a finale for Act Three, David decided.

After perhaps twenty minutes inside the tank, and just as David was noticing a brightening in the eastern sky where the full moon must be rising behind a heavy overcast of clouds and smoke, Benny emerged, looking grim. He paused at the hatch to tug on his fuse gently, peering within with his red light one more time. He snapped it off and scurried down. The night had grown noticeably lighter, but the moon remained hidden. All three checked and double checked their fuses.

According to their elaborate plan, David and Benny were to belly crawl back to their tank, and signal when they arrived that all were ready for the breakout. They would signal when all three tanks were ready to start, the shells were ready to explode in the embankment to blast a ramp out, and everyone was ready to fire back if discovered. Udi had already loaded his first shell in Yankel's tank and Greg was standing by to reload if necessary. David's tank was still pinned with the turret pointed backwards, unable to fire without moving. And Baruch Harel's tank would have to start and roll back up the crumbled bank they used to roll into the gully if it needed to fire. David and Benny crawled the long dirty tracks back to the three tanks hidden in the gully. Without the weight of shells and pyrotechnics, it was much easier, and they spent less time glancing towards the distant enemy with their campfire.

Sgt. Harel greeted them as they tumbled down from the track into the gully. "Those bastards are roasting a couple of sheep over there," he said, tossing the can of mystery meat called "loaf" he had just finished into the dirt. "Probably stolen sheep too," he muttered. "Everything is ready," he said, and swung aboard his tank, waiting for the signal to start. David went past his waiting tank to go confer with Yankel just to double check everything at his end. Yankel was tense and unusually quiet, obviously eager to begin. So David went back to his tank. The camouflage netting had been rolled up and stowed in its slings behind the turret, and all was shipshape. "Is everyone going to start OK?" he asked Sasha, who was stretching in the driver's hatch. Sasha nodded and yawned. "What time is it? David asked. "22:24" was his answer. "Let's go," David said. He whistled at Baruch, who was in the tank closest to Udi and their farewell fireworks.

He saw two quick flashes of light shined in the direction of the burnt tanks. A few moments later, he saw some tiny sparks in the distance that grew stronger and then disappeared for a moment. Then there was a tremendous flash and roar from the distant cannon barrel that he had so painfully turned. At that moment Sasha hit the starter and the tank rumbled to life beneath him. He heard, with much relief, the other two start as well, ragged, but running. He followed the track of the shell through the darkness and saw a scatter of bomblets burst in a fan shape about 300 meters short and well to the right of the Syrian sheep roast.

Another ten degrees of turn and a few more of elevation and they could have blown the roasting sheep right off the distant spits, he thought. A dark shape pelted down the dirt track and leaped down the gully with long sliding strides in the soft earth of the bank.

Udi paused, breathing hard, ready to light the fuses of the two charges dug into their exit bank between David and Baruch's tank. David had almost forgotten that step. But first, he had to see his mortars fire. A moment later the first tongue of flame shot up and he could see a shell, trailing fire from the incendiary powder, lob in the direction of the sheep roast. He fixed his binoculars on the distant camp to see what was going on there. He could see dark shadows running madly for their tanks and vehicles. His first shell burst less than 100 yards short of their encampment – right in line for a solid hit. Not bad for firing without a tube!

Machine guns were firing wildly into the night in all directions as rounds two, three and four hit – all well short, but in the right direction. Shell five was wide to the left, and shell six had just begun its flight when the first Syrian tank fired from its cover at the base of the wadi. Its shell was high and wild. The din of firing was the signal for Udi to light the two high explosive shells buried in the earth and run back to Yankel's tank. Sasha edged their tank away from the bank, but stayed well away from the coming blast. It came, less than a second after the second Syrian tank had managed to fire. David had ducked down in his turret, but not closed the hatch, and about a handful of dirt showered down on him.

By the time David was up, Baruch's tank had revved and was making a run for the broken bank. It looked too steep from David's angle, but he saw the underside of the big tank pitch up, treads clawing the embankment as it crumbled further under the weight. David had to tear his eyes away from urging the tank upwards with his will power and turn to see whether they had been spotted. The Syrian halftracks were spraying tracers into the night making quite a fireworks display themselves, but there was no real pattern to their firing. Baruch was right – they would keep right on firing into the dark until they ran out of ammunition or someone slapped them silly and told them to stop. The tanks were now firing more accurately in the direction of the burnt tanks sitting in the track. He heard the pitch of the engine change behind him, and turned to see the back of Baruch's *Gimmel* two, the white lettering pale in the brightening night, disappear over the lip of the gully, leaving a well churned, but quite passable trail behind him.

Sasha ran their tank in a rapid reverse right over the fan of earth of their blasted exit, backing almost to where Baruch had started his run. Stopping, revving the engine to the max, their tank slammed into gear. It was still rough shifting without the electronics, David thought as he hung on for dear life. The nose of their Merkava pointed to the sky. He could feel the churning treads clawing at the soft earth, and then a shudder as they gained traction again. The nose of their tank slammed down on solid earth and they were tearing up the dim track in pursuit of Baruch. Following Baruch was Sasha's job as the driver, David felt his perspective shift again as the turret swung around to face the wildly firing enemy. The tank shells were still blasting near the burnt tanks. Then, suddenly with an earth-shaking roar, the hulk that Benny had spent twenty minutes wiring went off in a pillar of smoke and fire. From his bouncing, jolting point of view as they raced away from their hiding hole, it looked like a direct hit on the magazine of a tank. He was sure that someone back in the Syrian camp was congratulating himself on a direct hit.

A few seconds later he saw the nose of Yankel's tank burst from their gully. Even to his practiced eye there had been no sign of a ten-meter long tank there moments before. His turret swiveled slightly so that their gun pointed away from the track behind them. Somehow he could tell that Benny was doing his best to keep his bouncing sights on the enemy camp – whether for practice to get used to their crippled system, or just to watch the action through the optical scope – or perhaps both.

It took less than ten minutes of driving up the gently rising, relatively straight track to reach the turn that marked the second half of their escape route that was known to only Yankel and his crew. The other drivers had walked this far just after sunset to mark the route in their minds. Baruch's tank had drawn up in a wide spot at the turn of the track and had its cannon pointed for a parting shot. David had been watching the tracers crisscrossing the dark minefield, and the enemy tank fire concentrate on destroying their own two hulks. But the latest two or three rounds seemed to be fired more in the direction of their escape track. They might have been spotted. He did not want to wait to find out. As Sasha drew up just past Baruch's tank, it fired, lobbing a shell at the entrenched tanks at the base of the wadi perhaps three kilometers distant. Benny was making fine adjustments in his elevation and bearing. David tensed for the coming recoil. Benny was taking his time. He saw Baruch's shell explode in the grove of trees that sheltered the enemy tanks – but it missed them. Then their own gun fired and David waited for the cloud of smoke and flame to clear to see the fall of their shell. It blasted a geyser of earth and rock just short of one of the tanks.

"Try that again," he said, as he heard the clang of a new shell being loaded. Yankel's tank drew up and came to a stop at a halfway level spot in the track. "We are bunched up too close," David shouted at Yankel's driver, but he was probably not heard. Baruch's tank to their right fired again, and this time they hit something – not a tank, probably a half track – for there suddenly seemed to be one less machine gun pumping tracer shells into the night. Yankel's tank fired and almost instantly began driving around them to take the lead and show them the way through the minefield. Baruch's tank swung in behind him. David waited for the flash and roar of their farewell shot. The long barrel in front of him was again wreathed in fire and smoke. He waited, binoculars trained on the tank they had fired on. A direct hit! A wild whoop went up from within the turret, and David yelled his triumphant defiance at the distant enemy. Their tank revved and jerked into motion. Within moments the firestorm of the enemy fire disappeared over the low roll of the landscape. He saw a shell burst perhaps twenty meters from where the three of them had bunched up for their final shots. That had been a mistake, and he and Yankel should have known better.

The turret swiveled to face the front. David could now watch their progress and try to take mental notes in case he ever needed to come this way again. He certainly hoped not.

Northern Defense Command, Mount Meron 00:30

It had taken twice as long as expected to download and analyze the satellite photos and data relayed via the US submarine. However, it gave Anna and the officers in the Northern, Southern and Central commands the first full picture of the war. The satellite reconnaissance was from early in the afternoon - compressed, translated and relayed in the mid afternoon over their limited secure data channels, and then unscrambled. They had been going over the data all evening, calling in the officers from the various branches of services represented at various installations their mountain top complex to interpret the images.

The picture that emerged was worse than anyone had had thought. Egyptian and irregular forces were pouring into Israel from the area of the Gaza strip – long a sore thumb that stuck into the soft coastal plain where the majority of Israelis lived. Their satellite pictures showed hundreds of tanks and heavy vehicles, and many more behind them streaming across the entire border. Egyptians were thickest at the edges of Ashkelon, the first large city to the north of the Gaza strip and the first of the seacoast cities that held the bulk of Israel's population.

Another mass of armor and supporting vehicles was striking eastwards from Gaza towards the air base at Ofakim and the desert city of Be'er Sheva. They could see little evidence of Israeli forces arrayed against either thrust. Reports from the air force was that nothing was able to fly yet. Not even a low tech scout plane because the fuel and ignition systems were all electronically controlled, as well as the navigation instruments and gauges. The only good news was that nothing appeared to be flying on the enemy side either. That was a mystery. This could be explained on the Syrian and Iranian sides perhaps by the few tactical nukes aimed at their command and control structure – but inexplicable for the Jordanians and Egyptians, whose air forces appeared unharmed.

Around their own positions in the north the map was totally confused. They could see large Syrian forces sweeping down the Hula valley at the base of Mount Hermon from Kiryat Shemona to Rosh Pina, and massing across the long border with the Golan Heights. The combined Syrian advances pushed as far as Katzrin, the largest town in the heights, and stretched in a dense smear of forces arrayed against the thin string of settlements that anchored the south of the Golan Heights.

A huge Jordanian force was swarming the southern end of the Kinneret and pouring down the Israeli side of the Jordan valley and arrayed against the town of Beit Se'an. The Jordanian forces were threatening to turn eastwards towards Afula and Megiddo that marked the start of the wide, fertile Jezreel Valley that led directly towards Haifa and the coast. Anna could not suppress a thrill and a shudder at thought of Megiddo – for its English name was Armageddon, the long-prophesized site of the final pitched battle at the end of days.

It appeared that Jericho, another fine Biblical name, was already in enemy hands. A force was massing there to push up the winding highway that rose from below sea level at the Dead Sea to Jerusalem in the Judean Hills rising to 800 meters above sea level.

There was no way that 48 or even 480 cruise missiles were even going to put a dent in that mass of invaders. That grim fact had been the subject of the past two hours of discussions being relayed through Anna's command post from the central command – which had now found its way to Jerusalem. The highest political level represented was still the Minister of Agriculture. The Minister of Transportation had been called away to deal with the defense of Jerusalem, and the rest of the cabinet was not in touch with any kind of communications. Street fighting and mobs of Palestinians, who made up more than a quarter of the city, was growing bloodier and more intense. Because of its unique status as the home of the world's three great religions, the city was largely demilitarized – and few Israeli forces could be spared to rush to its defense.

"We need air cover – and we need to neutralize Egyptian and Jordanian air forces and strategic assets," she pleaded over the scrambled voice link that was relayed to the Joint Chiefs of Staff at the White House situation room in Washington. "If anyone gets airborne before we do, it's all over," she stressed.

"I hear you, but the President is not prepared to attack any of your adversaries. That would blow the lid off the whole Middle East and put us at war with every Muslim nation on the face of the planet – and there are a heck a lot of them as you well know," the four star general on the other end of the scrambler told her for the nth time. "Air cover is out for now. The USS Eisenhower is halfway across the Indian Ocean. That's just about extreme range for a return trip, even if we could refuel. The Harry Truman is in the Northern Atlantic too many air miles away to do you any good.

And there is no way we can fly anything out of Europe without blowing the political situation there wide open."

"So we just get fed to the wolves?" she retorted.

"I'm sorry," the general said, "we are sticking our necks out far enough with satellite recon and Tomahawks – if word gets out – and it surely will, that we intervened on behalf of Israel… there will be hell to pay in the UN. Oil prices will go through the roof. And that would kill any hope of economic recovery for the next five hundred years. No president could survive that kind of fallout, as much as he likes Israel."

Anna was seething with anger, but trying to regain some slight degree of calm after her last retort. She couldn't afford to alienate their only ally in the world, however pitiful the help they offered. She relayed responses from the Minister of Agriculture while she tried to think of alternatives. She saw their point. The US military was thinly spread in a very hostile part of the world when it came to the Middle East. Europe only cared about oil, caving in to the most absurd Arab demands in the best of times. There was no help to be had there.

Ever since Turkey had grown more militant and started veering towards the Islamic extremist camp, NATO had been practically useless. A socialist party had taken over in the last Greek elections, eroding what little support Israel ever had there. Italy was useless even in the best of times. Germany was neutral to the point of ridiculousness. More to the point, Germany's studied inaction helped the Arab bloc. France was practically anti-Semitic, and fifteen percent Muslim these days. Britain was toothless and more than twenty percent Muslim minorities. There was no help there at all. Not even Czechoslovakia, an occasional ally and source of weapons and supplies – for a price – dating back to the Israeli War of Independence, had anything to offer. However some back channels hinted that they might be a possible conduit for re-arming if Israel had any hard currency.

She moved her conversation with the NATO commander over to a private channel. "OK, I understand you can't be seen as getting involved in the conflict. But how about this: you paint over the markings on a couple wings of F-15s and fly them in from Spain or somewhere fairly neutral. Bring them in over the Med to the Negev. We can get the runways repaired at Ramat Hovav in a couple of hours. In fact, forget the paint job, it's night time. Bring them in early this morning and we'll paint them ourselves with something fast drying. Just two or three wings would make all the difference right now as long as nothing else is airborne. We have the pilots, fuel and armaments – just not the planes. We'll even pay you for them – consider it a sale!"

"What about our pilots?" the general asked, obviously thinking it over.

"We could keep them underground for a few days and slip them out when we have something flying. They are re-wiring the trainers and observation planes and are making some progress on an overhaul of a Blackhawk," she said.

"That must be some overhaul," said the general, "everything is electronic – right down to the rudder controls." Anna now recalled that the general had some extensive Blackhawk flight time in the first Gulf War as a Marine pilot.

"Right, so you can see what we are up against – but if we had just a few of those babies flying, it would be shooting fish in a barrel. A dozen Blackhawks could stop the drive up the coast. Another dozen could turn the tide up north along the Jordan. Two or three wings of F-15s could strike anywhere they are needed. We are not asking for much, just a fighting chance," she could tell she was making some headway, so she pressed on. "Look, I don't know what you have in southern Europe right now, but I know it's less than two hours flight time from Greece in a Blackhawk, I flew down with some of your boys after briefing the NATO summit in '09. They wanted to see what ElOp was doing with our third generation heads up displays."

"Are you the short little lady with the charming Russian accent who gave us that outstanding briefing about EMP countermeasures?" the general asked.

"That was me," Anna admitted, blushing. She had worn a short, tight-fitting khaki uniform skirt instead of her usual slacks on the advice of her commander – so as to keep and hold their attention while she buried them in highly technical information. Apparently it had worked in his case. "And I think you must be the tall guy in the first row with the Marine buzz haircut and the two stars who stayed awake and asked about hardening the electronics on a Blackhawk afterwards and wanted to discuss it over drinks…."

Now it was his turn to hem a bit, for they had gone out with a crowd of brass to a restaurant. But she had smoothly evaded his attempts to continue the evening elsewhere. However, she sensed that they had finally made the person-to-person connection. They were now talking as people who knew each other, had sized each other up, and had some respect for each other's brains and skills. Perhaps something could happen.

He had been good looking, in a well-fed, self-confident, American military sort of way. The fact that he was married, was a fact that he did not see as an obstacle for his plans. And the fact that he was not even remotely Jewish, a point he (but not Anna) was oblivious to, made anything beyond dinner in Athens a non-starter. But the attraction had been obvious, and it was a card she was not loathe to play, since she had so few in her deck right now.

"I wish we had carried out the ideas you had for hardening the electronics on the Blackhawks. If I had not had that prior engagement with some more senior officers in the IDF, I would have been happy to have heard more about them," She more than half-lied. "But there was never any money and always something else was more important," she said quite truthfully. He said something sympathetic, and it sounded like his now four-star-sized masculine ego had been suitably assuaged.

Their discussion moved on to the technical and logistic problems of moving neutral aircraft into the war zone. Fortunately, there was a complete news blackout from the region. Reporters had no phones or even radios working to send what little news they had. Besides, most of them were hiding down in air raid shelters like everyone else, for there were still missiles falling in all the cities. There was complete chaos everywhere as people tried to find safety where nowhere suddenly seemed very safe.

"So, what are the major networks saying about the whole situation?" She asked, for she truly had no time to check on news broadcasts since catching the beginnings of the BBC world news earlier that morning.

"Well, with no one reporting in from on the ground anywhere nearer than Cairo, the news has been pretty much speculation, rumor. And, I'm sorry to say, nearly everyone is broadcasting the Arab version of things for lack of anything better to report." He said this almost apologetically, as if he could have done anything at that point to enlighten their reporting without compromising all kinds of complicated relationships.

"And what is their version that is coming across?" she asked.

"Naturally, they are blaming Israel for firing first and exaggerating the extent of the fallout in the region as a good excuse to keep everyone away while they do their dirty work in the dark. Al Jazeera said that Israel tried a treacherous first strike that seems to have backfired on their own heads. They are starting all sorts of dark rumors about hundreds of thousands dead, which is a perfect way to cover up their battle losses."

"I suspected as much. I just haven't had time to do anything but play telephone messenger for the civilians and relay as much information as we can collect to the boys in the field." She said, "And I hate to tell you that it looks pretty grim right now."

Their discussion moved along to things strategic, such as the odd lack of air cover. "Reports we have is that they have moved in with almost no anti-aircraft cover at all beyond some light stuff carried on APCs. So we could strike just about anywhere even without the smart munitions, if we had some planes in the air," she added, steering the discussion back to the subject of an emergency loan of aircraft.

"The big question marks we can't figure out is why Egypt and Jordan are staying on the ground. All our information says that aside from the radio interference and magnetic fluctuations to the compass, navigation should be possible within the EMP envelope."

"I might have a possible answer on Egypt," the general replied. "We have been trying to figure out what happened to ballistic missile number twelve launched by Iran. We show five intercepted, and five or six dispersed over Israel, but that leaves one or possibly two unaccounted for."

Anna said they had come up with the same count – two near Haifa, two near Tel Aviv, and one or two in the Negev. They either went off together, or there was a secondary burst slightly farther south, the data at that point was sketchy.

"Our satellite tracking has played the data a number of times. They are beginning to think that the last missile hit about the northern Sinai, and may have gone off at a lower altitude than the rest. They suspect that another one might have been deliberately aimed that way, air bursting perhaps as far as Suez."

Anna noted that down and tried to digest the information.

"Deliberately, you think?" she asked.

"Possibly. You know that Iran sees itself as the big enchilada in the region and doesn't want Egypt to take all the credit for the victory.

"But how does that explain Jordan?" she wondered.

"I don't know. Our Middle East desk had been chewing over that for the last eighteen hours. Their most plausible scenario is that Jordan may be holding back so that it can assert air superiority over the region as soon as everyone else has shot themselves back to the Stone Age. As long as Israel doesn't get airborne, and as long as they are making progress on the ground, there is no harm in holding their cards close and watching."

"That makes sense, actually, in a backwards sort of way," Anna admitted. "I swear if I live to be a hundred, I'll never figure out how these guys think."

"Let's hope you live to at least a hundred," the general said kindly, "Now let me see what I can find you in Europe. It won't be tonight, but check in with me about 1500 or so and I'll tell you what I found."

Anna thanked him and clicked off their private side channel. Hope at last. Now, to get through the coming day, she took her notes and called a quick executive conference. She met with Koby and the major who was now in charge of getting in touch with the IDF forces around them and keeping a conference line open to Jerusalem and Ramat Hovav.

Their efforts to get their meager number of EMP-hardened radio sets out to command units in the Northern Command were proving especially difficult. Messengers and couriers on motorbikes were able to zip back and forth between towns and military installations. But they were subject to ambush, interception or just plain getting lost. They had also been pinned down by firefights, or mis-directed for hours. A few sets finally got through to the Golani forces rallying near Rosh Pina. Anna and hoped to have some sets distributed up and down the Gallil and northern coast, but it was hit or miss. She had heard earlier that evening about a hair raising ride one motorcycle messenger had described. He had made a high-speed, back roads trip from Jerusalem to Haifa on one of those suicidal kamikaze Kawasaki bikes.

Amil the goat boy urged his plodding donkey up the hill from the highway to the smoking ruins of the Jewish settlement just across the border from his home in Syria. He had set off with his uncle Kassim on their two sturdy donkeys well before dawn so as not to miss the chance to get a car. Amil was thirty two or thirty three, no one was quite sure. But he was still called "the goat boy" because he spent his days in the fields with the family goats. He had never married. No one wanted to marry a half-witted club foot who spent his days in the fields with goats. He never learned to read or write, and neither had his father, or his grandfather before him. Goat herders did not need book learning. They needed to know where to find grass and water, and how to survive outdoors in all weather; and how to keep the flock together, and when to bring in fattened goats for meat, and bags of goat's milk for cheese.

His uncle Kassim could read, at least enough to follow the soccer scores in the newspapers and sports magazines that littered his barber shop. He was the only one in the family who could interpret the strange events of the past day. He told how the green flashes of light in the sky at sunrise the previous morning had been a strange secret weapon that had backfired upon the Israeli aggressors, and how the Syrian army had risen up to do battle like a lion, and had beaten the Israeli army – who were now fleeing from the Golan, leaving behind houses and cars and television sets, refrigerators and computers by the hundreds.

There was so much there that a clever fellow like Kassim, and a hard-working young man like Amil could make a fortune in one day. His plan was to load a car with all the merchandise they could find, and then tow it home with the two donkeys – with him steering and Amil – who was the best working with animals – driving the donkeys. And so Amil the goat boy would become Amil the rich man, and so he left his flock and led his uncle through the goat paths through the mine fields to where they cut a hole in the border fence and entered Israel for the first time in their lives.

Amil and his uncle were obviously not the only ones with thoughts of riches to be had for the taking, for there was a steady trickle of men, on foot and astride donkeys, one ancient Fiat sedan, and two men even on horses, who were making their way towards the town. Kassim had brought a pair of pistols, but he did not give Amil one, and he wore them in the belt of his pants in plain sight to discourage trouble. There were no soldiers to be seen except for a short convoy of trucks lumbering along from somewhere to the south. They could see that the backs of the trucks were covered in tarps – but obviously hauling heavy loads. Uncle Kassim spat as he guided his donkey back onto the road – "Soldiers always take the best for themselves – and they have trucks too."

However, they were nearing the blasted open gates of the settlement and could see the shattered ruins of the gate house and the first few houses of the hilltop settlement. These looked too destroyed to yield much. A lone car sat, blackened on the street. But never mind, there were many more houses, many more cars.

Somewhere in Syria 0645

Waking and dreaming blurred together in Chaim's dazed mind. He remembered only baking, raw and thirsty in the sun of a long afternoon, falling asleep towards evening, and then waking, only half conscious as a long, slow night passed in lapses of pain and wakening. But now, as the day had broken, dim and reddish grey, and the landscape had become more distinct around him, he knew he needed to start moving and find something to drink, or die. Putting it that way sharpened his thinking, and he rolled his head to the right to try to look around him. His left eye was swollen half shut now, and his temple was dry and crusted to the touch, but throbbing fiercely whenever he moved more than a tiny bit. He would have to ignore it.

His right arm ached from a nasty bruise, but could move OK. He felt around above his head and found the tangled lines to his parachute. He was still in his harness, attached to his chute. Still amazed at not being found, he decided that was good, because he could now use the chute to make shelter from the sun, bandages for his leg – still no feeling below his raw-feeling knee. His left thigh also complained at any attempt to move it. He lay there and studied what he could see in his field of vision to his right. He appeared to be near the bottom of some kind of dry, gentle grassy slope that climbed away to his right. In fact, he could feel the slight slope under him, more gentle still, which led him to think he might be near the bottom of a low hillock. He could hear the goats again, somewhere to his left and perhaps below him. One had a bell, and he found its occasional clank somewhat soothing. At least he was not completely alone – but what would happen when the goat's owner came to round up his flock? Wouldn't it be milking time about now? He remembered early mornings, before dawn in the goat shed in his uncle's kibbutz.

"I have to sit up and look around," he decided. He began to rock his body ever so slightly, right and left, feeling the warning pains from his left arm and leg whenever he applied any pressure. But he was getting used to the pain, and started to learn when it came, and when it backed off. He tried drawing his right leg up. He could bend his knee fine – his leg obeyed him. And as long as he did not try to move his left arm or leg much, he could move with his right side. He debated, should he attempt to roll all the way over off of his complaining left side, letting the momentum of the roll and the slope bring him up on his right elbow? Or should he attempt to lever himself up with his right arm and try sitting? He decided to go for sitting.

Gathering himself, he took a deep breath and held half of it. Chaim drew his right knee up, rocked to his right and let his knee fall to the ground and rolling his complaining hips and screaming left leg with it. He began levering himself up on his right elbow using the slight momentum of his roll to bring him over. His left arm now stabbed in pain as it fell uselessly to his side. But he did not pass out from the pain. All his years of pulling G-forces in a fighter jet had taught him how to tense and hold on to consciousness, pushing the blood back to his brain and forcing it to work.

He tucked his right leg under him, Indian fashion and levered his way up to a half-sitting position. He let his head hang down, fighting nausea and pain until his vision cleared and he could breathe easier. When he could finally look around, there was not much to see. He was near the bottom of a grassy slope studded with boulders – like anywhere in the Golan really. The sun had risen to his left, so he must be facing roughly south. All he could see was the other side of the rolling slope on the other side of his shallow valley. He was well hidden at least – he could see nothing, but nothing could see him. He still wondered at the lack of aircraft anywhere within earshot. He strained to hear if the artillery barrage was still rumbling in the far distance, as it had seemed to him the afternoon before – or was it a dream? No, it was real enough, he recalled hearing the rhythm it – just like artillery drill only heavier.

However, it was silent now. Was the war over – one of the short flare ups that came and went as quickly as they started? But, what about the strange green lightening that had burst over Haifa. What had knocked his plane out of the sky? What had caused his instruments to suddenly go blank, the stick dead in his hand? What had happened to Warbirds Two, Three and Four? He had no idea. He just knew that he needed something to drink and to take care of his wounds somehow.

He could now see why he could feel nothing below his raw left knee – his left foot flopped at an odd angle, and the leg of his flight suit was drenched in blood. He fought the urge to throw up. He sat rock still until his breath came evenly again. "OK," he thought, "I can deal with this – just one problem at a time." And he was glad that he couldn't feel anything from the mangled part of his leg – for the gashed and bruised knee was bad enough, and his left arm felt straight enough to his tentative touch, but was radiating sharp pains from somewhere just above the elbow, which he assumed must be a break. He continued his inventory of tentative exploration with his right hand, ignoring the throb of the bruises on his right arm. His head felt intact, but a gash had opened up a patch of skin over his left ear and temple, which was tacky feeling and achy.

He could see the goats now, perhaps a dozen of them, led by an older looking weathered brown doe with the bell. There were a trio of husky kids probably born that spring, and some older looking does. No bucks. Good, no Billy goat trouble here. They grazed away, paying no attention to him.

Chaim began to slowly gather his splayed out chute towards him, drawing in the parachute cords with his working hand. It came easily, snagging only once or twice, but relenting to gentle and persistent tugs. Soon he had the voluminous nylon folds of his chute next to his right side. It was tempting to lie down in their clean, inviting brown and grey desert camouflage folds, but he shook off the urge. Thirst and his aching body drove him onwards.

His first task, he had decided, was to cut a sling for his left arm, and tie it up so it would not stab him with pain every time he moved. That would be awkward, but he would get used to it, and it would probably lessen any damage to the broken bone. Then he would cut some strips for binding his head, just to keep the flies away if nothing else, and after that he would see what could be done for his leg.

From his sitting position, his survival knife slid easily from the cargo pouch on his leg. He had also eased out his .25 caliber survival pistol and set it within reach on his leg. He wondered if he should perhaps lure a goat close and shoot it, drink its blood and have raw meat to chew on – but the thought disgusted him, and images what a gunshot might bring kept him from seriously considering it – at least for now.

Cutting a large square out of the parachute proved trickier than he imagined, for it kept slipping under his hand and refusing to slice despite his razor sharp knife. He had to sit on a fold of the parachute and work away from his body to slice it cleanly – and eventually he had a ragged quadrilateral to fold into a triangle and slip around his useless left arm. The elbow protested sharply, but he managed to arrange it in the sling, taking it off and on to retie the knot behind his neck several times until he got the length just right. Eventually he found a position that was almost comfortable, and he cut another long strip to pass around his body and pin the sling to his body.

Tying a long strip around his head also proved difficult, so he eventually cut an even longer strip and wrapped it several times and tucked the end, turban style. That brought the only smile of the day as he imagined what his makeshift headgear would look like to Arab or Israeli alike. Working on making and wrapping his sling and bandages had taken a long time, but took his mind off his thirst and his pain. The sun was now well up in the sky and growing warm. For now that felt good, but he knew he would be baking by mid-day. He looked carefully around where he was sitting for anything that could be used to prop up a corner of his parachute to make a minimalist shelter from the sun. There was nothing but grass, weeds, dirt and rock. None of the weeds were thick enough to support any weight, and the rocks were not of a size that could be stacked in any way to make a pole for an awning. There were no trees or bushes in sight – not even a large boulder that could cast a shadow. He would just have to pull a fold over his head and sleep away the long hot afternoon – if he did not die of thirst first.

"Are there any bugs or earthworms?" he wondered. Survival training films had stressed that a body could live a long time on insect protein. He scratched half heartedly around in the dried grass and dusty earth next to him, putting a stem of grass in his mouth to chew. He saw only a few tiny reddish ants scurrying along – not worth the bother. He sat for a long time, desultorily digging in the dirt and thinking – of his wife and children, of his beloved Warbird One, of his friends and wing buddies, of the strange summer of constant alerts and stream of disheartening, alarming news. Each morning briefing seemed to bring a fresh batch of threats and worry. Well, they had been right. The war had finally happened – and at least he had hit his target. If he had to go down in enemy territory, losing his precious plane – at least it was after blowing a gaping hole in that half-kilometer-long sausage shape of a bunker. He wondered what was in it. Armor? Artillery? Perhaps it was those new assault helicopters that had been ferried in over the past few weeks? He hoped it was the helicopters, but why put them underground?

As he mused and dug, he noticed the funky odor of goat mixed in with the dry dirt and baked grass smell. Two of the does had wandered his way, and one of them paused to nibble curiously at his parachute cords. He almost shooed her away, but stopped himself. She had very full udders – with the veins standing out and droplets of milk at the nipples – well past milking time if his uncle's lessons in goat-ology were correct, and he had every reason to belief they were. Milk – on the hoof – and not two meters away from him!

He thought through several desperate options – shoot her and drag himself to the body and suck the udders dry – yech! That would be his last drink of goat milk ever, for the flock would scatter to the four winds, and the goat herder would come running – unless he had been called away to the war, or killed in the bombing... He started talking softly to her as his uncle had done, "hey girl, come over here – you poor thing, has nobody milked you today? Udders too full? Is it getting painful with no kid to help you out – where is your master anyway? Gone to war has he? Come to uncle Chaim and he can help you, yesssss....."

The goat had left off his tasteless parachute cords and was pulling at a stubborn weed nearby. Then Chaim remembered a crumbled nut bar that had been left in his flight suit from several missions ago. He patted a pocket on his flight suit – and was relieved to feel the lump. He drew out the smashed nut bar and nibbled a few nuts. The goat stopped pulling at her weed and sniffed the air. Chaim ate another nut, watching the goat who was now watching him. "AHA!" he thought, "now we're interested are we? OK, let's trade a bit of nut for a bit of milk, what do you say?" The goat didn't say anything, but remained standing there, chewing weed and watching with interest. Now, what did he have to put goat milk in? He couldn't quite see a way to squirt goat's milk into his mouth – although he had seen his uncle squirt his little sister as she drew up a milk stool to learn how to milk. Chani had hated that – but instantly wanted to learn how. Chaim had tried it too – and though awkward, had managed to squeeze a cup or two of milk before he decided it was too much like work. What about his water flask? He pulled it out and looked at it. There was no way he could hold it and squeeze off a teat and strip the milk out, and no way he could ever hit that small mouth if he stood the bottle up on the ground and milked with his good hand – not even his uncle could get more than a few drops there. Maybe he would just have to lie down and try to hit his mouth. What he needed was a pan or a bucket or…… a helmet! Where the hell was it? He had noticed it missing yesterday morning and not thought about it again. He turned painfully around and looked over his left shoulder behind him, for he had obviously fallen on his left side. There it was, large and rounded and perfect for milking a goat, even if the lining would taste like sweat. He was going for hydration and nutrition here, not taste. It was over three meters up the gentle slope, and he had already tried a test crawl – it would be excruciatingly painful and take him at least an hour.

He regarded the parachute cords around him and began to form thoughts of some sort of loop or lasso. "Well, if the cowboys can do it, so can the fighter pilots, because if you can fly an F-16, you can do damned near anything" he told himself. He cut a few long lengths of the narrow cords and braided them together to give them some extra stiffness and heft. His goat friend stayed close, and was tugging on another stubborn, low growing weed.

She did not startle as he tried a few test swings of his braided cord. He could send it out easily in front of him and down the slope, and even managed to rope a rock – releasing one side to draw his rope back. "Yee haw!" he thought – "Isn't that what they said in the western movies?" Now he began the task of turning his protesting body slightly to swing his rope uphill and over his aching left shoulder. That proved harder, and so he crinkled his candy wrapper and made sure the goat got a good whiff of candied nut before he concentrated his attention on throwing his loop over the upended helmet. Six tries later, he finally landed the loop beyond the helmet and began to carefully gather it towards him. He was afraid that the cord would slip right under the upside down flight helmet and not catch, but he was relieved to feel it catch, and see the helmet wobble and begin moving. Had he been trying to draw it uphill, he was not sure his lasso would have worked, but it came steadily towards him. As it rocked over a clump of earth, the cord pulled under and away, but now it was an easy toss away, and he soon had his trusty flight helmet at his side, ready to become a milk pail for the first time in IAF history.

He held out a speck of crumbled nut and nougat for the goat to inspect. She edged closer, sniffed it and nibbled it daintily. He could have grabbed her head and possibly thrown a few loops of parachute cord around her neck, but he knew how strong a goat could be – and he felt weak as a newborn lamb at the moment. He needed her closer, and so he scattered a few more crumbs on his useless left leg and waited. She stepped right up to him and began nibbling at the crumbs. "It's now or never," he thought, and reached slowly for his helmet and slid it under her as she stood, nearly astride him, seeking out all the tiny crumbs of dried nougat and nut. He sprinkled a little more on his leg and reached for her udder, speaking soothingly whatever nonsense came to mind. He might have mumbled a prayer – for she did not shy away from his hand, and he squeezed the full teat firmly with his thumb and forefinger as his uncle had shown him – and found it easier to do now that he had a man-sized hand. He felt the swelling milk below him and squeezed. The goat reached her neck over his leg, took another step forward, bumping his helmet, but not upsetting it. A warm, yellowish white stream of milk shot out, hitting the edge of his helmet and dripping down the lining. Chaim adjusted his grip and soon there was a steady whish, whish of milk spurting into his upturned helmet. As one teat became hard to work, he moved to the other and stripped it near dry, returned to the first and got a few more weak squirts.

The goat was finished the nougat and nut crumbs and almost stepped in his helmet before he steadied it and slid it safely away. He patted the docile doe weakly and drew the milk-slopped helmet into his lap and tried to drink from it. With one hand, and with the helmet's odd shape and padded brim, it was awkward. Finally he found that if he tilted it back and let the cup or two of milk collect near the longer back edge, he could lap it up without spilling much. The milk was warm and good and barely tainted with sweat, although the lining seemed to soak up a bit. He figured that he could cut the lining out with his knife and chew on it if his goats disappeared.

All his efforts had exhausted him so Chaim made a nest out of his parachute, twitched a few folds over him that would shield him from the afternoon sun, and soon fell into a dreamless sleep, aware that he had the stuff of life within him for at least another 24 hours.

In the Minefield 0530

Once out of the line of fire, the three tanks' run through the rest of the minefield was slow but uneventful. They stopped twice for Yankel to study his map, the tracks and various landmarks. Each time he was confident of his choice; and, since he was going first, so were David and Baruch and their crews. They arrived at the fence marking the southern end of the minefield not long after midnight. While they could hear steady shelling to the south, they were still some distance away from the fighting and not a thing was moving as they each carefully swept the sleeping landscape. Somewhere to their right was the highway that ran north and south from Mount Hermon to the southern tip of the Golan. But the question was, who held the highway? The shelling, they were fairly certain, must be around the northern most of the chain of settlements that were strung along the highway to their south. And if there was no shelling to the north or west of them, did that mean it was taken already, or still in Israeli hands? Or, perhaps the settlements were being shelled from two directions? The three commanders drew their tanks into the dubious shelter of a spinney of trees and stopped for a parley. They had come too far to guess wrong and roll right into a column of Syrian armor.

They studied their map and weighed their options carefully. Should they try to navigate the next large minefield to their south and go directly to the first settlement and hope to identify themselves before being shot? Swing west to the road and approach from that direction, missing mines and saving time, but running the risk of meeting a Syrian advance down the highway? Stay put and dig in until dawn? Or, swing east around the minefield and try to engage the Syrian attack from the rear and storm their way through to the moshav? The last two options seemed suicidal, the first seemed difficult, and so they were leaning towards making a run for the road.

"We should head for the road. I think someone should get out and walk point, say half a K ahead so that he can hear something. I'd like to volunteer," David said. Baruch protested that David had already crawled half a kilometer through the dirt that night with twenty five kilos of explosives on his back, and that he should go. Yankel argued that he knew the terrain the best. Tempers almost flared, but were quickly checked by the reality of their situation, and the fact that their men were depending on them. David acceded that Baruch should go – he trusted the wiry Sephardi and his sixth sense just as much as he trusted Yankel and his chutzpah, and so they agreed.

After giving Baruch about fifteen minutes to get well ahead of them, they edged out of the shadow of the trees and idled along, each commander sweeping the dark terrain around them, and Baruch's loader taking his place at the commander's hatch. Yankel's tank was in the lead, and David's at the back. It was odd to be rumbling along at a moderate walk after their frantic race the previous morning, and tearing out of their hiding gully earlier in the night. He looked behind him as they pulled out of the grove in order to imprint the lay of the land and the southern entrance to the minefield they had just left. One never knew when such information could save a tanker's life.

The night was overcast and smoky, with an orangish glow from many fires reflecting against the low cloud cover. The shelling to their south had grown intermittent, perhaps a boom every few minutes. After about half an hour of cautious edging along through the dark they could see the highway ahead of them that linked the northern Golan with the string of communities to the south. All three tanks paused and everyone scanned the roadway as far north and south as they could see, examining every shadow with their binoculars, listening for the sound of any approaching vehicles. To reach the highway they would have to cross open, exposed ground – at the mercy of any lurking ambush or any patrol moving along the corridor for a great distance. As they scanned the shadows and debated how and when to make their move to reach the exposed highway embankment and cross it, they heard the far off buzz of a motorbike approaching from the north. Each of the commanders edged their tank back into what shadows they could find in the open rolling landscape and watched and waited. The sound of the bike grew closer and closer. They could tell that the rider was having a bumpy time of it, idling around shell holes and gunning it up the occasional slope when forced to dip through a large crater.

In a short time, they began to see their late night courier – watching for any sign that they might have been spotted. All were tensed, ready to blast the lone biker with machine gun fire to prevent news of their presence reaching the Syrian command. Of course, there was an equal possibility that the rider was Jewish. But how could they tell? From watching the Syrian camp that day, they knew that the Syrian forces were communicating by motorbike. They had sent Koby and his motorbike out to reach their command center in the first hours of the war. Could that possibly be him, buzzing along on another message errand? There was no way he could have followed their track and found them without falling into Syrian hands. David studied the rider's dark silhouette as he bobbed and weaved along the cratered road. Impossible to decide.

Their lone rider racketed off along the road to the south, heading in the direction of the Golan Heights settlements at least. Perhaps he was Jewish. At least they knew he had not drawn any fire anywhere along his route, or been stopped and challenged by any patrols. When at last the noise of the bike died away, Yankel edged his tank out of the shadows and drove towards the road. David and Baruch, now both in their respective tanks, covered the dark landscape with their machine guns, while their loaders, gunners and drivers waited tensely for any order or sign. David swept the dark countryside to the north, while Baruch, since he was the southern of the two, faced any threats from the south. None appeared, and Yankel's tank reached the roadway, clambered up and over it, and pitched down the opposite side, using the embankment for cover. Baruch peeled off next and followed his path, and David signaled Sasha to follow suit as soon as he reached the roadway. Yankel was well ahead, with Baruch following at 100 plus meters by the time David's tank was over the road and lined out headed south at a moderate speed.

After fifteen minutes of easy cruising they reached the bridge where the road crossed the head of a long, deep wadi and stream that cut its way down in an ever deeper canyon until it reached the shores of the Kinneret. They were happy to see the bridge intact, for it would have meant a detour around the head reaches of the wadi to proceed further. It also meant that there was less chance of any attack from their right side, unless a column had driven south and was arrayed in a precarious position at the southern rim of the wadi. They could see the dark shapes of the crumbled water tower and heavily shelled buildings of the first settlement about two kilometers ahead. David wondered why there was no force guarding the bridge and its approaches. Had the community been overrun? The three tanks stopped and spread out within calling distance and regarded the darkened hamlet from a safe distance. There seemed equal chances that the heavily damaged buildings were held by Jews, Arabs, armed looters, bandit gangs, or just plain abandoned as the fight moved southward. Which was it? They could hear sporadic artillery fire well to the south, but nothing that sounded much less than ten kilometers away. They scanned all the likely defensive positions, wishing desperately for the thousandth time of the war that was not yet a day old, that they had a working radio, or their advanced night vision, infrared and motion sensing equipment operating. And they prayed silently that the enemy did not have all these things, and was not watching them, waiting for them to emerge for a clear shot that would end their war swiftly.

"Any ideas?" Eli called in sotto voice over to Yankel on his far left.

The dark shadow in the commander's hatch shook its head.

"Baruch?" he called to the head in the next tank. That helmeted head also shook. Eli thought for a while. There must be some way to signal the town from a safe distance; something that would not reveal which side they were until they could ascertain who they were dealing with. A safe signal….then his overworked brain clicked on "safety!" They could use the flare pistol in the safety and survival kit. He slid down the hatch and told Benny to keep watch while he rummaged in the emergency pack that was stashed in a cubbyhole beside the crew door that served as their escape hatch. He quickly outlined his plan to his crew and slipped out the crew door for a parlay with Yankel and Baruch, carrying the flare gun and six emergency flares.

Baruch climbed out of his turret and came along and the two commanders heaved themselves aboard Yankel's idling tank. They conferred in low voices around the commander's hatch, Yankel leaning on the rim, one hand resting on the machine gun just in case, the other two sitting on the low profile turret and gazing toward the dark town, hoping for a light or sign of life.

"Here's my idea," David explained, "what if I go a couple hundred meters away with the flare gun, stay behind cover and shoot off a flare in a neutral direction – say towards the wadi."

"Then what?" Yankel asked.

"We wait and see," David said, "and fire a second flare in about three or four minutes and see if there is any response... If there is nothing, I'll shoot a few more flares in the direction of the town and they might light things up so we can see something, and it may provoke them to fire. If nothing happens by then, I'll hike back here and we think of a new plan. Oh, and one tank should be watching the road to our back while the other two watch the town, we might attract some unwanted company."

The two other commanders considered the idea. To their two tired brains, it seemed to be as good an idea as any. "OK," Yankel said, "it's about two a.m. and nothing moving that I can see. We might as well try it. You keep your head down and we'll watch for any signs of life, or people trying to end yours..."

David climbed down and walked with Baruch back to the middle tank. They shook hands and exchanged a quick hug before Baruch climbed back to his spot. David walked on alone, retrieved his battered old M-16 and a few clips, a belt full of grenades, and his canteen, exchanged a few words with his crew, and left.

He picked his way carefully through the rocky landscape, dotted with bushes. Many of them were armed with thorns of various length and misery and there was the occasional prickly pear cactus and clumps of spiny sabras to lacerate him as well. Soon, however, he found some easier going as flat caps of rock offered bush-free passage for longer distances. After pacing off a good two hundred meters, he started looking for cover where he could see both the darkened town and the black shapes of the half-hidden tanks. He found a likely looking boulder, about chest high so he could see over towards the town, and open and visible towards his tank group. He took a long drink of water, and looked carefully all around to take in the lay of the sleeping landscape and look for escape routes back to his tank if his signal sparked a firestorm. He sized up a possible hummock in the terrain that ran parallel with the way he had come, and might offer a partly sheltered route back in case of a fire fight. He fitted the first flare into the tube of the pistol and aimed towards the sky to his right somewhere towards the dark land that fell away towards the Kinneret. He fired.

The flare whooshed up and away, bursting in a red starburst that faded as it fell in an arc and snuffed out before reaching the ground. He did not duck, but waited tensely, watching the dark shapes of the blasted buildings, looking, listening for any sign of activity. He could hear the deep thrumming of the tank engines a few hundred meters away. The town was nearly two kilometers away; an easy cannon shot if one had a clear target. He could see from his new vantage point that the tanks were partly screened by a rise in the land so that they were even less visible from the town than he had expected. From the turret he had felt quite exposed, but the drivers had chosen their stopping points well. They were practically hull down from view of the town. That, at least, was good news. He scanned with his binoculars, wishing for night vision and digital magnification, or, better yet, infrared that would pick up body heat or motors running.

And while he watched, he wondered. Wasn't it amazing the technology we took for granted all those years? How long would it take to build it all back? Would Israel ever struggle out of the deep hole of the recession now that its entire electronic infrastructure had been fried in a single morning? What had all the blasts taken, ten minutes from the first to the last? It took only ten minutes to go from one of the most technologically advanced nations in terms of computers per capita, broadband connections, more cell phones than people, world-class universities and technology parks, more published scientific papers and technology startups per capita than anywhere else in the world – all gone in an instant.

Damn them! He almost wished for another Syrian tank in his gun sights. Israel and David Engel refused to go down without a fight. There was no surrender possible without annihilation. The landscape remained dark and lifeless. He had no idea of the time, but he was sure from his long and wide ranging thoughts that much time had passed. Just to make sure he counted a full extra minute, fitted another flare in the pistol and fired again – this time bringing the flare somewhat closer toward the right side of the town, hoping it would shed a little light on the ruins.

He waited and watched. Still dark. Then suddenly a single light blinked on and off three times from a dark shadow near a wall. Then he heard the distant buzz of a motorbike. In about a minute he saw a dirt bike and dark-clad rider jockeying its way through the rough terrain roughly in his direction. He watched as the rider picked his way closer – stopping about 300 meters away behind a large boulder. He heard the motor shut off. A few seconds later a voice shouted in the distance, "Allo Allo."

The voice sounded familiar! "KOBY??" David shouted back.

"DAVID?!" the voice shouted.

He let out a whoop and shouted back. The whoop was answered by a wild yell, and the dirt bike started up again. It came ripping out of the shadow of the boulder and bounced and bounded over the rough terrain to where David stood waiting. He heard yells and whistles over his shoulder from the waiting tanks.

The two men embraced before his long-lost messenger could even swing his bike to a complete stop. He laid it down in the dirt, and they pounded each other with joy. They had last seen each other as Koby sprinted away in the pre-dawn darkness to reach headquarters with news of their situation as the bombardment was starting.

"I thought it might be you! We couldn't quite see a good profile of the tanks. But three tanks, alone in the middle of the night and not charging straight in – we knew they had to be Israelis," Kobi said as the relief poured out of him. "Damned glad it is you, too. We have barely a platoon left to hold the road here – everyone else had to go south to fend off another big push. I was stopped for coffee and waiting for the lieutenant to code a note when they spotted you guys approaching."

After exchanging more hugs and expressions of joy and amazement, Koby started up the bike again and David climbed on the steep, narrow seat behind him, drew his feet up as far as he could, and hung on for dear life as they jounced and roared the few hundred meters back to the waiting tanks.

Once again the commanders clustered on the turret of Yankel's tank – this time with addition of Koby. He explained quickly that the defenders had stuffed a culvert under the road just north of the town with explosives. Even though the charges were all wired to a detonator that would be set off manually, he said he would feel safer if they all drove around the booby trap. They quickly agreed to follow him into town.

After checking carefully for signs of movement behind them to the north, the tanks revved up and emerged back onto the road, following the jaunty dirt bike as it spun off the road again. They all swung wide through a field well ahead of the culvert that drained a small dip in the road. There was a ragged cheer from a number of dark forms hidden in the shadows as they rolled into the blasted town. There was not a single house or building left intact. After finding cover for all three tanks where they could command fields of fire overlooking the northern and eastern approaches to the town, Kobi, the three tank commanders and the lieutenant in charge of the platoon ducked down into a kindergarten's bomb shelter for a quick conference and a bite to eat.

There was much to tell as Yankel and David explained their running fight along the border and complicated escape down the wadi and through the minefield. Kobi recounted his day since leaving their camp just after the shelling started. He had found the command group readily enough, for none of them was moving. The eleven advanced Merkava IV tanks and half dozen mobile 155 mm artillery had then spent the day being towed, one by one into Yiftach and Yonatan to be rewired in the moshavs' agricultural workshops. Koby had spent the day buzzing here and there with messages. He recounted what he knew of the morning and late afternoon assaults on the northern settlements, and how the precarious line of settlements held as far south at the tip of the Golan Heights. However, the southern end of the line had been under attack all that afternoon and well into the evening. Kobi was headed south again to relay messages from a patrol that was exploring to the north trying to link up with forces near Katzrin. He said that a relatively small Syrian armored column had pushed its way down the road to reach the Kinneret, cutting off their access to Katzrin. However, the Israeli recon patrol commander thought it might be possible to encircle that force and eliminate it if they had some working tanks. Or, if they had some working radios, the reconnaissance group could call in coordinates on the enemy positions and they could be shelled from the heights.

He also told them of the desperate shortage of ammunition throughout the Golan, and how there were attempts being made to cross the lake and reach Tiberias and resupply. David saw Yankel's tired eyes light up briefly at the mention of fresh supplies of ammunition, for his tank was now down to five shells for the cannon. He had less than 1,000 rounds left for the machine gun, which was less than ten minutes of constant firing. David had 40 shells left – and Baruch's tank about 30, however none of their 105 mm rounds would work in Yankel's 120 mm cannon.

The lieutenant in charge of the platoon charged with defending the rubble heap of a town shared his long day as they devoured a pot of soup and a bag of cookies. Action at the northern end of the chain of settlements had been mercifully light since the first big push just after dawn that had pounded the town to rubble. While there had been a second massive assault in the direction of Yiftach and Yonatan, the little hamlet of Ami Am had been spared from the second wave. This was good, because there would have been precious little in place to stop it. He had been writing to beg for at least a tank or two, or perhaps some artillery to anchor the northern end of their thin line. If the enemy forced its way down the highway from the north, the remaining settlements would be caught in a deadly pincer. He was very relieved when the three tank commanders agreed to spend the rest of the night and to send Kobi out at dawn to check in with the area commanders for instructions.

The east shore of Lake Kinneret 05:45

After a short rest, the first of the morning prayers and a snack, Eli felt refreshed enough to contemplate the next step in their return trip – a steep climb back up the wadi to the top of the heights where their trucks waited. Since many of their volunteers were from Tiberias, they were familiar with the hiking trail, and had already shouldered their big sacks. With a large tank or artillery shell poking awkwardly from the top of each pack, they headed into the banana grove and towards the nature reserve track. Eli collected his knapsack and accepted a partial load of the much smaller and lighter mortar shells and headed off towards the rising sun. It was growing in intensity, but the sun was still unseen behind the rising escarpment to the east. Although it was still quite smoky and hazy, he was beginning to feel quite exposed at the lake shore, and so was everyone else. The boats had all disappeared back across the foggy lake to Tiberias.

The stacks of ammunition and supplies were quickly being shuttled to better cover at the edge of the banana grove.

Eli adjusted his heavy pack and trudged up the slope to the road, crossing it quickly and finding the beginnings of the track through the banana plantation. Although he had wrung out his socks and soaked pants and shirt, they were still quite wet and clinging to his legs while his feet squelched uncomfortably in his boots. He stopped to survey the lake behind him after he reached the safety of the first line of trees. The stack of ammunition had almost completely disappeared behind him. While there was still fog and smoke lying in low banks on the lake, the hills all around the lake were now glowing with early morning light. But the sky was an odd, smoky sort of overcast, and the normally clear northern air was now quite hazy. Ahead of him, just inside the banana grove, was the new stack of ammunition that was being covered with palm fronds and leaves from the banana trees while a handful of young men were packing the last of their lakeside cache up towards it. He squelched over to the cache and was mildly amused when one of the young men who was helping load other members of their human pack train gave him directions towards the track up the mountain. The kid had no idea he was talking to the person who had come down that very track in the dark and crossed the lake to recruit him for the job he was busily, and somewhat self-importantly administering. Eli didn't bother to set him straight, but trudged off in the pointed direction.

Even before it left the banana plantation the track began to climb, and Eli settled into a slow trudge. Eli was not a fast hiker even without a load of mortar shells. He preferred a slow and steady pace that gave time for contemplation and enjoying the view. But, as the trail steepened, his view was mostly of his feet and a few meters of the trail ahead. Every now and then one of the younger packers passed him as he plodded steadily upwards. So much had happened to him in the last twenty-some hours that he had plenty to think about, and he was quite absorbed in his thoughts. Since being awakened before dawn the previous day – was it only a day? – he had fought two desperate battles. He had killed who knew how many men who had the misfortune to enter the sights of his rifle scope. And after a dangerous night drive along the war-torn string of settlements, he had hiked down this very wadi carrying the pieces of his inflatable kayak. He recalled the horrible feelings of being lost on the lake in the dark, not knowing if they were paddling towards help or the enemy, and then their race through the dark streets of Tiberias. All in all, it had worked even better than he dared admit. Along the trail there were more than fifty young men bringing ammunition and hope to the beleaguered settlements on his side of the Kinneret.

Before he realized it, Eli reached the tiny stream and followed it up to the iron rungs placed to help hikers scramble around the steep rocks beside the little waterfalls that cascaded down the wadi. The falls were a bare trickle in summer and a small stream in the winter's rainy season. In this parched September, they were now quite dry. He rested a few minutes at the foot of the steep section, easing his heavy pack against a large rock and contemplated the scramble ahead. His pants and shirt were dry now, except for sweat, and even his socks were feeling less squelchy. Another young packer came trudging by and offered to help him, but Eli shook his head and said he was just resting a moment. The young man looked a little disappointed, like a boy scout who had just been turned down from the good deed of helping a little old lady across the street. Well, Eli was no little old lady, at least not yet. He cinched his pack more firmly and stepped up to the first rung.

After some puffing and pulling and not a little more sweat, Eli reached the top of the scramble in one piece. After catching his breath, Eli watched another packer clamber up the stretch with his precariously wobbling tank shell threatening to tumble out of the pack. He steadied the lopsided load and helped the young man straighten up his pack as he reached the easier ground, and both set off for the final climb to the rim of the wadi. They soon met the first packers headed down the wadi with empty packs.

Sam was waiting for Eli when he reached Woody, parked near the top of the trail. He had loaded half a dozen shells upright in the back of the pickup bed well away from the firebox. Together they helped Eli's companion unload his shell and offered him a drink before he disappeared back down the track for a second load. Sam looked tired, but he was eager to get going with this first load of shells back to Hespin, the largest of the Golan Heights communities. The rest of a motley collection of half a dozen trucks and tractors, including the old Dodge power wagon from the Yiftach dairy, now pulling a rickety open trailer, were farther up the hill where they were also being loaded.

"How many shells can we carry?" Sam asked as Eli cleaned the ashes from the wood-fired truck's fire box and carefully laid a new fire. The presence of high explosive tank shells made him extra careful.

"What do they weigh?" Eli asked.

"These big ones are 155's, they are about 50-55 kilos each, plus or minus depending what kind of round."

"Woody is rated as a 3/4 ton, so we could theoretically take up to fifteen – but I think I would feel safer with twelve. We're going to have to load them at the very back of the bed and leave plenty of space between the shells and the firebox, which will make us a bit tail heavy." Sam reluctantly agreed. Eli knew he wanted every last shell, but also saw the need for some margin of safety. They flagged down the next five packers coming up the trail and relieved them of their artillery shells. They were happy not to trudge the extra few hundred meters up to the other waiting trucks. Eli dug several heavy duty loading straps of nylon webbing out from under the front seat and set to work cinching their load securely in the back half of the bed of the big old ugly brown pickup.

It was perhaps seven-something in the morning by the time Eli put the old truck into the low range of its four-wheel-drive and they bumped and lurched their way up the rocky trail to the top of the wadi. The other trucks were still loading, so the two of them pressed on in Woody to deliver their shells and news of their successful night's work to the headquarters set up in Hespin. However, as they emerged from the top of the wadi into the open sweep of the plateau of the Golan Heights, they could tell that another assault was raging against the southern-most settlements. The sounds of a heavy artillery barrage boomed across the landscape, and they could see shells falling thickly around all of the settlements they had passed in the night on their trip south to the wadi by Kfar Haruv. The handful of soldiers and homeowners in the hamlet were busy digging better trenches and shelters as they watched the battle booming a few kilometers away. After talking with some of the soldiers and surveying the scene with his binoculars, Sam decided they needed to head straight for the nearest 155 mm artillery battery with their truckload of a dozen shells. He told Eli to steer for the hamlet of Geshur, a picturesque agricultural and tourist hideaway perched on the edge of a wadi that cut deeply into the Golan Heights that was just behind the main fighting at Moshav Eli Ad. It appeared that a large force was trying to push its way past one of the narrowest points of the heights where the uplands of the Golan squeezed between the deep *Nahal* Arakad that marked the border with Syria and the rocky gorge behind the hamlets of Geshur and Eli Ad.

They were able to follow the main road for a while until reaching the point where the plateau widened and they could dodge along a series of farm roads through the fields that offered better cover. Eli was able to make much better time in the daylight. Sam sat tensely in the passenger seat, his short-stock M-16 at the ready, poised to dive out the door or return fire at any moment. As they angled across the fields, the battle was thundering to their right just a few kilometers away. They could see that two Israeli tanks were dodging along behind some fieldstone walls that crossed some fields northeast of them. Sam said they were the older Merkava II version, though how he could tell that at such a distance, Eli couldn't figure. Israelis who served in the IDF seemed to have an eye for these things, the way a sports car fan could distinguish one year's Corvette from another.

Eli could now see the outgoing flash of firing from the battery hidden in a deep grove of trees near Geshur and he steered towards it, urging a little more speed out of Woody. He shifted now to high range but stayed in 4-wheel drive because of all the shell holes. Fortunately their load of artillery shells had not shifted more than an inch or two within the tight loading straps. He would have hated to worry about a loose shell bouncing around as they jounced and jolted along the shell-pocketed farm tracks. Here and there they saw the burnt tail pieces of rockets that had fallen in the first day's barrage.

He started beeping the horn as they approached Geshur, and soon a helmeted figure in camouflage and a flak jacket appeared from the trees and waved him towards to narrow two-track rut that entered the woods. He slowed down and turned onto the narrow trail. It quickly opened into a clearing, where they saw the big guns under camo netting strung between the trees. He could readily see there were only two or three shells left beside each of the four guns. The artillerymen barely stopped to cheer them and had the dozen shells off their truck in moments. Sam consulted briefly with one of their officers and dived back into the cab of Woody. Eli had already turned the truck around and was poised to run back for another load. "We have to steer some more trucks this way. They are the only battery between here and Hespin. These four guns, two tanks and a few mortars are all that is holding the pass here!" Sam said breathlessly.

Eli did not need any explanations. He revved Woody up and out of the clearing, charging down the two track through the woods and zipping up the bank and onto the lane that led out of Geshur, headed back to the precious ammunition being carried to the top of their human pack chain. Their boat had brought 72 shells, the other two boats of the night slightly more each. They knew it was not enough by far, but would have to do. They hoped that perhaps someone had dared to run across the lake in daylight since there were still no planes or helicopters in the sky.

Eli had spotted a less damaged track through the fields on their way over, so they made much better time going back without a load of deadly high explosives weighing them down, and with their urgency driving them forward. As they neared the highway leading to Kfar Haruv they saw the first of the motley collection of trucks pressed into service for their ammunition convoy. It was the Dodge power wagon pulling a trailer full of shells, and an ancient flatbed truck that belonged to one of the other moshavs. Both were laboring along under their loads. Sam flagged them down and gave directions to the battery at Geshur. Speeding down the highway the last few kilometers to Kfar Haruv, Woody hit about 50 miles an hour, its speedometer and odometer read in old-fashioned US miles. Their gas pressure was looking good, but Eli made a mental note to stoke up the firebox with some more wood before making their next run. They met the next three of the convoy leaving the gates of Kfar Haruv. They were two farm tractors pulling hay wagons and another antique truck that looked like a WWII surplus 6-wheel-drive 2 1/2 ton truck, the only vehicle of their fleet actually designed for this kind of convoy. Eli wondered if the old truck had fought in the war of Independence in 1948 as well. Sam gave them directions to the battery at Geshur and the back way into the besieged moshav of Eli Ad.

They reached the loading point at the head of the trail and caught up with news from the lake. Two more boats had risked the run across just after dawn, and they brought news of an armored column pushing toward Tiberias along the highway that encircled the lake. In the three minutes it took to load their shells, for Eli decided he could handle a few more now that he knew the route, they learned that the defenders had dynamited a large outcrop of rocks that created a landslide blocking the road and crushing the advance group of tanks. They learned that artillery dug in above the town was showering the attackers with well-aimed shells, while machine gun and anti tank teams covered the landslide area with deadly fire. Fortunately, as they had seen for themselves that night, the Tiberias defenders were well supplied with ammunition.

Within minutes they were headed back to Geshur with their fifteen shells and a couple boxes of 7.62 mm machine gun ammunition. As they reached the highway however, Eli remembered he had forgotten to feed the firebox. Checking all the gauges, he could tell that gas production was falling, and that they were slightly under optimum operating pressure. He told Sam about it and they stopped to feed the firebox just after leaving the highway at a point where Sam could survey the changing battle while Eli fed the fire. Sam filled him in on the news as they drove on, swaying under their heavy load as they navigated potholes and craters in the dirt farm roads. Sam said the assault seemed to be falling back. The two Merkava tanks they had spotted on their first trip could now be barely seen working their way farther north, almost opposite Eli Ad now, and the crash of shells seemed to be reaching slightly less far to the south. They could see the arc of outgoing shells from the battery they were feeding at Geshur, so he surmised that the next loads of shells had reached the guns in time. They made their zig-zagging trip through the farm tracks that crossed the fields in slightly better time, and soon met the Dodge and its companion from the neighboring moshav as they entered the lane towards Geshur. This time, when they arrived at the artillery battery in the clearing, there were at least a dozen shells by each piece and the tractor and 2.5 ton truck were just ready to pull out. A pair of older jeeps with jerry-rigged machine guns and their three-man crews were waiting and grateful for their machine gun ammunition. They peeled out of the clearing heading back to the fray the moment they got the last case from the back of Woody.

Eli could tell that Sam was itching to join the fight. As they jogged along the empty truck back through the fields Sam kept watch over his shoulder instead of looking ahead. The ammunition pile at the head of the wadi was beginning to grow again as they reached the trail head for the third time of the morning. They could see an intermittent line of young men trudging up the last few hundred meters of trail, each with a tall artillery shell poking from the neck of their pack. Eli fed a few more good sized chunks of wood into the fire box as Sam selected their next load. This time he chose the smaller tank shells and a couple more cases of 7.62 ammunition. He said they were 105 mm shells for the two tanks that were working to push back the tide of the assault as Ami Ad. He asked Eli if he would mind driving right up to the battle this time. Eli agreed, because he was willing to do anything to help – but noticed that Sam asked him after the tank shells were more than half loaded. They found room for 24 of the smaller shells, two cases of machine gun ammo, and still had room for the two soldiers, who had accompanied them in their morning hike to the lake, to perch on the sides of the bed. Eli was glad of a little more company if they were headed into the roar of the fight. All he had was a pistol. He asked Sam if there was an extra rifle anywhere, but there was no time to waste to look for one, so they left.

When they reached the point where the plateau broadened before narrowing to the contested battleground around moshav Eli Ad, Eli stuck to the highway until they approached the area where shells were falling. It was like approaching a cloudburst in the desert. One minute it was calm, and the next they were lost in the crash and boom of the thundering rain of artillery fire. Eli steered off the road and kept to the cratered ditch along side, sometimes having to gear way down and plow through the depths of a shell hole where there was no other way forward. Sam was now sitting half out the passenger side window, one foot hooked into the lap belt which he had pulled tight across the seat, peering into the firestorm ahead. After a while of threading carefully along the lee side of the road, he motioned for Eli to steer towards a small rocky hillock to the left of the road. Eli tried to see a clear way to get there, for the only way was through rocky fields with few tracks. After a few moments deliberation, he saw a pair of tank tracks that churned across one of the fields that seemed to steer reasonably clear of large rocks. He edged through the roadside drainage ditch and followed the freshly broken tracks.

As they drew closer to the hillock, he could see why they were headed there, for the two Israeli tanks were sheltering in its lee. As they drew closer still, he could see that the hillock was one of the many large abandoned bunkers left over from the earlier wars on the Golan, and he could see a tiny figure near the top who was signaling to the tanks. Their passage was difficult through the rocky meadow, used only for occasional grazing and strewn with boulders and now shell holes. Eli concentrated on picking a line in, through, and around the many obstacles. It was all first and second gear work in the low range, with the little truck plunging and climbing in and around craters left by the bombardment. Often enough a huge blast would fall somewhere nearby and gouge a new crater. Somehow Eli had no time for fear, he just concentrated on his driving, trying to close the distance to the two tanks.

Sam pounded the top of the cab and yelled something as he unhooked his foot and swung himself out the window and disappeared. Eli noticed a movement in his rearview mirror and saw both soldiers dive from the back of the truck – but he could not see what was making them dive for cover. He looked around just in time to see three huge tanks racing around the right side of the hillock coming full speed seemingly right for him. He threw the truck in neutral and opened his door and was about to dive away from the truck when he saw a huge shell crater dead ahead. Since he had forgotten to unbuckle his seatbelt, he was momentarily trapped in the driver's seat. Almost instinctively he jammed the truck back into gear and drove straight for the hole. The nose of the truck pitched forward and half slid, half rolled into the steep pit. At the bottom the engine stalled out and died, and Eli was unbuckling his seatbelt and attempting again to run for it when a tank shell whooshed directly overhead missing by centimeters. He half fell, half jumped out of the cab and sprawled on the dirt slope of the pit – which must have been nearly two meters deep, for only the top of the cab was above ground level where the truck had shuddered to a stop.

Eli regained his feet and sprinted out of the hole, away from the three quarters of a ton of high explosives. As he reached ground level there was a spray of machine gun fire that swept the hole, blowing away the bit of windshield that tilted up above the ground and swinging in an arc following him. Eli dived for the ground and pressed his head and whole body into the rocky dirt as the angry zip zip zip of shells whizzed just over his head and exposed back. Then he heard two booms somewhere to his left, and a crash and a kaboom in the direction of the three racing tanks. Eli saw a low rock that offered a shred of shelter and wormed his way to it, impervious to rocks, cactus and rough weeds. Another boom roared out to his left, with a third kaboom a half-second later, and the machine gun fire stopped abruptly. He lay still, ears ringing and adrenalin racing through his body and he heard the pop, pop, pop-pop of rifles being fired quickly, but in semi-automatic mode, answered by sprays of fully automatic fire from ahead of him.

Shaking, Eli unholstered his 9 mm pistol, chambered a round and slid the safety off. It took a moment before he dared raise his head a fraction to see what was going on. New, shorter bursts of machine gun fire joined the staccato symphony around him. He rose up slightly on his left elbow, bringing his eyes just above his sheltering rock, and swinging his pistol up at the ready. He couldn't make out a thing, just swirling smoke and noise and the burning hulk of what appeared to be one of the big tanks less than two hundred meters ahead of him. The semi-automatic fire, which he knew from experience must be coming from Israelis, was coming in choppy bursts from several of the shell holes behind him. If Woody had not been filled with high explosives, he would have been tempted to crawl back into its huge shell crater, for it offered the best cover around. He looked off to his left for some better cover, but saw nothing within an easy crawl. He looked behind him and could see nothing there either. He would have to make do with what he had. He dared another peek, levering up even higher on his elbow, risking almost his whole head above the level of his rock. Eli felt grateful for his helmet, which still bore the deep gouge in its Kevlar shell from the previous morning. He could make out nothing but the confused clatter of weapons and boom of shells.

Eli had begun to excavate his hiding hole a few centimeters deeper with his hands, switching the pistol from his right to left and back again as the digging progressed. Within minutes he had at least a slight cradle of earth to press himself into. The not so distant roar of heavy diesel engines and a fresh bursting of machine gun fire caused him to freeze again. Boom after blast roared out around him, seeming quite close and the earth trembled with each tremendous blast. He knew he must be in the middle of a tremendously fierce tank and armored vehicle battle, but he could do nothing but press himself into the earth and pray. Bullets ripped by overhead in both directions. He knew moving would probably be fatal.

The roar of engines and ratatatat of machine gun fire was pounding closer and closer until it seemed he was about to be run over. "Play dead!" his inner voice commanded, and it seemed like the only logical advice, so he buried his face in the dirt, slipped his pistol under his chest and left his right hand and arm sprawled in what he hoped was a convincing display of an unnatural angle and prayed. Another huge boom roared out practically over his head and the earth shook as a huge metal monster clattered right past – missing him by less than two meters. He dared not look.

The smell of diesel smoke and cordite enveloped him. He dared not look up, even a peep. The monstrous machine belted a burst of machine gun fire as it turned ponderously just beyond him, and in a few seconds it erupted in the flame and smoke of another round firing. Eli felt the heat of the blast on his exposed hand and arm. He felt like he was probably shaking like a leaf, but lay as still as he could. The huge tank rumbled a few more meters away – it seemed to be right about where Woody was wrecked in the shell crater – were they going to back off and blow the ammunition sky high? What had happened to the two Israeli tanks? Surely they had been overwhelmed in the second onslaught. He could only lie still as he could, pray and wonder.

He heard the clang of a hatch, and then voices off to his right in the direction of Woody. Were they speaking Hebrew? It sure sounded like it; but there was such a din going on all around with shells and gunfire that it was impossible to tell. Besides, Arabic sounded much like Hebrew, only a bit harsher and more guttural. He lay as still as he could and prayed.

Suddenly there were footsteps running towards him. He stopped even moving his lips in prayer, he had said his final *Shema Israel, HaShem Elokeinu, HaShem Echad!* Hear O Israel, the L-rd your G-d, the L-rd is ONE! The prayer said by every believing Jew, and quite a few non-believing Jews, when they felt their last moments upon them.

"ELI, you hit?"

It was Sam! He started laughing, his face still half buried in the dirt as Sam crouched down beside and prepared to turn him over, certain of a mortal wound. All Eli could do was roll weakly to one side, laughing with tears of relief as Sam knelt wonderingly at his side. Then, after a few wonderstruck moments, Sam leaned on his rifle and started laughing too. Eli rolled over on his back and laughed uncontrollably – and Sam punched him affectionately and doubled over his rifle in laughter and tears. An earth shaking boom of a falling artillery shell nearby brought them both to their senses, and Sam pulled Eli to a sitting position, where he could see soldiers heaving shells up and out of Woody and into the back door of a tank parked neatly in front of Woody's shell crater.

"We got here just in time, they were down to three or four shells each," Sam yelled over the din of the idling tank and the gunfire. "Our other tank took a hit on the treads and is out of action – but the crew is safe."

Eli just sat there and stared at the tank that he had thought was going to kill him. But he was beginning to realize that the fire fight was not over. He saw the tank's commander busy at the machine gun while three men with rifles fired bursts from behind the cover of its armored sides. Sam crouched and fired a short burst from his M-16 and tugged at Eli to follow him. He sprinted to the cover of the shell hole that engulfed Woody, and Eli followed, diving down the slope feet first, his pistol again at the ready. However, he was too disoriented when he edged back up to the rim to see anything definite to fire at. He missed his sniper rifle and its clear scope and his deep rifle pit with its commanding sweep of the battlefield. This running and jumping in and out of holes in a melee of fire was too confusing for an old man, he thought. However, when the tank slammed its door shut and roared off to carry its storm of fire elsewhere, he saw that Sam and their two companions were staying put, and had stopped firing.

"What do we do now?" he asked as Sam ducked behind the rim of their crater to reload.

"We make for that old Syrian bunker over there," Sam said, jerking his head towards the hillock that had sheltered the two Israeli tanks. Each of them grabbed their packs from the back of the truck, now empty of ammunition and frozen at a crazy angle where it had bounced partway up the far side of the pit and stalled. The windshield was completely shattered, and a neat row of bullet holes in the roof showed where the machine gun fire had exited. The back window was completely blown away, and beads and shards of broken glass littered the cab and the bed of truck. There was a jagged hole torn in the little chimney of the firebox, but otherwise the wood-fired system seemed intact. One front tire was flat, adding a twist to the tilt. If they could winch the truck out of the hole, Eli thought it just might run again. However, the middle of a firefight was not the time to think about that. He slipped on his nearly empty pack – for they had made room for packing mortar shells by stripping away all the non-essentials. Now he carried only water and a bite of food.

Eli and Sam crouched at the lip of their shell crater, looking for their chance to sprint to the next covering boulder that Sam pointed out about

25 meters away. The other two soldiers, working as a team, had covered each other to another rock nearby ahead of them. They both popped up and laid down a burst of covering fire. Sam gestured to follow him and sprinted, doubled over and firing a burst from his rifle as he ran. Eli followed, but saw nothing to fire at, so just ran as fast as he could, gun at the ready. His doubled over run was only half bent, and he pack flopped awkwardly until he dived for the cover of the boulder. As he gathered himself back up and readjusted his pack, Eli had the sneaking suspicion that Sam was busy trying not to laugh. Sam pointed out their next cover, this time at least 30 meters away and more to the left than forward. He zipped off a few quick shots and sprinted off. Eli cinched his helmet strap and pack tighter, took a deep breath and sprinted after him, paying more attention this time to speed rather than form. He arrived at the next rock breathing hard, but in less disarray. Sam fired a few rounds and ran off. Eli waited until he saw him flop down behind another rock before following. He could see the other pair of soldiers working their way slightly to the right and ahead of them. A few more sprints would take them into the lee of the looming hill of the abandoned bunker.

In this fashion, Eli and Sam sprinted and sheltered their way until they were at the base of the grassy hillock that covered the old bunker. Except for a pair of horizontal slits encased in concrete that were obviously designed for some kind of fixed artillery, and a pair of ventilation pipes sticking out near the top, it could have been a grassy hill with a few bushes clinging to its southern slope, which was protected from the winter winds that scoured the Golan from the north and west.

The hill cut off their view of the fighting, which had moved northwards. As they caught their breath, Eli counted four burnt out tank carcasses and the shattered remains of half a dozen armored troop carriers and half tracks that had made it past the imaginary line that ran from their hillock to the highway. Like seashells left behind by a retreating high tide, they marked the extent of the morning's Syrian assault. He could also see the disabled Israeli tank resting where it had been stopped, a large chunk of its left front armor and treads blown away. It was definitely in worse shape than Woody. However, a lone figure in its turret still plied the machine gun, firing short bursts into the roiling smoke of the now retreating Syrian advance.

They climbed to near the summit of the hill, each finding a perch where they could see the fight going on beyond, but shelter in niches behind the curve of the hill. Eli picked a spot near the top where he could see the embattled moshav Eli Am to his left. A trio of Israeli tanks and a pair of some kind of armored vehicles had edged out from the protection of the moshav and were pouring fire at the stalled mass of the Syrian advance. He could also see the huge bursts of the 155 mm shells as they fell among the milling tanks and armored vehicles. Then he noticed he was sharing the hilltop with a pair of artillery spotters he had not noticed before, because they were around more towards the southwestern corner. He could tell from a blinking light in the swirl of haze surrounding the moshav that they were signaling a relay point about halfway to the woods hidden behind the moshav. Eli could do nothing but watch the battlefield below him and wish for his trusty sniper rifle, for his pistol could do nothing at this range. He slid the round from the chamber, put the safety back on and snapped it back in its holster. He wished there was something he could do, but watching the roiling fight was so fascinating that he did not feel the need to move. His companions were firing less as the battle began to move out of effective rifle range. The tank they had reloaded had joined up with the other three and they were strung out in a loose line pressing the milling pack of the Syrian advance northward. From his vantage point, Eli could tell that they were still outnumbered at least 4-1 in tanks, and more than that in armored vehicles, but the artillery fire that continued to fall among the Syrian offensive was causing chaos as well as destruction. He heard the spotters to his left cheer, and saw something exploding among the confused cloud of dust, smoke and vehicles. He cheered hoarsely too.

It took perhaps another twenty minutes for the Syrian retreat to sort itself out and withdraw beyond the range of the Geshur battery and the tank fire from the spunky Israeli resistance. Their tanks did not follow further, but fell back to Eli Ad to regroup, and probably to reload. Eli wondered if there had been enough ammunition packed up the wadi to resupply them, even with the extra two boat loads. He saw a trio of Merkava tanks and a pair of half tracks emerge from somewhere to the east beyond the highway and head northwards, keeping to the far side of the highway. He had wondered what had stopped the Syrian advance from simply swinging around Eli Ad and pushing beyond it.

Sam came and joined him. "Nice perch you have up here," he said as he took in the view in all directions. From their hillock they could see the deep ravine that made their narrow neck of plateau such a strategic line. Had the Syrians pushed southwards, they would have been able to overrun all the communities at the south end of the Golan Heights and command the winding road that descended the southern end of the heights. From that road they could have linked up with the massive Jordanian force to the south of the lake, and together pushed on into the Israeli heartland. Eli and Sam could also see the Kinneret, or at least a blanket of smoke where the Kinneret lay, with the Galilean hills rising beyond. Sam loaned Eli his binoculars and pointed to where he could see the smoke and flash of a battle going on somewhere well to the south of Tiberias. He was relieved to know that the ancient city and their only source of ammunition and contact with the rest of Israel, was still fighting back. It was too hazy to see the north end of the lake, although on a normally clear day one could see as far as Mount Hermon to the north, as well as the hills of Tzfat and the mountains that marked the far edge of the Hula Valley.

They sat together for what seemed to be a very long time. Both were tired from being up all night and their constant race against the clock. Now, as the adrenalin ebbed from their bodies, they felt exhausted. Eli realized that he had hardly had anything to drink for hours except for a few sips as they drove back and forth on their ammunition ferrying trips; and none since entering the curtain of fire of the battle. He was parched. Fortunately, his pack held a couple liter and a half water bottles, and he and Sam drained one, and offered the other to the two artillery spotters, who were settling in for a long stay until relieved by others with fresh instructions.

Eli wished for a cell phone to call Natalie and reassure her that he was OK. He thought back over his scribbled note – gone to Tiberias in the kayak…. and felt he had certainly understated his mission. But who could predict anything any more? There was not a cell phone operating between Cairo and the Turkish border with Lebanon and Syria if last night's discussions around his sukkah table could be believed. His sukkah seemed a very long way away. Eli Ad was only a 15 minute drive away in a normal world, but the world was certainly not normal, and may never be "normal" again. That was too big a concept to think about with a tired brain that had been up all night.

"Ready to hike over to Eli Ad? I think it's safe," Sam said at last.

"Why hike, I think I can get Woody going again if we can winch it out of the hole," Eli said. Sam just stared at him uncomprehendingly.

"Really," Eli said, "Woody is fine except for the windshield, one front tire and the top of the cab. Nothing vital was hit. I have a come-along and a cable under the front seat, and the spare is underneath, so it should be OK. We could probably have Woody dug out and running again within the hour."

Sam looked relieved, "Well I'll be damned," he said, "that old truck is as tough as you are. It just keeps on chugging,"

"I'm not feeling so tough," Eli grinned, "In fact, I wouldn't mind a nap right now; too much excitement for an old guy like me."

"That makes two of us," Sam yawned, "But we better get going. What time do you think it is?

"Five minutes to ten exactly," Eli said, checking his watch. It had been less than ten hours since they left Eli's house on their night's expedition to Tiberias. It had been more than four hours since his wet and tired morning prayers near the lakeside. Their desperate resupply mission into the thick of the battle had been probably less than an hour. Eli felt like it was already a lifetime ago, even though the firing still thundered off to the north – in the direction of his home, he realized. He prayed that his moshav had been spared. They had already buried dozens of dead, moshavniks and soldiers alike, the previous evening.

Wearily and stiffly they got to their feet, said goodbye to the pair of artillery spotters, who waved thanks again for the extra water and were busy with breakfast. Sam whistled at their two companions to join them, and the four picked their way down the brushy south slope of the bunker's hill to where the battered truck sat crazily in the shell hole that had saved their lives. It seemed absurdly easy to just walk any which way through the weedy meadow, not worrying about deadly bullets flying overhead. However, Eli was noticing the extent of his scratches, bruises and abrasions from his dives and crawls through the dirt.

When they reached the truck the first thing Eli did was check to see if the two canvas water bags slung inside the bed by the tailgate were intact. They were, and he refilled his water bottle and washed his face, hands and arms of some of the dirt and debris of battle, being careful to use only a couple of cup fulls. Sam and their two guardians, whose names were Roee and Ronny – though he still could not remember which was which, did the same. With his face and hands at least somewhat refreshed, he could think a little more clearly, and Eli set about sizing up the task of resurrecting his truck.

The first thing to do, he decided, was to put on the pair of rough, leather palmed canvas gloves he kept by the fire box along with the portable saw and ax he kept in case he ever needed to cut some firewood for the wood burning system. They were right where they should be. The firebox was still warm, but he decided to wait until the truck was on level ground before rebuilding the fire rather than risk a poorly laid fire at the truck's steep angle. The tail of the truck was embedded in the dirt trapping the spare tire in its hanger underneath, so all four decided to wait to change the tire until after they had winched the truck out of it hole.

The cab of the truck was a mess of broken glass. Eli used his thick gloves to fish under the seat to get to the come-along ratchet he kept there. He handed it to Sam and pulled out the long steel cable that was coiled in an open box under the seat. He had to shake out shards of glass as he fed the end of the cable to Sam. However, Sam appeared to have no idea what to do with the cable, and stood there holding its stiff loops. So, Eli took one end with its hook and hooked it onto one of the two big tow rings attached to the frame of the truck below the front bumper. Sam seemed to get the idea, and pulled the other end of the cable up the slope of the shell crater and was standing around with it, looking lost again. Roee and Ronny stood around looking equally helpless. "City boys," Eli muttered, though the truth was he was also a city boy, born and raised in Chicago, but he had taken it upon himself to learn a few useful manual skills.

He took the come-along and its cable from Ronny, who was holding it, and looked for a stump or a solidly planted boulder within a few meters of the lip of the crater. He found a suitable rock and tried a loop of cable around it. The cable cinched snugly enough and looked like it would stay on solidly. The pull would be at about a thirty degree angle to the left of the truck's direction, but Eli figured that the driver's side tire was the full one, and it would steer towards the pull, counteracting the flat tire. He attached the come-along and its cable to the loop with a locking steel ring, slipped the ratchet off and paid out the cable towards the stuck truck. Sizing up the distance the truck had to travel to get out of the hole, and the amount of cable he had paid out, he decided to double the heavy cable on his truck back to the other tow ring on the bumper, and hook his come-along cable into the middle of the cable. That would give him a more even pull. The three soldiers watched in fascination, with a growing awareness of what he might be doing. Still, they eyed the long handle of the ratchet on the come-along with skepticism. How could something that simple looking pull a two-ton truck? He could see them wondering. Well, it was time to show them.

Eli engaged the ratchet and began to take up the slack. First the cable stretched out towards the truck began to tighten, and then the cable above his device that anchored it to the rock tightened up. Up until this point the long lever strokes of the come-along handle had been cranking easily. Now it took force to swing it through its 180-degree swing, and the cables were pulling piano-wire taunt, and the cable that hooked on to the loop through the truck bumpers was eating a groove in the soft dirt of the rim of the crater. Sam broke his trance and came over to help heave the lever. Now they made shorter strokes, not more than a 90 degree arc before letting the lever click back for another bite of cable. They felt a shudder in the cable, and saw the top of Woody's shattered cab move an inch or two. One of the two soldiers, Roee or Ronny whistled in amazement and came close to the cable to peer at the truck as it began to inch out of its hole. Eli shouted and motioned him back, saying more in pantomime than words that the taunt cable could snap and hurt him badly if it broke. After that the two soldiers came over to take over the winching. They all worked, almost impervious to the sounds of battle that were growing more distant as the morning went on.

Soon they had Woody winched out of the pit and the tire changed under Eli's instructions, for only Sam had ever changed a tire before, and that on a small Subaru. Eli swept much of the shattered glass out of the cab, and, using his thick gloves, pulled the rest of the sharp shards out of the windshield and back window. He spread a pair of coveralls on the seat, after shaking the glass fragments out of them as best he could. He had a fire lit in the firebox with almost the last of his wood supply, and was contentedly watching the pressure gauges climb as the two soldiers finished wrestling the flat tire back into the spare tire holder. With a final look at the shell crater that had saved their lives, for all thought that the explosion of their ammunition would have probably killed them all, they started up the truck and made their way towards Eli Ad.

Natalie woke in the dimly lit bedroom and wondered for a while what time it was. She could hear the regular breathing of Tali's kids on the mattress on the floor, but Tali, who had shared the king-sized bed with her, was not there; meaning that it was probably morning. The tightly fitting steel security window gave no clue whether it was light or dark outside. Only one of their clocks was working, and Natalie had stopped wearing a watch some years ago, relying on her ever-present cell phone to tell her the time. She listened a while, lying comfortable and not willing to get up quite yet. Yesterday had been such a long nightmare of a day – and yet she felt somehow insulated and protected from it in her home. She was lucky to get to stay home. Eli was out there somewhere, with his little rifle and his pack full of bullets, and his helmet and his pocket *siddur*. Where did he find the courage?

Tali was curled up with a cup of coffee in the living room, looking worried. "Eli left you a note on the dining room table," she said, pointing to a Shabbat candle stick oddly out of place on the table. It pinned down a note quickly scrawled on a sheet of paper from their printer's reject pile. She could see it was the last sheet of some internet pages Eli had printed. She read it aloud:

"Gone to Tiberias in the kayak for help with the IDF – back sometime after sunrise – love you dearly, Eli"

"What on earth?" she said aloud.

"Sorry, I couldn't help reading it," Tali said, "I have no idea… Is a kayak that little boat he brings to the beach with the kids?"

Natalie nodded, re-reading the note, "Gone to Tiberias for help…. With the IDF – at least someone went with him. G-d wish I had stayed up a little longer, I thought he was going out to do guard duty! Why didn't he wake me up to tell me he was going to Tiberias! He must have gone with that colonel – or maybe one of the officers here with him? There was that guy who borrowed the truck, what was his name?"

Tali shrugged. "Could he really go all the way to Tiberias in that funny little boat?" she wondered aloud.

"Oh, that part is perfectly reasonable, Eli and I have crossed the lake together once, and he has done it by himself a number of times. The kids used to think it was a big adventure to paddle all the way over in the summer for ice cream and falafel."

Natalie absently poured herself a mug of coffee from the pot Tali had made and peered out the shuttered doors to the patio. The sun was up, but just barely. "Back sometime after sunrise," she repeated. "I sure hope so. *Ribbono Shel Olam*, King of the Universe please protect my dear husband and all Israel…." she whispered aloud. "And help him learn to start acting his age," she thought to herself.

"Amen!" Tali said, she put her coffee cup down and came to the door and hugged Natalie. The two mothers watched the light growing stronger and listened to the not-so-distant sounds of war for a second morning in a row. The guns in their moshav were silent for now, but clearly a battle boomed and rumbled somewhere not far to the south.

The two women washed up the last of the dishes from the previous night's barbeque and surveyed the possibilities for lunch for whoever showed up at their sukkah, reminding themselves that it was the first day of the holiday. The first of the children were up by the time both had finished their brief morning prayers, for there was much to be done. Keeping busy helped keep Natalie from worrying too much, but as the morning wore on, she decided it was time to go see if she could find Baruch or any of Eli's companions in the northwest outer perimeter defense group.

Tali had been back and forth between their two houses, and gone visiting since the war started, but Natalie had not been beyond her house and patio. She was shocked at the destruction around the moshav that had been her home for the past five years, longer if you count the better part of a year they had spent building their house, or the times they had spent there as guests while trying to decide whether to join the moshav. Nearly every house had been turned into ruins, and all those that stood had shell holes in the walls or roof, and there were few intact windows to be seen. Even trees had been blasted and torn apart. Cars stood uselessly in some of the driveways – some damaged, some intact. How could Eli have been out in this kind of firestorm and survived? She wondered, or any of them?

She found about half of the community's men in the bomb shelter by the synagogue, and a few women praying in the small women's section by the entrance. They had reached *Hallel*, for all the men had their bundles of palm branches, myrtle and willows, along with yellow *etrogs* in their hands and the familiar melodies reverberated in the bomb shelter's walls. Eli was nowhere to be seen. She saw Gadi's oldest daughter and asked if her father was there. She indicated a short man wrapped in a *tallit* a few rows ahead of them. Then she asked if the girl had seen Eli. She shook her head as she sang with the *Hallel* – "*Hodu Adonai, ki tov... Ki l'olam chasdo* Give thanks to the L-rd for He is good, for His mercy endures forever." Natalie felt slightly comforted by the words. As Jews who believed in G-d and his Torah, Natalie and Eli knew that G-d supervised every element of his universe, even the smallest detail, and that whatever had happened anywhere, and what was happening to them now was not without meaning or purpose. There were no accidents in G-d's universe, even though the world might seem random or purposeless sometimes. Those thoughts reassured her somewhat.

Natalie stayed through the end of *Hallel* and the reading of the Torah that followed. Although the men were all in the same clothes they had fought and stayed up all night in, their white and black *tallits* gave them a strength and dignity that went beyond a mere woven shawl. There were perhaps a dozen soldiers in the shelter as well, with their olive drab uniforms. She always loved to see the men take out the velvet-mantled Sefer Torah, with its jingling crown of silver with pomegranate-shaped bells, and carry it solemnly to the *bimah* in the middle of the *shul*, even though this was a white-painted, very utilitarian bomb shelter. She looked around at its folding chairs, folding *mehitsa* dividing the men and women's sections. It had a small, but ornate *aron* with its velvet curtains for storing the Torah scrolls. In eight years of living in Israel, Natalie's Hebrew had progressed to the point that she could follow the Torah reading fairly easily. The men were tired and raced along through the readings, one *aliyah* following another in rapid succession. However she managed to keep up and followed along in the Hebrew-only *Chumash* she had taken from the shelf.

However, the harsh warning and dire words of the *Haftorah*, the section of prophet Zechariah read after the Torah reading on the first day of *Sukkot* leapt out at her even through the filter of her loose translation in her mind: "*Hineh yom ba...* behold the day is coming..... *v'asafti et kol ha goyim el Yerushalim l'milhama*....I will gather all the nations to war against Jerusalem....and the city will be taken, the houses plundered, the women violated, and half the city will go into exile...." She shuddered to think what might be happening in Jerusalem or indeed to the rest of Israel. They had felt so defenseless when they first found out about the nuclear strike that had rendered all their electronics and most of their cars and tanks useless. Only last night, after the battle subsided did she dare to think they were going to survive. She understood now why her husband had headed off across the lake in the night. They needed help – desperately.

"On that day there will be neither bright light nor thick darkness, but it will be one continuous day...." The reader went on. Day had flowed into night almost seamlessly. The night had been bright, the day had dawned ominously dark and dreary. "Is this the final war?" She wondered. It seemed impossible, but the recent views of her blasted community rose in stark testimony in her mind's eye before her. Who knows? Numbed and with troubled thoughts, she waited out the rest of the service for a chance to talk with Gadi, her husband's companion and group leader in their moshav defense force.

Gadi's teenage daughter helped her flag him down in the crowd as it milled around, talking and folding *tallits* and putting away their *lulav* and *etrogim*. She asked him what he knew of Eli's trip across the lake. Gadi looked apologetic and almost guilty, not looking at her directly as he said what he knew. Eli had worked something out about going across the lake with the young lieutenant who was working for Colonel Eschol. The colonel felt it was important enough to relieve Eli of guard duty that night and send a soldier in his place. Gadi didn't know much about the plan, except that they had all left in Woody and they needed to reach Tiberias and a large warehouse of ammunition that was stored near there. He was sorry he didn't have more details for her. He said he had heard the colonel and most of the IDF troops were somewhere to the south where the fighting was the heaviest.

Moshav Yiftach 12:15

Eli and Sam stopped in the bomb-shattered moshav of Eli Ad only long enough to check in on the state of their ammunition convoys. When they discovered that no shells had made it north of the fighting to the northern communities, including the battery at Yiftach, they quickly loaded another 15 shells for the 155 mm. howitzers from the small stockpile that was left from the morning's fighting and headed north. The old Dodge power wagon and its trailer were also being loaded for a trip north, but their little truck would travel faster by itself. They caught up with the roar of battle again at the embattled Yeshiva community of Hespin, but they bypassed the town well to the quieter western side, taking a series of dirt roads and trails until they were approaching Yiftach again from the west. There was only the occasional shell – perhaps one every ten minutes – as if someone had decreed that there should be no rest or security for the battered little community. They drove their load of shells directly to where they had last seen the three remaining howitzers. They soon realized that there were now only two, and that they had moved to new, deeper excavations dug for them by the hard-working moshav bulldozer.

The artillerymen cheered them like conquering heroes, making both Sam and Eli feel rather embarrassed. But when they saw that there were only three shells left for each big gun, and as they watched the artillerymen unload and practically caress each precious shell, they knew they had done something vital. "Now we can drop a few rounds on the heads of those bastards!" one of the officers said, as he flashed out new signals to their distant spotters who were relaying signals to even more distant spotters. Five minutes later his signals came back. After some calculations, the gunners loaded a fresh shell and turned their cranks and checked their indicators. One of the gunners offered to let Eli pull the lanyard to fire the big gun, but he decided he would rather have both hands over his ears. He made a good choice. The gun went off with a tremendous, gut wrenching boom. The gunners all had custom ear protectors and grinned with pleasure to be back in action.

Somehow Eli and Sam couldn't tear themselves away from the show. They were both dead on their feet, having been constantly on the go for hours. But somehow they each felt that they had a share in these outgoing rounds, having carried them in one way or another all the way from

Tiberias. Roee and Ronny seemed to feel the same way, and all of them perched behind a sand-bagged wall a comfortable distance away, swigging water and covering their ears whenever someone reached for the lanyard. There was a long pause after the fourth shell. Then the flash of distant signals brought the news – direct hit! Everyone cheered hoarsely. Now, perhaps, there would be some quiet!

"How about some lunch?" he asked Sam, Roee and Ronny. They all looked like they had somehow forgotten there was a thing called lunch.

"Lunch or nap?" Sam pondered, yawning mightily. "When was the last time I had a choice like that? I'll have a bite or two, then I need to grab some sleep." Roee and Ronny looked like they had come down on the lunch side of the question, for they quickly went and hopped in the bed of the truck. Eli had a little more than enough gas pressure left in the tanks to take them home through the cratered and pock-marked lane to his house. Thank G-d it was still standing, sukkah, orchard (most of it) and all.

Natalie met them as they rolled to a stop in the gravel drive in the shelter of the kitchen, which was still intact except for the one small shell hole from the previous day. Almost wordlessly Eli and Natalie hugged and wept on each other's shoulder for a long time. Sam and the two soldiers quietly slipped off to go inside and wash up.

"Sorry doll, I know you must have been worried out of your mind with a stupid note like that... we just had to get going in a big hurry and I couldn't think of what to say," Eli apologized. "We barely made it back across the lake with the first boat by sunrise. There was really not a minute to spare."

"I know you had to do it," Natalie said. "But I am going to frame that note in the Husband Hall of Fame."

Arm in arm they went into the house. "I need to tell you, we have four wounded officers in the spare bedroom. Dr. Shira asked if we could take a few cases off her hands, their shelter is swamped, and so is the community center. She sent Amy along to help care for them."

"Fine," Eli said, absently as he surveyed the extra people and baggage camping in his living room. Three soldiers slept while Tali's kids were playing quietly with several of the board games they kept for the grandchildren – it looked like they had combined three or more of them and it sounded like they were intent on making up new rules.

"Um, one of our wounded officers is a Syrian," Natalie said, "He's not getting out of bed any time soon according to Shira, but he seems stable enough."

"Is he a major?" Eli asked, as something clicked in his brain.

"Maybe, I don't know about these things and I didn't ask, but he speaks English."

"I think I met him yesterday morning... head wound, leg in a cast and a big bandage around his chest. Speaks a very British English?"

"That's him," she said, "Small world.

158   Golan! Day Two

"I'll go see him after I take a shower, has anyone been refilling the reservoir?"

"Two of the soldiers have been keeping it topped up – everyone had been really grateful for the showers, but I'm afraid there's not a dry towel in the house."

"Guess I'll recycle one, you know me," Eli grinned.

"Yes, I do know you, you grey-bearded eco freak! What happened to Woody's windshield?" Natalie said.

"Long story," Eli said with a yawn, "I'll tell you over lunch – what's there to eat for a small platoon? I invited Sam, Roee and Ronny."

"There's plenty – Tali brought over half her kitchen, and we've been cooking half the morning. Go get clean, I want to see if you are really my husband or just a walking dirtball that sounds like him."

Eli gave her another kiss and headed for the bathroom. Miraculously, it was free and only a little awash, with towels hung everywhere and every which way. He would have to carry most of them out the clothesline after he was done. He couldn't recall if the clothesline was still standing, even though he must have walked right by it on the way around the kitchen to the patio entrance. He checked the temperature gauge on the solar control panel next to the cupboard and was happy to see plenty of hot water left, and that the lever was in "Shabbat" mode, preventing the system from heating new water, but allowing a perfectly kosher shower as long as one was careful of the various do's and don'ts for bathing. He followed the most lenient opinions on this issue – and he was sure there were extra leniencies for a soldier just in from battle. As he peeled out of his dirty fatigues and boots, he took stock of the day's wear and tear. His hands were chapped and nails dirty and torn from digging, His forearms and elbows a mass of scratches and cuts from crawling in the dirt and weeds, knees too. A big blue bruise stared back at him from his left hip where he had fallen with the first rockets of the war. There was another pronounced bruise on his right cheek from the kick of his rifle and some scratches on the side of his forehead and face from who knows when. He ached all over, and took a couple of paracetamol capsules from the medicine cabinet before stepping into the shower. The hot water stung the raw scratches on his arms and knees, but the water soon felt soothing as they adjusted to the warmth. Since it was a *Yom Tov*, he made sure to use a dab of liquid soap rather than lather up with a solid bar – one of the finer points of Shabbat restrictions. There was plenty of shampoo in the array of bottles that normally inhabited his shower to use in lieu of soap. Several long luxurious minutes later, he stepped steaming from the shower and grabbed a halfway dry towel.

After he dressed in clean underwear and his other pair of camouflage fatigues, Eli remembered to take an arm load of towels out to the line – which was still standing. Heavenly smells were emanating from the kitchen, for fortunately the war had spared his two big propane gas balloons that ran the stove and oven. He followed his nose to the kitchen. Ronny or Roee had found the shower free after him and was singing away some what sounded like some lusty Ukrainian love song.

Natalie shooed Eli out of the kitchen after he sampled everything in sight and made a nuisance of himself smooching her at every opportunity. He dutifully carried a fresh tablecloth and a pile of plates out to the sukkah and began resetting the table for a festive meal. There had not been a shell falling in the moshav since their bulls eye on the enemy battery and he saw signs of people emerging from underground shelters elsewhere along his street. Aside from the neat line of bullet holes from the previous morning, the sukkah was untouched by the war. Although the day was hot, it was not as baking hot as the previous day, and a bit of wind was stirring from the north, bringing some relief to the heat. It was shady and pleasant under the branch-covered roof of his airy sukkah, for he had windows or doors on all four sides that could be closed against cool night breezes, or opened to pleasant summer airs. September weather in the Golan was usually still hot, but sometimes cool weather moved in during the eight-day holidays.

Seeing his *lulav* and *etrog* lying on the side table, where someone had left them after borrowing them that morning, he realized that he had not prayed the rest of the holiday morning services, or held his four required species. He stopped setting the table and went to get his *tallit* and a larger *siddur*. Natalie found him in the middle of *Hallel* when she came out to see what happened to him. He carried his palm bundle like an ancient sword, and she had the faint impression she was seeing a warrior from somewhere in Israel's distant past as he shook it right, left, up, down, forward and back like a martial arts dancer.

He finished up his prayers quickly, and helped Natalie and Tali carry heaping trays of food out to the sukkah. Then Eli remembered his wounded guests in the spare bedroom, including the Syrian major. He carried a pitcher of lemonade and a stack of plastic cups into the bedroom at the other end of the house, not quite sure what to expect. He found a lively discussion taking place in English and Hebrew between the Syrian major, and an IDF lieutenant who had both arms and most of his upper body in bandages. He looked like he had suffered some serious burns, but the bandages were mostly interfering with his using his hands to drive home his point. Eli quickly gathered that the subject was soccer, since the words Manchester United kept cropping up. Amy, one of the moshav's few single women over 30, was trying to calm both of them down, but clearly enjoying the energy of the debate. "Football!" she said, rolling her eyes in an exaggerated disgust as she accepted a glass of lemonade. Everyone had just finished lunch, but was grateful for more to drink, since the modest-sized bedroom was warm with five bodies in it and the windows mostly shut.

Eli poured the major a glass and welcomed him, asking if he needed anything else to be more comfortable. He graciously said he had everything he needed except for a working TV set to watch the day's match. He apologized on behalf of his government's Iranian allies for inconveniencing every football enthusiast in the Middle East. That met with hearty laughter all around.

Eli greeted the other two officers, both of them from the howitzer teams. He was relieved to see that they had survived the blasts that had destroyed their big guns. They were relieved to hear the whispered news that their comrades had silenced the last gun of the battery that had been shelling the moshav all day. Eli didn't want the Syrian officer to feel bad over the death of his fellows in arms. The artillery officers intuitively understood and kept their relief and celebration quiet. Eli collected a tray of dirty dishes and delivered them to the kitchen. He and Natalie carried warm loaves of fresh-baked *challah* and the first course of salads out to the sukkah and began to collect their guests. Amy had eaten with her patients, and none of them was ambulatory enough to come to the sukkah. Sam was comatose in an armchair, and Eli decided to let him sleep. Both Roee and Ronny, which ever was which, were both clean and had migrated to the table. Tali collected her kids, and the other three soldiers came along with them. It was a hungry looking crowd, so Eli made short work of the blessing over wine and for sitting in the sukkah. Everyone joined in for a rousing *shechianu* – "who has sanctified us, kept us, and sustained us until this day! Amen!" Then Eli led everyone inside to wash their hands for the bread. They all trooped back out and waited silently for the blessing for bread.

Eli relaxed in his comfortable wicker arm chair after he had sent the basket of warm slices of *challah* around the table and enjoyed the second moment of peace in the whole day of racing the clock – the first had been in the shower after the cuts stopped stinging. He smiled at Natalie and she beamed back as she passed the first of half a dozen salads. He took three kinds of olives, tabouleh, hummus, some Israeli cucumber tomato salad, something green with lots of fresh cilantro, sliced green peppers and cherry tomatoes from their garden, and something Tali must have made with half a dozen kinds of marinated beans.

With all the fresh bread, wine and salads, Eli was beginning to feel a tiny bit full when the chicken dishes began to show up – barbequed wings, Moroccan-style roast chicken with lemon and olives, leg quarters in some kind of teriyaki-style marinade. He was definitely full by the time he sampled everything being passed around the table. He had switched from wine to water after a glass and a half, reminding himself that they were still at war and he might be called upon to drive again, or at least shoot straight. However, even the distant thunder of the battle that had raged all morning to the south of them seemed to have faded into next to nothing, as if everyone had tired of war and taken a lunch break.

He told Natalie, and occasionally others at the table who listened in, about his midnight trip across the Kinneret, underplaying getting lost in the fog and the chances of being shot by either side. He described the *balagan* at the army depot, and their strange flotilla of tour boats filled with shells. He told of their human chain to carry the shells ashore, and of the pack train up the wadi to the top where their collection of trucks was waiting. He didn't mention driving straight into battle to deliver their shells to the two embattled tanks, only that they had come under tank and machine gun fire and were saved by driving the whole truck into a huge shell crater. He described watching the rest of the battle from safe atop the old bunker, their stops in Eli Ad, and their circuitous drive back north. All told, it made quite a tale.

After everyone had eaten, except for Sam, who had finally roused at the smell of roast chicken and followed his nose to the sukkah like a blind man only half awake, Eli asked for his guests' attention for a few words of Torah. What he had most in mind all that day were words of the *Haftorah*, the day's reading from the prophet Zechariah, which he had quickly reviewed in English – checking the Hebrew text from time to time to make sure the translation caught the exact meaning of the original.

"We sit in the sukkah each year to remember the Exodus from Egypt – how we all dwelled in temporary quarters for forty years in the desert. And we leave our secure houses – or in this year's case, our secure bomb shelters – and we eat and study and visit and often sleep in our sukkah. A sukkah is a temporary structure, open to the elements, or at least to the sky. And we remember that our trust and our real security lies in the will of the Eternal and not in any walls or roof made by mankind. And, indeed, we see that this little wooden sukkah is far more intact than most of the houses in this Moshav. We see that most of the sukkahs are still standing amid all the destruction, and we have to wonder – are we seeing an accident? – or a miracle in plain sight?" There was a buzz of comments and agreement and everyone had something to say about the all sukkahs that were standing.

He waited until the comments died down, and continued: "And each year on the first day of *Sukkot*, and on the Shabbat of *Sukkot*, we read the most amazing, frightening and awesome prophesies – from the prophets Zechariah and Isaiah – on the war that is to come at the "end of days," before the final redemption of all mankind. And frankly, it makes your hair stand on end to read about it."

"And so, the question in the back of my mind, and perhaps on the mind of every Jew this past amazing day and a half, is: is it happening now? Is this the 'Big One?'"

There were murmurs of surprise, but some of agreement as well around the table. Roee and Ronny were listening intently, and Sam had stopped inhaling chicken in a race to catch up on missed calories. Eli looked around the table and smiled. "I wish I had an answer to that, but I want to lay out some observations and ask some questions."

"If you read today's *Haftorah* from the prophet Zechariah, he describes a very detailed series of events. An enemy will be stirred up against Israel from the lands of the north, and indeed, Lebanon and Syria have attacked from the north; although Jordan from the east and Egypt from the south have also attacked. The prophet says that in fact, many nations will join in the attack. We have learned from talking to those who have interviewed captured and wounded soldiers that there are many mercenaries and "volunteers" from the former Soviet republics and many of the other Arabic-speaking nations among them from Somalia to Saudi Arabia. The prophet goes on to say that these nations will attack a divided Israel, and half of Jerusalem will fall, but half will remain. I have only rumors, but I have heard that there is serious fighting going on within the city."

"I hadn't thought of any of that," Sam said, but you're right. The parallels are chillingly exact.

"There's more, it talks of a long day, but one where it is impossible to tell day from night. And only in the end of the day one can perceive that it is afternoon. Many commentaries say this is metaphoric, that only towards the end of the struggle will some "daylight" or hope appear. All I know is that for me it has seemed like one continuous blur of day and night. We've had dim, dark days and bright nights lit by fires and an eerie glow in the sky all night. If I tried to tell the time from looking at the sky right now, I wouldn't have a clue if it was morning or evening. And, oddly, one of the most common things zapped by the bombs were everyone's digital watches, nobody but old geezers like me, who have old-fashioned, wind-up watches, know what time it is. For your information, it is now about 2:30."

"We all know the traditions from the *Medrash*, the *Talmud* and the prophets, like Zechariah that Armageddon, the final war to end all wars that sets the stage for the messianic age, is predicted to happen at *Sukkot*. And that after it is over, all the nations of the world somehow come to understand G-d in a new way, and all adopt the holiday. There's a famous story in the *Talmud* about how the other nations can't handle it, and kick the sukkah on the way out the door when the weather gets too hot."

"There are miracles and divine intervention at the end of Zechariah's account. And, if I were a Syrian or a Jordanian right now, I would seriously consider buying earthquake and plague insurance," There were chuckles around the table.

"And so, as I said, I raise the questions and leave them on the table. From where I sit, it doesn't matter if this is the "big one" or not. I'm going to do my best to make sure that Israel, or at least my little piece of Israel, survives."

Natalie clasped his hand under the table, and looked at Eli with tears in her eyes. "Me too," she said quietly.

For the rest of the meal there was a lively discussion. Was this the Big One? Some felt that the War of Independence in 1948 was even more miraculous and against even more desperate odds. Now at least the Jews had arms. It was their own shortsighted leadership to blame that their most sophisticated weapons did not work. The EMP damage had been, if not preventable, then at least able to be mitigated in many ways. There were countermeasures, and the possibility of having redundant, survivable systems. Clearly the Syrians had weathered the same blasts just across the border and kept most of their technology intact. The Israeli military had known about the bunker building programs for years, and it had been common knowledge in the lively free press. There were those observers, like a certain conservative Jerusalem Post columnist who could pass as a prophetess if her warning columns were read aloud today, Eli argued. There were religious members of the Knesset, called "right wingers" by the liberal press, who had been voices crying in the political wilderness for years about the effects of the constant appeasement of the Arab states and pandering to the myth that the Palestinian leadership was somehow "moderate," and not solemnly committed to the destruction of Israel. And what about all the repeated opportunities to build a workable missile defense system that had been frittered away in budget stalemates and pursuit of pie-in-the-sky technologies instead of available systems that could have reduced the damage if not prevented it?

Yawns eventually replaced arguments, and everyone sang the *Bircat HaMazon*, the blessings after the meal, together. Their mixed voices, accents and cadences blended in an odd sort of harmony. Eli and Natalie were putting away the last of the food as best they could with a non-working refrigerator when the moshavnik in charge of work details came around. He asked if they had any shovels or picks to loan. "Sure, what needs digging?" Eli asked.

"We are still collecting bodies from the field, and need help burying them," he answered, "And the backhoe and bulldozer are both down at Givat Yoav trying to reopen the road to the Kinneret."

Eli looked at Natalie, "Want a date?" he asked.

"But you need to sleep!" she protested.

"The colonel said I'm off until eight am tomorrow, and I want to stay awake until its dark." He said.

"OK, it's a date," she said, "let me go get some sturdier shoes on if we're going to be digging."

Anna and the Northern Defense Command bunker got their first good news in nearly two days — fighter jets were coming! By about 2300 that evening, two wings of US F-16s from Spain and one wing of F-15s from Portugal would be flying in, coming the last 150 km flying on the deck less than 50 meters above the Mediterranean. They had been stripped of markings, transponders, airframe and engine numbers, all armaments except four older-model, untraceable air-to-air missiles each, and just about anything identifying them in case of interception, crash or compromise. The pilots had all volunteered, and were flying without a shred of identification — not even dog tags. It was hush-hush up and down the line. In fact, all Portugal or Spain knew was that the wings were being moved to advanced positions in Cyprus in case of any spillover from the "Middle East Situation," as it was being called. Cyprus was a good destination to tell them, for radio, phone and TV communications were seriously disrupted there, and everywhere else within a few hundred kilometers of Israel.

Negev Command assured her that the runways at Ramat Hovav would be operable — if kerosene lanterns for runway lights and bomb craters patched with sand and hand-mixed, quick drying cement counted as operable. And, for the moment, it was relatively safe from attack. Fortunately the Egyptian offensive trying to capture the extensive IDF bases at Ofakaim had stalled completely as Israeli resistance stiffened on the second day of the lightning war. And the Negev bases were not being threatened by any major offensive.

However the massive push up the Israeli coast was another story. One thrust had bogged down in house-to-house fighting in Ashkelon, a city of more than 100,000 and the closest large city to the Gaza strip. Egyptian-led armored forces and infantry had bullied their way around the city and were now pressing Ashdod, the next large city up the coast. Raiding parties, for they barely resembled an organized military operation – more like well-equipped private militias and armed mobs — were everywhere. The majority of the mercenaries, and regular soldiers too, had become more interested in looting than fighting, except as a means to acquire more loot. Ironically, much of the booty being carried back to Gaza and the Sinai were TVs, computers and electronic toys — the very thing that had been destroyed in the first five minutes of the war. However with no working power to plug these things in, the irony would be some weeks or even months away from being revealed.

Anna also learned that a second nuclear sub, armed mostly with conventional cruise missiles, was now available in addition to the USS Sitka.

They had set up a situation room in the lounge of their underground living quarters and so several laptops were now arrayed on the coffee table. Maps were taped on the walls over the landscape and tourism posters, and the out-of-tune guitar was now banished to one of the mens' bunkrooms. However junk food, coffee and large plastic bottles of soda and fruit drinks mixed freely with the satellite intelligence data. Anna had brought in Koby and Shira from her group, the two majors from the mountaintop installation, and an air force captain who was in charge of the now-destroyed radars. Together they were soaking up coffee and data and trying to figure out the targets for their first air offensive. Negev Command estimated that the planes would be re-armed, re-fueled and ready to fly within about two or three hours of touching down. But flying night missions with the limited electronics that passed the American security restrictions would be iffy. They could, however, take comfort in the fact that the Arab advance had bedded down shortly after dark the previous night and that their troops appeared aversive to sustained night fighting.

"What kind of target list can we put together that would be safe to hit in the dark? How about the supply lines?" Anna asked, still feeling odd in the role as the senior officer in charge. "I'm a computer geek, for crying out loud," she thought to herself, "what am I doing selecting tactical targets for the air force?" But then, what had all the IDF senior brass done about preventing this debacle? Worse than nothing; they had frittered away ten years' worth of opportunities. So maybe she was going to have to use her best judgment, which perhaps wasn't so bad after all.

Nobody answered for a minute because everyone else in the bunker was someone else in the IDF constellation of command: an air force radar expert who hadn't flown since officer training days, one artillery major, one military police major, and another two computer geeks. The colonel on the radio link at Negev Command was in logistics. There was not a combat officer in the bunch.

"OK," Anna said, getting up and going to the big laminated wall map of Israel they had unrolled and tacked to the wall behind the two overstuffed armchairs. She took a red whiteboard marker from the board where they wrote the weekly duty rosters. She made a bunch of short red circles most of the way around the base of Mt. Meron. "These are the active enemy units we know about," she said. "At our base up here we have plenty of artillery up and running, perhaps a dozen jeeps, a few tanks and APCs, and plenty of guys on the ground. There is no heavy duty threat, but a lot of bloodshed and looting around the peripheral towns. They are overrunning wherever we can't be at the moment. That's our immediate neighborhood.

"Here are the main fronts as we know them circa 1400 today." Half climbing on the arm of the chair, she drew a series of short red arrows piecing the Lebanese border — ending where they knew there were active fronts and skirmishes all around the upper Galilee.

Then she drew a heavy dark arrow sweeping down the Hula Valley and ending at a zigzagging line near Rosh Pina, checking a laptop she had carried over and balanced on the back of the chair to show the disposition of forces as best as they had been able to discern from the satellite imagery. She drew a thin line in green around both fronts. "Here are the areas where we had 1.5 meter detail and pretty good data. Rosh Pina is touch and go. We have the better part of two brigades, but no transport, little armor, and the artillery is running very, very low on ammunition."

Then she sketched in the Syrian advance from Mt. Hermon to the line in the vicinity of Katzrin with another thick arrow joining it from the Syrian border in the neighborhood of Quneitra, and a third big arrow with branches stabbing at the line of communities along the Golan Heights. "Here's the Golan situation…" she said, double checking some new screens of satellite imagery they had marked up on the laptop. "We just got a few radios across the Kinneret on a speed boat about an hour ago, and the commander near Hespin has been in touch off and on since morning. Golan was able to re-supply with a few boat loads of shells last night.

"They tell me a couple guys actually paddled across the Kinneret in a kayak in the fog. One of them was an old man of about sixty, it was his idea and his boat, can you believe it?" Heads shook around the room. What a war this was turning out to be. "They are trying to open one of the roads from the Golan down to the lake here," she put a circle on the map across the lake from Tiberias. "They said there are eleven Merkava IVs coming online by tonight and they will send data on how they did it as soon as they link up the Tiberias again. That's damned good news. Colonel Eschol, anyone else remember him from Lebanon? Best tank guy in the IDF since General Tal. Colonel Eschol said he's planning to go on the offensive if he can get enough shells across the Kinneret. Of course, that depends on us hanging on to Tiberias."

There was a buzz after she mentioned the word offensive. Somehow it didn't seem possible to go on the offensive two days after your country suffered a crushing invasion on all fronts and a crippling electro-nuclear attack. But that was the way of all Israel's successful wars — take the battle back to the enemy, hit hard where it was least expected, and then keep on running and shooting until you won. Anna sensed the mood in the room change imperceptibly. Funny how twenty-four borrowed planes and word of eleven re-wired tanks in the hands of a respected commander could spark just enough hope to keep them all going, and re-inspire them to push the extremes of creativity and chutzpah it was going to take to keep Israel alive for another generation.

"Now for the Jordan Valley and Tiberias…" she said. There she drew in another big red set of arrows, one hooking around the southern end of the lake to threaten Tiberias, a second pushing down the Jordan Valley, and a branch of the second arrow that veered off towards Afula and Meggido.

The Jordan Valley branch of the second arrow ended in a jagged circle near the town of Beit Se'an.

"Tiberias and Beit Se'an are threatened, but holding. I'm afraid we'll probably lose Beit Sean and have to pull back to the hills, but it looks like we have a good hold on Tiberias. They were able to create rock slides at two of the pinch points north and south of the city and defend them successfully against the first wave. However, if Tiberias falls, there goes our re-supply for half the northern front, not to mention major civilian casualties. If Beit Se'an goes, it's clear sailing all the way up and down the Jordan Valley. However, the main force seems to be headed for Afula and the Jezreel Valley, and the big action seems to be pressing towards Megiddo — good old Armageddon. That's shaping in to a classic tank battle, except that we have less than three dozen running between Afula and Megiddo at the moment — all pre-1980 models.

"We've got to make sure we hang on to Afula, Tiberias, and Rosh Pina, and all three need help. I'm thinking our one flight of F-15s could hit the Jordan Valley and the Tiberias assault in the first wave, and then give some help to Rosh Pina on the second or third trip. I'm thinking of using the F-15s for the northern front because we still don't know what Jordan is holding back in terms of air force. F-15s would be better air-to-air if it comes to a dog fight, do I remember that right?" she asked the radar captain. He thought for a minute, and agreed with her assessment.

"Now for the south. We have a crossing and assault still forming near Jericho, but nothing heavy moving up the road to Jerusalem yet." She sketched in a red circle around the all-Arab city of Jericho. "We can hit them later if anything starts threatening to move out of the valley. And we can't do anything about street-level fighting with an F-16," she said, tapping the map over the holy city with her red marker, leaving a measles-like bunch of dots.

"Our biggest problem right now is this mass of Egyptian and mixed multitudes coming up the coast and making a real mess of the whole damned south." She angrily drew in arrows, zigzag lines and circles of concentrated forces around Ashkelon, Ashdod, Ofakaim, Kiryat Gat and other communities in the coastal plan and beginnings of the Judean Hills. "That's where I want our two wings of F-16s to start cleaning up first thing in the morning. But for tonight, or what's left of it after the planes get here, let's start hitting the coast road up from the Suez into Gaza. Here are the major points in the supply chain," she said, drawing red circles around a series of well-known places in the Sinai; places familiar to every Israeli school child, from Mitla Pass near the Suez end, to Raffah Crossing that served as the gateway to the Gaza strip. "That will stop the flow of supplies and fresh forces into the theater. I could just about give you the GPS coordinates of these by memory." There were some knowing chuckles from the officers who had been following her summary. They had also drilled in at least half a dozen Sinai war scenarios since their earliest days of military service.

"The Egyptians seem to have finally learned a thing or two from history — they bypassed the Negev entirely and came straight up the coast, just like the Pharaoh in King Hezkiyahu's time. And the worst part is that we have half our southern defense group stranded in the Negev with no transportation, or staring across the Suez from non-working tanks."

"Yeah, I'm sure if Ariel Sharon was still around, he'd have crossed the Suez again with whatever jeeps he could get started and be trying to drive to Cairo about now," the artillery major chimed in.

Anna stood back and looked at her artwork — the map of Israel looked stabbed and bleeding at more than a dozen points. She put the cap back on her marker and glared at the map. Three flights of borrowed fighters — twenty-four planes; that's all she had to work with — oh, and forty-eight Tomahawk missiles — what to do with them?

"OK, now, I'd love to use the Tomahawks on the Jordanian air force. But the ground rules are strikes only on "undisputed" Israeli soil, not even Gaza and Palestinian Authority. So does anyone have any nice big fat targets that are cruise missile-sized on Israeli soil inside of the Green Line, and that are going to stick round at least the next twelve hours while we clear targets and GPS coordinates with Washington, Norfolk and Langley? Bear in mind that using this option also means keeping about six hundred US sailors quiet about the intervention." Nobody had any good ideas. "OK. We hold those for later. If things start going really bad along the coast we might be able to hit places that are too hot for an F-16. Questions?"

It felt damned good to be able to hit back with something, anything. Anna assigned Koby and the radar captain to relay their targeting priorities to Command Negev. She needed to get back on the secure relay to her US contacts to coordinate the last minute details of the relief flight of fighter planes.

There were still no helicopters available, but there was a good chance of getting up to a dozen of their own propeller driven trainers airborne from a Negev training base by tomorrow that could provide better, up-to-the-minute reconnaissance for the jet fighters. They could also relay communications and people from front to front. There was talk that the old trainers might be able to be fitted with a pair of wing-mounted 20 mm cannon that could be used to strafe infantry and vehicle, but that was speculation at this point.

"Hello, General Taylor? This is Anna, you still on the channel?"

"Copy you there Anna, this is Frank." Still first names, that was good. She knew he had spent the last twenty-four hours begging, cajoling, threatening and bargaining heaven and earth to get them even three wings of borrowed planes.

"I don't know how to begin to thank you, or what you had to do to get us three wings of fighters, but thank you on behalf of me and everyone in

Israel. I think it might be just enough to turn the tide as long as everyone else stays on the ground," she began.

"I've been looking at the satellite pictures too. You have a lot of unwanted company right now, especially on the southern front. I wish I could get over there with a couple dozen Blackhawks or Apache Longbows. We could roll up such a high score on those sons of bitches it would go down in the history books."

"Wish you could too, only we have to win the war first to write the history books. Our next problem is going to be finding enough bullets, shells and missiles to shoot all of them. As you well know, we can only go about ten days before the warehouses are empty. And if you take away everything in our infrastructure and supply chain that was hit in the first two days, well, our logistics look pretty grim."

General Taylor was quiet for awhile. Maybe it was too early to start pressing on her next request, but the situation was truly desperate. Israel made only a small part of its ordinance, mostly specialized tank shells, some of the smarter smart bombs, and air-to-air missiles, plus a factory for the standard 5.56 mm bullets for the M-16 and Tavor rifles. For everything else, they used NATO/US standard rounds, from 7.62 mm machine guns to the 155 mm shells that they fired from their biggest guns. They generally had up to two weeks of ammunition in storage, sometimes less. After that, Israel always needed an emergency re-supply. Fortunately none of their defensive wars had ever lasted more than three weeks.

"Frank, you still with me there?" Anna asked anxiously.

"Yeah, I was just trying to think how to get some to you… What do you need most?"

"Good question," she replied, infinitely relieved that he was not pulling back. "Artillery 155 mm down to 75 mm for sure, the big guns are one of the few assets we have that were not shut down by the electromagnetic pulse. Mortars have been working overtime too, so all the standard sizes from 60 mm up to 122. Machine gun ammo is getting scarce on all fronts. Tank shells I think are not a big problem yet, given that we have so few running and shooting. I'll get back to you later with a complete shopping list if the store is open."

"Do that," Frank said. "It's going to take some time to make that much ordinance disappear without finding at least one friendly country to work with us."

"Try Czechoslovakia first," Anna suggested. "They generally will help for a price. They're close by, and they can be pretty discreet."

They wrapped up the final details of the incoming flights: code signals, frequencies for contacting them, and protocols for authenticating them as the real thing. She passed along the coordinates and limitations of the landing fields. He wished her and her pilots luck and they signed off after setting their next conference.

The ruins of Kibbutz HaGolani, late afternoon

Amil and his Uncle Kassim had loaded and unloaded the little Fiat Uno several times. After trying to tow a Mazda, and then a Peugeot, they had discovered that the little Uno was the biggest prize they could hope to roll home with only two donkeys. The growing competition for goods in the overrun kibbutz forced them to stake out one half-bombed house as their own and wave away any interlopers with a barrage of verbal abuse and, if that failed, a not-so-subtle display of Uncle Kassim's two pistols. The house they had chosen was modest sized. But, unfortunately, the kitchen had taken direct hits from several shells, for Uncle Kassim had dearly wanted a microwave oven to present to his wife. He had heard enough of her scorn and proud words about her father's house. But her father and mother had never had a microwave oven where you put in food and it came out cooked like magic a minute later. He had seen one at the banker's house at a wedding party.

Although the kitchen and one of the bedrooms were destroyed, there was plenty to choose from, and that was the problem. Not everything could possibly fit in the little car. Certainly the television was a must. It was not the extra-wide flat screen that Uncle Kassim had longed for, but it was a fairly new model flat screen. It would be the biggest one in their neighborhood, depending on what the others brought home or bought at the market. And there were six nice, matching upholstered dining room chairs tied to the roof of the little car with rope they had found in the basement. There were nearly new quilts and blankets but they took up a lot of room. None of the clothes looked like the right size. And besides, who wanted to dress like a Jew? Amil had picked up some toys for his nieces and nephews. That was the trouble, there was too much to carry in one load. Why didn't they bring two more donkeys? They could have pulled the Peugeot! Maybe even the Mazda.

And there was another trouble, the sun would be going down soon. There was no way Amil and Kassim were going to try the long trip back across the border in the dark. They would have to bed down in their half-pillaged house for the night. Uncle Kassim told Amil to gather wood and start a small fire on the tile floor near a blasted hole in the wall that would let smoke out while he took some towels over to the next house to barter for some food from their un-destroyed kitchen.

Moshav Yiftach 22:00

Eli and Natalie had helped dig the better part of two narrow graves in the rocky Golan earth. He had worked with a long pry bar, levering loose the many rocks and heaving them out while she scooped out the loosened earth and smaller rocks with the shovel. Were it not for the blasted and maimed bodies of enemy soldiers stacked near where they and a dozen of their fellow moshavniks worked, they could have been working together in their garden as they had on many such late summer afternoons. There were only a few mortar shells the whole afternoon, and the half dug graves served as their shelter whenever they heard the incoming whine of a shell. It was amazing to Natalie how a body became tuned to certain sounds when survival was at stake. Two days before, she had never heard a mortar shell. Rockets yes, plenty in 2006, but mortars no.

Eli was exhausted and worked slower and slower with his long pry bar until she made him stop. They helped lower six mangled bodies into the grave they had recently finished, attached the dog tags to six large wooden stakes borrowed from the moshav's vineyard supplies, and said a quiet prayer for the departed souls of their fallen enemies. Two young teenagers helped them fill in the graves, putting back in ten minutes what had taken them more than three hours to pry out of the rocky earth.

They left their tools which Eli had marked a long time ago with two blue stripes to make it easier to loan them out and get them back without getting them mixed up in communal projects. Some men guarded their tools jealously, even in the cooperative atmosphere of the moshav. But Eli was always happy to see his tools help someone else. In fact, Woody was off on another errand, this time without him, after he had cleaned the ashes out of its firebox and restocked its wood supply. It looked like a rolling wreck without its windshield or rear window, but it actually made it easier for a soldier to ride shotgun with a rifle or a grenade launcher.

After saying an exhausted and mumbled *Mincha* prayer with a *minyan* of soldiers beside the community center, Eli wandered home, washed the dirt off his face and hands, pulled off his boots and fell into bed. Therefore it was well after ten at night before he emerged from the bedroom in search of Natalie and food. He found both in the sukkah. The barbeque was going because the moshav dairy had slaughtered two older cows that were scheduled to have been shipped to the slaughterhouse later that week anyway. There was a *shochet* on the moshav trained in kosher slaughter and fortunately for the community he was home and not off with his reserve unit. They had delivered steaks and roasts to all the surviving kitchens in the community. Roughly half of them were operable in some form, either above ground in the ruins of the house or below ground in well-equipped shelters. Therefore there was a pack of soldiers grilling steaks over a wood fire, for they were out of charcoal and borrowed from Woody's supply by the shed. The roasting meat smell drove away the lingering smell of death that had haunted Eli since their graveyard duties.

Natalie and Tali had baked bread and pitas and found enough fresh vegetables and greens from their two houses and gardens to make a tempting array of salads. Both cooks were firm believers in buying in bulk and stocking up at sales so their supply of olive oil, spices and condiments were still coping with the constant guests. At least a platoon and a half of soldiers had rotated in and out of the sukkah since the barbeque started. Eli brought out an arm full of bottles of wine from his modest collection of Golan and Galilee wines and set out a dozen bottles of beer opened them and passed them around.

Eli filled himself a plate of steak from the grill, took some fresh pitas and salads and poured himself a glass of wine, and went to wash. Since it was now the first intermediate day of the holiday, he said the blessing for the bread first and ate some, then said the blessing for sitting in the sukkah. There was a mixed chorus of "amens" from those in various states of eating. He blessed the wine and drank some. Sam wandered out, looking still half asleep, and heaped himself a plate of food and stared at it in wonder. "Not a bad way to fight a war..." he said to no one in particular and dived into the heap in front of him.

Eli ate and ate. It had been a long time since he had a fresh cut steak done to perfection over a smoky wood fire, probably not since his hunting expeditions in northern Michigan with his cousin many, many years ago. Natalie had eaten earlier but found the salads and tidbits of steak trimmings irresistible and she kept Eli company. They presided over a mixed table of young soldiers with an older couple who lived three doors down whose bomb shelter kitchen was not up to the task of grilling a steak. The couple was telling the young soldiers at their end of the table stories of the Six-Day War. A soldier halfway down the table started one of the songs made famous during that 1967 war, *Yerushalaim Shel Zahav — Jerusalem of Gold.* One song led to another and another. They sang songs from *Hallel*, bits of psalms, and popular Israeli songs.

"*Sukkot* is the one holiday where we are commanded to be happy," Eli said, introducing a short *dvar* Torah as the meal wound down. "And it's a very odd thing to be commanded to be happy. We are told have *simcha —* joy and happiness. I mean, who doesn't want to be happy? But then, on the other hand, who can turn off or on an emotion like happiness at will? Especially at a time like this? How can G-d command us to be happy no matter what our circumstances, just because it is *Sukkot*?" Having laid out the question, Eli offered a possible way of looking at the issue: "Most of us go through life thinking that if we had maybe a little more money then we would be happy — or if we had a bigger house or a newer car — then we would be happy...We fall into the trap of thinking that materials things or our material situation can make us happy."

"But then, along comes *Sukkot* — when we go out of our nice houses and leave our cars in the driveway — and even our big comfy beds and our dining room tables with the chandeliers and the nice electric lights and air conditioning. We come out here in the yard to a little hut we set up once a year, and we are commanded to be happy about it. And, thank G-d, with good food and good friends, and even a little respite from the thunder of war...here we are, sitting on a patio with nothing but palm branches and some pieces of wood for a roof — and we are happy. We are sitting here, drinking a little wine, a little beer, and singing our hearts out, and we are happy. We have no idea what tomorrow will bring and we all know it took countless miracles for each of us to survive just one day today. But for the moment we can be content to be here, doing what our Creator commanded us to do, and being happy about it."

Eli went on with a few commentaries brought on the subject by Rabbi Moses ben Maimon, Maimonides; and by the medieval French scholar, Rashi. Shortly after he finished talking and another round of singing started, they heard the clatter of a motorbike work its way up their street and stop by their sukkah. Sam got up and went out to greet the rider, expecting it might be a courier with news from Colonel Eschol. He came back in with a young yeshiva student from Hespin with long *peyot* dressed in old jeans and a t-shirt from some hard rock group, with a large white knit *kippah*. Behind him was a small old man dressed in white in the Sephardic style. He had a cherubic, but yet deeply-lined face and stood barely five feet tall, and Eli instantly got to his feet as he recognized Rabbi Beniyahu from the yeshiva. Some of the young religious soldiers also stood up in honor of the elderly rabbi.

Rabbi Beniyahu was considered by some — but certainly not himself — to be the Sage of the Golan. Beniyahu was his first name. Eli had heard his last name once or twice and it was pretty much unpronounceable. Rabbi Beniyahu had been born in Morocco sometime in the 1930s and had gone to New York to seek his fortune sometime in the early 1950s. However he had stayed only long enough to add an incongruous Brooklyn accent to his English. He made his way to the Holy Land, studying with many of the great minds of the last generation before settling into a modest teaching position at the newly founded yeshiva of the Golan. He had been there since 1968, outlasting several *roshei Yeshivot* in those fifty some years.

The students both loved and revered him, hence his young escort on the motorbike. Eli offered the Rabbi his spot at the head of the table but the old man waved away his gesture and sat down a few seats away where a young soldier had been sitting before stealing off to bed awhile ago, leaving a plate of gnawed steak bones. Rabbi Beniyahu ignored the pile and motioned for someone across the table to pass him the wine bottle and a fresh cup. Natalie sprang to get a cup and spirited away the plate of bones in the process.

The rabbi poured himself a generous glass of Golan cabernet and said a quiet *bracha*, and downed half the glass. He looked up beaming, "now that is a very fine red wine," he said in his Brooklyn accent, "and made here in the Golan I see," he said peering at the label. He hoisted his glass to toast Eli and Natalie and drank a bit more. "Please go on with the singing, it sounded wonderful as we rode in. Perhaps someone knows the Sephardic version of that last song?" When no one volunteered, he launched into an intricate tune that gave the last song they had sung a whole different flavor. Rabbi Beniyahu helped begin several more *niggunim*. A few more neighbors drifted in to the sukkah, attracted by the singing in the still night. The artillery and mortars had been silent for at least the past few hours.

After awhile the rabbi stopped initiating new songs. He took a few more sips of wine and sat for a time, almost shining in obvious pleasure, and yet reflective and silent. All watched him, and after a few minutes he spoke again in his odd Moroccan/Brooklyn accent. "The weapons of a Jew are prayer and mitzvot. Tonight we are arming ourselves with mitzvot like the finest suit of armor ever made. Better than a ceramica," he said, referring to the bullet-proof flak vests worn by many Israeli soldiers by their street name. "By the mere act of sitting and eating and drinking, because we are doing so in a sukkah at the time that our Creator told us to do so, we acquire for ourselves a heavenly shield more powerful than any missile or tank."

He let those words settle in as he beamed at all present at the table and standing in the sukkah. "A mitzvah — carrying out *HaShem's* commandment or doing a good deed, such as an act of kindness towards your fellow human being — creates a heavenly smell, a wonderful odor that is both spiritual and physical. When the Creator of the whole universe commanded the Jewish people to bring sacrifices upon His holy altar, and they did so exactly as he had instructed them, the Torah says that it created a *Re-ach Tov*, a good and wonderful scent, that pleased the *Ribbono Shel-Olam*. And in those moments when the Jewish people acted on the instructions of their Creator, there was a *kesher* and a *devekus*, a tie and a drawing closer, between the Jewish people and their Creator."

He reflected another few moments, "there is just such a heavenly odor right here in this sukkah — although it may smell like wood smoke and barbequed meat to your nose. And here we have a dozen or so people singing — some of them off key like me — to your ears, and sitting in a small wooden booth and this is what appears to our eyes and ears — but to the Creator of all, there is a wonderful aroma and a powerful connection created wherever his precious Jews gather together and perform *mitzvot* and sing his praises.

"I found my way here tonight with the help of my *talmid* and his faithful motorbike because I heard that some men from this moshav helped save our yeshiva and perhaps the whole Golan this morning, and I wanted to thank them."

Eli looked embarrassed, Sam and Natalie looked amazed, and Roee and Ronny, who had been minding the barbeque most of the evening, looked awkward.

Rabbi Beniyahu nodded towards the head of the table where Eli and Sam sat. "Yes, I asked some questions when Colonel Eschol came to see me this afternoon and I asked some more questions when I stopped off at the *Shul* here. I was told that the owner of this sukkah had something to do with bringing several boatloads of ammunition from Tiberias this morning just in time to keep our little town from being overrun." He got up and came around to the head of the table in the crowded sukkah and put his hands on Eli and Sam's shoulders, pressing them to remain seated as they tried to get up, with a power that was amazing for such a diminutive old man. He beamed at the now-quiet group in the sukkah. "I had expected a slightly younger man upon hearing of rowing a boat across the Kinneret in the dark and not a grey beard like myself," he gave Eli's should a friendly squeeze. But I am not surprised to find him deep in the mitzvah of *chanachas orchim*—welcoming and taking care of guests, for it is the strength and protection of mitzvot such as these that enable our people to do amazing things in such difficult times. I understand that there are wounded soldiers being cared for in this home, both ours and our enemy, and that is an even greater mitzvah for it is said that the *Shechina*, the Divine Presence, is always found to be present in the act of caring for the sick.

"But there was an even greater mitzvah than all these that I heard said about our host and hostess." He left them to wonder a moment what he was talking about before continuing. "Burying the dead, and especially the dead of our enemies, is an act of pure *chesed*, a loving kindness that is so selfless that the deed cannot be possibly paid in this world in any fashion. I understand that the Kaplans chose to go help dig graves for our fallen enemies rather than spend the afternoon in well-deserved rest. The goodly odor of that good deed will surely help bring mercy and salvation for all of us."

The rabbi kissed Eli and smiled at Natalie and went back to his seat and started up another song and then another. The wine flowered freely again after Rabbi Beniyahu accepted another cup and the singing grew stronger and more passionate. Eli was still stunned to be singled out by the rabbi, for in his view every living soul on the moshav had put forth so much effort to help each other and to defend their beloved land that it didn't seem fair to point to his small contribution. Natalie looked happy, the kind words, the food and the song driving the constant look of worry from her face but not completely from her heart. She knew that Eli would be going away again. Even a trip to the community center was not necessarily safe.

Neither was sitting outside their earth-sheltered house. But for now, at least, she felt secure.

After midnight the party began winding down again as people drifted off to bed. The older couple had excused themselves awhile ago and left after exchanging hugs with Rabbi Beniyahu. Most of the young soldiers had wandered off to find a place to sleep, or reported elsewhere for guard duty, leaving Eli, Natalie, Sam, Ronny, Roee, two of the more religious soldiers, the Rabbi and his young *talmid*. They had broken out a large bag of sunflower seeds and all, including the rabbi, were engaged in the timeless Israeli pastime of cracking the thin shells open and munching the tiny inner seeds while schmoozing about everything from the war to the Torah, to food, friends and families. The Rabbi was recalling *Sukkot* holidays in his native Morocco and telling stories of the small seaside village where he was born and raised.

But Sam and the young religious soldiers steered the conversation back to their earlier topic of the night and asked Rabbi Beniyahu almost point blank: "Could this be 'the big one,' Israel's final war? And if it is, how can we know?" The rabbi cracked and munched another dozen sunflower seeds while considering the question. Finally he said with a long and soulful sigh, "I wish I knew." He gave a helpless gesture that showed both hope and despair. But before Sam and the young soldiers could press him further, he showed signs of continuing, and they fell silent.

"It is so difficult to know. The *Ribonno Shel Olam* only reveals His ways to us in passing—like looking at the wake of a ship in the ocean—we can see what is stirred up in our passing, but not what lies immediately ahead. However as you pointed out, He gave us the Torah and the Prophets as guideposts. And they can give us a few points of light to steer by, but not an exact map of the journey.

"We can know that the times of the *Moshiach* are drawing close. How can we know this? The Torah and the Prophets promised us that one day, after many years of exile, we could come back to this land and it would be fruitful again and blossom for us. And that is our sign. Watch the land and see. Just look out the window at the orchard planted around this house. It's hard to see in the dark but I remember two of my students talking about attending a celebration of first fruits here last summer. I must tell you they were very impressed and each of them vowed to plant their own orchards some day and I hope and believe that they will. Look at the land, everywhere the Jews settle becomes a garden with trees, flowers and orchards. The land blossoms to welcome us back. Yet for thousands of year this same land stood empty and barren, just waiting for our return. No other people could make it bloom the way we did. So if you want to see how close we are to *Moshiach*, look at the land.

"And also if we look around this table, we can see each of us gathered in the past few generations—drawn to come back to our ancestral land—a land the Jews have never completely left for there have always been as many Jews here as the land could support and the current conquerors tolerate.

"I can look around this table—I, a Jew from Morocco whose ancestors have lived there for more than two dozen generations—and I can see two Americans, our host and hostess who came here from Chicago. And their grandparents migrated there from Eastern Europe thinking they would become Americans and that being Jewish was something like their Old World accents, something that would fall away in a generation or two—am I right?" Natalie agreed, for it described her grandparents to the letter.

"And here are two young soldiers, Roee and Ronny who were both born in the Soviet Union behind an Iron Curtain that seemed so impressive during their childhood – but where is it now? Gone! And they came with their to Israel after many years of longing to be free of that dreaded regime. For them it happened so long ago that they can barely remember that other world, but it was very real for their parents. Roee, I remember meeting your father and grandfather in Petach Tikvah a few years after they came to this country. They were still amazed to be here." Roee looked surprised for he had only met the old rabbi that night and exchanged a few sentences of small talk.

"And you, Sam, your family went to America too, but your grandparents were from Poland and had come to Israel as *halutzim* long before the War of Independence, a war that is still going on today. Oh yes," he said, as the younger people around the table reacted with puzzlement. "This war we are fighting today, it is the same war as the War of Independence. It started long before 1948 and has never stopped. The War of Independence has only paused for breath in the last one hundred or more years. I myself have been here since 1955, just in time to see the Sinai campaign and the war over the Suez. Between then and now I have never seen a year without bloodshed and violence from our enemies—they have never let up. Oh, the names and faces and initials change: PLO, Hamas, Fatah, Hezbollah...the Torah knows their names...*sohnim*—haters of Israel."

Not a soul stirred at the table and he went on. "And so you ask me—are we so close that this could be the war of Gog and Magog that our prophets told us would come at the end of days...the final great struggle before mankind truly learns the meaning of peace—and the world is filled with the knowledge of G-d like the waters fill the ocean?"

"The answer to your question depends on what happens to our holy city of Jerusalem, and that, alas, we do not know...and we really cannot know until after this storm has passed over us and the sun comes out again. What will Jerusalem do? What will we Jews do with our precious Jerusalem this time?"

He gazed into space and cracked and ate more sunflower seeds. "I remember so well, remember as if it was yesterday, the excitement we all felt when Jerusalem was reunited in 1967. It was a miracle—an open miracle--that a handful of paratroopers could come in and retake half the city in just two days! These were Jordanian regulars, mind you, not some *fedayeen* with old rifles. And we were some upstart, nineteen-year-old country, young and cocky like any nineteen year old. We had next to nothing.

"I lived through the bombardment in those first days of the war. It was almost like yesterday, only without the rockets. Mortar shells by the hundreds. I was living in a tiny flat in Yemin Moshe, right opposite the Old City walls. Today it is a high-priced art studio—then it had no hot water, and cold water that came in a trickle from a tap only when G-d willed it. For years there were snipers firing from the walls of the Old City—often enough that I would take the long way to synagogue in the morning rather than cross an open street where people I knew had been wounded while just walking down the street. It was truly a miracle. Have you ever walked on Ammunition Hill and looked at the trenches and the bunkers there? They had everything! We had a few hundred soldiers to spare—and somehow they were enough.

"And when we did finally see what had happened to our precious Jerusalem behind those walls, what a shock that was. The Jewish Quarter had been behind walls and barbed wire since the Old City fell in 1948. What destruction we saw there—where our Jewish homes had been. Our synagogues all destroyed, houses left in ruins. Just left in a heap. But what hope we felt. The Old City was ours again!

"But alas! We took our holy Temple Mount back only for a moment, and then the cursed politicians hauled down our proud flag within hours, and handed our holiest site over to the most unholy scoundrels who ever set foot in our holy city! And half the city with it.

"So what do we have today? A wall. Not even a wall of the Holy Temple, just the Western Wall of the Temple Mount. And not even the whole wall, just a portion of it. While on top of the Temple Mount, the place so holy that a G-d fearing Jew would tremble with awe just to set foot there—what do we have? A golden dome set down by some one-time conqueror—one that has fallen and been defeated repeatedly. But we keep giving it back to our sworn enemies...why? I wish I knew. The Arabs couldn't understand it then—and they still don't understand it today. If you win a war—what are you doing handing back what you won? They figure we must be weak or afraid somehow and so, every ten years or so, they try again.

"What can I say? Have we Jews learned our lesson yet? How many times do we have to fight for our lives, fight for our right to live and breathe in our own land, fight and win, and then have the blind politicians hand over what our people and soldiers have won back with their blood and suffering? Are we ready to say, 'ENOUGH!' Are we ready to stand up and be the people that G-d knows we can be? Are we ready to learn and live by our Creator's holy Torah? Alas, I wish I knew. Watch Jerusalem. Pray for Jerusalem. Pray for Israel's brave soldiers and long-suffering people."

Rabbi Beniyahu was lost in thought awhile longer. "And yet, here we are, sitting in a sukkah in the middle of the most desperate fight since the War of Independence began and we are together, celebrating and doing *HaShem's* holy commandments. And because of this there is hope. No, not only hope, an assurance, a promise from the Almighty that we will survive. No matter what, as long as there are Jews ready and willing to follow the Torah and its commandments, there will be Jews."

Sam and Roee and the two younger soldiers jumped in with what seemed like dozens of questions each – mostly in Hebrew, but sometimes switching to English for Eli and Natalie's sakes, for it was clear that they struggled to keep up with the flow of the discussion. Rabbi Beniyahu filled out his points with quotes and sources from the Torah, *Mishnah*, *Midrash*, *Talmud*, *Tanach* and Prophets. He showed them clearly how many of the prophesies about the history of the Jews had been fulfilled to the letter: The exiles, the scattering among the nations, remaining perpetually few in numbers – never greater than 16 million at any time in history, and yet being an amazing light to the nations of the world – inspiring two of the world's great religions which had somehow grown to more than a billion followers each while their source never became a majority anywhere but tiny Israel.

They marveled again at the tremendous ingathering of Jews, just as prophesized in the Torah. Even in little Moshav Yiftach there were Iranians, Moroccans, French, English, South Africans, Americans and Canadians, two families from Ethiopia, one from Yemen, and families from Russia and all over the former Soviet states, from Moscow to Azerbaijan.

It was well past midnight when they heard the Moshav's ancient Dodge truck that was serving as Col. Eschol's staff car come rumbling and bumping up the shell cratered lane. Sam excused himself from the discussion and went out to greet his commander. Eli was torn between going out to greet his new guest or staying with Rabbi Beniyahu. He stayed in the sukkah, but got up to greet the colonel when he came in.

Colonel Eschol had three extremely dirty, tired-looking captains in tankers fireproof coveralls with him and an equally exhausted lieutenant who had been running up and down the Golan with him since well before sunrise. But, the thing that caught everyone's notice almost immediately was the portable radio the colonel had clipped to his belt which fed an earpiece in his right ear. They could hear the faint garbled chatter of radio traffic, and could tell that he was keeping half an ear on the messages as he greeted everyone. He paused to hug the rabbi and bent down to accept a kiss on both cheeks. He saw Eli and the soldiers all eyeing the radio and patted it with pleasure with one hand while accepting a cup of coffee from Natalie with the other and giving her a grateful half bow.

"Yes, it's real and it works! We got four of them from Tiberias via speedboat this afternoon. I have one long range one, the artillery has two short range sets, and the Merkava IV force has the other long range. Home base for this network is on Mt. Meron. If we relay via operators in Tiberias or Tsfat, we can reach Northern Defense Command up there." He held up a finger for quiet and paused to concentrate on a message. "Golan One – affirmative," he said into the microphone.

"Allow me to introduce our captains," he said when his attention came back to the people in the sukkah. "This is Captain Tsvi Goren who now has eight of his eleven Merkava IVs in running order, and hopes to have the rest operational by tomorrow morning." Captain Goren shook hands all around, except for Natalie, for it was clear she was a religious woman. "And these gentlemen are captains David Engel and Yankel Klein who just joined us with what is left of the tripwire force from the border north of here. Eli, I think you might have seen part of their daring breakout yesterday morning when you called attention to those tanks you saw on the ridge to the northwest. Their story and the timing match almost perfectly. They spent most of the first day hiding out in a streambed that cuts through a big minefield north of here. If they could use your shower, I'm sure they would be most grateful. I brought some towels with me from what's left of the *mikveh* in Ami Ad. I could use a splash too if there is any warm water."

Eli, who was up adding small sticks of dry cedar to the barbeque, said that of course they could use the shower. He led the shorter of the two tripwire force captains into the house and showed him where to find everything he could possibly need for a shower. The man was a walking zombie, but when he saw the stack of clean towels and the array of shampoos and soaps, he showed a spark of life and mumbled an effusive, if barely audible, thanks.

The colonel was deep in conversation with Rabbi Beniyahu, and Eli noticed that Yishai, the old Iranian Jew who had introduced him to the wounded Syrian major was part of the conversation, which sounded like it was half in Arabic to Eli's half-trained ears. Colonel Eschol had grown up on a kibbutz in the Galilee back in the days when Jews and Arabs mixed much more freely, he recalled.

The tall tripwire force captain washed his hands, said a blessing over a pita and the blessing for *l'eyshev b'sukkah*, and Eli made a mental note to offer him the use of his *lulav* and *etrog* if he were still around in the morning. There was something familiar about him; then Eli remembered the tank that had nearly run over him that morning as he played dead. Apparently the captain didn't recognize him, since Woody was away on errands and Eli had been mostly dazed and shell-shocked as the tankers had quickly loaded the shells from his truck and roared off back into the fight.

The tall captain pulled up a chair in the sukkah and was soon splitting one of the last of the beers with the other tanker captain. They were deep in shop talk when Eli came back from the house carrying a plate of steaks. He put half a dozen on the barbeque as it was coming to life again, and seasoned them with a dash of garlic salt and a light sprinkling of pepper. He tended the fire and his steaks awhile and then went into the house to scrounge a blackened cast iron skillet and some olive oil to cook some eggs to go with the steaks, for it was now closer to morning than to midnight. The moshav's egg production was down severely with the shelling and the loss of power to the hen houses. But then, as there was no way to get eggs to market, there were plenty of eggs to go around for the moshav. Natalie busied herself with clearing and resetting the table as best she could around all the people and freshened up the salads and brought out cool drinks of homemade lemonade made from concentrated juice canned from last summer's lemon crop. She also had made a fresh pot of coffee and set out a few pitchers of iced tea.

By the time the eggs and first of the steaks were ready, all three of the tankers had showered and were back in the thick of the military plans that were being spun around the colonel and his radio. Eli brought the whole pan of scrambled eggs to the table with a big serving spoon so that everyone could help themselves, and he set a plate of steaks down within reach of the colonel and his captains. Everyone dug in with as much gusto as their tired bodies could manage, which was enough to make the eggs and every scrap of the steaks disappear within minutes.

"Reb Kaplan, I'm seriously considering making this sukkah my headquarters for the rest of the war," Colonel Eschol said and he devoured the last of his steak and mopped up the juice with a roll. There were mutters of agreement from the assembled officers.

It was close to two in the morning by the time their guests had finished their meal and had sung the blessings and a few more songs led by the indefatigable Rabbi Beniyahu. The rabbi's motorcycle driver had expired in a chair in the living room along with a few assorted soldiers and a heap of Tali's kids in a blanket tent they had erected by one of the bookshelves. Colonel Eschol unfolded a pair of laminated maps of their area of the Golan and spread them out on the unused end of the table and was soon plotting the next morning's strategy with Sam and the three tanker captains and, Eli was surprised to see, with Rabbi Beniyahu and Yishai, the old Iranian Jew. The younger lieutenant had crawled off to sleep in the Colonel's jeep long ago. But then, the rabbi had been in the Golan for nearly 50 years he reasoned, however it looked odd to see the small, white clad rabbi and Yishai with his three days' worth of white stubble and big *kippah* bending over the map with the soldiers, several of which towered over them by more than a foot.

Eli helped Natalie clear the table and put away what was left of the food as best they could with no refrigeration. However he was curious to follow snatches of the planning. From what he could gather between trips, the first mission of about half of the rebuilt Merkavas would be to break out to the north and join up with a beleaguered force somewhere near the town of Katzrin, which he understood had been overrun in heavy fighting. They would trap and eliminate some forces that had broken through to the northern end of the Kinneret thus relieving at least one half of the siege of Tiberias. It would also open up a new supply line.

"By the way, Eli," Sam addressed him at one point, "you'll be happy to know that we were able to open the road from Bene Yehuda to the Kinneret late this afternoon. So we can haul our ammunition by truck instead of knapsack. Oh and our Druzi friend says hello. He's doing a great business and he dropped his price to two thousand shekels per trip after I told him we were practically family and the colonel signed a note promising that the State of Israel would buy his boat if he got bombed."

"That's great!" Eli laughed. "I'm glad to hear that capitalism is alive and well and that I'm off the hook for buying the boat. How is the Kinneret squadron of the Israeli Navy doing?"

The colonel beamed at Eli and said, "Thanks to you and your kayak — and a couple dozen speedboats — I can now say we rule the Kinneret. Our friends in Tiberias have done some marvelous things with mounting rapid-fire anti-aircraft cannon and machine guns on boats and making raids against the Jordanian forces at the southern end of the lake. Before the sun was fully up this morning they had shot up everything that could possibly float and harassed the armored column trying to push its way into Tiberias so much that it withdrew to Deganya. We're shelling them from the heights at Poriya and have them pushed back to the southern end of the lake. If we can hold out here and open up the north end of the lake, I'd say Tiberias will be safe by this time tomorrow, G-d willing," he said with a nod to Rabbi Beniyahu who was now half dozing in a chair by one of the lights with a volume of one of Eli's books on his chest and Yishai, the old Iranian Jew, sound asleep sitting up next to him.

"I'm glad you're still awake because Sam and I have another job for you and Woody," the colonel said, motioning Eli to pull up a chair next to them.

"OK," Eli said, "but whatever it is, I have to talk about it with Natalie first this time."

"Of course!" the colonel readily agreed and he waited while Eli went to find Natalie in the house. Eli found her mopping up their heavily-used bathroom and brought her back to the sukkah. Rabbi Beniyahu and Yishai were dozing serenely in folding camp chairs and the Colonel and Sam had spread out one of the maps on the table and were studying it. The three tanker captains had left awhile before.

"Ah, Mrs. Kaplan! Thank you again for another wonderful meal," began Colonel Eschol.

"It's Natalie, please," she protested, "and you are most welcome — you and every soldier of Israel."

"Natalie," the colonel said, "thank you and your husband for everything you have been doing...opening your home, feeding everyone who comes by, the showers, the use of your truck. And I must say, your husband has proven a very brave, creative and ingenious soldier. We would be out of bullets without him and his ideas right now."

Eli looked embarrassed but Natalie looked both proud and surprised. The extent of the benefits of Eli's nighttime trip across the Kinneret had not fully sunk in on her with all the busy demands on her time and energies running the household and managing their many guests in addition to her community duties on the moshav. Eli had been very matter of fact in telling her of his travels.

"Really, we had our backs to the wall and were starting to plan last-ditch tactics when your husband offered us a way across the Kinneret we never thought of. I have to admit I was not sure I would ever see him again until the moment the first hiker showed up with a knapsack full of mortar shells and the news." Eli had not heard that admission before.

The colonel revealed a little more of the full extent of the Golan's peril before Eli's pack train of ammunition began to arrive — some of which Sam might have been hearing for the first time, for he looked impressed at several points in the narrative.

"And so, Mrs. Kaplan, I mean, Natalie," the colonel concluded after coming back to the point in his story when Eli and Sam had re-supplied the two stranded tanks at a critical turn in the battle — even more critical than either Sam or Eli had gathered before now. "Your husband is not only a wise and resourceful soldier and very good at thinking outside of the box as they say — but he is also very lucky — although Rabbi Beniyahu here," he gestured towards the dozing rabbi, "thinks it's more than plain luck. Either way we need some more of that resourcefulness and luck right now."

Except for a wonderful marriage, two beautiful and talented daughters and happily married daughters, six grandchildren, and a modest income, Eli had never thought of himself as particularly lucky. He and Natalie looked at each other wonderingly, exchanged a shy smile, and turned their attention back to the colonel and his mysterious mission.

"Rabbi Beniyahu and Mr. Yishai Haran have volunteered already," the colonel said. Eli noticed that Rabbi Beniyahu was awake now and watching him quietly. "And Sam is going too — since it is a bit of a reconnaissance mission and that is his expertise. And actually all three of them have suggested that their chances would be better if Eli came along as the driver." Sam looked a little sheepish.

Eli and Natalie looked truly puzzled, wondering what Eli was supposed to reconnoiter with two elderly Jews and Sam.

The colonel spread out the edge of the map further, weighting it down with an empty wine bottle. "Here we are," he said, pointing to a dot near the main highway that ran the length of the Golan, "and here is the Syrian border and over here is Kibbutz HaGolan which was overrun in the first hours of fighting. The main force came down along this valley here — and also crossed the border here, here and here," he said, tracing various thrusts and breakthroughs along the border.

"Our new problem is over here," he said, circling a group of markings on the Syrian side of the map. "There is a huge complex of hardened bunkers just across the border from where our tripwire force was positioned — and that's where at least two Syrian divisions were bunkered when the EMP went off.

"Now at this point I have to share a little state secret with you," he said gravely, meaning Eli and Natalie, "but I know I can trust you to be totally discreet about it even after this war is over. The Americans have been sharing their satellite surveillance with us and they turned up something that could threaten everything we have managed to do up until this point." He stared grimly at the map and even Rabbi Beniyahu looked grave.

"The satellite imagery they shared with us showed that we managed to hit at least four of these huge bunkers at the start of the war — and to give you an idea of scale here, just one of them would fit the better part of an armored brigade. None of the planes came back — they were caught in the electromagnetic event and probably crashed wherever they were flying. They are not our concern now, may the Holy One have mercy on them, but one of the bunkers they bombed This afternoon's satellite pictures showed some extensive digging going on at one end and what looked like at least one helicopter sitting next to the excavations. We think they might be salvaging the attack helicopters that we have been missing so far in this action. The Americans think that there could be up to one hundred helicopters underground in a bunker that size." Eli felt a shiver up his spine at the thought of even half a hundred helicopters swarming the Golan.

"Of course we all know what they could do it if even a few of them were able to get in the air. It would change the whole situation up here. We hardly have any anti-aircraft defenses working bigger than those rapid fire cannons we used for the Kinneret navy, and, of course, none of them is up here yet. We are bringing in a few with the road we opened up, but it's not enough to defend more than a few of our groups."

Eli peered at the map trying to imagine what he and an eighty-something rabbi and his seventy-something friend could do even if Sam were a one-man commando team. Natalie looked worried but solemn, waiting to hear what all this had to do with her husband.

The colonel cleared his throat and took a drink of cold tea and looked at Natalie. "Now you are probably wondering how your husband fits in all this and why I'm about to ask him to go above and beyond the call of duty once more — not that I asked the first time — he volunteered.

"What Rabbi Beniyahu and Reb Yishai have in common is that they are both native Arabic speakers and Reb Yishai used to visit across the border back in the nineteen fifties and sixties when such things were still possible. We know from our scouts and the satellite that there are a lot of civilians coming across the border here near what's left of Kibbutz HaGolan. They are clearly looting everything that is not nailed down and perhaps a few things that are — and carrying them back across the border somewhere near our bunkers…not where the army came through but somewhere more, shall we say, discreet.

"Sam and our Arabic speaking rabbi have volunteered to disguise themselves as looters going back home with a truckload of spoils and find out where it is they are getting through the minefield. They'll also see how much of a force there is guarding the bunker complex — and show the way for a group of tanks and jeeps — also volunteers — to slip through and hit those helicopters." He thumped the map.

"Now our plan is for you to approach the border near Kibbutz HaGolan through a minefield on our side — Captain Klein, who you met earlier, will escort you that far. They'll help retake the kibbutz and be waiting for your return along with a company of infantry to hold the kibbutz in case any of our Syrian friends object."

"OK," Eli said, "I know Sam here is a one-man commando team and Rabbi Beniyahu and Yishai can pass for Arabs — but what about me? I can't even speak Hebrew worth a damn and know about three words of Arabic…If I open my mouth with my big fat American accent, we're all dead. And why Woody? How many wood burning pickup trucks just happen to be driving around in Syria, looting or no looting?"

"We've thought about all that," the colonel said, "The plan is basically for you to keep your mouth shut and drive — with a little mud and charcoal and a *keffiyah* — you can at least look the part — and with the back piled up with furniture and empty boxes, it won't be very obvious. Sam tells me that you rigged the truck according to the plans to use either fuel — gasoline or wood. I would expect that this run could be made using gasoline — we have plenty at the Moshav and it gives you more power and range than wood, right?"

Eli admitted that he was right about the truck being able to run on either fuel — although he had not run it on gasoline for months. "So I sit there with a towel over my head with the two rabbis in the front while Sam navigates our way through a big Syrian minefield and across the border into this big fat military camp with brigade-sized bunkers — and I just drive," Eli said dubiously.

"Well now that you put it that way, it does sound a little far-fetched," the Colonel said looking at Sam for help explaining the elaborate but fantastical-sounding plan.

Sam looked at Eli and Natalie who were looking rather unconvinced by the plan which was obviously mostly his concoction of ideas. However Sam was, at heart, a natural-born salesman as well as an entrepreneur and reconnaissance officer. He was not going to abandon his plan without hearing a better one.

"It's like this, Mrs. Kaplan, I mean Natalie. We're turning back as soon as we find the route through the Syrian side of the minefield…we'll be spending less than an hour in Syria if all goes well…" Somehow spending even a minute in Syria didn't look appealing to either Eli or Natalie…not to mention driving through minefields on either side of the border, so he switched tacks.

"I guess I have to call it something more than luck," Sam said, looking almost pleadingly at Natalie. "But ever since I met your husband, this has been a very different war for me. I've got to tell you that I was thinking about how to build tank traps with picks and shovels and use grenades and Molotov cocktails, and near-suicide missions to take out their tanks and artillery when I first came to your sukkah to confer with the Colonel. I didn't think we had a chance, to tell you the truth, and I was prepared to take down as many Syrians as I could shoot before they ran right over the top of us.

"But here in the moshav I found a very different spirit. I stepped out of what felt like a losing battle and the worst artillery and missile barrage of my life into a beautiful, secure-feeling little house—with hot food and coffee and—more importantly—hope! Not some sort of 'everything will turn out fine' sort of hope but more of a confidence that the *Ribbono Shel Olam* was still running things point of view. And that as long as one could do the *mitzvot* and help a friend and neighbor that somehow there would always be an Israel.

"And when I left your house, driving off in this amazing pickup truck of yours, running on wood smoke…well I did a lot of thinking on the way to the brigade and back. Maybe I had my priorities wrong and maybe there were more ways to save Israel than shooting an M-16." He looked embarrassed at the disclosures but went on.

"We both had a pretty long day and when I came back late at night after running all over the Golan in this magical old truck that ran when even the IDF's best were still in the shop being re-wired, there were Eli and Natalie, feeding half a *pluga* of soldiers and neighbors and sitting in the sukkah with five kinds of salads, three kinds of chicken and a dozen bottles of fine Golani wine! I thought that there is definitely someone watching over these people!

"Hot showers, hot, home-cooked food! And not a dozen hours before I was sure that a package of crackers and some warm tuna was going to be my last meal on earth.

"I've got to tell you—even after seeing the hospital they have rigged up in the doctors' basement a few streets away—which is truly amazing, stepping into your house is like stepping out of the war and back into what Israel could be...should be really. And I've given a lot of thought to how I want my home to be after this war is over...." The colonel was looking restless for he clearly had to be somewhere else soon but he also listened to Sam with a certain feeling of agreement — as if he were articulating many of his own thoughts.

"And since then I've had the pleasure of paddling across the Kinneret in the dark of night with your husband. And just when I thought we were hopelessly lost and going to have to float around until daylight and certain death, he showed me how to read waves and the water. He showed me the direction again — and helped me realize that G-d always gives us choices and options no matter how bad they may seem, and that we have to be aware of the information He is giving us at every moment in time.

"And just a few hours later, we were crossing that same lake on a big tourist boat, carrying back enough shells to save the Golan for another day. And now that the road is open and the Kinneret is ours again, all we need to do is keep those helicopters buried in their hole and keep those shells coming and by G-d, we'll win this war yet.

"So that's why I want your husband as our driver," Sam said, summing up. "Because somehow I know that whatever happens, Eli is going to make the right kind of choices because that's the kind of man he is."

"I don't know," Natalie said, feeling the truth of Sam's words, the depth of his pleading and a quiet pride in her husband of more than thirty years. "All you say is true but none of it says that it has to be Eli. Anyone can drive his truck, we are happy to volunteer Woody. I mean, for awhile there is sounded like you wanted to take Eli along as some kind of lucky rabbit's foot or something — not to belittle anything you said, because I understand about having trust in *HaShem*. Eli what do you think?"

Eli thought for awhile. He could feel the colonel's and Sam's confidence in him and felt Rabbi Beniyahu watching him too. While he was eager to do anything to help out, he knew how hard it was for Natalie every time he left. And frankly, the idea of driving into Syria scared him, because it was almost completely unknown to him even though he lived just a few kilometers away. Syria had been closed to Israelis for decades. And Syria had been increasingly closed off to most other Western travelers for a number of years. He turned to Rabbi Beniyahu. "OK, this is not a *shylah* and I won't take your answer as binding — my question is not should I go, but more, why should I go?"

Rabbi Beniyahu looked as if he had been expecting and perhaps somewhat dreading the question. His friend, Yishai was awake now too, and Rabbi Beniyahu looked at Yishai for a moment before answering. "I must admit that I asked if you would be available to come with us when Colonel Eschol told me about your adventures this morning and now that I have met you properly, I feel even more so. I certainly don't claim to have *ruach ha kodesh* or any prophetic abilities — but I do claim to be a student of *HaShem's* holy Torah. I know that when the Creator of the world makes a promise for the good, that it is always kept. I am also a student of *midos* — the manners and measures of a Jew, and by these measures you are a man worthy of an extra portion of Divine protection. I would certainly like to have such a man with me on such a mission."

Eli felt both flattered and burdened by the answer, for it clearly made refusal difficult. He turned to Natalie for support, but she was clearly moved as well. "If you want to go, I won't stand in your way," she said simply.

"OK," Eli said, "I'm in. When do we leave?"

"We need to be rolling by five — it's two-thirty now — that gives us perhaps two hours to sleep," Sam said, consulting Eli's watch.

Eli remembered how helpless and lost he had felt in the middle of the tank battle near Eli Ad. "One more thing though," he added, "can I take the sniper rifle, just in case?"

Sam looked surprised but raised no objection, saying they could keep it hidden behind the seat. The Colonel looked relieved and rounded up his lieutenant and two escorts and set off into the night to put his part of the plans into action.

Day Three

Ramat Hovav Airfield – the Negev 01:11

Major Yossi Green was like a braided rope stretched just short of its breaking point. There was no more room for giving or waiting another moment to get his wiry tense body into an airplane and off into the night sky to carry the war back to the enemy that was ravaging his homeland. But the three flights of stripped down US fighter planes that promised to turn the IAF back into an air force again, instead of a bunch of frantic electricians, were four hours late getting off the ground in Spain and Portugal. They were another half an hour longer than expected in flight with their zig-zagging course up the Mediterranean Sea. Their errant course was designed to fool whoever might be looking at a radar screen and conceal their final destination. In those four and a half hours he could have made perhaps five round trips to his targets in the Sinai, wiping out bomb loads worth of tanks, trucks, grounded aircraft, anti-aircraft batteries, radar stations and supply depots.

But at last he heard, and felt in his gut, the deep thunder of high performance jet engines flying low. A ragged cheer went up that was soon drowned out by the roar of incoming F-15s. Yossi's heart was pounding by the time he saw the shadowy, twin-tailed shape of the first F-15 as it came in low, flared and settled on their freshly patched runway. Ground crew signalmen and women guided it quickly to a taxiway as the next bird thundered in.

As wing commander, this first bird was his, and Yossi was bouncing up and down on the toes of his flight boots as he watched the hot jet being guided in, its powerful twin engines rippling the nighttime desert air with their heated blast even as it idled. Yossi knew that there were more than two hours to go re-arming and reprogramming the bird before he could be airborne. But now that the jet was tangible at last, and not an imaginary one, that time would pass in a flash. He was up the crew ladder and congratulating and quizzing the American pilot the moment they rolled it to a stop inside his half-buried hanger. His fellow pilot was equally high and wired from flying at Mach .7 less than two hundred feet above the deck, and making a night landing at a lantern-lit, strange desert airfield. He was happy to tell him everything he could about what controls, systems and capabilities were operating in the stripped-down, un-identifiable aircraft he had just smuggled into a war zone. He tried to tell it all at once. He also fervently wished that he could be flying the upcoming missions instead of Yossi. He wanted to go not only for the thrill of action, but for the chance to strike against an enemy who had broken every treaty and convention ever made, and who was in the act of overrunning Israel's borders at nearly every point. He had been briefed on the satellite reconnaissance reality of the situation.

Yossi was soon happy to hand his fellow pilot off to a pretty, young IAF cadet, who led him away to the debriefing rooms and underground safe area that would be his home until the American volunteers could be safely smuggled out of the war zone.

The plane and its swarm of ground crew were the sole focus of his attention for the next hour and fifty two minutes as they reloaded and rebooted all the software, checked all the hardware, and armed it with an array of air-to-ground missiles and conventional bombs. He carried only a light pair of air-to-air missiles at his wing tips in case of interceptors. At the same time, a team of workers sprayed on IAF insignias and touched up the camouflage in desert tones with fast-drying paint, making everyone in the hanger more than a little light headed.

Only two of his wing of eight planes would be equipped for air-to-air fighting on this first flight. They were counting on getting in and out quickly, and inflicting the maximum damage to the nearest depots and choke points of the main supply routes from Egypt. So far their ground radar – sadly decimated by the electronic assault as well as the heavy missile and artillery bombardments – had shown nothing flying over the Sinai. Those two would fly cover high above while Yossi and five others would thunder in low and fast to hit their first mission's targets – mostly radars and command and control sites to blind the enemy and pave the way for future hits.

They gave him slightly over half a load of fuel to compensate for an aggressive bomb load, and because it would be a very short trip to his first two targeted missions. He could refuel between the second and third strikes with a full load and plan to be in the air most of the morning once daylight hit. Between three and six am the plane was to be his. Then he would be handing it over to the next pilot before he lost any of his fighting edge. Yossi thought he could make four or five trips into the near Sinai by then. There might even be time for perhaps one or two passes over enemy forces invading Israel just a few dozen kilometers away from their desert airbase once it was light enough to tell friend from foe. There were three other top pilots waiting their turn for the warm cockpit behind him. He would get his next chance to fly again that afternoon, assuming the plane was still in one piece.

Although it felt normal to be in the cockpit of an F-15 again, it was not his bird. His faithful plane was in pieces at the back of the hanger as electricians and mechanics tried to replace and test each electrical component in its complicated innards. This was a slightly newer model with a few changes to the side stick controls that he would have to relearn and adjust to as he flew. It had and a totally different radar and fire control system than the souped-up Israeli version he had come to know over the years. It almost was like being back in flight school, only this time lessons needed to be learned while on the fly – literally.

And, in the last few days, he had come to appreciate in a new and keener way, simple things like a watch that worked or radios that connected him to his wing mates. In his world up until yesterday he could also take for granted a radar system that showed him what he needed to see, and the reassuring roar of a jet engine that followed each nuance of his flight stick. That reality came to him clearly as he rolled out of the bunkered hanger and out onto the parking apron and noticed once more the gasoline lanterns that marked the entrance to the taxiway. They looked primitive from the cockpit, though he had gotten used to seeing them from the ground as he had paced, waiting for the US flights.

As soon as the first four birds were ready, he eased his throttles and began his taxi to the runway. Wheeling around smartly at its near end, he barely paused before making a final glance at his instruments and stamping on the brakes as he revved the engines. Releasing the brakes as the pitch reached the right degree of thunder, he rocketed down the freshly patched runway and roared skyward. Airborne at last!

His wing was all airborne within minutes, and their two watch dogs climbed up and away to cover their flight. As soon as their escort reached three thousand meters in altitude, Yossi barked a command to his wing, pulled back on his throttles and felt the G-forces piling up as he accelerated towards the Egyptian border. He timed their eight sonic booms to begin as close to the border as he could – partly to inspire fear and awe, but mostly because it felt good to rattle them. He hit Mach 1.5 before it was time to throttle down and settle into his attack run for their first targets – a radar and communications complex surrounded by anti-aircraft batteries. His first longer-range missiles flashed away towards the still-silent batteries. Seconds later, he was hammering the command bunkers with special bunker-breaking bombs, and watching his spread of air-to-ground missiles make a fan of destruction among the radar and radio towers. As soon as his gun cameras had recorded the scene, he flipped over in a tight loop and headed home for the next load. Only a single SAM had launched before the blistering attack of their six F-15s had hammered most of the complex into rubble.

Near Kibbutz HaGolan 0510

Needless to say, Eli and Natalie did not get much sleep between three and five a.m., but Eli finally dozed off for at least an hour before their ancient wind-up travel alarm woke them. He found that Sam was back with Woody, and that the back of his truck was piled high with junk furniture. It looked more like the work of refugees than looters to Eli, but he decided not to comment on it. Eli noticed that they had some strange license plates which must be Syrian on his truck. He wondered how they found time to acquire such things.

Natalie looked on the verge of calling the whole mission off and he knew she wanted to. As a Jewish wife and mother, she out-ranked the colonel by a moral mile, and both she and he knew it. That is why he had carefully asked her permission to "borrow" Eli. And, having given her consent, she felt at least partly bound by it. However as a wife, she knew she had ultimate veto power over such a plan. That was one of the beauties of Israel, Eli thought to himself. No general, no matter how many stars, would dare to argue certain issues with his mother or mother-in-law – or any Jewish mother for that matter. There were areas where he was clearly out-ranked by greater wisdom and higher authority.

Rabbi Beniyahu, who had slept overnight at Yishai's house, showed up just in time with his friend in tow. Both were dressed as rural Arabs, with nondescript belted robes and *keffiyah*-style head coverings. Sam was dressed as a secular Arab militia-type, which is to say, tight jeans and a camouflage-style t-shirt and a menacing old black Kalashnikov assault rifle. Sometime in the past couple hours he had arranged to get or give himself a really bad haircut in a crude style favored by Arab street toughs. Yishai and Rabbi Beniyahu checked over his outfit, right down to the battered sneakers, and approved.

Eli felt silly stashing his long sniper rifle behind the bench seat, kind of like the kid who wouldn't leave home to go on vacation without his favorite toy. He felt a little guilty for depriving the Moshav of half its long-range sighted rifles. But somehow he felt safer knowing it was there if, G-d forbid, it came to a fire fight. He recalled how lost and helpless he felt the previous morning, stranded in the middle of a tank battle, and how he had sworn that he never wanted to feel that defenseless again. Sam looked at it approvingly, and that gave him some encouragement. And, he reassured himself, there had been no shelling since some time around midnight that he was aware of, so perhaps the moshav defense group could spare it for a few hours. But, of course, he knew that the shelling could start up again any time, and that another attack could be imminent.

Since they would be operating on gasoline power this morning, he threw the lever that switched from wood gas to gasoline, shutting down one carburetor and opening the second on his customized engine. The truck coughed and ground its starter a bit before catching hold and idling roughly for a little while, and then began running more smoothly with the occasional hiccup. He figured that the last bits of the wood gas had to work through the fuel system and the engine needed to get used to gasoline again. His gas gauge read less than a quarter of a tank, so they would have to stop off by the Moshav agricultural equipment barn for fuel before meeting their tank escort.

They tried a variety of outfits and headgear on Eli from a duffle bag that Sam had brought. They decided that he looked most authentic, and slightly menacing, in a faded Syrian military-style fatigue jump suit that was missing the insignias and markings. Natalie chose a big black beret for him. Sam darkened Eli's face and hands with some sort of brown stain. Sam, Natalie and the two older men admired their handiwork. They decided he could pass for a retired officer if he kept his mouth shut and looked ferocious. Eli practiced a scowl, and evoked laughs from Natalie and Sam. Looking in the side mirror of the truck, he tried again. They were even more amused. "Just stay in the cab and look bored and impatient, and you'll pass," Sam said. "We can always say you had your tongue cut out by the secret police – that's not so uncommon, especially among officers who voted for the wrong party." Eli was not very reassured.

Eli kissed Natalie one more time and climbed into the cab. He accepted an extra thermos of coffee to go with the large traveling mugs she had poured for him and Sam. With their costumes arranged, extra weapons hidden, thermos of coffee and sacks of lunch stashed, it was time to go. Sam climbed up to a secure perch not far behind the driver's side of the cab. Since the back window had been blown out, he could now reach Eli and yell in his ear if needed. Rabbi Beniyahu had climbed in and was sitting in the middle, his feet scarcely reaching the floor by the gear shift. Yishai took up only a little more space next to him. Eli felt like a giant next to them. He glanced in the rearview mirror and tried another scowl. A swarthy, bushy-bearded, slightly over-the-hill desert warrior scowled back at him. Sam caught his look and snickered before putting on a truly intimidating imitation of an itchy-fingered militia guard. Every troupe must have at least one amateur, Eli decided, he would do best to keep his mouth shut and not try to go for an Oscar for best supporting scoundrel.

He eased the truck into gear and pulled out of the drive, all four waved to Natalie, and he imagined it must be quite a sight, for she looked torn between tears and mirth. Sipping coffee carefully around the bumps and pot holes, they made their way to the moshav machine shops where there were gas pumps. However, a sleepy-looking soldier waved him away from the regular pump and over to a hand pump and hose they had rigged up by the underground tanks. Eli unlocked the gas cap, trying to remember how many months ago he had last put gas in Woody. It must have been last spring when he drove down to Jerusalem to help Rivka and her husband move some furniture. It seemed like an age ago, and it set him to wondering how his daughter and grandchildren were faring in the war-torn city. The soldier worked a small hand pump, and the gas flowed slowly up the rubber hose and into his tank. It must take a really long time to fill a big truck or tank, he thought. His two seat companions dozed as if they had no cares or worries about driving into Syria in a bullet riddled pickup truck. Sam had made himself comfortable in his nest amid the furniture, his arm wrapped around tall piece of what looked like part of a wooden bed frame, and his Kalashnikov held loosely in its sling.

Eli thanked the soldier for the gas, and headed out for the main gate of the moshav where two tanks and a pair of jeeps with jerry-mounted machine guns were idling. Sam hopped down and scrambled up to confer with the commander of the first tank. Eli waited in the cab, practicing not talking. He sipped coffee though his nerves were decidedly on edge. The dark face and strange beret that scowled back at him in the mirror was someone else, not Eli Kaplan, semi-retired communications consultant and grandfather of six. He distracted himself by trying to figure out the differences between the two tanks. One was supposed to be a Merkava III, and the other an older Merkava II. Sam had rattled on a bit about their escort last night – how these were two of the tanks Eli had seen escaping over the hill far to the north on the first morning of the war. He mused how it was odd that there were more older tanks running than the newer ones, but that just went to show what an upside down and backwards war this was. Grandfathers and eighty-some-year-old rabbis were pressed into service as scouts, and the moshav teenagers and old men and women dug graves for strangers.

Sam hopped off the tank and jogged back to Eli's window. "That's Yankel Klein," he said, as if it was some famous name Eli was supposed to know. Eli thought he recognized the shorter of the two captains who had visited his shower and his sukkah last night. Sam climbed back into his nest as the first big tank in front of them, with the white characters *Alef* 1 emblazoned on the back, pulled out amazingly quickly for something that large. "Follow him!" Sam yelled from his perch, and so Eli put Woody in gear and raced to catch up with the speeding tank. Until he reached third gear, it was a bit of a race, but the dark mechanical monster topped out at about fifty kilometers an hour as it tore down the road to the highway. The two jeeps swung in behind them, and the second tank, *Gimmel* 1, Eli noticed, brought up the rear of their strange procession. They reached the main highway and turned north.

Rabbi Beniyahu and Yishai were definitely asleep despite the dusty wind pouring through the open hole where the windshield had been, or the bumps and swerves as they sped up the shell-cratered highway in pursuit of the tank. Sam was scanning the passing, pre-dawn shadows from his perch. The sun should have risen by now, Eli thought, seeing that it was slightly after 5:30. However the smoke and haze made it hard to tell day from night, and he thought with a tingle in his spine of the prophesies of Zechariah. A little while later, though, he could tell that the sun had risen, for the eastern sky was an angry red with streaks of light, and the sky overhead had definitely lightened. He had an easier time seeing the scenery now as it emerged from vague shapes into details that only daylight could show.

Somewhere a few kilometers north of the last town in Jewish hands the tank turned off the highway and headed up an ordinary looking dirt road that looked like any of a hundred jeep trails and farmers' tracks in the Golan. Eli had been too busy following the speeding tank and dodging pot holes to notice any particular land mark, and he vowed to pay more attention to where they were going. However, it was hard to do much more than stay on the tail of the fast moving tank and keep from smashing into any of the large rocks that it rumbled over with its higher clearance, or bottom out in any of the holes in the track that it easily spanned. Glancing in the mirror, he saw that the jeeps were bouncing and careening around too, and perhaps falling a bit behind. Eli hoped the big tank would slow down a hair, but it forged on, slowing only as they began to climb up a long draw, and then angle up the side of a sweeping swell in the landscape.

Pretty soon they flashed through a fence line, ran over a broken gate, and sped right past some yellow and red signs that Eli knew must warn of a minefield. He tightened up his watch on the track ahead, and made sure to follow inside the wide tracks churned up by the tank. He shifted down into the lower gear range and began to fall behind the still-charging lead tank. The jeeps were farther behind still, with the rear-guard tank crowding them along. Rabbi Beniyahu woke up and looked serenely about. He conferred with Yishai a few moments and they both gazed all around them in wonder, as if tourists on a jeep tour taking in the sights. But he was wrong, they were taking their bearings, for Rabbi Beniyahu pointed to a cluster of mounds and some ancient olive trees near the crest of the long hill they were climbing. "That's Beit Ramot HaBashan, where there was a yeshiva after the fall of the Second Temple. We'll stop there for *shacharit*." Eli had been so busy worrying about being pressed into an expedition to a Syrian minefield that he had forgotten all about morning prayers, and had completely forgotten his *lulav* and *etrog* required for prayers on *Sukkot*. And what about their IDF escort – were they going to stop to let three old men pray? They had a war to fight!

But, to his surprise, the tank pulled to a stop just beyond the trees, and two men jumped out of the back, holding *tallit* bags and their long palm frond bundles. Eli glanced at Sam, who seemed aware of the stop too and looked unperturbed. Eli parked the truck in the shelter of some trees and got stiffly out of the cab. At least he had a small travel *tallit* and his pocket *siddur* in the knapsack he carried everywhere since the war started. That plus lunch, water, some clean socks, a thermos of coffee, and the last 300 rounds of high-powered rifle ammunition.

The two jeeps and the other tank pulled up and took positions around the grove of trees and mounds, making a sort of perimeter. Within two minutes, there were eleven men, counting Eli, Sam, Yishai and Rabbi Beniyahu, all pulling on prayer shawls and beginning morning prayers. They gathered in the shelter of a large spreading tree by some large building stones that had once held up a long-gone structure of many ages past. They had perhaps five sets of *lulav* and *etrogim* set aside for when they would be needed for *Hallel*, so everyone would obviously have to share, and Eli didn't feel so chagrinned about forgetting his. Besides, he knew his set would be getting regular use as soldiers stopped at his sukkah for meals and visits.

A young soldier led the prayers in the Ashkenazic style, which struck Eli as odd because most of their impromptu *minyan* looked Sephardic. He raced along, and Eli, though used to the "businessman's special" speed of weekday morning services in many *shul*s around the world, found it hard to keep up, and *davened* at his own pace. Eli kept being distracted by the peaceful beauty of their remote spot, and his thoughts wandered ahead and behind, wondering what this day would bring on the other side of the hill, which was surely overlooking the Syrian border.

As their young leader raced through the *Shemoneh Esrei* and started to blast through a tuneless *Hallel*, Rabbi Beniyahu subtly put the brakes on by starting a well-known melody for the first and second parts of the *Hallel* psalms. Their voices all joined in as they allowed themselves a musical interlude in the rapid-fire *davening*. He allowed the young leader to race on a bit more, before introducing some more melodies for some of the last few psalms. These were some of the more widely known and popular tunes for the words, for there were many possible variations to choose. This not only returned their prayers to their inherent beauty, but it also gave those with *lulavs* and *etrogs* time to pass their sets with those who did not have them. Eli accepted the four species from Rabbi Beniyahu with a smile, and said the blessing over taking them up before finishing *Hallel* with them. Since they did not have a Torah scroll, they skipped the Torah reading for the day – which described the animal sacrifices brought on that third day of the holiday. They raced on through the *Mussaf* prayer, which mentioned the day's sacrifices as well, so Eli felt they had done their best. The impromptu service was over in well under an hour, which was record time for any synagogue holiday service Eli had ever attended.

Everyone packed up in an instant and Eli barely had time to fold his *tallit* and sling his knapsack back into the truck before the lead tank took off with a roar again. He jumped into the cab and waited only until Yishai had closed the door and Sam had swung up to his perch before he took off in pursuit. He caught up with the big tank when it stopped just short of the crest of the long hill. He saw that the commander had climbed out and was walking ahead with his binoculars to peer over the top of the rise and see what was afoot on the other side.

"Tell me more about Beit Ramot HaBashan," Eli asked Rabbi Beniyahu and Yishai as they waited for the tank commander to finish his reconnoitering. They told him that the town was much older than the time of the Second Temple, possibly going back to the first settlements in Israel in the days of the *Shoftim*, the Judges. However, it had not been mentioned in the *Tanach* at all, and the *Talmud* only once. There was a reference to a small yeshiva during days of turmoil in the century that followed the fall of the Second Temple in the year 70 of the common era. Yishai added that Phoenician pottery and beads, and early Greek era coins had been found by amateur archeologists there. These finds inspired several years of illegal, clandestine digs that sold whatever artifacts they found on the black market, so the true history of the site may never be fully known, he sighed. At that point in their conversation, Sam, who had been half following the discussion through the broken back window, hopped down and went off to confer with the tanker captain, who they could see was now coming back to his tank. The three older men waited quietly for his return.

After just long enough for Eli to start feeling drowsy again, Sam came back and asked them to come follow him on foot to the crest of the hill. Eli shook himself awake and climbed out and walked along the fresh tank tracks with Rabbi Beniyahu and Yishai. As they approached the crest of the hill, they followed Sam's example and kept low, bent almost double and following in a slight indentation in the broad hilltop until they came to a clump of bushes where the short tanker captain was studying the landscape ahead with his binoculars. They kept their voices down too, although it was probably not necessary, for they soon saw that there was little action on the other side. A few loaded donkeys were moving along the rural highway that ran along their side of the border, but they were far away and hard to discern even with the binoculars that Sam offered them.

First Yishai looked through the binoculars, then Rabbi Beniyahu as Sam pointed out the landmarks and made sense of the scene before them. He pointed to the broken houses of Kibbutz HaGolan far to the south on a hill along the border, and to the highway between them and the overrun kibbutz. Then he pointed out some small figures and few old cars that were slowly picking their way through the no-man's-land between Israel and Syria. "That's where our looters are coming through – and there's a steady stream of them going back right now. See those two donkeys pulling a car? They're about where they have been turning off the road to head through the border. We don't see any organized patrols – just the occasional army truck or jeep running along the road – and there doesn't seem to be a checkpoint anywhere – even on the Syrian side."

Eli finally got his turn with the binoculars and looked at the ruined settlement in the distance. He had known a few young families who lived there. G-d, what if the same thing had happened to Yiftach? He shuddered. He then followed along the road, adjusting the glasses as he moved along further. He could see a few straggling groups of men and donkeys, all loaded with as much as they could carry. He paused to watch the car pulled by the two donkeys roll off the road and down the embankment, almost upsetting its load of chairs and junk tied to the top. He looked back at Woody and its bogus load of loot. Sam had done a good job, it looked just like one of those creeping carts and cars. Sam stood next to him and showed him the route down from their broad, low hill crest that would join the road slightly north of the gap where the looters were returning. "Yankel and his buddy are going to cover us from up here. The extra troops to take back the kibbutz weren't available, so they are going to hang out up here and lay down some fire if we get in trouble." Eli was disappointed to hear that news. It seemed like the plan was unraveling somehow.

"Ready?" Sam asked.

"No," Eli replied truthfully, "but let's get going, because I'm never going to be ready for any of this Purim parade. I wanted to be Queen Esther this year, not Haman." He gave Sam another attempt at a fierce scowl. Sam laughed and started back down the hill to their waiting truck.

However before they got back in, Sam made all three of them go through their pockets and knapsacks and the truck for anything identifying them as Israelis, wallets, ID cards, even dead cell phones. He asked if their rings had any Hebrew inscriptions. "We should have done this before we left your house," he apologized. Eli reluctantly handed over his *tallit* and prayer book, and his wallet with all his hard-earned ID cards and Sam placed them in the empty knapsack. He checked around the floor of the cab for any trash that would identify them. Eli pulled his insurance card and some Israeli CDs out of a pocket in the visor and handed them oven. Then he cleaned out Woody's glove box and dumped its entire contents into an empty knapsack. Sam carried the pack off to *Gimmel* One and handed it to the commander with a short word or two with him. Eli wondered when and if he would ever see it again.

Eli's stomach was churning over the two cups of strong coffee and muffins by the time they all piled back into Woody and pulled out. The tankers saluted them respectfully as they rolled by on their way over the hill and down the other side, and that braced him up a bit. Soon they were picking their way down the trail on the other side of the hill, in full view of anyone driving the road, or guarding the Syrian border for that matter. He hoped their disguise was convincing – a muddy old truck without a front windshield or back window, piled high with furniture and an odd collection of people.

After a long and tense ten minutes they reached the road. There was no traffic to the north, and to their south they saw only carts and donkeys. Eli looked at Rabbi Beniyahu, who shrugged and motioned him on. So Eli gunned the truck up the low shoulder of the roadway and headed south on the highway at a moderate speed in deference to their broken windshield and Sam's perch on the side of their load. He could see a pair of donkeys pulling a rubber-tired farm cart turning off the highway ahead and idled up to the spot. Another pair of loaded donkeys, with one rider, was a few hundred meters farther on the highway, but did not seem to be paying any particular attention. The donkey cart that had just turned off ahead of him was plodding along not far from the road.

"Pass him slowly on the left, and pause if Yishai starts up a conversation" Sam said quietly over Eli's shoulder. Eli downshifted and eased the truck with its load of old furniture off the highway and along the path that was being worn by donkey carts and the occasional car. He ground along in low gear and swung left to pass the slow moving cart, which he could now see carried a refrigerator, stove and washer. No wonder it was moving so slow. He concentrated on his driving as they passed. Although they were on the Israeli side of the border, and there had been no minefield warnings on the wire fence they passed, he could not help noticing that all the tracks kept close together through the grassy plain.

Yishai called out something guttural sounding as they passed the driver and a teenaged boy with an old rifle. They just muttered something back and concentrated on their load. Eli drove on a little faster until they reached and passed the next donkey load. In a few more minutes they passed the broken-down fence that marked the first of three on the Israeli side of the border. A second, taller fence with razor wire had been broken down and lay on the plowed up swath of sand and fine dirt that marked the area between it and the next fence. In normal times, Israeli soldiers patrolled a dirt track between the first and second fences and checked the cleared, brush- and grass-free zone between the second and third tall fences to see if there were any tracks left by an infiltrator. Right now there were plenty of tracks through the clean strip – all leading to Syria and the next broken section of fence. He could see that a little car piled high with chairs, a television ("Why bother?" he thought) and household goods was stuck on a piece of fence that had wedged under it. The donkeys were apparently refusing to back up and let the car roll free, and the driver who was steering the vehicle with barely room behind the wheel to move, was hanging out the driver's side window yelling a constant stream of abuse and perhaps advice to the befuddled donkey driver, who seemed like a slow-witted fellow on a good day.

Eli studied the situation as he slowed down and approached the donkey-towed car – a battered Fiat Uno with Israeli plates. "Some prize," he thought, but then immediately wondered what had happened to its rightful owner. The car probably came from the nearby kibbutz. Well, it was mostly blocking the way through the fence, and there would soon be a donkey-jam if it did so much longer. Eli decided that there was enough fence lying down to the left of the stuck donkeys and car, and that perhaps if he drove over it slowly, passing as close to the car as he dared, he could get safely past. It might perhaps also free the struggling donkey and Uno combination as the fence was pressed down by his passing. He started to swing left, wondering if it was right to help a thief in such a way. "What would a real Syrian do?" he wondered. Rabbi Beniyahu and Sam offered no advice, so he went ahead and pulled carefully onto the downed wire fence. There was a screeching of metal on metal, but apparently the trick worked, for at the same moment, the donkeys and Uno lurched forwards. The driver gave a startled yell, which might have started as invective and turned to thanks, which Yishai returned.

"Pause a moment. Let Yishai find out some information," Rabbi Beniyahu whispered. A three-way conversation ensued, with Yishai leaning out the right window, the driver hanging out the window of the jammed Fiat, and Sam contributing some sharp remarks from his perch on the load. Eli, the rabbi and the awkward looking donkey driver were quiet. The fat little man jammed in the Fiat had the most to say. But as the slow moving cart with the appliances began to catch up and clear the first fence, everyone wrapped up their gab fest and Rabbi Beniyahu nudged Eli to go ahead.

Their next direction was obvious: head straight for the broken fences on the Syrian side of the border. While all the warning signs on the Israeli side had been in Hebrew, English, Arabic and symbols, the Syrian signs were fewer, and all in Arabic. Apparently if you wanted to come to Syria by this route, you had better read Arabic, Eli thought. Uneventfully they rolled through the two fences on the Syrian side and followed the well worn trails through what was most probably a minefield. Eli couldn't read Arabic, but he could guess well enough.

Rabbi Beniyahu filled him in on the conversations with the donkey-driven Fiat's driver – or steerer and brake man, since the car was being towed. The two gentlemen were from a nearby village and had been helping themselves to their government's recently liberated property in Kibbutz HaGolan. "They wanted to know if we had a microwave to trade for anything. We should let him know if we found one, just look for the barber in Sur El Arik. Oh, and the big base where they are digging out the helicopters is straight ahead past the minefield, only four kilometers to the gate."

"So, it's true about the helicopters," Eli said, glumly.

"I'm afraid so," said Rabbi Beniyahu.

"So, what do we do now? We've confirmed the track across the border and the helicopters – can we go home now? He said, more than half in earnest.

"Let's see what else we can learn in Syria," the Rabbi said simply. So, Eli drove on along the bumpy track and crossed into Syria for the first time in his life. He knew pitifully little about the huge country of 21 million people – except that they had gone to war against Israel in one form or another ever since Syria became an independent state in 1946. By driving a few hundred meters across the border, Eli knew he had left behind a modern, lively, democratic state with a free press, unfettered economy, and five times the gross domestic product as its backwards neighbor. He knew that literacy rates had dropped to perhaps 75% on this side of the border – worse for women – and that Syria did not participate in the world in the same way as its effervescent neighbor. It was not quite as closed to the west as the Soviet Union had been during Eli's childhood, but it was very much a dictatorship ruled by the unpopular, but all-powerful Baath Party. With those thoughts, he drove them into Syria following the stream of donkeys, carts and battered cars. Apparently on this side of the border as well, only the antiques were running.

In Sam's briefing, he had said they would blend in with the stream of local traffic until they could see or find out the extent of the forces guarding the big military compound that held the helicopters being dug from the bomb-blasted bunkers. He almost wished Sam was sitting next to him instead of the silent Rabbi, but he checked himself, and decided that perhaps Rabbi Beniyahu was the best protection in this kind of situation. Funny, the Rabbi seemed to think that of him.

Eli knew he was a long way from Jewish sainthood. Eli had lived a largely secular life for his first thirty-some years, and had grown more religious and involved in Jewish life only in the past twenty five or so years – enough to raise his girls a Zionistic form of orthodox. Now they were both living an Torah-observant life. One live in Jerusalem. She tended to be the more of a dati – more a sort of modern orthodox in outlook but very orthodox in practice. And the other daughter lived back in Chicago, was married to a yeshiva-educated kollel rabbi, and lived a very ultra "black hat" lifestyle. It was odd how life worked out for them that way.

Eli soon reached the first real road in Syria, and followed the trail of carts and donkeys of looted goods towards what looked like a medium small town, perhaps a little bigger than nearby Yonatan. Only it looked run down, dirty, and had only a handful of dusty palms, no real downtown, and three minarets of various sizes. Eli guessed this might be Sur El Arik, but there were few signs – and all of them in Arabic. He was tempted to ask the rabbi, or turn around and ask Sam, but he was practicing keeping his mouth shut, and knew if he couldn't keep it shut when they were alone, it would be hard to keep quiet when they were being talked to. He had caught himself tempted to toss in a "l'hitraot – see you later" when they left the donkey-powered Fiat."

Keeping his mouth shut, Eli drove slowly into the run-down town. It had no shelling damage, in spite of being just two kilometers from the border. He mentally compared it to the scenes in his mind from driving out of Moshav Yiftach that morning. That might have helped his glowering, sour look. As it was, their truck and its load gathered only a few sharp looks by idlers and watchers in the street who were merely curious to see what was being carried by. As they passed the center of the town, denoted only by a few larger buildings and a traffic circle, Eli circled the run-down open space that appeared to have had a fountain once a long time ago. Yishai muttered something and Rabbi Beniyahu pointed to one of the streets leading away from the opposite side of the circle. He turned that way and began to pick his way through slow-moving traffic. It was mostly donkeys, a few camels, a few bicycles, and a large number of pedestrians, some of them wheeling carts. Ahead he could see a congested area that looked like a typical middle-eastern *souk* or open air marketplace. He slowly negotiated the crowded narrow street, using his truck like a wedge to ease around slower moving traffic and force on-coming donkeys and carts to squeeze aside. Eli had enough experience with driving in Jerusalem and Tel Aviv at rush hour to feel confident playing the never-ending game of "chicken" and brinksmanship to see which driver would yield last. He noticed that this traffic jam was somewhat less prone to use its horns than its Israeli urban neighbors, possibly because half of them were broken, or perhaps because they didn't work on stubborn donkeys. There was plenty of yelling and cursing out of drivers' windows, most of it ignored. But some led to shouting matches over a point of etiquette that would block the street until each had made his point several times, causing others to be drawn into the fray in their frustration to get around the two or more who had stopped to shout.

On the other side of the *souk* he could see a large dusty park where carts of loot were being unloaded and displayed for sale. There was plenty of action going on here, though the crowd was mostly men and boys. Few women were present, and most were dressed from head to toe in shapeless dark burkahs. All the women wore full head scarves, but almost none were covering their faces. Everyone was engaged in the hubbub of buying and selling, and the action was heated in places. Rabbi Beniyahu casually motioned Eli to an open space towards the fringe of the action, and signed for him to park. "So this is how Israeli spies work!" Eli wondered to himself, "they go to the *souk*!"

Sure enough, Sam jumped down as soon as Eli stopped. He started to untie the load. Eli was tempted to help him, but only Yishai got out. Rabbi Beniyahu stayed sitting quietly by Eli, taking in the chaotic scene with serene, calm eyes, missing nothing. Before Sam had finished untying the first articles, several men had come up and begun bargaining with him. Rabbi Beniyahu kindly gave Eli a running summary of the discussions, speaking quietly out of the side of his mouth while keeping his eyes casually on the scene going on behind them with the rear and side view mirrors. "They want to buy the whole load and rent the truck to go back for more... he's offering a fantastic sounding price... but to be paid on our return.... Nothing doing. Now Sam is telling him to get lost, his venerable grandfather is not going to rent his truck to the likes of him.... There's a little comment on Sam's ancestry... and mine, I guess I'm his new grandfather now.... I always wanted a son in the IDF. Now, these two are looking for silverware.... The other guy is buying computers, not too bright, obviously. Ah, this one actually wants to look at the other chair on top of the load, sure he does, he's just sizing Sam up.... Yishai got rid of him."

The wheeling and dealing went on for nearly an hour and Eli was beginning to wonder what they were going to get from sitting there, besides a few rumpled Syrian notes for the two wooden chairs and side table that Yishai sold. Now, at least, they could make change if any was needed. But after a while, he noticed Sam having more lengthy talks with some younger men, some of whom were armed and dangerous looking – possibly from a local militia, Eli guessed. A little while later, Eli was not only sleepy and bored, but he needed somewhere to get rid of all the coffee he had drunk that morning. He suffered in silence for awhile, and then whispered his problem to Rabbi Beniyahu. Fortunately the Rabbi had the same problem, and gave Eli a quick lesson on what to expect in an Arab public restroom. However, as they got out of the cab, and told the briefly idle Sam of their mission, he gestured towards some dusty bushes over in a nearby corner of the *souk* that were apparently being watered after a fashion, there being no restroom for this makeshift market.

That made Eli's job easier, and he and the rabbi sauntered casually over towards the bushes, with Rabbi Beniyahu keeping up a monotonous sounding monologue in Arabic, to which Eli appeared to be following raptly. When they finished their business and were sitting back in the cab again, Eli asked him what he had been lectured on. "Oh, just verses from the Koran guaranteed to bore any listener and make them think there was nothing interesting going on unless they wanted to hear more." Eli was quietly amused. So Rabbi Beniyahu could recite ten minutes of non-stop Koran, perhaps more. He was an amazing little man.

Sam had unloaded most of the junk from their truck, leaving only enough to mask the odd wood-burning contraption, which could pass for an old wood stove or some boiler parts. Pretty soon he and Yishai had a buyer engaged in a loud, hand waving, passionate discussion, which ended with smiles, handshakes, and some money being passed. Rabbi Beniyahu whispered that the middleman had just bought the rest of their pile of goods for about half a year's average salary, and that he would have first right of refusal over their next load from Israel. He said also that Sam had politely refused an offer to come to lunch at the man's house – saying that they deeply regretted missing the hospitality and good company, but that they had to get back to Israel while the pickings were fresh.

Yishai, looking quietly proud of himself, climbed back into the cab and had a few words with Rabbi Beniyahu. Sam soon scrambled back into the truck and motioned Eli to start up and head out of the market, back in the direction they had come. Apparently they were done. He felt infinitely relieved. After nearly three hours in the noisy *souk*, it was a relief to be moving again. It was after eleven in the morning, and the day was growing hot and sultry. Although the sun was dimmed on this side of the border, it was not nearly as smoky as Israel where fires burned unchecked. The wind was still coming from the east, but had nearly died away to nothing. Eli edged their mostly empty truck through town. Sam now sat on the edge of the pickup box where he could see him plainly in the driver's side mirror. At a glance, he looked nothing like the IDF lieutenant who had borrowed his truck a couple days ago.

On reaching the edge of town, Eli accelerated once he was clear of the congestion and started rolling home with great relief in his heart. He found it impossible to maintain his scowl, but it no longer seemed necessary. There was little traffic on the one-and-a-half lane, broken-down asphalt road. It was a road that appeared to have little normal traffic, which made sense, since it swung so near to the Israeli border. He could see what he could now recognize as tank tracks on the berm. Every now and then he had slow down and squeeze over for an oncoming cart or ancient car. Eli had to concentrate on the road, with its many potholes and broken edges. And at one point perhaps halfway to where the path across the border fences began, he had to stop and let a herd of dusty brown sheep be driven across the road. They were just about done crossing – there must have been a couple hundred of the dirty, dispirited looking beasts, drooping along in the midday heat – when he heard a roar and a prodigious honking behind him. Looking in his mirror, he saw a jeep with flashing lights and a long line of supply trucks with canvas tops rapidly approaching. Eli squeezed Woody off the road to make way for the convoy. The jeep came roaring past, blaring its horn and scattering the last of the sheep while the three scrawny boy shepherds scrambled out of its way. There was one boy and most of the sheep on one side where Eli pulled over, and the older looking two boys on the other side, suddenly having to work hard to keep their handful of sheep from crossing over the stream of big trucks rumbling past. There must have been fifty or sixty trucks; big, boxy-looking, Russian-built military trucks with six wheels and big, canvas covered canopies – probably five or six ton capacity each, Eli guessed as he watched them silently.

In the mirror he saw Sam watching them pass. While he was trying hard to look bored and disinterested, Eli could tell that it was like a cat watching a bird through a window. He could almost sense the twitching tip of a tail. Rabbi Beniyahu and Yishai looked grim. None of them was happy to see that many supplies headed for Israel. Eli was acutely aware of how they had struggled to bring in the first few wagon loads of shells across the Kinneret and up to the embattled Golan. It was such an unfair fight!

The supply column finally passed. Eli turned around and checked the road behind before pulling onto the roadway again. Half a dozen sheep lay dead, run over by the convoy, the boys were dragging the carcasses off the highway. Eli fought his natural urge to stop and help them, and carefully drove past, not looking. Rabbi Beniyahu let out a soulful sigh and looked sad. Yishai was shaking his head. They started to drive on slowly, but the dusty wake of the huge supply convoy, and their missing windshield persuaded Eli to slow way down to let the line of big trucks pull away.

After a few minutes of this, Rabbi Beniyahu nudged him in the ribs. "Pull over at that farm track up there and head for those bushes, I need to relieve myself for a few minutes, and my dignity requires some proper cover," he said quietly. Although he was anxious to get out of Syria, Eli was equally anxious to let the Syrian military get a long way ahead of them. He drove up to where a little-used rural dirt track exited their road and meandered off up a low hill. Sam called something softly in Arabic, which the rabbi answered as they pulled off the highway. Sam returned to his vigil in the back of the truck, looking nervous. It was a moderate distance up the soft dirt track to reach the dusty greenery that Rabbi Beniyahu required. Eli pulled to a stop and the rabbi climbed gratefully out of the cab. Eli parked and shut down the engine, since the rabbi hinted he might be more than a few minutes. He looked off towards where the long column of ammunition trucks seemed to be heading for the same gap in the border where they had come through on their way to Syria. Apparently it was a local shortcut. Sam was standing in the pickup bed, also watching the disappearing convoy.

Suddenly Sam stiffened up and stared to the south, beyond where the trucks were milling as the first of them started to navigate the narrow track across the border. Eli couldn't see anything, so he climbed up in the truck bed beside Sam and looked again in the direction he was looking. A cold panic gripped him too, and he froze like a statue next to Sam. There was a tremendous mass of tanks in a line coming up the highway on the Israeli side of the border, the one they had crossed on their way to the gap in the fences. At the distance, without any binoculars, the tanks were just a mass of shapes for Eli, but the effect was just as daunting. There must be hundreds of them! He stared at them dumbly. What could it mean? Were they coming this way back to Syria? He turned to Sam.

Sam was now looking at the top of the hill where their tank escort had left them – a long way away. Yishai, who had climbed out of the cab to stretch his legs and shake some of the dust out of his clothes, was just beginning to take in the news that something was drastically wrong. Sam quietly explained it to him in Arabic, and helped him climb up to the truck bed so he could see. They dared not pull out binoculars or the scope on Eli's rifle, lest they be taken for spies or someone being too nosey in the wrong place. The tanks were moving quickly, throwing up a cloud of dust in spite of the asphalt highway, as well as smoke and a shimmering haze of heat in the baking mid-day sun. The effect was as an approaching dust storm. And soon they were hearing the distant rumble of the tanks, like rolling thunder coming closer.

Eli could see that the supply train was halted, lined up part way through the border crossing, with half the trucks still parked on the narrow road on the Syrian side, waiting to cross through the border openings. That somehow reassured Eli that the tanks were probably not coming this way. Mutely they watched the mass of force in motion arrayed before them. The leading tanks of the column were now close enough to begin to make out individual shapes. Sam whispered that they were the latest model Soviet main battle tanks, with reactive armor; anti-aircraft-capable, land-mine resistant, top-of-the-line machines. There were dozens of them in the first ranks, moving up the road at perhaps 70 – 80 kilometers an hour. Eli could tell that they looked bigger and tougher than the ones that had nearly blown him to bits two days earlier – and those had been big and bad enough.

Rabbi Beniyahu came and joined them. Sam helped boost him into the back of the pickup, and the four of them stood quietly, as if in a reviewing grandstand. Their little hillside gave them a spectacular view, with the border fences beyond and below them, and the parade of armor rolling along above and beyond the thin strip of no man's land, and above it all, the hill where they and their two ancient tank escorts had surveyed the whole scene. Eli wished they were up there now, even though such safety seemed a very thin reed indeed.

The parade of forces went on and on. After the first phalanx of late-model tanks came armored personnel carriers by the score, each chock full of troops. Then more tanks, a bevy of jeep-like vehicles, some supply trucks, and then it seems the pattern of tanks followed by APC's started all over again – perhaps marking another division or unit. Where were they all going? Sam seemed to be wondering the same thing, for he jumped down and began walking up the two ruts of their farm track to go higher up the hill to find out. Eli decided to go with him, anything to break the spell of dread and doom he felt watching the overwhelming panoply of tanks and infantry rolling by.

Slowly they climbed the track towards the top of the hill where some dusty looking goats grazed, completely unconcerned. Eli wished he could care only about grass and weeds, and not about everything else in the world right now. However, he suddenly realized that it would be a bad idea to encounter a friendly or curious shepherd right now – even if was a boy like the ones with the sheep. But, Sam walked along beside him, and curiosity urged him on. The head of the column had disappeared from their view around the curve of the hill. Even at the distance of more than two kilometers, the rumble of the moving army was oppressive. Below them on the road leading to town, Eli could now see groups of men and donkeys, and perhaps a dozen cars and trucks stopped along the highway to watch and wait for their passing. There was also a cluster of carts and cars gathered around the tail end of the supply column, waiting to cross the border as soon as they moved. "The carrion crows are gathering for another feast," Eli thought grimly.

It was a longer way to the top of their little hill than it had seemed when they started out, and it was not so much of a hill as a hummock that marked the edge of a slightly higher area of small hillocks and grassy dips, not altogether unpleasant. It was very much like the Israeli side of the border, only a little lower perhaps, and somewhat less lush vegetation. The goats seemed happy enough with it though, there were about two dozen brown and speckled ones grazing calmly about. Eli looked around anxiously to spot any shepherds before they spotted him and attempted a conversation. There appeared to be no one in sight. Sam was headed higher still, walking quickly towards the next higher hillock to follow the route of the enemy army, whose rumble seemed somewhat fainter as they left the edge of the first hill. Eli hurried after him so as not to be left alone, feeling odd to be walking through a Syrian goat pasture in the unfamiliar military style fatigues. The black beret was hot, but it was keeping the hidden sun from baking his head and shading his eyes slightly from the mid-day glare.

He trotted up the next hillock behind Sam, glancing around every now and then to see if the end of the Syrian march was in sight. It kept coming in a mind-numbing array. The supply trucks were still stopped waiting for their turn in the doomsday parade. Eli shuddered to wonder where they could be heading, for they were going north along a track they had already conquered. Sam was obviously wondering the same thing. Sam jogged up the next rise and hopped up on the tallest boulder in sight to gain another meter of height in a vain attempt to see farther. Eli could tell he was itching for binoculars – not that they could tell him much more from this distance. No radio, no binoculars, no map, just a single gun between them, the black Kalashnikov that Sam carried as part of his costume – they had hardly any of the tools of a soldier's trade. Eli felt completely helpless.

Eli climbed up on the big, lichen-covered basaltic boulder beside his friend. Together they strained to see the front of the column, which was pressing farther north along the Israeli – Syrian border, following the highway that they both knew ran north all the way to Mt. Hermon. The question was, where would this menacing army be going when it turned westward? Eli and Sam traded speculations: Katzrin? But it had already been overrun. Perhaps they were circling their northern-most positions to press a new attack towards the north end of the Kinneret, But then, they had already driven one column back from that path with heavy losses from the advantage of the remaining Israeli artillery on the heights. They would be foolish to try that again – even with this huge force. Sam bet that they were circling even father north to come down the next highway that drove through Katzrin.

That means they are combining forces with the army that overran Katzrin – Sam speculated. They would be aiming for the north end of the Kinneret – coming out somewhere near Capernaum. The more Sam chewed that idea over, the more convinced he became that he was right. Such a combined force could go south and take Tiberias without much trouble – or force their way westward and break out towards Korazim and roll west for the coast. Once they pushed through to the big east-west valley that ran past Carmiel, it would be easy to reach the coast at Akko. Both stood and numbly contemplated the effect of driving an armored wedge through the northern quarter of Israel. They could only assume that the force that had broken down just past Katzrin was equally as massive as the column that was now rumbling past.

They stood a long time in mute horror, feeling cold in the oppressive heat of the day. Summer had not released its baking grip on the Golan yet, even in mid September. As Eli stood next to Sam, staring at tank after truck rolling past in the distance, his ear was hearing a persistent and almost pleading bleat of a loud goat not far away. Afraid that it might mean the approach of a curious shepherd, Eli turned and scanned the rocky meadows behind them, looking for the source of the alarm. Although the blaating and bleating was nearly constant, it took him a while to spot a dusty, brown speckled goat standing by what looked like a camouflage tarp or perhaps a sleeping bag perhaps less than a hundred meters away in a hollow behind them. He tugged at Sam's elbow and whispered that there appeared to be a shepherd sleeping nearby.

Sam turned casually around and gazed off in the direction that Eli surreptitiously pointed. He then looked a long time, shading his eyes squinting to see better in the glare of the midday sun. "By G-d! I think that's a parachute, not a sleeping bag!" Sam said. Swinging his Kalashnikov off his shoulder and chambering a round, he whispered for Eli to start moving slowly back in a circle towards the truck, and to take off running if there was any shooting. Eli sat down on the boulder and slipped to the ground and started reluctantly moving away, watching Sam as much as he could while watching his feet so as not to make too much noise. Fortunately his hunting skills were only unpracticed and not lost completely, and he felt he was moving with a suitable amount of stealth. However, he was fascinated to watch Sam.

It felt like he was watching an IDF training film. Sam moved with speed and stealth, gun at the hair-trigger ready as he slipped through the meadow, going from cover to cover, but never taking his eyes completely off his target. Eli was less than halfway to the hill that marked the way back to the truck when Sam drew close to his target, creeping slowly and checking carefully in an arc around him, gun at the ready. Then just as quickly, he lowered the gun and ran to the sheet of camouflaged nylon. Eli froze, ready to run like hell – or go help Sam, he wasn't sure which. Sam knelt out of sight for over a minute, and Eli began to edge towards his escape again.

Then he saw Sam stand up, look around, spot him and wave urgently for him to come over. Eli ran heavily now through the grass and weedy meadow, dodging boulders until he came to where he could see Sam crouching beside the camouflaged nylon, which he could now tell had a tangle of cords and was a parachute. He arrived, panting and dry in the heat to see Sam trying to rouse an unconscious airman, still strapped in his harness, wearing an odd, bloody, turban-like wrap on his head, and his arm in a makeshift sling cut out of the same parachute. "He's still alive," Sam croaked, his voice choked with emotion. Eli felt tears come to his eyes as he too knelt down to see better. The name tag stitched into the breast pocket of the man's flight suit was in Hebrew and English. Eli's brain read the English first, Tzippori. He saw two bars on the one shoulder of the flight suit not wrapped in a sling – he was a captain – IAF.

"G-d bless you and keep you," Eli whispered as he took in the man's pale, blood streaked face, his awkward sling and bandage-like turban. However, the state of his left leg below a makeshift tourniquet stabbed him with pain and sorrow for this fallen captain. His left boot was turned at an odd angle and the ragged flight suit where his calf should be looked blood stained and not quite right. He could see that the man was breathing shallowly, and responded very faintly and weakly to pain as Sam pinched his good arm and tenderly touched his left knee above the crude bandage. Eli's eyes were running freely with tears of relief and sympathy to see the shadow of a response. He looked at Sam. Sam's dirty face was streaked with fresh tears too.

"Go get the truck – bring it as close as you can, hurry!" Sam choked out.

Eli took one last look at the fallen airman, looking in awe at the jagged bandages cut from the parachute and beginning to comprehend the pain, loneliness and fear the poor man must have suffered – for he surely must have come down before dawn on the first day of the war. He got up and began running towards the truck as fast as he could in the heat and rough terrain. He was winded by the time he reached the lip of the hillock where they had left the track to walk further. Eli slowed to a determined jog as he started down the track towards the truck, which was still almost half a kilometer ahead. Rabbi Beniyahu and Yishai, who had reclined in the meager shade of an ancient olive tree near the truck, looked up in alarm as he appeared over the rise, running. They got stiffly to their feet and were back at the truck, possibly reaching for the weapons they had hidden. Eli waved as if to signal that it was OK, and jogged on, panting, down the track.

"Get in!" he croaked as he came close enough to be heard, forgetting that he was not supposed to speak as part of their charade. He was barely conscious of the vast army that still rumbled by over his shoulder on the other side of the border. He had numbly checked to see if there was any new action on their road, or if the supply train had moved on yet. While there was a larger collection of camp followers behind the stopped column now, the supply trucks had not yet moved.

Eli ran, panting raggedly, hot and winded to the driver's side of the truck. He got in and started the engine as Rabbi Beniyahu and Yishai settled in next to him. He put the truck in gear and was grinding slowly up the road before he could speak again, still breathing heavily. Rabbi Beniyahu offered him a bottle of water, which he drank awkwardly between heaving breaths.

"We found an Israeli pilot – he's in bad shape, but still alive," Eli managed to gasp between sips and pants. Somehow Rabbi Beniyahu and Yishai did not seem as stunned by the news as he thought they should be. But then, all they had were his words. They had not seen the bloody makeshift bandages, cut from a parachute, or the pale airman with his horrible injuries, still in his parachute harness.

Eli glanced at the distant mass of trucks moving along the highway, and the nearer, but still quite distant cluster of the supply convoy. He told himself that chances of anyone being concerned with their battered little truck were small, unless perhaps some of the would-be looters were looking to upgrade their transportation. He drove slowly and deliberately to the top of the hill where they had left the track and paused, surveying the rocky meadows and rising hillocks beyond, looking for a path he could pick with his truck. He made sure he was in low range and 4-wheel drive, took a long sip of water, and eased off the track, following the cleanest line he could see.

After climbing awhile and jouncing up and down over frame-twisting rocks and dips, he decided that they had gone as far as he could safely drive without risking being stuck. He also didn't want to subject their unconscious airman to quite such a jolting ride if it was not absolutely necessary. Rabbi Beniyahu volunteered to watch the truck, and produced a 9 mm automatic pistol from a pocket in his robes. It looked bigger than any five-foot-tall Rabbi should be able to hold, but Eli didn't doubt that he knew perfectly well how to use it. Eli could see nothing left in the bed of the truck that would make a suitable litter, and he decided that the parachute would probably do just as well for transporting the pilot as anything he could think of.

Eli and Yishai took water and the rudimentary first aid kit that Sam had allowed to remain from their papers and supplies, and jogged off. Although he was at least seventy, the tough old moshavnik had no trouble keeping up with Eli as he led the way back to where he had found the airman. Fortunately it was not far from where he had been able to bring the truck.

Sam had arranged the remains of the parachute into a neatly folded long rectangle next to the airman, which would make a perfect litter if they eased the man onto the middle of it and each grasped a corner, with perhaps Eli or Sam taking two. The bleating goat that had drawn Eli's attention to the airman was still complaining, but less frequently, practically stepping on the parachute that Sam had spread. Sam waved at her in annoyance. He had picked up the airman's helmet and stuck it on his head, and had stuck the bloody survival knife they had found next to the airman in the back pocket of his jeans. The three men knelt down on the spread parachute and prepared to move the injured airman. Eli took the hips, Sam took the head and shoulders, and Yishai took the delicate task of moving the mangled leg. The goat nuzzled the back of Eli's head, and he shrugged her away, but with gratitude for calling his attention to the downed airman. She seemed concerned somehow for the man's welfare. Were goats as loyal as dogs? Eli wondered as he eased his hands gently under the man's hips.

When each was satisfied with their grip, Sam whispered, "On three," and counted. The slender airman felt surprisingly light as Eli eased him up and shuffled back slowly on his knees, lifting the man only a little bit in order to shift him over to the waiting nylon folds. Gently, slowly, they moved the unconscious pilot and were relieved to hear a faint groan as they settled him in the center of the folded chute. Sam dampened his fingers and moistened the man's chapped lips with a few drops of water. The goat nudged his elbow and he shooed her away in annoyance.

Sam volunteered to take the feet if Eli and Yishai felt strong enough to take the head. They did. So they all knelt at their respective corners of the rectangle of nylon and gathered hand holds by rolling a bunch of the slippery material and testing their grips. When they were all ready, Sam counted again and they slowly lifted until all had gained their feet, and Captain Tzippori was cradled in the bunched parachute a little less than waist high. "Eli, you set the pace, nice and easy," Sam suggested.

The goat followed, bleating in complaint as they made their way slowly and carefully up the slope of the little depression that had sheltered the airman from the sight of the world for the past three days. They made their way a few steps at a time, picking an easy course around boulders and dips towards the next rise, and over to where the truck waited. Eli had the sense of seeing their odd procession as from afar in his mind, two older Arab-looking men, a blood-stained injured Israeli airman sagging in a swath of nylon chute between them and a swarthy, tough looking younger man with a rifle and a bloody knife stuck in his back pocket, and a brown speckled goat bringing up the rear, and occasionally nudging the young man's behind. Eli could hear him swearing at the persistent goat in Arabic. "Easy now, Sam," he said over his shoulder, "I wouldn't have noticed him if it wasn't for her." After that the muttered curses sounded just as annoyed, but less dire. In fact, Yishai, who was struggling manfully his third of the load, smirked at one of them.

As soon as they came within sight of the truck, Rabbi Beniyahu came to help Yishai with his side and to gaze with alarm and deep affection at the unconscious pilot. He touched the man's bloodied head bandage at one point and said a quiet prayer which Eli could not quite catch.

Since it was still hot mid-day and there was no shade in the bed of the truck, they eased the wounded pilot down in the meager shade of the truck and all sat down next to him and rested a while, passing a pair of water bottles between them. After sitting and resting a while, Sam got up to reconnoiter, walking up to where he could check on the track and the road behind them, and take a quick look at the Syrian forces waiting in the border gap and along the highway in Israel. He came back and sat down in the shade with the rest of them.

"We're going to be here for a while They are still moving troops along the road and haven't even started with the supply and ordinance yet," Sam said bitterly. "What can we do for our friend Captain Tzippori?" he asked.

Yishai had already gently probed the arm in the sling and decided to leave it be. He gently washed some of the blood from the man's temples and begun to delicately peel back the makeshift turban-like bandage. He said that the man seemed in better shape than one would expect for three days alone in the hot sun.

The goat bleated about a meter from Sam's ear, and Sam irritably flapped his arm at her, "Stinking goat, get out of here, he's going to be OK," he muttered.

"Have a little *rachamim*," Yishai tisked gently, "The poor thing hasn't been milked in over a day. Her shepherd must be off playing soldier – or looter, whichever the case may be." He pointed to her full udder, which was literally dripping with milk. "That must be painful."

"Pass me that helmet there," Yishai said, pointing to where Sam had set the airman's helmet beside his place in the grass. Sam passed it, questioningly, over to the old moshavnik, who peered at it, sniffed the insides, and scraped at something in the crown. He looked wonderingly at the goat, and back at the helmet. Eli and Sam stared at him, at the helmet and at the goat, who let go an annoyed sounding blaaaaah again, as if trying to reason with these thick headed men

"Well, wonder of wonder, miracle of miracles if our pilot didn't have a goat for Rabbi Eliyahu's ravens…" he said simply.

"Or the Rashbi's carob tree…." Rabbi Beniyahu offered. Eli's mind raced to catch up. Obviously, Yishai was referring to the ravens who miraculously fed the prophet Eliyahu (Elijah to the non-Hebrew-speaking world) in the desert while he hid from the evil king Ahab. Rabbi Beniyahu was alluding to an equally miraculous carob tree and a stream that nourished the great sage Rabbi Shimon Bar Yochai in a later age as he and his sons spent years in a cave hiding from the Romans.

Sam was a couple heartbeats slower on the allusions and wondered what they were talking about.

Yishai pointed to some dried milk scum on the bottom of the helmet Sam had salvaged. "It looks like our airman was able to milk our little goat friend at least once. I guess the IDF is slightly behind today's air force in their agricultural survival skills..." Yishai said reprovingly.... "and perhaps we had better milk our kind-hearted little aromatic friend instead of hurl insults at her like "son of a knock-kneed donkey and a cross-eyed billy goat, for our friend is most definitely female."

Yishai took the helmet and moved towards the goat, clucking soothingly and calming her with a much sweeter sounding Arabic. Sam looked thoroughly chagrinned, and watched as Yishai expertly milked the little brown spotted goat. He got almost half a helmet full and offered some to Sam, who refused to touch it. Eli tasted a finger of the warm, strong smelling milk. Rabbi Beniyahu and Yishai each took a small sip, which they savored. Sam got up to reconnoiter again. Yishai said they should save the milk in case the airman gained consciousness, for it was the most perfect nutrition they had on hand for him besides water.

The three men discussed the miracle of the goat and the airman for a long time. Even Sam had to admit, after he came back from his look around, that although one could see it was a perfectly natural chain of coincidences – together it began to strain credibility. The airman had to parachute to the ground at the beginning of a war, without being seen or found – despite the fact that his plane must have crashed somewhere, though perhaps many kilometers from this spot. Here they were, less than two kilometers from a heavily manned border, less than a kilometer from a well-traveled road, right in the middle of an abandoned flock of goats. The coincidences when on and on – right up to Rabbi Beniyahu needing a relief stop and pointing to the bushes along this road, Eli and Sam walking farther to see where the enemy was going, and Eli hearing the goat and turning to look for a shepherd. It seemed too much to accept as a perfectly natural chain of events, and yet each turn seemed quite plausible in itself. "Just like the Purim story," Eli commented. "Nowhere do you see the name of *HaShem* in the whole Megillah, but His hand is seen constantly..."

Sam went to check the Syrian movements again, and came back to announce that the supply trucks were beginning to move again through the border as the supply caravan of the vast army was beginning to sweep past. It was now three in the afternoon, another two hours to go before sunset. The four men quietly debated how to try to slip back through to Israel, now with an unconscious Israeli airman. They all agreed it would be too risky to try to change his clothing, or put something over his flight suit. No one thought it was wise to mess with the mangled leg, or pull the bloody turban of parachute scraps farther than Yishai had been able to clean – for there were unknown head injuries beyond their secure wraps.

All remembered scenes of what happened to Jewish soldiers or captives if they fell in the hands of an Arab mob. The video images of the two lost Israeli reservists who drove down the wrong street in Ramallah came readily to mind. They had escaped a mob to take refuge in a Palestinian Authority police station in the early years of the century – only to be killed and their bloody bodies thrown out the window to a raging mob – and this only a few miles from civilized Jerusalem. These images were seared into the minds of any Israeli who contemplated the dark side of relations across the tense border with their neighbors. They recalled the lost airman Ron Arad, captured at the start of the first Lebanon war. Arad had been a mystery for years, and his final end was still unknown.

"We need to wait until dark," they all agreed. But to get their airman to a hospital as soon as possible, they decided to head across the border at sunset or a little before, needing just enough twilight to find their way back. With that decided, Eli and Sam were told to take naps for the remaining hours, for they had barely slept the night before. Yishai and Rabbi Beniyahu volunteered to keep watch.

In the Air, Jordan Valley 1650

Major Yossi Green's second turn in the "borrowed" F-15 came sooner than he expected, but not sooner than he wished. Action was so intense after the first two sorties that pilots were rotated after only two hours in the cockpit instead of the planned three. There was no need or time to run a full preflight check on an aircraft that had just touched down and been refueled in fifteen minutes. The only thing that mattered was to get back into the skies again. Since Egypt's advance air bases in the Sinai had been disabled with the same EMP that had taken down the IAF's eyes and ears – or perhaps an errant EMP aimed for Israel – their first opposition of the day had not appeared until his third sortie. Yossi had played it in his mind endlessly in his six and a half hours on the ground as the next three pilots pushed "his" plane to its limits to fend off wing after wing of Egyptian fighters while trying to do as much damage as possible to the Egyptian and irregular forces scattered on the ground across southern Israel.

Even Yossi's limited tactical radar could tell him that there were a dozen MIG 25 Foxbats streaking up the Sinai Peninsula to meet his air wing as he had lifted off on his third pre-dawn sortie at about oh five hundred that morning. Only a Foxbat would be flying at more than Mach 2.4. Twelve on eight were not bad odds for a normally equipped wing of Israeli F-15s. In fact, they might be almost called even. Though the Foxbat could hurtle through the atmosphere at speeds approaching Mach 2.5, it was not quite as agile a fighter as the wily F-15 Eagle. With Israel's state-of-the-art sight-guided air-to-air missiles, eight F-15s should have been able to make a fine breakfast of a dozen Foxbats – especially when flown by Egyptians who had far less in-the-air combat training and experience than their Israeli cousins. But, armed with old-fashioned, heat-seeking sidewinder-style missiles, getting a clear shot up the tailpipe of a supersonic Foxbat was a different story.

Yossi was glad to have had his two unopposed bombing runs for getting used to the different side-stick controls. The lack of the in-helmet, heads up display refinements that had been the best that Israel could offer, and the completely different fire control system – all that had taken every moment of his two fast runs to hit the Egyptian command, control and intelligence sites that were first on their target lists. With the C3I infrastructure down, the fighters would be able to work free of interference from the most sophisticated layers of the Soviet-style air defense network.

Fortunately, Southern Air Command had an inkling there might be fighters aloft – and for his third flight, Yossi's hard-working bird was loaded with eight of the sidewinder-style missiles and enough fuel to stay in the air as long as necessary. Only fifteen minutes were needed for the first wing of Foxbats – but what an intense fifteen minutes! Yossi had split his wing into four working pairs and scattered them to draw the neat formation of MIGs apart. They designated two "home bases" for any pair to run for if they needed help. As he had anticipated, the Egyptians split into groups of three for every two Eagles, something they had probably not trained for extensively since their instructors preferred flying in perfect two- and four-plane formations.

Yossi and his wing man had led their trio out over the Mediterranean, causing them to drop most of their advantage in speed and altitude before Yossi flipped agilely over and raced them back to home base, arriving with his wing man just enough ahead of their pursuers to help pick off one of the trio pursuing their designated partner pair. It was a beautiful set up and a good clean shot. However, Yossi and his wing had to pull back on their sticks and climb for the sky in a climbing race with the clumsy but fast Foxbats on their tails. Again their agility and turning edge trumped the powerful Soviet-built jets. They were able to split near the top of their arcs just in time to dodge the missiles fired behind them, swoop down and become the pursuers themselves. Again, it was a maneuver as clean as the diagrams he had chalked for his wing in their tactical planning sessions the evening before as they waited for the Americans to deliver the planes. The technical limitations of their lower-tech, but reliable missile choices dictated all new plans.

Two more hits and now he had only one Foxbat to deal with. That pilot, suddenly finding himself alone in the sky with two deadly Eagles on his trail, fired up his afterburners and headed home; counting on his superior speed to take him out of harm's way. Yossi let him go and followed his radar to where he had left his friends dueling in a two-on-two dogfight. By the time he arrived a minute and a half later, his services were no longer needed. Their other four planes were not quite so lucky. One of Yossi's friends lost a wing and had to bail somewhere over the Med – which was a better place for an Israeli airman to go down than the current Sinai... but dangerous with their limited communications. There were no choppers for a pick up, and so the Israeli navy, the half of it that was running, would have to race the Egyptian patrol boats for the prize. However, the six-to-three advantage soon dwindled to five-to-three, and when Yossi's four Eagles showed up to help out, the odds were suddenly seven Israeli birds to five Foxbats. Three of the Foxbats might have made it home... they were doing Mach two by the time they left Yossi's tactical radar screen.

Thanks to the morning's action, Yossi's wing of F-15s was down to six for their second turn in the cockpits. Another bird had gone down in the next pilot rotation and their hot and heavy dog fighting action. The two wings of F-16s were down three planes lost, and one grounded for repairs. The total operating IAF was now Yossi's six F-15s, and twelve F-16 falcons. That is, unless one counted the four prop-driven IAF trainers that got off the ground that morning. They estimated thirty confirmed Egyptian kills, and two maybes. They knew Egypt must have more planes, but none had come to greet them in the last two hours. Perhaps it was tea time – or perhaps there was a really tough half-time pep talk going on in their flight rooms right now.

However, Jordan was on Yossi's mind as he lifted off, for he was headed north for the first time that day in a long overdue mission to relieve the intense assaults on IDF forces in the upper Jordan Valley. And, the question top-most in his mind was, where was the Jordanian Air Force hiding, and would they come out to play? Once again, he left armed for air-to-air combat – though the sidewinders would do perfectly well if fired at a nice warm tank or fuel truck. He wondered which the eight pointed arrows would pierce – bird or beast?

The answer to that question was not long in coming. A dozen birds showed up on his radar, gaining altitude and closing rapidly. He would need visual on them, but Yossi suspected they were the pride of the RJAF – US made F-16s. His twin-engined, twin-tailed F-15s were bigger, heavier, more powerful and perhaps a shade newer – but not enough to give him an edge in technology. The F-16 could match him turn for turn, climb for climb, g-force for g-force. Their edge would have to be their greater experience and natural Israeli chutzpah.

Yossi barked out his game plan in their scrambled voice link: "We're splitting three and three, home base is Mt. Pisgah – I'm going high and east, Yair, you are with me and Uri, Yoni – you go see Mt. Hermon and come back to see what kind of pickings you can find at about 10,000 meters....One, two, three split!"

He headed straight east, firing a pair of sidewinders to confuse and rattle the oncoming enemy – even though the chance of hitting something head-on was nil – it worked. At the same time he began to climb and accelerate to threaten to drop in behind any Jordanian who persisted on their original course, or vectored north to go after Yoni's group. The tactic worked, his three were climbing cleanly away from the pack of 12, who had to slam on their figurative brakes and slew around to the south in order to keep him in their sights. His maneuver also drew the pack of enemy jets back over their own territory, where they had an equal chance of being shot down by their own over-eager air defenses as he did. Unfortunately, nothing launched from the Jordanian landscape below him, so he would have to sow his own confusion. Now, to lead his pack of hounds in hot pursuit; but not too hot, back over Mt. Pisgah – the final resting place of Moses overlooking the Jordan Valley and Jericho.

Yair and Uri were right on his wing tips as they prepared for their next split. They had been steadily accelerating and climbing to near their 20,000 meter ceiling. Yair would stay high and trace a broad loop, trying to fall in behind and pick off any of their pursuing pack, while Yossi and Uri would pull a diving turn and hurtle back through the hounds, guns blazing and lead them on another fast chase, spilling altitude and gaining speed until they led right back to the killing zone over Mt. Pisgah. If they timed it right, Yoni and friends would have a couple shots at evening the odds, and Yair might get lucky on their fox and hounds run to Mt. Pisgah.

On Yossi's signal, he and Uri slammed into a hard, gut-wrenching, diving turn while Yair thundered away to gain his freedom. Two birds went after Yair... he would have to shake them himself. Ten scattered as he and Uri blazed back through their pack. As soon as they regrouped on his tail, it would be a straight speed contest until Yoni showed up. He felt the slight shock wave as they crossed the sound barrier on their way to Mach 2+. Windows would be breaking all over Jordan, too bad he had to fly so high. He could really rattle them good if he could fly lower. Uri split wider on his wing as they thundered along their 10,000 meter down slope. A pair of Jordanian missiles flew overhead high and wide. Once they hit Mach 2, there would be little chance of an air-to-air catching them. He could see the brown and faint green map of Jordan unroll beneath his wings until the rounded hump of Mt. Pisgah and the Jordan Valley beyond appeared dead ahead; 12,000 meters, 2,000 more to go. Radar showed the chasing pack strung out behind him, panting for the kill, too many blips to count.

The split second he blazed over the Jordan River at twice the speed of sound, Yossi put his hard-working bird on its tail and climbed again, splitting northwards. When he finished his loop and came down again looking for his prey, there were at least two less Jordanians, for he could see their smoke where a sidewinder had done its work. He had no idea where Yair was with his two playmates, but counted on him to take care of himself. His quarry was scrambling to get out of his sights by dropping to the valley floor and rolling left and right. He chose the right-hand pair of planes, for it would take him back over Jordan. He much preferred dead airplanes falling on Jordan than his beloved Israel. The thought of ejecting over enemy territory did not cross his mind as a worry now. Two more sidewinders, one less Jordanian. He and Uri relentlessly pursued the remaining plane of the pair they stalked. The nimble, single-tailed F-16 dodged three missiles before being run to earth and nailed by their coordinated effort.

Climbing back for altitude and a view of the situation, Yossi and Uri found themselves alone in the sky with their four companions. From their reports, the score was quickly reset to Israel 6 – Jordan 0. The other six birds had scattered towards the interior.

"Everyone OK?" Yossi asked. Getting five resounding yeses, he led his pack north up the Jordan Valley to hunt some armored prey on the ground. Their instructions were to use their 20 mm cannons to strafe and burn, while saving their side-winders in case of trouble on their return trip. Twenty minutes of hot strafing action on the highways and troop concentrations north of Beit She'an took them to their safe return margins – with room for another dog fight should any pups come out to challenge the top dogs. Yossi could tell from the massed targets on the ground and the totally uncoordinated anti-aircraft fire, which was surprisingly light, that their appearance in the sky over the Jordan Valley was completely unexpected. Two birds took turns flying cover against interceptors as the other four shot their magazines empty, evening out a very lop-sided situation on the ground as best they could.

Although Yossi talked a tough chatter over the radio, he was secretly glad not to face another fresh wing of Royal Jordanian Air Force jets on the way home. Their return trip took them within sight of Jerusalem, and almost on impulse, Yossi took his wing directly over the beautiful city, low enough for their IAF markings to inspire courage in any Jewish hearts, and gladden any Jewish eye that lifted its sight to the heavens to greet their thundering pass. It risked their lives, but felt like perhaps the most important thing he had done all day. The thrill of air-to-air combat kills was dampened by the choking emotion he felt in making his aerial salute to Yerushalaim as it sped past him in the golden haze of dust and smoke.

Northern Defense Command, Mt. Meron 15:00

Anna and her staff followed the news of each flight of their "borrowed" fighter jets with anxious elation. Each loss struck them hard, some to tears even, and each victory was cheered despite their many other tasks. Her hard working group was now coordinating all radio traffic for the northern districts. Given the relatively short ranges and few possible frequencies of the EMP-proof radio sets they had sent out by perilous motorcycle messengers, they had to relay between command groups that were often only a dozen kilometers from each other, but a long way away from the more powerful base stations high on Mt. Meron. This tied up practically every available non-combat soldier on the mountain top – those who were not already involved in keeping the radars and various antennae in one piece and working order. More and more, her operators were falling into the daunting task of logistics – getting food, fuel, medical aid, and most importantly, ammunition to where it was most needed.

She herself had been working their international communications, coordinating with US command groups to fill a seven-page "shopping list" of essential items to keep their war effort alive. A few tramp freighters were being chartered out of minor ports in the Adriatic – mostly from Yugoslavia and Croatia – and at least one of them was now on its way from Cyprus and hoping to make landfall near Haifa tomorrow. It would be a small but welcome drop in a very large bucket that needed filling. It would be met by a pair of patrol boats and escorted in.

Anna had never given much thought to the Israeli Navy. It was the most overlooked and least glamorous of the Israeli armed services. However, in this war, it proved the most reliable. Thanks to the foresight of some unsung admiral and various technical advisory committees, slightly more than half of Israel's small fleet of patrol craft were EMP-hardened. Their reliable conventional engines started, their radars and radios worked, and together they formed an off-shore network of communications and support that was stretched to the limit up and down the Mediterranean coast. In fact, Anna heard via her growing network of radio links, that it was the Navy, with its offshore guns, that was keeping large areas of Ashkelon and Ashdod in the south from being completely overrun. They had also raided the attacking forces wherever they dared approach the coastline – forcing them to turn to rougher interior roads to move supplies through the Sinai. And just recently, one of the speedy little boats had out-raced its Egyptian counterparts to pluck an F-16 pilot from the drink off the Sinai. That had provoked cheers as the news spread around their mountaintop command center.

Every six hours they held as brief a "status and update" meeting as possible – just so that everyone got the bigger picture beyond the link in the chain they were busy trying to hold together. The news from the south of Israel was almost unanimously bad – except for their victories in the air over everything that the Egyptian air force had tried to fly against them. The score, assiduously kept by the IAF radar captain, was now something like Israel 38, Egypt 6 – if you count the plane that limped home so full of bullet holes that one could see daylight through the fuselage. And the latest news of the first sortie up the Jordan Valley was just in: Israel 6, Jordan 0. That sent cheers resounding in the crowded cave command groups in the trailers, situation room and jury rigged radio relay rooms.

Their local neighborhood was much improved. Missile strikes on the mountain had dropped dramatically. The IDF groups on the base and at the neighboring bases were able to get more and more equipment running, including a few newer model tanks, a growing number of APC's, jeeps and half tracks. The garages on each of the bases were becoming expert in re-wiring and re-fitting as fast as their mechanics and electricians and various volunteer crews could manage. However, there was ominous news of a large armored force swinging away from the Golan Heights and threatening to join up with the Syrian armies that were pressing south already against a shaky line that was holding, but just barely, between Rosh Pina and somewhere south of Katzrin,. The retreating IDF had been pushed out of the latter town after two days of bitter, street-to-street fighting. She would have a clearer picture when the afternoon satellite intelligence was relayed through their American friends.

Anna had another battle on her mind as well, the inevitable PR battle in the world press – which was always eager to condemn Israel as the aggressor and villain no matter what the facts were. She and Kobi were doing their best to get the facts out: that Israel did not strike first, that there had been a coordinated, vicious and overwhelming attack launched at her civilians from all sides: and that Israel was defending itself and needed help from anyone who cared to preserve freedom, democracy and an open society in one of the darkest, most dangerous corners of the world.

As always, the worldwide Jewish community had rallied to the cause, but was confused as to the actual facts on the ground. Some feared a complete disaster, and others assumed that the situation was overblown and would sort itself out in a few more days as one more bloody scrap in Israel's battle-scarred history. She had hastily formed European and American committees apprised of the facts as best she could get them out, and each was working at top speed to round up as much support as possible.

Anna and Kobi had another project dear to their hearts – getting Radio Israel back on the airwaves. In his spare time… which was minutes here and there, Kobi had scrounged the bare bones of a broadcasting studio and located it in one of the men's bedrooms. He had inspired his antenna team to wire them up to one of the AM transmitters still operating. They had assembled an ad-hoc group of volunteer disc jockeys, and the last part of each quarterly status briefing was devoted to deciding what news they could safely broadcast without compromising the security situation. They were filling the air time between their hourly news broadcasts, which started that morning at 0600, with the very eclectic music collection that made its way down into the intelligence bunker in peacetime. Thanks to Kobi, much of the choices were heavy metal and Israeli rock bands, and a soldier from the topside group had contributed a vast collection of oldies. But it was better than dead air, and any Israel with a working radio – they had no idea if there were many or just a few – would find a signal coming in as strong as they could make it on the traditional national news channel.

Eli had just finished *davening mincha* and lay down to nap until it was safer to cross the border. As he lay there, stretched out in the warm shade of an ancient olive tree that was more gnarled trunk than branches, he became aware of a rhythmic beating sound. Sam, who had dropped off for a nap while Eli *davened*, jumped to his feet and started anxiously scanning the sky to the east. Then Eli realized what he was hearing – helicopters – definitely more than one. By now the thumpa thumpa thumpeta of a cruising helicopter was unmistakable. Sam looked around to size up the available cover and options – and chose to take a few steps and lean casually against the twisting trunks of the old olive tree. He kept his AK-47 only a short shift from being at the ready. Eli remembered that they were supposed to look like a truck load of Syrian locals. He glanced around to see if Captain Tzippori's parachute looked anything like a chute. He didn't think it would be noticeable from a distant helicopter, even if they had a pair of field glasses on them.

Of course, they might be mistaken for deserting soldiers – for there had been a certain number of young men at the *souk* who looked suspiciously like they belonged elsewhere, and who had kept in the background whenever an official looking army vehicle had passed. Eli wouldn't have noticed it if Rabbi Beniyahu had not pointed it out in his half-whispered commentary. The Rabbi was certainly looking the part of an older Arab, and sat apparently unperturbed by the approaching helicopters. Soon they could see a low-flying formation of three menacing dark helicopter gunships approaching from the east, following their highway. Eli nearly fainted when he saw Sam cheerfully wave at them as they passed. The door gunners, quite visible as they passed nearby, waved regally back.

All four of them followed the flight of helicopters, and realized, each in their own moments, that their path, angling north and west to follow the track of the army, would take them right past the hill where they had left their tank and jeep escort. Eli found it hard to breathe as he watched the three deadly choppers fly over the mass of supply trucks squeezing through the border and saw them angle northwards towards the head of the column, which had long ago disappeared out of sight. They did not vary their speed or the pitch of their rotors, and he could breathe easier as they began to slowly disappear from sight.

Sam, however, grew more agitated as they faded into the distance. He scanned the eastern sky for more. Then he turned and tried to take in every detail of the supply column making its way through the winding narrow track across no-man's-land and the border fences. "Got to risk it," he muttered. He went and pulled Eli's long-range sniper rifle from where it was rolled up in the coveralls behind the seat of the pickup. He carried the rifle, still hidden in the bundle of coveralls, over to his olive tree, climbed up into a crotch of the tree where the branches began to spread, and unwrapped the rifle and its scope. With the high powered scope, he began to study the road back towards the village, the various army trucks and scavengers milling through the gap in the border, and up and down the road. Eli watched as he scanned the hill where their escort had been hidden. He also peered off towards the north along the line of trucks of the advancing Syrian forces. After checking nearly all directions at least two or three times, he wrapped the rifle back up and climbed nimbly back down to come over to where Eli, Rabbi Beniyahu and Yishai sat, watching over the unconscious pilot who lay wrapped in the folds of his parachute, breathing shallowly, but easily whenever they bent low to check.

"I need to get back to Captain Klein and start figuring out how to get to that bunker," Sam said urgently, "assuming that he is still there. How three helicopters could miss two 65-ton tanks and a pair of jeeps at that range – no matter how well camouflaged – is almost beyond me. If there are three choppers flying – that's two more than yesterday's satellite photos showed, which is seriously bad news. Traffic is clearing up through the crossing, and nothing else is coming from the direction of the village and base – so I'm thinking we can slip through at the tail end of the looters. There's only an hour and a bit until sunset, and maybe half an hour of twilight to work with after that…. I'd like to be back over here with a commando group by then. What do you say about moving now?"

Eli looked at Rabbi Beniyahu and Yishai, who looked thoughtful, but not to the point of speaking yet. "I've been thinking about how to transport Captain Tzippori in the truck," Eli said. "The problem is that the bed is eight feet, but the wood burning apparatus takes up about the first two and a half feet. The captain is maybe five feet eight – I forget what that is in centimeters, because I still think in feet and inches when it comes to height … but you see the problem. I don't think we want to bend that leg. And we still don't know much about neck or spinal injuries, except that he must have had a fair bit of movement to cut the bandages – and milk a goat for that matter. So I think putting him diagonally would not be very good – which might mean driving him with the tailgate down."

Yishai, who had adopted the captain as his patient, though he was a farmer, not a doctor, agreed with most of Eli's assessment, but thought he could arrange the pilot more or less diagonally without injuring him. "I've been trying to think what we could put in the back of the truck to hide him better. It wouldn't make sense to be headed into Israel with a load of firewood at this point – or hay, or goats, or just about anything I could think of." Yishai said. "All the donkeys, cars, carts and trucks we saw headed for the border were pretty much filled with men and boys – except for two I noticed, that had women aboard. Maybe they were being taken along to choose what to bring back? I don't know, but it got me to thinking…"

Rabbi Beniyahu spoke up at this point… "I think you are on to something there. A properly dressed woman is something that your average Syrian man will not look at – if her husband is around, that is. Unfortunately, they are more polite than the average Israeli on that point. Perhaps if Yishai and I pulled our robes over our heads and arranged some kind of veils – we could make a reasonable resemblance to a chaddur, especially if we are sitting down in the back of the truck. We could cover up the captain and make him perhaps look like a sleeping woman... that way we might be OK even if someone looked directly into the bed – which I doubt."

Sam thought about it and agreed, and they quickly moved into action. Sam stashed the rifle behind the front seat again after taking a last long look around with the scope, especially studying their route back though the border – which appeared to be cleared of supply trucks, and starting to empty of its swarm of looters. Most of the mob headed back south towards the overrun settlements, but a fair number headed north, following at the heels of the disappearing army. That would make their short jog to the north along the highway to the trail that led back to their hilltop rendezvous look less suspicious.

Eli lowered the tailgate and arranged their bundles so that they could ease the wounded pilot carefully into the bed of the truck. Then Rabbi Beniyahu and Yishai climbed in after him, one on each side and arranged him so they could lift the tailgate again. Once their patient was settled, the two men began fixing their bulky robes. There was some chuckling and even a giggle or two as they tried various ties and wraps – looking more and more like a pair of dumpy, aged Arab women with each invention. Rabbi Beniyahu padded his getup with some strategically bunched up extra clothes – provoking a roar of laughter from Yishai – who proceeded to outdo him in enhancing his unnatural endowments until he looked quite buxom himself. Sam, who was busy being anxious and worried throughout their loading and preparations, doubled over with a good, tension relieving laugh as well. Eli was still smirking as he climbed into the driver's seat and eased the truck around. He couldn't help breaking into a big grin every time he glanced in the mirror to see his two wives and sleeping lady in the back. It totally spoiled the effect of his darkened skin and big black beret.

However, as they rolled slowly down the track back down to the road, all of them had sobered up considerably. To any prying eyes, the two ladies were looking modestly down at their sleeping sister, though the road was empty when they reached it. Sam had settled into the passenger seat, his AK-47 held just below the window level, ready for quick action. There were only a few donkey riders and donkey cart drivers plodding their way towards the border. No one gave them more than a second glance. The sun was getting low in the western sky as they reached the now well-traveled track that wound through the minefields and through the fences. Someone, probably the ammunition convoy, had taken the time to cut away the fallen fences and mark both sides of the passage with upright posts here and there. Eli made as good a time as he could without rattling their injured passenger. Nobody gave them more than a passing look over, even a jeep full of soldiers that was parked by the road where they reached the highway in Israel. They appeared to be waiting for someone or something, and looked away as soon as they saw the two "women."

Eli turned north and was glad to accelerate away from them, feeling the first flood of relief to be back into Israel – even though it was still overrun with more enemy than he had been able to count. They passed a lone ammunition truck pulled over on the narrow shoulder, tipping somewhat precariously as they tried to change a driver's side tire in a spot that Eli thought was plain stupid. The truck was threatening to topple over onto them and their mis-placed jack. Had they merely pulled off the highway a few dozen meters further, there was a far better spot for changing a tire. Sam eyed their load greedily as they slowed to edge past – it looked like the big artillery shells that they had ferried across the Kinneret two days ago. Eli could hear the driver and his mate arguing loudly as they slowly passed.

Sam pointed out the track where they had come down the hill a few hundred meters past the still-tipping ammunition truck. He kept stealing glances back over his shoulder. He fidgeted and kept peering towards the truck as they shifted into low and began to worm their way up the hill, until they disappeared over a shoulder of the hill and the truck moved out of sight. However, they could now see the tail end of the looters and army still streaming northwards. The sun was getting near the horizon behind the hill, occasionally flashing in Eli's eyes – but the smoke and haze made the setting sun much dimmer than it should have been, and he was able to see fine with no windshield between him and the setting sun. Now that they were safely away from Syria, Eli and Sam began to talk again, enough to ask the "women" how their patient was doing. "Still breathing," reassured them slightly. But, Sam was so absorbed in his thoughts that he answered absently – and soon Eli gave up and concentrated on following the two tracks that led up their hill.

They were past the top and quite near where Eli was sure they had left their escort early that morning before he spotted some movement in a clump of bushes. However, when he looked back to see what it was that moved, he saw two camouflaged figures emerge from the vegetation, and then he saw cogged wheels and a bit of tank track where he had just seen bush. Sam was already waving at the figures, and told Eli to drive closer to the huge bush. It was the tall and the short tanker captains. He noticed a smaller bush beyond them begin to move, and saw there was a jeep underneath. No wonder the helicopters had not spotted a thing as they flew by. They greeted the two captains, and quickly told them of their situation with the gravely injured pilot – news which both saddened and cheered them.

A few minutes later, Eli, Sam, Rabbi Beniyahu, the two tanker captains and a lieutenant from the jeeps were gathered in their observation bushes overlooking the Syrian border and holding a brief council of war. It was nearly five in the afternoon, and the sun was getting redder in the western sky as it prepared to set in perhaps half an hour. The day had already grown somewhat dimmer. Their meeting was startled by a pair of deep booms in the sky almost directly overhead, followed by the faint roar of jet engines and more distant booms to the south. Eli looked straight overhead in alarm, looking for the source of the sound – but Sam and his companions had already adjusted their gaze to scan the skies to the north – recognizing the sonic boom of a supersonic aircraft – and knowing it was already far ahead of its sound wave.

The tall captain, who Eli recalled was named David something, was first to spot the disappearing specs with his binoculars. "Twin tails – F-15s unless they have some of the newer MIG 31s flying," he said as he followed the vanishing specks. He watched them until they almost disappeared, and then appeared to climb even higher, come to a standstill in the distant sky, and turn back towards them. This time they were prepared for the new sonic booms that rattled them and resounded from the hills around them, and Eli was able to discern the high-flying planes as they raced south again.

"What on earth are they doing?" the soldiers wondered, "Think they're ours?"

"I sure hope so, because we have a helicopter problem," Sam said, drawing the discussion back to their starting point. What is the best way to complete their mission and keep the Syrians from resurrecting any more attack helicopters? Sam challenged the group. Their original plan called for another group of tanks to join them, and sweep down on the loosely guarded camp in a lightning raid. But the other squad of tanks and the company of soldiers and artillery batteries that had been picked to take back the overrun kibbutz to their south had been needed urgently elsewhere, so they were on their own.

Sam took a moment to check up on the progress of the tire change on the ammunition truck – and on the waiting four soldiers in the jeep at the border – both of which were in plain sight from their hill top. Satisfied, he quickly outlined a new plan.

"I think I can get into that camp with that ammo truck and a jeep full of soldiers if we can find a couple more Arabic speakers. We can pass ourselves off as bringing in some special equipment for the excavations and recovery. We might be able to drive right up to the hole and do a little demolition work."

"You trained in that?" the taller captain asked – "because I have the perfect man for the job if it involves blowing something up..." The shorter captain, Yankel, chuckled. Sam admitted that his reconnaissance training had involved some minor demolition, but nothing too complex. He said he would be glad to have an expert along. Yankel snorted at the word "expert," but no one asked him to explain, for the jeep platoon leader cut in.

"I have two Haifa kids who speak a passable Arabic, and I can at least understand most of what's being said.

Yankel jumped in at this point and said, "OK, I think I see where you are going with this – but I'm not going to sit here looking like a bush while there is a big fat juicy supply train not five K from here and all their tanks twice as far ahead of them. David and I are going hunting until we run out of shells again. You can have his gunner for your demo work. We'll grab one of your team for a loader. Now, how do you plan to borrow that truck and take out the squad in the jeep?"

Sam told them about the sniper rifle, and Eli strained to understand the clipped, fast moving Hebrew, which was so full of jargon he could hardly follow. Less than five minutes later, the plan, which involved a two-tank charge after the disappearing supply column, and Sam and one of the tankers and the soldiers from the two jeeps heading into Syria – this time with destruction in their hearts, not a quiet trip to the *souk* and some intelligence gathering. Sam asked Eli if he felt up to returning to the Moshav with the injured pilot, the rabbi and Yishai – without the sniper rifle, but with the AK-47 just in case. Eli looked at Rabbi Beniyahu for assurance. He was still wearing his robe in a womanly fashion, without the headscarf and veil – but with his added endowments still stuffed in his bosom. It made an oddly discordant sight with his perpetually disheveled white beard. However, seeing the old Rabbi's calm face still looking serene, and yet perfectly aware of each of the complications – Eli agreed.

They climbed back in the truck after a quick change over of weapons. Sam showed Eli how to load a clip, chamber and unchamber a round, use the safety lock, and the lever for switching to automatic fire if needed. Sam drew out the sniper rifle and scope – leaving Eli's coveralls and taking the small pouch of shells – down to less than 300 rounds now. He gathered up his knapsack, and they paused a moment for a silent hug of goodbye. They heard the tanks rumble to life as their crews threw off about half of the camouflage – for there were still three and possible more helicopters somewhere in the skies. As Sam turned to leave, a powerfully built tanker jogged over, calling to them and holding up a familiar looking knapsack – the belongings they had left ages ago that morning. Sam collected his few personal items, hugged and kissed Rabbi Beniyahu, shook hands with Yishai and trotted off to put his plan into action.

Yishai climbed in the back to ride with his patient, and Rabbi Beniyahu climbed into the cab, cradling the AK-47 in a familiar way that let Eli know he knew how to use it. Eli restarted the truck and headed for home. They had not gone more than fifty meters when the first rifle shot cracked from the bushes on the hilltop. Others followed in a deliberate succession. Eli had no doubt that Sam was well on his way to picking off the two truckers

– who were probably cut down in mid-argument, and the four soldiers in the jeep – who would be dead before they knew what hit them.

Given the setting sun and the urgency of their injured companion, Rabbi Beniyahu said that they should say their *mincha* prayers while driving – and he offered to say them aloud with Eli so that he could concentrate on his driving. All of them added a silent prayer for their companions, their safety and success, and for the fragile health of their brave pilot.

Syrian Border 17:15

Benny nearly skipped away from the brush-covered tank, clutching the "mad bomber" toolkit he had quickly thrown together within minutes of David telling him his new mission. He gave Greg a few last minute pointers on their improvised and improved optical gun sights, shook hands with the big soldier recruited from the recon group to be their new loader while Greg took over as gunner, and ran to catch the jeep that was about to go to Syria. It felt good to be able to move again.

Captain David Klein felt the same as he watched his pyromaniac gunner run towards the waiting jeep. Yankel's tank, still trailing about half its brush covering, pitched forward and out of sight over the crest of the hill, and Sasha threw their tank into gear and they were off with a roar. The diesel engine was running smoother thanks to a pit stop in the moshav potato barn the previous evening. David could feel the fuller power surging through his steel chariot as they rumbled down the hill in pursuit of Yankel. As they reached the road, he could see that Sam and the first jeep's crew were well on their way to changing the flat tire on their commandeered ammunition truck. A few hundred meters beyond them, the Syrian jeep at the border crossing showed no signs of movement. Benny, hanging on with his box of goodies and grinning from ear to ear as the second jeep peeled off, gave them a wave as they pulled onto the road. David's *Gimmel* One headed north in pursuit of Yankel's *Alef* One, and the jeep raced south to see what could be salvaged from the ambushed Syrians. He silently wished them luck and turned his attention to the road ahead of him.

David was plenty familiar with the highway running along the Israeli Syrian border, and so was Sasha, his driver. They caught up with Yankel a few kilometers north as the big, brush covered tank slowed to bully its way through the confused crowd of looters donkeys and vehicles. Yankel's tank was blowing its horn – an odd sound coming from a big pile of armored brush – and he was letting go a few rounds from the machine gun over the startled heads of the largely civilian crowd of would-be looters. They were so amazed at the sight of a pair of Israeli tanks in their midst that they milled and got tangled up with each other getting off the road. However they scattered much faster when the cannon of Yankel's tank boomed with a fiery blast over their heads, and a few seconds later he heard the multiple blasts of a direct hit on an ammunition truck.

David kept one nervous eye on the milling mob as they edged through the last of them. He saw the barrel of his own main gun angling up for a shot. He didn't see anyone daring to point a weapon at them – although there were rifles and pistols aplenty in the nasty looking crowd. All appeared too astounded or too afraid to shoot, and equally amazed that they were not being slaughtered on sight. A different scene flashed through David's mind as he imagined two Syrian tanks coming across a mob of Israelis in a similar strait. He felt angry at the mere thought, and turned his attention to the line of supply trucks that stretched out ahead. He called down to Greg to aim for the farthest trucks in his gunsights. He wanted to cut off the hindmost segment of the column from escape. Armed looters were disgusting – but not his immediate enemy. His shells were meant for the truckloads of death and destruction intended for his homeland. At the blast of his cannon firing away over their heads, donkeys scattered dumping their riders and upsetting carts. The minute the road was clear ahead of them, Sasha accelerated to close the distance to the ammunition column.

Once clear of the milling mob of camp followers, the two tanks fell upon the tail end of the long supply chain like a pair of ravening wolves upon a flock of lambs. The Syrian commander, in his ignorance or arrogance, had neglected to follow his supply train with a rear guard capable of dealing with a pair of Israeli tanks. The two armored personnel carriers that followed in the dust of the supply column were dispatched in the first few rounds from Yankel and David's tanks as they closed to within less than half a kilometer of the now burning end of the line of trucks. Once they had taken care of any threat from the armored personnel carriers, Yankel shelled as far forward in the column as his gunner could see – cutting off escape in that direction with burning trucks and exploding ammunition. The tactic was absolutely ruthless and completely effective. In the next twenty minutes, the two tanks pumped more than forty shells each into the milling mass of stopped trucks full of tank and artillery shells with no where to go but sky high as round after round of the two tanks' fire hit home.

The havoc they created and the element of surprise was so great, and the Syrian's communications and decision making was so poor, that it was twenty minutes before the first handful of tanks began firing at them from amid the smoke and confusion. Doubling back against the traffic jam of their stalled convoy, the Syrian rear guard could only reach the point where the line of destruction began. There was a mass of burning or fleeing trucks in between them and the Israeli marauders.

Golan! Day Three

Night had fallen, adding to the chaos. Instead of retreating, Yankel and David pressed forward along the left flank of the stalled, burning and exploding column of trucks, staying well away from the effective range of any accurate small arms fire. Soon there were tanks burning and exploding in the firestorm of confusion where the column had been cut off from the rest of the advance. David kept his machine gun busy as sporadic shots pinged off their armor from soldiers lucky enough to escape the devastated supply column, and level headed enough to return fire. An occasional rocket propelled grenade challenged them, but all were fired wild or short of the ever-moving pair of predators.

Pausing only to take better aim with their makeshift optical sights, the pair of tanks leapfrogged each other, moving cross country and ranging along the flanks of the column. As they neared the point where their shells had first bisected the line, Yankel was able to concentrate his fire further forwards, cutting off another segment for destruction, while David kept any resistance at bay. Greg was proving a very capable gunner, and the loader borrowed from the recon group was keeping up with him fine. They gained a high point opposite the carnage of the highway and saw the next mass of armor beginning to turn and race back to beat off their attack.

"Time to run," David thought to himself, and the rational side of his brain seconded the motion when there was a tap on his leg from the loader, who shouted "Last ten shells!" They had left that morning with a fairly full load of 56 rounds. Thanks to the well-stocked caverns near Tiberias and their improved cross-lake shuttles and trucking, there were still a couple cases of machine gun ammo left. He bent down and told his gunner to begin aiming to sow confusion in the mass of turning and oncoming tanks as best he could, while David began scanning the dark landscape for an escape route. With his machine gun, he kept firing short bursts into whatever trucks he could see still intact – and was often rewarded to see their cargo catch fire and begin to explode. Several gasoline tankers had been hit and were sending towering flames into the dark sky, which was making their targets stand out in stark relief.

Yankel was still firing mostly at the stalled convoy – for he knew that such an opportunity to destroy the enemy's supply line so completely only came once. He was making every shot count, and plying his machine gun with a vengeance. David, however, was able to keep part of his mind clear of the race to destroy and kept it firmly on the need to survive. He spotted his line of retreat at the same moment that Yankel's tank took a devastating hit less than 100 meters away. The energy of the impact between shell and onrushing armor sent a shockwave that hit David in the chest like a sandbag. He staggered on his firestep and clung to his machine gun to recover. In the next few moments, fire engulfed the front of Yankel's tank, as it was stopped in its tracks. It had taken a direct hit to the front – where the engine, slow-burning diesel fuel tanks and heavy armor protected it best, but a 125 mm direct hit none the less. A second later the crew door opened and the loader staggered out, his fire-proof suit ablaze with burning fuel.

Without being told, Sasha, who had been sizing up David's shouted escape route, gunned their tank over to pick up the crewman, who had the presence of mind and training to drop and roll in the dirt to put out the flaming fuel. In that instant, David saw Yankel slumped over his silent machine gun, not moving, garishly lit by the flames that consumed the front of the tank. Their tanks had closed to within a dozen meters. Not thinking, he vaulted out of his turret and ran to the burning tank. He took a gulp of air and entered the open crew door at the rear, and groped for the gunner where instinct told him he should be. He felt a pair of coveralls, grabbed a handful and pulled with all his might. An unconscious weight slid toward him, and he grabbed a second handful and tugged the gunner free. Then he did something that his brain told him was useless, dangerous and would probably get him killed, but he did it anyway. He left the unconscious gunner on the ground and leapt up on the back of the tank, staggered forward against the heat of the blaze, and seized Yankel's inert form by the back of his tanker's suit and hauled him by sheer force out of the now-burning hatchway and onto the rear deck.

Bullets flew around him, and the air was alive with shells, but David did not care. He could not leave his friend's body there, even if it meant dying together. Sasha apparently felt the same way, for he had parked in the lee of the burning tank, grabbed the lifeless body of the gunner, fireman-carried it to their tank, and heaved him onto the front deck. The dazed loader had managed to stagger to the back of their tank and was dousing his face and arms with water from one of the sacks that hung by their rear hatch. David dragged Yankel's body to where he could load it onto his shoulders. It smelled of diesel fuel and burnt flesh, and he dared not look at its face. He carried it to his waiting tank and heaved it onto the front quarter. Fortunately, their borrowed loader had the presence of mind to climb up and take over David's duties at the machine gun, for the small arms fire was growing intense in its absence, and a pair of rocket propelled grenades burst against the side of the already burning tank.

David ran around his stopped tank as Sasha vaulted back into the driver's hatch. He pushed the dazed loader in ahead of him and had just pulled the crew door closed when their tank spun on its treads and raced away. The turret swiveled 180 degrees, and the loader slid down to make way for David to climb back up to his perch. Tears streaming from his burning eyes, David emptied the machine gun's magazine into the blazing darkness, mechanically reloaded and forced himself back into the discipline of look, aim, fire again. All he could see was darkness and flame, there was little to aim for, except when the bright blasts of tank cannon revealed their positions in the growing darkness. He was grateful that the turret was facing backwards, and he could not see his two dead friends where they had been dumped on the front. Sasha must be at eye level with them, he thought between bursts. Sasha was bowling along with no regard for bumps or breaks in the rough terrain, and it was impossible for Greg to even think of hitting a target.

Their borrowed loader soon appeared at the observation hatch and began to ply that machine gun as they left the burning column in their wake and struck out cross country at top speed. After another minute or two, David told him to stop – for the blaze of their machine gun fire was probably doing more to show the enemy their whereabouts than it was preventing pursuit. They both stopped firing and peered behind them in the darkness to see how close their pursuers could be. A few times they saw flashes light up dark shapes of tanks where they fired their cannons. Every now and then a shell burst near enough to them to tell him they were still in the enemy's sights. He silently urged their 27-year-old Merkava onwards.

Syria 17:50

Sam elected to drive the ammunition truck himself once the jeep's crew had changed the tire. He had spent those few precious minutes poking around in the spacious, canvas covered cargo bed taking stock of the load of artillery shells with Benny, the demolitions expert he had borrowed from the tankers. Benny knew his shells, fuses and timers and was delighted to have a good selection for the work at hand, including some incendiary rounds that caused him to chortle with boyish delight. Sam liked a man who was enthusiastic about his work. Unfortunately, the uniforms they had hoped to borrow were severely bloodstained, but khaki is khaki, and camouflage is camouflage, so Sam had to satisfy himself with collecting the truckers' hats and insignias. Fortunately one of the drivers had left a uniform jacket hung on a hook behind the bench seat which was big enough for Sam. The driver was apparently a sergeant, which perhaps explained the endless argument that Sam had passed less than an hour earlier. A sergeant's stripes would do just fine for his new position. Benny had the presence of mind to bring along some generic-looking fatigues with no markings, and he had given his replacement gunner his fireproof tanker's coveralls. The two of them tied the rear flaps of the cargo bed's canopy closed.

Satisfied, the two climbed into the cab and Sam drove up to where he could turn the ponderous truck around on the narrow road. A few minutes later they pulled up to the borrowed Syrian jeep. The two Israeli jeeps had been stashed a good two hundred meters from the busy road, and had gone back to looking like bushes. Sam regarded the four men in the jeep in the gathering twilight and in the headlights of his tall truck. They managed to look like a presentable crew of nondescript Syrian soldiers – with perhaps a certain special look of competence and pride that went with being demolition specialists – which is what they were to be. Sam waved them forwards towards the obvious track through the border. There was no need for scouting now that hundreds of trucks had rolled through the gap between the fences.

When they reached the highway on the Syrian side of the border, he pulled ahead to lead the way through the now dark town, for there was still no electricity working anywhere in the western two-thirds of Syria. It felt odd to be headed back to the sleepy little Syrian town again. It hardly seemed like the same day. And the view from the tall, lumbering six-ton truck was decidedly different than from the back of Woody. Sam wondered how everyone was doing, and if they had reached the moshav safely. To distract himself, he began getting to know his demolitions expert in the minutes that remained before they arrived at the Syrian depot.

Benny, he found out, was a reservist who had crewed with Captain Klein for more than ten years. He knew his ammunition and explosives like any good tanker. But as they talked, Sam began to gather that Benny's actual demolitions experience was, well, somewhat freelance and self taught. However, as he probed deeper, he was treated to a story about the tanker's fireworks display for the amusement of the Syrian sheep roast. He began to think that maybe this grinning, overgrown boy might know something useful on the subject. He was certainly impressed with the makeshift mortars and Benny's finale of blowing the tank and the path out of the gully. Unfortunately, he also learned that Benny knew only the most rudimentary street-level Arabic, and had no sense of the accent. Sam pointed to the generator-run lights of the camp gate ahead and advised Benny to keep 100 percent quiet from this point on. Sam would do all the necessary talking, and Benny would pretend to have an excruciating toothache. Benny produced a few realistic moans and a fairly convincing pantomime. Sam counseled him not to bury himself in the part.

Sam deliberately rolled up to the gate and its bored-looking sentries at a thundering pace, pulling to a stop in a cloud of dust. Hanging out the driver's window and not waiting for the challenge, he yelled a burst of rapid fire Arabic at the dust-choked and annoyed guards. He waved a sheaf of papers gathered from the glove box at them and berated them in a universal fashion reserved for obnoxious NCO's the world over. Without waiting for them to respond completely, he threw the truck in gear and lumbered through the gate, treating them to a foul blast of exhaust. The jeep followed in his wake, barely deigning to glance at the guards, who roundly cursed them but let them pass rather than ask for any more abuse.

Sam drove deliberately towards the southeastern corner of the camp, heading for where he had seen the damaged bunkers and excavations marked on a poor quality fax of a satellite photo that had been sent over the only working fax machine in Tiberias, motored across the lake and motorcycled to Golani headquarters the previous evening. The camp was huge and he was thankful that it had recently emptied out of more than 200 truckloads of occupants. He guessed that the only bright clusters of lights he could see ahead of them were for the excavations for the buried helicopters and he steered towards them. Fortunately, security within the sprawling camp was nonexistent, and he drove the big ammo truck up towards the excavations unchallenged. He paused before entering the lighted area to take stock of the situation. The jeep drew up along the driver's side and together the six Israelis sat taking in the scene.

At first glance, it was pure confusion. There were mechanical shovels of various sizes clustered around, and inside a large crater of earth, rock and broken concrete, and over top of all of them there was a large construction crane set up. Bulldozers, scrapers and earth movers trundled around almost at random, getting in each other's way half the time. Some were loading a line of dump trucks almost at random. However, there was a small wooden shack with a group of officer-like men standing idle and drinking from small cups. Behind them a large crew was busy cleaning dirt and debris from the dusty - but dangerous looking - black body of an assault helicopter. Another appeared chopper to be getting new rotor blades, while a crew worked within the machine as well. There were only the two helicopters in sight and there were no other lighted areas in Sam's area of view anywhere else in the dark camp.

"This is the place," Sam announced to Benny, who started to answer, but checked himself and rubbed his jaw, emitting a noncommittal moan. "Show time," Sam said quietly to the occupants of the jeep. "Follow me and keep quiet," he added in Arabic. Sam put the big truck into gear. It was big, but not quite right in scale with the massive earthmoving equipment lumbering around the site. This time he rolled slowly up to within hailing distance of the shed.

Benny couldn't follow much of what Sam said, but he had to admire the man's chutzpah and style. Sam bellowed something out the window of the cab. Not bothering to get out, he lectured the confused looking group of half a dozen officers with a long and exceptionally loud tirade that included many sweeping and wild gestures. A few attempted to answer him, but he brushed off all explanations and launched into a new barrage of words and gestures – every now and then gesturing to the men in the jeep pulled up beyond them. At one point one of the Arabic speakers in the jeep stood up in the passenger's seat and pointed at various things all around them and yelled something equally forceful. There was a full-fledged argument and shouting match for a good fifteen to twenty minutes before one of the more senior-looking officers threw his hands up in the universal gesture of despair. He called a few noncoms over, who went off and began giving orders. After that, Sam just had to give a few bursts of rage and wrath to keep things moving. Almost an hour later, he began to back the truck down a dirt ramp that led to the bottom of the excavations where a hole and a shaft had been punched through to the damaged bunker.

Benny had not been completely idle while nursing his fictitious toothache. He was surveying the equipment at hand, the layout of the pit, and the probable dimensions of the huge bunker from the mounds of its monumental mates nearby. Apparently the bomb had burst at one end, sealing the exit and collapsing nearly half the huge structure, from what he could read from the contours of the ground by the glare of the construction lamps. They waited near the mouth of the excavated shaft while a gang of tired-looking workers trooped out of the hole.

"You want the site lights on or off?" he whispered to Sam in an idle moment.

"On for now," Sam whispered back, then backed the big truck almost right to the very edge of the open shaft. The underground workers had climbed out by a series of wide wooden ladders. Sam told the two Arabic speaking recon men from the jeep to seal off the area – not letting anyone in, while he led Benny and the other two down into the pit. Fortunately he had found a working flashlight in the cab of the truck. When they reached the bottom, this came in especially useful – because the departing workers had rudely turned out the makeshift working lights. Benny was able to turn them back on after a few moments of searching for the master switch in a confused mass of cables and junction boxes.

The lights showed that they were near the end of a cavernous bunker. They could quickly see how the first four helicopters had been pushed along the concrete floor to the open shaft and winched up with the big crane. Two more severely damaged choppers sat where the not-so-careful demolition crews had blown the shaft open through the meter-thick reinforced concrete roof. They could see it had a metal netting as an inner layer – the EMP protecting envelope that had sheltered its contents even at a depth of ten meters below ground. There was a partial cave-in that was blocking the access to what appeared to be dozens of mostly undamaged choppers. "It's your show from here," Sam told Benny, "just tell me what you want – we have about thirty minutes before they find out my song and dance up there was totally bogus."

"What did you tell them?" he had to ask.

"That we were demolition specialists sent directly from Damascus, and that we were here to speed their work along big time." Sam chuckled.

Benny forgot about the toothache. This was going to be his masterpiece. Thirty minutes was barely enough, but considering what he had to work with, he would have to go for just a plain big, humongous bang. He told Sam to get their helpers handing down the half a dozen incendiary rounds from the truck – the ones with the green caps, and at least three or four of the aerial rounds – for they had three minute fuses. Then he happily scampered off through the fallen debris to see what kind of ordinance the helicopters contained that could add to the show.

Sam recruited one of his two posted sentinels, and the four of them selected the required 55 kilo shells from the back of the ammunition truck and carried them precariously down the wooden ladders. Sam wished he had been able to finish the afternoon nap that had been interrupted by the fly-by of the three menacing dark choppers. Between pauses to catch his breath and check on Benny, who scurried around with various bits of timers, fuses and powders, Sam could see at least two dozen medium-range assault helicopters in the dark vault. There were clearly more at the other end beyond the lights – though how many had been damaged by the bomb strike, he could not tell. Benny sent him climbing back up to the truck and jeep to search for a better pair of pliers – which he found in a tool box near the winch that they should have perhaps used for lowering their high explosive shells. Sam was just plain tired and looking forward to getting out of this strange hole in the ground. He sat down for just a moment and accepted a water bottle proffered by one of the hard-working soldiers who had brought it down after their last shell – for Benny had asked if there was a fifth illumination round available.

The two of them watched Benny carefully ladling the contents of an open shell into something he had rigged up with the timers and a trio of incendiary shells wired together. Finally Benny straightened up, and looked with obvious satisfaction along the row of shells, wires, powder trains and devices he had arranged leading off into the depths of the cavern. He dusted his hand off and came over to Sam.

"Are you ready to split?" Benny asked.

"Sooner the better," Sam said.

"We'll have exactly fifteen minutes from the moment I start the first timer. You two go upstairs and start the truck – I'll set the timer the second I hear the engine rev and I'll be up in a minute. We need to be out the gate by the time this baby blows – though it's a damned shame to miss the show."

"Maybe next year," Sam said, getting to his feet and heading for the ladders, "Make me proud."

"No worries," Benny said.

Sam climbed wearily up the ladders and took a brief look at the situation topside. Evidently everyone had decided that a break was a good idea, and most of the workers had disappeared and equipment had stopped running. It was, after all, well past eight or nine at night. From the weary faces of the pit crew as they had trudged past, he had been sure that the crews had been pushed hard. Sam heaved himself into the cab as the crew of the jeep got in and fired up their engine. The engine rumbled to life and he gave a couple loud revs, blowing a cloud of diesel smoke. A minute and a half later Benny popped into view climbing out of the pit. He paused to surreptitiously push the top ladder over, blocking anyone from easily getting into the pit. Sam watched in the mirror as he jogged up to the passenger side of the cab. They were rolling the moment his feet left the ground.

Moshav Yiftach 19:30

Eli and his friends made what was, for war time, an uneventful trip home with their injured pilot. During the bouncing ride home, Yishai had changed his robes back to a more masculine form, while cradling and protecting Captain Tzippori from the worst of the lurches as the truck picked its way down the dirt tracks to the highway home. About dark they could hear a large number of explosions, and could see the glow of pillars of fire in the night to the north of them. They did not realize that the two tanks they had left on the hilltop could create quite such havoc in the supply column they had watched go by on the Syrian side of the border that afternoon. Eli and Rabbi Beniyahu speculated that other tanks must have joined the battle to create the conflagration that lit up the skies for miles. They whispered personal prayers on behalf of the Israeli forces.

During the slow, two hour journey home, they passed only one Israeli patrol consisting of a pair of armored personnel carriers that they recognized from the company that the Moshav's mechanics rebuilt. They were cheered by the sight of their armored vehicles back in action and exchanged news. The soldiers told them that the moshav had been quiet since a pinprick of an attack that afternoon, and that the main action appeared to have shifted to the north. They confirmed this with their news of watching the huge army rolling by heading northwards, with the supply train in the van. Eli and Yishai told them of the three attack helicopters, of the attempt to raid the Syrian camp and other information that had not been able to be passed along because of the lack of radios. The patrol was too small to warrant one of the precious radio sets, so news of the war was still being relayed by contacts such as theirs, and motorcycle messengers who buzzed back and forth between groups. They expected to rendezvous with the larger group of newly re-wired tanks that had gone north earlier in the day to help relieve the Israeli forces pinned down near Katzrin.

The moshav was indeed quiet when they finally turned into the broken main gate. The sentries recognized Woody, and they paused only to relay essential news before taking Captain Tzippori straight to the makeshift hospital in the bomb-shelter basement of the Levine's house. They found the basement even fuller than before, but still calm and with no new incoming cases thanks to the afternoon and evening's quiet. Two ambulance service volunteers came out to the truck with a backboard and a proper litter, and together all five of them gently transferred the wounded airman and carried him down the stairs.

Tired as he was, Eli could not tear himself away from the side of the unconscious pilot, as if by sheer, dogged will he was keeping the man alive. Eli had found him, and somehow in some unconscious code, that seemed to make feel responsible for him, though he knew he was now in expert hands. However, he did tear himself away from watching the doctor's exam long enough to go wash up and ask one of the young teenage volunteers to go tell his wife that he was home safe and sound – and to ask her to join him at the clinic.

When he came back to the bedroom examining room, somewhat cleaner and sipping a mug of coffee, he watched as the two doctors, an army medic and a nurse from the local health clinic finished peeling off the bloodstained flight suit. They had already started an IV, having apparently matched the blood type from their limited donor supply gathered from the moshav and soldiers who had given over the last few days. Eli tried to remember the last time he had given blood. Perhaps if he could ever get a full night's sleep and a rest day, he would see if they needed his common A-positive blood, he told himself.

The pilot's injuries were not quite so terrible looking once cleaned up – except for his lower left leg, which was looked crushed and dead of life. He gathered from the doctor's comments that they were debating an amputation versus an attempt at reconstruction.

He heard Natalie in the outer room and went to greet her. They hugged in quiet relief and gratitude to see each other again, each unharmed. Then Natalie came into the examining bedroom with him to see the pilot as Eli whispered the story of finding him. "Come home," she urged as his narrative began to ramble and become confused.

Day Four

Moshav Yiftach 0810

Eli woke up wondering what time it was. He rolled over to hold his watch up to the faint light coming from the doorway to his room, and was surprised to find Natalie snuggled up next to him. He peered at his watch. Ten after eight. It was the first time he had slept through the night since the war began – was it only three days ago? He lay back and took in the peace and comfort of his own bed, his own bedroom, and his own thoughts. He felt like he had lived outside of his normal self for so many days he was becoming someone else. He didn't feel like the same Eli who had lain in this same bed just a few mornings ago, thinking more about what was cooking for the upcoming holiday of *Sukkot* than being invaded Syria, Jordan, Lebanon or Egypt. Not that the possibility of war had ever been far from his mind, In their hostile Middle Eastern neighborhood, possibility of war was never completely absent from any thinking Israeli's mind for very long. But for now it was quiet. Eli realized his ears had been tuned in for the past few minutes, listening for gunfire or shelling.

He thought back to that first morning when he had been roused from a deep sleep with a confused story about the lights being out, and the Syrians coming. It was another Eli who had spent that day lying and crouching in a rifle pit dug under an outcropping of rock. He remembered the crash of shells shattering the rocks and the machine gun bullets digging furrows in the earth too close for comfort. Yet he thought of them all with an odd detachment. He found it hard to believe that he had alternated between desperate, against-the-odds missions with Sam and Woody, and playing host in his sukkah. Inside its familiar walls, there was only a line of bullet holes to remind him of the war that raged around his home for the past three days.

He recalled meeting Sam. Now he could not imagine not knowing Sam. He smiled to recall the lieutenant's eager incompetence with a paddle in the kayak, his really bad haircut, their mission to Syria, his finding Captain Chaim Tzippori – for they now knew his first name as well as the name stitched on his flight suit pocket. Where was Sam now? Had he really gone back into Syria and driven straight into the enemy's camp with their own truck? Was Sam dead – or alive? He felt guilty wondering such things while luxuriating in his own comfortable bed.

Natalie felt him stirring and asked if he was getting up. "Not quite yet," he said.

An hour later they were sipping coffee together in the sukkah. Eli had already missed the first and second *minyan* at the moshav's two synagogues, and he needed, as he put it, a little "liquid *kavanah*," some caffeine in his system to improve his concentration for the extra long morning prayers for the intermediate days of the week-long holiday. He felt like he could easily go back to bed and sleep for a week, but he poured a second cup and went back into the house and brought out his *tallit*. His *lulav* and *etrog* were already out in the sukkah, laid on the table for any soldier who needed to fulfill the *mitzvah* of the four species.

Natalie would have normally wandered off to her household chores, Internet correspondence or hand crafts. But she was not letting Eli out of her sight. She picked out a book to study and brought it to the sukkah just to be with him. The morning was warm and quiet. If she didn't look out the windows of the sukkah at the shattered shells of the neighboring houses, she could almost believe the war never happened – was not still happening. She wondered what WAS happening? How could Israel fight a war without the Israel national news on the radio? She stole glances from her book to watch Eli *daven*. The coffee and the poetry of the psalms that began morning prayers were beginning to make him look like her real husband, not the exhausted shell that drove back into the moshav last night.

Tali, their neighbor, who had discreetly spent last night with her children in the bomb shelter she shared with the neighbors on the other side of her, wandered in with a basket of fresh whole wheat and bran muffins for them. Amy, the woman who was nursing their four patients and had slept on one of their couches, came out to greet her – for they had arranged for Tali and her oldest daughter to spell Amy for a while so that she could go home and rest and get away from the constant work for a little while. The three women made their way into the kitchen to catch up on whatever tidbits of news they had to share and not to distract Eli, who was still praying.

It was Friday morning and the three women needed to decide what and how much to cook for Shabbat, which began at sundown. There was no way of knowing how many people they would be feeding – beyond the four injured patients in the guest room, and Tali's children. Who even knew if Eli would be around from one minute to the next? Most of the IDF soldiers had left the kibbutz the previous afternoon and evening. Word was that the battle had suddenly shifted to the north, with threats of a combined force breaking through all the way to Tiberias. It was maddening having no radios – even the soldiers had no news. Colonel Eschol, who had been such a frequent guest the first three days of the war, had not been seen since the previous afternoon. And yet what little news that did filter in was mildly encouraging. Israeli fighter jets had been seen over the Jordan valley. There had been a major battle to the north last night that ended with an entire Syrian supply convoy being virtually wiped out. Someone else reported a helicopter or two shot down near

Tzfat. There had been no major attack on any of the Golan Heights settlements since early yesterday. Tiberias was still safe.

So, what to cook for anywhere from twelve to fifty people between now and Saturday night when they could cook again? And, what was left to cook after three days with no refrigeration? Would there be any more cows slaughtered? How about eggs and milk? All the cows were being milked by hand, for the computerized panel that ran the milking machine was down, even though they had emergency power in the dairy. The only answer was to bake up a storm of *challah*, pitas and rolls, make big salads out of whatever their gardens offered, and put on the biggest stew pots they could manage. Natalie had finagled a big roast out of the dairymen, and had salted it and soaked it so that it could be kosher for baking. Their fresh steaks had been kosher roasted directly over an open fire without soaking and salting, but baking a roast required the blood to be drawn from the meat. She decided it made sense to do all the bread baking early in the day and have the roast done last.

Once it was settled what everyone was making and when, Tali and Natalie shooed Amy out of the kitchen and told her to go home and rest. Amy insisted on checking on her patients one more time before leaving. The kitchen settled down to a companionable hum of activity, and Eli came in and asked if he could help chop, wash or prepare anything. The two women tolerated his assistance for the sake of his company, and the talk turned back to the war – the lack of news about the war, and the difficulties of coping with no power, bombed houses and no communications. Tali's children roamed in and out, mooching snacks and hanging around to listen to the adults telling about the war. Eli settled into a comfortable chair and shelled peas from Tali's garden at a leisurely pace while telling about his odd trip to the *souk* in the town across the border. The two women wanted to know every detail – what people wore, how many women were on the street and in the *souk*, how many cars they had running, whether there were any phones working. They were somehow surprised to hear that there was absolutely no war damage just a dozen kilometers away. And yet it made sense, the war had not come their way. All the fighting so far had been on Israeli soil. There had been no counterattack against the invading army – yet. Would there be one? How could they ever know which way things were going?

Their talk wandered to wondering what it would be like after the war – assuming of course that Israel survived these days of trial. They couldn't imagine any other alternative, even though they knew they had been within minutes of being overrun. For all they knew, a third wave of invasion could be forming across the border, and they would have no way of knowing until it came. How the poor IDF forces were spread so thin! And how many had fallen – moshavniks and soldiers together, women and children along with the men. They named the ones they could remember and knew that there were many more they could just not find the names for. In the Kaplan's kitchen it seemed impossible it could have all happened. How would they ever be able to reach Tali's husband – wherever he was. And what about Ruthie, Eli and Natalie's oldest, who would be worried sick back in Chicago? How much news about the war was reaching America, they wondered, and how distorted was it – even with cell phones and instant communications? The TV pictures of what was happening in Israel were hard to match with the reality in normal times, and these were not normal times at all.

Eli wondered aloud how his handful of communications clients were doing without him? It was the first time he had time to even think about them. Were they still thinking of him? Or had they written him off as dead? At least three of the companies had Israeli R&D shops. The minute the war was over, they would need to reassure their customers their operations were still sound – but were they? Did he even have a business anymore? Funny how little that all seemed to matter at the moment. He finished shelling the peas at last, and took up a basket of snap beans, popping off the ends and munching on a few as they talked and talked. They could have gone on forever, cooking and enjoying each other's company, but the Shabbat was approaching, and there was much more to do to put their much-used little house in order.

Tali went off to take care of the wounded officers. Eli and Natalie followed after a while. After greeting their guests and checking on each, asking about their progress and comfort, Eli and Natalie decided that the metal shuttered windows could be opened all the way to air out the room and let in more light. It had been more than 24 hours since the last shelling. Tali promised to close them at the first sign of trouble. Everyone was glad to see the sunshine. Although it was still not clear of haze, the day was mild and sunny. Eli was standing at the window, gazing at the view when he heard the rumble of an approaching tank. "It's one of ours," one of the injured artillerymen said. Eli pushed the soldier's bed over so he could see out the window better. The man pronounced it a Merkava II after peering at the distant shape a while.

"I wonder if they have any news of Sam," Eli wondered aloud. Everyone, including Major Basri the Syrian, agreed that Eli should immediately go to wherever the tank was going to stop and get fresh news of the war. Eli was reluctant to leave Natalie, even for a short walk to the dairy or community center, and so he demurred a while, until they all realized that the tank had passed the center of the moshav and appeared to be turning up their street. By now, Eli could read the *Gimmel* 1 painted on the tank. It was David Engel and his crew. He had left them to go hunting the Syrian supply train with Captain Yankel Klein – was it less than a day ago? They would surely have news. As Eli told the sick room who it was, he noticed two odd wrapped bundles on the front of the tank, which was driving slowly for an IDF tank. Eli knew how Sasha, David's driver, liked to blast the big machine from point A to point B. Something was wrong.

The big, dark, camouflage-painted tank came to a stop at the end of Eli's short driveway. Eli and Natalie came out to greet their tanker friends, sensing that something was terribly wrong. They soon realized that the two wrapped shapes on the flanks of the tank were bodies. Captain Engel pulled off his helmet and climbed wearily out of his hatch. The driver, Sasha, sat woodenly in his heads-up driving seat, barely nodding a greeting.

"It's Yankel," Captain Engel said, "and Schmulik, his gunner. We couldn't get to Tzvi. Only Charlie the loader made it out – and he is pretty badly burned. We dropped him at the clinic," he explained as he climbed down and greeted Eli.

"I need to find Rabbi Beniyahu. Yankel and Schmulik would appreciate some words of Torah as we bury them. Perhaps you'd like to help?" he said without emotion.

"Of course we would," Eli answered, embracing the smoke-stained, battle weary captain. "He's staying for Shabbat with Yishai. Give us a lift and we'll show you the way, OK Natalie?" he asked. She agreed, and the two of them climbed up on the turret of the tank.

"I've never ridden on one of these, but I've wanted to ever since my first Yom Hatzmaot parade..." Natalie whispered, settling in next to Eli on the low slope of the turret as Eli gave the driver directions to find Yishai's house two streets over. "I guess you've been on a dozen by now," she added.

"Actually, this is my first time too," Eli said, "but I've spent a fair bit of time chasing after these things in Woody the last few days." However, the sight of the two wrapped bodies dampened any possible enjoyment of the ride. A few minutes later they climbed down with Captain Engel to go check the bomb shelter behind Yishai's house. Savory smells of spices and herbs greeted their noses, and the three of them made their way down the stairs to the candle-lit shelter. They found Yishai's wife and three other women cooking a feast on a pair of kerosene burners. She told them that Yishai and the rabbi had gone to the clinic and then the cemetery. She offered the captain a taste of a spicy lentil and rice dish that sat steeping on a table filled with such tempting smells. He took a taste and thanked her.

The three climbed back up the concrete steps of the shelter back to the world of sunlight. There were a few dozen children gathered around the tank, staring shyly at the big machine, the two silent bundles, and the exhausted soldiers, who managed to crack a faint smile at the sight of them, and croaked out greetings. Greg and the scout they had borrowed as a replacement loader had emerged to ride on top, hot and grimy after a long night of war. The older children wanted to know where the fighting was now, and who was winning. "Nobody is winning – everyone is losing in this war," Sasha told them. They accepted his answer.

Eli, Natalie and the captain climbed back up. The children went back to their games when they drove off towards the clinic. Not surprisingly, the rabbi and the older moshavnik had already left the clinic. They drove slowly and solemnly to the edge of the moshav where the small cemetery was surrounded with trees and flowering bushes. It was a beautiful spot. They quickly spotted Rabbi Beniyahu sitting on a stool by a row of graves in being dug at the far end of the graveyard, in the section separated from the Jewish graves. There were two new long rows beyond the spot where Natalie and Eli remembered digging less than two days ago. Rabbi Beniyahu was reading a page of *Talmud* to Yishai and a small group of young men from the yeshiva who were too young to join the war, as they dug graves for a large stack of bodies, covered with tarps waiting for their turn in the freshly turned earth.

All of the tankers followed their captain, Natalie and Eli to where the Rabbi sat, and all waited silently for him to finish the lines he was explaining. Eli was surprised to realize that he was reading from a section of laws about *mikvot* – ritual baths. It seemed an odd topic for burying enemy dead, although it was traditional learning material for a Jewish house of mourning. The Rabbi looked up from his sefer at last, although he had acknowledged their arrival with a silent glance earlier.

"It's Yankel," David said, "Will you help us bury him and Schmulik?"

The rabbi quietly agreed to help. He told Yishai to keep working with the young men on the graves they had in progress. He left his book on the stool, kissing it goodbye like a dear grandchild, and went with the tankers back to their tank. The volunteer who was keeping the graveyard records for the moshav came and joined them, and he walked them over to a row near the entrance and pointed out an open place for two new graves in the Jewish section. He came back to the tank with them, asked to see the men's dog tags, and began to carefully record their names, ID numbers and Jewish names in the cemetery record book. The soldiers fetched shovels and tools from the back of the tank, and Eli and Natalie collected shovels from the tool shed by the gate, which included their own. "Wartime makes for very unusual dates," Natalie whispered when they were alone.

The four tankers, including the borrowed one, Eli and Natalie set to work digging two new graves. Captain Engel worked with Eli and Natalie. Though they could tell he was exhausted, he threw himself into the work and they had a hard time keeping up with his pace, pausing to rest and drink water far more often than he did. Tears as well as sweat streaked his smoke-stained face. After a while, as he began to slow down as the hole deepened and the throws from each shovelful grew longer, he began to talk of his friend, Yankel.

The two had gone through basic training together, fought in the first Lebanon war together, and gone their separate paths after David had left the IDF and gone into business. Yankel had always been the best – the smartest, the most clever, the most brilliant tactician, the wiliest warrior.

He knew the Golan like his own backyard, every stream, every minefield, every hill top and track. Whenever David's reserve duties took him to the Golan, Yankel had been there. He had been a fierce competitor and a dedicated friend, moving IDF heaven and earth to make it for both David's son's *brit* and the boy's bar mitzvah thirteen years later – just last year about this time of year. David had always been more religious, in the traditional sense, than Yankel; whose personal life, marriage and three children had always revolved around his IDF service. Yet Yankel's religion had been Israel – and he had insisted on passing a deep love for Jews and the Jewish land along to his children.

"He was on a very high level to have had the merit to have been such a warrior for Israel," Rabbi Beniyahu said gently. They had not realized that he had come and sat down beside their now-waist-deep hole.

"I agree," David said, "but how do you know that?"

"Think about it," Rabbi Beniyahu said, "We have all kinds of laws about what kind of animal is acceptable as a sacrifice in the Holy Temple when it was standing – and may it stand again someday soon. The animal had to be of a certain age, healthy, without any disqualifying blemish. The *Talmud* goes on at great length about what constitutes a *"mum,"* a blemish that invalidates a sacrifice. You recall the whole debate in the Sanhedrin about the sacrifice, brought on behalf of the Roman ruler. The bullock was secretly damaged by Bar Kamsa in a way that was not obvious to a casual observer. He did this in order to discredit the Jews by forcing them to either reject the emperor's sacrifice, or compromise on the law."

Eli and David agreed that they had heard the story – which was said to be the initial reason for the beginning of the eventual destruction of Judea by the Romans and the Jews' long exile.

"And so," the Rabbi continued, "if a sacrifice that we mortals bring needs to be without blemish, think a moment, what does it mean when the Holy One, blessed is He, who is perfect in all His ways, chooses His own sacrifices? Must they not also be perfect?"

David thought a while. "Yankel was a good man, but he himself would say that he was far from perfect."

Rabbi Beniyahu paused a moment, "Perhaps perfection is the wrong word – it is more like *shelemut* – a wholeness or completeness. It comes by achieving something in perfecting or correcting an aspect of one's character or accomplishing a certain task in the world. You know that we all come into this world with all the abilities and opportunities we need to complete tasks that are uniquely ours. These are things that needed completing in order to raise the world to a slightly higher level, our own special contribution. For instance, a baby who comes into this world, grows sick and dies in a few days somehow needed to be here to complete only perhaps one thing. Or a handicapped person has something to overcome in this world beyond their physical defects – and they obviously have what they need to do so, for the Creator of all made the world that way."

"And so Yankel, Yaakov ben Abraham, completed his piece of creation last night. His work done, his soul is now free to leave. Our souls are still working on something, and their tasks are obviously not done yet."

"I suppose I could try thinking about it that way," David said, as he paused for his first real rest, and a long drink of water.

It took another hour to finish the graves. When they were close to done, David sent Sasha and the tank to go get Charlie, Yankel's faithful loader for the past dozen years, from the clinic, and bring him, bandages and all, to attend the burial. They finished their holes and washed off with a bucket of water and some hand towels. The young men came over to help them form a *minyan* of ten men over age 13 and, together, they all bore the wrapped bodies to the graves and gently lowered them in.

Rabbi Beniyahu said the prayers for a burial, singing some Psalms together with the small group, and chanting others. Rabbi Beniyahu gave a short eulogy, addressing himself to the *Ribbono Shel Olam* as much as to the handful of people present. "*Ribbono Shel Olam El Maaleh Rachamim*, L-rd Master of the Universe, G-d who is filled with mercy, we are burying today two brave and loyal mighty men of Israel: Yaakov ben Abraham, Yankel to his friends; and Samuel ben Heskiyahu, Schmuelik to his friends. They gave everything they had to give in the defense of your beloved Israel, they can give no more. We are saddened by their passing from this world, for their life touched us all. And we are afraid, all of us, to have lost two who were so brave and strong at a time when our borders are still overrun with those who breathe violence and hatred against Your people, Israel. We stand here under a sky darkened with the smoke of many fires, and land shaken and torn with overwhelming forces and violence."

Rabbi Beniyahu paused before going on, "And *Ribbono Shel Olam* we can't help wondering, how long? How much longer must we bury our sons and daughters? How much longer must we be surrounded with those who seek our destruction? How long until the light of Your Torah enlightens the whole world? Until we realize the words of Your prophets that they shall beat their swords into plowshares, and study war no more? Your servants Samuel ben Heskiyahu and Yaakov ben Abraham, Schmuelik and Yankel, were forced to study war – for the sake of your people Israel, so that there could be those who learned your Torah night and day and not take up the sword. I understand that Yankel became a genius at the study of war on the level of your greatest scholars. Out numbered, out gunned, blinded by a cruel sneak attack in a time of peace, Your servants Yankel and Schmuelik and their brave crew hit back at more than forty iron chariots built for destruction in the past three days his friends have told me. One against forty. Where does Israel get such men?

"The *Tanach* tells us about one such a man. This moshav is named for him, and so it is appropriate, perhaps, that Yankel and Schmuelik came here to Yiftach to be buried. In the times of the Judges, the Children of Israel were oppressed by the Philistines and the Children of Ammon for many years. And for eighteen years they had no leader to stand up for them. So who did they finally choose? The mightiest warrior of the time was Yiftach, the son of Gilead and a harlot. So, when Gilead's wife had other sons, they banded together and drove out Yiftach, and he went away to live with the other rough characters of the age in the land of Tob.

"But when Ammon came to make war, the Jews begged Yiftach to come and lead them. They chose him not because he was wise, or a great scholar, but because he was a strong and skillful warrior – and because he loved this land, perhaps more than any of them. He sent messengers to the king of Ammon and asked 'What is between me and you that you have come to me to fight in my land?' 'My land,' he called it. You should read the King of Ammon's long winded reply. It is like reading last week's newspapers.

"In times such as these, the G-d of Israel sends us such men, and when their work is completed, he takes them back again.

"And so, *Ribono Shel Olam*, we are weary of war, we have few such men left to lead us, and we are waiting for Your deliverance, may it come speedily in our day. Amen."

All too soon it was time to replace the earth in the grave and cover the silent forms. Tears flowed with the dirt cascading into the two graves, and they filled them back up in near silence. Then they washed again from the buckets, and the students and soldiers said the afternoon prayers together by the quiet graveside. It was now midafternoon, and Eli and Natalie invited the mourning tankers back to the house for Friday night dinner. They were due back at the northernmost community in their section of the Golan by midnight in order to reinforce a secondary line of defense, but they were entitled to a decent dinner first, and showers.

The tankers parked their bullet scarred tank at the foot of Eli's driveway again for the second time that day. It was getting late in the afternoon, and Eli and Natalie rushed to the kitchen to make sure there was enough for four more hungry, tired warriors. Eli checked the hot water and towel supply in the bathroom and set the Shabbat timer on their solar hot water system. The tankers sent the new guy in first, for he had been loading 30 kilo shells and digging graves for the past 24 hours. David and Sasha asked if it would be OK for them to unroll their sleeping bags in a corner of the sukkah for a nap until it was time for the prayers welcoming the Shabbat. Eli found some nylon covered ground pads for them and went to visit his patients.

Friday night dinner was a relief from the war for everyone at Eli's table, except that each carried a sadness within that dampened the mood. Eli could not help thinking of his first night's talk about the commandment to be happy during the whole holiday of *Sukkot*. But the death of Yankel Klein had drained all the happiness from this group. The two artillery officers who were recovering from their burns were able to come to the sukkah for a meal for the first time, but needed help eating. Amy, who had been their volunteer nurse and companion for the past two days, fed them each in turn, provoking the only chuckles with her "open wide for the airplane" imitation of feeding a toddler.

Captain Engel looked forlorn without his friend Yankel. He had come back from synagogue late because he stopped off to visit Charlie in the Levine's basement clinic. His burns were too bad to allow him any more excursions other than his stretcher-carried visit to Yankel's funeral.

However, as the wine and food began to have their effect, the mood lightened somewhat from misery to reflection. "You remember the rusty hulks of the armored columns left over from the War of Independence that are scattered on Highway One going up to Jerusalem?" David asked Eli.

"Of course," Eli replied.

"I've been thinking of them a lot lately," Captain Engel said. "I remember when I was a kid hearing the stories of the supply columns trying to relieve the siege of Jerusalem, and of the ambushes and the bravery of the Palmach fighters who died there. But they were just that, stories. They were stories from another time, another world. Try as I might, no matter how good my imagination, they all seemed like they happened in black and white like all the newsreels from the War of Independence. Even the sound seemed distorted in my imagination.

"A few years ago they collected a couple groups of the rusted remains, painted them up with some kind of preservative paint, all in a neutral olive color and lined them up in rows on concrete as a memorial. But I remember them best when they sat where they had been hit, rusting away, along the roadside.

"Even in recent years, in our exercises in the Golan, we would always come across these rusting remains – jeeps, abandoned field guns, every now and then, the body of a tank or a truck, most of them from the '67 war or the Yom Kippur war. Both those wars happened before I was born. I grew up knowing all kinds of stories about them, but they were from another time."

"When I saw Yankel's tank burning as we left it, with the shells flying all around us, I couldn't help seeing a vision of one of those memorials. Only this time it was in color, and I was living the story. I knew the people in those doomed armored trucks, knew their stories and knew their wives and husbands and children.

"And so I wonder, what will my children think when we drive up to the Golan some day and I point out the burned out remains of Yankel's tank – assuming I survive this war, which is not at all for certain – what will they think? I'll be the old soldier with the memories. The young can never fully understand.

"You know we started out this war, two groups of tanks, Yankel's eight and my group of four. Now only mine is still running, and Baruch's is still in the shop. Charlie is the only one of Yankel's group of forty to survive that I know of, and this war is only four days old. What kind of odds are those?

"And yet somehow, we keep going. When you and Sam showed up with your little truck load of shells, and two of the Syrian tanks wasted their first shot aiming at you instead of me, that made the difference between life and death for us. We lived and they died, and because you drove into a shell hole and they missed, you lived too. I am starting to lose count of how many times we have been one shell away from flaming death in the last three days. But we keep going. Tonight, after pausing for a few hours of precious Shabbat in your sukkah, we have to get back into *Gimmel* One and go back to the war. And when I do, I'll be thinking about Rabbi Beniyahu's words: *"Ribono Shel Olam,* we are weary of war, we have few such men left, we are waiting for your deliverance, may it come speedily in our day. Amen."

Eli was not sure what to say. He had been trying to think of some appropriate words of Torah, but somehow nothing seemed to fit the mood or the company, which ranged from fairly religious to quite secular. Natalie was looking troubled by the description of his close encounter with death, and looking at him as if to question what else about his war stories had been under-reported. He was about to launch into something from the prophet Isaiah when they heard the rumble of a jeep coming into the moshav and soon realized that it had passed the community center and had turned up their street. He and Captain Klein stepped out of the sukkah to see if it was a messenger from headquarters. They watched a boxy, Soviet-style open jeep approaching for a moment before realizing where they had seen that jeep before. It was Sam!

Sam let out a most un-Shabbat-like beep of the horn, turned off the engine and hopped out of the driver's seat, while on the other side, a very tired, dirty looking Benny climbed out, grinning from ear to ear with pleasure.

Eli grabbed Sam in a bear hug and waltzed him into the sukkah, which was well lit with candle lanterns and oil lamps, so that he could see his friend better. David and Benny hugged, and then were joined by a joyous Sasha and Greg. The loader they had borrowed from the recon group stood there grinning, and greeted the tank's proper gunner with mock formality. "You can have your bloody tank back, I never want to see the inside of a Merkava again unless it's Independence Day at Latrun with my great grandchildren!" he swore.

"Colonel Eschol gave me twelve hours off for good behavior, and I couldn't think of anywhere else in the Golan I would rather be than Moshav Yiftach with my lucky friend and rabbit's foot Eli," Sam said, with a wicked wink at Natalie. "Oh, and I promised David I'd give him his demolitions man back – this man is wasted as a gunner. I think President Assad himself must have felt that boom in his hidey hole of a bunker in Damascus. What a trip!"

Sam and Benny interrupted each other, pausing in their triumphant narrative only to shovel in more food. Their story sounded like a madcap college prank, except that Eli and David knew that six Syrian soldiers had been shot from long range with the rifle that Sam returned to the moshav. The story of Sam's abuse of the guards at the gate, and his out-arguing a drinking party of Syrian officers that he was a demolitions expert on an urgent mission from the high command, provoked roars of laughter, lifting the pall of sorrow from Yankel's death at least for the moment.

Benny described the elaborate series of explosions he had rigged in the underground bunker, starting with a cluster of incendiary shells brought down from their captured truck, and leading by various trains of powder and fuse to set off the missiles and ordinance carried in at least a dozen of the attack helicopters. They both estimated that there were at least twenty five or more choppers that could have been salvaged. Benny had rigged a series of five three-minute fuses from illumination rounds to make the initial timed explosion that set off the chain reaction. He was rightfully proud of that bit of ingenuity, for it gave him fifteen minutes from setting the first timer to climb out of the bunker, get in the truck and drive like hell with Sam to get out before the big bunker blew.

"I wish we could have seen it properly," Benny said, wistfully. "All I saw was a pillar of smoke from their excavation hole, and the whole camp shook with the first series of booms."

Sam chuckled, "I just remember watching the guards at the gate staring back at the show while we rolled the hell out of there. They had no clue what hit them."

They described a tense ride back through the border, fortunately unopposed because of the great shoot out going on to the north thanks to Yankel and David's tanks let loose on the rear of the supply train. Because the big supply truck would not have made it over the route they came, and because they still had better than half a load of precious 155 mm shells that would fit an Israeli howitzer just fine, they detoured south until they could cut through a minefield path to get back to Israeli lines. Sam and Benny had delivered their shells to the first Israeli battery they could find, now mostly shifted north to meet the new threat. Sam and Benny had spent the rest of the night and Friday ferrying supplies and equipment in the stolen truck until they met up with the other half of the recon patrol. They swapped the captured truck for the captured jeep-like vehicle, and went back to working for Col. Eschol until getting their twelve-hour reprieve from the war.

Sam wanted to know all the details of Eli's trip back and how their pilot was doing. They agreed to go pay the clinic a visit before Sam had to leave. It was nearly eleven before they wrapped up the meal with a few songs – a more solemn mix of tunes than the night Rabbi Beniyahu had first come to meet them.

Natalie came along to the clinic, not wanting or daring to leave Eli alone with Sam for fear he would disappear on another dangerous trip. Captain Tzippori was still unconscious, but his color and breathing seemed better. Unfortunately, the doctors had to amputate his left leg below the knee. "If we had a proper hospital and a couple good neurosurgeons, I'm sure it could have been saved," Dr. Levine told them. "But this is the best we can do here, there was not enough circulation left to keep it from turning gangrenous on us, it's a wonder it didn't start festering already in this heat. The good news is that there is enough there to make a good attachment for a prosthesis, and he should be able to walk pretty well. I'm afraid his jet fighter days are over, though, poor man." The doctor whispered in the quiet stairwell, where he had accompanied them. He escorted them up the stairs and out the kitchen door, saying that he had not been outside in over a day and a half.

It was getting close to midnight when Eli and Natalie said goodbye to the crew of the tank. The soldiers' Shabbat respite from the war had ended, and they disappeared into the warm night. Eli and Natalie watched their shadows disappear, and listened for a long time as the deep rumble of the tank engine faded into the distance. Sam was already asleep on one of the ground pads vacated by the tankers, leaving instructions to wake him before 0600. Speaking little and working quietly, they cleared the many dishes, put away what was left of the food, checked on their various sleeping guests and collapsed into bed.

Mount Meron Northern Command 23:45

Anna arranged for the loading of four more freighters in as many different Adriatic ports by the time she finished up her night's scheduling with USCOM Europe. The first shipment, a mere 450 ton-grab bag of munitions and electronic equipment scavenged from the arms dealers in Yugoslavia, would be arriving sometime the next morning, assuming that the old rust bucket of a tramp steamer did not sink beneath its load. Her dockside contact had expressed some concern for its seaworthiness, but it was the first ship available. The other four loads would trickle in over the next two days; five ship-sized drops in a large and fast-leaking bucket. She needed to find a bigger source of supplies – such as Athens, Naples, Gibraltar or even perhaps Marseilles.

She pulled her headset off and sat for a moment to clear her head for the upcoming midnight briefing. Peeling her scribbled notepad to a clean page, she tried to sum up all she knew of the situation in the last six hours since their 18:00 update, which had been quite brief because of the pressures of juggling so many demands. She had not even realized it was Shabbat until she heard one of the religious officers making *Kiddush* over a plastic cup of grape juice produced from who knows where.

Since she had been focused on shipping, she started with the situation at sea and on the coast. There the situation was relatively stable. The Israeli Navy was in firm control of the coastal waters, and had even sent raids up the Lebanese coast and down well along the Sinai. They were keeping the attack in the south at least a kilometer or so back from the beaches, and giving the strained ground troops and reserve groups some cover and support they could count on. They had been very effective in resupplying units along the sea coast, and their ammunition situation seemed secure for a few more days at least. She had a lead on a source of two and four inch shells that might keep them in business.

In the air there was good news and bad news. The bad news was that the 24 planes borrowed from the Americans were down to 14 after so many hours of constant sorties. The good news was that they had been incredibly lucky and effective in keeping the sky clear of challengers. To Israel's ten planes downed, there were now at least sixty less Egyptian fighters flying, three dozen less Jordanians, and even a half dozen Saudi fighters that had ventured forth to join the fray had been shot down; over 100 planes by her radar captain's meticulous count. However, even a 10-1 win-loss rate was a slow attrition that would bring an end to the IAF in another 48 hours unless their ground crews could finish re-wiring some of their EMP damaged planes. Three Israeli pilots had been rescued, but that still made a staggering mortality rate for the pilots who flew against the odds.

There was hope of getting perhaps a dozen planes or so in the air over the next day or two. But Anna had her doubts about getting a supersonic fighter jet flying again in less than a week, even with their talented ground crews. She was placing more hope and reliance in the reports she was tracking from three different air bases that were overhauling perhaps thirty Blackhawk and Apache Longbow helicopters in the first batch being pushed through the maintenance hangers. Even though their control systems were every bit as complicated as the jet fighters, perhaps even more so, there was a larger margin of safety and more room for error in the slower moving, lower flying choppers. Besides, she knew more about the Blackhawks from her earlier training than she did the sleek jets. She knew it could fly. She made a note to prioritize targets for the first missions of choppers starting the next morning if her sources at Ramat David and Palmachim were reliable, and she felt they were.

On the ground, it was impossible to sort out the quickly shifting situation. The south was a morass of fighting, with nearly every town and settlement under attack in some form or another, and no large groups of attackers or defenders sorting themselves out in the melee. The largest coherent unit of command was at the company, or even platoon level in most places. Even low flying helicopters would have a difficult job of sorting friend from foe in that confused mess. She jotted a note to herself to ask the group for possible ways they could think of to alert Israeli ground troops to identify themselves quickly and easily to approaching helicopters without tipping off their enemies. Perhaps they could broadcast something on Radio Israel that would make sense only to Israelis who had served in the IDF.

Jerusalem was still reporting active street-to-street fighting in some contested neighborhoods, but fortunately no enemy troops had stirred from their massing in the Jordan Valley near Jericho. She wondered what was keeping them from marching on Israel's thinly defended capital. Perhaps the arrival of the IAF and their vigorous actions up and down the valley had changed their minds.

Up north, the situation had shifted dangerously in the last twelve hours, with a new combined force beginning to push the strained Israeli lines north of the Kinneret and threatening to break through along Highway 85 in a dash for the coast. However the few remaining IDF armored forces in the Golan had proved exceptional in rolling up the supply convoys creeping along in the wake of the huge force, and now threatened to cut them off from their most direct line of retreat. Without supplies, the combined Syrian forces could not push much farther. She wished that the Jordanian and irregular forces that were still pouring across the border and pressing towards Afula and the Jezreel Valley could be cut off as well, but their supplies were being harassed only by air at this point, and there were just not enough planes to do the job.

The Lebanese border was bloody and nasty fighting, but not the mortal threat of the Syrian, Jordanian or Egyptian advances. At worst some small towns might fall, but there were no masses of tanks and armored vehicles threatening to roll into Israel's coastal heartland from that direction at least. She jotted a last bullet point to cover, flipped her tablet back to the first page of her notes, rubbed her tired eyes a moment, pulled her hair back and reclipped it, and headed off to the status meeting. She had scheduled herself a four hour nap afterwards, and she was looking forward to it. She hoped for another quick meeting.

Day Five

Moshav Yiftach 0010

David was both serious and sad the moment he set foot out of the warmly lit sukkah and remounted his waiting tank. There was none of the usual banter or levity that usually accompanied firing up the old Merkava. Even in Lebanon there had been a kind of grumbling gallows humor. Now he found every time the engine started to be a small miracle. How long would it take for him to take a simple thing like starting an engine or making a phone call for granted? What would it be like to call Anat and the kids again? How were they? He had heard no news, good or bad, about her home town of Zichron Yaakov where she had gone to stay with her parents. From what he could gather from the general news, there had been no invading forces reaching that far. Trouble with the neighboring Israeli Arab towns like Faradis could be another matter. However, for the most part he had heard that many Israeli Arabs – like those in Faradis, had been keeping their heads down, and only joining in behind any Arab victories. In fact, he heard that most of the Arabic-speaking population of Tiberias had rallied to help the Israelis. However, chronic trouble spots like Khan Yunis or Jenin that were controlled by the PA were a different story. He had heard troubling tidbits about sniping and armed gangs roaming in the streets of Jerusalem.

Yankel's death weighed like a slab of concrete on his heart and oppressed the whole crew who had buried him that afternoon. However, they had a war to fight, the question was where? He watched the familiar country roll by in the night as they picked up the main road and headed north to their rendezvous point with the hodge-podge tank group that had formed from the remnants of a dozen units scattered up and down the Golan. Between them, they had a half a dozen working tanks now that the moshav shops had finished putting Baruch's *Gimmel* Two back together. It now ran on half treads on both sides. It might not be able to handle tough terrain, but it would be able to shoot even more accurately with the improved optical sights that were being fitted during its down time. It had its interior cooling and positive air pressure restored against the possibility of any biological or chemical weapons being used as the enemy grew more desperate. Baruch's driver could now operate without being heads up – although at night, the vision was much better out of the hatch.

David had not given much thought to biological weapons since the start of the war. It had begun and continued for the past four days as a straight-on, intense, grinding, force against force combat using very traditional, mostly last-generation weapons. However, he found himself wondering about a tidbit of rumor mentioned at the brigade security briefing held before their trip to the Syrian border, before their savage fight with their two tanks against the supply column for an entire army; before Yankel died. One of the logistics people had warned the tankers not to neglect their biological hazard systems – because there were rumors of some strange sickness cropping up behind Syrian lines in the very area Sam, Rabbi Beniyahu and his host that night had visited. There was speculation that one of the bunkers bombed might have held chemical or biological shells that had broken open.

Dirty warfare was not a novelty in the Middle East. In the long Iran-Iraq war of the 1980s there had been recourse to chemical weapons on both sides. There were documented cases of Saddam Hussein's regime using experimental germ warfare on whole Kurdish villages. Syria certainly had biological and chemical warfare capabilities. Israeli intel was fairly sure that many of Saddam Hussein's "weapons of mass destruction" had slipped quietly over the border into Syria in the weeks and days before Iraq fell to the American-led invasion. David was quite sure that these nasty toys could be brought into play if the utterly ruthless regime that ran Syria with an iron fist felt its grip was slipping.

Arab and Palestinian propaganda accused Israel of all kinds of biological devilry, from super-rats infesting East Jerusalem (but not, curiously, the adjacent Jewish old and new city), and sterilizing chewing gum or cigarettes being sold to unsuspecting Gazans – which clearly were not working based on the birthrate – if anyone could even believe such a preposterous notion.

David knew that while Israeli research in these areas was quite advanced, perhaps the most sophisticated in the world, it was all carried out with the intent to protect its soldiers and citizens from the schemes of its neighbors, never to use such weapons in war or peace. He thought, with a sympathetic ache in his left arm, of the frequent cocktails of immunizations he submitted to as an IDF officer. He hoped that whatever may have been unstoppered across the border was something he and his fellow soldiers had been inoculated against.

With such worrisome thoughts, they rolled northwards up the highway to rejoin their unit. When he got there, he was surprised to find everyone getting ready to move out back the way he had just come. The major in command of their group flagged him to come over and ride along while Sasha maneuvered their tank around to join the column as it began to roll.

Their orders, David quickly learned, were to retake Ramat Magshimim, the community that had been overrun opposite Hespin and the only remaining major thorn in the way of retaking their sector of the Golan Heights. A mechanized company had finally materialized in the wake of David and Yankel's costly victory over the Syrian supply train, and had easily retaken Ramat HaGolan, what little was left of it. He understood from the major that they had found evidence of brutal killings of the Israeli civilians caught in the rapid early Syrian advance, as well as various horrors inflicted upon the dead Jewish defenders. While most of the civilians had made it out of Ramat Magshimim, he should prepare himself and his men for some unpleasant surprises in the town, which had been reduced to rubble in the past four days of intense fighting.

The mechanized company, another company of infantry, his tank group, part of a reconnaissance company, and some *Sahal* special forces were preparing for the assault, which would take place late in the morning. The plan was to wait until the sun was high enough in the sky not to limit the vision of the attackers, who would be approaching from the west and south, with the tank group swinging around the town to the east to cut off the defenders. Fortunately, most of the enemy armor had been pulled out of the town, and it was held mostly by irregulars and plain infantry – not any of the elite or super-well-equipped Syrian units. Unfortunately, there was expected to be some grim close combat. The tanks were not to encircle the town completely, just threaten enough so that the defenders might decide to flee rather than fight.

David hopped off the lead tank as it paused to negotiate a large group of bomb craters in the highway and climbed back aboard *Gimmel* One as Sasha slowed to pick him up. He told Sasha the new orders and ducked down into the turret to tell Greg and Benny. All greeted the news with a certain grim anticipation. They reached their bivouac site on the western side of Hespin at about two in the morning. There was time to bed down for some quality sleep for all hands, with perimeter security being provided courtesy of the town's defense group.

In the air over Jordan 0100

Major Yossi Green's wing of F-15s was down to four planes, and he was determined not to lose a single one of them on this mission, even though flying at night with their limited instrumentation was difficult. He knew his bird by now, and the pilots of his wing were the best in the business. They would take advantage of the night to hit every Jordanian air base known to exist and make sure there would be nothing flying from that sector by the time the sun rose in less than five hours. The first three raids would be his responsibility. If they survived until 0300, the next group of pilots in rotation for the hot seat would have a crack at what was left. Yossi and his wing man Uri were flying as low as they dared over the Judean hills while the other surviving pair, Yair and Yoni, were sweeping along a little farther to the south. He could not see them with his tactical radar turned off to avoid detection, but he felt their presence in the night sky to his right. Once they had passed the first perimeter of what was left of the Jordanian air defenses, they would turn on their radars and go in hot for the final two or three minutes, staying low and fast then climbing suddenly before releasing their GPS-guided bombs to find their targets.

Their first target was the air base closest to the Jordanian capital of Amman, only a few air minutes from the Israeli border. It was a "showcase" base that housed some of the newest of Jordan's several hundred jet fighters, but most of them had been flown only for air shows and a few very formal joint exercises with other desert nations, mostly Saudi Arabia. However, in the past two years, he knew that most of the hangers had been buried and hardened to withstand a "casual" bombing with conventional armament. Therefore he had a pair of 400 kg "smart" bombs slung under his belly, and hoped that they had indeed retained their guidance system where they had been stored in deep bunkers that had survived the EMP blasts. His ground crew assured them that they tested out as OK, so he should believe them instead of his gnawing worry that preceded every first sortie.

They thundered over the Jordan River, hilltop high, on a track taking them just south of Amman and its still formidable air defenses. He could see ground radar sets locking on until the left side of his heads-up helmet display was a mass of orange lights. He spoke a brief word into his com link and both planes jinked right and dove closer to the dark hills that flashed by. A tone in his earphones told him that there were SAMs launched, and he flipped on his tactical radar. It took four long seconds to give him his first glance of the incoming threats, and they were easily the four longest seconds of his life. He almost plowed straight into an onrushing ridge as he was so distracted waiting for the display to come on. He heard a low whistle in his earphones and gathered that Uri had seen his near miss. However, he was relieved to notice the flash of an exploding warhead somewhere behind him, presumably on the ridge he had just missed. Two more SAMs were tracking on a collision course with him dead ahead, he slammed into a hard left turn, climbing just a little before rolling back to the right almost parallel to his original course and climbing steeply.

His radar display showed the deadly blips bearing away to his right after passing right under or over him; he did not have time to check their altitude readings. More SAMs were locking on and launching as he swung back on his course to the airbase. Amman was a dark mass to his left instead of the fairyland of light that it had been on all his fly-bys up the Jordan River in night maneuvers in all his training missions but one. He had run past it one wet winter night during a regional power blackout that had scrambled half the IAF as a precaution. Ahead he could see white bursts of old-fashioned-but-deadly flak from conventional antiaircraft batteries that told him he was on course for the air field. Checking his wingman's position, right where it should be as always, he pulled back the stick and the throttle to climb above the fireworks. They would release their hanger-busting bombs from about 10,000 meters and trust their four bombs' "smarts" to find their way to their pre-set targets. There were no aircraft in the sector. He couldn't imagine an air force that was not flying a rotation of interceptors over its air bases in war time, especially at night. Although there was no one home at Ramat Hovav at the moment, it was only because all fourteen planes were in the air or refueling on the ground with no one left to fly cover for the base. It would have to rely on its ground to air missiles working in case of a bombing raid. So far only one flight of Egyptian bombers had tried.

The moment he reached 10,000 meters he released his two presents for the RJAF and climbed up and away, heading for home. Two more SAMs were incoming, but with his increasing speed and rate of climb, he felt he could outrun them. Uri was snug on his wing and the two birds accelerated homewards for another load. He wished there had been time and planes enough to hit the Jordanian air defenses harder before going after their airfields, but it was that kind of war – no time to spare to go by the book, just keep fighting and staying alive.

He was just beginning to relax and think ahead to a quick landing and new bomb load – if anyone flying a supersonic jet fighter can ever be described as relaxed – when a tone in his earphones alerted him to an unidentified aircraft in radar range. A quick glance at his tactical screens told him the bad news, multiple bogeys in the air over Eastern Jordan, probably launched from one of the remote bases targeted for one of his next bomb loads. "*Heverim* … friends," he told his wing mates. Each of them confirmed contacts approaching from the east. "Ground radar, how many royal friends do we have?" he asked.

"We're confirming eight for dinner," the ground controller said, "but we can't see anything lower than 200 meters without a Hawkeye in the air."

"Any 16's available?" He asked.

"Negative, not for another ten minutes minimum," ground replied.

"Dealing with it." Yossi thought for a few seconds – not in words but in patterns, fluid, moving, three dimensional sorts of thoughts that were abstract on one level, but quite grounded in his current airspeed, direction, altitude, mood and experience. It was something he could never explain to his wife or friends who didn't fly, but it made him an ace near the top of the IAF deck.

As he and his wing pulled a sweeping 180 degree turn and gained altitude, he began to lay out the plan that had suggested itself the strongest out of the many options that raced through his brain. "Ok, here's our game. Let's shake up this pack of cadets. Run them around the sky. Two laps and we break the first one that gets dizzy." There were syllables of agreement from his three companions.

"Yair, you G-force king – you're pack leader. Yoni, look for places to park and pick up some points. Uri and I will keep their pants wet until we see a target. Good hunting!"

He fell in behind as Yair shot ahead and accelerated on a tangent designed to pull the oncoming pack away in pursuit. Yoni was playing a loose wing position, taking a microsecond longer than Yossi knew he could to respond to his leader's moves. He watched the on-rushing blips begin to angle towards them on his radar display. They were still too far away to discern a pattern, and he could not spare the attention to count them, but the group looked like a round eight or so. As soon as they picked up on the trail, he would begin a series of feints designed to pull the pack apart.

Yair's fox and hounds chase took them high and looping deep into Jordan. No tones warned of SAM launches, although he could see amber spots indicating radar lock on as they sped through the night skies. At this point, a SAM had an equal chance of downing a Jordanian fighter as one of the high flying Israelis. Yair was doing a fine job of pulling the dozen fighters into an intense chase, with little chance of locking on long enough to fire a missile.

"Tango number two," Yossi tipped his wingman two seconds before rolling right and threatening to loop away from the lead pair. At the last second the two birds settled back on the leader's trail, having moved a little higher and farther right in the process. He could see their pursuers clearer on the tactical screens now. There was no chance of a visual ID at this range and nighttime conditions, but his second sense told him they were a pack of F-16 Falcons on his tail. Something about their apparent acceleration, rate of climb and ability to follow their turns told him just as clearly as a fly-by visual.

"Think our friends are 16ers, let's go a little higher and faster," he suggested. Yair climbed and accelerated into a gut-wrenching climbing turn in response. Yossi filled his lungs and tightened his legs and stomach muscles as he entered the high-G turn. As his vision blurred for a moment he could sense Uri falling off a hair from his tight wing position. "Bogie down with a twist," he grunted as soon he could speak, and he pushed the stick forward to initiate a dive. As he twisted left then right to reassume his follow the leader he checked the display behind him. It looked like the last two were beginning to loosen from the pack.

The two Jordanian leaders behind him chanced a pair of missiles each from a range of about five or six kilometers, only to watch them go wide as the chase cut a hard left turn that looped back towards Israel. Yossi followed Yair's winding trail with half an eye and watched for any sign of weakness in the pack behind them. In a flash he saw the gap he was looking for. "Exit four," he barked in code to Uri and the two of them suddenly split into a pre-planned arabesque figure that brought them down neatly behind the pursuing pack with the two stragglers in their sights. Two missiles each, two quick kills and the pack broken up nicely. He was now the pursuer, and despite the efforts of two planes that he now visually confirmed were Falcons to roll away and get on his tail, he soon had another plane in his kill zone. He fired two more ARMs and flipped over to support his wingman pursuing the next kill. He was now down to two air to air missiles, for he had carried only six along with the pair of medium bunker busters. However he did not regret spending four of his missiles to down two planes, it made the odds a lot more even.

At this point, combat experience and intense training trumped numerical advantage and a few short minutes later, three remaining F-16s fled towards the nearby Saudi Arabian border. Yossi was torn between the urge to follow them and the need to return to base for another bomb load. He decided to leave them – too bad there was no way of knowing which buried hangers were now missing their RJAF birds so as not to waste a bomb on them.

Five minutes flying time took them back to their approach to Ramat Hovav. "Still looking for helpers?" an incoming Israeli F-16 pilot asked him over the common channel as he waited for a turn to land.

"You're welcome to come along next trip," Yossi said, then swung around for his landing approach.

Mount Meron 0500

Anna felt ready to start another endless day after four hours of deep dreamless sleep, a shower and a sit-down breakfast with Kobi where at least five minutes was spent talking about something besides the war. For some reason, perhaps the chronic lack of sleep, they reminisced about their university days in the Talpiot program for high-scoring technical and scientific recruits. Each of them had finished their eight-year commitment and re-enlisted because the IDF offered them fascinating real life challenges that neither of their mathematical minds could pass up. Although Kobi had dabbled in a high tech startup as technical adviser for awhile – the horse he backed in the Internet sweepstakes had turned out to be a technical success, but a market failure. He had shown Anna the business plan a long time ago, and all the flaws she had pointed out had come true with a vengeance.

They added their dishes to the tottering pile in the sink and made their way back to their computer screens and headphones. It helped to remind herself there was a world outside of their secure cave. She would have to remember to make a trip topside sometime to see a little sunshine before she turned into a true troglodyte.

She scrolled quickly through the night's major events in the common network blog they all fed with tidbits to keep each other up to date as her command team carried out their wide ranging tasks and communications. The number one headline was that the Prime Minister had been located at last. He had died sometime on the first day of the war, buried deep in the collapse of a political crony's private bunker near Be'er Sheva. It had taken so long to locate him because it was an unscheduled stop and all of his bodyguards had died in the surface blast that had caved in the private shelter. It solved the war's biggest mystery when one of the tycoon host's sons had come looking for his parents and started digging. The Defense Minister had been seriously wounded by shrapnel and was out of the war in the first hours. He had been inspecting home defense shelters in the south, but was not in one the first hour the rockets began falling. The Minister of Foreign Affairs was stuck at a conference in Sweden and unable to get home. The Ministers of Agriculture, Finance and Interior were still arguing over who was the acting PM. The Agriculture minister had the most seniority in age and government service, but the Interior Minister out-ranked him in the coalition-leading party. The Finance Minister didn't have much of a claim except that he was obviously more important than anyone else because he controlled the money. However, the electronic bank and financial records had all disappeared in the first three minutes of this war.

Anna wondered if the banks kept disaster recovery tapes in EMP-proof vaults or offshore. She doubted either scenario. What a mess it would be sorting out a whole economy with few reliable records. If she was lucky, maybe they would lose her credit card balance from her last trip to Europe. Not likely. Alas, her pension and savings were probably blipped away in a nanosecond, but her credit card debts were probably engraved in triplicate somewhere, never to be erased.

She clicked ahead to notes on the air war, and was sad to note the loss of four more planes overnight. No matter how spectacular their air to air combat scores, they could not keep up this attrition. The good news was that the first four re-wired F-16s and a pair of F-15s were due to be ready for a test flight later that morning. Even better news was a note about air-readiness testing of a dozen re-wired Blackhawk helicopters being done at the nearby Ramat David and perhaps another dozen in progress at a base in the Negev. Two more sets of arrows in her quiver, and not a moment too soon.

On the ground the picture remained muddied, and it was hard to assess what had moved in the night. Radio reports were incomplete, but told of hard fighting at both ends of the country, and plenty of turmoil in the middle. Apparently the blob of forces gathered in the Jordan Valley were spreading out from Jenin and Jericho and threatening settlements up and down the West Bank. There was still no direct attack on Jerusalem, but there was chaos in the streets along the neighborhood boundaries between

Arab and Jewish areas. A large, well-armed Palestinian paramilitary group had tried to close Highway One between Tel Aviv and Jerusalem, operating out of villages along the narrow corridor that connected Jerusalem to the plains. However, they had been pushed back by reservists from the armored forces headquarters at Latrun using a hodge-podge collection of museum piece tanks, trucks and armored cars. From the tidbits she read, it must have looked like a remake of a '48 war movie.

And even better news was a line that noted contact between the Israeli Navy and the first incoming freighter of supplies an hour earlier. She made a mental note to query the 6 am briefing about where to send the load of shells and ammunition. However, where it was most needed and where and how it could be carried there were all equally pressing problems.

Turning to the international reaction, she was pleased to see that Koby and friends had managed to establish several Internet connections via satellite phone hookups. Expensive yes, but who was counting costs? Already a few *hasbara* – information and media relations officers in the Jerusalem headquarters were beginning to feed accurate information to the world media and encourage questioning of the most far-fetched claims.

Except for their satellite connections, there was a virtual Internet blackout from southern Turkey all the way to Cairo. Even in the high-tech Persian Gulf emirates the EMP effects crashed servers, networks and hardware for days afterwards. It was making accurate news coverage almost impossible. Jerusalem was having a major impact by uploading some of the first clear pictures of the fighting – including video clips taken by some of the few cameras to survive the electromagnetic pulses. For once, there was no blitz of misleading, propaganda-ridden film pouring from the Palestinian side. They were stuck in the Stone Age again.

But world opinion was largely undaunted by the few facts filtering out of the region. All but Israel's handful of friends in the world believed the Iranian story that Israel had launched the first nuke and that there were massive Arab civilian casualties. Without tipping their hand about Israel's remaining satellite coverage, its missile detection capabilities (still operating, thank G-d) and other critical details, this was proving a hard claim to refute. However, except for bombing supply lines, depots, command and control structures and air bases, Israel had not taken the war to its neighbors and their civilian populations. Those who had not poured across the border with guns and carts to haul off the loot were unharmed. This kind of "fact" would only come out weeks or even years after the war.

Could Anna indeed contemplate the concept of "after the war?" This morning, for the first time, she could think about the war ending. Today, with the helicopters and their own jet fighters beginning to come on line, the first supplies beginning to trickle in, and their limited victories in the field – perhaps there was hope after all. In the past 24 hours, there had been no major breakthroughs by the invading forces. In fact, Israelis were counter-attacking everywhere they had a few people to spare. For instance, the southern Golan Heights not only was holding, but a pair of tanks – no more – had attacked the rear of a Syrian supply column and nearly wiped it out. Already the commanders were pressing ahead to roll up the rear of the massive Syrian advance that had joined up to push past Rosh Pina and Korozin and threaten Tiberius from the north by breaking through to the Kinneret in a new place. The Syrians were also trying to push west along the highways toward the coast. She noted that front as a prime place to use the newly re-commissioned Blackhawks. She checked the clock on her screen. Time for the 0600 meeting.

Moshav Yiftach 0600

Natalie and Eli both tumbled out of bed early – even though it was Shabbat – to take their turn at guard duty. They had dutifully woken up Sam from his borrowed sleeping bag in the sukkah, fed him breakfast, and shared coffee from the big air-pump thermos they prepared before Shabbat. They wished him luck, for he was due back at the command group in a few hours, collected their weapons from the gun safe, and headed out to their assigned patrol beyond the perimeter of the moshav.

Like almost all the women on the moshav, Natalie had learned how to handle a rifle and a hand gun. Today she had a battered, IDF surplus, single-shot carbine that was probably almost as old as she was. However unlike about half of the Yiftach women, including most of the women her age, she had never served in the IDF. Her training was limited to basic firearms safety training, and some shooting on the target range on the Golan base that had been open for training the moshavniks during the last few red alerts and crises. She and Eli had gone shooting together a few times and companionably, and a little competitively, blasted away at a few target scenarios. Though Eli was just as nearsighted as Natalie, his vision was more correctable with glasses for distance. And so, though her aim and gun handling were good, she could only hit the targets she could see at fairly close range. On the two times they got to fire in automatic mode, because of the high cost of ammunition, Natalie's 15-20 meter targets had at least four or five more bullet holes in them than Eli's. Eli used to joke that he could shoot anyone trying to attack from a distance, and Natalie would finish off anyone he left standing.

Though Natalie was not part of the trained moshav defense groups, every healthy person between about sixteen and at about seventy-something had gone through at least basic defense drills and emergency practice. So she had asked to share Eli's guard duties with him, and the group leader agreed that they could work together. It was only a three hour hitch anyway and their area had been quiet for more than a day. All the intense fighting seemed to have moved north.

Their duties for this fine morning were to walk between the various checkpoints and pickets set up in a perimeter extending several kilometers from the moshav fence. It was not too hot yet, but the Golan was still blanketed with an eye-watering smoke and haze. They packed extra water, snacks, prayer books, and reading matter for the pickets, who found themselves suddenly quite bored after days of intense, any-moment-could-be-our-last fighting followed by a day of sporadic shooting, but no serious attacks.

It felt good to get out and walk together and talk. They found they could not quite get used to the shell ravaged landscape and the odd brownish yellow haze that kept the usual vistas from opening up before them. It made the odd shapes of blasted tanks, trucks and armored vehicles appear surreal – in stark detail when they were close to them, and somehow blurred and unreal when they were farther. Every now and then they had to pause and reorient themselves to the changed countryside, familiar in its contours, but strange in its twisted metal flora.

They reached the first picket post and chatted awhile with two fellow moshavniks. Eli knew them from the dairy and the synagogue, but they had already passed well along to the next picket outpost before he remembered their names. They continued on their leisurely stroll, enjoying each other's company, and beginning to feel a bit like they were on a pleasant Shabbat morning walk – except that they were toting rifles and rucksacks. At the rate they were going it would take them their whole three hour guard duty to make one circuit of the posts in their sector.

The next two pickets were IDF soldiers from a reserve unit that had been called up, but stuck with no transportation after the EMP hit. They had started their war at the bus station in Tiberias and helped fight off the attack from the south along the Kinneret on the morning David and Sam had kayaked across the lake for help. Somehow they had heard the story about the two kayakers from Yiftach and appeared impressed to meet Eli, and wanted to hear the whole story first hand. Since they were in no hurry, Eli and Natalie sat down on the edge of one of their fox holes and told them, sharing some of Tali's famous muffins and the small thermos of strong hot coffee they had poured for themselves before setting out. The coffee was most welcome, for the two were stuck at their post with no stove to boil water – and besides it was Shabbat.

"It's odd," Natalie said as they wandered on to the next outpost on their circuit, "I never thought I would ever be married to a war hero."

"For crying out loud, all I did was paddle across the Kinneret. With the kids in the summer it's called recreation," Eli protested.

"Yeah, and in the middle of the night in a war zone, with no idea what's going on and the enemy all around, it's called being a hero," Natalie argued.

"I just made the suggestion. They were trying to figure out how to get to Tiberias. The next thing I knew, Sam and I were packing the truck."

"Well, you've always been MY hero," Natalie said.

Eli stopped walking, wrapped his arms around her, rucksack, rifle and all, and kissed her. "Hmmm, I always wanted one of those cute soldier girls – maybe we should get you some khakis to go with your rifle."

Natalie held him awhile and they stood in the middle of the bombed out barley field that contoured around the hill beyond the moshav. Only a kilometer away, it was already blurred in the morning haze from brush fires and the war that was raging somewhere to the north of them. For now it was quiet. They held hands and moseyed along to their next stop at the top of the field where the nearby apple orchard ended. They were sorry to see that perhaps a third of the trees had been damaged by the shelling.

Their next checkpoint was a group of five reservists from the same stranded unit. They were clustered around a machine gun. They had an older-style bazooka resting where it could be grabbed quickly. They also wanted to hear the story of the kayak mission to Tiberias once they figured out who Eli was. They had also heard of the trip to Syria and finding the pilot, for one of them had been in the basement hospital visiting a wounded friend when Captain Tzippori was brought in. Two of them had stopped into the Kaplan's sukkah to borrow the *lulav* and *etrog* on their first day after being shipped across the lake. Unfortunately Eli and Natalie were out of coffee, but there were still muffins enough to go around and home baked cookies from another home in the moshav that still had a working oven.

"They really look up to you," Natalie told Eli after they excused themselves and began their trip back towards the moshav.

Eli shrugged modestly.

"No, really," She insisted. "It gives them hope somehow, to know that ordinary people are doing extraordinary things. And it's a great story – although the Kinneret is getting wider across every time I hear this tale."

"Well, if you follow the zigzag route Sam and I paddled, it's almost twice as wide," Eli said.

"I've been wondering, just how lost were you? Now that we're alone you can tell me. If I listen to Sam you were drifting lost and G-d knows where. If I listen to you tell it, you were just a little unsure about where you were going to come out on the other side for a while."

"You want the truth?"

"Nothing but the truth. I'm your wife, after all."

"And that means I have to tell you the truth all the time?" Eli queried.

"Absolutely, it's in the Torah."

"Ok, where?"

"Well, you remember that G-d himself told Abraham to listen to Sarah about sending Ishmael away from the camp."

"That doesn't mean he had to tell her the truth. It means he had to listen to her advice – although it seems we are still having trouble with cousin Ishmael in spite of that advice," Eli said, waving his hand at a nearby tank carcass, with the Syrian marking plain on the unburned half.

"And what about the commandment to the sons of Adam to leave one's parents and cleave to one's wife?" Natalie asked. "You are avoiding my question – just how lost were you?"

"Maybe I can cleave to my wife sometime this afternoon if there is some quiet in the house," Eli suggested.

Natalie gave him a swat with the hat she was wearing to keep the morning sun out of her eyes.

"Ok," Eli relented, "the truth is there were no stars or moon to steer by, no wind that I could make out, and I was beginning to wonder if we were not going to have to sit there until the sun came up. But I didn't want Sam to freak out. I was still getting to know him and he seemed a little hot headed – always rushing off to do things. It's funny how we've grown close in these few days – and done some pretty amazing things together. "

"I'm thinking of getting the kayak bronzed some day," Natalie teased. This time it was Eli's turn to give her an affectionate swat with his hat.

"I still don't know how Sam talked me into driving into Syria with him and the Rabbi. I felt like his lucky rabbit's foot as you so succinctly put it. If it hadn't been for Rabbi Beniyahu agreeing with him there is no way I would have gone. Somehow I trust the Rabbi's instincts – and I generally don't believe in those kinds of things."

"Yes I know," Natalie said. "And yet somehow when he said all those things about you – and they are all true, you are way too modest to see the good you do – somehow I felt everything was going to be OK. And look what happened – you found Captain Tzippori! If that wasn't a miracle waiting to happen, I don't know what is."

"Actually, I was trying to keep up with Sam and turned around when I heard a goat carrying on, thinking there was a shepherd nearby," Eli said.

"Still, you know what I mean. It's almost as if HaShem is giving us a little reassurance every now and then that we are on the right track."

"I suppose you are right. I just know I was so damned impatient and anxious to get out of Syria at one minute, and then the next minute I was so busy taking care of this Jewish pilot who fell out of the sky and who needed my help that I hardly thought about being scared."

"I know how much you regretted making aliyah too old to serve in the IDF," Natalie said. "You never talked about it much, just the little remark or expression now and then, but I've always known that these guys were your heroes."

"I did read every book on Israel and the Palmach and IDF that I could get my hands on from a pretty early age," Eli admitted. "And the stories about the old days with the Palmach and the Hagannah and the Irgun always amazed me. The things they did against incredible odds with practically nothing to work with... I guess we're still having to do that. Especially in this crazy war. You know I have to stop and remind myself several times a day that this war is less than a week old, and yet all of a sudden our whole world has changed."

"I have to stop and think that too," Natalie said. "And it's really strange to think that for all we know, life is going on in Chicago just the same as normal: same traffic, same TV and radio, same insanity about baseball. People are shopping and going to work as normal. Israel is just a three-minute segment on the nightly news, if even that much. Ruth must be absolutely frantic with worry though."

They stopped at another outpost, chatted with another moshav couple they both knew and joked about making husband and wife guard duty mandatory. By now their three hour shift was over, and it was time to head back to the moshav to catch the late *minyan* at the *Beit Knesset*. They were still more than a kilometer from the moshav fence line when Eli noticed some movement out of the corner of his eye. He stopped suddenly on the trail and Natalie nearly ran into him. He stood staring off to his left.

"What?" Natalie asked, unslinging her rifle, nerves suddenly tense and hands prepared to work the bolt and chamber a round.

"I thought I saw something move," Eli said, scanning the debris-strewn swath of destruction that lay a few hundred meters behind the high-water-mark of the enemy advance on the moshav. There were blackened, burnt-out armored vehicles and the gutted remains of tanks. There were still dead bodies this far away from the moshav. The burial teams had only advanced the first hundred meters or so, and had paused for rest on the Shabbat. Had there not been so impossibly many to bury, they would have worked on the Shabbat – for tending to an unburied corpse – friend or foe – was a commandment that overruled the Sabbath prohibitions. Packs, rifles, radios and equipment were scattered where they dropped, mixed with shreds of tires and odd pieces of vehicles blown off. It was a forlorn and chaotic scene, showing in sharp detail in the near ground and dusty haze in the middle and far distance, giving the impression of a gruesome tableau that went on forever.

He stood, silently gazing at a not-so-distant area where something seemed to have caught his attention. He saw the half-blasted side door of a half track swinging in the hot dry wind that had begun to blow during their return walk, promising another baking afternoon. That wasn't it. He also saw some stalks of tall grass waving, but that wasn't enough to catch his eye either. What was it?

Natalie felt the eerie silence and a chill of foreboding creep up her spine. "Eli, what do you think it was?" she asked to break the silence.

Eli stood staring a few more moments before answering. "I saw something – maybe someone moving – just a bit." He too had eased his rifle off his shoulder and now began to use the telescopic sight to sweep the area where he thought he saw movement.

"If it was a 'someone' don't you think we should find some cover instead of standing here like two statues in plain view – or get some help?" she asked, wishing she had some binoculars or something to sharpen the sights around her.

Eli looked up as if breaking a trance, looked around them and spotted an overturned something with three out of four wheels left, some sort of a jeep perhaps, though the top had been blown mostly away and the rest crushed where it landed. It was about 30 meters away. Keeping his rifle at the half ready and his eyes mostly on the spot of ground he suspected contained the something that had caught his eye and flashed a message to his brain, Eli sidled slowly over to a partly sheltered spot behind one of the intact wheels. Natalie cautiously followed him, glancing around to make sure of her footing on the uneven ground.

He rested his rifle on the edge of the upturned chassis and resumed his search through the scope. Following his line of sight, Natalie could tell that he was sweeping an area less than 100 meters away and appeared to be going from body to body, studying each for movement. She shuddered at the sight of all the several-day old corpses, her imagination filling in what her eyes could not quite make out. Together they stared for some minutes. Then Natalie turned to re-orient herself to the moshav fence line, for the fence was blasted apart and overrun in places. They were perhaps a kilometer from the moshav. She couldn't quite see the outposts she knew should be there near the boundary fence.

"Eli," she whispered.

"What?" he answered absently, still peering through his scope.

"Isn't this a minefield?"

Eli pulled himself abruptly from the scope and looked around as if for the first time. He looked toward the moshav fence, looked back at the trail they had left to take cover, and looked at the debris around him. Natalie could see a look of shock and horror and complete chagrin steal over his face in millisecond turns.

"My G-d you're right, I think it is!" he said, also in a whisper as if a loud voice could set off one of the hundreds of defensive mines sewn in fields around the perimeter of the moshav over the past fifty years.

They stared at their feet and looked behind them, trying to see their footprints where they had angled off the trail. It was impossible to tell. Neither of them had been paying much attention. Then they turned and looked around the littered scene surrounding them. As if in confirmation, they both found themselves staring at a shallow, wide blast crater not far away that looked for all the world like the aftermath of a landmine.

"Could have been a shell..." Natalie murmured, unconvinced. Eli shook his head.

He bent down and peered under the overturned frame and examined the ground around his feet. "I'm pretty sure this would have blown anything within at least a meter when it flipped," Eli said, still in a low voice and working to convince himself as much as Natalie. "See those marks over there? I think that's where it was when it was hit and blown over this way. Something blew half the top clear off it and scattered it there behind us." Natalie nodded, still unconvinced. She did not dare move her feet, but did lean on the overturned oily steel frame for support.

Eli sighed and turned back to his scope, as if to take him mind off the immediate problem with something he could do. "Let me just finish my search grid while we try to think of a way to get out of this mess," he said quietly.

Natalie fought back an urge to thump him over the head with her rifle butt. Eli could be maddenly methodical and impossible to budge at times and this was one of them. But in the next few breaths she calmed down and reminded herself that it was precisely his methodical and analytical qualities that were going to get them out of the fix that his single-minded curiosity had led them into.

Eli was clearly tense and his mind working while he slowly moved his scope from point to point, sweeping his mental search grid. He fixed a while on a spot, moved away from it and back again. Natalie strained to see, but she could see nothing but a jumble of bodies and wreckage too far away to make out clearly with her unaided eyes.

"There," he said quietly, "there is someone moving, just an arm, but he's clearly still alive." He passed the long rifle and scope over to Natalie who handed her rifle to him rather than set it down on the dangerous ground.

She took a few moments to get used to the new perspective of the high powered sight and Eli pointed it in the direction of his find. Mangled, dirty and dismembered bodies jumped into sharp relief as she zeroed in on the spot he pointed out. Then she saw it too, a tattered sleeve, a faintly moving arm, barely lifting from the ground. She could not make out his head or feet in the jumble of dead surrounding him, only part of a torso and the weak movement of a forearm, fingers limp and unexpressive. After gazing at the movement awhile watching the arm fall loosely then lift feebly again in a few seconds, she forced herself to study the pile around him. Then she mutely handed the rifle back to Eli. She felt both pity for the poor suffering soul who must have lain there for perhaps two or three days as his life ebbed away and revulsion for the carnage and bloodshed all around her. All this had happened while she drank tea and comforted scared children less than a kilometer away in her snug, earth-sheltered house. All this ugliness was heaped and broken on what had been a beautiful field of grass and flowers that had been protected by the landmines from grazing and any other uses.

Eli stared a while waiting for another trace of movement. He wondered for a fleeting moment if this unknown soldier had been shot with the very rifle that found him. But the pile of death around him suggested a mortar or artillery shell nearby. However he did not recall firing in this direction much. He had concentrated on a section farther to the north. He watched another feeble slight raise of the arm, this time there was a hint of a movement of a finger. He had the impression the man was praying and punctuating his prayer with gestures as he sometimes saw in *Shul*.

"I'm going to call out to him," Eli said, passing the rifle with the scope back to Natalie, "watch him and see if there is any response." Natalie swapped rifles with him again.

Eli took a deep breath, cupped his hands and yelled, "Salaam."

Natalie shook her head, still concentrating on the scope. Eli called a few more times, mangling the few Arabic phrases they had been taught in defense group training.

Natalie studied the distant figure in the scope. The arm raised again in its silent rhythm. There was no change to its motion: just up, a vague flicker of the fingers, and down again. She passed the scope to Eli again, taking her rifle back. He watched the intermittent motion for a long while. Finally he lowered the rifle and slung it back over his shoulder and turned to study the gentle slope behind them, looking again for a landmark between them and the trail thirty meters away.

"Mines are sown about every ten meters here, but in a pattern that was forgotten years ago. Even if we knew the pattern, we couldn't be sure of the grid or where we are in that pattern," he thought out loud. "That means a possibility of perhaps three mines between here and the trail – or none, or maybe six. There is no way of telling."

Natalie scowled at his encouraging words. "Ever play minesweeper?" She asked.

"Not too often. I always lost about three out of four games…" Eli mused, staring at the littered ground ahead of them.

"My point exactly. What about him?" she asked while thinking over all the possibilities she could think of in her mind – both for getting out of their pickle and for getting help to the wounded soldier.

"I'm sure we came on a slanted path, but a fairly direct one that ended here. If I could only be sure of the angle we could probably retrace our steps fairly accurately," he said.

"I've thought of that too, but I think we angled off a little bit at first, and then more sharply as we approached the wreck here," she replied, "and those are not good enough odds for me. What if we fired a few shots and tried to signal one of the outposts?"

"I can't think of anything better," Eli said after considering the idea, "we just have to make sure that no one follows us down here. I hope they have enough sense to stick to the path. Unlike me," he added. "Do you want to do the honors? I think the standard distress signal is three shots evenly spaced."

"With pleasure," Natalie said. "You watch our friend and see if there is any reaction to the shots." She chambered a round, aimed high in the air away from the moshav and the outposts and prepared to fire. Eli found the figure in his sights again, waited until the arm moved again and signaled her to start. Natalie fired three slow, deliberate shots into the hazy sky. Then she ejected the last spent round from her chamber and waited, watching and listening back in the direction they had come, and back towards the moshav where they had been going. Eli paused from his vigil in the scope occasionally to peer around.

He checked his watch. "Let's try it again in about three more minutes, and then about five minutes apart," he said. "They will need some help zeroing in on the sound because we are not very visible here off the trail." After an interminably long three minutes, Natalie shouldered her rifle and fired three more, keeping her gun aimed in roughly the same direction so as to be consistent, and wondering if it mattered.

There was not much to do for the next five minutes but stand, leaning on the blasted chassis behind what was once a back wheel and wait. They spoke little, wondering about the wounded man, and wondering how anyone could survive three or four days in this dry heat. Both noted little discernable response to their shots except for perhaps an interruption in the rhythm.

For the third five minutes Eli retold the story of finding Captain Tzippori. He reviewed all the signs left by his taking care of his wounds: the makeshift turban, the strips and sling cut from the parachute, the goat's milk dried in the helmet lining. And they wondered again at his determination and ingenuity. At last report he was still unconscious, but responding to stimulus and light, and even moaning and mumbling in his coma. His color and skin tone was much better and the doctors were confident he would recover consciousness in the next day or two as long as they were able to push fluids. However, they would be making their own Ringers solution soon if no fresh medical supplies could be found. The hospital in Poriya had none to spare and neither did the IDF field hospitals. And so the radiologist and pathologist were making plans to cook and bag their own solutions.

They were lost in this conversation when the time came around for their fourth set of gunshots. Natalie was chambering a fresh round when they heard helloing from the direction of the moshav. Both of them shouted together in attempt to guide their rescue party.

In a short while, they could see six figures hurrying up the trail from the moshav. They yelled until they got their attention. As they approached to within calling range they could see that there were five with guns at the ready, and one carrying what looked like stretcher poles. There was nothing that looked like a mine detector, but then, why would there be?

When the squad of IDF soldiers, three men and three women, approached to the nearest point on the trail to them, Eli and Natalie fumbled over their Hebrew trying to explain that they had entered the minefield because they had found a wounded soldier. Finally one of the women replied, "You can just tell me in English if you want, you say you found someone alive out there?"

Feeling both relieved and embarrassed at their poor grasp of the mother tongue of the land they were defending, Eli and Natalie took turns explaining what had happened while the soldiers took turns casting about and studying the distant wounded figure. At length the leader decided that three should return for mine detection equipment – there was one working set that the burial groups had been using – and a medical corpsman. There was no consideration given to leaving the poor man – even though he appeared very far gone, and it would be risking a number of lives to retrieve him.

Two of the women soldiers settled down on the trail to wait and keep the Kaplans company although Eli felt that the need for a babysitter had come and gone already. They were glad enough for the company, for a half hour stretched into more like two hours before the trio returned with two mine specialists and a medic. "They were just sitting down to lunch," the leader explained, "and I had to wait for them to collect the mine gear after telling them,"

One of the mine specialists put on her earphones and calibrated the magnetometer while the other shushed the chattering group. All eventually stopped talking and watched her work. As soon as it was calm and quiet, the sweeper began her slow and methodical way, swinging the detector loop slowly from side to side in a wide arc in front of her, watching the meter and listening for tones. After working her way perhaps ten meters towards Natalie and Eli, she paused, worked her instrument in shorter swings around a point to her right, reached into her pack, and pulled out a small red piece of tape stuck to a straight wire stake. Gently she poked it into the ground to her right so that the flag stood upright, its bit of red tape swaying in the wind, which was now hotter and drier and feeling a bit dusty and smoky under their eyelids. Eli and Natalie sipped at their water bottles and watched. The soldiers on the slope above them mostly watched the mine sweeper, but were also taking turns with a pair of binoculars watching the wounded man. Soon the hum of conversation returned to their group, but no more shouting back and forth to Eli and Natalie.

The minesweeper began to work left away from her flag, planted a small green flag behind her, and continued working her way towards them. She stuck a little green flag every few meters to mark the safe trail. She did not hurry, even the last little bit. She checked around Natalie's and Eli's feet in an elaborate show of being extra careful – which Eli thought was serious at first, until he saw his own footprints nearby being elaborately checked over. Eli lifted up one foot in a dumb show and pointed for the soldier to check under it. Eli grinned at her, and the soldier broke into a huge smile at last, and they hugged with relief and pleasure.

"Actually, it is hard to tell about a mine when you are near such a big chunk of metal as this with so many fragments lying around," the soldier explained as they followed her carefully flagged trail back. Even though the footpath through the mine field was probably little safer than their wrecked jeep, both Natalie and Eli felt much safer on the known path, and vowed never to wander into another minefield again.

However, their little group of soldiers and medic were planning to do just that. Together the squad's sergeant and the two minesweepers, both noncoms as well, walked up and down the stretch of trail, peering at possible paths through the debris to get to the pile of bodies that contained the lone survivor. Finally they settled on a likely path with not too much metallic debris, and yet fairly direct. The second minesweeper took the headset and detector, fiddled with his settings a few moments, and set off. This one worked noticeably faster, until he found and flagged his first mine and then he settled into a slower rhythm. By the time he was halfway to their goal there were four little red flags outside the green trail he had flagged.

As Eli stood with Natalie and the group of soldiers they began to hear sounds of distant artillery breaking the calm of the early afternoon. They glanced at the group leader in alarm.

"What time is it?" the squad leader asked Eli, pointing to his watch. "About 1400," Eli said.

"They're taking back Magshinim. The plan was to hit them in the heat of the afternoon when everyone is tired, bored and most of them sleeping. No Shabbat naps for them today," the sergeant explained.

"Any chance of the fighting reaching here?" Natalie asked. Magshinim was less than a dozen kilometers from Moshav Yiftach.

"We're back on high alert," the sergeant said. "In fact, my group was headed out to reinforce the perimeter when we heard your shots. We had to report back to command first before coming out to investigate. Otherwise we would have been here sooner."

"Do you need a sniper?" Eli asked, not daring to look at Natalie.

The young sergeant glanced at Natalie before answering. "You had better check in with the Moshav group first. I'm sure they'll have orders for you."

They turned their attention back to the minesweeper. He was now approaching the tangle of bodies that contained the man Eli had spotted hours earlier. Eli unslung his rifle and zeroed in on the spot with his scope. The sergeant took his binoculars back from the group and was also studying the minesweeper.

Eli made a half-hearted gesture to Natalie as if to offer her the scope, but she demurred, and he went back to watching the distant figures. He could not see the wounded soldier now, for he was behind the minesweeper. They heard the minesweeper calling out in Arabic as he put down his wand and took out a hand gun that he kept ready, but not pointing at the prone figure beyond him. A few more phrases in Arabic came in bits over the hot, dry breeze that was blowing across the field from the east. Eli recognized one that he had used earlier when calling out to the distant casualty. He now recalled that it meant "keep your hands in sight" not "raise your hands." He was having a hard enough time remembering the Hebrew he already knew without trying to remember Arabic that he never knew.

He caught a sudden move in his scope. The minesweeper dived or fell to the ground and there was a flash and a muffled boom beyond him. Eli heard the sergeant gasp in amazement and both concentrated on the minesweeper, who rose slowly to his feet, clutching his neck. Eli saw a reddening of his hand, and realized he had been wounded. He stared through his scope back at where the fallen soldier had lain. There was little recognizable as men there now, just a smear of blood and torn flesh. The wounded man must have set off a hand grenade or a bomb just as the minesweeper approached. The minesweeper had gathered up his dropped detection wand and was beginning to walk back towards them, holding his bleeding neck. The leader yelled at him to stop. He took a few more steps and stopped.

Two soldiers and the medic, led by the minesweeper who had rescued Eli and Natalie, picked their way quickly but carefully along the marked trail and hurried to where the wounded minesweeper stood, bleeding and muttering himself.

In barely a minute they reached him. The medic took over the neck wound, applying a large field dressing and quickly checking for other injuries. By the time the two soldiers had the poor minesweeper lying and swearing vigorously on the stretcher, the medic had his helmet and half the man's shirt off and had applied squares of gauze to his cheek, temple and a spot on his arm. Eli watched in fascination at the quick and expert work unfolding before his eyes, until he suddenly felt like a peeping Tom and lowered his rifle.

"How bad is he hurt?" Natalie asked as Eli took his eyes from the scope.

"The neck is probably better than it looks from here because the medic is not putting much pressure there and is letting the soldier hold it himself. The rest looks pretty minor," he said.

The sounds of the distant shelling had grown more intense. Not long after the stretcher bearers joined them and changed places with two fresh bearers. They set off at a moderate pace towards the moshav. A few minutes later they met another squad of five coming out to replace them at their post on the perimeter. A few words were exchanged, just enough to relay the news.

As soon as the path was wide enough to walk next to him, Eli approached the wounded soldier, grabbed a hand hold on the litter to help carry, and asked him how he was doing, and what had happened.

"I'm going to be OK," the young man assured him, "But that crazy jihadist just blew himself to heaven and back. His seventy virgins are not going to find much left to love."

The squad leader came alongside and also wanted a fuller story. And so, as the group walked together towards the moshav perimeter, the young soldier held his blood-soaked bandage to the side of his neck where a piece of shrapnel had grazed him, and told his story. Their collective pace slowed as everyone strained to listen.

"I'm not sure what didn't seem quite right," the soldier began. "As I approached and called out to him, I could tell he was somehow aware of me, but wasn't responding. He appeared to be reciting Koran and yet paused a bit as I spoke and almost seemed to be on the point of responding. He had his eyes shut tight and was moving that hand you saw, as if measuring time – and I realized I'd seen the gesture before, when they showed films of suicide bombers praying the morning before their killings. He had his other hand inside his jacket, and something about the jacket and the whole way he was lying didn't seem right. So I yelled for him to put both hands in sight, and began to back up a bit. That's when he blew. Didn't say Allah this or Allah that or anything. It was bigger than a grenade. I think someone wired him and left him for us to find."

"I've heard of that happening to the US guys in Afghanistan and Iraq," the squad leader said. The wounded man began to nod his head in agreement, but stopped himself and put a little more pressure on the seeping cut. "I've heard about those too," he said.

"First I nearly blow myself and Natalie to bits trying to find him, and then he almost takes you with him," Eli exclaimed. "We were damned lucky today."

"How long do you think he had been there set up and waiting for us?" the leader asked.

The mine specialist shrugged his unhurt shoulder. "No idea," He said.

"My guess is that their field medics decided they were too full up to treat whatever was wrong with him, and his commander offered him a chance to die a hero," the medic said. "What kinds of injuries did you see?"

"It looked like one leg was pretty well mangled, but come to think of it, looked like it had been dressed and his head had a bandage too, no helmet. Although in thinking about it, I wonder if it might have been one of those white headbands that martyrs wear now that I play the tape back in my mind. What I thought was a bloodstain might have been letters in red. Son of a bitch, he tried to kill me – for having the nerve to try to help him!" the soldier on the litter swore a string of surprised profane observations under his breath as they walked along.

A fresh quartet of soldiers met them at the perimeter fence and offered to help with the stretcher, but the medic, Eli, Natalie, the soldiers and the other minesweeper waved them off and continued their trek to get their friend to the clinic in the Levine's basement. All of them were still turning the suicide / attempted murder over in their minds and trying to get a grasp on it, asking more questions and wondering various theories aloud.

Ramat Magshinim 1400

David Engel and his crew woke from hot, troubled naps less than an hour before the rescheduled assault time which had been moved from mid-morning to the heat of the afternoon. If the plan was to catch the defenders hot, sleepy and disoriented, it had a good chance of working, except that David felt the same way. He poured some lukewarm water from his canteen down his neck and took a few gulps and tried to clear his head. Baruch's Turkish coffee seemed to be lacking its usual heart-palpitating punch this afternoon. Perhaps the fragmented dreams where he knew that his friend Yankel was dead, but where Yankel kept appearing sporadically, were depressing and confusing him. He needed some of Yankel's sharpness now as their tank edged closer to the shattered community they had begun to retake.

The half dozen tanks in his newly formed unit swept in a ragged line, perhaps 150 meters apart and angled towards the small town. Mortar shells still burst in a rain of covering fire within the half dozen streets of the town. There were few shreds of red tiled roofs left and no houses even halfway intact above the first story. What the Syrians and their mercenaries had taken by force four days ago, the IDF was beginning to take back, one devastated house at a time. Commanders had warned about booby traps, mutilated bodies of the community's overrun defenders and other shocking sights. Five days of war and seeing his best friend cut up by machine gun fire in front of his eyes had left David feeling numb and almost apathetic. He had needed this Shabbat to recharge his emotional and spiritual resources, but there was to be no soul restoring nap this afternoon. He had a job to do.

The crew of *Gimmel* One was subdued today too. Any other time going into action had always sharpened their senses and brought a charge of energy. He wished for a second cup of coffee and a long, really cool shower after first steaming away the smoke and stench. This was no way to feel going into a close battle. Lives depended on his wits. David swept the oncoming edge of the community carefully with his binoculars, looking for any movement, any sign of resistance or booby traps. His driver, Sasha, was heads down using their rebuilt periscopes for the first time of the war. So far there was no fire in their direction, although David could hear small arms and machine gun fire at the southern edge of the town where the infantry was making their approach.

In "normal" circumstances, his tank would be firing too at this point, just to increase the shock and thunder of the attack. But tank ammunition was still scarce and they hoarded their forty five rounds for real targets. He studied the mostly downed perimeter fence line again, looking for points where machine gun nests, bazooka or RPG teams could be hiding. He lowered his binoculars and swung the machine gun into action. There were a few possible lurking places – the kinds of places where he would be hiding if he were defending instead of attacking. He fired a test burst at a pile of rubble where some sort of outbuilding had collapsed near the broken perimeter fence and looked for any response. The action brought a welcome sense of purpose and direction. He blasted a few more rounds at the shadows underneath its slabs of concrete and shreds of metal siding. As if in answer, an RPG round blasted from beneath one of the slabs and arched towards them. Sasha spun left and the turret spun right as his gunner kept the target in sight. The rocket propelled grenade fell short and to their right. Two seconds later their cannon erupted in flame and smoke and the pile of rubble jumped on the impact of a 105 mm high explosive round.

The other tanks began probing and firing as well. David searched for his next target. He tested other points of the oncoming edge of the community with bursts of machine gun fire. The turret turned slightly beneath him as his gunner, working his optical sights, spotted something worthy of a shell. David tried to follow the line of the cannon barrel to see the threat and gave the general area a hosing with the machine gun for a second before the cannon fired again. In the two seconds before their smoke cleared enough for him to see, he heard the staccato of several heavy machine guns firing at them. As bullets stitched the dry ground in front of their tank he spotted one of them and began to return fire. Sasha sped up and the turret moved again pointing straight towards the source. The fire was coming from the blasted upper story of a crumbling house near the fence line. Another shell from his tank silenced the menace just as its bullets were beginning to rattle off the front of their Merkava.

One of their supporting tanks, possibly Baruch's, silenced the other machine gun as they rolled across what was left of the settlement's outer fence. At this point their orders were to created a toehold within the settlement, just enough to give them cover and to block any escape in their direction. Their orders were to engage anything that moved while supporting the main assault coming from their left. Once the ground troops joined up with them, they would begin the final sweep of the settlement, pushing the invaders relentlessly back. Now it was time to start picking a spot to push in and pause. David sized up the half dozen houses that presented themselves as the nearest candidates. He didn't like the look of the one that had held the machine gunners. It was too big to be sure of what was on the other side. He picked a pair of one-story, older-style bungalows, or what was left of them, that were just a little closer.

David yelled down the hatch to his gunner. "Clear out those two bungalows – one round into each – foundation high. Tell Greg – two anti-personnel mortar rounds – just on the other side."

David went back to probing and challenging the nooks and crannies of the shattered houses that were now less than 100 meters away. He heard the occasional ricochet of a rifle round hitting the turret, but nothing larger was firing back at the moment. He looked for signs of fresh digging in the back yards behind his selected bungalows that might contain mines or booby traps. One had a trampled looking garden patch, to be avoided at all costs since its dirt could easily conceal a fresh mine. The other had the remains of a laundry hanger and colorful plastic play house. He hoped Sasha would pick that back yard for their approach. But first a high explosive round flashed out from beneath him as Benny punched a gaping hole in the nearest bungalow, the one with the garden. David could see clear through the demolished house now. With its stucco-over-cinderblock construction exposed, he could be relatively confident it contained no enemies capable of surprises. He continued to work his machine gun at any remaining windows or gaps in the neighboring houses. He noticed the outgoing whoosh of Greg's first mortar round and watched its arc out of the corner of his eye while he worried the neighboring house with his machine gun. He saw the blossom of its burst just clear of the house. That should take care of anyone hiding on the other side.

Another cannon shell and mortar combination put a hole and a dusting of explosives into the other bungalow next to their intended parking spot. David forced himself to look away for a few seconds to make sure that their supporting APC with its squad of soldiers was in sight and prepared to come in their wake. He saw the half dozen APCs working their way towards the tank group. Glancing around, he saw that Baruch was headed for the other side of the neighboring bungalow. He would be protected by the remaining walls of a taller house to their right, but vulnerable to anything that might be behind it. "Greg, give them a mortar round next door to the right," he shouted down the hatch, wishing for the thousandth time that day for a working intercom and radio.

As they edged towards their toehold between the houses he heard the flooop and whoosh of the covering mortar round and was relieved to see another blossom of dust and smoke arise behind the taller house. If he put his tank directly between the houses, he could cover beyond Baruch's flank as well. He crouched down again and yelled the direction to Sasha.

As they crunched across the backyard and approached the two smoking ruins of the bungalows, David fired short bursts into the smoke and rubble beyond the gap between them just to keep anything down that might be lurking there. He eased a hand grenade from his belt with his left hand while his right plied the machine gun, ready to pull the pin and lob it before ducking into the hatch at any sign of trouble in what was left of the two houses. Sasha pulled the huge tank neatly between the two ruined bungalows and paused, engine revved though, prepared to sprint in any direction. David sprayed a protective arc at street level in all directions in front of them and the turret turned in a slow semi-circle as Benny studied the scene beyond with his sights.

Nothing moved or fired back to challenge them in those first tense moments. David heard the rumble of their supporting APC and the clank of its crew hatch opening. He peered into the swirling smoke and ruins of what was once a peaceful rural community street. Across the street the houses were half destroyed with the shelling of the past five days. There was no knowing whose rounds had done the damage at this point. There would be little left to rebuild by the time it was safely back in Jewish hands at this rate, he thought bitterly.

They had a few minutes to study their street and what they could see through backyards of the next parallel street. Then the first groups of fleeing soldiers began to appear from their far left – apparently flushed out of their bunkers and trenches by the determined ground assault of the reconnaissance company. Sprinting groups and single figures emerged from the smoke and falling shells, scurrying away towards the far side of the community. David was very selective with his machine gun fire. He rained destruction on any who appeared still intent on turning to fire their weapons, and spared those in full flight, especially ragged youths who appeared to have flung away their weapons for greater speed. There did not appear to be any civilians in the mix, although many of the fighters seemed to be militia with no particular uniform. Panic and flight are powerful allies. Better to let them spread despair and defeat in the lines behind them. The operation orders were very specific about letting the enemy run and spread panic and confusion, rather than spreading slaughter and death for no reason. It was a very Israeli approach, practical and yet compassionate to the greatest degree possible.

Soon they saw the first teams of recon fighters appear – moving in coordinated squads and now recapturing ground quickly. They were moving from one shattered house to the next, being careful not to leave any surprises to their rear. As soon as he caught the attention of one of the nearest squad leaders, he signaled for Sasha and Baruch and their squad of covering force to move forward another row of houses. They had only one brief firefight with a pair of armored car-type vehicles and another machine gun nest before they emerged at the last row of houses on the northern side of Ramat Magshinim. From there they could see the fields scattered with discarded loot and equipment, burned vehicles and fleeing irregulars. For some groups, David deliberately fired just short of their fleeing feet or just over their heads. Benny spent one shell only on a fleeing halftrack, stopping it in a burst of flame.

Within the next hour, the streets, bomb shelters and remaining houses of Ramat Magshinim were all secured. Various handfuls of injured or stranded soldiers were captured and held in the remains of a picnic ground. They were immediately given water and the seriously wounded taken away for treatment. A ten-minute commanders' meeting at the northern edge of the town quickly assessed their casualties: six dead and perhaps twice that number wounded. Overall it was very clean operation against what appeared to be more than twice their numbers in fairly well entrenched positions – at least at the perimeter. Several platoons of recon troops joined their six tanks and six APCs. Their blocking force had suffered no casualties beyond one shrapnel wound. They reformed to pursue the fleeing enemy at a safe distance – keeping up the pressure and preventing looting. They planned to chase them all the way to the Syrian border crossing a dozen kilometers to the northwest.

David and his crew were just finishing up a welcome stretch and water break beside the shattered remains of the community center when he saw a familiar figure approaching, perched on the back of a motorbike, with his white beard flowing from beneath a helmet, and his long white shirt and *tzitzit* tucked in his pants. Rabbi Beniyahu recognized the two tank crews and waved as he dismounted. This time his driver was a young soldier. Another smoke stained, battle weary figure also waved hello to Rabbi Beniyahu. It was Lt. Sam Hirsh, who had just led a platoon of reconnaissance soldiers from his old unit through the streets of Ramat Magshinim, fighting house to house until the resistance crumbled and fled.

David half filled his helmet with water one last time from the one working hose that had been spliced into a pipe that drained the remains of a water tower. He dumped the half-full helmet on his head and let the water cascade down beneath his hot flak vest and T-shirt. Then he went over to see Sam and the Rabbi. "Back on the feet again, I see," he remarked to Sam.

"Good to see you. Thanks for the assist, tanker man" Sam replied, "Nothing makes a hole in a house big enough to walk though like a 105."

"Shalom Rabbi," David said, smiling for perhaps the first time that day.

"Shalom Aleichem my brave Merkava friend," Rabbi Beniyahu replied, "We have begun to take back our land. Your merit in Heaven is great today. May you be blessed with success and may your enemies continue to flee seven ways before you."

Coming from anyone else, that blessing might have sounded contrived to David's ears; but from Rabbi Beniyahu, like everything else about the elfish old man, it seemed natural and even matter of fact. "Thank you Rabbi," David said quietly.

"My group is going to stay here for the rest of the afternoon to secure the place and see if we can pick up anything useful in the way of intelligence," Sam said. "You guys take care of yourselves." He gave David a handshake that turned into an arm around his free shoulder since both men had automatic rifles slung over their the other.

David collected his men and reboarded their tanks for the careful pursuit. Looking back as they prepared to push off, he saw Sam and the rabbi sitting down with a prisoner at one of the few intact concrete picnic tables. He saw them offer him a cigarette and a canteen. The glum looking young man took the cigarette, but refused the water.

Moshav Yiftach

The afternoon sun, muffled in a smoky sky, was baking the moshav in waves of sultry, dusty heat. Eli and Natalie quickly gave up their plans to spread their late Shabbat lunch in the sukkah, and opted for the cooler interior of their house, which had been closed up on the sunny sides to preserve the morning's relative cool. Even so, it was hot, and their two twelve-volt fans that had miraculously survived the EMP and worked on the solar system did little to stir the stifling air. Besides, both fans were in the spare bedroom with the wounded, for their bandages and burns made it hard to stay cool. Natalie and Eli had a fairly quiet meal with the two somewhat ambulatory artillery officers and their afternoon caregiver, a shy young woman who was relatively new to the Moshav and who spoke little English.

Eli was feeling upset and discouraged. He was upset because he had nearly caused the death of a fellow Jew that morning by calling in help for a suicide bomber planted among the wounded. He was discouraged because of all the death and destruction that lay beyond the tattered boundaries of their once-beautiful community. Although the tide of the short, brutal war was beginning to turn, with Israel beginning to regroup and counterattack – he feared their tired and ammunition-short soldiers would not be able to deal anywhere near the crushing defeat that would end Syria's war mongering for more than a few years. It would take nothing short of a resounding defeat to silence their foes, and he did not feel that kind of decisive outcome was in the making.

He shared his concerns with the two artillery officers, who knew much more about the relative strengths and weaknesses of the forces than he did, and they shared his doubts. "Bashar and his kind know only power," one said, "and without technology and advanced weaponry, we don't have that kind of power any more. It will take years to rebuild, and in this depressed world economy, maybe decades. Meanwhile, the oil money will start to flow again in the Arab world as soon as they have power and transportation up and running. The oil companies will see that they at least have power and fuel for the oil fields."

"And yet you can't help seeing the miracles happening under our noses each day of this war," Natalie said, taking the other side and trying to lighten the glum mood. "Here it is Shabbat and we are already taking back the Golan. Three days ago we were nearly overrun, right here in this house. Now the guns we hear in the distance are mostly ours."

"You're right," Eli said, "and I know we are not supposed to be down hearted on Shabbat or *Sukkot* – but I wish I could feel more optimistic. I wish I could believe that this whole war won't just happen again in another ten years like it has for the last century and more. Why can't the world just leave us alone?"

One of the artillery officers gave as expressive a long-suffering shrug as he could with both his arms still in casts. The gesture cost him a few moments pain from his healing burns and broken bones.

"I wish I could do something besides sit here and listen," the other said, indicating the one tattered ear that was not bandaged on the shrapnel torn half his face.

"I know what you mean. I felt better when I was out there doing something," Eli said with an apologetic glance at Naomi.

Together they all paused and listened to the gunfire. It seemed to have grown closer in the past minutes. Eli glanced at his rucksack ready by the patio door and felt the sling of his sniper rifle secure on the back of his chair. He was considering bentching quickly and going to see if he was needed on the perimeter when he heard hurried footsteps outside in the garden. He picked up his rifle and stepped to the door in time to see Gadi rush past the sukkah heading for the door.

"Checkpoint *Kedem, kulam!*" he shouted and dashed away to the next defense group member's house.

Eli kissed Natalie, gave the two soldiers and their nurse a quick wave, scooped up his pack and was about to run off towards the gathering point on the eastern perimeter of the moshav. Then he stopped, for Natalie was scooping up her pack and bolt action rifle. "*Kulam!* They're calling for everybody," she said, breathless as they both hurried away. Both of them whispered the long holiday after-meal prayers aloud as they jogged along, bobbing their heads to acknowledge various neighbors who came running, packs and rifles in hand.

"*Ma matsav?* What's going on?" Everyone was asking. But no one had answers, except that the sounds of automatic weapon fire and explosions now appeared closer, possibly between Yiftach and Yonatan, the next community to the south. There were no shells falling in the moshav, so they all took fairly direct paths to Checkpoint Kedem – the eastern rally point.

When they got there, Eli and Natalie were a few dozen paces behind the younger moshavniks. They slowed and came to a stop as they reached the outer edge of the knot of about a dozen people getting directions from a young IDF soldier with a captain's bars on her shoulder. She dispatched three teenagers to one of the near perimeter bunkers. They headed off at a run and Eli and Natalie edged closer in the clump of moshavniks waiting for their directions. She saw Eli's long barreled rifle and that of Nir, the other older marksman who trotted up as the three teenagers left. "Snipers, we need you out at that hilltop there," she said pointing far to the east, "dig in behind the machine gunners and cover them."

Nir headed off immediately for the minefield path that would take them to the far hilltop. Eli, after an awkward peck on Natalie's cheek, started after him. He wished he could hear where Natalie would be stationed, but knew he couldn't linger. He started off after Nir, but paused half a second and turned just in time to see her being waved back towards a fence line bunker. He waved, and was relieved to see that she saw him and waved back. Turning back, he concentrated on trying to catch up with Nir. Though shorter and stouter, Nir was charging up the faint footpath with determination and a far more rapid stride than Eli's longer lope.

Eli was soon sweating profusely and parched in the dry, smoky afternoon heat. He had packed four water bottles inside the pack but had not left one in an outside pocket that he could reach, so he huffed on, growing drier and more worried with each passing minute. The hilltop was a good two or three kilometers from the moshav. It stood outside of the defensive minefields and commanded a view of the not-so-distant Syrian border. Eli had sat there several nights and a couple long hot afternoons during red alerts and drills earlier in the year. However with the wreckage of the earlier Syrian advances, the multiple shell craters, and some newly placed spirals of barbed razor wire, he was beginning to lose his bearings as they chugged up the last part of the hill. Fortunately, Nir seemed to know the way better and had slowed his pace to something more reasonable for a man the far side of fifty.

"How many shells do you have left?" Eli asked him as he caught up to him for a third time as their track zigzagged up the brushy slope.

"*Meot, plus / minus* Nir answered – about 200." "*V'atah?* And you?" He croaked.

"About 120," Eli said. "About ten minutes of heavy shooting," he thought to himself. Of course, he had a 9mm side arm – but only four fifteen-shot clips – another few minutes of close range shooting. "Then what?" he wondered.

As they neared the top of the rise, really just a rounded bulge in the long swales of land rising in low waves along this part of the Golan, they saw an artillery spotting team dug in under one of the larger dry shrubs that had lost most of its dusty green dispirited leaves. Nir whistled and one of them turned around. Taking in their weapons with a glance, an officer motioned them to pass to the right and appeared to point a little ways over the hilltop.

The now-familiar sounds of battle had been growing steadily closer as they had approached the top of the rise. Eli and Nir unshouldered their rifles and each chambered a round as they more cautiously approached to where they could see over the crest. Both were crouching lower and inching forwards, so that as they got lower and lower, they had to move farther and farther forward to have a chance of seeing. They were practically prone before they could see the downward slope. They saw perhaps a dozen soldiers, including a machine gun and a bazooka team, dug in behind whatever cover their side of the hill afforded. None were firing at the moment, but all were watching tensely towards the southeast. Nir whistled again to get their attention. One looked up and pointed towards a moderate sized boulder farther along the hill's crest that offered enough protection for two and a good view.

Eli had taken in a fair bit of the situation before them by the time he slipped his pack off in the lee of the boulder and reached for a water bottle for a welcome drink. He could see distant figures and vehicles moving amid falling shell bursts and smoke well to the east and south of them. He assumed they were the retreating Syrians from Ramat Magshinim and communities farther south. Apparently the IDF offensive had been successful, and he prayed that Sam and David and his many new friends in those units were OK.

After drinking half a bottle of water that was still somewhat cool from the house, he propped his rifle in a handy notch in the rock and began to study the fleeing troops with his high powered scope. Nir did the same and they both scanned the distant scenes before them. It soon became apparent to Eli that the distant figures were indeed fleeing the sporadic fire behind them. They were being driven northward on a path that looked like it would pass within perhaps a kilometer of their position. The Syrian border was only two kilometers away from their hill. But at that point the border consisted of the edge of a steep wadi topped with double fences and extensive and thickly strewn minefields. It would be suicidal to try to go that way, so the Syrians were fleeing northwards towards one of the many easier border crossing areas.

"*Ein l'chem tankim,* they have no tanks" – Nir muttered gratefully. Eli agreed. He had not seen a single tank, though there were a smattering of half tracks and miscellaneous trucks. "*Kamma hatzi trackim? Sheva, shemonah?* How many half tracks – seven, eight?" Nir asked. Eli hadn't been counting, but the number seemed about right. Feeling negligent, he quickly swept the retreating ranks again and made a summary count.

"Maybe eight – and one APC – I can't tell about that far right one," Eli said at last. Could just be truck with some guys waving a bazooka."

"Allo, Allo"

Eli was startled to hear a loud voice call them from nearby. He looked up to see a swarthy reservist with a dark beard and a pair of binoculars in his hand jogging up to them. The sergeant quickly introduced himself as their friendly neighborhood NCO in charge of their hill for the moment. He appreciatively took in their two long range rifles and scopes, and squatted on his heels for a short briefing behind their rock, keeping half an eye on the unfolding battle that was drawing steadily closer. For Eli's sake, he spoke mostly in English, for Nir could follow it well enough.

"Our guys drive Syrian out of Magshinim about three-thirty. They chase them out of all of southern Golan. They get them running and we keep them scared. Chase them all the way to border in north of here. Our job - make sure nobody come this way. Nobody. We don't want any, how you call them -nogoodniks - getting behind us making problems. Orders - shoot just enough keep them moving – shoot anyone comes this way closer than say than half-kilometer – what are you sighted in for?" They told him 300 meters. "Good – anyone even approach 500 meters is dead. Anyone wants to run north or east, you let him run. Priorities: One, hit armored vehicle if you can. Two shoot trucks - stop truck, not engine. Shoot truck tires good target. They go bye bye, we keep what left of truck. *Harosho?* Good?"

He asked them how many shells they had and winced at the numbers. "Stick to easy shot – and don't kill anyone you don't have to. Anyone firing at you – dead. Anyone coming this way, dead. Anyone shooting back, really dead. Shooting at Recon guys, really really dead. Got it?" They repeated his instructions. "Good hunting," he said, patting them each on the helmet before snaking his way back to his bazooka team.

Nir and Eli settled back at their respective scopes and watched the distant figures growing closer and somewhat more distinct. They watched a long time in the hot afternoon sun, drinking a lot of water, and talking a little. There were more men and trucks and the occasional half track or APC, loaded to overflowing with riders hanging on the sides, all streaming northward in the hot afternoon sun. Every now an then an artillery or tank shell burst among them, causing a hurried scramble, but mostly a resigned detour around the damage. Few stopped to render aid. At one point a pair of not-too-loaded-down armored personnel carriers appeared to be heading their way and Eli and Nir agreed on dividing their targets right and left – sighting in and trying to steady their crosshairs on a miniscule window or a vulnerable front tire. However the two distant vehicles turned back northwards well before their imaginary half kilometer point of no return.

They watched the straggling stream of men flowing northwards, generally about a kilometer away. Every so often they tore their eyes away from the distant spectacle to scan the hills and dips in the landscape to the south of them to search for any stragglers or attempts at infiltrating behind Israeli lines. On about their fourth or fifth sweep they picked up a trio of distant figures who had swung well to the west of the retreating columns. They appeared to be attempting to stick to the limited cover afforded by the brush and small gullies. From Eli and Nir's vantage point, perhaps a kilometer or more away still, it appeared they might be hiding as much from the retreating Syrians as from the Israeli communities they must know lay to their west. The three appeared to be carrying automatic rifles, but not carrying more than light rucksacks. As they continued to draw steadily away from the retreating Syrians, Nir and Eli took turns keeping a constant watch on them. Nir was of the opinion that they might be deserters – possibly Ukrainians, Georgians, or even Russians. For they appeared in the occasional full-face view as they bobbed up and down over the rough terrain, to be lighter skinned and perhaps taller and broader than the average Arab.

Since there was nothing threatening to break away from the main column, which was doggedly retreating and barely firing back at the still unseen Israelis behind them, Nir said he was going to go get the sergeant for a consultation about their three break-away stragglers.

Eli settled in to watch the three steadily moving men and try to look for clues about their identity and intentions. Somehow he felt that deliberate infiltrators would be greater in number. They were now less than a kilometer away, and on an angling course that would have them crossing the gentle ridge behind him, perhaps half a kilometer away. It did appear to be a fairly direct path to their Moshav. But did that suggest deserters or infiltrators? He studied them through his scope. They were now within range of a moderately long range, but fairly straightforward shot.

The trio had worked their way much closer by the time Nir returned with the sergeant, Sgt. Moskowitz, if one could believe the name above his left hand pocket, and his high powered binoculars. He studied them a few moments, spoke a few words with Nir in Hebrew, and announced that they certainly looked like former inhabitants of the Soviet Union to him.

"See, that one on the left carries his Kalashnikov just like Russian army manual – nothing like Arab. And the middle one is fattest Syrian I ever saw in uniform." When the men had approached to with a few hundred meters and there was still not a sign of a threat from the main retreat, Sgt. Moskowitz sidled a about a dozen meters back down the hill. He picked a spot where he could stand by a tall rock, yet duck behind it in half a step if needed. "Cover me, and shoot if anyone raise weapon," he told Eli and Nir. They sighted in on the slighter two figures on the right and left of the big fellow, who they could now see sported a huge black beard.

"Стоп теперь! Stop Now!" The sergeant bellowed in Russian. Eli saw his man freeze in his tracks. The sergeant shouted some more. Eli watched his target, a thin, wiry man in a tattered but not-too-dirty-looking set of fatigues cautiously raise his rifle over his head with both hands in a sign of surrender. Then, as Sgt. Moskowitz barked instructions, he saw the man awkwardly pull the clip out of his Kalashnikov, throw the clip away, and stick the rifle sideways through the straps of his backpack. He put his hands on his head. All three men complied readily with the Russian orders. At Sgt. Moskowitz's command, they walked slowly, hands on heads, until within a dozen meters of the sergeant. There they stopped again on his command, looking nervous but weary and relieved. A four-way conversation ensued in rapid-fire Russian as Sgt. Moskowitz interrogated each of them.

The interrogations sounded sharp, but grew friendlier, and the Sgt. clearly began to answer a few of their more urgent questions. No doubt about it, they were deserters from one of the former Soviet bloc countries. But Nir and Eli kept a close watch and held a bead on them even though their sniper rifles were awkward weapons at such close range. After some more discussion, the three men carefully eased their rifles out of their pack straps and laid them on the ground pointing away from any harm. Then they placed three long knives and a handgun on the pile, after gingerly ejecting the clip. Then, one at a time, they approached to within a few meters of Sgt. Moskowitz and thoroughly emptied their packs on the ground where he could see all the contents. Each in turn took off his pants and shook them out and held them up for him to see front and back, and did the same with their shirts before being allowed to put them back on.

As he casually, but carefully watched each of the three go through this ritual, the sergeant periodically asked Nir what was happening with the retreat. Nir filled him in several times before the three were done reloading what was permissible in their packs. Then Sgt. Moskowitz lined them up, and used the one-way nylon plastic locking strips that IDF soldiers used to secure prisoners. He linked each of the smaller men to the big one in the middle, who was therefore forced to carry his pack without being able to take it off without undoing all the straps. Sgt. Moskowitz seemed somewhat apologetic at this measure, but the three men were so relieved to be in safe custody and away from their mercenary units that they accepted it with easy resignation.

"Georgians," Sgt. Moskowitz announced as they approached. He arranged their prisoners in a dip in the hillside between his own group and Eli and Nir's boulder, where they were protected from any stray shots from the retreating column, yet in his full sight as he joined Nir and Eli in watching the retreat. He gave the prisoners a bottle of water and Eli offered them food from his pack, which they took with grateful words that were mostly unintelligible to him. He smiled and nodded, but kept a close watch on his pack and rifle. "They can stay here until we can go back to the Moshav," the sergeant said, setting the arm load of rifles he had collected from them on the ground next to Nir.

Eli offered Sgt. Moskowitz a sandwich made of homemade bread and a chunk of cheese with tomatoes from his garden. They ate together, with the deserters a few meters away, but within conversational distance. The sergeant was amazed to see fresh food. Even though he had been stationed near the moshav for the past two and a half days, he and his men had been living mostly on "loof" and canned rations since a few days before the war began. Eli dug out a couple of nectarines and offered them too. The sergeant took one for himself and tossed the other to the big Georgian a few meters away. The three prisoners carefully divided the precious fruit.

Once everyone had eaten, a conversation started up between Sgt. Moskowitz and the three Georgians. For Eli's sake, he translated bits of information as they went. Eli learned that the three claimed to have joined a militia for the sake of having a job in their depression-ravaged homeland, never knowing that their commanders would be selling their services to a Syrian warlord. There were originally about a hundred in their company, mostly Ukrainians (all three spat at the word) and a handful of Moslems from Tashkent. They had been in Syria for a few months, nearly starving and roasting to death in the summer sun without even tents for shelter. No one had been paid in weeks. It was a good thing their unit was one of the last to cross into Israel, for none of their sorry lot had the stomach for a real fight. They had marched into Ramat Magshinim a few hours after it was captured, took part in a half-hearted assault on what must have been Hespin from their description, and settled in to the ruined town to dig fortifications.

At this point in the narrative, there appeared to be a three-way argument in whispers among the Georgians. Eli looked at them curiously, waiting for the story to continue. "They are trying to decide whether to tell me something, they're afraid I might possibly hold it against them," the sergeant said. He waited for them to finish their argument, scanning the retreating troops in the distance from time to time with his binoculars. Eli took a few sweeps with his scope too, but was too interested in the unfolding story to pay much attention.

Finally the big man with the bushy black beard spoke up, and addressed Sgt. Moskowitz in a hesitant, but confiding manner. The sergeant listened intently, asking only the occasional short question and not pausing to translate for Eli and Nir. The two other Georgians began to supply what appeared to be confirmation and details. After much back and forth, growing more intense and urgent sounding, Sgt. Moskowitz broke off to ask Nir to go down to his unit and fetch Amnon. He described him as the tall skinny guy with the corporal's stripe. Nir slipped quietly down the hill to where the bazooka and machine gun teams were dug in and quickly found Amnon, and the two came up the hill at a run.

"They say that the big *Shul* in Ramat Magshinim was booby-trapped before everyone pulled out. They say that four families were shot dead in the basement of the *Shul* the day after the town was captured, and left there, and that they are also wired as part of the trap," he told Amnon. "I think these guys are credible, at least on this point. I need you to run back to the moshav and get to the first radio you can find and warn them." He asked a few more details from the three deserters. They appeared to answer with a fair bit more details, leading Eli to wonder if they had perhaps been part of the wiring. What else had these men done? He wondered, and suddenly felt less friendly towards them.

As Amnon sprinted off, Sgt. Moskowitz shook his head. "It's *mishugah* fighting a war with no communications. Runners – what's next – pigeons?"

They all went back to watching the retreating Syrians and mercenaries. Eli tried to think of the big *Shul* in Ramat Magshinim. He had been to a bar mitzvah there once a long time ago. It was a big building with several classrooms, and, he recalled more classrooms in a spacious basement. He shuddered to think of four families caught hiding there and shot. It must have happened on the first or second day of the war. What had happened to them in the hours in between? He didn't want to think too hard about that. He watched the three deserters in the hollow in the hillside below him. They had scrunched around in their awkward line so that they too could watch the distant retreat. Were they some of the executioners? He wondered. And who were the victims? He ran his mind over the various families he knew in Ramat Magshinim. He didn't know too many. He recalled three people from there who he had met on the outskirts of Hespin following their firefight there on the second day of the war. That was a long time ago.

Northern Command Mt Meron 18:35

General Tchernikovsky collected her notes from the 18:00 briefing and tried to organize the main points in her mind as she sat down to her computer screens again. She was now running on three systems – one for Internet only that was separated from all the other networks and firewalled to the maximum, one for inside her command center, and one that interfaced with the rest of the IDF systems. The news that changed her life the most was that Central Command, Jerusalem and the Southern Command had all finally come online, meaning that her mountaintop was no longer the sole link to the civilized world. There would be a meeting of the Knesset tomorrow, assuming that enough of the 120 members could make their way to the secure bunkers near the Knesset building in Jerusalem. They would then ratify an interim government and take over the diplomatic and political roles.

However, logistics and begging supplies and materiel from the Americans, NATO and other nations still fell heavily on Anna's shoulders. There were now half a dozen supply ships enroute. It was not nearly enough, but it was more than there were yesterday. The first ship had already landed in Haifa bringing much needed tank and artillery shells, and several hundred secure radios. She now had nearly two hundred of the precious radios placed with commanders and artillery teams in her northern district, and base stations operating out of Haifa, Afula and Tzfat. However, the radio traffic load on her small staff was still overwhelming, not counting the intelligence, satellite data and logistics work that was simply staggering. No one had more than four hours of uninterrupted sleep since the war began. She sipped at her nth cup of coffee – now black for all the milk and sugar had gone by the end of Shabbat, and told herself that she needed to slow down on the caffeine intake soon, or she would not get the full benefit of the five hour rest period she had penciled for herself starting after the midnight briefing.

However, her chief worry at the moment was disturbing news from the air force and satellite intelligence that suggested that there was a new wave of forces beginning to flow across Syria from the east. Apparently many of the helicopters that had been held in reserve for a second wave, the ones that the Syrians had supposedly stationed outside the EMP damage zone, were now repaired and beginning to maneuver across the country in short hops. They were escorting new columns of armor and mechanized infantry and truck after truckload of soldiers and supplies. Clearly they were not all Syrians, for there were as many again as the first waves on days one and two of the conflict. It was hard to tell at this point of their ponderous but steady progress across the countryside exactly where they were going to strike. They appeared to be heading to reinforce the columns that were struggling to break free through the hill country to the coast. But they could easily turn south and join Jordanian forces trying to do the same thing.

Air cover was being provided at least in part by the Saudis, who had largely stayed out of directly participating in the war so far. Their intelligence suggested that a large contingent came all the way from Iran, suggesting that they too had hardened their military sites in advance of the EMP attack – which made perfect sense.

Was it a desperate last roll of the dice? Or a coordinated attempt to drive a fatal wedge through the heart of Israel? And it came in the face of the first real Israeli offensives of the war, pushing most of the Syrians out of the southern Golan Heights. The IDF was expanding their pocket of resistance around Tiberias, beginning to stop the tide of advances in the south, and even counterattacking at points from the Negev. All of this had left the IDF exhausted, stretched thin, and always perilously low on ammunition, food, parts, fuel, supplies and reserves. Thanks to their network of 200 radios, the area commanders were at least apprised of the looming threat. Best estimates had the tide of destruction set to break the next morning – as early as dawn if they travelled all night. Against this onslaught, all they had new to bring to the table was a handful of Blackhawk and Cobra gunships and a dwindling Israeli Air Force that could not bring new planes on line faster than they were being lost.

Fortunately it appeared that Egypt was running out of steam. Between the effects of the errant EMP pulse and the successful Israeli air strikes at the long supply lines and airfields, Egyptian supplies flowing to the southern front had slowed to a trickle. Several unsuccessful naval forays had been beaten back by Israeli patrol boats. The exception was a pair of light Egyptian cruisers that had muscled past long just enough to shell Tel Aviv for a frightening, but unremarkable half an hour before being sunk. They were hit by a pair of anti-ship missiles hastily loaded onto a flight of F-16s at the last minute. The Egyptian air force had been largely unsuccessful, with a few exceptions. They too had succeeded in bombing Tel Aviv and its suburbs with some random hits, practically suicide runs for most bombers never made it home if they made it to their targets at all. Fighter forays generally ended in dogfights, with the score heavily in favor of the IAF. But even these victories cost dearly. Of the original twenty four planes flown in from Portugal, there were only ten still in the air and two in the repair hanger. Promises of the first IAF rewired fighters had been pushed off until evening, or perhaps tomorrow morning. Tomorrow morning might be too late.

Outside Moshav Yiftach

The late afternoon wore on with no let up in the retreating troops. Eli swore he had seen several thousand go by. But now there was somewhat more intense firing to the rear of them, leading him to believe that the Israeli advance was approaching at last. He redoubled his watch, and was careful to sweep the sides of the march and to scan the landscape to the south of them to guard against infiltrators taking advantage of the confusion. There was still no firing in their direction – although their positions were not as well hidden as they could have been.

There was a buzz of comment and excitement among the Georgians, who were peering at the retreat quite unconcerned for their safety at this point, as if they were watching a parade. Eli followed their gazes and swung his rifle scope up to see better. He saw a clump of half a dozen newer looking armored personnel carriers and a black, humvee-type vehicle pulling rapidly through the slowly walking troops. He followed the humvee in his sights, looking for an insignia or sign of rank. He sensed a fairly high ranking commander in rapid retreat. There were half a dozen trucks following the group, and these were loaded, but not overloaded with soldiers. Unlike every other truck passing that afternoon, there were no freeloaders clinging to the sides. Clearly an elite unit.

Sgt. Moskowitz had apparently noticed the same thing and was studying the group with his high powered binoculars. He asked a question in Russian of their prisoners, and received some emphatic answers, followed with a spit of disgust at the mention of a certain name.

"That's the general in charge of this sector," Sgt. Moskowitz said, "Let's see if we can nail him. Eli, what's the range?"

Eli took an educated guess, "just under a kilometer, and moving maybe 30 klicks an hour in that crowd."

"See if you guys can put some holes in that humvee and bring it to a stop," the sergeant said coolly, then he waved the three Georgians to take cover and shouted down the hill to alert his squad that they were about to open fire.

Eli could see only a bare shape of the moving humvee in the dust and distance, but he drew a bead just ahead of the left front tire should be and squeezed off his first shot, using the rock as a solid rest. The bang of the first shot always nearly stunned him, setting his ears to ringing. After that first round, he got used to the sharp concussions. He chambered a new round and studied the target for a hit as Nir fired off to his right. This time he aimed for where the driver's side window would be and eased off another round, followed by the report of Nir's rifle to his right. Wiping the sweat that threatened to drip into his eyes, Eli lined up another try for the front wheel. He noted that the humvee was now slowing down, not moving faster. He fired again and again before he noticed that the APCs were beginning to return fire. Machine gun bullets stitched tracks up their knoll, causing their deserters to flatten themselves into their hollow as the bullets whizzed over and around them.

He abandoned his comfortable position firing over the top of the boulder and lay down prone to fire around the side, with a smaller rock offering him some additional shelter and a cushion of earth that he had prepared as a rifle rest. He could hear bullets hitting the other side of their boulder and smell ozone and see fragments of rock and dust flying. He gave up shooting at the humvee and looked for an open turret on an APC to silence. It took only a second to find one, line up a shot and fire. They were much closer than the shadow of a humvee he had been trying to hit. He pulled his head and shoulders completely behind their sheltering rock as he worked the bolt and eased back into firing position in a lull in the splattering impacts. He saw another man shoving his way into the turret he just hit, and Eli fired again, feeling fairly sure of hitting the replacement gunner as well.

The fire on the other side of his rock intensified and he dared not edge back for a new shot as rock fragments flew in the gap he had just left. As he lay wondering what to do, he heard the outgoing whoosh of a bazooka, and within a second, the shattering fire against his rock stopped. Eli edged back over and looked for his next shot. The next gunner that he saw was hunched way down in his turret, presenting a scant target, so Eli decided to aim for the poorly protected magazine of his 50 caliber machine gun. He popped off another shot, chambered a quick round and peered through the scope to see his target. The gunner appeared to have stopped firing and seemed to be trying to unjam his weapon. Eli sent another shot towards the turret and reloaded. Sighting in again, he looked again for the black humvee and had to sweep the cluttered field before he spotted it sprinting away towards the north, with two of the APCs following close behind. However, it appeared to be running flat on at least one rim, he noted with satisfaction. Now, for the remaining three APC's. The bazooka had smoked one, would they stay and fight? Unload their truck loads of elite troops and charge their hilltop? Did they even suspect that they had more than a five to one advantage over the squad on the hilltop? Or would they run?

He sized up the nearest truck. It was a big Russian-built six-wheeler. The troops were staying on board. Although most were firing away, Rambo-style, over the side, none of their shots seemed to be coming anywhere near him and the IDF group nearby. Eli recalled their orders about perhaps disabling a truck or two, and he had a clear shot at the two back tires. He settled into a comfortable prone position and fired. He was happy to see when he looked back after his second round, that the truck had tipped precariously, and that the soldiers were swarming away to the next vehicle. They were running. Soon the last two of the retreating six-wheel-drive trucks looked more like the rest of the retreat, with soldiers from Eli's disabled truck clinging to the sides. He saw the driver get out, check the blown tires for a moment, and then scurry off after his companions as a shot from Nir pinged the truck near him, raising a small mushroom of dust.

Sgt. Moskowitz scuttled down to check on his squad and soon came back grinning. The three Georgians had gotten up and were standing and shaking their fists at the retreating Syrian commander, who was now just a black smudge in the distance.

"Nice shooting, *Sava*, looks like you bagged us a 6-wheel-drive KRAZ transport – tougher than a rhino. Here come our guys, let me send them a signal." He pulled out one the thermos-shaped plastic containers that Israeli soldiers use to keep their *tefillin* clean and waterproof. Unscrewing the lid, he used the mirror, normally used for seeing that the head piece of the *tefillin* were on straight and centered, as a signal mirror. He caught a ray of the late afternoon sun and reflected it towards a group of distant tanks. After a few minutes of playing the fickle beam of light across them, there was a winking of an answering reflection. Then the sergeant pulled a flare pistol from his pack, and shot a blue flare in a high arc over their heads. "Now they know where we are," he said, as he stowed all in his pack again.

Eli and Nir were put to work making a careful scan of the path of the retreat and scouring any possible avenues of escape behind them. They divided the terrain with overlapping assignments and set to work, using their gun sights as the small telescopes they were. They could hear the rumble of the first advancing tanks drawing near as they finished their sweeps, finding nothing alarming in the hazy landscape. Eli stood and straightened up and stretched and shook the kinks out of his shoulders from holding the rifle steady. He glanced at their prisoners, who were growing apprehensive at the approaching tanks and APCs. They were sitting down in their sheltered spot and trying to look inconspicuous. He looked at the approaching tanks. The near one looked familiar – and the second one in the sweeping line was running on half treads, could it be Captain Engel and *Gimmel* One and Two? Eli was sure of it. He had seen *Gimmel* Two in the moshav machine shop being refitted. He watched as the familiar tank ran easily up their hill and stopped just downslope of Sgt. Moskowitz and his squad.

"Watch these guys a minute, I need to go say hello," Eli asked Nir. His fellow moshavnik agreed, casting an appraising glance at their quiet captives.

Eli shouldered his pack, lighter now for having drunk three out of the four bottles of water, counting the one given to the Georgians, and having used perhaps another twenty-odd rifle shells. He studied their captives a moment, decided they would be crazy to start any trouble with a fully armed tank not fifty meters away, and walked down the hill to join the conference going on at the commander's turret. With the tank now facing away, he saw the white painted *Gimmel* 1 and knew it must be his friends. Perhaps they had news of Sam.

"*Shalom Aleichem* Captain Engel!" he called as he approached the side of the tank. The dusty, smoke-stained commander turned and flashed a quick smile of white teeth through a grimy face with three days beard and the smoke of battle thick upon it.

"Reb Kaplan, nice to see you. Misha here was just telling me about some fancy shooting. Too bad we missed the big kahuna in the humvee, but maybe I'll catch up to him before the border crossing."

"Any word about Sam?" Eli asked anxiously, for he suddenly remembered the booby-trapped synagogue, and he had heard that Sam was going in on foot with the recon company.

"I saw him just after the shooting stopped. He came through fine – and you would never guess who else? Rabbi Beniyahu!"

Eli shook his head in wonder. How did that old man get around night and day with barely a rest?

"And the strangest thing happened right after that, as I was just telling Misha," Captain Klein continued, as though it was perfectly normal to stop a strategic battlefield conference to gossip about old friends. "There was a group of guys from Ramat Magshinim who showed up and wanted to *daven mincha* in the *Shul*, and they asked Rabbi Beniyahu to join them."

Eli's heart almost stopped, but the captain continued. "But the rabbi stopped them at the door and wouldn't let anyone go in. He said there was an unholy odor – and perhaps great danger inside. Everyone was really fired up about getting their synagogue back. It was almost intact except for some shell holes in the classroom wing. But Rabbi Beniyahu was absolutely unmovable. And when some joker went and started prying open a basement window since he wouldn't let anyone go in the front door, there was a stench bad enough to knot your socks. We called for sappers and they found the whole place was wired." He paused a moment and looked grim, "and the basement was full of bodies – some of them were wired too, I heard later from messengers catching up to us."

Eli and Misha looked at each other with relief, and cast a sharp look at their prisoners, sitting miserably about fifty meters away. Eli made a move to go back to Nir and watching the prisoners, but Sgt. Moskowitz motioned him to stay a moment.

"We need to see how many of those trucks we can get running before nightfall. Use them to pick up our guys. They had to walk most of way from Ramat Magshinim. I hear you moshav guys good with tools and trucks – yes? So I take prisoners. You get Nir two of my guys help. You start with that six-wheeler. Use to fix thing you find that can get run. Think you can do that?"

Eli reluctantly agreed, glancing at the sun which was perhaps an hour or two away from setting. He had certainly changed Woody's tire in battle conditions, a Russian transport with a pair of huge all-terrain wheels was just a whole lot bigger. Fixing things – well, he could try.

Misha selected two riflemen from his squad, briefed them and introduced them to Eli and Nir, who had been relieved of watching the prisoners. Eli sized up the two soldiers. Ari was tall and strong looking, but did not look delighted at the assignment, while Barak was wiry and restless looking. He wondered how much either of them knew about mechanics, so he asked them what sorts of vehicles they had worked on. Ari looked blank, but Barak said he had messed around with an engine or two. Nir, he knew, had driven most of the moshav's heavy equipment, and had probably done some of the maintenance, but he wasn't sure how much. That made them a decidedly amateur crew of mechanics, although he felt sure that Barak was probably understating his experience out of modesty.

They said quick goodbyes to their group, shouldered their packs and headed off towards the tipping hulk of the truck Eli had hit. Out of curiosity, he tried pacing off the distance, but was interrupted by detours around clumps of brush and rocks too many times for an accurate attempt at measuring the distance of his shot. However, after nearly fifteen minutes of heavy walking, he decided that it must be just short of half a kilometer. Damned good shooting for an old four-eyed greybeard, he congratulated himself with satisfaction. He had managed to hit the front left tire and the forward of the two huge back tires, causing the big truck to teeter precariously.

The two younger soldiers went first, alert for any sign of survivors, booby traps or lurking ambushes. When they had swept around the truck adequately, the four of them fell to work searching their abandoned prize. They quickly found the over-sized jack and one good spare, a large lug wrench, and the driver's rucksack, which yielded a nice collection of wrenches, screw drivers, vice grips, and a bottle of arrack. "See if it starts first before we tackle this tire," Eli suggested. Barak swung up in the driver's seat. Finding the key still in the ignition, he cranked it over twice before it started with a satisfying roar. Meanwhile, Eli and Nir were sizing up the ground around where the truck had come to a stop. They decided it would be easier and safer to get the jack under the frame if Barak could pull the truck a few meters forward. Nir explained the situation to him and stood by the driver's door while Eli watched from a safe distance. The truck tilted alarmingly with two of its three left side tires in shreds. Replacing the front tire would give them a drivable, steer-able truck, but not one that could take heavy loads until they found a replacement for the shredded middle tire. Barak revved the engine and eased the clutch, coaxing the big truck forwards on its other four driving wheels. Eli winced as he saw the brake drums threaten to be ground in the dirt as the shredded tire peeled off the forward rim. He motioned them to stop the second it was clear of the obstructions.

The three of them set to work jacking up the truck and pulling the front and middle wheels off – which were fortunately not damaged except for a gouge in one of the rims. Ari kept a lookout and swept an ever widening perimeter around them, going as far as examining the nearby APC that had been burned out by the penetrating round from his team's bazooka.

The three worked quickly and easily together, with little talk needed. However, following Murphy's law, there was one stuck lug nut that threatened to break even their big lug wrench, and they took turns jumping on it, applying a few drops of oil from the dipstick, since there seemed to be no spare oil cans, and cooking the nut with Barak's lighter to try to expand it just enough to give. All the wheel studs were severely rusted, but this one was practically destroyed. They were contemplating how to safely shoot if off with one of the high-powered sniper rifles when Barak gave the lug wrench one more good stomp and it turned a fraction. With some more oil and sweat, it came off. Soon they were fitting the spare wheel with its tire on the front hub. The tire was fairly solid, which was lucky because they had no pump to top up the air. They stripped the other rim of the rest of its shredded tire, lowered the truck and stowed their jack, and cleaned their hands with some dry dirt and their shirttails.

The sun was now close to setting. The four of them climbed into the back and stood on the railings of the bed of their truck to survey the field for their next resuscitation effort. They saw another truck perhaps half a kilometer away and decided to drive over there to see if there was another usable wheel. It appeared to be a slightly different model of the same kind of truck. They would cruise by a disabled half track on the way.

"It's your truck," Nir said to Eli as the four of them looked at each other to see who would drive. Eli grinned and climbed into the driver's seat. Nir climbed in the cab next to him, and the two soldiers took up spots in the back. Eli laid his rifle on the floor of the roomy cab, looked for a seat belt and found none, and sized up the gauges and gear shift. He felt for and found the emergency brake release, slid the gear shift into what he felt sure was first, for the shift pattern was worn completely away, and eased the truck into gear. The truck responded ponderously but evenly. He soon had the hang of driving it, being careful to baby the left side around any dips and bumps that would endanger their one lone rear tire on that side. However, Sgt. Moskowitz was right, the big KRAZ truck was as solid and powerful as a rhinoceros, at least in the lower gears. He checked the gas gauge and was happy to see more than half a tank.

They drove slowly by the wrecked half track, decided there was nothing to salvage and drove on to the next truck. It had taken a hit to the cab, taking all the controls and perhaps a bit of the engine compartment with it. However, it had a nice pair of dual wheels on the back that were untouched. Barak hopped down and pried open what was left of the hood and checked out the engine. Shaking his head, he came back to where Eli and Nir were sizing up the spare tire and the dual wheels, measuring against themselves and walking over to their truck. "Worth a try, they are both eight lug nuts, and I'd swear they are within an inch," Eli said. They found the jack, brought the other jack from their scavenged truck, blocked what was left of the front wheels, and set to work stripping the hulk of all six wheels and the four usable tires – one never knew when they might be needed. All four worked quickly, with Ari acting as lookout whenever his extra hands were not needed. It was sunset by the time they fitted one of the scavenged wheels on Eli's "new truck." They were calling it Comrade Rhinoceros by now. The wheel fit fine, and having six working wheels gave them a greater feeling of security as they prepared to move off to find their next salvage job. However, Eli and Nir asked for five minutes to *daven* a quick *mincha* prayer before the sun set all the way, and the two soldiers, who were not religious, poked around the area for anything useful.

Finding nothing even remotely repairable in the vicinity, they piled back into Comrade Rhino and set off to overtake the Israeli advance which had passed perhaps two hours earlier. It was growing dark but Eli could see well enough to follow the plainly rutted trails made by the retreating army. The truck, a Russian-made brute that rattled and roared its way over the rough terrain, was solidly made and powerful enough to make driving relatively easy. It had a super low "granny" gear that could grind along, and a second gear only enough higher to afford another mile or two an hour. Third got them going too fast for the tedious terrain, and fourth and the higher range on the gearbox were out of the question until they could reach some sort of road. This beast didn't really need a road, and after driving it for a while, Eli started to feel like Woody was a mere windup toy truck. He wondered for the first time what it must feel like to drive a tank. It must be an awesome feeling of raw power.

Every time they came near a wrecked vehicle they slowed or stopped and appraised the salvage possibilities. Unfortunately, the Israeli shells had done too good a job on all of them. They did make a mental note of a half track that seemed to have thrown both rear treads. That could be a possibility worth a return trip in daylight, with someone who knew how to retread a half track.

It grew slowly darker, and Eli found himself driving with his head out the window half the time to see better, for headlights were out of the question. They all followed the sounds of battle and saw the occasional belch of flame from the tanks off in the distance ahead of them. Barak gave a sharp whistle and Eli paused while he shouted something off into the darkness ahead of them. There was an answering shout from a dark shape in the near distance that he had taken to be a large rock, but quickly realized was one of their own trucks. They had caught up with the infantry part of the advance. The roaring tanks with their long flashes of muzzle blast were a good half a kilometer ahead. Eli drew carefully up to the dark shape and saw the outline of a jeep and an APC emerge from the darkness ahead of them. There was also a knot of men on foot. Eli eased their truck to a stop nearby. He and Nir waited in the cab while their two IDF escorts scrambled down to go and parlay with the command group by the jeep.

Eli glanced at his watch by the dim instrument panel lights of his truck. They had been running without headlights for over an hour. It was now close to 2200. He was beginning to feel sleepy as he and Nir waited for the two soldiers to confer with the commander. It had been a long day. Had it only been that morning when he and Natalie had set out on a light hearted walk, chatting with the perimeter outposts and handing out coffee and cookies? And then they had wandered into a minefield to try to save a wounded man who turned out to be a suicide bomber. It seemed like another month already. A few hours at home then a long jog to the hilltop with Nir. Capturing the deserters. Getting in a fire fight with the retreating command group – and bringing down a six-ton-truck, he patted the utilitarian metal dash. "Welcome to the IDF Comrade Rhino," he said aloud.

Nir chuckled, "*Salut,*" he added.

"Wonder what the gas mileage on this baby is?" Eli asked.

"I think there is a reason only our Arab cousins are driving them," Nir answered. "It's probably in the range of liters per kilometer – you saw the size of those fuel tanks. If I could read Russian, I'd go looking for a service manual." He gave a half hearted poke in the glove box. With the dark and not daring show a light with live firing going on not far away, he could not identify anything, except for a pair of stinky socks he tossed out the window with a disgusted noise.

Day Six

Somewhere Northeast of Moshav Yiftach 0015

Eli shut off the big diesel engine to save fuel. Both he and Nir were dozing by the time Barak came back, climbed up on the step outside the driver's window and spoke: "We're going to be transporting prisoners as soon as we can get rigged for it. Can you drive back to that last roll of barbed wire we saw? I think it was a little ways back. And weren't there some heavy gloves and some wire cutters in the toolset we found?" Eli answered in the affirmative. He had made a quick mental catalog of the tools when they first found them. He had not noticed any particular barbed wire rolls along the way – but was sure they could not have driven a few kilometers through this battle torn land without finding some.

"Here, you remember where you saw it – you drive a while," Eli offered, and he slid over on the wide bench seat. Barak swung aboard, felt out the shift pattern, waited for Ari to climb back on, and backed a half circle away from the command group. Apparently his night vision was better. He seldom needed to poke his head out the window as they bounced back across the dark landscape. A few long jouncing minutes later he pulled up next to an unmistakable roll of spiraling razor wire. Barak parked the truck, found the heavy gloves and wire cutters, and climbed into the back of the truck with Ari. Eli and Nir clambered down to go help, unsure what he was up to. He sent them back for a crescent wrench from the cab, which Eli fetched. They saw the two soldiers working to unfasten one of the tubular metal frames that held up a canvas cover on many transport trucks, but the canvas was missing on this one. They pulled it free and handed it down. Eli and Nir stood there holding it, somewhat mystified while the two soldiers scrambled down and took if from them. However, when Barak took his end over to the spiral of barbed razor wire and started threading it through the middle of the loops, Eli began to grasp that the two intended to use the U-shaped piece of awning frame for a spindle to hold the roll of barbed wire. Since there was only one set of tough gloves, they stood by until they could be of assistance.

Once threaded, the two soldiers used their makeshift spindle to pick up the spirals of wire and drag them over to the side of the truck. Eli was about to help them lift the spool into the back of the truck, but soon realized that Barak had something else in mind.

"I want to make a barbed wire roof – stretching it from side to side, close enough spaced to discourage anyone from climbing out easily. So I want you guys to pass me the free end and I'll start making passes back and forth, tying it off here and there as I go. Two of you hold the spool, and the other one feed me wire off it."

They set to work on his plan by the dim light from the cloudy night sky. There was a fragment of moon somewhere above the clouds that cast a faint light. But Barak had all the hard work. They took turns gingerly feeding him the stiff wire bare handed since it involved frequent cuts and scratches. Barak was muttering curses as he occasionally got sliced by his own handiwork in spite of the thick leather gloves. However, he was slowly and methodically weaving tight bands of razor wire at about the waist height of the truck's low side walls and side bars. It would mean sitting slightly stooped for a six-foot person Eli's size not to get tangled in his spiders' web. That was probably part of his plan.

"Transporting prisoners," Eli wondered as he idly took his turn holding up one side of the makeshift spool and nursing a nasty slice across his index finger. He had some first aid plasters in his knapsack, but there would be time for them later when the work was done, it was probably not his last. The job was just past half done and he had taken two turns as wire feeder already. Since the beginning of the war he had been face to face with a number of prisoners of war. Some of the uneasiness had passed, but he still wondered what it must be like. What if they were quietly plotting escape, revenge, or perhaps a crazy plan to start a fight and hope for the best? In fact, there was a prisoner of war living at his house right now. Natalie was probably home by now, since the retreating army had passed their moshav without further incident. The Major was a model prisoner, polite, pleasant even. He was quite a conversationalist and an independent thinker who seemed free from many of the common stereotypes of the Arab mindset – at least according to how it came through in the media. Some of the others in the hospital in the Levine's basement looked like tougher customers, more of a security risk if not downright disagreeable. And he thought of the Georgian deserters. Granted, he would not want to meet the big burly bearded fellow in a dark street, or in a bar on the wrong side of an argument, but he could easily imagine working side by side next to such a person.

His thoughts were interrupted by his next turn as wire feeder. They had salvaged a couple greasy rags from the tool kit, which they wrapped around the feeder's hands to make the job a little safer. Now he had greasy cuts, but somewhat fewer of them. They were all tired by the time they finished up their barbed wire roof by wrapping turns enough over the tail gate to keep anyone from easily slipping out without lowering the gate. The four of them contemplated their makeshift prisoner transport with a critical eye, and pulled apart several strands looking for weaknesses. However, Barak had been careful to keep his turns taunt and close enough spaced that one could only pry them apart with difficulty. He debated aloud the wisdom of making some longitudinal wraps, but decided it was good enough.

Eli checked his watch again, it was after one am. They hardly noticed the sounds of tank fire any more as the running, or rather walking-speed battle moved steadily northwards. Since standing in the back riding shotgun was now impossible, the four of them jammed into the big bench seat. Eli was elected to drive again. His hands were a little tender where they had been ripped by razor wire, but he had managed to put first aid plasters on the worst of them, and shared his supply with the others. They looked like four guys who got the worst of a cat fight. Eli hit the glow plug on the big turbo diesel engine, cranked it and it roared to life. Barak, as the smallest of the four of them, was smashed in the seat next to Eli, straddling the gear shift levers. Nir dozed, and Ari was perched, his arm and shoulder out the right window.

"Hey, think this radio works?" Barak asked, turning it on. It produced loud static.

"It's 1:30 am in the middle of the biggest Middle Eastern war of the century. Every semiconductor chip within a thousand kilometers is toast, and you think you can get a radio station in the Golan?" Ari kvetched. But he said no more as Barak began patiently twirling the tuning knob. There were no preset buttons on this rig.

A few distant signals made a blip or two, probably AM stations in Europe at that hour of night, but Barak could not pull them in. Large chunks of the dial were blank. Then, a pop and a burst of sound, hastily he dialed back, missed the sweet spot and slowly edged it forwards. Then the cab was filled with the unmistakable sound of a woman reading news in Hebrew. Nir was suddenly wide awake, and Eli slowed the truck to ease the bumps and concentrate. In a half minute it was over. They had caught the tail end of a news break from Radio Israel Tsafun – Radio Northern Israel. The announcer was no professional, but sounded like a young woman in the military from the jargon she used in her newscast. They caught the vital information that the station was broadcasting news on the half hour before the announcer introduced another set of Beach Boys tunes, starting with "Surf City USA."

For the next three minutes, the big KRAZ truck was filled with the sounds of surfing guitars, followed by "Hey Girl" and "Little Deuce Coupe." Eli felt a mind/time warp happening to his brain.

"Ever been to California?" Barak asked.

"A long, long, long time ago," Eli said. "Mostly San Francisco and the Bay area."

"I did a road trip with my brother after he finished army service," Ari said dreamily. "I was sixteen, he was twenty one. Man we had some babes there. And I thought Tel Aviv girls were easy!" he said with enthusiasm.

Their anonymous DJ finished up her Beach Boys set and then jumped decades ahead to something long and awful sounding by a German grundge band Eli had never heard of. Even Ari didn't like it. But they merely turned the sound down rather than lose their link to the rest of the world. They all kept checking Eli's watch to see when the two am news would come around again.

It was a few minutes before two when they caught up with their support group with the prisoners. Ari bounded out of the cab and announced to every soldier standing around that they had a working radio, that news was coming up at 0200, and that the prisoners could f—g wait a few minutes. That drew a fair crowd to their truck, including the CO, who was as hungry for news as anyone. At his nod, Eli turned the radio up for the benefit of the two dozen soldiers standing around in the dark. After another American oldie whose title Eli couldn't remember wound to a close, the young woman's calm voice came booming over the dashboard set.

"*Shalom Israel zot segen Tali b' Radio Israel l'tzafun* Shalom Israel, this is Lieutenant Tali with Radio Northern Israel!"

"Shalom Lt. Tali!" a few enthusiastic young men said.

In a calm, unhurried voice, Lt. Tali Ashkenazi read a news script of bullet points jotted down by various people at the Northern Air Defense Command on Mt. Meron.

The top item was the recapture of Ramat Magshinim in the Golan Heights, and her account, with the occasional aside – like "*kol ha k'vod* - way to go!" was fairly up to date and factual. The troops around the truck cheered so loud and long that they almost missed the next item, news of the first shipload of supplies from the International community that landed in Haifa that afternoon. There were a few remarks about the air war, but nothing very specific. There was news of heavy fighting in the south of the country. She read the news of the prime minister's death and that the minister of agriculture was convening the Knesset for the first time later in the day. A blood drive in Haifa, announcements of milk, eggs and vegetables available at certain collection points and at various kibbutzim, a warning against all non-essential travel, advice on storing foods without refrigeration, directions for how to coordinate finding missing persons. Post offices were now open for that purpose wherever postal workers were available. Lieutenant Tali wished her listeners a pleasant good morning, and went back to spinning CDs.

It was close to three am by the time they had the prisoners loaded. It was a sullen, suspicious, slow-moving group of nearly two dozen. Several of them were lightly wounded and nursing their field dressings with exaggerated and touchy care. The back of the truck was a bit crowded, mostly because of their scavenged spare tires. Otherwise there would have been ample room for a few more had there been any. As they were loading, Nir was reassigned to another squad and sent ahead to the recaptured moshav of Ramat HaGolan where Eli was apparently slated to join him after delivering their prisoners to the nearest border crossing.

However, the retreating Syrians were only now beginning to reach the various crossings, and they might have to hang back a while until it was safe to approach within unloading distance of the border under a flag of truce.

Barak and Ari took care of the loading arrangements with some other soldiers, and Eli stretched out on the front seat for a very welcome twenty minute nap. He was sorry to have to wake up and drive again in what seemed just a few moments later. His brain ached for coffee. Then he remembered his last chocolate bar hidden in the depths of his pack. As they pulled out of the makeshift camp and followed a jeep of extra guards to the border crossing, he told Barak where to find the buried treasure in his pack. The three split the precious dark chocolate bar three ways. Barak and Ari were taking turns sitting halfway out the passenger window to watch the dark mass of prisoners in the back.

Barak gave a weary and worried sigh and began briefing Eli on the news from the command group. "I don't know any good way to put this, but there is a huge mass of men and armor headed across Syria right now – with helicopter and air cover this time. They are expected to be here shortly after dawn. They could turn south and hit at the southern end of the Kinneret. But everyone expects them to try to roll straight though here because this is the shortest route to the coast. They could also swing north and come around behind us on their drive for Haifa and the coast."

All of a sudden the last bit of chocolate was very dry and dead in Eli's mouth. He couldn't speak but only nodded dumbly at the devastating news. All their hard won gains could be wiped out with the coming morning sun, their homes overrun, and nowhere to run to. And his mind moved dully reviewing the overworked handful of IDF that were left in the whole Golan. Ari apparently had heard the news, for his reaction was stony silence.

"How many?" Eli croaked.

"A lot – almost as many as the first waves. We think they are the "B" team – not as up to date as the elite groups that hit us on days one and two, but more like the cannon fodder they threw at the settlements. But this time they have air support: helicopter gunships, at least fifty or more of them, and fighter coverage. IAF will be hitting them with everything they have – but we're really thin in the air right now, really thin."

Eli considered this. He recalled the waves of oncoming men and armor breaking, but just barely, against all the firepower that the IDF and his moshav had been able to muster. He had started the war with 600 rifle shells, now he had barely 100. When those ran out, then what? Was Natalie being warned? Were they evacuating women and children from the Golan communities? To where? Tiberius? But there was still only one way to get there with enemy forces holding the northern and southern tips of the lake. Crossing was too risky – even at night, especially with helicopters on the loose.

"What are we supposed to do?" Eli asked.

"Our orders are to race back to a supply depot set up near Maaleh Gamla that is shuttling supplies from the lakefront. They are still running boats across, but it's getting really dicey now that the Syrians are on to us. There are only a handful of boats fast enough to make the run without getting blown out of the water by shore based artillery sitting there waiting for them. And of course, to make that kind of speed they can't bring much over in one trip. We're supposed to shuttle all the available ammunition we can carry and perhaps tow an antiaircraft cannon back to Ramat HaGolan. That's where we'll be posted. Another driver will take the truck back for more supply trips – we need you and your sniper rifle on the hill there in Ramat HaGolan. Nir is supposed to start working out our fields of fire. There may be two more long range rifles joining us from Hespin – the rest are needed for watching the border by the settlements. With any luck we'll join him sometime after 0500 and dig in like crazy too.

The small lift Eli had experienced from his short nap and third of a chocolate bar had ebbed completely out of his system, replaced by a deadening weariness and heavy sense of resignation. All he could do was concentrate on picking a course over the dark tracks that revealed themselves from the back of the dim jeep ahead of them, as if it was being rolled from a big roll from underneath it somewhere. Fortunately he could drive on autopilot pretty well after more than forty years behind the wheel.

As if reading his thoughts, Barak broke in "I asked for you as the driver and Nir to scout the new positions because I didn't know how many English speakers might be there right now. But mostly because I never met a Sephardi moshavnik who didn't drive like a maniac..."

Eli snorted. "Actually, he's pretty good, but he has never driven anything this big – he told me that a while back when we were changing the tires. Me, I've driven some fair sized trucks in my time, but nothing like this brute. It must have nearly half a meter of ground clearance."

"I haven't driven anything bigger than a van either," Barak admitted, and Ari drives a motorcycle, so you know he's brain damaged. I need a few minutes shut eye. Make sure Ari wakes me up in thirty minutes and doesn't try to play the tough guy," Barak said with a jab at his friend's ribs.

"Do that again and you get ten minutes," Ari growled.

Eli checked his watch by the dimmed dashboard lights. A little after three am. Not much time to sleep thirty minutes, unload a truck load of surly prisoners and shove them across the border, and get to Maaleh Gamla and back. This monster was built for strength, not speed. At least they had roads from there on, bomb craters included.

At three thirty he prodded Barak awake just as the jeep in front signaled for them to pull ahead and stop. They had just pulled up to the crest of low hill. On either side of him he could see small groups of men digging in, and near them were a pair of tanks. As Eli pulled the truck alongside the jeep, Barak hopped out and went to talk to the other driver while Ari and three men from the jeep fanned out around the back of their prisoner transport.

Eli leaned wearily on the big steering wheel after engaging the emergency brake and peered at the dark landscape ahead, dimly lit by moonlight filtering through the smoke and haze. Firing had stopped, for he realized he no longer heard any gunfire at all. As he concentrated on the scene before him, he began to make out the dark shapes of retreating soldiers, with the occasional truck or jeep, loaded even higher than before, streaming in thin lines through the gaps in the minefield where they had advanced so confidently just five or six days ago. Across that invisible line was Syria. And somewhere a few hours to the east where the sun would rise, was a fresh wave of insanity rising and threatening to burst on the thin line of Jewish soldiers he saw grimly digging in. Perhaps a couple kilometers to the north, he could see the dark hilltop that had once been the vibrant young *yishuv* of Ramat HaGolan. Had they asked him, he would have preferred to be here on the ridge where at least Moshav Yiftach was in his line of retreat. But was retreat even possible? Probably not.

He found he felt little fear, just a numbing weariness, a choking feeling of despair that he had to hold in check or cry and scream in frustration, and a sullen, dogged determination to just keep on going until he could do no more. If he died, he died. In some ways, that was almost a relief – a release from responsibility, from caring, from trying and trying without the means to succeed. How would Ruth, his daughter in America, handle it if her family were wiped out, Israel broken in pieces, and the Middle East a nightmare of the new Middle Ages? It was a thought too bitter for thinking.

A wiry dark-skinned soldier banged on the metal side of the back of the truck and startled Eli from his grim thoughts. He began yelling in an angry sounding Arabic – obviously giving the prisoners their instructions. From somewhere else another soldier had appeared with a white bed sheet or table cloth on a pole and was wedging it so that it flew above the right hand window. The wiry dark soldier hopped up on the step of the cab outside Eli and told him, in perfect English, to pull slowly down the hillside ahead about two or three hundred meters at walking speed so the guards could keep up, and to be prepared to jam it into reverse and gun it back up the hill if anything was fired at them.

Eli took a last swallow of water from his bottle, slipped it back in his pack and took off the brake. On the soldier's signal, he put the truck in granny gear and crawled forwards. He found it impossible to try to watch for muzzle flashes at the border and the bumpy terrain too, so he concentrated on his driving, with his guide pacing the truck a few meters away. At last he signaled Eli to turn around and stop with the tailgate downhill towards Syria. He pulled the truck in a neat half circle and stopped, his foot firmly on the brake, for the hand brake could not be trusted even on such a mild slope.

With much yelling and shuffling about, the prisoners climbed out and were given a pair of stretchers for their moderately wounded, although all could walk if they had to, Eli noted. They marched off in a straggling knot down the hill. After about a hundred or so meters the guards began to fall slowly back and return to the truck.

"OK, lets go get some ammo," Barak said with relief, climbing in through the window around the pole of their makeshift white flag.

They ferried the men from the jeep to the top of the hill. As soon as Eli got his bearings, the three of them set off on a course to intercept the rural highway that followed the Israeli side of the border.

Ari had the next nap. Thirty minutes was decreed this time which was their estimated running time to Maaleh Gamla, barring detours or delays.

Once on the highway, Eli shifted into the high range and got a feel for what the truck could do on the road. It ran pretty well, he decided, but the big oversized tires were a chore to steer even with the power steering. It didn't seem to coast at all like a two-wheel-drive down hills but had to be plied with gas to keep all six driving wheels turning at speed. There were fewer shell craters in the highway that turned southwest towards Maaleh Gamla than he expected. The roads along their settlement strip had been pretty well pock-marked. They reached Maaleh Gamla at close to four in the morning.

Barak steered Eli to the makeshift depot in a highway maintenance garage tucked into the hillside on the winding road leading down to the Kinneret just outside of town. As they backed the truck up for loading, a score of sleepy soldiers emerged from various points and sprang to loading as two men cut their hard-won barbed wire roof away with a pair of large snips. In a few minutes they were sitting few inches lower with a hefty load of shells and cases of ammunition. Barak told him that the antiaircraft gun had been sent ahead with a jeep already.

"Take us to Ramat HaGolan driver, and don't spare the horses" Barak said sleepily. He was snoring before they even pulled fully out of the small community perched on the rim of the Golan Heights. Ari was now sitting at the window seat while his friend curled up between them. He dozed off a few times in spite of the open windows and the cool night air pouring through the cab. Eli fought to stay awake. Dread at what they were approaching and a fatalistic realization of what a single stray shell could do to the tons of ammunition clanking in the bed behind him kept his eyes mostly open all the way back. The return trip took a good forty minutes and they were directed by jeep to half a dozen artillery placements up and down the border defenses for the next hour, unloading their precious cargo. Both Ari and Barak got another nap, and Eli was wishing for a chance to snooze too. He had his hands full following first one jeep, then another, and then a motorcycle, and finally a tractor to the various gun placements. He was happy to see over a dozen big guns, for he well remembered their protective umbrella of fire in the desperate fight to save Moshav Yiftach. It seemed an age ago.

Finally they were told to take the rest of their load, now down to half a dozen crates of mortar shells and a few dozen boxes of rifle and machine gun shells, over to the hill where the shattered and looted remains of the settlement stood. They unloaded at a sandbagged bunker not far inside the blasted gate of the community, turned their truck over to a fresh team of drivers, and walked following a young soldier up the hill to where their positions would be.

It was getting close to sunrise, for the eastern sky had lightened considerably in the last half hour. Incongruously with the blasted houses and grim shell holes, the morning chorus of birds was singing in the many bushes and what was left of the trees of community. Eli dimly thought of the *Shacharit* prayers and he walked wearily up the road past house after house torn apart by shelling, fire and looters. He wondered how he would have the strength to dig, much less fight in the hour or two ahead.

Their guide took them along a street that wound around the top of the hill, and left them off at the first of a half a dozen houses which would have had stunning views to the east had any of their upper stories and balconies been left intact. All that was left was basement- or ground-level rubble. Nir found them quickly. He was overjoyed to see them and eager to show Eli the warren of trenches and reinforced shelters that constituted their sector. Eli numbly tried to take it all in. When he found out there was no digging left to do, he asked to be allowed to sleep at least an hour if possible. Nir understood immediately and led him to a nest of blankets in a secure small room-sized shelter with two exits. "I'll wake you up well before anything shows up," he promised.

Ramat Hovav Airfield 0300

Major Yossi Green was awakened by an urgent whisper. "Wake up, we're ready to try her again," said his ground crew chief. It took only ten minutes to hit the bathroom, wash his face and upper body, pull on a clean flight jumpsuit and be climbing up the cockpit ladder, chugging a can of energy drink. With his crew chief giving him a running narrative of the last few hours of tests, modifications and changes, he began working the long version of the preflight check. As he did, the previous evening's test flight came sharply to mind: problems with the fuel pumps, sluggish response on the flaps and ailerons, warning lights that turned out to be false, and no warning lights at all for the near stall that almost cost him his life. Instrument readings had been misleadingly low, high, or just plain false for altitude, attitude and air speed, leaving him to fly by the seat of his pants and ease his troubled bird back home.

It had been such a disappointment after such hopes. All afternoon and evening there had been one delay after another. Finally he got the go ahead about eight the previous evening. He remembered the breathless feeling of seeing his beloved F-15 put back together and waiting for him to climb aboard and fly away into the black night sky.

What could he expect this time? Could they fix even half the bugs in four hours? So far, so good. He watched his trim tabs respond to the controls with a critical eye. They appeared smooth and immediate, but what did that feel like in the air? It didn't feel like his beloved bird anymore. Too much had changed. The same sleek body but a different, alien brain and nervous system, "I want my baby back," he mused.

Preflight check done, double checking all the critical systems, he steered the nose wheel as his ground crew pushed his bird out of its sheltering, half buried hanger. Once on the tarmac he fired up the twin engines and felt his excitement mount as they roared to life.

Now under his own power, he rechecked all his control systems again, feeling the rolling plane wag from side to side in response to the rudder, and bob and dip in response to flaps and ailerons. Nothing for it but to power up and give her a try. Maybe the old girl was in there somewhere.

Cleared for takeoff he lined up on the runway, jammed on the brakes and powered up before releasing the pent up thrust and hurtling down the air strip. So far, so good. He glanced a last time at his indicators. The altitude was correct for Ramat Hovav, fuel read one quarter. No sense burning himself up with more if they met the landscape coming down. Compass heading true so far. Time to pull flaps and fly.

The nimble bird leaped into air like as if let out of a cage and climbed in a satisfying moderate G-force curve towards the night sky. Above the haze within the first minute, he burst into a clear night sky, Orion setting brightly to the west. The Dipper dipping to the north seemed to beckon, but he held to his flight plan of taking it out over the Med for a series of test maneuvers that would soon tell him what he had to work with. The shoreline rolled by beneath him and soon he was in the clear air over the dark sea.

He rolled gently left, right, banked left, banked right, and tried some easy turns. He climbed gently at first, then dropped the tail and shot skyward at full power. His baby had come back to him. He let the nose fall over at the top of the loop, did an extra loop the loop for sheer joy, and dived for the deck with the pure pleasure of flying. A half an hour of maneuvers later he felt she was ready for a taste of live action. He vectored off to the easy target he had been given to test the weapons systems, a sleepy depot just off the coast road where the Egyptians had been creating a network of trails to try to bypass the much-bombed primary supply routes. He radioed the news back to base, checking again for any radar traffic. Two minutes later, he caught a group of four trucks sneaking north along a road snaking through the dunes, strafed them twice, and headed for the depot a few kilometers away to test the pair of missiles on his wings. Two clean hits later he left a fuel tank blazing and an armored personnel carrier in pieces and turned homeward.

Only after he landed and headed for the pilots' briefing did he remember the details of the last briefing. Massive forces with air cover were crossing Syria and heading for the northern fronts. With his own bird back, there were going to be a whole lot less of them flying home that day, he could promise that.

The pilot's briefing room, with its big comfortable chairs and clipboards with mission details being handed out was packed even though only twelve pilots would be actually flying the first strike teams. Everyone first wanted to know how his test flight had gone and he was asked at least times before he could sit down, where he was badgered with four more eager questions.

With his and Uri's bird back it the air, along with a pair of Israeli F-16s, the twelve planes on this next strike was two-thirds of the combat ready IAF fighter force. Six more would be standing by close to home for any further attempts to bomb Tel Aviv or any of the coastal cities. Everyone was sure that something had been coordinated this time despite the declining spirits on the Egyptian side of the border.

Unfortunately, infrared satellite information was not getting to Israel anywhere close to real time, so their location reports on the various columns were several hours old. However, compared to a reliable roadmap of Syria, their course and destinations were beginning to seem clear. They appeared to be heading to hit the border somewhere just north of the Kinneret. The thrust was most likely aimed at reinforcing the faltering Syrian offensive that was trying to bully its way through the hill country between Tiberias and Tzfat and break through towards the coast.

The Israelis' flight plan should take them about thirty kilometers into Syria to hit the huge mass of men and vehicles as they rolled for the border. With luck, they would have time enough time for two or three strikes before the Syrian forces could reach Israel. The massive force had been creeping across the breadth of Syria in stages of approximately thirty to fifty kilometers. They were taking at least four hours to make each stage, with helicopters, mobile anti-aircraft batteries and armor shuttled ever farther forwards to protect the vulnerable mass on the ground.

Their plan was simple enough, Yossi and his team of six F-15s would provide the air cover, and the six F-16s would pound anything on the ground, plus cut up any helicopters they found in the air.

The last of Yossi's group was airborne by 0430, an hour before dawn still. With luck, they would be back to re-arm before sun up. Breaking into three pairs, they scattered high, higher and still higher in stair steps of altitude, with Yossi taking the middle level at about 7,000 meters, Yoni and Yair higher at 10,000, and the new kids cruising at about 5,000 meters. All were watching their long range radar sets as best they could, there was no need for secrecy, their target was not going anywhere, and any company in the air would be most welcome.

They were somewhere north of Jerusalem when the first interceptors showed up on their screens, perhaps eight or more of them, They asked for a count from ground control and were told ten blips. Yossi could see the group of F-16s on his screens a couple dozen kilometers behind him. If any more interceptors showed up, he could pull a few off them into air to air mode to help out, for they carried half air-to-air and half air-to-ground missile loads. His group was loaded with birdshot only.

Sure enough, as they neared the Syrian border another flight of interceptors appeared on their screens, another ten at least. Yossi hailed the F-16 leader and asked for two pairs to come forward to play ball. The remaining pair slowed and dropped back, intending to sail through once the dogfight began and hit their targets, with a priority being to blast the choppers wherever they could find them – in the air or on the ground.

In the two minutes remaining before they met the interceptors Yossi outlined a simple plan to his five pairs. He intended to throttle up and blast straight for the first pack of ten with his wing man Uri, scattering them like ten pins and trying to fly right through their formations in the wake of a spread of missiles fired from long range. After that, it was every pair for themselves, and good hunting.

He checked the tactical radar and instruments one more time before powering up and cutting on the afterburners for his mad charge. He set a course to meet the first group, which appeared to be in neatly stacked formations five high and five low. He told Uri to aim for the high five while he took the low road at the last minute. As soon as he could acquire even the most tenuous targets on his air to air system, he fired two Israeli modified ARMS at the upper pack and then dived suddenly to release two more in the general direction of the lower. He had to throttle back a hair not to risk overrunning his own missiles as he hurtled towards Syria at something approaching Mach 2. He was making a window shattering boom if there was any glass down there left to break down there.

As expected, his tactical heads-up display showed a wild scattering of missiles in return, and a quickly dissolving formation. He concentrated on the five lower planes looking to see any pattern to his break. Then her returned his gaze to the night sky ahead to see if he had any visual contact yet. He saw the trails of his four missiles fanning out above and ahead of him and followed the lower two as best he could. His helmet view showed collision alerts and he caught the flash of wings ahead just above. He shot underneath the oncoming jet, clearing it by more than 300 meters, but it felt like 300 millimeters. Yossi pulled into a hard looping turn to go after it. By the time he cleared his vision from the brutal g-forces of his turn, he discerned three targets ahead and two part way through their turns in an attempt to get behind him. They could wait. He had a good radar lock on the middle plane. He chanced a single Israeli-style ARM and banked a hard right to see if he could out maneuver the turning plane on that side. A bright fireball ahead told him his missile ran true. There were too many bandits in the air to go by the book and fire two for one target – certainly not when they were painted that bright in his sights. His first two salvos had cost him half his arrows. However, his earphones told him that they had been well spent. At least two more Syrians were on the barroom floor besides his kill.

"Uri, where are you?" Yossi asked as he sized up the turning arc of his chosen prey.

"Right behind you Green Machine," said his earphones. "High and right and half a klik inside of your turn so far,"

"This one's yours. I'll keep him running," Yossi replied coolly and eased his turn just a fraction to let Uri move into position.

Their target, realizing he now had two on his tail, jinked left then attempted to spiral away and right. Uri's missile caught him before he could shake free.

"Good one, let's get upstairs," Yossi said, initiating a steep climb to gain altitude and perspective. It was hard to read his tactical display from the attitude of 90 degrees, for ahead and behind meant something totally different. But as he topped out of his loop and pointed his nose back towards Israel, he realized that the action was now behind him. They both pulled tight turns through the thin upper air and vectored off towards the thickest action. Only a coded transponder told them who was who among the blips. They sized up the situation and headed off to help a pair of F-16s that appeared to have their hands full. Indeed, missile tracks were criss-crossing the sky at crazy angles as they approached the nearest pair of bogeys. Two Syrian pilots attempted to break off their chase of the two F-16's and respond to the new threat. Their maneuver was too textbook plain to fool either Yossi or Uri, and the pair were soon in flames. However, a fireball in the sky, paired with the disappearance of a blue transponder blip, told them they were too late to save one of their countrymen. With no time for regret, they were soon on the tails of the killers.

These two were good, clean in their maneuvers and just enough pages ahead in each chapter to stay alive. The four planes soared through an aerial chessboard ten kilometers high by fifty kilometers wide before one of the Syrian pilots missed his cue and took an air to air missile up his tailpipe for his mistake. The other turned for home, but never made it.

Out of missiles, Yossi and Uri headed for home. Radio checks told him that Yoni and Yair were half way there already with the youngsters in tow. One of the young pilots was having fuel flow problems, but control systems were working well enough to take the plane in. Tone in his headphones alerted him to another pack of bandits at the edge of their tactical field behind him to the northeast. He was sure he could outrun them easily and alerted the teams at home base to look sharp for incoming fun.

"Green team, we have probably stealth fighter signatures bearing southeast 135 degrees – range 50 K," the voice of their squadron commander broke over his earphones.

"Good G-d no!" Yossi whispered. He had been afraid of this moment the whole war. Due to the tremendous influence of their oil money, the Saudis had taken delivery of the first group of six next-generation F-35 fighters sold outside the US. With all the red tape and politics, Israel had to wait another year before getting more than a few test flights of the new birds. Not even a trainer could be spared. He had flown an earlier test model two years ago out of Nevada. Sleek, fast, harder than hell to see with a radar until too late, and deadly.

"How many?" he asked.

"More than one," was all ground could tell him. Thanks to some sophisticated diagnostics on their new generation ground radar, something to do with signal backscatter, they at least sense that there was a stealth aircraft and plot a rough course. Altitude and speed readings were unreliable at this point. Ground told him that their course appeared to intercept his path somewhere over the Dead Sea. Good, that was hill and canyon country, with some well-known wadis that an experienced pilot could fly if he knew their peculiar twists. A deep wadi south of Masada came to mind. Going high and wild was useless against a faster plane he couldn't see. Getting low and slow against a confusing ground pattern was their only hope.

"We're going for *Nahal* David," Yossi told both his wingman and ground control, "see if you can get us some covering fire where we come out." If the steep desert canyon had been good enough for King David to hide in three millennia ago, it might work for a Jewish air warrior of the twenty-first century.

He and Uri pushed up their airspeed and headed for the deck. He was more angry than scared. He knew what he was up against and he was just plain mad about the unfairness of it all. Given a level playing field he knew Israeli pilots could out fly any fighters in the world, including the Americans. They had beat the Yanks, NATO, Aussies, Argentineans and Indians hands down time and time again in air-to-air competition. But this was unfair. Dirty money politics and bad faith had kept Israel from getting a fair shot at the new generation fighters they had helped develop and refine. And now an unknown number, somewhere between two and six, were closing in on him.

Reaching the deck somewhere north of the Dead Sea, he and Uri sped low and fast, looping around the familiar Judean hills with the plan of hitting the eastern edge of the remains of the Great Rift Valley. It contained the Dead Sea, the lowest point on Earth and getting lower as the sea level dropped in successive drought years. He saw a flash of light on his heads-up display as they shot over Jericho just above rooftop level. The bandits were closing from the southeast. "Fire your missiles now and hit a mosque why don't you? he taunted them in his mind. Too late to change the plan he could only hang on and fly like the maniac he was.

Their two birds nearly skimmed the dry shoreline of the Dead Sea in the growing predawn light, practically following the contours. The green smudge of Ein Gedi blurred by at eye level out his cockpit window, followed by a blink of the familiar shape of Masada. Two more wadis to go. A pair of missiles blinked in his visor display and flashed into the rocky cliffs ahead and to the right as he slowed in preparation for his hard right turn into the oncoming Wadi David. He had done this wadi half a dozen times over the years, practicing for just such an emergency, much to the objections of the Israeli Parks and Nature Reserve officialdom.

He banked and rose at breakneck speed into the mouth of the deep wadi, pulling up just enough to clear the first dry waterfall, swinging left then back hard right to stick to the floor of the wadi above the falls. He saw the upper end of the wadi directly ahead, pulled neatly up and out and immediately turned to dive into the head of the next wadi to the north. The flash of friendly F-16 beacons greeted him in his headset display, as well as a fan of friendly missiles aimed behind him. Uri was half a second on his tail. They dived down into the adjacent twisting canyon, letting their airspeed drop suddenly, but ready to power up the split second they emerged over the Dead Sea again. "Got the bastard!" he heard in his earphones, "He thought he could fly high and pick you off when you came out."

"The park service can clean up the other at the first waterfalls, big, big mess," said another voice.

"Sector clear" announced ground control. "Time to go home."

Northern Command Mt. Meron 0550

Anna winced as she took a sip of hot bitter black coffee. None of the many couriers up and down the mountain had responded to their pleas to bring up a bag of sugar, or if they had, it hadn't made it down to the command center yet. She was not one of those who put heaping tablespoons of sugar in a cup and called it coffee, but she liked just a little sweetness in her life. There was little sweetness now, cooped up in a high tech cave for a week straight. She'd been outside once as the war was breaking to see if they were radioactive. Since then, nothing but work,

work, work, worry and exhausted sleep, and not nearly enough to knit the raveled sleeve of care more than a stitch or two. She had slept until the last possible moment, wolfed a tasteless breakfast of old rolls and something that passed for cheese, and now screwed up her face for another sip of the necessary stimulant. She had no time to check her workstation, only to go directly to the 6 am status meeting and pick up the situation as best she could. Given the ominous news – as black and bitter as her mug of strong coffee – that loomed over the six pm and midnight briefings, she expected little better and possibly worse for their morning roundup.

She greeted the assortment of group leaders as they filed into the conference / dining room. She hadn't even had the energy to study the maps on the walls with their hodge podge of new notes scrawled on their laminated plastic covers. Koby, who had been working nearly opposite shifts as her for the past few days, led off with the overnight news. Their first two wings of fighters had been intercepted by substantial numbers of Syrian and allied planes. There was possible confirmation of Saudi markings on some of them. It was definitely two brand new Saudi F-35 next-generation stealth planes that had jumped the returning Israeli strike force. Both had been destroyed in a clever trap in a desert canyon south of Masada, leaving four left in Riyadh. However, only two Israeli F-16 made it through to the targets, and they had found very few helicopters within striking range. The Syrian attack helicopters had apparently gone to ground at news of their approach and been well hidden. The F-16s distributed their bomb loads on antiaircraft and tank units the best they could before the approach of a third wave of interceptors forced them to race homewards. Israeli losses were one to air to air, and one down for serious maintenance. The second wave strikes, begun a little while ago, were apparently hitting stiff anti-aircraft fire and missiles from the ground, as well as new waves of interceptors. IAF was doubtful of hitting much on the ground until these were dealt with. Unfortunately, the promised re-wired Blackhawk helicopters were going to take at least another day. However, several had been in the air briefly for testing, which was a good sign.

Two more supply ships were being escorted from their rendezvous point 50 kilometers off shore, and there had been no further attempts to shell the Israeli coast by the Egyptian navy in the past twelve hours. The Knesset meeting was set for four pm, with at least 60 MKs accounted for and more showing up every few hours as jeeps and trucks and antique cars brought them into Jerusalem from wherever they had been scattered. One MK had reportedly made it up from Rehovot in his neighbor's 1967 Volvo, with his neighbor's wife riding shotgun with the Uzi she had carried in the Yom Kippur War. The wounded Minister of Defense was fighting a nasty secondary infection and would not make the meeting. Education, Finance, Interior, Transportation, Labor, Religious Affairs, and Taxation were all accounted for. The Minister of Agriculture, the most senior member of the party forming the government, would be presiding as acting Prime Minister, although half the meeting was expected to be spent arguing that point alone.

On land, the mass of armor that had joined forces from the northern and southern Golan invasions had succeeded in breaking through the IDF lines between Tzfat and Tiberius and had broken loose as far as Carmiel, where their drive had stalled again as fresh IDF forces from the interior and coast stopped them. The Syrian advance was trying to dig into the handful of Israeli Arab villages across the valley from Jewish-held Carmiel. They were apparently running low on ammunition and fuel after their supply trains had been shot up and bombed mercilessly behind them.

The Jordanian advances in the Jordan Valley and their attempts to use the historic invasion route through the broad Jezreel Valley over the hills beyond the Jordan River – which had been followed for centuries by Babylonians, Assyrians, Arabs and Turks – were being held up outside Afula. Much of the Jordanian army had withdrawn towards Nazareth to seek cover in that almost exclusively Arab city. The tank battle of the millennium that had promised to develop at Megiddo – known to Christians as Armageddon, had so far failed to happen. This freed a few of the collection of Israeli tanks that had been scraped together to oppose them. They were able to shift north to help stop the Syrian thrust. However, Jordan still held a broad strip of Israel between the south end of the Kinneret and most of the west bank of the Jordan at this point. Their threatened advance on Jerusalem had been badly diluted by their attempts to grab and hold such a long strip of very vulnerable territory. IDF pin prick counter attacks were threatening to cut their strip of West Bank gains in several places.

The Southern Command sectors were reporting a few mixed successes, but a general lack of progress as the hard-hit IDF forces there attempted to coalesce into larger units and begin pushing back. Only a few small communities had been taken back. Ashkelon was the site of heavy fighting as the Israelis tried to dislodge the hordes of armed looters and militias that had streamed there from Gaza to the south. They could only keep a few kilometers along the coast clear with the constant help of Israeli navy gunboats, who had to guard against attempted Egyptian naval adventures as well as help their comrades on shore. The elite armored Egyptian forces that had made it halfway to Tel Aviv at points were being slowly driven back as they too ran low on supplies and ammunition, thanks to the stranglehold the IAF had kept on their long Sinai Desert and coastal supply lines. As they spoke in their command bunker meeting, the second and third waves of IAF were hitting the looming Syrian advance again, and ears were strained towards the doorway to catch any sounds of triumph or despair.

On the diplomatic front, the PR war was going poorly. Most of the world believed the Iranian and Egyptian claims that Israel had attempted a nuclear strike. Accordingly, they believed that there were massive civilian casualties, devastating environmental damage. They were buying the story that Israel's neighbors were in desperate need of immediate and substantial international aid, including more arms. Saudi Arabia and the Persian Gulf states were unusually quiet, mostly echoing the same threadbare lies. She sensed they were waiting to see the outcome without committing themselves openly. However, the Saudi Air Force apparently felt free to come and go as they pleased. Anna hoped that the wreckage of the two F35's in the Judean Desert south of Masada would be convincing enough proof of their complicity. However, it was a time where perception was everything, and facts were few, and largely ignored by those with the luxury of ignoring the facts. Israel had no such luxury.

Near Ramat HaGolan 0700

Sam had been up most of the night running orders to and from Colonel Eschol's mobile command group. The colonel was no longer in charge of the entire Golan, just the armored forces. A lieutenant general from the Golani Brigade had arrived after someone even higher ranking was able to relieve him elsewhere. He had arrived, weary and battered from five days of trying to keep the overwhelming Syrian forces from breaking through from Rosh Pina to Tiberius. The general was smuggled by high speed ammunition courier boat across the Kinneret, and Sam had picked him up in Maaleh Gamla in Woody and ferried him to the defense lines forming on the high ground behind Ramat HaGolan. He'd borrowed Woody at the moshav after retaking Ramat Magshinim with elements of his old recon company.

After an afternoon of hard fighting, interviewing captured soldiers, and learning of the hidden horrors in the synagogue and other execution sites around the once green and peaceful rural town, Sam was running on sheer determination to see the job done. He briefed the general on their way to join the Golan headquarters group.

After hearing the general's details of the other end of their front, Sam could detect signs of weakening in the enemy's massive assault. It had taken the Syrian's withdrawing from his sector of the Golan and throwing all their combined forces at the strip of hill country that ran between Tzfat and Tiberius to finally break through, but at tremendous cost. And part if that price tag was losing most of their supply train to a pair of enterprising Merkava tanks. Sam knew that story well.

And now this new equally massive offensive was taking its sweet time lumbering across Syria with its reserves. Even though there was intelligence about a large force of assault helicopters, they were sticking close to their anti-aircraft batteries for fear of the tiny IAF. The IDF had the whole night and precious hours of daylight to prepare. There were now more than a dozen of the most modern Merkava IV tanks, fast and ferocious even without their advanced electronics, more than a dozen of the older Merkava IIs and IIIs, six or seven big 155 mm mobile howitzers up and running, and an equal number of towed ones. The Golan had a good collection of smaller anti-tank and anti-aircraft cannons, and two surface-to-air missile batteries that had been brought online thanks to the ingenuity of the Israeli mechanics. Even given the size of the force headed their way, they had a fair chance of stopping it – or at least forcing it into a long and dangerous detour.

The general was using his artillery and older tanks to set up what amounted to a roadblock in the way of the Syrian advance. If the IAF could help them with the helicopters, they could lay down a convincing barrage of fire. Their ammunition stocks were reasonably adequate for a least a day of hard fighting. They hoped that this roadblock would make the Syrians decide to retreat, or try to swing north around though the land they had captured. That northern country was fairly rough, with limited places to cross the Jordan River, and was very lightly held. Mostly militia and looters were running loose there, with little organized defense. The general was holding his dozen advanced tanks and about 25 APCs and half tracks on his northern flank to press and harass any attempts to bypass their lines to the north. If the Syrian mass had to make a wide detour to the north, it would stretch their supply lines through some difficult country. It seemed like a good plan, if they could deal with the threats from the air. There was also the possibility of a fresh Syrian missile barrage, with short range, more accurate tactical missiles forcing the IDF troops under cover while they pressed the attack. Sam sincerely hoped that these had all been used up the wholesale bombardments in the first two days of the war.

However, the part of the plan that bothered him was Ramat HaGolan. The hilltop community, now in ruins, was a full kilometer and a half from their main line of defense. It stood, isolated and squarely in the path of the Syrian advance. Relatively speaking, it was being lightly defended. There was no more than a company of infantry and perhaps a hundred unattached reservists and civil defense riflemen. His wartime friend and owner of the battered, wood-fired pickup he was driving, was one of them. The infantry company had machine guns, both light and heavy, a large collection of field mortars, and a handful of anti-tank cannon. But they had no air defenses, and nothing but the protective umbrella of the heavy guns two kilometers away to keep them from serious harm. Admittedly, they were well dug in. The hill was important psychologically, but not necessarily strategically. It could be easily bypassed, but it was a bad hand of cards to be holding. Sam didn't like it. They had zero chance of retreat once the shooting started.

Sam thought of his friend Eli as he dozed in the cab of Woody waiting for either the general or the colonel to tell him where to go next. He had met Eli Kaplan the first night of the war. In fact, Sam, the colonel and a dozen soldiers had requisitioned Eli's snug, earth sheltered house as the perfect headquarters for their defense of Moshav Yiftach. When an older man had wandered in that night, in dirty fatigues with a salt and pepper beard, graying hair, and a long sniper rifle, Sam had not realized for a long while that this old man was the owner of the house. The man just went about his business like it was normal to have an IDF headquarters in one's living room. And he had handed over the keys to his one-of-a-kind wood powered truck without even learning Sam's name or when he would be back.

Over the next few days he had gotten to known Eli and his wife while the command group used the house as a headquarters, field hospital and cafeteria. Where else could one find fresh steaks, home baked bread, fine kosher wines, fresh fruit and garden salads in the middle of a war zone? Somehow this miracle seemed to come naturally to Eli and Natalie, and indeed, to most of the moshav families. Sam was beginning to reassess his wholly urban lifestyle. If nothing else, this war had shown the fragility of the energy intensive, high density life he was used to. He had little idea how people were coping in the cities, especially with nearly every able-bodied person pressed into wartime service.

But the clincher had come early the next morning as the two of them floated lost and directionless in the foggy, smoky Kinneret with nothing but an inflatable kayak between them and G-d knows what lurking in the fog. Sam realized that he had been minutes away from being a completely helpless, despairing wreck. Somehow Eli's calm assurance and quiet competence had set them straight, and delivered them within a few dozen meters of their landing in Tiberius. Was it the fact that Eli was religious? Sam wondered. But he had known dozens of religious men, soldiers and civilians. What was it about Eli that made him glad when the old Rabbi had urged him to go along on their madcap mission to Syria to blow up bunkers containing the dreaded assault helicopters? He shook his head. Whatever it was, Eli was now his friend, and Eli was sitting somewhere over there on that hilltop with nothing but a rifle and a hundred rounds of ammunition between him and the Syrian army. He wished he could be with him. Maybe the colonel would let him go in with some volunteers if he asked.

He closed his eyes and tried to rest, but he couldn't. He made up his mind. He couldn't sit by and watch a wave of 50,000 or more Syrians and mercenaries smash against that shattered hilltop over his friend's head. He grabbed his knapsack and short M-16 and strode over to where the colonel and the general were just wrapping up their conference with the other staff officers.

"Natan," he said as he came up to Colonel Eschol, "I want to go help them out in Ramat HaGolan. I can't sit here and watch while they get overrun. Is there anything else we can spare them?"

His long-time commander didn't need more than a glance to see there was no arguing with Sam on this one. He also agreed that it would be tough to watch the pounding they were sure to get, even if the advance retreated in short order.

"Tell you what," he said, "has that truck got a trailer hitch?"

Sam thought a moment. "Yes, I must have banged my damned kneecap on it twice while loading shells, why?"

"I've got an old 88 mm anti-tank gun over there that won't be able to do much good from here," he said, waving at a small cannon farther down their ridge. "I was thinking of moving it south to the other end of the line, but it could probably do more good on the hill if they could use it. Why don't you run down there and see if the crew will volunteer to join you. And if they will, load up their shells and tow them over to the hill as fast as you can hump it, because I hear the advance groups have been spotted less than an hour from here."

Sam started to run back to the truck, and heard his commander yell after him, "And if you want to stay with them, just don't get anything blown off you can't grow back!"

He waved and was off in Woody leaving a faint scent of wood smoke and a spray of small rocks.

As he expected, the four man crew of the older anti-tank gun was eager to volunteer. They were happy to get a chance to be in the thick of the coming action, even though none of them were sanguine about their chances of surviving the day. Thankfully, it was the right sized trailer hitch, and their supply of shells fit snugly in the bed of Woody. Two men squeezed into the cab and the two other reserve artillerymen perched in the bed as best they could. It was chock full of shells. There was nothing but some flak jackets stuffed in between to insulate the front row of high explosive from the hot firebox. They drove almost straight down the hill and pelted pell mell for the road into the shattered kibbutz.

The sentries at the gate cheered their arrival, and gave them quick directions to a suitable firing pit dug near the top of the hill. They had the gun man-handled into the enlarged mortar pit within minutes, the ammunition unloaded and ready to go. They were soon expertly surveying their new field of fire. Sam took a few minutes to find a sheltered place to park Woody on the side of the hill away from the Syrian border, facing towards the exit for a quick getaway should one be possible. He was banking down the fire in the firebox and thinking whether to cut some more wood from a nearby blasted tree, or go find a unit to join when the first incoming artillery shell landed well short of their hilltop. Forget the wood.

Sam slung his pack over one shoulder and checked the clip on his rifle. It was full. Then he jogged around the hilltop road to the first infantry group he found.

"Morning lieutenant," one of the smoking soldiers greeted him.

"Any more recon people with you?" A reservist sergeant asked.

"Just me, with greetings from HQ and an 88 and crew for some last minute help," he said. "I'm looking for a couple of moshavnik snipers: a couple of old guys, fifty plus, tall guy with a grey beard and a shorter guy."

"They're about two or three houses down," one of the younger soldiers volunteered. "I met the short one when he was setting up. They have some really good cover and a great trench system – dug by yours truly and friends. Tell them Motti says hi."

Sam thanked them. He looked over their network of deep foxholes and trenches approvingly. Sam made his way past a heavy machine gun group and found a back entrance to a bunker that appeared to feed into a trench that snaked its way over to the next house. It was amazing what a motivated group of soldiers could dig in one night. He followed the trench that emerged from the other side of the protected bunker made of roofing scraps, earth and sand bags. Then he duck-walked along the narrow trench and slipped through a hole under the foundation of the next house and found himself in another makeshift bunker. This one had slabs of reinforced concrete artfully arranged in the shell of the basement. Along the way he greeted various defenders who were warily watching the falling curtain of artillery shells ranging in on their hilltop.

The next slit trench between the houses was shallower, due to rocks, and he crawled around behind the shell torn basement walls and popped into what was left of the basement. Someone had ripped up the tile flooring in the rubble-filled basement along the far wall and dug a trench inside the thick footer of the foundation. There he saw a familiar battered helmet and a long rifle poked through a hole hammered through the wall. Eli was studying the Syrian border just a kilometer away.

"Hey old man," Sam said as he slid into the comfortable trench next to him, "I brought your truck in case you want to go to town and get a beer after this is over."

"Sam!" Eli said, startled by his sudden appearance. A huge shell boomed on the slope below them, shaking the house and causing a loose chunk of concrete to fall somewhere nearby. "What the hell are you doing here? Last I heard you were cleaning up in Ramat Magshinim."

"It's clean enough. I thought I was needed here, and I brought an anti tank squad with me, compliments of the colonel."

"Good to see you," Eli grinned, grabbing him by the shoulders in a bear hug. "Why didn't you bring the beer with you too?"

"No room, too many damned shells," Sam shrugged. They hugged again and settled in to watch the bombardment. Each peered through a separate hole in the foundation that was just the right size for a rifle and scope with a clear view, and dug down to a comfortable standing height.

"Nir spent the morning bashing these through with a hammer and a piece of drill steel," Eli explained. "We've spent the last couple hours customizing them. He's in the house next door with the same kind of setup. I got a ninety minute nap when I got here, how about you?"

"'About the same, maybe two hours worth of cat naps," Sam yelled back. "I picked up General Irani at Maaleh Gamla and have been running him all over the country in Wood. But he's got a proper jeep now."

Shells were soon pounding the hill with great regularity as the barrage that heralded the Syrian advance had found their range. Sam got out his binoculars and studied the storm of smoke and fire before him. He was glad to see the answering fire from the Israeli big guns was beginning to make some hits in the distance, emphasized by the eruption of the occasional column of smoke and fire from exploding ammunition.

Then a familiar but dreaded sound cut through the din. Helicopters. They were flying fast and low, so low that their own barrage probably threatened them as much as the light fire from the Israeli anti-aircraft batteries that were beginning to fire in a staccato clatter somewhere in the distance. He saw the dark shapes of several sleek, fast Soviet assault helicopters come slicing through the banks of smoke with their rapid fire cannons blazing. Sam drew back from his view hole and crouched under the angled slab of concrete that served as his overhead shelter. Twenty millimeter cannon shells tore at the remains of the outside wall in a deafening hail.

He could hear the helicopters wheel away, climb, bank and come back for another pass. There was nothing he could do with his little assault rifle but stay out of their way and hunker down until there was something on two feet to shoot at. They would be a long time in coming, if they came at all.

As the helicopters roared in for their second pass, Sam was surprised to hear the sharp crack of Eli's high powered rifle a few moments before the hail of 20 mm cannon fire rattled the rubble around them again.

"You crazy?" He yelled, deafened as he turned to face Eli, who had withdrawn now under his own sheltering chunk of concrete.

"Must be," Eli shouted back with the remains of a wild look of defiance on his bearded face.

"Don't do that again!" Sam shouted.

On this second pass, the helicopters flew low overhead, spraying fire from their side door gunners. They hit the ridge behind Eli and Sam with a spray of missiles and cannon fire before looping back to hit the isolated hilltop from the back. Before he crept deeper under his tilting shelter, Sam saw two choppers go down. He wondered what kind of damage their pass at the IDF formations behind them had done. The IDF had precious little they could afford to lose and still face the massive ground assault that was grinding its way westward. He could see Eli crouching low in his trench and well covered by his concrete slab, which was probably a chunk of the remains of the upper floor. Eli offered no heroics this pass. The line of choppers wheeled back and passed low overhead, guns blazing. A small missile hit what was left of the back wall of their house, spraying concrete bits and shaking the ground beneath them, but causing no harm.

They returned to their view slots. Eli was not poking his long rifle barrel out to use the scope this time. He was cautiously looking out without its aid. Sam saw the ground assault forming up in the distance. They were perhaps a medium-range cannon shot away. The IDF artillery was nicely ranged in, for they had spotters with radios now working from the hilltop. He saw several wings of assault helicopters wheeling for another pass. And in his gut, almost more than in his ears which were still deafened from the cannon fire and the nearby rocket blast, he felt the deep throaty rumble of jet engines. Sam couldn't see where they were coming from, his north and south views were blocked by rubble. He stepped back from his peep hole and stood up and looked at the sky overhead and behind them, but quickly abandoned the effort and scrambled back under his overhanging shelter. He whistled and motioned Eli to do the same. Eli straightened up and scanned the sky for a brief moment before scuttling off to his hiding hole.

Sam's question was answered a few moments later when the blast of air-to- ground missiles crashed into what was left of the house next door. From the one-two sound it was a well-aimed pair. He prayed that they had missed the artillery spotters in their hilltop neighborhood. A few shards of red roof tile clattered to the ground nearby. Two seconds later the deep bass rumble of fighter jet engines grew to an excruciating crescendo and roared almost directly overhead and faded quickly in Doppler-shifted lower tones. He heard the roar of the jets climbing and banking somewhere behind them, and soon doubling in sound as a new wave of fighters roared in. This second group did not fire any missiles in their neighborhood. Sam guessed that the second wave was targeting the IDF forces arrayed behind them.

However, when he looked over at Eli a few moments later, he saw him grinning broadly and giving the thumbs up! Eli had a view to the south from his hiding hole further along their basement trench. He was shouting something, but Sam couldn't make it out with his ringing ears. Were they really IAF?

Sam listened to the now distant roar of jet engines rising and falling in pitch and volume. Whoever they were, there was a lot of maneuvering going on. It was either strafing runs or a dog fight, it could be either. He peered cautiously out from beneath his covering slab, scanning overhead and behind for more helicopters, and peeked quickly out his view hole for a half a minute before forcing himself to scurry back to shelter.

That thirty-second glimpse did not tell him much, and he thirsted for more information. However, Sam told himself to calm down and be cautious. He took a swig of water from his canteen and found his throat was dry to the point of cracking. He drank deeply and put the bottle away. He wished he knew what time it was. Sam whistled and pantomimed looking at a watch for Eli, who held up nine fingers. Nine o'clock, and no ground attack yet. So much for the Syrian's not-to-be-taken-lightly advantage had they attacked at sunrise. It was devilishly difficult to fight back with optical sights and a big red Golan sun in your eyes. He had been through enough drills that summer to know that for an established fact.

Checking overhead and behind again, and motioning for Eli to alert him of any danger, Sam crept back to his loop hole for a longer look. Jet engines still rumbled, but not close by. He took a few moments to regain his bearings, and had time to take a decent sweep with his binoculars. Again, he was reluctant to pull away from his viewpoint, but this time he crab walked over to where Eli was sheltering, for his overhanging slab was big enough for two.

The artillery barrage, both incoming and out-going over their heads continued steadily throughout the helicopter and jet assaults. Sam had to put his helmet up next to Eli's to converse. "They aren't moving any closer," Sam yelled, "maybe even edging away a bit. I couldn't tell. I'm pretty sure I saw a downed helicopter in their ranks, and possibly a plane burning off to the southeast."

"They were IAF, the second wave, I could see their markings," Eli yelled back. "And I could see a few loops of a dogfight going on to the south – definitely jet on jet."

"They came through for us, *Baruch HaShem!*" Sam said.

"*Baruch HaShem,*" Eli agreed.

They sipped water and shared an apple that Sam had scrounged sometime during the night at one of his many stops. After about five more minutes, both of them took turns at Eli's nearby and slightly larger loophole.

"Definitely moving back to get out of howitzer range," Sam said after studying the situation for awhile.

"What's next?" Eli asked.

"Not sure," Sam said. "They could probably afford to pound us with artillery all day and night and then come at us fresh in the morning. Or they could bypass us to the north, leaving a blocking force here to guard home base. Your guess is as good as mine." He nibbled the last bits from his half of the apple core, sliced neatly with his long combat knife. "The general thinks they'll bypass. Their main objective is to relieve the force that is stalled out near Carmiel."

"Good grief, you mean they got that far?" Eli shouted back, for he was still well deafened by the pounding artillery.

"Broke through early yesterday," Sam said.

"Damn."

"They're stopped cold in a trio of Arab villages across the valley from Carmiel – almost out of ammunition and digging in. If this column doesn't get there, they're history."

"And if they do?" Eli asked.

"If they do link up, they could easily break through to the coast and hold on for a couple days. And if they do that, we're history." Sam said grimly.

They contemplated this horrible scenario for a few moments, then went back to their loop hole to watch some more. "Definitely moving back," Sam yelled. "Taking the big guns back to about the ten to fifteen kilometer range I'll bet. They want to be able to hit us here, but get out of range of the big guns 2 km behind us. We have maybe 200 meters worth of elevation advantage on them, so all things equal, they won't find much of a safe zone."

However, the front at this point was only about two or three kilometers beyond them, which means they were still taking a heavy barrage of tank and smaller artillery fire as well. Sam suddenly yelled "incoming!" and dived to the floor of the trench, pushing Eli down too. Their sheltering wall shuddered with an ear-splitting boom. Dirt and concrete fragments showered on their heads. Moments later, as they began to pick themselves up, a large chunk of wall south of them, including the slab of concrete that had sheltered Sam earlier, collapsed in a dusty "whumph."

Sam realized that not fifteen minutes earlier he had been crouched in the spot that was now buried in rubble. His desire to move over and talk to Eli had saved his life. He clapped the older man's shoulder and dusted him off as they sat up, half-stunned by the concussion. Another round landed somewhere behind them, and two more downslope from them, but they had nowhere near the impact of the one hitting their basement wall.

They spent the next hour and a half crouched in their trench. They checked the slab over their head for stability a few times, but decided that if it fell, it would leave a safe gap where their makeshift trench passed beneath ground level. Nonetheless, they sat on the floor of the trench with their heads at or below ground level, except for periodic peeks at their loop hole. Eli got out his pocket prayer book and prayed a while, and said some *Tehillim*. Sam envied him for his faith in this time of doubt and danger. But after some thought, realized that it was his faith too, even though he had let his practicing it become watered down. Now he was lucky if he showed up in a synagogue two or three times a year. Once to say *kaddish* for his beloved grandfather, once for his grandmother, and maybe to attend a bar mitzvah or two.

By the time Eli's watch was reading 11 am, the invading force had withdrawn several kilometers from the border and were obviously shifting the bulk of their thrust northwards. Both could hear more intense tank fire in that direction now. The howitzers kept up their regular pounding of their hilltop, but it had grown so regular as to be almost predictable. The two or three shells a minute suggested to Sam a battery of six firing at a moderate rate. And the spread of shells had grown more erratic, suggesting moves in their location and withdrawal of the close-in spotters to a safer distance. A slightly slower rate of fire returned over their heads, perhaps a shell or two a minute, suggesting that the IDF was conserving ammunition and just keeping the threat at bay.

They were taking turns with twenty or thirty minute naps each in the mid day sun when a runner from the field artillery group Sam had brought in found him. He told Sam that he and the pickup were needed at the command group again. The gunners were ordered to stay at least until the next morning, the runner, a middle aged reservist, told them. In real life he was a corner grocery story owner from Tel Aviv. They traded news of the war for a few moments. Sam was sorry to say goodbye to Eli, but relieved to know he was probably not facing being overrun by half the Syrian army. Not that three fifty-kilo shells of high explosives a minute going off in your neighborhood was something to be taken lightly, but it was certainly easier to bear than imminent annihilation. They said a manly goodbye, just a tear or two in the corner of the eyes, shook hands, and Sam set off to zig zag his way back to where he had parked Woody for a quick escape. He hoped it was not a smoking shell of metal after all their hilltop had been through in the past few hours.

In the air over the Jordanian border 0920

Major Yossi Green was the last of his flight group to take off that morning. An idiot light had kept aborting his abbreviated flight check. Uri had hung around the base flying cover and fighting the urge to go strafe a few Egyptian ground forces not far away. Finally Yossi had a green board and hurtled down the runway to take his place in the latest wave of the air battle that was being fought all morning over Syria and Jordan.

As the two jets pounded northwards, gaining speed and elevation at nearly full power, they listened to the terse reports from the dogfights in progress, and ground control's updates of new developments. Flying nonstop, the IAF jets had returned again and again to the air theater over Syria, with a good chunk of Jordan and northern Israel thrown in. Ground fire had been vicious and had taken its toll of every attempt to punch through and hit the massive armored columns inching towards the Golan. Three more F-16s down and an F-15 from their wing. Moshiko had been a promising young pilot who had collected five air-to-air kills so far, as well as being one of their best air to ground attack pilots. He had pressed in for the kill on one helicopter too many, and had paid for his zeal when jumped by a pair of MIGs.

However, now that the columns had reached the Israeli border where a pitched battle was being fought on the ground, the IDF ground fire gave them just enough running room. They could now get close to the helicopters that had been their prime objective for the past day and a half. Between the concentrated surface batteries and successive waves of fighters vectoring in from Syria, Jordan, Saudi Arabia and other points unknown, they had their hands full.

Yossi picked up the familiar call signs of Yair and Yoni, the other two aces in his group of four F-15s still flying. He and Uri were now in their own IDF jets, rewired and hardened for the rough electronic environment that was still playing havoc with their radio and navigation instruments. The other two were still flying a pair of borrowed, remarked US planes that had been smuggled in from Portugal on the second day of the war. A few more IAF fighters had come out of the testing hangers, but they were not being finished as fast as they were falling from the sky. Yossi heard of only one more flight working the area now. A group of four F-16s were cleaning up any attack helicopter that dared push its ugly nose beyond the protective cover of the Syrian antiaircraft batteries.

They were about to clear the northern end of the Kinneret when he began to get an accurate read on his tactical radar. Four bogies were coming in low and slow, apparently bombing the hilltop community of Ramat HaGolan where he had heard that a brave group of a few hundred volunteers were holding against the brunt of the Syrian threat. They were too low and too slow to get away from him now. Yossi gave Uri a course that would intercept the enemy fighters as they finished their pass over the hilltop, and pick up their tails whichever way they turned. In seconds he had visual. He saw four MIG-21's making a low bombing pass at the tiny hilltop in the rapidly closing distance. They would have him on their radars now. Which way would they break?

His instincts as much as his eyes saw them break south, and in a microsecond he was adjusting his approach to cross their trail at a speed they would not be able to attain for a full minute after their slow strafing run. Four missiles, two clean hits and he hurtled past the breaking up pieces of MIG. He pulled up hard so as not to stray into Syrian ground fire. Tone in his headset told him there were SAMs. A glance in his visor showed them now behind him. He slammed into a hard banking turn that dropped in altitude and would take him back over the hilltop he had just passed at 600 km/hr. The SAMs blipped off his tactical view. "Got one," Uri said in his earphones.

Getting some altitude and looping back, he noted the remaining MIG high-tailing it homewards. No new jet threats in view. Ground Control confirmed, with its usual caveat – no AWAC, so watch the floor. Anything crawling along the floor would be visible now as he took in a spectacular view of the Golan, with the mass of Mt. Hermon to his left with its streaks of leftover snow near the summit; the expanse of the Kinneret, gleaming like brass in the late morning sun, and the rugged plateau of the Golan spread before him. Now, where was his next target? From his eagle's eye perspective, he could see the Syrian army spread out just over the imaginary line that formed the border. He could tell that there were columns swinging northwards bypassing the stubborn little Israeli hilltop. He recalled the morning briefing saying that such a swing was to be expected. The northern Golan was in Syrian hands at this point, so they had no resistance that way, but some rough and badly torn up country to traverse to get to their goal: the stalled column in the wide valley near Carmiel.

The lead elements of the assault were well past the imaginary line of the border, meaning that they were beginning to pull beyond the umbrella of the heavy duty SAMS. Now they were protected only by what they could truck along with them. "Let's notch up a few tanks and AA trucks," he said to Uri.

Two minutes later they were swooping down on the advanced armored units inching down a bomb-shattered road. Ten minutes later, at least four tanks and a pair of truck mounted missile launchers were blocking the road, and Yossi was headed back to base for another load of missiles.

Day Seven

Northern district command Mt. Meron 0030

Anna had a welcome problem to work out as she settled back into her cluster of computers after the midnight briefing. There were a few hundred English, French and Italian Jewish volunteers steaming across the Mediterranean on a chartered cruise boat, with the intention of helping Israel in her hour of need. There had been much talk earlier in the war of a similar group embarking from Miami, but the transit time across the Atlantic promised to be more than a week, so the plan had not gone anywhere. However, their European brethren were only a two-day sail away from the small Italian port where they had embarked. They could dock at Haifa sometime tomorrow morning, but she needed to schedule suitable air and sea protection for them. They were carrying mostly food and medical supplies, for getting arms aboard past the Italian authorities had proven a difficult challenge.

She had spent the whole of the day on the radios and computers relaying messages and coordinating information flowing from the fluid situation in the Golan. It was a relief to have only her own sector to manage now, but her area of responsibility and command had grown more and more complex as their communications net extended wider and deeper. However, the situation appeared to be unfolding roughly as General Irani had hoped. The relief force made up of nearly sixty thousand men had poured across the border late in the morning, and had swept north. As expected, they had elected to detour around the ten thousand or so men and women mustered by General Irani, from IDF units, local defense forces and volunteers. Anna had gnawed her fingernails to the quick while sweating out the morning's advance on the tiny group of volunteers holding the reclaimed wreckage of Ramat HaGolan only two kilometers from the border. There had been cheers of relief when the IAF showed up on the scene, and further celebrations when the first Israeli-rigged Apache helicopters joined the fray late in the afternoon.

Together the IAF and helicopter teams had kept the Syrian air force and helicopter forces at bay, and had notched up impressive gains as the day wore on.

Now the Syrian advance was bunched up and having to fight its way through the hill country between Tzfat and Tiberias. The Jewish defenders were instructed to extract a steep price, but to let them pass if it was too costly to hold them. She expected the second wave to link up with the fifty thousand or so mixed troops from the first Syrian invasion who were stalled in their advance in the wide valley that lay only a dozen kilometers from the coast.

This first Syrian wave had started the war with more than twice those numbers. The Syrians were clearly running low on ammunition and fuel. They were taking a pounding from the increasing numbers of Israeli artillery batteries being moved into the area. They were also being subjected to regular raids from the IAF and reconstituted helicopter forces, yet their anti-aircraft fire had fallen off considerably in the past hours.

If the IDF could wear down the relief forces in the second wave and exact the kind of the high casualties that had destroyed the effectiveness of the first wave, they could prevent the combined army from breaking through to the coast. Anna felt there was finally a good chance of stopping the Syrian invasion and turning it back on itself. In the hills and valley beyond the Syrian advance there were now perhaps fifty thousand or more regular and reserve IDF troops, plus strong contingents of local defense groups. However, any number of things could still go wrong. Any loss of air cover over Israel would be fatal. Any drying up of the Israeli supplies would be just as deadly. Any way one looked at it, up to more than one hundred thousand armed men in the heart of one's homeland was just plain dangerous.

There was also the problem of dislodging the tens of thousands of looters and irregular militias that had poured across the open border and had spread out behind the lines. They would have to be dealt with as quickly and as efficiently as possible, or else Israel would be mired in an endless guerilla war and a long, bloody struggle to get her lands back. Fortunately there were several combat groups formed and beginning to do just that in the Golan.

She was following two in particular by their call signs on the radios. Her radio favorites were very capable and highly successful young leaders from the early days of the war. One, known by his call sign "*arbeh minim*, four species," had initiated the supply ferries across the Kinneret and then led the cross-border raid that took out the bulk of the Syrian helicopter threat. He had helped retake the southern Golan and was just now leaving Ramat HaGolan for a new force being formed to retake the northern Golan. The other, named "*Gimmel* One," was the commander of a tank and a half who had survived being overrun in the tripwire tank forces and had managed to shoot up half a major Syrian supply convoy with one other tank. If these two commanders lived through this war, they would be the new Israeli IDF heroes of the day. Anna had never heard of either, an ex-recon lieutenant from the reserves, and a reserve tanker captain. She silently wished them well, and set to work trying to assure them of their next day's supplies.

She was typing up a list of supplies to be faxed to one of the depots when there was a happy shout from a few consoles down in their underground operations center in the caravan underneath the mountain. "AWACS!" the air force liaison was shouting with glee. "Two AWACS from Australia – a lend/ lease deal by the Jewish communities in Sidney and Melbourne! Someone down there has some real connections! Two AWAC and two Hercules are making the haul – and there is a leased Qantas cargo jet flying in F-16 electronics kits and parts from Hawaii as we speak!"

"Can we keep the Hercules?" Anna yelled over the din of the celebration echoing in the trailer. A couple curious faces appeared at the doorway and had to be told the news. "Don't know" the jubilant officer said, "I'll find out when they call back."

AWACS! What a different war it could have been if they had a couple AWACS in operation coordinating the air war instead of the bank of desktop computers in her trailer. To see what was happening in the air in a thousand kilometer radius was a dream that had disappeared in the first minutes of the war. God bless the Australians!

Ramat HaGolan 0020

Eli was surprised to be awakened by a pair of short, somewhat rounded little sergeants telling him he was urgently needed on an important mission due to depart an hour ago. With their urging and yammering in his sleep addled ears, and their less-than-useful help, he dressed in a mental fog. He found his kit and his rifle and almost forgot the *tallit* and prayer book he had on a box beside his pack. Eli stumbled out into the darkness still wondering what the hell this was all about. The sergeants each slightly overweight and about four and a half feet high, seemed like a pair of misplaced munchkins. Neither spoke more than a word or two of English; and their Hebrew was not the best. From their accents, he guessed that they were immigrants of less than a few years standing from somewhere in Eastern Europe.

It was not until he climbed into the back of a two-and-a-half-ton truck and found a place in the stack of bodies in the back that he found Nir, and got some inkling of what was going on. He learned that they were supposed to go somewhere with Sam, and that this truck was filled with people collected for the mission. As far as Eli could tell, there were some irritable old guys in the back, most of them much older than himself, and that they were intent on sleeping.

The two sergeants drove like hell through the darkness, often tossing everyone in the back half a meter in the air and from side to side as they careened through the middle of humongous pot holes. Somehow his companions in the back of the truck, with the exception of Nir and a young Ethiopian recon man who looked more scared of the driving than the war, managed to cling to sleep, or at least a resting position.

The truck stopped at a busy roadside depot where a crew of soldiers was sorting loads, fueling trucks and dealing with the supply needs of an army that had passed them some hours before in a tearing hurry. There, shaken and still half stunned from waking to this uproar, Eli climbed from the back of the truck, helped solicitously by the young Ethiopian, who had recovered his equilibrium. Stretching and checking for fresh bruises from being slammed against something hard in his pack and the sides of the truck, Eli looked around for Sam or anyone familiar. He spotted a big Russian Kraz transport parked under a grove of trees and headed towards it, wondering if it was the one he had helped capture. Indeed it was, he recognized the numbers on the door, and one of the soldiers milling around by the cab. They exchanged greetings, and Eli asked about Sam. The soldier pointed off in the direction of another truck, some sort of pickup with a roof mounted machine gun emerged from the darkness – missing a windshield and suddenly he recognized it was Woody!

Sam was nowhere around. Eli checked out the machine gun mount. He found it was bolted solidly through the roof of his cab with four stout bolts and a pair of angle iron braces inside for stiffness. Then he climbed in the back and looked over the smoke condenser and fire box for damage as best he could in the dark. It was in good shape, all things considered. No new bullet holes in the short smokestack since the last set acquired when delivering tank shells in the southern Golan. Then he wandered back to the small supply truck that had brought him. He arrived and milled around the tail gate, enjoying the relatively cool night air. The weather had cooled noticeably since the hot afternoon baking in the trenches at Ramat HaGolan. He was extremely grateful for the relief from the heat.

The older men had stayed on the truck. There appeared, from the dim light that filtered through the trees from the night sky, to be only three of them at the moment. Several must have woken up and wandered off. Eli was beginning to wonder if he should crawl in the back and join them. The two sergeants had been so strident about not losing a moment, and in hurrying him to get dressed and out the door with them. They kept saying that they were due somewhere before midnight and it was already nearly one am. Well, hurry up and wait seemed to be very much in effect in the Golan for the past few days.

He climbed into the back and was just arranging his pack for a nap when one of the sergeants – Tweedle Dee, Eli had named him in his mind, having not caught his name or heard any clue – climbed up the tailgate and stood in the back shouting to his companion, Tweedle Dum. Another of the old guys climbed in the back, the sergeant sat down. Suddenly the engine started up, the truck backed up, and then rumbled off at a more reasonable speed. Eli could definitely tell someone else besides T-Dum was at the wheel. They pulled out of the depot and headed north, as near as Eli could tell from the waning moon he saw far to the southwest and the dark hills in the distance that marked the far side of the Kinneret and the hills of Tzfat and Rosh Pina.

After a while they slowed down, and eventually eased to a stop. Eli heard the buzz of a motorbike approach, some rapid conversation with the driver and the sergeant with its rider, and it buzzed off again. They remained stopped. "Catch any of that?" he asked Nir, who was sitting opposite him in the back of the truck. The older men had the best places towards the front were they were protected from the wind and dust, and had a smoother ride. Funny, Eli realized that he had gotten used to being one of the elders in the pack since leaving the moshav two days before. And although he chafed at the deference the younger men were showing him, he had gotten used to it. He was surprised when one of the older, white haired guys opposite him sat up and suddenly addressed him in English with a strong American accent.

"They say there is a small Syrian column heading down the road, and that they have maybe five minutes to set up an ambush. Our job is to run like hell and warn the guys at the depot that there are two tanks coming down the road.

Indeed, the truck was turning around and stopped again pointing back the way they had come. After a moment they started rolling back the way they had come at a moderate pace.

"Um, thanks." Eli said, and after a moment of digesting this news, asked, "I'm Eli Kaplan from Moshav Yiftach, have we met?" For the man's accent was definitely American.

"I know a lot of people there. My name is Josh Cohen from the Nimrod Lodge, nice to meet you,"

Eli had heard of him, and his lodge, a fairly upscale mountain chalet about halfway up Mt, Hermon. He had stopped in the restaurant a couple times with Natalie, but they had never spent the night there.

"Wonderful food," Eli said, "Natalie and I ate there once, but we haven't been up to Mt. Hermon in at least two years. Come to think of it, I think that might have been you who came by our table, and we talked about the wine. I think I asked you why there were no Burgundies, Bordeaux or Beaujolais grown in Israel, something I have asked the vintners at our moshav a few times, and never gotten the same answer twice."

"I understand it's too hot here, for Burgundies or Bordeaux for that matter," Josh said, "As for Beaujolais, I've often wondered that myself, I love a fresh young wine." Eli remembered the conversation now, and was about to say something more when they heard a burst of machine gun fire and explosions in the distance. It was over in less than a minute. About two minutes later they heard a radio crackle in the cab of the truck, and their truck stopped as the driver answered it. Very un-Israeli not to talk on the squawk box and drive, Eli thought, But, a second later they were turning around again and heading back the way they had been originally headed. "*Kol b'seder*," T-Dum called back to his fellow sergeant.

"So, do you know what's going on? Eli asked,

"Sort of," the lodge keeper said. "My friend up there in the cab, who owns the rental shop at the ski lodge and does the snow cat tours knows more. That's Barak Saguri, by the way, one of the platoon leaders who helped take the heights in '67, maybe you've heard of him. What I hear is that we are heading up towards Mt. Hermon, and dealing with all the checkpoints and strongholds along the way, because central command really wants the mountain back in the next couple days. We'll be joining up with a tank force that is sweeping the border a few kilometers east of us. We're supposed to meet up by the time we reach the town at the base of the mountain. There is talk of us taking up positions around the base, maybe even climbing up as far as my lodge. Then they are talking about having a group of commandos do a helicopter drop near the top and sweep the mountain from the top down. That's what I've heard so far, and why Barak and I are along – a little local knowledge goes a long way up there.

Eli had certainly heard of Barak Seguri, in fact, he had possibly read about him in one of his grandson's fourth grade school books. He recalled a picture of a big, lanky man in a kibbutznik hat leaning on an artillery piece with another of a camouflaged soldier sitting on top of a burnt out bunker. But the man must be in his late seventies by now, surely? He had already been the father of perhaps six or seven children in the sixties when two were killed by shelling from the heights.

Temporary supply depot 0200

Sam finally found the one piece of equipment he had been looking for since Colonel Eschol gave him his assignment a few hours earlier. He had hoped to recruit his volunteers and jump off by midnight, but he couldn't see going on a scout and secure mission without at least one motorcycle. He lucked into two – owned and ridden a pair of *Hesder yeshiva* students who knew the Golan well, since they were studying in the yeshiva in Hespin, They would have been starting their eighteen-month military service next month had the war not come along. He recognized one of them as the young man with the white *kippah* and the long blond *peyot* who had delivered Rabbi Beniyahu to his friend Eli's *sukkah* a few nights ago. Upon inquiring about the welfare of the Rabbi, Sam found that he was fine, and still very much in demand among the Golan communities. His wisdom and knowledge of the Torah law was being put to the test in difficult cases, such as how to rededicate a vandalized and bombed synagogue, or what to do when burying unidentifiable dead.

He had sent two of the sergeants he had recruited off to Ramat HaGolan in a two-and-a-half-ton truck to collect his two senior snipers, Eli and Nir, as well as a few enterprising young soldiers he had spotted there during the brief siege. Right now he was nominally in charge of thirty six men. It was the largest command that he had ever had to deal with on his own, and it was straining his organizational skills to think of how to make the maximum use of all his assets. He found it easier to sort and think though his task groups by vehicle. He had the two eighteen year olds from the yeshiva as his point men – zipping out and back on their fast dirt bikes to scout the way. Then he had his one armored vehicle, a Russian-made APC with its twin 50 caliber machine guns for muscle. He entrusted his precious night vision binoculars with the master sergeant in charge of that group. He mounted a 7.62 mm machine gun on the roof of Woody, and loaded the back with a hand-picked group of recon men. He had been lucky also to get Roee for the gunner, and Ronny to ride shotgun. They were two of the ten men from his old recon unit who had volunteered to join him. Sam would drive Woody for now.

If the situation called for looking like a gang of irregulars, Sam and his crew would come up the road in Woody. With the horn blasting, headlights flashing and much shouting and firing of guns in the air they would try to provoke a panic and headlong retreat.

However, if the situation called for looking like Syrian regulars, they could approach the checkpoint or stronghold in the big Kraz transport truck and the APC. He had the rest of his recon men and a mixed group of regular soldiers – nearly twenty men – divided between the two vehicles. They had enough fire power and men to take out a fairly well guarded strong point. Then, his Golan reservists, Eli and Nir and the local volunteers were assigned to the older model transport truck – which was nondescript enough to pass for either side. Right now he was pulled up along side of the small transport talking with two of the older Golanis and his two dirt bike daredevils.

The moment his two scouts spun off on towards their first objective, Sam climbed out of the cab of Woody and went around to each of the vehicles in his small armada. He started with the APC group. "Last chance for a stretch, let's huddle up over here in the moonlight and I'll tell you the plans," he called to the men in the armored back of the carrier.

Sam had to wait a couple minutes while a string of trucks rolled past their road junction depot where his odd collection of vehicles had been assembled. When the last one passed, he signaled to his waiting group for quiet and began speaking.

"Our job is to clear the bad guys out of as much of the Golan as we can in the next two days. We're going to be rolling in a few minutes and meet the scout bikes on their return. I just wanted to tell you that we have one of the heroes of the '67 war here with us – the white haired kibbutzik driving the small transport. Barak Saguri lost a son and daughter to Syrian artillery shelling in '65, and he was one of the infantrymen who took the heights for us in '67. So he knows this country – actually all of them do, we have six civilian volunteers in that truck, and they could probably whip us all in a straight up fight, so give them some respect. We are playing three cards here – you guys are our only ace – we have Woody over there as the joker, and that big Kraz transport as the jack. If the situation calls for muscle, you guys are it. When you get the chance, drive in as close as you can. Make sure you shoot first, don't wait to be recognized. Good luck." Sam shook their hands one by one as they climbed into the APC, and he gave the driver the thumbs up to pull out on the narrow, barely two-lane country road going north.

He gave pretty much the same talk to the men in the big Russian transport. He would send them in first if it looked like a situation where it might be possible to fool a squad of soldiers into thinking they were friendlies. At the signal they would jump out and try to take the surprised enemies prisoner before a shot could be fired. He still preferred to avoid bloodshed if at all possible, no matter how difficult taking and dealing with prisoners could be.

The older men in the supply truck needed no pep talk and knew the plans already since they had been involved in working them out.

Sam jogged over to where Woody was parked ready to take off. He had the truck running on gasoline for the night so as to look and sound as normal as possible. However, they carried no spare fuel, and would have to scrounge what they could if they ran past their reserve tanks on the second day. Then Woody's wood burning firebox might come in very handy. He waved goodbye to the depot master and headed north up the country road behind the dark shape of the APC already a half a kilometer ahead. It felt good to be moving again.

Their spread out convoy had run up the dark road for perhaps ten minutes when he saw the APC stop. Leaning out the window, he could hear the two stroke engines of the dirt bikes as they approached. He pulled up behind the APC and jogged up to where the two bikers had stopped.

There was, as the two young men quickly explained, a Syrian convoy headed south on their road just a few minutes away to the north. It was a jeep and two tanks leading a pair of loaded transports and a fuel truck. There was probably less than five minutes to plan an ambush. Sam thought of the unprotected supply point ten minutes south, and of the tank force well away to the east. Think fast. Just then the Kraz transport pulled up, which gave him an idea.

"Park that baby right in the middle of the road and look like you just finished changing a tire. Soldiers, look like Syrians and be prepared to jump the two tanks with grenades as soon as they stop and pull open their hatches. Amnon – keep them amused in Arabic best you can.

"APC," he called to the master sergeant who was studying the road ahead with the night vision binoculars, "You pull over to the right, look casual and prepare to rake the jeep and any soldiers you see with the .50 cals. Wait until we have hatches open on both tanks. There's no way we can stop two tanks without getting some grenades inside. Our RPGs won't do a thing against Soviet armor."

He told one of the riders to go back and flag the small transport and tell them to stop, turn around and run like hell back for the junction and warn the people at the depot.

"Ok, my guys. We're going to pull off the road behind the APC because we don't fit the regular army picture. We come out, guns blazing as soon as there is shooting, got it?

He heard the low rumble of tanks as he pulled Woody to a stop on the blind side of the APC. He wished he could watch, but instead he had to rely on listening rather than risk being seen at this point.

The deep throated tank engines rumbled closer and closer. They were running without lights in the pale moonlight, with the moon obscured by smoke, but casting an indistinct light across the dark landscape. There was no real cover available. As soon as the tanks topped the next small rise they would see everything. He counted on everyone to play their parts well. But he had never been director of a show this big, or quite this impromptu. He heard the dirt bikes buzzing in the distance to his south.

The tanks slowed as soon as they topped the rise, but did not stop. Sam agonized as his ears strained for a clue to their reactions. He could see the beam of flashlights coming from his fake tire changing gang at the truck, and hear shouts in Arabic. They were still too far to hear anything though, he surmised. The tanks continued to slow, but kept coming until they pulled within easy shouting range. Sam heard a harsh voice shouting something in Arabic about getting the beep out of the middle of the road. Then came Amnon's cheeky reply about needing a level spot for his tire change, and why didn't they just go around, there was plenty of the infidels' land free for the taking.

The voice then wanted to know how far to the east-west road and the Syrian army. Amnon answered that he was almost there, just go straight ahead and turn right at the junction, and if they reached the Mediterranean, they had gone too far. "Could they spare some number two diesel?" Amnon asked.

The reply was the equivalent of "no way, go to hell you lazy thieves, get your own fuel."

Sam heard the lead tank gear down and the clank of its treads change from pavement to soft dirt. Any moment now. Amnon kept up his plea for fuel, saying that any honest officer in the holy fight against the infidels would be blessed with good fortune by Allah if he shared a hundred liters with his fellow comrades in arms.

The unseen officer heaped more scorn on the disabled truck and its idle troops, saying that they were running from the enemy. A second voice joined in the invective, higher pitched and using even saltier language, inspiring Amnon to throw in a few remarks about tankers and camels and their common ancestors. At one of his choicer insults, Sam heard the tanks stop suddenly and several more voices join the chorus of abuse.

"Now!" he thought. As if in answer to his thoughts, the voices changed suddenly from anger to surprise. He heard the echoing bang of several hand grenades go off. At once the machine guns in the APC beside him chattered into life – dealing death at a hundreds of rounds per minute between them. Sam revved Woody and pulled out of the shadow of the APC and raced for the back of the convoy. He wanted to capture the fuel tanker intact if possible, and had told his crew as much while they had waited for their break.

As he pulled around the APC and accelerated towards the road, Sam saw flame and smoke spewing from the hatches of both tanks. The concentrated fire from the twin machine guns had cut up and decimated the jeep. The pair of menacing machine guns now fell silent, pointed directly at the cab of the first transport truck. He saw dark figures of the recon soldiers from their decoy truck approaching the cabs of both trucks, guns drawn and ready to shoot. Sam gunned Woody along the roadside until they were opposite the fuel truck in the rear of the surprised convoy. He drew up a few meters away alongside. Roee had the machine gun pointed straight at the driver. Ronny and the soldiers scattered from the cab and back of Woody. He saw the scared faces of the driver and his relief holding up their hands in surrender.

Within minutes, they had secured their three prizes, two trucks laden with food and ammunition and a medium-sized fuel tanker carrying a full load of number two diesel if his kibbutzniks were right. Sam flashed the all-clear signal with a flashlight to the bikers to recall the older Golanis in the supply truck down the road.

They took a few minutes to top up the tanks on their three diesel trucks, but the tanks were almost full from their recent stop at the road junction depot not far behind them. They made the half dozen prisoners cling to the outside of canvas cover of the first truck. Sam prepared to dispatch their three captured trucks back towards the Israeli supply junction they had left less than a half an hour before.

The transport truck rolled in at this point, with his older volunteers. He sent he two dirt bikes buzzing back up the road to scout their next objective. He had to keep moving and cover as much ground as he could in the cover of darkness. No telling what the next day could bring in this crazy war.

All the men in the back of the transport truck stood up to look, hanging on the slats of the sides. They were all peering out as the truck slowed down and they smelled the smoke of burning fuel and heard the shouts of soldiers ordering prisoners to line up.

They saw the smoking ruins of a pair of tanks and what was once, perhaps, a jeep a moderate distance away. The prisoners, half a dozen of them, were being hurried from the remaining vehicles, a couple supply trucks, which were pulling away from the burning tanks. Suddenly one of the burning tanks erupted in a huge explosion as the fire reached the ammunition. At that, the prisoners suddenly began to hurry forwards away from the danger. The explosion blew out the windshield of one of the captured supply trucks. Fortunately, there was no driver assigned to it yet. However, the lumbering fuel truck that had just passed the two tanks rocked in the blast but kept going.

"Quick work!" Nir marveled, and Josh agreed. They stood in the back of their truck a long time while the soldiers sorted out the prisoners and chose drivers to deliver the captured trucks to the depot. There was nothing in particular needed of them at the moment. Pickets had already been set up and the APC sent ahead to block the road ahead.

Eli studied Josh's face in the light of the still burning tank. He was older than he first thought, although athletic and deeply tanned from living high on the mountain and running a lodge that catered to sports people, he was perhaps in his mid to upper sixties, perhaps even a young seventy. The other two men lined up behind the cab and peering over at the scene, were also silver haired with the weathered faces of lives spent in the harsh Israeli sun. Eli said hello.

They watched the prisoners being guided to the side of one of the captured supply trucks, the one with windshield intact, and saw them climb up on the outside of the canvas cover, and be driven off, clinging to it, guarded by the windshield-less truck behind, with the tanker in the lead. Eli saw a familiar wiry figure jog over to their truck – Sam!

He took a moment to chat with Eli and Nir and apologize for not speaking to them sooner. "Sorry I have to borrow both your trucks, you can have this one after the war if anything happens to Woody," Sam told Eli. "And we had to use bolt holes for mounting the machine gun, I hope they don't leak when the rains start. Other than that, no new holes in the old beast."

"No problem," Eli said, "Can I just keep the machine gun and call it even? It would come in handy for traffic jams and finding a place to park in Tiberias." Sam said he would consider it.

"What's next?" Eli managed to ask before Sam ran off again,

"There's a checkpoint run by regulars a couple K up the road," Sam told the group in the back of the truck. "We're going to roll up with the APC and Kraz and see if we can capture them without any shooting. But after that tank blew, they might be a bit nervous. Tzfat command didn't pick up any radio traffic going outbound from our little skirmish here, so they don't know we're here yet as far as we know."

With that, he jogged back to Woody and peeled off with the APC and big Russian truck in his wake.

After that, there was nothing for them to do but wait and wonder again. The two older kibbutzniks settled back in their nests of packs and blankets and went to sleep, Nir settled in for a nap, along with the sergeant, but Josh Cohen sat up with Eli and talked.

"Where were you when the war broke out?" Eli asked.

"Oh, I was down in Kiryat Shemona with Shira, thank G-d. At first we thought it was a power outage. We were in a zimmer up behind a friend's house. But then the sirens went off and the missiles started falling. We headed for the shelters and spent a less than an hour there before the orders came to evacuate. We actually got out of town on a pair of mountain bikes with our hosts. I keep a rack of them as rentals at the lodge for guests, so I was in good enough shape to keep up with the youngsters. We huffed up the hill to Rosh Pina and they gave me a gun when the front reached there. Shira had done her IDF service in artillery, so they pressed her into a gun crew as spotter. About three or four times we thought we would be overrun, and I ran out of shells twice banging away with the AK 47 they gave me. But eventually we pulled back to near Caanan. That's where I was when the special forces guys found me. They actually ferried me over here with some other guys in an Apache. It was great to see something of ours flying."

Josh wound down his story and they sat there in silence, listening to the regular breathing of their companions in the back of the truck. Eli could tell by the setting orange half moon that it must be getting near morning. It was too dark to see his watch still.

Eli was dozing off when he heard the approach of the motor bike. Standing up and peering at the dark road ahead, he saw the bike weaving its way around shell holes and pot holes. As it pulled up and the rider pulled off his helmet to talk to their driver, Barak, Eli saw the white knit *kippah* and long *peyot* of the yeshiva bocher who had delivered Rabbi Beniyahu a few long nights ago. He wished him Shalom and asked about the Rabbi after the young man had delivered his message. "*Baruch HaShem*, fine. I saw him yesterday," the young man replied, "I came to tell you to join Sam and the rest about two kilometers north of where the checkpoint used to be. They were no problem, just seven more prisoners to deal with," He said matter of factly. With that, he put his helmet back on and buzzed off, *peyot* flapping from underneath.

The truck started up again, and soon they were crawling slowly up the pot holed road. Eli must have dozed off again. T he next thing he knew, they were stopped again and people were climbing out of the back. He found his pack and shouldered it and his rifle and climbed down. There was no tall young Ethiopian scout to help him this time, and he found it a long last step from the bumper to the ground. Eli nearly stumbled over backwards with the weight of his pack shifting on him. Fortunately no one was watching, for he felt old, slow and awkward as he trudged around the emptied truck and walked over to where everyone was gathered, talking in low voices as they stood in a wide place in the dirt track where their group had stopped. Eli noticed the main road silhouetted against the night sky some few hundred meters behind him.

Sam was talking with Barak Seguri and the two older men from the back of his truck. Eli realized he had definitely been sound asleep, for he didn't remember turning off the main road, or stopping. He saw Woody parked at the head of their little column, with the APC behind it, he could see the shadow of someone manning its turret. Just ahead of where they had stopped was the big Russian Kraz transport. The knot of soldiers stood in a wide spot in the track behind the Kraz, screened on the northern side by a row of tall cypress trees making dark tall shapes against the night sky.

"Form a *Chet*," Sam called to everyone milling around. They immediately formed a three-sided "U" shape like the Hebrew letter *Chet*. Sam stood like a dot at the open part at opposite Eli.

"Here's the situation," Sam said. "We have the only sizable settlement in our sector a few kilometers ahead. Scouts say it is full of irregulars, and that they are definitely trigger happy. There is no rolling up and jumping out and saying 'boo!' this time. There are too many of them, and the community is too big. It's maybe thirty to forty houses spread out in a circle on a low rise, surrounded by fields. The non-natives are definitely restless. They took pot shots at our bikes twice, so they have some sort of watch system and a perimeter set up."

"So, here's what we're going to do. We have three small field mortars with us, and about twenty rounds each. It's not a lot of fire power, but enough to make plenty of noise and see if we can make them run. We are going to circle around to the southwest. Benny here knows the layout of the fields and out buildings. And we hope they decide it's time to run and head out the main road."

"We'll run through all our shells in about ten minutes; and if that doesn't work we will need to apply a little more force. Woody and the APC are going to create a diversion to the south and the recon crew is going to attack on foot from the west. That will be just before sunrise, so our snipers can start firing from a little rise to the east. The rest of you will be by the supply truck at our rendezvous to cover them in case of a breakout in that direction. Questions?"

There were quite a few, dealt with quickly and clearly. Within about ten minutes, everyone pretty much knew their part. The vehicles pulled out a few minutes later, running slowly and carefully down the dirt tracks between orchards and fields and a large vineyard. At one point they all stopped again, and parked in the shelter of an apple orchard. Eli saw the different groups disperse, some lugged the mortars and their cases of shells to the north side of the orchard. Sam and a file of recon men slipped off to the west. Woody and the APC edged around the orchard to be between the mortars and the low hill Sam had indicated for the snipers.

"You guys are with me," one of the older kibbutzniks told Eli's group. Another older kibbutznik had joined the file of recon men going east, and one had taken over driving from Sam. That left Eli, Nir, Josh, and another older man who had been in the cab for their ride, and Tweedle Dee. Eli now felt guilty for calling him that in his mind, since he was about to go off to a fire fight with him. However, the time did not appear right to ask his name, since they were in a hurry and talking in whispers.

As they filed out of the shelter of the orchard, Eli could see they were following a hedge row between fields, and headed for the not-too-distant low hill that was to be their vantage point. In the lee of the hill he saw some long, low open sheds that looked like they used for storing agricultural equipment. Off in the distance he finally saw the dark buildings of the small settlement they were going to attack. It felt good to be moving after a few hours cooped up and rattled around in the back of the truck. As the five of them moved along at an easy walk through the dark fields, the smell of earth and vineyards, flowering hedges and green growing things filled his senses. He found his hearing and vision sharpening as they left the world of mechanical things behind. Despite the tension, Eli was enjoying the predawn darkness. It brought back memories of helping with the harvests on the moshav, and going out in the darkness to where the grape harvesters worked all night in the glare of lights, clearing row after row of ripe grapes. The grapes in the vineyards they walked through tonight were not yet ripe, but had a faint odor of sun-drenched grapes still hanging about them in the cooler night air.

They climbed stealthily but calmly up the far side of the hill. The five were spread in a makeshift skirmish line, ready to drop and fire at the sight or sound of anything untoward.

They took up positions at the top of the low hill. Eli could tell this was a favorite spot of the settlement farmers when he found himself at nose level with a hefty pile of cigarette butts. He found a different spot and began to dig himself a bit of an earth berm with the heels of his boots to shelter him and rest his rifle. After about fifteen minutes of scuffling around in the dirt and arranging a few small rocks, he was satisfied with his post. He settled in and wiped the heavy morning dew off his scope, checked the action of his rifle, pulled out two more loaded clips and arranged them at the mouth of his open rucksack within easy reach. He peered through his rifle scope to see what he could see. Every now and then he heard the faint crackle of the T-dee's radio as the three groups checked in with each other.

"Five minutes," the young sergeant called softly. Each answered with a quiet acknowledgement. Nir had nestled in under a large bush at first, until he discovered he shared it with a large colony of the biting kind of ants. Now he was a little way the other side of the sergeant, with Josh and the older kibbutznik sitting behind a circle of stones that had obviously been used for a fire pit.

Eli wiped the dew off his glasses and his scope again and pulled the rim of his battered helmet down to cover the eyepiece and peered at the dark settlement on the nearby hill. It was less than three hundred meters away, and the dark, detailed outline of the houses came into sharp relief against the lighter night sky behind them. He studied the near perimeter, house by house. The settlement had just a low, five-wire barbed wire perimeter fence, with a dirt track on the inside for the night watch to drive around. However, they had been negligent in clearing brush from their free fire zone. Eli could see several places where Sam and his recon squad could approach with a moderate amount of cover on the far edge of the hill. The houses appeared to be undamaged by the war. He found that unusual, but then, this little hamlet was off the beaten track, and had probably been abandoned without a fight. He caught the glow of a cigarette by the corner of one building, and soon made out the dark shape of a lounging, bored guard with a rifle slung casually over one shoulder. He would be an easy shot now, but he would probably disappear once the mortars started, which should be soon. Eli swept the rest of the perimeter, saw nothing else moving, and zeroed back in on his guard lighting another cigarette from the butt. "Smoking is bad for your health," Eli lectured the distant shape as he chambered a round and returned the sights to his target.

"Ok to pick off the guard once the mortars start?" Eli whispered to the sergeant in the most precise Hebrew he could manage.

"Hold your fire until phase two," came the emphatic whisper.

Eli returned to watching the distant shape smoke. He was wiry and short and moved restlessly like a younger man. He was obviously bored and irritable. He wouldn't be bored for long. Too bad they had to shell an intact settlement though. It seemed a waste to think what sixty mortar rounds would do to the clean, light colored, stone-faced bungalows. The settlement was only about fifteen years old, and the trees were not very big, although the fields and vineyards seemed well established.

A moment later he heard the distant whump, whump, whump of three mortars fired and soon heard the now familiar whistle of falling shells, outgoing from the sound. His shadow guard heard too, stiffened and then froze as the three shells landed one, two, three just within the perimeter fence. Eli felt the faint shock wave of the blasts ripple the still morning air, and soon heard the outgoing whistle of more rounds. They fell among the first row of houses, one blowing a meter-wide hole in a roof, the other two falling in the yards. His guard had ducked out of sight behind the corner of his house. By the third round of shells there was pandemonium within the settlement. He saw dark figures rushing out of most of the houses, and much shouting. It took another minute and a few more rounds before a machine gun opened up, firing a wild arc into the night roughly in the direction of the orchard where the mortars had been set up. More shells and then another machine gun started up, this time zeroing in more on the orchard. Eli hoped they had dug adequate cover. He saw dark figures running to and fro, and saw many diving down into trenches dug just outside the perimeter of houses. He could have picked off a couple by now, but he dutifully held his fire.

A few RPG rounds sailed outwards from the trenches, but fell short of the orchard, which was a good kilometer and a bit distant. Two more heavy machine guns, apparently placed in the basements of two of the larger houses, firing out of ground-level windows, added to the cacophony. And not long after, he saw the flash of mortars from somewhere inside the ring of houses and heard the boom of heavy mortar rounds falling in the direction of his comrades in the orchard. Bad news.

But worse news came to his ears not long after as he heard engines starting within the compound, large diesel engines. Were they preparing to pull out in trucks? He wondered briefly, but soon saw the familiar shape of an APC stick its armored snout between two houses. In moments it had driven across the perimeter fence and another one popped up in its wake. These guys must be regular army. No bunch of militia would have been able to go on the offense within five minutes of a mortar attack.

He followed the lead APC with his sight, but it was too dark and moving too fast to get a clear bead. It was buttoned up tight. The turret gunner was well protected with half wing shields. Soon it was blasting 20 mm cannon rounds at the orchard. Eli felt a gripping fear for his companions; there were only a half dozen of them there, and four more with the trucks somewhere behind them at the other side of the orchard. Were they pulling out and running for it? Or did they have some counter measures planned? There was no way to hit a fast moving APC with a little field mortar without more time and a lot of luck.

Just then he heard the rattle of automatic rifle fire at the other side of the compound and the bursting of grenades and RPGs. Sam had decided to attack with his dozen recon men!

"*Esh! Esh!* Fire!" the sergeant cried out, followed by a short burst of fire from his rifle. Eli could only take a "best guess" shot at the gunner's turret of the lead APC. He chambered another round and tried to find a clearer view. For a split second his cross hairs passed over a figure in the open turret. The APC had advanced far enough toward the edge of the orchard that he could see past the wings shielding the gunner. Eli steadied, found the image again and fired, loaded, found it again much farther off and fired again. He pumped a couple more quick rounds towards the back of the turret before the lead APC reached an irrigation ditch near the edge of the orchard. He couldn't tell if he had hit anything or if the gunner stopped firing for a moment as the tracked vehicle pitched forward and then reared skyward crossing the ditch. At that moment he saw bright flashes of two RPGs hitting its near side. They must have been very close range, for the metal monster shuddered to a stop a few meters past the ditch, and he saw crew bailing out the back hatch. The sergeant and the other rifles on their hill made short work of them.

Eli turned to the second APC and saw it had slewed off in a high speed turn and was running off to the west where Sam and his team had attacked. Eli had no time to think, he just tried to find the bobbing turret in his sights. He had only two shots before it roared off out of range, so he turned his attention to the dark settlement. He studied the dark houses and tried to pick out exactly where the machine guns were nested.

The nearest one was not hard to spot, for it spat a fairly constant stab of flame raking the distant orchard where the now silent mortars had been. Eli knew the mortar team had shot off all their rounds and were probably scuttling back to the trucks, hiding behind the skinny tree trunks for the shred of cover they provided. He studied what he could see lit up by the muzzle flash of the heavy machine gun. It was a basement window, the kind that was only about half a meter high to let in light. It had been sandbagged around the edges. But there was a good sized opening, and the snout of the machine gun was thrust well beyond. The gun had some leeway on both sides and Eli knew that if he fired at the near side, he would be very likely to hit either the belt feeder, the gunner, or at least scare the crap out of both of them. He settled in for a very deliberate shot, waited for their next long burst and fired. The gun stopped half a second later. Bullseye! He watched the opening for a short while, waiting to see if anyone would step up to man the gun again. But realized he was wasting time, and scanned for the other heavy gun that was similarly placed.

However, in the interim he noticed two things. One was incoming fire in their direction, both rifle and mortar, and the other was the lack of fire from the far side of the settlement. What had happened to Sam? He thought they had made it inside the perimeter from the sounds earlier, but now there was only sporadic firing over there as near as he could tell, but the line of houses blocked his view.

Thinking of Sam and the battle hardened recon men he had come to respect took his mind almost completely off of the incoming fire. He did not have a good angle on the second heavy machine gun, which fortunately meant it did not have a good line on him. But the other two lighter machine guns were pouring fire at their hilltop, and that had to stop. There was no way he could hit the hidden mortar teams who were walking rounds of shells backwards towards their hilltop, having overshot with their first rounds by a lot. But he did see where the nearest machine gunner was. He was firing with only a few sandbags for cover from within a shallow trench. Eli noticed his eyepiece was steaming up and wiped it clear and settled in for a deliberate shot. Something that sounded like an angry hornet had buzzed his sleeve and he cocked his elbow to rub the objective with a bit of the cuff of his camouflaged shirt. Rifle bullet, a dispassionate voice said in his brain. He found the head and shoulders figure of his machine gunner nicely outlined behind the flame of the muzzle, which appeared to be greatly foreshortened in the scope, as if pointed right at him. He let out half his breath and fired. A buzzing of bullets whizzed directly over his head and then stopped. He chambered a round, feeling the heat of another angry wasp prick at his sleeve again. A burst of rifle fire clattered off to his immediate right, and he heard the sergeant yelling at him and mentally translated the Hebrew. "Get the beep out of here! *Achshav!*" He realized he had being hearing the voice for a while now.

Eli hooked his elbow through his pack strap and began to snake his way backwards. More bursts of fire came from his right and in the flash of a mortar shell exploding beyond them, he glimpsed the outlines of Josh and the older moshavnik firing from a crouch as they scuttled backwards. He kept worming his way backwards, pulling the pack and cradling his rifle in front of him. Soon he could no longer see the roofs of the settlement and he stopped to gather his pack together and prepare to get up. He found he was shaking too bad to do up the drawstring at the top of his pack.

"*Kol ha kavod*," a voice shouted in his ear, and a pair of strong hands helped him to his feet. "*Acharei alai!*, After me" the young sergeant yelled, and scuttled off half bent over, running down the hill they had climbed so leisurely not an hour before. Eli got shakily to his feet, cradled his rifle in his arms and began to run. After he ran down the hill for a minute, he realized he could stop stooping over. He swung his pack on his back and set off after the dark shape of the sergeant and his other three companions at a dead run. They all ran, stumbling through the dark fields of something dry and about knee high. Hay, barley, oats or wheat, he couldn't tell. They ran until they reached the grove of trees that sheltered the rusty sheds. Eli was the last to arrive, puffing hard and feeling the burn in his legs from a hard run. They all stood around blowing and gasping and looking behind them to see if there were pursuers. The sergeant, younger than the rest of them by a good thirty to fifty years, was the first to recover his breath, and he was on the radio finding out what was going on.

The good news was that Eli could hear Sam's familiar voice. He wasn't dead!

Once they stopped heaving and sweating like mad, the water bottles came out and they shared some brief remarks. "Close one, damned close, too damned close! What the hell did they wake up over there? Half a brigade of regulars? A full company strength at least. What, two APC's, two heavy and two light machine guns, mortars and rifles by the score – had to be at least a regular light infantry company!" The old timers surmised. Now what? Were the hunters about to be the hunted?

"We got any RPG's with us?" Josh asked anxiously. The older kibbutznik shook his head. "Hand grenades?"

"Maybe the sergeant," Nir wheezed and coughed. Eli was still breathing hard too between gulps of water. He was eyeing the hilltop behind them and both sides of it looking for any sign of movement. He also suddenly realized that the firing had stopped. He held the face of his watch up to the sky and barely made out the hands, a little past four am. There was less than two hours to sunrise; it would be pretty light by five-thirty. Hiding did not seem much of an option, especially since they left five obvious trails through the field behind them.

"What's the story?" Josh asked the young sergeant as soon as he put the radio back in his pocket.

"No tanks to be had anywhere. Engel's group has its hands full with a settlement three times this size and a tank brigade threatening to cross the border somewhere beyond him, Golan South has nothing to spare from the blocking force, and General Irani has everyone else tied up with the 100,000 troops still trying to break through to Carmiel. Not even a howitzer to spare and nothing in transit," the sergeant summarized.

"I meant what's the story with us?" Josh said, rephrasing the question.

"Sam's thinking," the sergeant said.

"Anybody hurt?" the older kibbutznik asked.

"Two down from Sam's team – Minkov and Hadar, and one hit by shrapnel on our mortar team, not sure who," the sergeant said flatly.

"Wait a minute, aren't you Minkov?" the kibbutznik asked.

"Alexei is my brother," Sgt. Minkov said, "I'm Sergei Minkov."

"Oh my G-d," Eli gasped.

"*Baruch Dayan Emet,*" said the older kibbutznik.

Eli felt a wave of guilt for missing the strong family resemblance, calling them in his mind Tweedle Dee and Tweedle Dum all this time and never getting to know his comrades in arms, though there had been ample time while milling around earlier in the night. How could he be so cavalier even in his thinking?

"He fell near the fence line. They dragged him back to the bushes when they pulled back, but he wasn't moving. Hadar caught a bullet just after they opened fire. Right through the throat, nothing they could do for him. They managed to carry him back to the trucks." Sergei said.

They all hugged him in turn, while careful to keep one eye on the horizon beyond.

They stood around numbly, waiting for Sam's radio call. There was nothing they could say really.

The radio crackled in Sgt. Minkov's pocket, he put in the earpiece and listened.

"Pull out," he said.

He led out of the grove and headed back down the track towards where they had left the trucks, and the other four followed him.

However, as they passed near the sheds again, Eli called out to slow down a minute. He was curious what kind of equipment was there, for he had spent the past week scrounging whatever would run, or might run, for the moshav mechanics to use. He had worked around enough kibbutz and moshav fields to know that this was the kind of shed they used to park seasonal equipment, like hay bailers and combines. And it was harvest season for hay and some of the field crops. The older kibbutznik, who he had finally learned was named Dror, had the same instinct, and jogged over to the sheds with him. The others pulled up to a stop near the cover of a hedge and waited impatiently.

"Look, if they were coming after us, they would be here by now – you saw how fast they came after the mortars!" Dror had argued. Eli had to admit it seemed logical to him, and some of his apprehension fell away.

The sheds were open on the other side, facing south and they walked quickly around them, rifles brought out and at the ready. Eli's was more for show, since hitting something at such short range would be luck indeed. Sure enough, there were four dark shapes of machinery inside. These shapes soon resolved themselves into a pair of old John Deere tractors and a pair of bailing machines. It was a well set up little shop for being in the middle of nowhere. Eli wondered why everything had not been stolen even in peace time, for cattle, sheep and agricultural equipment rustling had been common in the Golan for years. However, he vaguely remembered something about a new young moshav up this way that had a reputation for being trigger happy at night. He recalled that the moshav barely avoiding a lawsuit from some innocent cattle rustlers who were only thinking of borrowing some cows when two of their number had been ventilated by the moshav's night patrol. Their argument had been that until they actually carried off a cow, they were merely night time sight seers. Since the rustlers were local Arabs in good standing with the village head man, their plea was almost taken at face value. The settlement offered medical expenses, and a warning that the next rustlers would be killed on sight.

The best thing about old John Deeres was there were no fancy electronics for an electromagnetic pulse to disrupt. The real questions were: what kind of shape they were in? and were the batteries left in? "Think they'll start?" Eli asked his companion as they stood gazing at the bonanza of farm equipment.

"Let me go talk to Sam a minute," Dror said, and waved for Sgt. Minkov to bring the radio. Eli wandered into the shed as Dror argued with Sam on the radio. Sure enough, there were batteries in both tractors. They were old, but in good shape, good tread on the big wheeled tires, grease in all the fittings he touched. He had to wipe his hands off after checking them over. One had a front loader bucket, the other had some kind of rake attachment at the back on a hydraulic lift. If nothing else, the front loader could help them dig shelters for their trucks faster than anything they had brought with them. But where were they going next?

He strolled back to where Dror and Sam were wrapping up their conference, and it sounded like Dror had prevailed.

"We're to meet them back at where we set up the first ambush," Dror said, handing the radio back to Sgt. Minkov. "If we can get them running in the next three minutes, we take them. Otherwise we hoof it back double time."

"I'll take the front loader, you take the rake," Eli suggested.

A minute later he was feeling for the key – which was thankfully in the ignition, saving a few minutes of hot wiring and much aggravation. The engine turned over three times and caught. The roar of the tractor filled the shed and Eli suddenly felt very vulnerable, but he put the big Deere in gear and eased out the clutch. The machine lurched forwards, but the bucket of the loader started to drop. He frantically tried the row of levers to his right and found the one that raised the bucket up and out of the way before it dug into the earth and stopped him cold.

He heard the roar of the second tractor revving up behind him as he wheeled out of the shed and into the brighter predawn dark. He soon had the roaring beast under control. He pulled it to a stop and waited for Dror to pull along side.

"What about the bailing machines?" Eli yelled.

"Not enough time," Dror roared back. "Head south across the fields until we can pick up the highway out of sight of the settlement."

Sgt. Minkov climbed on the hitch of Eli's tractor and clung to the back of his spring-mounted metal seat. Josh and Nir clambered aboard the bar of the rake behind Dror. "Hang on," Eli shouted over the roar of the tractor. He let out the stiff clutch again and they bolted off.

For the first two kilometers, Sergei Minkov spent most of his time trying to peer behind them without falling off. After that he gave up and hung on for dear life as the tractor jounced and bumped across the fields, following a rough track that Eli spotted. After a long while, Eli saw the track end at an irrigation ditch that looked too big to cross, so he hauled the tractor around heading east towards the road. Now they could both look behind them without risk of falling off for Sergei, or missing a bump or smashing into a rock for Eli. The morning sun was just catching the top of Mt. Hermon above a bank of clouds in the distance. Eli pointed to it, and saw Josh and Nir looking at it while bouncing up and down on the cross bar of the hay rake.

"*Tov meod*, very beautiful," Sergei said. Eli saw his face was streaming with tears, and he felt the coursing of tears down his own cheeks as well. He watched the scene as much as possible, while navigating the now trackless pasture, slaloming around more and more rocks as they approached the highway. Finally they ran over a roadside fence, and Eli gunned the tractor up the embankment and emerged on the highway. On topping the next rise, he saw the burnt out shells of the two tanks not a kilometer distant. The sun burst above the horizon not long after they gained the road and Eli almost missed seeing Woody and the APC way off to the east of the road in the blasting light of the rising red fireball of the sun.

Near Ramat HaBashan 0500

David Engel fingered the oak leaf pinned on his epaulette. Both he and Colonel Eschol had wept openly as the colonel pinned them on, making his field promotion to major official. Both knew that it should have been Yankel receiving the oak leaf. But Yankel was now turning to earth back at a moshav to the south. His trusty tank was beginning its long career as a rusting landmark in the Golan. With the oak leaves came a heavy burden of responsibility, in his case for nearly 1,000 men in the makeshift armored brigade tasked with clearing the Syria-Israel border and advancing toward Mt. Hermon. He could see the tip of the magnificent mountain warming to a pre-dawn glimmer of light above the smoke and clouds that obscured the Golan. He was conferring with his counterpart, the major in charge of perhaps another 1,600 men, mostly reservists and settlers, assigned to infantry and support roles. Together, they were trying to retake the overrun moshav of Ramat HaBashan. In peacetime it was a green and lovely hilltop with trees, flowers and neat whitewashed houses with red tile roofs. Now it was a stubborn hill of rubble and trenches harboring three times as many Syrian regulars and irregular looters than its normal Jewish population.

Rather than get bogged down in a slogging match from settlement to settlement along the border, David had dispatched most of his rag tag collection of armor northwards to the third Israeli settlement along the border, with the plan to meet up on either side of the next community between them. He wished he was with them and not here. Siege warfare was not part of IDF doctrine. IDF was get in, hit hard and get out. Drive through, drive around, skip over and cut back. Not sit there and pound a hilltop to further rubble, especially when each shell was hard to replace. However, after three hours of shelling and probing assaults, this nut was refusing to crack. True to Biblical military doctrine, he was attacking on only three sides, leaving the side facing the Syrian border free for an easy retreat. But the defenders were not taking that option, at least not in considerable numbers. David's troops had held their fire as some stragglers left that way, so as to encourage the rest to give up and go home.

David wondered if he was cut out for this kind of command. He wasn't even regular IDF and hadn't been for years. And he had lost half his unit in the first hours of the war. What kind of leader was that? But Col. Eschol, and by extension, General Irani, had confidence in him. That part was good. But he was trained to lead a tank platoon, a company at most, not a whole brigade, and certainly not one he could only reach on four radios for crying out loud. Not only that, but the Colonel had expressed his confidence in David in yet another way, one that was chafing a bit at the moment.

"David, I want to ask you one more favor," the colonel had said, as if giving David a field promotion to major was not a "major" favor going in the other direction. His extra polite tone had alerted David to the fact that this was not necessarily the kind of favor it would be easy to refuse, or to carry out.

"There is a young journalist, a writer with the Associated Press, who has found his way to our headquarters – G-d knows how. He said something about being on a bus to Tzfat that was stranded in Tiberias for the past week. He wants to see where the action is. Since there are only about three foreign reporters in all of Israel right now who have crawled out of their cozy shelters and sought out the action, I thought you might be able to show him some, and perhaps keep his head from being blown off as best you can."

And so, hunched over David's spare pair of binoculars and snapping away with a knapsack full of disposable Kodak cameras – the only cameras that seemed to be working –was a skinny, four-eyed, twenty something fresh out of journalism school with a head full of misconceptions about the Middle East. He was sporting an expensive pair of hiking boots and the usual photographer's khaki vest with a million pockets. His now worthless digital Nikon was weighing down the bottom of his big red hitchhiker's mountaineer-style bag,

David was pondering a possible feint with the half dozen tanks in his group, followed by what? Not another probe with infantry. They had already lost fifteen men that morning, with three times as many wounded. There had to be a better way.

He was therefore happy to see Corporal Natan Andreyev, the chemical physics lab tech from Haifa who served as Baruch's gunner, as he dashed over to David's tank. He hardly saw his surviving companions from *pluga Gimmel* lately. It had been run and shoot, wait and sleep, drive here, drive there for the past few days. Natan gave him an unusually snappy salute. Natan usually forgot saluting completely. But he was grinning broadly when he said a cheery "Good Morning, Major Engel, sir!" So that was it! He was celebrating David's promotion as much as the rest of the *pluga*.

"Morning corporal," David managed to return with a hint of a smile.

"I got a brainstorm I want to run past you," Natan said, way too awake for five am.

If Natan had a brainstorm, it must be a good one, for he was so brilliant in chemistry and physics and things scientific as to be almost unintelligible to ordinary human beings. David hoped he could follow this one. Natan's lessons on electromagnetic pulses at the outset of the war had been equal parts illuminating and obscure.

"What if we gave these pests a little whiff of bug spray?" Natan enthused.

"You mean chemical warfare? What are you talking about?"

"Well," Natan said, thrown off his spiel a little bit, "not chemical warfare exactly, but a little chemistry, yes."

David closed his eyes and rubbed them a minute and prompted Natan to explain what he had in mind.

"So, I'm sitting there in the tank and thinking about what kind of shells to throw at them next – armor piercing – no good on stone, high explosives – big boom, big deal, anti-personnel – not so good against someone dug in that tight, incendiary – not much left over there to burn. So what does that leave?"

"Illumination, marker rounds, tear gas…." David filled in, "assuming we had a full kit, what do you have left over there?"

"I've got all three, which got me to thinking, you know, what would happen if you mixed tear gas, say with one of the colored smoke markers."

"Something green and stinky?" David ventured.

"Exactly!" Natan said triumphantly.

"OK, so how does lobbing some pretty colored tear gas on them clear the hill? They have chemical kits – at least the regulars do, and so do we."

"Think about it a minute," Natan continued. "They have chemical weapons out the wazoo, biological weapons too. We know that, we trained for it. So why haven't they used any? Why hold them back? Forget the Geneva Convention, these turkeys don't know from Geneva Conventions. And besides, they did a first strike with nukes already. So why not pull out all the stops and use their ugly little secret toys?"

Why indeed, David wondered. It certainly wasn't from a sense of humanity or fair play from what he had seen so far in this ugly war. "Why?" he asked.

"The only way I can figure it is because they can't handle them – they would kill as many of their own guys as ours – maybe more. Plus, they are afraid of what we have. They know we're smarter and have better technology. They probably believe that we can probably wipe them out five times over if they were to start something really dirty."

"So you think if we lob in some tear gas with some green or blue smoke in it they will panic and run?"

"Actually, I was thinking that fogging might be more effective than shells," Natan said.

"Explain fogging."

"You know, like the kind of atomization and fog making that they use when dusting crops or fogging for mosquitoes. Have you ever watched one of the mosquito control trucks in action?" David had to admit that he hadn't.

"Well, if it's working right, it puts out a big white cloud that slowly drifts downwind and dissipates gradually, knocking out all the flying skeeters in its path and delivering a safe dose of malathion or whatever they are using these days."

"Where do we get an insect fogger at five am in the Golan?"

"Any vineyard or any orchard would have at least one," Natan said.

"How long would it take you to set something up?"

"Not long. I think I have a good mix going out in back of the tank right now. I've been atomizing using the exhaust, the spare fire extinguisher and some hoses and water bottles, want to see?

"Definitely," David said. He called down to his loader to take over the con of the idled tank for awhile and told his driver and a field artillery lieutenant where he could be found for the next few minutes.

They jogged over to *Gimmel* Two, which was still running on short tracks, but otherwise intact. Natan had collected a couple amateur chemists and tinkerers, who were standing by to help with the demonstration. David greeted his friend Baruch, who also made a point of saying "Good morning, MAJOR."

After a few moments of fidgeting with his reaction vessel, into which he spooned a teaspoon of powder from a marker round, Natan signaled the driver to rev the engine. Collecting and concentrating the exhaust in a Rube Goldberg tangle of tubes and bottles, Natan was soon shooting a vile, almost fluorescent green fog from the nozzle of a small hand fire extinguisher. It indeed made a small but impressive bank of dense fog that rolled away towards some very annoyed soldiers in an APC, who drove off with some curses echoing behind them. David caught a whiff of the choking, noxious odor of tear gas, with perhaps a more emphatic chemical smell. "Enough!" he gasped, eyes tearing.

The chemists and inventors were also choking and dashing water on their eyes, but looking happy that their demonstration worked.

"OK, what's the weather forecast for this morning?" David asked, pondering the possible effects of their cloud, and how to safely release it upwind of the entrenched hilltop. In picturing this, he suddenly wondered about the effects of using chemical weapons – however innocuous. Would Syria respond in kind? And would they for generations accuse Israel of unleashing unspeakable biological horrors, never mind the truth? A lie repeated enough times becomes the truth in certain corners of the Middle East, and Syria was clearly just such a corner. The bigger and more outrageous the lie was, the more believable, especially if it involved the Jews.

"The wind has shifted over the last couple days, and is now coming out of the west so the predictions are northwesterly or westerly. That's what is bringing the cooler weather," Natan said. "And unless it picks up a lot after sunrise, it should be pretty gentle. Sunrise would be the perfect time to fog – either early morning or early evening."

"We don't have until early evening," David said irritably, his eyes still tearing and stinging from a mere whiff of Natan's colorful concoction.

"And I'm worried about how it plays out on the Arab street over the border there. Do they suddenly decide to get out the nasty stuff because they think we did it to them? This could also get our supplies cut off from the US and Europe in a heartbeat if there was even a shadow of suspicion. Not that they are lining up to help us right now, but any excuse NOT to help would be seized and trumped up."

"Well, that's your call. That's what comes with the gold leaves," Natan said matter-of-factly and without malice. "I'm just saying its possible."

"I'll think about that while you and whoever else you need *zuz* out of here and find the nearest foggers and get back here as fast as you can. This could save a whole lot of lives if we can work it right." David signaled the artillery field lieutenant to bring over the jeep they were using to run orders where there were no radios. He instructed him quickly to take Natan and his three apprentices anywhere they needed to go, in a hurry. If they needed any people or equipment he should know that it had number one priority.

As he walked back to his tank, which was serving as his mobile command post, David was developing the germ of an idea into a plan.

He checked in with Greg, his loader, and Sasha, his driver, and answered the questions of a young infantryman sent over to inquire about the status of his unit for the next hour. David then called over to the young reporter, startling him completely and rattling him more than a little to be summoned by the big, battle hardened tank commander who was apparently held in so much awe and respect ever since he had begun to follow him around. David had been able to spare few words and little time for the young man since agreeing to take him along. David had let the reporter ride along in an ammunition truck, not exactly designed to follow his order not to let the young journalist get his head blown off, but certainly designed to instill some fear and respect in the young man. He had managed to survive the trip, and interview the driver as much as the driver's limited English would allow.

David saw the younger man's trepidation, and tried to attempt a reassuring smile, which probably came out as an unnerving flash of white teeth in a smoke blackened face. However he sized him up further in those few moments and decided that he appeared intelligent enough, and certainly enough on the ball to find his way into the heart of a field command group in wartime.

"Where did you say you were from?" David asked, trying to think how to put his request.

"Columbus, Ohio," the reporter said, wonderingly.

"And you work for the Associated Press?" David probed.

"Actually, I'm working for them as an intern – six months for the experience – I get a small stipend for expenses," he explained.

David began to wonder if his idea would work.

"And how have you been able to file stories with all the phones out?"

"There is one satellite phone in Tiberias I found, so I managed to get a couple stories out a few days ago."

"About what?" David asked, not being able to come up with something better.

"You know, the war... like the EMP and how it started with Syria attacking the whole Golan and Jordan pouring in over the border, and the fight to save Tiberias. And what little I can find out by pestering everyone in a uniform...."

"I see," David said, "How long have you been in Israel?"

"About three months."

"Have you been here before? Do you know any Hebrew or Arabic?"

"*Efo Sherutim*? where are the bathrooms?" the AP intern grinned sheepishly. No, I've only been to Canada before, oh, and London once. I just finished my BA in Journalism at Ohio State."

"I know the colonel introduced us, but I haven't had much sleep in the last week, tell me your name again."

"Tom. Thomas Edward Warren."

"Are you Jewish?" David asked.

"No, nothing religious really. My parents were some kind of Protestant, but they didn't do anything much and didn't pass it on to us kids."

David pondered a minute, and the young man stirred uneasily. He was not used to being the one answering the questions.

"I mean it's pretty obvious I'm not Jewish. I really don't know much about religion really. Why do you want to know? Tom asked.

"I wonder if you could act as a kind of... what to call it in English... a witness, is that the word?"

"You mean like in a court case?"he asked, mystified.

"Sort of," David began, "like in the court of world opinion, you would see something we are about to do, we would explain it to you, and you would simply report the facts of what you saw."

"I don't know, I have to stay neutral really. Reporters really shouldn't take sides or anything..." he protested.

"But you would report on the facts as you saw and understood them?"

"Well, yeah, that's my job, right? To be as objective as possible and to try to give the whole story, as much as possible..."

"Good enough," David said, "I'll let you know in an hour or so if we need your, um, objectivity."

"Can you tell me what is going on? I mean right now, or since I joined your group? I think I found this place on the map. Is that Ramat HaBashan or this other place, Kiryat Yonah?" he asked, pointing to a page in a small motorists guide to Israel he had pulled out of one of is many pockets.

"Ramat HaBashan. Until last week, it was a peaceful Israeli town with kids on vacation for the holidays and parents working in the city or doing something agricultural. Right now it has been destroyed, looted and occupied by Syrian regular army troops and various militias and irregulars. We are trying to take what's left of it back and convince them to leave Israel and not come back."

Tom took out his reporters' notebook and began to scribble quickly... "Wait," he said. But David had already hurried off to see a field ambulance, actually an old pickup truck scrounged from the streets of Tiberias, and find who the latest casualty was.

Northern District Headquarters, Mt. Meron 0620

Everyone had a lot of updates, so the meeting was threatening to go well beyond their self-imposed fifteen minute limit. New uplinks were coming on line, more than tripling the amount of voice and data they could handle. Better encrypted radio sets were being delivered to their key field commanders, albeit by motorbike once again.

The Australian AWACs had arrived about an hour ago and were being refitted to communicate with the IAF planes they had flying. The two C-130 Hercules cargo planes brought welcome communications and medical supplies. A skilled team of Australian Jewish volunteers had slept on the plane as best they could during its long fight from Melbourne. They went straight to work in the electronics and communications shops in the Negev. Best news of all was that they had nearly forty jets of various kinds airworthy, plus a growing number of short take off and landing propeller planes now in the air. It was now possible to move from one end of the country to the other.

On the helicopter front the news was promising too, there were somewhere around forty choppers flying, many of them armed Blackhawks and Apaches. There were a few airlift and medivac choppers in the air too. One was due at the summit of Mt. Meron with relief communications and technical crews and fresh food sometime that morning. Even Anna was getting tired of junk food and black coffee.

The morning session stretched on because everyone was eager to talk and had much to say. They reviewed the ground war in the Golan and Gallil, their two areas of command. They would know more in a few hours if the combined Syrian forces that had just linked up were going to be able to blast through the IDF forces arrayed against them. Depending on how effective their growing air superiority was at hitting the ground targets and stopping them in their tracks, it could be over very soon. If not, it would be a bloody mess.

There was also this crazy plan to scare the Arabs out of Ramat HaBashan with fake nerve gas made up of tear gas and colored chemicals. They had nearly overruled that one, but after much debate deferred to the ground commander's assessment of the situation. Rumors of anthrax-like or Ebola-virus-like symptoms kept cropping up on their limited intelligence assessments from the cross border areas of Syria. It would be just the IDF's luck to be blamed for what the Syrians did to themselves. Many argued not to give them even the shadow of an excuse. But on the other hand, how many Jewish lives would it take to recapture a burn out, bombed and destroyed hilltop, and the one after and the one after? Those kinds of questions were impossible to answer really.

Another combined IDF force had formed up near Rosh HaNikra at the northern tip of Israel on the coast and was preparing to make a drive along the Israel-Lebanon border. Their goal was to cut off the supply lines and force the irregular Hezbollah raiders to pull back or be surrounded and eliminated one by one. The troops based near Tzfat had begun to clear the area between their base and Mt. Meron, bringing much relief from the hit and run mortar and rocket fire. But now they were all taken up in blocking the Syrian second column from swinging northwards, and pushing them back wherever possible.

Anna had just returned to her array of monitors when a communications aide signaled that her "boyfriend" the NATO commander was on the secure link to NATO headquarters in Brussels. Apparently he had hopped the Atlantic since the last time she talked with him. She glanced at her little time zone popup, it about 0440 in Brussels about now. Didn't this guy get any sleep either?

"Hey Jack, what's up?" she answered as the call patched through to her headset.

"Mazel tov on your AWACS," the general said in a friendly way.

"Good intelligence there," she countered. "I thought our highly placed friends in Australia had kept the lid tighter than that."

"Actually, I had something to do with persuading them to OK the transaction, so you might say they have some small strings attached," he said.

"How long are the strings?" Anna asked, growing wary.

"One mission long – otherwise they are yours for the duration," the general said pleasantly. For someone who probably slept in the seat of a transatlantic jet sometime in the previous twelve hours, he sounded chipper enough.

"Those kinds of strings I can probably handle. I was afraid you might say they were off limits for any targets outside of Tel Aviv or something," she said, realizing as she said it that her joke might have come across as hostile or bitter. However, there was an understanding chuckle at the other end of the fairly clear scrambled voice line.

"Only on Friday the thirteenth, otherwise it's open season," he joked back.

Anna was relieved her joke had not misfired completely, and she laughed along with him.

"Ok, copy that, no Friday the thirteeners. Are you going to tell us about this one mission of yours?"

"I'll give you the general idea – get it, General T?" (he, and most Americans couldn't pronounce Anna's last name, so she was know at NATO as General Anna T) He took a moment to chuckle at his own joke, and she managed a titter or two to keep him company, waiting for the other big size 49 shoe to drop. He was quickly back to business. "As I said, I'll give you the general idea and then you can call together everyone you need in the next couple hours and we'll conference on it say about 0900 your time."

"OK," she said, taking a deep breath and waiting to hear what the most powerful nation on earth for the past half century wanted little, war-torn, battle-scarred, limping Israel to do.

"You guys did a nice job of knocking out Iranian command control and information, and in blinding their missile system, but there are still plenty of hard assets still on the ground. As soon as this war is over, they are going back to hiding them and shuffling the deck so that we may never have them clear in our sights again like they are now. We have identified two critical spots that – if you hit them now – like in the next 24 hours – there would be no long range threat for a number of months or perhaps years."

"And these are places you can't hit with a Tomahawk IV? I thought those things could fly up to a bunker, knock on the door and say 'Boo!'"

"Except for the 'say boo!' part, yeah. Trouble with Tomahawks is that they leave fingerprints behind that say 'Uncle Sam was here' in big letters."

"So you figure we are in deep enough with Iran already that the bomb fragments might as well say 'made in Israel' on them?" she asked as neutrally as she could.

"Well, basically, yes. Except that the only bunker busters you have that will make that trip say made in the USA on them… but everyone knows we gave them to you, so it goes on your tab, not ours."

"The price of those AWACS just went up a lot. I'd better tell the boys not to scuff up the carpets or leave any butts in the ashtrays," Anna said, thinking hard.

"Actually, you can probably keep them if you can do this one little strike for us. You have all the mission planning done. It just needs updating for the current post EMP reality.

"How many planes are you talking?"

"Eight with bombs, minimum. Maybe four for air cover should do it. Twenty hours estimated mission time taking the central route flying high, one fueling each way. We can supply that from Turkey.

"What are the targets?

"I'll save that for the conference. Just say they are two places already identified in the Henhouse Three scenario we drilled on the simulators last year. Target two is pretty far northeast, but not at the end of the line."

"Henhouse Three, gottcha," Anna recalled the absurdly named scenario well. It looked like Israel was supplying the foxes for the raid.

"Think you can round up your team by 0900 or should we give you another hour?" he asked.

"Let's shoot for 0900, and if I have to move it back, I should know in the next hour," Anna said.

"Excellent. The heavy loads should be 3,000 kilo Buster Browns. How many do you have?"

"At least three dozen left, I think. We used a few to blow bunkers in Syria before the EMP.

"Good. Say, I'm really sorry to have to take twelve planes off the flight line for twenty four hours just when you got on top of the air game. We think they're afraid to put anyone in the air at the moment because nobody is flying more than airfield cover at the moment. Word is the Saudis were scared shitless when two of their F-35's went down. How in the hell did you do that?"

"If we ever see a day of peacetime again, I'll tell you over the best bottle of wine in Naples, promise," Anna said.

"Looking forward to it," the general said. Anna could practically hear him lick his chops at the thought.

"But I'll probably be an old married lady with six kids by then, and you'll be a grandfather," She said to calm him down.

"I'm a grandfather already, my little Emily had a baby last Fall." He said proudly.

"Mazel tov *Sava!*" she said, "Get back to you by 0900, looks like I have a little more work to do.

"Me too, bye for now."

So, that was why the Australian Air Force was willing to let a couple of Jewish businessmen and minor government functionaries make a cash deal to get two surplus AWACS out of retirement. Someone in Washington wanted a job done that needed AWACS, however old. In fact, in this case, older was probably better. She heard that some of the instrumentation was still vacuum tube technology, which was immune to EMP, though not to age. However, what was the old adage? Never look a gift AWAC in the mouth? She buzzed Koby, they had a lot of work to do.

Sam was glad to see Eli back in one piece. Sam had spent the past half hour waiting nervously for his two snipers and their three companions. Dror and Eli so excited about salvaging two working tractors that Sam almost forgave them their delays in getting back. The Azerbaijani regulars he had expected at any moment since stirring up their hornet's nest at the moshav a few kilometers to the north had not materialized. Now that the sun had risen a full hand's breadth above the horizon, his little ambush was losing any chance of effectiveness.

Sam and the older men led Sgt. Minkov over to the back of Woody where his brother lay along with corporal Hadar. Four of the men had already started digging graves in the rocky earth near the top of their hill. He hugged the short Russian and murmured some words of consolation. Sam felt devastated at the loss of two good men and mad at himself for underestimating the enemy and not probing further. He had gotten too far in this war by winging it, using spur of the moment inspiration and on the fly tactics – except for the battle for Ramat HaMagshinim. That had been planned by his boss, Colonel Eschol, and it had been executed in textbook fashion with few losses despite stiff odds. Sam needed to rethink his plan. If the enemy was not coming to him, he had to come up with a new and safer way to get the job done.

Unfortunately, there was not a spare tank or any other armor or artillery to be had anywhere in the Golan. Every available gun was being used to keep the massive Syrian advance contained and to stop the threat of a breakthrough towards the sea. His friend, the newly promoted Major Engel also had his hands full. Air cover was working overtime elsewhere. He would have to either bypass the hornets nest or improvise. But he was drawing a blank. Sam handed the radio over to his second and decided to take a few minutes for a quick cup of coffee and some breakfast where the kibbutzniks had boiled up a billy can of coffee and fried up some eggs. G-d knows how they had preserved a few dozen eggs through all the commotion they had been through that night.

He accepted a mug from Eli, who had just cleaned it out after using it himself. "Thanks," he said.

"We're really supposed to make it all the way to Mt. Hermon today?" Eli asked.

"That was the plan," Sam said grimly. "We could sure use a tank or two. It doesn't have to be anything fancy. Just a little armor and a cannon and we could have those bastards cleaned out of there in an hour flat."

"Nothing available?" Eli asked.

"Nothing.

"Air support?

"All busy stopping the big push. There's nothing to spare to move a mere hundred guys out of a little moshav in the middle of nowhere," Sam said.

"Damn." Eli commiserated.

"Wonder what they're doing up there?" Sam wondered. He had sent the scouts back out on their bikes as soon as they had set up their makeshift ambush. But he wasn't satisfied with their cover, or their positions anyway. So it was probably time to either figure out a bypass plan or a safer plan of attack. But how did one safely attack a force at least twice his size?

"Hey Sam, have you ever seen the Rose Bowl parade or an American high school homecoming?" Eli asked.

"Not sure about the Rose Bowl, but I've seen some parades," Sam said absently, sipping his too hot cup of coffee, desperate for the reviving jolt of caffeine to his brain.

"I was just thinking about a float we made back in high school, the sophomore class float. We made an old tractor just like that John Deere over there look like a submarine, with a big sign, 'Sink the Hornets!'"

Sam looked at the old tractor and tried to picture it looking like a submarine. He wondered what Eli was doing reminiscing about American football and parades. "How to you make a tractor look like a submarine?" he asked, blowing on his coffee.

"In our case, it took some scrap lumber, a lot of chicken wire and crepe paper flowers. It was hard finding enough silver and grey crepe paper in Evanston, but we found enough to make a 25 foot sub, with a couple cheerleaders in the conning tower. I was the driver and they were practically standing on top of me. I had a real crush on one of them. Never saw such great legs before or since," He chuckled.

Sam yawned and smiled just a fraction. This was a side of Eli he was not aware of. He saw him as an older, dati, married moshavnik with a grey beard, not an American sophomore driving cheerleaders around in a tractor submarine. "Why are you telling me about this?" he finally asked.

"Well," Eli said hesitantly, "I was sizing up that old falling down shed over there, and the chicken wire fence and wondering if we might make a couple tanks – or at least a couple things that looked like tanks."

Sam looked down the slope at a falling down pair of sheds and a wire enclosure he hadn't thought of since he first noticed them in looking for a spot for his ambush. Apparently there was a water tap down there where the coffee and breakfast makers had gathered water for washing up.

Sam looked up at the brightening sun. "Dunno, maybe before the sun was up we could pass off a couple tractors as tanks. They had some pretty good spotters there, and one pair of binoculars would be hard to fool."

"Yeah, but you remember what the guys did to the tanks up on the ridge while we prepared to go into Syria?" Eli persisted. "They looked just like a big moving bush. I almost didn't notice the tank inside they were so well camouflaged."

Sam stopped a moment to remember. He too had been impressed at the tanker's art, as well as how fast they put their camouflage together. His brain started to click and visualize how to create a pair of moving bushes that might imitate a disguised tank.

"What about the shape and the profile underneath? How would you make it about the same bulk and dimensions?" he asked.

"Well, I haven't thought this through completely," Eli said, "but those sheds are nothing but corrugated sheets of thin metal, easily pried off with a hammer and wrecking bar. I always keep a hammer and crowbar in the back of Woody along with some other tools, just in case, you know. And they could be shaped with the shears we collected from the depot after our experience in making the Kraz into a prisoner transport. So I was wondering if we made a wood frame and could cut out the siding in roughly the profile of a Merkava – you know, low and flat and pretty dark – coating it with some soot and dirt should take care of the coloring – and put a good layer of branches and leaves on the outside, it just might pass, especially if you were up-sun of them."

"What if we meet a real tank?"

"We're screwed. Of course, we would be screwed anyway, but they would blow up the tractors first while the rest of you ran like hell," Eli said.

"True enough," Sam mused. He sipped at his coffee and let the vision grow in his brain.

"How long do you think it would take?" he asked.

"Well, the sophomore class took a month… but most of that time was screwing around and going out for supplies and pizza. I could probably knock up the frame and a mock up of one side in an hour or two with a couple helpers. If someone pulled the sheds apart while we worked, taking care to keep the pieces pretty much intact, the whole thing could take less than half a day," Eli said.

One of Sam's recon men had wandered over in search of a cup of coffee, and had perked up his ears at the word "cheerleader." He had been to college in the US. He looked dubiously at the old tractor and the falling down shed. "What would you use for the cannon barrel?" he asked, joining their conversation.

"Dunno," Eli said, "maybe we could use an actual cannon barrel from one of those two tanks we burned."

The three of them stood in the warming sunshine and contemplated the three wrecked vehicles on the road below them.

"You know," the soldier said, "the one tank torched on us and blew off all the ammo, but the other one didn't catch fire. I used a fragmentation grenade to clean out the inside. I wonder if anything still works?"

No one moved. The two soldiers imagined the after-effects of a fragmentation grenade in a tank interior. Eli casting his scavenger's eye afresh over the intact tank body. "Let's go see," Sam said finally. He handed the coffee cup over to another soldier to finish and whistled to the master sergeant from his recon group. He told him to keep a sharp eye out while they looked at the tank wreckage.

Eli grabbed a flashlight, pliers, a hammer, screwdrivers and a slim wrecking bar from his tool box in Woody. Sam collected another soldier who had served briefly in the armored forces before deciding he would rather walk around in the fresh air and sunshine than be cooped up inside a metal can all day.

The four of them approached the burned out tank and the fragged tank slowly, each of the soldiers remembering every detail of their previous night's ambush. Sam recalled the feeling of invincibility that had followed the apparently easy win. Wiping out a command jeep and two tanks, and capturing three valuable supply trucks in less than two minutes had made Sam feel that luck was on their side. Therefore he had gambled in a very risky fashion with his three-pronged attack on the settlement, with far too little firepower to pull it off, and lost two good men. He could have lost everyone. Being a captain was proving tough going so far. Sam could tell from how his three companions moved slower and slower the closer they got to the disabled tank, that none of them was especially eager to go have a look down the open hatches, especially the young soldier who threw one of the grenades. Leadership had its disadvantages, he decided, and motioned for Eli to hand him the flashlight.

Sam recognized the low, flat profile of a Soviet built T-72. Syria had hundreds of them. The open driver's hatch was close at hand and easy to reach with a short hop up to the sloping front deck. Sam pulled himself up even with the open hatch and gave a lightening fast glance inside. He did not want to risk a chance shot from a wounded tanker. However, his glance told him enough to take a slower, more deliberate look. What was left of the driver was slumped and splattered over the controls. There had been an instrument fire in the panels he could readily see. His hopes of driving off in a "free" tank were quickly dashed. However, it might not be as bad as he imagined.

Sam clenched his jaws and climbed up to the turret with its two open hatches. The right side hatch had a machine gun; the left looked like it had been the delivery point for the grenades, for it showed some jagged tears and blast marks. He opted for the right side, and looked inside. In the brightening morning sun, he saw a blood spattered gunner's compartment, but no body. He paused, puzzled, but then realized that his hand was resting on a sizable swath of dried blood on the open rim of the hatch. Pulling his eyes away from the bloody interior, he saw splatters of blood in a trail that led over the side of the tank. Raising his eyes further, he saw where it stopped. A pair of crows were picking at a bloody corpse in the ditch a few meters away. Sam lost his coffee.

Looking in the third hatch was also gruesome, but taught him why the ammunition had not caught fire and cooked off. The flak-jacketed assistant gunner or tank commander had fallen over the loading apparatus and kept any sparks from igniting the shells. What kind of insanity brought men to die in the middle of the night in the middle of nowhere and be picked at by carrion birds in the morning sun? Sam couldn't understand it. He was fighting for his home, family, country and the 3,600-year history of the Jewish people. What were these men fighting for? Were they mercenaries fighting for a day's pay and food with the promise of plunder? Or did they just hate Jews because they were taught to hate Jews for a lifetime, having probably never seen one close up until stopped by Sam's patrol last night.

Sam's ex-tanker recruit had gathered enough courage to climb up and was studying the mess in the driver's hatch. "Let's pull him out of there and put him on the road for the burial detail," Sam said grimly. "If we each grab a shoulder strap on his ceramica, he might come out in one go."

His companion braced himself and grabbed a shoulder strap and waited with a clenched jaw until Sam got a grip and a good stance. On three the two men heaved up and out, and what was left of the driver moved bulkily at first, then lifted smoothly. They lifted his feet clear. The man was barely five feet tall – a good height for a tank driver in one of these cramped Soviet beasts. Eli and the other soldier came to help, and took the body and lay it on the pavement in the shade of the tank.

Without more than a word or two, the four men did the same with the gunner who had died shielding the high explosives that would have made the tank an exploding torch like the burned out shell next to it. Once the bodies were removed, the ex-tanker clambered down all three hatches while Sam sat wearily on the turret and looked off into the sun-washed expanse of the Golan. He stared at the massive bulk of Mt. Hermon rising above the haze and thought, "*Elo-kim* it is a beautiful morning."

Tal, the short-time tanker, was taking a long time inside, or at least it seemed that way. Sam was about to ask Eli what time it was, but Eli and the other soldier had wandered over to the shot up wreckage of the jeep. They had pried up the bullet-riddled hood and were poking around for usable parts. Sam suddenly noticed that the turret beneath him was turning slowly to the right. He leaned over to peer in the hatch. Tal was bent over some steel wheels, turning them by hand. The turret started moving back left again. "*Kol ha kavod!*" he told Tal, who grinned at him.

"Watch this," Tal said. He stood next to the big breech of the 125 mm cannon and turned a new set of wheels. The long barrel of the cannon rose gradually. Then Tal opened the breech, showing Sam a big shell inside. "We have radius and elevation. Even if we can't start this thing we have a field piece we can tow up to the settlement and start shelling the crap out of those bastards. I saw at least forty rounds back there, maybe more."

"What are the odds of starting it?" Sam asked.

"Pretty much zilch," Tal said, "The ignition and control systems are all fried, as well as most of the steering and all of the electronics. But the treads and gear wheels are all OK. So if we can get it into neutral, it should be towable by the Kraz or perhaps even one of those tractors."

"Best news I've had all morning. You keep working on what you can figure out, I'll send down a cleaning crew and burial detail."

Sam climbed down and waved Eli over to him.

"OK," Sam said, "here's the situation, we have one real tank that we can tow at least, and use as a field piece. But I like your idea about making a fake tank too. And we'll put the brush work on this one too so it looks like we have a pair. We want this one to look like a Merkava, not like a T-72. I'll get you a couple guys to start pulling apart the shed and getting the materials for your... what do you call it... floating thing. You and Nir get to work on that while I work the radio and try to come up with something more orthodox. But you know, it just might work. I don't care if they come out to meet us. We can deal with an APC or two, we just can't storm an entrenched village with machine guns and mortars dug in. It would be suicide."

Ramat Hahovav airfield, the Negev 0900

Major Yossi Green was pacing the hanger, trying not to annoy his ground crew as he wondered why he had suddenly been ordered off the flight line for a mandatory twelve hour rest period. He knew there was a briefing coming up in about an hour, but in the meantime his CO was being mysterious and very quiet. Did he really not know what was up? Or was he shutting him out of something top secret until the last minute? All he knew was that he needed to rest up for a very long flight. But to where? Egypt? There were still airfields operating at the southern edge of Egypt, but they had not been a threat. Was it retaliation for the Saudi incursions perhaps? Too risky. They had plenty of hardware left, including the other four stealth F-35s. That left Iraq or Iran. It had to be Iran.

He stopped pacing and regarded his ground crew as they tested equipment and moved ordinance around to get ready for instant loading while not knowing what would be next. His bird was out on a mission with the number three pilot. He had better bring it back intact because Yossi had a hunch it would need a good going over if he was indeed flying to Iran tonight.

Twelve hours from a half hour ago would make it, what, 2030? And six hours flying time to somewhere the other side of Teheran would make it what? 0200 or so – a night strike. They had trained for a wide variety of Iran missions. Which one?

Yossi smiled at the nearest aircrew member who looked relieved to smile back. He realized that his pacing had set them all on edge. They were used to him being in the air or in the pilots quarters except when performing a preflight check. He would stop in for a few minutes upon arriving at the base in the mornings and that was the only time he ever said hello. He should spend some more time with his ground people sometime. They were a great group and he relied on their expertise and support in more ways than he could count every time he hurtled skyward in that complicated jet fighter. "Great work," he said, "I'll be back when I know what kind of load we'll be packing."

He headed off to a late breakfast with a clearer mind and a sharper appetite. He remembered the simulation runs – ten to twelve hour missions in a narrow little cockpit. Better a big breakfast now and something lighter later on.

Ramat HaBashan 0630

"OK, we're ready for our demonstration," Natan said to Major Engel.

David looked at the contraption Natan and his group had created to be towed behind Baruch's tank. It resembled a compressor on wheels, but it had a variety of small makeshift tanks and tubes and miscellaneous parts stuck on.

"Send the reporter over," David called back to his tank crew.

A few minutes later, a wary but very interested looking young American AP intern showed up, led by an even younger soldier who had been entertaining him and keeping him out of the way with stories about the Tiberias navy.

"Good morning Tom," David Engel said, "I want to tell you what we have here, and what we plan to do with it. Feel free to ask any questions you want."

The reporter pulled out one of his pocket cameras and snapped a couple pictures of the contraption then pulled out his note pad.

"OK, what is it?" he asked.

"This is an insecticide sprayer we borrowed from a nearby vineyard, but we are not planning to spray any insecticide today. We've made a few modifications so that we can spray tear gas."

"How do I know its tear gas?" the reporter challenged.

"Well the smell for one thing, have you ever smelled tear gas?" David countered.

"Um, once, I covered a labor dispute that got ugly, and the cops used some," Tom said.

"So you remember what it smells like?"

Tom nodded. "But that's not proof," he said. "Never mind that for the moment though, why are you using tear gas? Are you hoping to attack using chemical suits?"

"Not exactly. Besides, they have chemical gear too. The Syrian army has trained using all kinds of gas," David said. This was proving a little more difficult than he expected. "We have added some color to the smoke for visual effect and basically what we are trying to do is fool the Syrians into believing that we are using some new kind of nerve gas." He went and explained Natan's theories about why the Syrians were prepared for chemical warfare, but had not resorted to any dirty tricks despite their reputation for ruthlessness.

Tom followed the arguments fairly well, challenging a point or two. "So this is a *ruse d'guerre* so to speak, a little deception, and you are hoping they will panic and run?"

"Exactly," David said with relief.

"Then, why are you showing me all this now? And why are you wanting me to write it up? Wouldn't that spoil the whole deception? I mean suppose my story gets filed tonight or tomorrow. It might not be too late for them to strike back."

"Our first concern is to save lives, mostly ours, but theirs too. It would cost a lot of time to lay siege to the hill, which we don't have, or a lot of precious lives to storm it, which we never have. But, our other main concern is what our allies will think? We don't get slammed in the court of world opinion. We want the truth out there. This is tear gas and colored smoke, nothing more. I got an eye full of it earlier this morning and I can tell you it's the real thing as far as the tear gas goes. Here, you can even see the English label on the shells we used." Natan and his chemists showed the emptied shells, and which container was which, and where they were stored ready to mix once the atomizer got fired up.

"OK," Tom said at last after one of Natan's crew unscrewed a lid and offered to taste the brew to show that it wasn't poisonous nerve gas. "I'll believe you on that part. But why care what America and NATO think of a little tear gas – this is war after all. It seems legitimate to me."

"I guess you are too young to remember all the *balagan* about our allegedly using white phosphorus as illumination shells in Operation Cast Lead," David said wearily. "Even though every modern army in the world uses some sort of phosphorus shell for illumination, it is an international incident and a UN investigation if Israel fires some. Everything Israel does is done under a microscope – magnified a thousand times. Have you ever stopped to count how many journalists there are in Jerusalem?"

Tom shook his head.

"When I served a rotation in central command, someone told me there are about one thousand five hundred credentialed foreign journalists in Jerusalem at any one time. Twice as many if there is something going on, like a nice safe war like Cast Lead. Do you know how many foreign correspondents there are with credentials based in Beijing, a city ten times the size of Jerusalem and capital of the most populous nation on earth?" Tom looked blank. "Would you believe three or four hundred?" Tom looked puzzled.

"But not many journalists speak Chinese. I thought of asking for a posting in Japan, but without Japanese, there didn't seem much point, even though most Japanese speak some English," Tom said lamely.

"How many journalists do you know who speak Hebrew – or Arabic for that matter?" Major Engel challenged. Tom shrugged, he was beginning to see his point. "Why Jerusalem?" Major Engel asked again. "OK, so we are a holy city for the world's three greatest religions – although the Koran never mentions the name Jerusalem or its Arabic names anywhere. But how many stories written with a Jerusalem dateline have anything to do with religion? And how many reporters care a rat's patootie about religion?" Tom looked guilty as charged, for he had said as much when the major had quizzed him earlier.

"It's not about religion. It's about the Jews."

"But Judaism is a religion," Tom protested.

"But most Jews are not religious. Look around my company if you have any doubts. How many guys did you see wearing their *tallit* and *tefillin* this morning? Maybe a fifth of them? And this is war time, no atheists in a fox hole and all that… No, it's the Jews. The world either loves us or hates us – mostly hates us these days. But anything the Jews do is news. And it's not because we own all the media either. We don't. How many Jews do you know working for the BBC? Or how about for Al Jazeera, the fifth biggest news network on the planet these days? They keep a studio with ten people in Jerusalem. Security is a nightmare with them around.

"What do the Palestinian school teachers teach their little kids each day using your taxpayers' money? 'Death to the Jews!' It's in all the text books. there is no Israel on their maps. What's two plus two, four? Wrong, it's death to the JEWS!"

Tom was beginning to look overwhelmed, so David wrapped up his history of media relations course. "Basically, what ever we do, it's wrong. Even when we are being more humane than any other army on the planet, we are accused of being inhumane and compared to Nazis. I'm sorry to get so worked up about it. It's just something we have to live with here. When I have to make a command decision whether to blow a little smoke and save some lives, I have to think about what are the consequences for the next week's headlines."

"Sorry," Tom said. "I've heard some of this before, but no one has made it quite as clear as you just did. Anyway, I'll report what I see as best I can. Let's see the show. And good luck. This could really save a lot of lives on both sides if it works."

Soon Tom and David Engel were watching from separate hatches of David's tank. David was in his commander's hatch, and Tom perched with a borrowed pair of binoculars in the left hand auxiliary gunner's hatch. They watched as Baruch's tank rolled on its absurd looking three-quarter-length short tracks to a point upwind of the hilltop community they were trying to retake. It was a brilliant morning, clearer than previous days, although pockets of smoke still clung to the low ground and valleys. The summit of Mt. Hermon shone bright and clear above the low-lying haze.

The gunners on the hill were watching the single tank too and some howitzer shells bracketed its path not far behind. David ordered a response from his artillery team, only to hear the booms almost immediately behind him, and watch the flight of the answering shells arcing overhead. Baruch's tank speeded up for awhile, but slowed down again and stopped when no more shells fell in its vicinity. They watched a pair of figures scramble from the crew door and start tinkering with the towed sprayer. A couple minutes later a spurt of green smoke emerged. Within seconds there was an impressive cloud of glowing green tear gas forming. David chuckled as he saw the distant figures hurry back into the tank, grabbing a water sack from the back as they went. Natan probably had overdone the hands-on final adjustments and gotten an eyeful of gas in spite of his mask.

Soon the tank began rolling slowly forward with the trailer emitting a great and growing rolling cloud of psychedelic green gas behind it. Another artillery shell fell far beyond it and the big guns behind David's tank responded almost instantly.

They watched in fascination as the green cloud roiled and rolled across the open ground towards the base of the hill. After about ten minutes, the tank turned around and began to move slowly back along its path. The first snaking clouds of green gas were drifting lazily towards the fence line of the moshav. Now the tank stopped for more adjustments, and now a cloud of bright blue-green began to blow from the sprayer behind the tank. David could see his friend Baruch now, standing up quite plainly in the commander's turret of his tank wearing his full chemical suit. The effect was almost overdone he was standing so far out of the turret, something no tank commander would do in wartime conditions. "Get down you idiot!" David swore, but they had no radio link to the tank.

The fog was now a bright electric blue and began to form and drift eastward. Meanwhile the green cloud rolled past the kibbutz fence line and approached the first row of shattered houses. David concentrated his binoculars on the distant community, straining to see how the defenders would react. A cheer went up from the neighboring tank. Then he caught the sight of a distant soldier scrambling out of a trench and running. Pretty soon he saw figures in full flight all around the hilltop. The banks of blue smoke were beginning to reach the fence line of the kibbutz as the green smoke coiled lazily towards the first line of houses. More and more figures were beginning to be seen fleeing in panic on the distant hill. There was a muted cheer from the group around the command team. "Hold your fire!" David ordered into the radio. "Let them run."

Somewhere south of Tel HaBashan 1040

By ten-thirty Eli was putting the finishing touches on a scrap wood and corrugated roofing tank body by covering it with a layer of chicken wire scabbed out about ten centimeters from the panels so that the brush cutters could begin weaving stems of leafy branches in it. They had done a sample corner, stood back and admired their art, and had gone back to work with even greater vigor. Everyone in the small company of thirty some men had contributed something. Eli could tell that it felt good to them to be making something for a change, instead of blowing things up. Seven days of constant death and destruction had weighed on their psyches, and an artistic shop project had proved just the thing for morale. Although most had been up almost all of the night, and much of the preceding nights and days, few opted to sleep long, and at this point, almost all were working on either the fake tank or the real one, or standing guard.

Eli had heard bits of news that straggled up the low rolling valley that contained the small animal and hay shed, long since abandoned. He heard that the cannon on their real tank was quite functional. Not only that, but the tank was towable, and might even be fixable if they could send it back to a shop like the one at Eli's moshav, which had already fixed more than a score of crippled tanks and armored vehicles. But for now, they needed the big 125 mm cannon and its forty two shells. They had all been identified, counted and re-loaded in their fire resistant containers. Eli heard that the compartments of the thirty-some-year-old Soviet-built tank had cleaned up fairly well, that the turret could turn 360 degrees. It had full elevation and depression; in short, it was a fine, portable cannon for their next assault on the entrenched company in the settlement a few kilometers to the north.

Sam came by to admire the work of Eli and his crew. Two fairly skilled and artistic soldiers were applying a second coat of a mud, ash, dirt and oil mixture they had concocted to mimic the dark camouflage of a Golani brigade Merkava tank. Sam complimented them on their artistry, for it was a good likeness, and the spackling of mud evened out the corrugations of the sheet metal. Someone else had carefully snipped out a fairly good likeness of the angular front and back fenders of a Merkava. With a good layer of green and brown leaves and branches, it would look just like the real thing at a few hundred meters, which was all they asked. Eli had brought the tractor down next to the shed and paddock so they wouldn't have to schlep their scavenged materials up the hill to where they had been parked.

Sam had sent one of his radios ahead with a foursome of soldiers piled on the two motorbikes. He now had a running report of everything going on in the settlement. They had surprised a company of Azerbaijani infantry that had decided to settle in for the long haul and take over their own chunk of the newly liberated Golan. That is what their updated radio intelligence from Mt. Meron told them, and he had dispatched one of his pickup crew of volunteers who spoke the language, having made aliyah from a neighboring part of the former Soviet Union. His spy had confirmed the fact by getting within earshot of a general meeting of the company going on in one of the buildings with wide open windows. He had been tempted to lob a few grenades and make their upcoming job easier. However, it would have been a difficult throw, and would have meant breaking cover and sprinting away before being shot at by the now-quite-alert guards.

Fortunately nothing had come down the road from the north to reinforce the settlement. The Syrians were throwing everything into the massive battle for breakthrough or bust going on a few dozen kilometers to the south and west of their route. Every now and then they heard or saw jet fighters in the skies in that direction. Nothing came close enough to send them scrambling for cover, though all had chosen in advance where they would scurry if the sound of helicopters or jet engines grew too close.

Eli was proud of his ingenious frame, which was an improvement on the one he had helped design as a high school sophomore some forty odd years ago. He had managed to securely wire a pair of stout rafters to the frame of the old tractor running on each side of its long snout of an engine. Then he used them to support a series of fairly strong cross pieces. He had scavenged and straightened with his hammer enough nails to make a stout, stiff frame. Unlike the crepe paper and two-by-four contraption that had served as their second-place winning float, this fake tank would be fairly solid, and not sag at the ends. It would have farther to go than the main street of Evanston and over some much rougher terrain. However, the judges for this parade were much more expert and had more at stake by far. Instead of a cheerleader with great legs there would be a smelly, unshaved recon scout directing him where to drive, for his vision would be minimal under all that vegetation and chicken wire.

And, to answer the soldier's question of much earlier in the morning, the barrel of their fake tank was a piece of the real thing. They had been able to unbolt the end section of the badly burnt barrel of the destroyed tank, and a piece of drainage pipe scrounged from the junk pile next to the sheds to make it to nearly the exact length of a real T-72 cannon.

Applying the camouflaging branches went quicker than Eli expected, and soon he was starting up the tractor again to give it a test drive. It had gained considerable weight with the final coat of mud. He was worried that whole chunks of it might fall off as they bounced along. But his frame was holding up admirably, and they had allowed just enough ground clearance to be able to maneuver in fairly flat ground, such as the played out meadow and overgrown fields between their workshop and the road. Except for the amplified roar of the old tractor motor and the visibility problem, Eli felt fairly comfortable driving the rig. Someone had suggested that they remove the muffler and reroute the exhaust through a four inch piece of flexible PVC irrigation hose they had found in their junk pile. That made their thundering bush not only sound like a tank, but, to a distant observer, there would be a realistic plume of hot exhaust vented skyward just like the real thing.

With the guidance of his scout perched on the frame to his right as if commanding the hidden tank from a turret, Eli took his place in their improvised parade lineup. The APC would go first in their decoy parade. It was not only their greatest firepower and most convincing armored vehicle, it was necessary in case of a counterattack from the settlement. They had partially camouflaged it so as not to look like a Soviet APC, but to be possibly an Israeli model. Next came the Kraz transport, also partially disguised, for both sides used similar big six wheel drive trucks. It had Sam's recon men ready to dive out and set up a counter-counter attack. It was towing, by means of a long chain that they hoped would not be too noticeable, their newly camouflaged T-72. Next came Eli in his wood and chicken wire dummy, followed by Woody, also sporting a good layer of branches and cover, and the two and a half ton truck bringing up the rear.

Their plan was to be seen coming up the highway from a good long distance, and then disappear behind the hill they had used as a sniper post, but keeping a good distance from the settlement. They planned to begin shelling from safely behind the hill and hope the enemy assumed that there were two tanks firing. They would use the spotters already deployed from their motorcycle gang. If the enemy came out in force, they prayed they had enough firepower to deal with it. It was too bad their cannon fire would make a further mess of what was still a fairly unscathed community.

It took twenty minutes of chugging along in their absurd parody of a convoy. It was not fooling anyone up close. Eli could plainly see the outlines of a T-72 in the bush ahead of him, but then he had a close in view. From a distance he hoped it could pass for a Merkava. His spotter leaned down and yelled that the settlement was now in view. That was Eli's signal to elevate the barrel of their "gun" slightly, using the hydraulic bucket on the front of his tractor. He concentrated on the touchy hydraulic controls, too much would tear the camouflage away and reveal their deception. He raised and lowered it just a bit for show. Then he followed the real tank in front of him as their convoy pitched off the highway and made its way across an open field to shelter behind a rolling hill in the terrain.

Sam had taken up a new station next to his master sergeant in the APC for this maneuver. They gave each other worried grins. Sam had his APC maneuvered to near the break in the hill where they could almost instantly respond to any sallies from the settlement. Meanwhile, the big six-wheel-drive Kraz towed their captured tank to a reasonably level spot in the lee of the hill where it could begin its bombardment. Tal, the former (and very short-time) tanker, was hunched in the cramped turret of the T-72, cranking in the compass bearing fed to him by a second set of spotters they now had on top of the near hill. As soon as he was ready and had raised the barrel to what he hoped was somewhere near the right elevation, he signaled Sam.

Sam checked one more time with their forward spotters, again with the near spotters on the hilltop, and gave him the go-ahead.

Tal gave the elevation wheel one more bit for good measure, checked his breech, signaled his loader to clear, and pulled the firing trigger. He could see nothing but sky in the clear optical sights. The laser sighting system was not working, but laser sighting would be almost useless in an over the horizon shot like this anyway. The long cannon barrel erupted in a cloud of smoke and belched flame. Tal remembered why he hated tanking. His ears were ringing in spite of the padded headphone / earmuffs. The tank intercom was fried, but the earphones worked moderately well for ear protection. He felt claustrophobic in the hot steel turret even though they were working with both hatches wide open. However, he and his loader selected another high explosive shell and eased it into the breech while they waited for their spotters' report. Too far by a good half kilometer, and bring it half a degree right, came the report. Tal cranked in the corrections and fired again. The turret was engulfed in eye stinging smoke again. A faint breeze seemed to be blowing most of it back into their faces. "Hit." came the spotters' report. "Another quarter degree right, same elevation."

"*Mama minim*, this is baby *minim*, they're buying it!" came the excited message from their spotters. Tal fired again, feeling the visceral boom and recoil as if he were part of the big cannon. Another hit. This time the spotters told him to shorten the range a bit and come back left a half, they were going to try to hit one of the perimeter machine guns. Three more shells with minimal corrections between them brought the cheer of a direct hit, and another piece of good news, the APC had pulled out with a string of five trucks and two jeeps. He was directed to chance a shell two degrees higher and three degrees farther right to follow them with his fire.

A miss, but a satisfying increase in the speed of the last jeep, his spotters reported.

Sam and his sergeant pounded each other on the backs of their flak jackets and cheered. "One APC, let's go get the bastards," Sam yelled to his driver, and getting on the radio, he told the radio man in the Kraz to send Woody and his recon men after him.

They hung on as their APC roared to life and tore off in pursuit, angling off across the field to regain the highway and try to overtake the fleeing column. If they could eliminate the enemy APC, the rest of the trucks and jeeps would be sitting ducks for their powerful twin machine guns. Turning to check behind him, he saw Woody bouncing through the meadow in their wake, Roee clinging to the machine gun, four other recon men hanging on in the back, and Ronny and a rifleman driving. They would probably pass him when they reached the road, for their truck could reach highway speeds, while the low-geared APC topped out at about 60 kph.

Looking back at his fleeing prey, Sam quickly saw that the enemy APC was aware of the threat and was maneuvering to place itself between the trucks and the oncoming Israelis. These guys are professional soldiers, Sam concluded once again. He warned himself against getting too cocky. The APC, as he recalled from the previous night's battle, was armed with a 20 mm rapid fire cannon, just as deadly as his pair of .50 caliber machine guns. It was much more than a match for the little 7.62 pop gun he had mounted on Woody. Unfortunately, no one in Woody had a radio, so he would have to rely on hand signals. As they approached the highway, he signaled Ronny to keep Woody behind the cover of his APC as best he could, and so the pickup truck fell in behind him when they reached the highway.

The Azerbaijani company gained the main road about a kilometer north of them, and Sam's gunner tried a burst of machine gun fire aimed high and long. It was well wide of the mark, and soon fell short too as the retreating column accelerated. Sam's APC soon reached its top speed on the highway, and within minutes it became clear that they were not going to catch up. The newer model Soviet APC was pulling away gradually, and its test bursts of 20mm cannon fire tore up chunks of pavement a few dozen meters ahead of them.

"Fine," Sam yelled. "We pursue two or three kilometers and turn back. We haven't scouted anything north of that, and I don't want to charge right into a trap," he yelled at his sergeant.

Sam got on his radio and told the group behind of the situation. He made arrangements for a group to scout the settlement, being wary of booby traps, and to tow the tank in. As an afterthought, he told the scouts to go in accompanied by their fake tank, to flush any ambushes.

Eli was stretching his back by draping his head and shoulders over the big steering wheel of the tractor when the word came for him to pull around the hill and head slowly for the settlement. The two and a half ton truck followed in his wake. When they neared the point where they would be in sight of the settlement, he was instructed to wait while a squad climbed down from the truck and fanned out in a skirmish line to approach the settlement. For good measure, Sgt. Minkov decided their real tank should lob a fresh round at the near side of the community using an antipersonnel round to discourage snipers. Eli could see Nir back up at the top of their hilltop where the two snipers had fought the night's attack on the settlement. Another soldier had Eli's sniper rifle out, and he felt a tinge of possessiveness. However, he had to admire the group's handiwork surrounding him on the tractor. The box like structure that turned his liberated tractor into an ersatz tank was really a solid piece of work. The mud job seemed to have stayed on too.

None of their precautions proved necessary. The settlement was quite deserted and still fairly intact in spite of being shelled twice, once by mortars and once by their captured tank gun. After triple checking for booby traps, Eli and a group of the religious soldiers gathered in the undamaged synagogue, whose two Torah scrolls were intact and apparently untouched. Perhaps these invaders knew the market value of an undamaged Torah scroll (about $50,000 and up for a good quality scroll) and had decided not to destroy them. Or perhaps they just thought they were pretty.

The group had three sets of *lulavim* and *etrogim* among them. Since it was still morning, they soon had a makeshift service going in the liberated little *Shul*.

Sam came back as they were wrapping up *Shacharit* and beginning *Hallel*. He looked in approvingly and disappeared back outside. Eli was swaying as much with exhaustion as with religious feeling by the time they reached the final few prayers. He took off his *tallit* and folded it neatly in the small bag, thinking over their strange night and odd morning. Who would have thought that he would be praying in a real synagogue this morning, freshly vacated by a company of fierce mercenaries from somewhere around the Caspian Sea? And all this thanks to building a tank "float" for a thirty-minute parade? Where was he this time yesterday? Oh yes, waiting out a bombardment and air attack in an under-defended, Alamo-like hilltop with little chance of survival. Perhaps he should have put more *kavanah* into his *Hallel*!

Eli was one of the last ones out of the neat little synagogue, for he had to stop to marvel the collection of books untouched by the occupiers. It was quite a contrast to the completely trashed and vandalized *shul*s at Ramat HaGolan and Ramat Magshinim.

When he found Sam again he was sitting on a bench outside the community center, which was intact except for windows shot out in their attack. He was surprised to see Sam talking with a pair of dirty, ragged-looking children, perhaps aged seven or eight. Eli slung his pack and rifle down on an adjacent bench and tuned into their earnest conversation. Having just finished praying in Hebrew for the past hour and a bit, his brain began picking up their conversation fairly well.

The girl was nine, apparently somewhat older than her brother, but smaller. With no adults around, the two of them had been hiding out in the fields near the community for a week. Their father was somewhere in the army and their mother had been killed in the first night of rocket attacks. The children had run away to a hiding place in a haystack. When they came out the next morning, everyone in their community had left. They then spent the next week dodging around the edges of their former home. Eli's heart went out to them, so solemn and brave. He marveled at how they had kept their heads and taken care of each other. They had plenty of water from the irrigation systems for the vineyards. She described how they had eaten handfuls of ripe wheat, figs, which grew in abundance, various greens. They had even crept into a henhouse near the edge of the community to steal eggs a few nights. Since all the dogs had been killed by the soldiers, it was easy to sneak around at night, they said.

Soon Sam had raised the Northern Command operators on Mt. Meron and had them looking for the children's father and an uncle. Sam sent the children into the community center for the lunch that was being cooked up on its gas stoves by some of his more culinary-minded soldiers. He stretched, noticed Eli listening to the children's stories, and ambled over to give him a slap on the shoulder.

"Your fake tank worked like a charm, along with about a dozen shells from the real one. We're going to leave it here, parked under some trees near the perimeter to discourage marauders. By the time we finish lunch, there should be a platoon or two of volunteers here to take over the community while we carry on north. My bike patrol is about ten K north of here. They say smooth sailing for that next bit of our sweep."

Eli shouldered his pack and rifle and clumped after him to the welcome smells emanating from the kibbutz dining room. Someone was frying up onions, herbs and vegetables with a heavenly aroma. There was now a spread of crackers, cheeses, jars of pickled herring and various pickles and condiments scrounged from the still reasonably cool walk-in coolers of the kibbutz. Eli set his pack on a chair next to him and went to work on putting together a plate of food to take outside to the undamaged sukkah. He wondered what the occupiers had thought of the oddly decorated shelter.

An hour later they were heading north again. Lined out along the rural highway, the APC went first, followed by Woody, then the Kraz towing their disabled tank, which kept the speed of the column to about 20 kilometers an hour. Eli was napping in the back of the two and a half ton truck with the other "old guys" when something woke him and he began to notice the signs of fear and apprehension growing in the men around him. He was too sleepy to catch their rapid remarks in Hebrew, but soon heard what was throwing them into a panic: there was the steady choppeta choppeta choppeta of oncoming helicopters not far away!

Eli stood up to look around and get his bearings. They were spread out on a barren and lonesome stretch of highway that ran steadily northward on a section of high plateau. There was absolutely no cover to be had. But the truck was pulling off the road anyway for the benefit of whatever protection the berm of the road offered. The older kibbutzniks and Josh Cohen were now diving off the tailgate and scattering in the ditch along the highway. Eli was about to jump after them, but his leg was asleep and his foot tangled in the webbing of someone's pack. He fell sprawling on the jumble of packs and gear in the back of the truck. By the time he had unhooked his foot and begun to pull himself to his feet, the first of a flight of dark, menacing helicopters was in plain sight. Eli froze, not knowing what to do.

He could not take his eyes off the oncoming V of half a dozen darkly camouflaged attack helicopters. They could easily be firing by now, but they weren't. Could they be Israeli? Eli heard someone, probably Sam, shouting into a radio nearby in the ditch. Clearly, the helicopters were checking them out, for they passed quite close and wheeled around for another pass. Eli thought a minute. If they were Israelis, what did his group look like from the air? A Soviet tank, a transport and an APC, accompanied by a pair of non-descript trucks. They had no way of identifying themselves. Their only hope was to somehow relay a message through one of the command groups in Tzfat or Mt. Meron in the next three seconds before these helicopters unleashed their awesome firepower.

"Arbeh minim, Arbeh minim, Highway 938 north of Ramat HaBashan, Call off the helicopters! Over!"

Arbeh minim, the four species. Eli could see the long pointy cluster of a palm branch sticking out of one of the older men's pack right in his face. He drew it out and reached in the pocket where he has seen the *etrog* stashed earlier. Taking the palm branch bundle and the big yellow *etrog* in his hands, he stood up in the bed of the truck and started waving them like crazy at the lead helicopter, which had just completed its leisurely banking turn. It was now coming in lower with a serious rake to its menacing dark body like a wasp about to sting.

"Scorpion leader, we have some idiot waving some vegetables at us from the back of the truck," the pilot at the point of the Apache patrol radioed. "Holding fire, might be a surrender, over"

"Scorpion Three, this is Scorpion One. You need to go back to primary school, over"

"Why is that Scorpion One?" the first pilot asked.

"Scorpion Three, those are *arbeh minim*: palm branch, myrtle, willow and an *etrog*. Over."

"Scorpion One, how am I supposed to know that at five hundred meters? Over."

"Scorpion Three, It's still *Sukkot, chag sameach*, over."

"Copy that, Scorpion One, I told you the haredim were going to take over the Golan, over."

"Scorpion Three, you need a whack on the back of the helmet. Over."

"Copy that Scorp One."

Kiryat Yonah 1300

News of the strange and deadly green gas had obviously reached Kiryat Yonah. It took only a few moments from the starting up of the agricultural sprayer before the Syrians were pouring out of Kiryat Yonah as fast as they could travel. Major David Engel had left a company of reservists back at Ramat HaBashan to clear any booby traps and secure the ruined community. Now he had to send at least two platoons into this small agricultural kibbutz that commanded another hilltop near the Syrian border. By the time he reached the real resistance in the Israeli Arab towns farther north on his sweep of the border, he would be running low on manpower. However, Natan's fake nerve gas idea was certainly working – even better than expected. And, if Ramat HaBashan was any indication, the enemy was clearing out too fast to even set much in the way of booby traps or last minute sabotage. He prayed that their clean sweep would continue.

Tom, the young journalist intern they had taken into their confidence with the background about the teargas with added colors, was eager to go back to Tiberias to file his story. But he was even more eager to see how the day played out. He wanted to cover the recapture of Mt. Hermon even more, so he stayed with Major Engel's command group. David could tell from the more thoughtful nature of the young man's questions, when they could be asked, that he had been thinking over his lecture on the dilemma of Israel's media relations in war time. However, he knew by now what the average desk editor did with any original stories sent in from the Middle East. Everything had to fit the black and white, politically correct stereotypes that passed for journalistic objectivity these days. He silently wished him luck in getting his story through.

Right now, David was more concerned with meeting up with the group of his armored forces he had sent ahead to secure the major road junction and small Israeli community at Ein Zivan. This was a particularly sensitive spot because it faced the large border town of Quneitra, which was on the Syrian side. The town served as the official gateway to Syria. It had a large UN presence in peacetime. David was wondering if any UN peacekeeping officers would emerge from the ruins and try to broker some kind of ceasefire. He and his government were not interested in a ceasefire until all of Israel was back in Israeli hands, and the armies that had poured across their borders were sufficiently crushed not to be a threat for many years to come. That was not going to happen any time soon, he felt.

Still, some UN presence could prove useful, such as in setting up prisoner exchanges or perhaps arranging for a peaceful withdrawal from Arab occupied Israel. He laughed ironically at that thought.

But, what preyed on his mind was the advisability of using their colored tear gas strategy anywhere near a large population center, like Quneitra, where it could set off a dangerous panic. He called the captain he had placed in charge of his advance armor group.

"*Gimmel* One, this is Machete, over"

Good, his captain was now in direct radio range. "Go ahead Machete."

"*Gimmel* One, it's past lunch time and you have all the sandwiches, when do you get here, over.

"Machete, no bread for sandwiches, but we got some great green soup, you want some?"

"Negative *Gimmel* One, too spicy for me.

"Machete, how's the view at the upper picnic grounds?"

"Clear weather, no mosquitoes, and the ants have all gone home for a nap," Machete replied.

"Glad to hear it. Be there within the hour," David replied and signed off.

The last bit meant that his advance team had retaken the two steep hills packed with bunkers and communications towers that stood back a little way from the Israeli side of the border. That was a relief, for even a small force dug in on those two landmark hills would have been a very tough obstacle.

He called his command group together to make final plans for securing their string of three small communities further, and for assuring their tenuous supply lines. David's small counteroffensive had cut directly across the path of the Syrian advance of the previous day. If the mass of Syrian troops ever decided to turn around, their pitiful few thousand men and women would be cut off.

He also got an update from the commanders who were facing the fairly substantial blocking force left the Syrians had left behind on the their side of the border. He was relieved to hear that they were staying put and not threatening a break through anywhere. The IDF was spread dangerously thin. Even with substantial numbers of armed volunteers from the Golani communities and elsewhere, there were not enough people to watch every inch of the border.

He heard good news of the Israeli attack to retake Katzrin, the largest community in the Golan. The local volunteers had practically led the charge and had quickly swept the once-overrun town clear of looters and Syrian rearguard forces. The shooting had been over by mid-morning. A sizeable number of surrendering Syrians and their irregular mercenaries were now safely incarcerated in the town's middle school playground. If the UN observers wanted to make themselves useful, they could find some way to ship all these unwanted invaders home.

Less than an hour later, David, riding in his trusty *Gimmel* One with *Gimmel* Two on his flank still towing the sprayer rig, spotted Machete's tank group waiting at the base of the nearest of the two hills near the Ein Zivan junction. He was happy to count them and find the group intact so far. However, as they drew closer, he was not so happy to see a pair of baby blue helmets bobbing in the back of one of Machete's armored half tracks. Sasha drew up next to Machete's newer Merkava IV for a turret to turret talk between the commanders. The drivers as well as the gunners and the loaders exchanged news too.

Machete was a forty-something reservist captain that David knew well from training sessions in the Golan as well as staff refresher courses. He gave a quick but glowing report of their surprise flanking attack that caught the defenders of both hilltops off guard and unprepared. They had captured a number of officers and an extensive amount of communications equipment and computers that might tell their experts back at Mt. Meron just what kind of capabilities the Syrians had in the field at the moment. There could well be the possibility of valuable codes and passwords. The two of them debated how to get a truckload of the equipment safely through the fast-changing battlefields to their command and intelligence groups based on the distant mountain. "I think there might be safer going tonight if all goes well," David said, "So let's just wrap them up and put something together for the evening dispatches. Helicopter might be an option too. We had one quick sweep of Apaches this afternoon. There should also be some Chinooks available within the next day or two."

Machete climbed stiffly out of his turret and came over to sit on the edge of David's command hatch. The two of them studied a laminated map of the terrain ahead. There was one more small Israeli community before they reached the first of several small agricultural towns that were mostly Druze and Israeli Arab. The Druze would mostly welcome them. The Israeli Arabs would present a mixed picture. Some would be quietly relieved to see law and order and some semblance of an economy restored with the return of the Israelis. But they could never not say so without becoming the target of a drive-by shooting or an unfortunate accident in the near future. Others would be resigned to whatever fate came their way, for all they cared about was who would pay them for the next crate of apples they picked. And some would be mighty disappointed not to become citizens of Syria. This last group and the young hot heads, who had soaked up jihadist rhetoric since their kindergarten days, might pose a serious threat of dangerous guerilla warfare.

David described the effects of "gassing" the two towns liberated earlier that morning, and the two debated the wisdom of staying with the tactic.

They were inclined not to use the gas, especially with two UN officers noisily demanding their attention from the not so distant halftrack.

"I guess I'd better acknowledge the representatives of the United Nations and see what they want," David said wearily.

"All yours," Machete grinned.

David was surprised to find that one of the baby blues he had thought from a distance was an Indian officer was, in fact a woman captain from the Nepalese elite mountain rangers, who spoke a very correct, but charmingly accented English. The other blue helmet belonged to an apoplectic colonel from Poland who demanded a vehicle and a satellite phone to be put at their disposal immediately.

"Colonel," David said as calmly as he could manage. "See this little radio? I have exactly five of them to command this group of 1,000 men. And as for vehicles, I could not in all conscience give my own mother a skateboard if I had one. I'm sorry; I am in no position to help you with your request."

The Colonel blustered on for awhile, but eventually ran out of steam. In the meantime, David and the Nepalese captain quietly sized each other up. When the Colonel finally ran down for a few moments to catch his breath, David directed him over to the supply truck where he had parked Tom the young journalist, promising that Tom knew of a satellite phone and might help him find it again.

With the Colonel gone, David spoke to the short, compact Nepalese captain. "Do you know the borderlines up on Mt. Hermon?" He asked her.

"Yes, I've done a lot of time in that sector, how did you know?"

David wanted to say, "Nepal – mountains ..." but he held his automatic reply in check, and just said, "Lucky, I guess. I need someone who has a clear idea of where the lines are."

"Are you going up there?" she asked, looking mildly impressed.

"Hope to by tonight," David said.

"What's this I hear about nerve gas," she suddenly said, looking at him intently.

"I see misinformation travels fast, even with no phones. It's tear gas, with a little color added," David said, deciding to be absolutely straight with her.

"How can I be sure of that?" she asked, looking at him keenly.

"Two ways," David said simply. "Our apparatus is right over there behind that tank with the short treads, *Gimmel* Two, and you can ask our chemist who thought of the idea. And two, you can go see that AP intern if your Colonel friend hasn't dragged him off to Tiberius yet. We gave him a demonstration beforehand, and he watched everything and took pictures and notes."

The captain opted for seeing the sprayer and talking with Natan, so David introduced them and slipped away to continue his planning for the next hop northwards. He was also at a road junction that led directly west towards where his friend Sam was working the small country roads behind the border. He had tried to raise Sam on the radio earlier, and had left word with the communications group in Tzfat to notify him the next time Sam came online.

In the Air over Mt. Hermon 1300

Sam gazed out of the nose of the rapidly climbing helicopter, still stunned to be aboard instead of shot to pieces by its rapid fire cannons. His tiny group of vehicles quickly vanished in the crazily tilting landscape and soon the Apache was climbing with a gut wrenching acceleration towards the bank of smoky cloud that shrouded the base of Mt. Hermon. Sam hung on to his hard-earned lunch, but just barely. In a moment they were through the layer of cloud and emerging again in bright sunlight. The pilots had dark aviators' goggles, but Sam was temporarily blinded by the blazing light. Beside him, straining at the harness in his jump seat, was the silver-haired Barak Saguri, wild and wide-eyed as if he was preparing to take back the whole mountain himself.

Not ten minutes before, Sam had been hugging the rocky earth in a shallow roadside ditch praying that the helicopters were both Israeli and not about to shoot them to smithereens before discovering they were also Israelis despite their unorthodox choice of vehicles. However, word had reached the commander of the helicopter group at almost the exact moment that their point pilot had spotted an older man waving a bundle of palm, myrtle and willow branches at them and had taken his thumb off the firing button. Now the three helicopter group was tasked with taking him and his local guide, the infamous '67 war hero Barak Saguri, on a quick reconnaissance tour of the 2,800 meter tall mountain. They were expected to be one of the first teams to reach its base and begin securing it again for Israel.

The helicopters flew straight for the huge mountain until Sam, gripping the back of the pilot's seat in front of him, was sure they were going to crash into the mountainside. But, at the last minute, they veered off, the horizon tilting crazily, until they were skimming along not far above treetop level. Their nearness to the ground made their speed seem reckless, although Sam could tell from the easing of the throttle and the pitch of the engine that they had actually slowed down. His eyes would not make his brain believe it.

Barak Seguri, confused for only moment by their sudden shift in perspective and direction, resumed his running commentary of their progress up the mountain. "Now we should be crossing the access road real soon, there it is, looks deserted... We're dropping over the shoulder towards the Syrian side now, careful, there are some spotter posts up ahead, could have machine guns.... There's one over there! Man do they look surprised!" The helicopter behind them sprayed the scattering Syrian soldiers with cannon fire as the three dark shapes whirled overhead. The three choppers spun at full tilt down a deep ravine that split the mountain, "This must be the landslide track from the seventies," Barak announced. "Yeah, you can still see tree trunks pinned in the debris fan down there. Wow it was a big one! I've never seen this side of the mountain from the air. Impressive. What are you doing, coming up on Shemesh from the Syrian side? Good idea, their guns will all be pointed the other way. Here she comes. Oooh ah! What a ride!"

The three dark shadows raced over the jumbled town and Sam, Barak, the pilots and crews all tried to take in as much information as possible on their fast flyover. There was comparatively little action on the sleepy mountain town streets below them. They could see a large number of houses shattered by gunfire, but very few military vehicles around.

Their whirling tour continued on up the mountain. Soon they circled the ruins of Nimrod's fortress, rebuilt as recently as Crusader and then Ottoman times. They passed low over a cluster of lodges and guest houses, which included Josh Cohen's Nimrod Lodge. It looked relatively intact, but had a cluster of jeeps and cars parked outside as if it were being used for a headquarters. Following Barak's directions, their ship took the lead and the three choppers zigzagged up the mountain, checking various border strong points, potential road blocks, and of course, the ski lodge where he ran his ski and snowcat rental business. It was buttoned up tight, except for perhaps a platoon of startled looking soldiers surprised in the act of setting up a communications tower, which they quickly knocked out with a small bomblet. From there the choppers shot skyward and scouted the maze of ridges that radiated from the summit slopes. Here and there they drew anti-aircraft or machine gun fire, carefully noted the location, and maneuvered around to hit the installations from their blind side. Sam was impressed to see how well the three worked together, with a minimum of chatter over the radios. They rounded off their tour with a high speed pass of the backside of the mountain, traversing Syrian territory, to look at the supply roads and infrastructure dug into the Syrian and Lebanese sides of the mountain. They saw only small groups of soldiers and few armored vehicles. Sam hoped he was seeing everything, and not missing a battalion or two dug into deep bunkers waiting for the signal to come out.

Fifteen minutes later, having flown down at dizzying treetop level, this time scanning the complete length of the main access road, Sam and Barak hopped out safely, but still swaying, on the ground by their column. Their group had advanced less than a kilometer in the meantime. "Time to get back to tank hunting. It's a real duck shoot back over on *Kvish* 85," the pilot said. "Good luck, see you from the top tomorrow afternoon, G-d willing."

Anna and her communications teams had no break from their headphones and computer monitors since early morning. Messages, requests and pleas poured through their overtaxed network, which still required all long-distance communications to be relayed once or even twice. Through this barrage of communications, they followed, bit by bit, the relentless press of the huge Syrian relief force as it blasted its way towards the stalled advance column. They were harassed the whole way by small, fast, hard-hitting IDF mobile forces stinging at their flanks; and by wholesale sweeps of helicopters and jet fighters whenever they could suppress the mobile anti-aircraft batteries enough to get through. The two forces began to merge about noon, and for the last two hours, they had surged forward in a combined, all-out attack down Highway 85 trying to reach the coast.

Against them was everything northern Israel could get to the scene. Fortunately that included a solid collection of field artillery and not a few tanks. Backed by Israel's growing air superiority, and with increasing numbers of aircraft coming into play almost hourly, the lines were holding. The Israelis have been forced to give a few kilometers of lightly defended open ground, but they were standing firm on the hillsides of the broad valley. It was all the command and supply groups could do to keep the supply of shells coming to the hot barrels of the big guns and to keep the waves of gunships from running into each other.

A little while ago, the air raiders reported hitting the last two antiaircraft batteries. Since then, air support had been able to hit at even closer range, with devastating effect. Anna could not even imagine the carnage that must be left on the killing fields, but she could tell it was beginning to sicken some of the pilots. They had stopped announcing their kills with anything like satisfaction, and were now reporting the hits with a grim efficiency. Anna was raised by avowed socialists, and had no religious upbringing at all beyond what one naturally learned in Israeli schools, but the slaughter was beginning to sound like a defeat of Biblical proportions.

For the past two hours, she had two of her Arab speakers working on getting through to Syrian High Command, or to any of the field commanders to urge surrender. If the Syrians were listening, they were not yet responding. So the pounding continued, slackening only as temporary shortages of bombs and ammunition slowed the deadly cycle. Their crippled depot system and shortage of transports was making it impossible to keep up with the demand.

The fighting was still brisk on the northern border with Lebanon. The sweep there was moving slowly, village to village. There was much work to do clearing snipers, entrenched bunkers and roving bands of guerillas from the hilly border country. The general in charge of that sweep had only advanced a dozen kilometers, but had been careful of his troops and equipment, and was doing a thorough job.

News from the northern part of the Jordan Valley still reported the main Jordanian force holed up in Nazareth and the various Israeli Arab villages. It looked perhaps if the Jordanian plan had shifted from conquest to perhaps some kind of annexation of as much adjacent territory as they could occupy. Israeli commanders wished they would come out from their civilian cover again and fight in the open, but it was beginning to look as if the IDF would have to go in after them. Going into built-up civilian areas full of noncombatants was the last thing the Israeli military wanted to do. For now they were content to wait until the Syrian and Lebanese threats were neutralized.

Then there was the problem of getting back Mt. Hermon. The afternoon's quick helicopter surveillance showed the mountain fairly lightly held. However, aerial surveillance could easily be wrong. She had a pair of satellite photo experts going over detailed pictures of the mountain from the last week, running time lapse images through their computers to see if any significant forces could be detected. So far the numbers of units overwhelming the mountain in the first two days of the war were nowhere to be seen. About half could be traced moving on to other fronts – such as joining the big southward push down the Hula Valley and the sweep down the Syrian-Israel border on day one. But somehow there still seemed to be at least a battalion or more unaccounted for. She hated to pull the precious helicopters off of their busy bombing missions. The massive invasion stalled in the heart of northern Israel was their largest concern. Right now, her priorities were stopping the main Syrian drive, cleaning up and sealing the Lebanese border, dealing with the Jordanians, and lastly, retaking Mt. Hermon. Of course, there were dozens of smaller concerns, and maintaining the flow of supplies equaled all of them.

Village of Najur 1500

General AlHanasrallah was only three or four kilometers from the tantalizingly lovely, red tile roofs of Carmiel, and even less from its rich industrial park at the foot of the hills along Highway 85. But he could only gaze longingly at the rich prize, and curse the lack of tank, anti-aircraft and artillery ammunition that kept it from his grasp for the past day. Worse, the local Arabs were not exactly being helpful – hiding food, not even sharing water if they could help it – all in the past day as the mighty conquering army that they had cheered two days ago had overstayed its welcome. Worse, from the local point of view, the conquerors had stopped conquering and now were acting as magnets for the worst sort of bombardment imaginable.

The general and what was left of his staff had retreated up the steep mountainside to a cave-like bunker that was serving as their command post. But, he could see very little to command; even with his high-powered binoculars. His entire force had dug into a handful of small Israeli Arab villages scattered along the valley, and were trying not to get blown up by the relentless Israeli air raids or their constant barrage of artillery. The generals in command of the first army to reach this wretched impasse were holed up in proper bunkers deep under the larger village of Beit Jan, a bone crunching jeep ride up and over the hillside, which would be quite suicidal now.

Even the day before, it had seemed so easy – join forces and smash through the stubborn Israeli defenses, overwhelming them with sheer numbers and firepower. For a few confused but heady hours, it had seemed possible. They were less than 25 kilometers from the seaside north of Haifa. There were only a few towns and little in the way of natural obstacles to stop them. Just a little more push, and they would have been through, rampaging their way to the lush coast and driving into Haifa. Once there, they could have fought their way house to house until the seaside port, perched on high hills around the harbor, would have been Syrian.

But no, it was the same story as the first day of the war. For the first hours he had ridden near the front of an invincible force, with armor so deep that it made hours-long traffic jams getting through the border crossings. So many cannons and long range guns, and backed with short range missiles that it seemed nothing could stand before their onslaught. But, somehow his front line had ground to a halt along a stubborn line of small settlements. Jews were stubborn by nature, and Jewish settlers even more so. And once the first wave had failed to push past the curtain of fire – feeble by the standards of today's barrage – he could have swept the whole Golan free of Jews and marched into Tiberias at the head of a victorious army. Now look at them, cowering in holes and caves, down to their last few rounds of ammunition, and waiting for the end.

It couldn't end this way. It was impossible. A jet passed low, dumping another load of high explosives where the some of the last of his tanks were dug in and covered with what dirt and camouflage they could find. Finished.

As if they were reading his dark thoughts, his staff stayed at the back of the cave and kept out of his way.

There was no way out. He could not retreat. His way back was blocked by a phalanx of Israeli tanks and guns that had snapped at his heels all the fifty kilometers or so from the Syrian border. Their numbers had grown from a nuisance to a real menace. Ahead were more IDF regulars, at least a full division or more. He had tried to break through to the south to the larger Israeli Arab town of Sakhnin, which was often a hotbed of Palestinian unrest. However, that assault had been met with stiff resistance and beaten back. He also tried to move northwards, over the mountain and through the hill country to reach the relative safety of the Lebanese border only a couple dozen kilometers to the north. However, his force was too broken up to make any progress in that direction. Had he gone that way twenty four hours ago, there would have been little to stop him. Now the armored noose was closing in that direction too. Damn the Israelis!

He heard the Israelis on the radio for the past hour, urging surrender and an immediate cease fire – but that was not an option. He could never surrender. It was not the way of his family of desert warriors. However, his wife's family, that was another story. There was his rotten brother-in-law safely in charge of the blocking force back at the Israeli border. He was sitting snug and fat on the Syrian side of the border and doing nothing with the 30,000 men at his command to keep the supply route open to the invading heroes? Less than nothing! A few days ago a small Israeli tank force had decimated a supply train practically within view of the border. What had that slinking dog done? Nothing! A few measly tanks – one armored patrol could have stopped them! By Mohammed's beard, he would have to fix that slithering snake of a brother-in-law. If those supply trucks had made it though, he would still have anti-aircraft cover. He would have shells for his tanks and shells for his artillery. He would have taken Carmiel and driven on to Haifa! The plan would have worked. It was all that miserable snake's fault!

At least now he knew what to do. He stalked over to the radio set and glared at the operator. "Get me through to Damascus. I need a secure private channel to the Minister of Finance!"

Map of Mt. Hermon

Google Earth map of Mt. Hermon with the vertical relief exaggerated 3X showing the fictitious Nimrod Lodge and route climbed on the eighth day.

Mas'ada Junction 1720

When Sam's motorcycle scouts reached Mas'ada Junction near the base of Mt. Hermon, they found a jeep with a few soldiers waiting for them This was a surprise because they had expected to arrive at the rendezvous first, having heard that Major Engel's column was running into difficulties with the large Arab and Druze town of Buq'ata a few kilometers down the road. Their radio communications had been spotty for the last several hours. However, by the time they sped back down their lesser-used country road to rejoin Sam's group, he had heard the news via the radio.

"Heck of a war where the commanders are telling the scouts the news," they grumbled. The motorcyclists were tired and sore from riding back and forth with little rest since the previous evening. Sam was cheered by the news that Buq'ata and perhaps the larger town of Majdal EsShemes – or Shemesh in Hebrew, was back in Israeli hands thanks to the ingenious invention of the gunner in Major Engel's tank group: green tear gas, delivered in a menacing cloud from a borrowed agricultural insecticide sprayer towed by a tank. Whatever worked, thank G-d. There would be no house-to-house fighting to clear these two border towns.

Now Sam had to play catch up. He decided they would leave their broken Soviet-built T-72 with the small garrison left by the road junction, to be towed into the nearest workshop to be fixed when possible. Their towed tank had served its purpose now, routing a moshav full of Azerbaijani infantry and helping chase a small garrison out of a tiny hamlet that lay along their route. He consulted briefly with David Engel on the radio. The road was clear at least as far as Shemesh. After that, his recon unit would probably be given a sector of the mountain to clear, on foot whenever the roads became impassable.

They changed drivers around at the junction. Eli was happy to be back at the wheel of Woody and not bouncing around the back of the smaller transport truck. He had collected a new set of bruises to add to his collection of foxhole black and blues. There were also the barbed wire scars on his hands and forearms, scraped knees and elbows from crawling around in the dirt at night, and some nasty cuts on his face from flying bits of rock and concrete from the bombardment of Ramat HaGolan. If this war went on much longer, he would need a new set of skin. He could still feel an aching, tender spot on his left hip where he had first fallen, pack, rifle and all, against an unforgiving Golani rock when one of the first missiles of the war exploded not far away. It seemed like both yesterday and forever ago at the same time.

Fortunately, he had caught up on a little sleep since finishing up his fake tank project that morning, for his sniper services were not needed for the second community after the initial reconnoiter. But he was sure Sam had not slept a wink since taking over command of their group more than 24 hours ago.

Eli was happy hear the report of a clear road to the next rendezvous and to see that at least this part of the Mt. Hermon road still looked the same. There was nothing to shell for a long way until they reached Shemesh. His new companion, Josh Cohen, the mountain lodge owner, was also getting to ride up front, squished in the middle, with Ronny snoozing at the window. There was a motley collection of soldiers in the back, some sleeping, others alert and taking in the beautiful mountain scenery in the golden hour before sunset. It was truly magnificent. They were now bringing up the rear of Sam's odd convoy. Sam was up front in the APC, followed by the Kraz, now loaded with as many soldiers as it could carry, followed by the loaded smaller truck. With the two motorcycle scouts' bikes piled in the back of the two and a half ton transport, there was less room for people, but somehow everyone managed. All who could sleep were sleeping in spite of the golden rays of late afternoon sun. They knew there was a night ahead of who knows what. Perhaps fire fights, perhaps a counter attack, perhaps moving up the mountain in the cover of darkness. Sam had not had an opportunity to brief anyone since is talk with Major Engel. Chances were that he really would know nothing for certain until they got to the jumping off point, wherever that was.

Every now and then, Eli could see a pair of APCs chugging up the road far behind them, visible whenever the turns in the road revealed a long stretch in the rear view mirror. Word was that Shemesh was secure, or soon would be, depending on who you listened to, Josh or Ronny. Eli hoped it was secure already. He did not relish trying to shoot after dark, especially with his dwindling number of rounds. No one they had encountered in the past few days had 7 mm magnum ammunition, so he and Nir had perhaps forty rounds apiece. Hardly worth carrying an awkward, long, five-kilogram rifle for that.

Eli downshifted and looked for a way around the upcoming shell crater. The truck in front of him had gone right, so he looked for a promising line in that direction. It meant easing partly into the edges of the hole to squeeze by a big tree stump, so he slowed way down so as not to dump his passengers in the shallow crater. It was the first shell hole in awhile, which meant there must be something coming up to be a target for shelling. Sure enough, he could soon see the outskirts of Shemesh, a few shell shattered houses. He recalled they had once sold tourist goods. As he slowed down, he began to hear the now-familiar sound of cannon fire, tanks if his ears were tuned in correctly. But how far was hard to tell because the sound was rolling off the shoulders of the mountain and echoing. The firing was slow, and not very intense, perhaps a shell every minute or two.

He drove on a few minutes more. Josh was quiet and listening to the cannon fire too. Outgoing, was his opinion. Eli concurred. It was odd how one learned such things almost unconsciously. He would be hard pressed to explain to anyone how he knew the shells were outgoing. Perhaps there was some kind of Doppler shift in the sound that receded. Whatever it was, his ears and brain had worked it out days ago. Outgoing meant that the Israelis were probably the ones who were doing the shelling this time, which was good.

They were entering the hodge podge streets of Shemesh now. Like any mountain town, roads ran where they could, following contours or climbing crazily and zigzagging up and down slopes. After a few turns, they arrived at a large parking lot in the lee of a big, partly bombed building that looked like some sort of government office. There were a handful of trucks, APCs and a pair of tanks parked in its relative shelter from the Syrian side of the border. Sam had pulled up next to a Merkava that looked familiar. *Gimmel* One, Eli read the now filthy white lettering on the back – it was his old friend Captain Engel. No wait, it was now Major Engel. Eli would have to go over and congratulate him if he got the chance. He pulled in next to Sam's APC, leaving room for them to back out in a hurry if needed. Since everyone else, except for a couple sleepers in the back, jumped out and began milling around the commander's tank, Eli put the parking brake on and climbed out to join them, hoping to get in a quick mazel tov to the new major. He didn't see Major Engel in his usual spot in the turret of his tank, but he quickly spotted him sitting at a big folding table someone had dragged out of the building. He was studying maps with a gaggle of officer types. He heard someone farther down the wall of the building shouting "*Mincha, Mincha!*" and saw a *minyan* of soldiers gathering, using the window ledge of a ground floor window as schtender to hold a prayer book for the leader. Eli reached for his pocket *siddur* and went to join them. Sam would figure out where to find him if he needed him.

A moment before the leader started, Eli saw Major David Engel and his Sephardi sergeant in charge of the other tank disengage themselves from the table and come to join the prayer group. The sun was close to setting completely. There were about thirty men gathered for the *minyan*. Even Sam came over to join them. Eli saw Josh standing around uncomfortably over by the trucks. Although Josh kept strictly kosher in his lodge, and identified as Jewish to the core, he was basically a secular guy who saw kosher as a marketing edge, not a way of life. Odd mix. As he was finishing up the *Shemona Esrei*, Eli noticed an awkward young man, looking too clean to be a soldier, wearing a photographer's vest and high tech hiking boots. He was snapping a picture of the *minyan* with a disposable film box camera. Very odd. He also noticed both Sam and David Engel saying the mourners' *Kaddish* prayer for the dead. Perhaps he should be saying it too, for who knows how many friends had been lost. But as far as he knew, Naomi and his daughters and grandson and grand-daughters were all alive, *Baruch HaShem*. Perhaps they were saying it for Yankel or one of the other men they had lost, since it was impossible to notify families who would take over the remembrance.

As the *minyan* broke up, he saw his chance to get to David Engel. "Mazel tov, Major Engel," he said, reaching out his hand.

"Eli, I should have known Sam would schlep you up here!" David said, lighting up in a brief smile. He started to move on in the phalanx of soldiers and officers vying for his attention, but stopped, as if struck by a sudden thought. "Hey, I have a job for you too, if it's ok with Sam," he said, casting a sidelong glance at Sam, who paused to listen. "You see that guy with the instant cameras over there – he's an AP intern reporter looking for stories. Why don't you let him ride with you up to the lodges and tell him about some of your adventures with Sam?" Sam grinned and shrugged. He knew he had just had something foisted on him, but it seemed harmless for now. There was no way that the guy could go where they were going past the end of the road.

The gaggle of officers and information seekers moved in the reddening sunset back to the table with the maps. David called over a man that Eli recognized as Sasha, his tank driver. After a few moments, Sasha extracted himself from the knot of people around the table and collared the reporter in the photographers' vest, and steered him over to Eli.

Sasha was smiling broadly as he introduced Tom, the AP reporter. He was effusive enough so that Eli knew he was glad to see the young man go. Oh well, what harm could this guy be? Eli did not know any state secrets to spill. "This is man who make boat cross Kinneret in night to get shell for tanks and big guns. We see him drive in middle firefight. We have three shells left. We very happy to see him and brown truck. Then Syrian tanks come and tries to blow him up, but truck falls in hole and everybody safe – shells too. We kill two tanks, have one shell left and go take more from truck that fall in hole.

"Amazing man this Eli, builds bomb-shelter house himself, makes goodest steak in whole Golan, makes truck himself that run on smoke – no kidding. You ride with him, ask him all about it." Sasha beamed.

Moshav Yiftach 1950

Natalie was cleaning up the dishes because Tali had done all the cooking that night. Joan was taking care of their wounded soldiers as usual; changing dressings, turning over bed linens to get extra mileage between washings, and emptying the makeshift bedpan for the Major, who was still unable to move around much due to his extensive internal injuries. Tali had done all the cooking that night because Natalie was tired, uninspired, and worried. Her brain could not picture a meal out of the odd collection of ingredients that faced her a few hours ago, so she had swapped chores with Tali, who managed a couscous and vegetable concoction that made a credible and tasty meal. She worried that another sundown had come and gone with no Eli, and no real word of Eli except that he was off somewhere with Sam. Being with Sam generally meant being in the thick of whatever was going on, or about to go on. That didn't feel like a very safe place for a 58-almost-59-year-old, semi-retired, business communications consultant.

Natalie was fast coming to hold the opinion that wars should be fought exclusively by young people… a thought she knew was inexcusable and indefensible. It was her generation's mistakes that had let this war happen, no reason to burden only the younger generation with it.

However, looking at it another way, perhaps it was a young people's war – in that more than half the population of Egypt and Syria were under 21. What did they know about Jews or Israel, except as an outlet for their discontent? The past decade had been hard for their Arabic speaking neighbors, made worse by incompetent leaders.

At least Israel had an economy that worked to the extent that there was a world economy for it to work within. At least Israel educated its young people and had built one of the world's most caring, compassionate societies despite its spiny Sabra personality. At least Israel had been trying to do something besides burn fossil fuels until they ran out completely.

She peered out the window and could see the shadows of two young men taking turns filling buckets and water cans from their garden well. That was actually a bonus feature of the lot they chose, and like everything in their hand built house, it reminded her of Eli. He had discovered an old iron pipe buried in a corner of their garden was a fifty-foot-deep test well that had been sunk nearly a generation earlier. He had looked up the well logs, no small feat for someone who could barely read modern Hebrew, and convinced the moshav council to let him use it on the quiet for irrigating his little garden. Eli had it tested a few times and found that it was indeed drinkable – if needed. In fact, it had a lower bacteria count than the municipal water system.

The town's two deep wells were struggling to keep up with demand since the moshav's water tower had been blown to bits in the first morning of the war. One pump had burned out, and the second was not running very well on their generator power. So people in the northern half of the town had been relying on the Kaplan's garden well for their washing water. Pairs of young men had been taking turns pumping and filling for most of the afternoon, and were now back at it working into the evening. They were perhaps just catching up to the evening wash-up rush. She herself had used a bucket or two on the night's dishes, toilet flushing and cleanup chores. They and most of their neighbors were also filtering it for their own drinking purposes.

She sighed and rinsed the last of the cups. She missed Eli right now. There was so much going on as the war swept back and forth across the Golan. She checked the little windup clock they kept in the kitchen. It was time for the eight o'clock news on Tali's radio.

Tali was dozing in an armchair in the living room, so Natalie moved the radio to the other end of the room and turned it on. She just caught the tail end of what must have been the lead story, something about a massive battle that stopped the Syrian advance somewhere outside of Carmiel. A lot of the place names were not familiar, but she pictured the broad valley hemmed in by steep hills on both sides. It sounded like quite a blood bath despite the announcer's calm description of the events. She prayed that Eli was nowhere near that mess. Closer to home, there were reports of a string of border moshavim and kibbutzim to the north being recaptured, which cheered her considerably. Perhaps Eli was somewhere up there. She knew that Sam worked for Colonel Eschol, and the colonel was assigned to their sector of the Golan. Perhaps her husband was not so far away. She wished the brave, patriotic and thoughtful idiot would be careful tonight.

The rest of the news was taken up with the slow motion drive to sweep the invaders from the south of the country. There were too many of them by far, and they were giving up ground slowly. Even Israel's miraculously recovering air force was not moving them along much faster. They could not be everywhere at once. There was also news of the cities, food rationing, water systems damaged and people standing lines for water, like the pump outside her kitchen window only more so. Transportation was for emergencies, the war effort and essential supplies only. She wondered how Rivka and the kids were managing in Jerusalem. They had little stocked up in their small, overpriced apartment, but at least they had a bit of a shared garden with a fig tree and a pomegranate. Figs were still ripe, at least in the Golan, did the season end earlier for Jerusalem? She couldn't remember. "Oh don't be silly," she scolded herself, "there was no way they were down to eating figs, they were in the middle of the holiest city in the world – there had to be food to eat at least, even if they had to carry water in buckets from a tap somewhere." It was summer, there would be no rains for a few weeks or even months yet. Still, they would manage. She could count on Rivka to make do.

To take her mind off worrying about Rivka and the grandkids, she decided it was time to go see the patients in their spare bedroom. The moshav had finally arranged transportation for the poor tanker with the badly burned arms. A speedboat took him across the Kinneret as soon as it was safe enough to transport wounded without fear of shelling from the north side of the lake. The south end of the lake was still problematic, but the Jordanians had been less dangerous since the IAF had showed up. They limited themselves mostly to sniping and firing the occasional wildly inaccurate artillery shell at boats speeding across. The northern end of the lake was safe enough from snipers, and the chance of an artillery shell hitting one of the small boats was slim. Natalie was sad to see him go, for she knew he would not get the same personal attention in the overcrowded hospital as he did in her home. But of course there was more they could do for his severe burns, and she heard that some reconstructive surgery might be possible.

In his place, the Kaplan home had taken in Captain Chaim Tzippori, the pilot accidentally found by Sam and her husband – except that she was too religious to believe in pure accidents. The pilot had soon learned that her husband had found him where he lay in a goat pasture the other side of the Syrian border. He let her know how grateful he was by being a model patient – something that was rare in Israeli soldiers in general, and pilots in particular. He had given up smoking in flight school years ago, but still had the fidgety habits of a smoker, so he got good at eating sunflower seeds – so much that it was getting hard to keep him supplied. Captain Tzippori had few recollections of the mission that had sent him over the border in the first minutes of the war, except that he had hit his target. He remembered only floating through the night sky in a daze, and waking up to pain and sun, and making friends with a goat. He declared fervently that he was going to join his uncle's kibbutz and love goats for the rest of his life, because he knew with his severely broken leg and arm that he would never fly again – walk someday soon, G-d willing, but not fly, at least not fly a jet.

Eli was getting sleepy waiting for Sam's assault team to send the all-clear after their attack on the Nimrod Lodge. It was owned by his companion from earlier in the day, Josh Cohen. Josh, Barak Saguri and another of the "old timers" had gone with the attack groups, because of their intimate knowledge of the lodge and the area, and their more extensive military training. Eli had felt left out and left behind. But he had to admit that his night vision was not what it should be, and that he was dog tired after a wearing week of fighting and driving around at all hours of the day and night. He had no place in a nighttime commando-style raid. Besides, he was babysitting the reporter, who had plied him with question after question ever since Major Engel had handed him off to Eli at Shemesh.

Tom was a good interviewer, Eli realized, once his awkward veneer of self-importance and complete ignorance of most things Israeli had opened a bit to reveal an open curiosity and a sincere desire to hear another's story. In their stop-and-start trip up the mountain from Shemesh to the scenic overview where they were parked, the AP intern had heard Eli's story in various pieces from the first hours of the war. He heard about the desperate fight to keep Yiftach from being overrun, about his pre-dawn kayak trip across the Kinneret, and about the ammunition ferries and pack train up the Golan Heights. He had listened to Eli's matter-of-fact account of driving shells into the battle for the Southern Golan, and heard his second-hand accounts of what he knew about Major Engel's escape with two other tanks from the trip wire force. He had learned of Eli and Sam's "spy" mission into Syria, and of Sam's demolition of the bunkers that ended the threat of attack helicopters. He heard about their finding the downed IAF pilot and how he had dressed his own wounds and survived on goat's milk until Eli and Sam found him. He even managed to hear a bit about Eli's family, his life before the war, the story of helping find arms for the moshav, and about Eli's hand-built house. Tom declared that he really wanted to visit the moshav sometime. And he had insisted on examining the wood burning alternate fuel system, including a tour under the hood of the dual/fuel carburetor system that could switch from wood gas to gasoline with the flip of a lever. They had been running on wood fuels since Shemesh, mostly to conserve gas, and since downed wood was plentiful. Tom had helped cut deadwood branches to replenish their wood supply, and had kept the low key questions coming, just enough to keep Eli talking.

Eli had described the incident with the suicide bomber planted among the wounded, as well as of burying the war dead, both Israeli and Arab. He had told him of the final hours of Yankel's life, as he and Major Engel had nearly destroyed the Syrian supply column until being driven off by superior firepower from the rear guard of the tank columns. Eli told Tom of the tearful funeral for Yankel and his gunner, the painful injuries and courage of the one surviving member of Yankel's crew. He told him of the long and close friendship between the tankers, and indeed, of all the long-standing reserve units who fought and trained together over the years. Tom had not fully appreciated the extent to which the reserves were more than half of the Israeli army in war time. He learned that nearly all able-bodied Israelis served in the IDF and that annual reserve duty was as much a part of Israeli life as vacation and taxes.

It had now been more than an hour since they had heard the short bursts of gunfire coming from the vicinity of the lodge, and still no word on the success or failure of the attack. The transport truck was parked nearby, and the two pickets posted nearby were fighting to stay awake in the cool night air of the mountainside. The rest of their group was sacked out in the back of the two trucks.

"So, how do you think it will all end?" Tom asked sleepily. He too was wearing down.

Eli thought about all they had discussed, and all he knew about the progress of the war. He had a somewhat broader view in the last few days since they had discovered the lone Israeli radio channel. And working near Sam and his radios had added to his knowledge of the overall picture. At the moment, it was beginning to look almost positive. The massive Syrian advance and relief effort was stalled some few dozen kilometers away. The helicopter pilots had told of the round the clock bombardment of the holed up Syrian advance columns, and word of their pounding had filtered out to the rest of the group after Sam and Barak came back from their flying trip around the mountain. Eli had few doubts that Sam's crack recon team and volunteers would quickly blow any opposition out of the Nimrod Lodge. The only question was how much of Josh's precious lodge would be left standing when they were done. Eli was pretty sure that Sam would spare as much of the luxury lodge as he could without risking his men.

Eli summarized these thoughts with Tom, in a slightly disjointed order. "How will it all end? There is only one way we can let it end at this point – and that is that all the invading armies, looters and mercenaries are driven completely out of Israel. There will be no stopping until the last one is over the border. We won't pursue them any farther than we need to. Israel does not want one square inch of ground that was not ours in the first place. You can quote me on that one," he said.

Tom gave him a tired smile and put away his notebook at last. "I believe I will," he said. "You have been through a lot in the past week. I should shut up and let you sleep."

However, sleep was not destined to happen for either of them, for a few minutes later they heard the buzz of one of their motorcycle scouts zipping back from the direction of the lodge. The two sentries shook themselves awake and prepared to challenge it, but recognized the rider immediately in spite of the dark. The helmet with the long *peyot* flapping in the wind could only be their yeshiva friend back with the news.

"What took you so damned long?" the soldiers left with the transport truck were demanding while firing questions at him a mile a minute as the young yeshiva student killed his engine. He pulled off his helmet, shaking out his long hair and letting his *peyot* flap. Someone offered him a water bottle, along with three or four more questions, and all waited while he glugged the better part of a liter and got stiffly off his bike, which he been riding almost continuously since the previous night. Everyone sat him down and crowded around. Eli noticed that the reporter still had an American concept of personal space, for he sat somewhat apart from the dense pack jammed around the weary messenger.

"Piece of cake," he grinned.

"Then what took so long?" demanded several at once.

"A bunch of them ran off into the woods and we had to track all of them down before we could be sure we had everyone. The owner of the lodge knew just where most of them would run, so we surrounded them in one neat sweep and they surrendered. We have about fifteen officers locked up in the walk-in cooler. Too bad it was empty though. Not a drop of beer, wine or whiskey left in the whole place. The owner said he had about $60,000 of wine, beer and liquor in stock, plus about another $10 grand in food – all gone, damn their greedy little hides."

Eli translated the gist of it for Tom, who scribbled in his notebook.

"The place is completely trashed, but at least they didn't burn it down or blow it up. Hardly a window left. The bar is all shot up – not by us – and the bedrooms are shredded. Hardly anything left. They carried off most of the beds, chairs, tables, lamps. All the art is gone, except the Jewish stuff, which they ripped up and shot at. Josh was heartsick."

His audience wanted to know more about how the attack went. The scout told them how they had burst in simultaneously in three teams: ground floor, second floor and kitchen, driving the startled officers out into the parking lot where most of them were caught. Only three had been shot in the fast moving raid, the rest captured, most of them unarmed. The Syrians had been using the lodge as an officers' quarters. The group had captured some maps and communications equipment that could prove valuable. In fact, the radio expert in their group was using it to reach Mt. Meron and Jerusalem direct, and was studying their voice scrambling setups to see if they could be decoded.

"Wait," he said, "it's even better than that. There's a pair of working satellite phones! Natan tried one and got hold of his cousins in Los Angeles. Sam figures that as long as we don't blab any important military information, we can all make free calls on Uncle Bashar's phones until they get smart enough to turn them off. Or perhaps they'll figure out how to use them to target a smart bomb. For that reason he had us make all our calls from a guest cabin a couple hundred meters down the road. I couldn't reach any of my yeshiva friends on either coast, but they would be learning right now."

Tom perked up with that news as Eli passed along the tidbit.

They all piled back into the two trucks, and moments later were pulling up to the bullet scarred sign for the lodge. The "o's" in the English half of the Nimrod Lodge sign showed evidence of extensive and poorly aimed target practice.

Tom hurried off to find the two satellite phones, and Eli walked stiffly into the shambles of the main lodge dining room in search of Sam. He found him upstairs in what must have been Josh's office, which at least had the desk and a few chairs intact. Sam was studying a stack of maps with his sergeants and other interested parties.

Josh was slumped in a large armchair looking dazed and at least ten years older. "I'm going to rebuild," he said to Eli, "it's really not as bad as it looks, mostly glass and trim... the structure is sound.." he said, encouraging himself. But he didn't look encouraged.

"What's next?" Eli asked Sam when he caught his attention from the maps. Sam gave him a weary, welcoming grin.

"Sleep," he said, "Four hours worth, then we are off an hour and a half before dawn to climb our sector of the mountain. You can stay here if you want, I don't want Natalie saying I forced you to go up a 2,800 meter mountain."

"I've climbed it twice – once in summer and once in winter – and a whole lot of mountains higher and tougher, although none lately," Eli said. So if you want me along, I'll try not to slow you down."

"OK Daniel Boone, bring your squirrel rifle and we'll see you at 4 am. And look here, I finally got myself a watch, at least until I can return it to the colonel's widow in Syria. Genuine Rolex."

"Nice," Eli said. "Where do we sleep?"

"I have my guys sleeping out in the woods across the road to the east of the lodge. Password tonight is "*Senir*" one of the old names for Mt. Hermon from the *Tanach*. It means snow in Aramaic or some such language.

"*Senir*," Eli repeated, "I'll try not to pull a Colonel Marcus," he said, recalling the American who had volunteered to train Israel's Palmach until shot by a young sentry for not knowing the Hebrew password.

"With your American accent, I think they would give you a second chance... besides you smell like wood smoke, how's old Woody running up at this altitude?"

"Pretty good, but I can feel about a ten or twenty percent power loss when pulling uphill with a load."

"Would you mind if Josh borrowed Woody tomorrow morning while we're up the mountain? He wants to pick up his wife."

"No problem. Hey, is it true about the satellite phones?"

"You bet, I called my cousins in New York and left a message. You want to call your daughter in Chicago?"

"Can I really? You don't believe that stuff about targeting a phone with a smart bomb?

"Oh, it can be done. We did it all the time to nail bad guys in Gaza, and even Beirut. But is Syria capable of putting something that sophisticated in the air right now after the EMP and the pounding they have been taking from the IAF? I doubt it. And besides, we hit them so clean and fast, they don't know we're here yet. There are half a dozen ladies locked up in the cooler with the big shots, and most of the brass is in there with no pants."

Eli snorted at the mental image. "Too bad the refrigeration system doesn't work, they could use some cooling off."

Sam chuckled and went back to his maps, and Eli got directions from Josh how to find the guest cabin with the two hard-working phones. He walked down the neatly trimmed garden path while trying to remember his daughter's phone number. The trouble with cell phones and speed dials was that nobody remembered a number these days. Well, at least he could call directory assistance for free.

Ramat HaHovav Airfield, the Negev 2000

Major Yossi Green fidgeted in the soft, executive style briefing chair, eyeing his fellow pilots and navigators. There were to be sixteen planes on this mission, nearly half of Israel's airworthy fighter jets. Twelve of them would be F-16s toting one 2500 kilogram bunker busting bomb each, designed to penetrate up to three meters of reinforced concrete or ten meters of earth. The remaining four would be Yossi's group of F-15 pilots flying with a mixed load of tactical missiles for air to air combat to protect the group, and air to ground to take out any anti-aircraft batteries causing trouble for their mission. There were expected to be both. Even their worst case scenarios had more than twice the number of aircraft for one target, and this mission was aimed at two.

He forced his attention back to the *Ramat Kal* (Commander in Chief) of the Air Force, who was tapping the map again pointing out their targets one more time. First up was the heavy water nuclear reactor and plutonium production facility at Arak, about 200 kilometers southwest of Tehran. Since the majority of the site was above ground, only four bomb loads had been earmarked for its reactor dome, cooling towers and central control facilities. Their goal was to create enough damage to take if off line for a few years, but not enough to create a danger of radioactive spills. After hitting this target 1,400 kilometers away, the four bomb-free F-16s would then be flying light enough to join the antiaircraft fire suppression efforts for the second target, some 200 kilometers deeper into Iran.

The plutonium fuel enrichment plant at Qom was buried under a mountain just beyond the huge Natanz uranium enrichment facility. It had remained secret for more than a decade before being revealed to the world in 2009 as the US and UN pressured Iraq to come clean on its nuclear fuel capabilities. Eight of the big bunker busters were slated to shake rattle and roll the deep rock entrances to the secret facility and collapse enough of the mountain that it too would be off line for at least a decade. Two of the big bruisers actually weighed in at 3000 kilos, about the maximum load for an F-16 full of enough fuel for the long trip.

The only good news was that the havoc they had wreaked against the Jordanian air force and air defenses over the past week allowed them to fly the most direct route to their targets – straight over Jordan. They would then fly straight across Iraq, which fortunately had not rebuilt much of an air force since the US pullout. Then they would blow straight on into Iran for a good 350 kilometers more before reaching their first target. The US Air Force was confident enough of Iraqi airspace, having owned it for years even after the pullout, that they promised a trio of K-130 tankers, protected by a squadron or two of F-15s, to refuel them enroute both going and coming home. That made a major difference in their projected fuel loads, and enabled them to slip in a few tactical missiles each.

However, the part of the whole mission that rankled Yossi was that the Americans – who were threatened by Iran's nuclear capabilities just as much as Israel, in terms of the economic fallout, were offering fuel, but no help where the going was tough. "Too delicate a geo-political situation," in the words of the *Ramat Kal*. Their logic was that, since Israel was already in over their collective heads, the Yankee fly boys could stay dry on the riverbank and watch. Bullshit. This was everyone's mission. The bloody UN should have stopped this nonsense decades ago, but nothing had been done. Hundreds of bureaucrats and diplomats had wined and dined and debated in venues from Geneva to Stockholm, and every five star hotel in between, and peace had blown up in their faces last week. Now they were probably wringing their hands and wondering when the next opportunity for a fancy dress summit might emerge from the ashes.

Somewhere over Jordan

Major Green was still climbing to reach the high altitude flight path the mission planners had calculated would give them maximum speed with their heavy bomb loads. At least his bird was relatively light. Though carrying a full load of fuel and a pair of discardable wing tanks, he had only a rack of air to air missiles bristling from the wings of his F-15, with a few air-to-ground visually targeted arrows in his quiver for taking out pesky radar or SAM sites in the way. He was flying top cover, a good fifteen hundred meters above the heavily laden F-16s. He had watched their pregnant profiles while climbing past them to his station above and ahead. Each of them carried a huge, bunker-busting mega bomb of at least 2,000 kilos slung from their bellies. Their take off roll must have been all the way to the end of the extra-long runway to get airborne in the still-hot desert night.

Even now, almost twenty minutes later, his cockpit was just beginning to lose the last of the heat of the desert night and assume the chill of high altitude flying that would be with him for the next few hours until they dropped down for their low, ground-hugging approach to the final target. He unrolled his mental map from the countless briefings and simulated missions. This was the real thing, though, and that was the real Jordan unrolling in the pale quarter moonlight below him, not a virtual one. Somewhere another thousand kilometers ahead, slightly under two hours flight time with a refueling pause, was their first stop, the heavy water nuclear reactor at Arak. It was not their main target however. Their job at Arak was simply to hit it hard enough to make sure it stayed off line for a good number of years. A minor hit on the reactor dome, knock out a few cooling towers, a direct hit on any of the associated plutonium processing facilities would be enough to cripple any nuclear weapons program for a few years at least.

Their main target was buried in a mountain another 150 kilometers farther east: a secret plutonium enrichment and weapons trigger making facility that was discovered by international observers only a few years previously – although it had obviously been there for at least a decade. This was the wild card that had enabled Iran to build a much larger and more advanced nuclear arsenal than anyone had suspected. Israel had prepared for a conventional nuclear standoff, but not a crippling electronic first strike. They had been under the mistaken opinion that Iran's obviously aggressive nuclear program was based more on big nukes than the EMP-producing weapons that had hit seven days ago. Breaking open this sprawling and well buried complex, much of it deep under a fair-sized mountain, would be difficult, but not impossible. There is no way that even the biggest bunker buster could destroy the deepest recesses of the mountain where the nuclear trigger facility was no doubt buried, but they did have reasonably good intelligence on four very active entrance complexes, and two more that showed sporadic use. If they could hit the openings of all of the entrances with the powerful, delayed-shockwave bombs, their assault could collapse hundreds of meters of tunnel. With luck, it could fill the deepest tunnels with enough debris, smoke and dust to isolate and ruin much of the high-tech equipment. For good measure, there was discussion of a second strike in a week after observing satellite intelligence closely to see where the focal points of activity were forming in the aftermath of their visit this morning.

His altimeter now read 10,000 meters, time to level off and boogie. He appreciated the calm, reassuring voice of the AWAC controller confirming his altitude, speed and heading, as well as the news of clear skies ahead. It was a relief to have eyes in the sky again after a week of flying blind. Clear skies, in this case, meant clear of Jordanian jets as well as dirty weather. He checked the position of his wingman and the other pair of eagles flying top cover, and glanced at the two formations of F-16s winging their heavily laden way below and behind him. *Kol b'seder*. He enjoyed the wide open night sky spread out before him. Cassiopeia was bright overhead and in front of him in the clear desert air. Behind him he could catch Ursa Major setting; the great bear would have set by the time they reached the Iranian border.

"Eagle One, I have an update on your pitstop."

"Go ahead K-bear."

"Eagle One, come about four more degrees south to a new heading 097. Juice will be served in 40 minutes."

"Thanks K-bear, not even thirsty yet, but a guy can always use a cold drink in this heat, good to have you back."

"Likewise Eagle One, have a nice visit."

Day Eight

Approaching the Iraq – Iran Border 0045

Less than five minutes after refueling, K-bear informed Major Green that there were interceptors vectoring in on his course from the Saudi border. Their speed and altitude could only mean one thing, fellow F-15s, of which the Royal Saudi Air Force had plenty. And, of course, K-bear's antique radar could not rule out the possibility of the remaining four of the F-35 stealth fighters sneaking along in their wake. Yossi informed his squadron, even though he knew they were all tuned in to the same channel. He wanted them all wide awake and focused on the incoming information and orders.

"What's the current intercept point?" he asked, switching his heads up visor view to a large scale tactical screen.

"It's hard to plot at the moment; they're making a long arc through Iraqi airspace, and appear to be trying to run past just south of your course. Unless they slow down, that puts them right over target one. They should get there about five minutes before you do, plus or minus a minute or two," was the reply from the AWAC gathering the data from its parking figure-eight loop in the sky a few hundred kilometers behind them roughly straddling the Jordan – Iraq border. There were a pair of F-16s keeping that track clear of any interference, and so far none had been offered.

"How many?"

"At least six, maybe eight."

Yossi concentrated a few moments on the display showing the remaining distance to their first target, the heavy water reactor complex at Arak. Possibly if he and his small group of F-15s could head off the interceptors well to the south of their projected flight plan, the F-16s could take out the first target without his help. However, that meant taking on eight hostile aircraft that were nearly identical to his own craft with his group of four. That made roughly even odds in his book, but they were now more than 1,000 kilometers from home, and any Israeli pilot who had to bail out over either Iraq or Iran could look forward to captivity, possible torture, guaranteed mistreatment, and the probability of many years or even a lifetime in a very ugly prison.

He seriously doubted that Iran had any fighter defense left to challenge them if it had not shown up already. And anything that Iran had to put in the air would be definitely less of a threat than the American-built fighters streaking towards him from Saudi Arabia. Given their speed, the Saudis were obviously running on afterburners and nearly full throttle – close to Mach 2.4 compared to the sedate and fuel-conserving Mach .8 of his attack group at the moment. He weighed the options for a few moments, a very few. The clock was ticking.

Hitting the targets on the ground was their main priority and would buy them a nuclear-free neighborhood for at least a few years if the strategy jocks were right. That much made perfect sense to Yossi. And there were enough F-16s to deal with what was left of Iran's mostly blinded air defense system. Therefore, the only answer was to try to head the Saudi interceptors off at the pass, tying up all of them for long enough for the F-16s to hit Arak and keep going to their next target.

"K-Bear, give me an intercept time and bearing to head them off south of the target if we vector off in about five minutes and rev up to about Mach 2.6. Falcon leaders, let's throttle up to 1.5 now and break some windows downstairs for the next five minutes. Prepare to blow a little chaff and drop to the deck on my signal. We split south; you stay on course and drop off their radar. Got it?"

His plan would take everyone closer to the target while flying higher and faster than planned, cutting the time he had for intercepting the Saudis, but getting his F-16s to the target faster. Releasing a cloud of chaff should confuse the Saudi's tactical radars long enough to cover the splitting up of their groups. He expected that the F-16 groups low-flying final approach to the target would be hard to track.

"Eagle One, our friends have an AWAC too. I can see it near the edge of the Gulf. Your friends will have to go down to 100 meters or less to keep them blind."

"Copy that K-Bear, you hear that my Falcon friends?" There was a checking in of affirmatives.

Yossi sped up, but dropped back in the multi-layered formation so that he was over the main body of F-16s now flying less than 1,000 meters below him. From time to time he tapped his chaff release control to let a sprinkling of the highly radar-reflective metal foil bits fly off in a thin stream behind him. He hoped it would have the desired effect of beginning to confuse the Saudi AWAC and tactical radars of the incoming fighters. He told Uri and a pair of the lead F-16s to do likewise.

"OK Eagle One, I have an intercept course. They're now running almost parallel to you and 100 K south, closing at an angle. Their speed is down to Mach 2.2 but, still on track to reach Target One three minutes ahead unless they try to pick up your tail."

"We'll see what we can do about that. What's my time and turn?"

"Time is two minute. Turn on a heading of 135 degrees. Switch on the afterburners and speed up to Mach 2.6. The hostiles' altitude is 9,000 meters and steady. We now confirm eight planes in the pack. You should reach them about 40 K southwest of the target."

Forty kilometers at Mach 2.6 meant only about one minute of flying time, it was cutting it mighty close. "When do the falcons show up?" he asked.

"Falcons should be on target four minutes after you." That meant he had perhaps one pass at the Saudis before the lower and slower strike force of F-16s arrived.

"What's our plan big guy?" Yair asked. Yair and Yoni were his other pair of Eagle pilots, Yair as Eagle Three and Yoni as Eagle Four, his wingman. He knew that Uri, his own long-time wingman, was dying to ask the same question, but never would. He always let Yossi pick the plays unless he had something new to suggest.

"What do you think of a quick slap and slide?" Yossi suggested,

"I can do that, give me the specs."

"Slap one AMRAAM at 15 kilometers and go high. I want to draw them up to 15,000 meters or better if possible so there is less chance of them noticing our friends creeping along the deck. Then we both slide right and flip around, going higher and faster. If they don't budge from their course, we're on their tail in seconds."

"Slap and slide right and upstairs, right behind you."

The F-16 group had gone to radio silence ahead of their split, coming up in less than a minute. Yossi forced himself to review the target area map and check the tactical screens which were now showing the Saudis ahead and south of his path. They were on a direct course for the target and had not veered or slowed to engage the Israeli planes. That seemed very odd. There must have been some loose lips on the American side. It was like someone had deliberately handed the Saudis their whole flight plan. But why had they made a plan to meet up over the target area? Was it to make some obscure political or propaganda point to the Iranians? There was little love lost between the other two most powerful nations in the region. The politics and strategy didn't figure, but eight F-15s going nearly two and a half times the speed of sound was something he could handle, if he was lucky, very lucky.

Yossi took a few calming breaths and prepared for the hard banking, climbing turn, reminding himself to dump a couple seconds worth of chaff. He heard the time signal beep from the AWAC, ten seconds to the turn and split. "On my mark, turn to 135, climb to 15,000. Turn on the afterburners and power up to 2.6. Don't forget your chaff. Ready five, four, three, two, one Mark!"

Throttling up smoothly he powered into a climbing turn, spilling a few seconds worth of metal chaff and keeping half an eye on the tactical screen as he went. He engaged the fuel guzzling afterburners and felt the surge of power as they boosted his thrust to near redline levels. Within seconds, the bright blips of the F-16s were growing intermittent and blurred with the ghost echoes from the scattered chaff falling through the skies showing up in odd patches. He powered up and climbed with Uri right on his wing. Yair and Yoni were following slightly below and left of them. A few more seconds and he could see no sign of the sixteen F-16s that had dropped to the deck. The Saudi formation did not budge from its course. In fact, K-

Bear told him that they were descending to 7,000 meters. He watched his altimeter climb past 12,000 meters.

"Eagle One, I have a shimmy developing in a control surface. Powering back," he heard Yoni break in.

Damn. His airspeed indicator was not quite up to Mach 1.8. "Copy, chill down to what feels good," he ordered. He concentrated on dropping his speed to match the blip to his left on his area screen. Yoni was spilling speed while maintaining the rate of climb. They were now at 14,000 meters, but had dropped back to about Mach 1.2. That was bad news.

"I'm OK below 1.3 to 4," Yoni told the group. "Time for a plan B."

Yossi checked the flight of Saudis. He was now on a course to pass behind them, for they held steady to their now arrow-straight flight path. They had dropped another thousand meters and slowed to nearly Mach 2. It was almost as if they didn't know the Israelis were there. But how could that be, even in this FUBAR age of post-EMP electronics? They had an AWAC in the theater as well – a much newer one, he was sure, than the retired Royal Australian Air Force bird code named Koala Bear, or K-Bear for short, that was watching his back. And he had been using the radio often enough to alert them even if their radar was broken. Something didn't make sense.

"Yossi and Yoni, you slap, we slide. Fire two each, good spread. Eagle Two and I will try to pick up their trail." That would make the odds 8-2, because his other pair of Eagles would soon fall behind the fast moving action. His quick glance at the target area map showed the Saudis getting there in the next few minutes.

"Going high and right," he said, powering up rapidly and banking into a broad, climbing arc. Uri was right on his wing. In moments they had reached Mach 2.0. Yossi kept his throttle close to wide open and climbed to 16,000 meters at Mach 2.6 before leveling off. He was soon hurtling through the thin upper air at more than two and a half times the speed of sound, but it was smooth and easy, giving him no sense of the speed this far from the ground. He could almost see his fuel gauges dropping before his eyes at this rate of burn, but that was not a concern yet. He had to blow this group of eight Saudi F-15s apart and keep them from falling upon the bombing group streaking to the reactor target somewhere to the north of his new position.

The Saudi formation stayed tight and steady. His tactical readout showed they had dropped to about Mach 1.4 and were now down to under 4,000 meters and still descending, almost like a landing approach. What in the world was going on with them? Were they bait for a pair of stealth F-35s silently dropping in on his tail? There was no way of knowing.

Twenty seconds later he saw the alarm and new radar tracks showing that Yair and Yoni had fired their spread of four AMRAAM missiles at just under extreme range. Finally the two perfect diamond shaped formations of Saudi F-15s split. One diamond dropped towards the deck, spreading out into a ragged bunch of four blips, but the other maintained its shape and was arcing around to meet his new course. A few seconds later he heard Yair announce a hit. It must have been on one of the diving four, for the climbing diamond shape was a perfect foursome. He could read their game plan like an open book, slide in under and behind him. Well that was certainly NOT going to happen. He pointed his nose skyward towards the starry canopy above and went into a full power climb, chewing up the next few thousand meters of altitude quickly as he approached the operating ceiling of 20,000-plus meters. The Saudi formation was well below and behind him now. Feeling the powerful climb begin to fade, he flipped over and flew inverted at the top of a broad loop, trying to concentrate on his instruments and not the spinning landscape far below or the whirl of stars in the direction where "down" had been a few moments ago. He caught a glimpse of Uri flying nearly along side, also inverted. Counting to ten silently, he completed the loop and spiraled down in a thundering dive which should drop him, if his seat of the pants reckoning and instincts were correct, smack on the tails of the Saudi formation.

It took a few moments to reorient himself and check the relative positions. It appeared he was behind the flight of Saudis, but several kilometers farther behind than he had planned. He would now have to catch up to them, and they were already splitting and looping right and left. He decided to follow the right hand pair since they were closest to the target area, now less than a minute's flight time ahead.

"Holy camel! They just bombed the reactor!" came a startled cry from Yair, who must have followed the remaining three Saudis the target area.

"Who?" echoed K-Bear.

"The Saudis. They went straight in and dropped three big ones before we could catch up," Yair marveled.

"I have visual now, they're strafing the admin buildings – I see secondary explosions from a gas depot too. Ground fire is heating up – got to dodge."

What in the world could be going on? A staged show to make the Israelis think the reactor was out of action? But that was so convoluted and risky. Yossi could briefly imagine it as one of half a dozen possibilities that raced, only partly formed, through his mind as he concentrated on catching up to his zig-zagging pair of targets. A moment later he had a visual glimpse of his quarry as it jinked suddenly up and right. He could see distinctly that it was carrying some large heavy ordinance slung underneath that was cramping its maneuverability. How in the world had they flown at nearly Mach 2.5 with that kind of load? Yossi wondered as he veered for a possible shot.

As he relentlessly closed the gap with the desperately dodging plane, he noticed something even odder than its bomb load as he almost overran his target and had to throttle way back to regain his trailing pursuit,. He caught a glimpse of the blue and white Star of David and IAF markings – very well done – on its tail and wings. However, its by-the-book combat style and lack of a confirming coded transponder, as well as its flight path from the Saudi border gave away the charade. He squeezed off an air-to-air, visually guided missile and tried to keep the target firmly in sight. But the Saudi pilot finally tried something more radical and he momentarily lost contact in a cloud of smoke flares and chaff. When he found his prey again, it was weaving too much for a visually guided bird, so he launched a radar-homing AMRAAM, which could close on the target at a blistering Mach 4. At this range he had about a 50% chance of a kill.

Somehow the Saudi pilot shook the AMRAAM too, and for a few moments he threatened to maneuver in behind Yossi. A burst of cannon fire from Uri, his wingman, convinced the Saudi pilot to try something else at the last second. He dived for the deck and Yossi followed, keeping a discreet distance and waiting for another good shot. Suddenly, he noticed the familiar – from endless drills – cooling towers of the Arak reactor in the spinning moonlit landscape. His quarry leveled out at a few thousand meters and accelerated straight for the complex – clearly he wanted to be rid of his heavy bomb, which was slowing his craft down enough to give Yossi a distinct edge. Yossi could have tried another AMRAAM, but he held his fire on a wondering hunch. Sure enough, he saw guided smart bombs drop and ignite from beneath both the Saudi planes and they immediately split into much more aggressive turns. He followed the right hand plane, sensing a weaker wing man than the leader to the left. The planes were accelerating much faster now, free of the drag of their bombs. In fact, both Saudi planes were showing an uncommon amount of acceleration. Perhaps Saudi oil money had found a way to soup up the F-15 engine beyond known limits. In a few seconds it was now obvious that these Israeli Air Force painted imposters had a distinct power edge on Yossi's bird. Within two minutes, it was equally clear that the Saudis were heading for home, and a few minutes later they were out of range. Pursuit was worthless.

"Eagle One, do you have that on film?" K-Bear inquired.

"Affirmative," Yossi sighed. At least they had some good data for the computer and aviation nerds to dissect.

"Good, 'cause otherwise I wouldn't believe it," K-Bear said.

"What do you see on the ground?" Yossi asked, checking his screen to make sure the Saudis were not coming back for more fun and games.

The IAF had managed to get a very long-range, unmanned, slow and high flying recon drone over the target area and had been watching it for nearly an hour before the jets showed up.

"Damage appears to be real, four good hits and collateral damage to fuel and admin. Big Bird wants you to drop down for a look and to take care of the AA batteries on the western side if you can."

"On it," Yossi said, checking one more time on the retreating blips still showing on his tactical theater view. "Let me know if any more company comes this way K-Bear."

"Skies are still clearing," K-Bear confirmed.

Yossi wondered afresh at what his group had just witnessed, and the recon drone had confirmed. The seven remaining Saudi planes had bombed the older, heavy water "experimental" reactor at Arak, ending for them as well the threat of a quickly re-armed Iran. They had gone in at nearly the exact same time as the Israelis, with planes painted to fool anyone noticing them into thinking they were also Israelis. Very clever, cowardly, but clever. Well, Israel, since statehood had taken the rap for everything that went wrong for anybody in the old Middle East. It seemed like the pattern was going to remain unchanged in the new Post EMP era.

Yossi took a fast, high pass over the complex, slicing across the southwest corner at an angle to see what batteries were tracking or firing at him. He knew that the recon drone's handlers back in the AWAC would also be watching and could tell him what he needed to hit on the next pass. He tried to concentrate on taking in all the information he could, but his brain was buzzing with wonder and questions over the Saudi strike that had left craters and cracked open buildings in the familiar complex spinning by below him. He took a long leisurely loop to turn around, made sure of the location of his other pair of Eagles, and got his targeting information from K-Bear. It seems there was a SAM site about a kilometer southwest of the reactor vessel that showed signs of radar life. The drone's controllers had spotted a pair of truck-mounted AA missile launchers farther along the western perimeter about a half a kilometer from the SAMs. The SAMs would warrant a missile each from Yossi and Uri. The trucks they would hit on a low strafing pass, too low and close for their battery of rapid firing missiles to lock on and fire.

"Ready, approaching on a heading of 350 degrees, coming true north and dropping down to hit the truck mounts," he cued Uri. He heard a syllable of confirmation, something like a "yo." Yossi checked his air to ground missile firing switches again, chose one and armed it. He glanced at the status of his 20 mm cannon, took in speed, altitude and attitude readings, flexed his hands on the controls a few times and plunged into his dive for a low and fast approach. Uri followed like a shadow. As soon as he had radar lock he fired his air to ground, seeing a flash go by to his right as Uri fired too. In a mere moment he was straightening his course to due north and peering into the onrushing scene to see where these two trucks were hiding. It took him a moment to spot them, tipped off by the frantic rush of men running away from one of the vehicles, and the movement of the rack of multiple launcher tubes on the other. He adjusted his course, dropped lower and readied his finger on the cannon trigger and waited for the moment. In another second he fired and watched the arc of shells streaming away towards the truck that was attempting to lower its launch tubes enough to fire at him. Microseconds later he caught the truck square in his optical sights before it disappeared beneath his speeding plane. He swung low and fast, climbing to make a hard banking turn for a second pass. "Nice shooting," he heard from K-Bear a few seconds later as the high altitude TV cameras on the drone zeroed in for the damage assessment. "Go back for the empty one now. Have your wing stay high and watch for secondary targets."

"Copy that, Uri?" Yossi asked his wingman. He heard a reassuring affirmative grunt in response from his wingman who was still in the last moments of a moderate G-force turn. Lining up for another low pass, he took his time approaching, dropping his speed enough to get a good run over the abandoned truck, and was gratified to see a burst of flame from some hits. He sensed that there was ground fire coming from somewhere and decided to flip up and power away skyward.

"Boss, you're trailing some smoke off the right wingtip," Uri told him. Yossi checked and saw a hint of smoke from one of his two disposable wing tanks. Something had hit his spare fuel. However, to fly even, he needed to jettison both. Too bad, he had not touched the fuel in either of those tanks yet. Yossi released the safety switches and announced that he was preparing to drop both wing tanks. On three he released them both, feeling a miniscule surge in air speed with the decreased drag and weight. Unfortunately, losing his wing tanks at this stage meant that he absolutely had to refuel on the return trip in order to make it anywhere near home. Any glitch in their rendezvous with the USAF tanker over Iraq would mean a long walk home. With the wing tanks he could have theoretically made it home if he turned back just short of the next target.

The four F-15s regrouped high and south of the reactor complex and compared notes while they waited for the bomb damage assessments. Yoni and Yair had been hitting air defenses on the east side of the complex while Yossi and Uri had worked over the western side. "Yoni, any more flutter out of that control surface?" Yossi asked, trying to assess everyone's status. Everyone had already heard his announcement about dropping the wing tanks.

"I feel something just a touch odd when banking hard and right, I'm thinking a slight loosening along one of the trim tabs, or else a bird strike," Yoni said, "Yair hasn't been able to get a visual on anything though."

"I might have to send you home," Yossi said. "You and Yair climb upstairs to about 5,000 and keep an eye on that thing. Our falcons should be showing up very soon. K-Bear, how long until falcon time?"

"*B'seder*, see you upstairs."

Yossi could tell that Yoni was disappointed to miss the rest of the flight. It would leave them with only three highly maneuverable birds armed for air to air combat for the most critical part of their mission – hitting the hardened nuclear fuel processing plant another 150 kilometers away.

"Eagle One, what's your assessment of Eagle Three?" K-Bear asked.

"These things generally get worse, and never get better. I think I'll be sending him home – anyone from falcon force need to go back?"

"Eagle One, we are thinking of sending one bird with some instrument problems home. We have everyone slowed down while the big boys look at the Saudi strike again. Current wisdom is drop two big ones for insurance and send those two home to join the party up at Carmiel. We have two more SAMs showing signs of life to the north. What's E-3 got left on his rack?"

"Three air, three ground," Yoni replied.

"Copy that, Eagle One. Can we send E-3 to take out the SAM and save the rest of your surface ARMS for Qom?"

"Yoni, you OK with that? You have two friends for the homeward trip."

"On it. Give me the target info K-Bear."

Uri and Yossi powered up and away from their ground attack level and joined Yair upstairs at about 5,000 meters. They had grandstand seats to watch Yoni make text-book perfect bombing and strafing passes on the two doomed SAM sites. Two minutes later he joined them in their top patrol upstairs where they were all were treated to two more picture-perfect medium altitude bomb runs by the pair of F-16s. One of the big smart bombs hit near the main reactor vessel, and the other blew a huge hole in the largest fuel processing building on their target overlay maps. That should keep the facility off line for a good number of years.

Then they watched the two birds wheel and zero in on the still-intact cooling towers. A spread of air-to-ground missiles brought two out of the three hour-glass shaped towers crumbling halfway to the ground. Yossi and his F-15 group cheered their two F-16 companions and wagged their wings at them as they joined the party upstairs to wait for the bomb damage reports to be checked and double checked. The six pilots were treated to a spectacular high desert sunrise as they waited, leisurely checking their instruments, controls and responses, all the time keeping a close watch on their fuel. Without his wing tanks, Yossi realized that he was shaving it pretty fine to make it to Qom and back to the refueling rendezvous after all the extra air time over target plus his air-to-air maneuvers and their higher speed approach.

Five minutes later they got the all-clear from the Target One task group. Yossi's remaining three birds each took a moment to slide up alongside Yoni and give him a farewell wave, and watch him join the two now much lighter F-16s for the homeward trip. Then they sped skyward and eastwards in pursuit of the larger F-16 strike force that was winging its way towards Target Two.

Eli was breathing hard and had settled into a steady, determined trudge as they climbed up a rocky gully and worked their way higher and higher towards the tree line on the south side of Mt. Hermon. They had risen well before dawn and struck off on a faint trail that took them contouring around the well-wooded base of the massive peak. Sometime after about an hour's hiking they had crossed into the Syrian sector, denoted only by a pair of broken down, rusting barbed wire fences. They were now climbing towards their target for the morning: a Syrian observation bunker that commanded a large portion of one of the massive southern shoulders of the mountain. Eli was lagging well behind at this point, but the last man of their recon and reservist team was still in sight. There had been little danger of ambush in this fairly open scrub and rocky terrain since leaving the woods. They kept to the cover of a deep and brushy gully, which made the going slow at times as he had to thread through tangles of undergrowth. His long rifle kept getting snagged so many times that he had finally unslung it from his shoulder and was carrying it in one hand or the other as he puffed along.

Trudging upwards in the predawn cool, although he was sweating heavily at this point, the air was delightfully fresh on his overheated face. He noticed also that his eyes, which had been feeling dry and gritty and irritated for days since the beginning of the war, were now streaming with clear tears from the cool morning air, and were feeling fresh and clean after a night on the mountain above the layer of smoke and dust that lay at the lower elevations like a soupy sea at his feet. He paused to take his bearings and enjoy the view for just a moment, draining the first of his three water bottles for the day to replace the sweat that was pouring freely with their steady upwards climb. In the predawn light he could see most of northern Israel spread out below him. The Kinneret was veiled in a pool of smoke that had collected in the depression, much like the early morning mist that had engulfed him and Sam on their kayak expedition. Was it only a week ago? It seemed like two or three lifetimes at least. In that week his whole world had changed, and that of all Israel and its neighbors, who were now sunk in the bloodiest Middle Eastern war since the days when Iran and Iraq had slugged it out for eight deadly years more than two decades ago.

This point had been brought home to him when he reached his daughter and a grandchild on the telephone last night, courtesy of a satellite phone captured from the Syrian officers billeting at the Nimrod Lodge. Her voice sounded perfectly normal, once the surprise began to wear off. Eli could picture his daughter's neat, West Rogers Park bungalow on a quiet, tree-lined, all-American city street in Chicago. His daughter was flabbergasted to hear him from the middle of a war, a war in which very little news had made it out of the smoke and action, hardly any of it first hand. The first still and video pictures were only beginning to show up in news clips and online news sites and blogs. Lack of internet access, as well as no electrical power in the wider Middle East region, from Turkey to Libya to Pakistan, had kept first-hand news to a minimum. Speculation was rampant and abundant, and some of it being reported as news for lack of any hard information. She suspected, rightly so, that the US government and military knew far more than they were letting on. Though he knew a fair bit at this point having had Sam for a regular companion, as well as having various staff meetings taking place in his house, his truck or his sukkah, Eli was not liberty to set her straight on that subject. He had agreed to complete secrecy as a price for using the phone, and could not give any information, including his location. They chatted for about fifteen minutes until Eli's extreme fatigue and the soldiers waiting for a turn brought their miraculous connection to a close. Of course, she had heard no word from her sister in Jerusalem either. He signed off with reassurances that he and Natalie were OK, that the war appeared to be winding down somewhat, and that he felt sure that her sister was all right in their relatively safe neighborhood in Jerusalem.

Eli spent the night, what was left of it, in his sleeping bag rolled out on a ground pad beside his trusty pickup truck parked at the edge of the woods across from the lodge. The next morning, Sam briefed his motley collection of troops over coffee in the somewhat intact lobby of the Nimrod lodge. The owner had located his personal supply of Kenyan Arabica coffee beans untouched in a secret drawer in the otherwise trashed out kitchen, and treated the lodge's liberators and their accomplices to the best cup of coffee of the war so far, despite the absence of milk. It was strong and hot and had just the right amount of sugar to energize Eli's tired system. Sam had explained their objectives in that four am briefing. The IDF, with the backing of the provisional government, had decided that recapturing Mt. Hermon was a high priority – both militarily and symbolically. Its massive bulk commanded the northern extent of Israel's territory, and its sources of water, its strategic heights and its psychological value were inestimable. However, securing the mountain in a sustainable and defensible way meant at least temporarily capturing some of the network of Syrian fortified bunkers that overlooked and commanded large parts of Israel's third of the mountain.

Their target that morning was one of the Syrian bunkers that controlled a large swath of Israeli territory and made Israel's hold on the mountain tenuous at best. To reach it, they had to cross a massive rockslide gully that scarred the lower southern part of the massif, and then work their way up a series of minor gullies in Syrian territory to come at the well-entrenched, fortified bunker from the rear. The mission planners felt that Sam's rough and ready group of two and a half dozen recon regulars and reservists could tackle it, with helicopter backup if needed. Two companies of paratroopers were scheduled to be airlifted to the summit ridges a little before dawn, and they would work their way down the mountain, catching the Syrian defenders between two fires.

Eli mulled over all these thoughts as he put one foot in front of the other. He remembered their odd trip up the length of the Golan Heights, capturing three hamlets along the way. He mused that he had spent the previous morning building a tractor into a fake tank. They had used the fake tank and a disabled real tank to dislodge a stubborn company of Azerbaijani irregulars from the first Israeli community on their way. They had pushed on, eventually meeting up late in the afternoon with the main column in Shemesh on the slopes of Mt. Hermon. He chuckled as he remembered getting assigned to babysit the reporter, and waiting with him while the regulars stormed the lodge. And from there his mind returned to his daughter's voice, so delightfully clear and warmly familiar over a satellite phone owned by some recently captured Syrian officer. He wondered what they would make of their next phone bill... if it even arrived in EMP-stricken Syria. Their aggressive neighbor was also without electrical power in most of the country, or perhaps all of it. That meant that the phone must be working on someone else's satellite phone system. Perhaps somewhere in the former Soviet Union some clerk would be puzzling over a sudden rash of calls to Chicago, New York, LA, London, Moscow, Pretoria and Sydney last night.

The next time Eli stopped for an extended puff and wheeze, he sat down on a cool, flat boulder lying at a perfect sitting height and contemplated the view some more. He was definitely feeling the workout in his legs, back and shoulders now. He recalled climbing the mountain for the first time, what, about eight years ago. He had just turned fifty and was enjoying a bit of a rebirth in his newly adopted country where he was suddenly free from all the ingrained routines of thirty years in the workforce and beginning to redefine himself. He had not yet started building his handmade house, or even selected moshav Yiftach as his next home. However, he had always felt drawn to the Golan area, and today's airy perch confirmed why. He could see almost half the length of Israel, or at least its hilltops.

He slipped the heavy pack off his shoulders for a moment, leaned back to rest, and awoke to the rattle of gunfire sometime later. The sun was fully up, but not over the eastern shoulder of the mountain yet. Startled, he looked up the gully for the soldier in front of him. He was nowhere in sight.

Eli picked up his rifle, tightened up his pack and rolled off his comfortable rock to take cover below it. He listened intently to the different bursts of fire reverberating in the still mountain air. The gully and the echoes made it impossible to tell where the firing was coming from, except that it was generally above him. He chambered a round, made sure the safety was still all the way on, and tightened his helmet. Then, staying low and taking care to keep in the lowest point of the rocky gully, he crept slowly upward to where he had last seen the last soldier in his group.

After several tense minutes of climbing, he reached the point where he had last seen one of their group. Eli cautiously peered over the low rock ledge. There was intermittent firing, seemingly from two directions. Almost in confirmation, a spray of automatic weapons fire zinged off the rock walls of the right hand side of the gully a few dozen meters above him. He heard an answering quick two shots of a rifle on semiautomatic not far above him. Then he saw two soldiers from his group flattened on the scrap of ground between two protecting rocks. One, who appeared to have just fired, was facing left, while the other was in firing position aiming up and right. He fired a three shot burst and ducked. Half a second later there was a ripple of bullets kicking up dirt and rock around the two Israelis in response.

Eli looked up and right to try to spot the threat, but it was out of his view. From the height of the next burst of bullets that rattled against the moderately steep rock wall above him and to the right, the Syrian position to the left was lower down and had a poor angle of fire. However, the one above and right could fire almost to the bottom of their shallow gully.

Eli studied the situation awhile, still letting his breath slow down and his head clear from his involuntary nap. The coffee had worn off long ago, but the analytical part of his brain was working fine, taking in the two angles of fire, studying the slope of the gully and the availability or lack of cover. He could tell he was safe where he was for now, unless something changed, such as the Syrians sallying forth from their secure bunkers. He could also see that the gully deepened above his two companions and offered more shelter for all of them, but little chance of firing back from its depths without climbing up one side or the other. He needed to let the two soldiers know he was there below them. Perhaps they could direct him how to use his sniper rifle to their advantage to help extricate them from their perilous position. He tried to whistle, but his lips were too dry and cracked from the days of smoke, sun and dirt. He couldn't remember either of their names, for they were from one of the groups of soldiers who had joined them the night of their drive up the Golan. So he used the standard, effective but obnoxious Israeli call for attention – "Allo allo!"

It worked, he held up his sniper rifle over his head in greeting as both turned to see. It appeared to be the first good news they had in a while. He waited while they conferred a moment, fired another burst at the unseen bunker above and to the right, and talked some more, gesturing for him to wait. Eli was happy enough to wait rather than enter the zone of fire from either of the unseen bunkers. There had been no mention of a bunker above and right of their target, of this he was quite sure. So perhaps it was not a bunker, but a moving patrol, in which case, he might soon come in view of them. He could not see anything beyond the rim of the gully and the sky beyond. It appeared that his two companions had come to a decision. In a moment, the one on the right fired a five shot burst, waited for the answering hail of fire to splatter around his crevice, and suddenly gathered himself up and sprinted upwards to the shelter of the deeper gully above. A few moments later the one who had been firing left fired off a burst up and right and did the same scurrying sprint. This time there were a few bullets chasing him until they splattered the rock on the gully above where he nearly disappeared into the shadow of sheltering walls.

Soon the two soldiers were motioning to Eli to follow them, which meant leaving the safety of his hiding place out of sight of either bunker, and sprinting upwards in the bottom of the steep gully. With a pack and rifle weighing him down in the thinning mountain air, covering perhaps only ten meters of exposed ground seemed a very long ten meters from his point of view. However, there was nothing for it. Their gully widened and was relatively much shallower and less protected below them, broadening so much that there would be no escape back the way they had come. That left only one option. Eli took a few deep breaths, checked his boot laces, adjusted his pack straps one more time, eased the rifle's safety off in case there was a chance of a shot, and heaved himself up on the ledge that had been protecting him. He knew he was still below the line of fire from either Syrian position, but he now felt fully exposed none the less. The danger from the left hand bunker, their original target, was minimal, unless he stood up all the way. However, he would be running into view of the unseen shooters above, and that scared him. He knew he needed to make his sprint before the fear gripped him too tightly and he lost his nerve completely. He began to run upwards, straining to see both his footing and get a glimpse of the unseen menace to the right of him. He saw for a moment that indeed it was another bunker, well camouflaged into the side of another rocky shoulder of the mountain, and that it commanded both the first bunker and their gully very effectively. He saw the muzzle flashes of what appeared to be a machine gun before a stumble made him tear his eyes away and pay attention to where he was running – if his hurried, lumbering trot could be called a run. However, it was fast enough and he pulled into the deeper part of the gully above at a good clip and almost had to be stopped by the bear hugs and back slaps of his two companions.

In spite of Eli's huffing and gasping for air after his sixty meter uphill sprint, he could still hear firing above them: the clatter of a machine gun, the same one that had fired a burst at him, and the staccato barks of IDF-style answering fire. As soon as Eli caught his breath enough to move again, the three of them climbed slowly upward in the steepening rocky gully. It closed in steadily as they climbed until it was scarcely a couple meters wide on the bottom, with nearly vertical walls on either side. While they were quite safe from either bunker, they were also quite trapped like fish in a barrel. A little more climbing brought them to the rest of their group. The return fire was almost directly overhead when Eli spotted a pair of agile young soldiers who had climbed a broad crack on one side of the deep rocky chimney and were firing at the bunkers from a relatively safe niche in the rocks. Their main danger was from flying rock splinters being kicked up by the machine gun and automatic rifle fire that was rattling back at them trying to pick them out of their safe hiding holes.

Down on the floor of the gully, the walls of which had narrowed to form a rock chimney perhaps two or three meters wide and now quite vertical, the rest of the group was resting or clustering around Sam and his radio. A few young soldiers were attempting to climb higher up in the gully, but their way was blocked by about a ten to twelve meter high cliff. It would be a waterfall in the rainy season, and showed stains where a trickle of water ran down most of the summer. It was now only damp and mossy.

Sam was happy to see Eli, but not happy about anything else. "We're trapped," he said. "We can't go up, and it would be suicide to go down. Worse, the commando teams that were supposed to drop on top of the mountain were canceled. They needed every available body to stop a breakout of the Jordanians near Nazareth and the Syrians near Carmiel." Sam went back to his radio.

Eli tried to take in the situation, which was a confusing sprawl of nearly thirty soldiers jammed together over perhaps a fifty meter stretch of rocky gully. He also realized that he was hungry, so he put his pack down next to a group of resting soldiers and dug into it for some food. He found a handful of fruit and nuts and pulled the bag out to munch on them along with another water bottle. The firing overhead had slowed down to the occasional exchange. Eli could see bright morning sunshine overhead as well as a sliver of mountainside and landscape below them.

Like the rest of the resting soldiers, Eli soon found himself watching the efforts of Roee and Ronny and another pair of soldiers who were attempting to negotiate the slightly overhanging waterfall, or to scale either of the vertical sides of the neck of the rocky chimney that blocked their upwards progress. They needed to get higher on the mountain to have any chance of outflanking and taking out the upper bunker.

From the soldiers around him, Eli heard about their failed attempt before dawn that had left one of their number dead nearly at the doorstep of the bunker, and had wounded two, who were being tended below him. The second bunker had opened up fire just as they were preparing for the final rush to storm their target bunker, and its raking fire had taken its severe toll before they could retreat to the temporary safety of the gully again. There were only half a dozen lightly-armed soldiers in the bunker below and left of them, but at least two heavy machine guns and a perhaps ten to fifteen soldiers manning the one above and right of them. If they could get some men higher up the mountain, there might be at least a chance of out flanking the Syrian positions. Or perhaps they could capture the bunker that was their original target, which would at least open up a safe retreat down the Israeli side of the mountain.

Eli watched Roee try standing on Ronny's shoulders in an attempt to reach a secure set of handholds that would enable him to get up the overhanging waterfall. They were a nearly a foot too short, and Ronny was one of the tallest soldiers in their unit, standing about the same height as Eli's six feet. Perhaps if he and Ronny could boost him an extra foot together…. Eli packed up his snack and water bottle and walked around the resting soldiers to the head of the gully and studied the fairly blank looking rock walls that half a dozen young and fit soldiers had attempted to climb already. There were simply no good hand or footholds, and the damp rock in the shady gully and their wet boots from tromping around in the mossy floor of the chimney were not helping.

Eli had done some moderate rock climbing in his younger days, and so he studied the problem from a climber's point of view. Dry shoes would help, but it would not solve the short pitch. It would take a very advanced climber to scale either of the vertical side walls, and the moss-slick overhang of the waterfall itself was impossible. Eli cast an appraising eye farther out along either of the side walls, since their angle lessened somewhat away from the waterfall, but there was no chance of climbing the easier rock and then traversing back into the chimney above the waterfall. One side was overhanging, and the other would put the climber squarely in the line of fire of the left hand bunker. Besides, there was nothing but a blank stretch of wall to traverse back to the waterfall. They appeared to be cliffed out. Eli tried a lower hand hold on the right side wall. It was too small to do much. He turned around to study the opposite wall again and absently scraped some mud from his boot against the wall behind him. He suddenly realized that the span between the two rock walls was about his height, meaning that he could possibly put his feet on one wall, his hands on the opposite wall and climb up, bridging the gap with his body. It might work.

He took off his pack, took off his muddy boots and socks, put down his rifle and tried it at a spot where the chimney flared enough to give him a little traction. Bare feet were the next best thing to specialized climbing shoes for friction, he had learned once upon a time on a camping trip in Colorado with some more experienced climbers many years ago. He had to put one foot on the wall behind him, and stretch forward almost his full length and put his outspread hands on the wall in front of him, bringing his body nearly horizontal before the opposing forces of feet and hands gave him traction on the two walls. He felt funny, arching his body to bridge the gap between the two walls, starting out at about waist high. He flexed and experimented until he found the right tension and angle. Eli worked his way up like an inch worm, first hands, then feet, spreading his feet and hands to stabilize himself and keep from slipping. He had to creep up a couple inches at a time, maintaining constant pressure on hands and feet to keep from falling. It started to feel a little more secure as he found his balance point between the opposing forces, and he recalled a deep chimney of rock half a world and half a lifetime away somewhere on a sunny mountainside above Boulder, Colorado.

Suddenly, he noticed everyone had stopped their clambering and had begun watching him. Soon he was more than head height. "Way to go Spiderman!" someone cheered. Ronny and Roee positioned themselves below to spot him in case of a fall. Now the climbing actually got easier as the two walls narrowed a bit, and then opened more to a more comfortable distance. With steady work he was able to crab his way up to nearly the level of the lip of the waterfall. Now came the tricky part. The two walls widened too much to allow him to keep going upward, and he was not quite high enough to get a purchase on his goal at the floor of the waterfall. He looked down. He was now an uncomfortable way above the anxious heads of his friends. The thought of inching down the way he had come was not very appealing, but certainly more so than a sudden fall. His feet were feeling cold and clammy and slipped occasionally against the cool, unforgiving rock, but his hands and the rest of him were hot from the effort and concentration.

He saw a solid hand hold a little farther to his left. It was the kind of big, secure hold that climbers called a "bucket hold" – nearly impossible to mess up, and good for two hands and a pull in several directions. If he got both hands on it he realized that he could easily scramble the last bit. However, to leave the safety of his hands and feet arch, he would have to spring forwards and let his knees and feet smash into the wall in front of him while he clung to the hold for dear life. Once he recovered from the shock and impact of his lunge, he could then scramble to safety at the bottom of the next section of the gully. His body would probably twist around and thump into the wall too, even if he managed to absorb some of the shock with his feet. That might be painful, but as long as he kept his secure, two-handed hold, he would be fine. Before he did that though, he thought he had better take a good look at the upper part of the gully to see if it was worth the effort. He could see a long way upwards, enough to gather that it was negotiable for a fair distance ahead, perhaps enough to get them even with or even above the right-hand bunker. He regretted not having his boots on for this next move, for it involved letting his feet and the rest of his body fall against the wall in front of him while his hands clung to their solid "bucket hold" of a grip. He got his left hand on the hold and prepared to grab it with his right, letting his right leg fall free. He felt his body pivoting for a moment, hanging in a precarious bridge between his right hand and his left leg. Then he made a grab for the hold with his right hand, letting his foot fall at the same instant, and felt his body swing forward and smash into the wall in front of him. He hung on a moment until the force of the blow had subsided and he clung by his hands on his big hold. Then he leaned out on the rocky knob and brought his cold and battered feet back into play and walked them up the wall to where he could get one knee up to the level of the ledge. Gratefully he found another hold for his left hand and heaved his body onto the lip of the waterfall. A little more scrambling brought him to a secure heap on top of the waterfall in the basin carved by ages of dripping water. A faint clapping sounded below him.

"I've got to lose another five or ten kilos," Eli thought to himself as he picked himself up and brushed himself off. He stood up and looked down at the faces below. "Someone toss me my boots," he called. He saw Sam's among the upturned faces and saluted.

Ronny followed his example and came inch-worming up the chimney a few minutes later, trailing from his belt a bunch of rifle slings and webbing belts hooked together. He covered the distance in less than half the time it had taken Eli, but he too stopped when he reached the awkward spot at the top where Eli had made his ungraceful exit. But this time, Eli was able to grab him by the belt from above and help him negotiate the last bit without smashing into the wall quite as hard. Even so, he finished off in a mad scramble. Ronny grinned broadly as he too pulled into the safety of the empty pool. He had done the climb with his boots on, and they quickly pulled up Ronny's pack, with both rifles and Eli's boots clipped to it. Eli pulled on his boots as the next climber crabbed his way up between the rocks. Ronny went on ahead to scout the upper part of the chimney while Eli remained to pull in the soldiers as they finished the hands and feet chimney climb. There were three more soldiers in the upper part of the gully by the time Eli had finished lacing up his second boot, having been interrupted every minute or two to haul in another body.

However, it appeared that Eli's technique only worked for people who were at least five feet seven or taller, for the chimney was simply too wide in places for a shorter person to negotiate. That would leave the group about half up and half down. Unfortunately, no one had a rope, and their webbing and rifle sling makeshift rope was not safe enough to haul a person up. Sam was one of the last of the soldiers to make the climb, and sat there chuckling after Eli performed his now customary office of pulling him the last few feet.

"I'm not sure what to call you now, Daniel Boone or Spiderman?" He shook his head wonderingly, and looked timidly back over the edge of the precipice he had just inched up.

Sam crouched near the edge with Eli, watching the next of their group squeeze his way up. "I don't know what would this war would be like if I hadn't met you, but I know my ass would have been dead at least three times by now without you and your bag of tricks," he said with both good humor and appreciation. "Thanks for showing us boy scouts how it's done."

"Old Indian trick," Eli said.

"Come on," Sam said, getting to his feet after the two of them hauled up his pack and rifle. "Let's see if we can shoot our way out of this hole in the ground."

Sometime after midnight General AlHanasrallah had been able to get through to his brother in the Ministry of Finance. It was a poor connection, and things had to be repeated four or five times to make sure they were understood. But fifteen minutes of shouting over a satellite phone with a fading battery was enough to ensure that his traitorous brother-in-law would never survive his return to Syria, and that AlHanasrallah's second wife and her children were to be turned loose without a single Syrian pound of his wealth. Not that a Syrian pound had been worth much lately. It took about 1,500 of them to make one euro the last time he had gone to Switzerland. He gave his brother the numbers of three of his four Swiss bank accounts. His best mistress had the fourth and would probably clean it out shortly after he was gone if she hadn't already.

He did not bother sleeping that night. Few officers did. After midnight because of the Israeli-declared, unilateral ceasefire there was no more shelling to keep him awake. Except for some drunken Croatian mercenaries firing off tracers into the night sky, all had been quiet. His financial and family affairs set in order, the general and most of his command staff bathed and prepared themselves for martyrdom, the supreme sacrifice of the jihadist for Allah. He found his mind, which had been troubled, irritable and roiling with anger for the past week as his magnificent army failed and unraveled around him, was unexplainably calm and almost serene. He found new insights into some of the verses of Koran he had learned and repeated almost completely by rote almost all his life. He had chosen the path of a Muslim warrior, and he would follow it to the very end. There would be no surrender.

After the predawn prayers, said under a secure night sky with the first faint lightening of the eastern sky beginning to dim the stars, he and a half a dozen of his colonels and majors had gone to see the richest man in Najur– or rather, gone to see his beautiful stable of purebred Arabian horses. All but one of them was untouched by three days of bombardment. They had been moved to the shelter under his verandah. The accuracy of the Israeli gunners was amazing. The village's three mosques and their minarets were untouched by the blistering barrage. Only the houses that had been the source of gunfire had been flattened, in this case, about half of them. The largest building in town flew a red crescent flag, and it had only broken windows from the blasts, but no direct hits.

The rich man had argued, pleaded, offered plans of escape, anything but his precious horses. However, seven determined officers, all washed and wearing white robes donated by villagers eager to be part of their glorious martyrdom, and each of them armed to the teeth, soon sent him away without a bullet between his angry eyes.

There were only enough saddles for five of them, so the youngest two majors mounted bareback and struggled mightily to stay on. Israel's announced cease fire was due to end at six am. At perhaps a minute before six, the seven of them pranced their spirited horses out from behind the rich man's house and into the main street of Najur as it wound down the hill to the highway. Despite the threat of a new bombardment, soldiers by first the dozens, then by the hundreds, and soon by the thousands cheered them.

Mounted on a magnificent black stallion, General AlHanasrallah felt like Saladin must have felt. The cheering filled each of the seven with pride and overflowed their hearts with a wild happiness that felt like freedom and unlimited power. This was jihad as it was meant to be. Their mounts felt the excitement too, and snorted with eagerness to be out of the confines of the village and out in the country with the roaring and booming stopped. They glistened in the bold light and the glorious splendor of a sun rising in a blazing red above the banks of smoke. The air was sharp and clear where the banks of smoke had cleared in the six hour truce.

Soon they had cleared the village and were descending the road to the main highway that had been their route to conquest, and now marked the limit of their dream of a conquered kingdom. It was well after six and the guns were still silent. The general allowed his horse to break into an easy canter, and his six officers hung on to follow him, finding the robes a little slippery in the saddle, and their city-dwelling behinds unused to a moving horse. One of the bareback riders had fallen off twice while clearing the village and had lost his horse the moment they cleared town. He strode purposefully but painfully behind them, brandishing a submachine gun and trying to look dashing in spite of his mud-stained white robes and bleeding chin. All Muslim warriors should learn to ride, it was the only true path, Alhanasrallah thought briefly as he glanced back in the aftermath of the hapless major's second tumble, which had unleashed a burst of automatic fire from his weapon.

Gathering his reins into one hand, he pulled his automatic pistol from its tooled leather holster and fired a burst of shots in the air. Fortunately his mount was used to gunfire, having celebrated more than a few local weddings, and he did not rear. He cantered up to the road, walked his horse across the hard and shell shattered pavement and down the other side, and broke into a gallop. His troop of now five other riders followed as best they could. There was only one other trained horseman among them. The other major took a hard tumble as they descended from the highway, and his horse ran off, tossing its head and galloping away from their group to enjoy its freedom.

Now the industrial outskirts of Carmiel were only a few hundred meters away. Somewhere ahead the Zionist infidels were waiting for him. Were they too amazed at his bravery to fire?

In truth, they were amazed. Five hundred yards away in the fox holes of the picket line of IDF advanced positions, a group of soldiers were enjoying the show and waiting for their officers to figure out, with consultation with the command group, what to do with these clowns.

"Think any more will fall off?" one wondered.

"Bet you the one on the white horse does if he tries firing off that RPG launcher," his companion answered.

"Hey, what do you call five Arabs on horseback in the middle of a war?" challenged a third. "History," he said, after enough grudging "What's?" He got a couple clods of dirt thrown at him for his attempt at wit.

In another bunker a couple hundred meters behind them, two company commanders were watching the horsemen's progress with binoculars. "Think they shot Old Yasir to get his horses?" one asked.

"I can't imagine him letting that black stallion go without at least a clip of bullets in his skull," opined the captain, who had also grown up in the area.

"I remember seeing him drunk as a lord galloping down the highway one time. I was just out of the army and back from India. It was before the second intifada and so he could carry his pistol outside of the village then. But he's a wily old fart. I imagine he backed down just this side of a bullet.

"I wonder how close they'll let them come before someone has to shoot the bastards? They could be a danger to someone if they got within a stone's throw maybe.

"Watch and see," the older one said, keeping a field radio to his ear. "OK – time to shoot the sons of bitches, just make sure Old Yassir's horses don't get hit." His companion relayed the order to the unit's snipers, who were delighted to undertake the challenge of leaving the villager's horses unharmed. Seven deliberate shots later all five horses were running free, and the three snipers were arguing over who had missed their first shots.

General Hanasrallah's jihad came to an end in an empty, trash strewn field about 100 meters short of a plastic bag making plant. He died happy. Black Lightening, his horse for the occasion, enjoyed a gallop along the highway with his companions before heading back to the village.

Northern District Command Mt. Meron 0720

Kobi and Anna were working their first shift together in more than two days, and both were closely monitoring the situation near Carmiel whenever they had a moment in their other command and communications duties. "We have a Syrian captain on the channel who wants to know if we can continue the cease fire until he reaches someone higher up," one of their Arabic speaking radio operators called out at last.

Anna hurried over to the console while motioning for Koby to get one the generals in charge of the Carmiel battlefield on another link. "Tell him we are willing to keep the cease fire going as long as there is no moving troops or heavy weapons, and no firing on their side." Her operator relayed the message. There were a few exchanges further, but even to Anna's ears, the man on the other end of the radio sounded relieved, but very, very stressed.

"Ask him where he is, and how many are under his direct command at present." She waited while the two Arabic voices worked out the question and answer with various circumlocutions and side issues.

"It's complicated," the translator said. "If I understand it correctly, he is the highest ranking person left in the combined general staff of the Syrian Fourth Armored and Seventh Mechanized Divisions. Everyone over the rank of major is either dead or rode off on some horses this morning – there's something weird there I didn't quite get. Anyway, he is the senior of the four captains left from the general staff, though there might be some others in field positions that he can't get in touch with."

"Yeesh! That is complicated. Schmooze with him awhile and get as many facts and details as you can while I relay that to our battlefield command and see what we can do for him." Koby had them on a secure satellite link. "Who is it?" Anna asked.

"Crembo," Koby grinned.

Crembo was really General Abraham Kraemer, but ever since third grade, most of the world called him Crembo, although most of them did it behind his back ever since he reached the rank of lieutenant many years ago. The story, which no one doubted, was that in third grade Abraham Kraemer had won the respect and admirations of his classmates by eating fifty six marshmallow-filled chocolate Crembos in under three minutes. He could have eaten more, but there were only fifty six to be had in the entire lunchroom that day. Crembo had stuck – for life. And it sort of fit, because, unlike the lean and athletic types that tended to become generals in the IDF, Crembo was a big, solid, easy-going lump of a soldier who just happened to be a whole lot smarter and more ambitious than he looked. It was rumored that he still had a passion for the puffy chocolate treats, but had to eat them in secret to avoid outright mirth or complete insubordination on the part of his subordinates.

"Tchernikovsky here," Anna said, picturing the big man at the other end of the signal being bounced off one of their few satellites unaffected by the EMP at the beginning of the war. The massive pulse of electromagnetic radiation had passed right on out into space, taking the inner vitality of at least a dozen satellites of all nations with it.

"Anna, how are you doing? How's your father making out?" Crembo said.

"Dad's fine. He and mom have a good shelter in their building and the neighbors are looking after them. Thanks for asking," Anna said.

"They should be proud of what their daughter has being doing for her country. Really, Anna, you've done a magnificent job putting us back together."

Damn, is he running for Knesset after the war? What's gotten into old Crembo? she wondered to herself. "Thanks, um, we have a Syrian captain on the radio who says he's most likely the senior surviving officer of the combined general staff of the Fourth Armored and Seventh Mechanized."

The deep voice on the other end of the satellite phone chuckled. "I imagine he is. I watched General AlHanasrallah and the rest of his cronies go down this morning. An inspired bit of horseplay it was too. White robes, turbans, weapons waving, and seven magnificent horses. Old Yasir raises the best Arabians in the whole Galilee."

"General, I'm not quite following you. What are you talking about with all the horses? We couldn't quite get the whole story out of our Syrian senior captain."

"Oh, it will make quite a story for the generations of young hot heads to follow this bunch," Crembo said. "Basically, Hanasrallah and six of his general staff rode out in battle against us this morning mounted on the village headman's prized Arabians. Yasir Husseini, the richest Arab in at least four of the villages across the road from here raises Arabian horses and we've bent over backwards not to blow them to *shemayim* and back for the past three days because old Yasir is a good old boy and always treated the locals right. Anyway, we shot the sons of bitches and they are now all upstairs with their seventy virgins – or so the story goes. And the horses all headed back home after a bit of a frolic. It was worth prolonging the cease fire just to see them galloping free."

Anna had a hard time picturing what he was talking about, but Koby, who had spent more time in the field around there, was having a good laugh at the story. "So, what do I tell our captain?"

"Tell him we'll keep things quiet until, say, noon. What happens after lunch is up to him."

"Got it," Anna said.

"Oh, and tell him to keep trying to reach his comrades from the first wave force. They are holed up just over the mountain from him in the bigger village up there. You can give him a few radio frequencies to try if he's too dim to reach his own people. They have been cranking out the calls to Damascus like there's no tomorrow. Actually in the case of General Bandur and his bunch, there probably is no tomorrow."

"I'll patch him through myself if I have to," Anna promised.

"Keep me informed," Crembo signed off. "And give your dad my best when you see him. G-d willing, it may be soon."

All the fuel gauges on Yossi Green's beloved plane were a hairline away from rock bottom. In fourteen years of flying this bird, Yossi had never taken it anywhere near the limit on all four tanks. With their wartime rewiring job in the past week, who knew how accurate the gauges were in the first place? "K-Bear, what's the word on *delek*?"

"Two more minutes to rendezvous," K-Bear replied.

"Could you give me a gas-saving glide path and have the tanker meet me near the floor of the fueling zone?" Yossi asked anxiously.

"We've just finished the numbers there Eagle One. Start descending at a rate of 40 meters per second and throttle back to 600 kph and you should arrive at 5,000 meters about the time you see our three friends. You're first in line at the eastern most tanker."

"Dropping 40 meters per second starting now, speed 700 dropping to 6." Yossi replied, feeling some sense of relief.

He was tired after being in the cockpit for seven hours of hard flying, There had been the morning fuel stop. Refilling a jet fighter in flight was never a piece of cake – especially when the tanker was American and the bird was Israeli. It always felt like the subtle steps of the dance needed to close and clamp on to a dangling fuel nozzle in mid air were just a little out of synch. It involved negotiating all the while with a fueling specialist watching from an aft-mounted TV camera. Somehow Americans needed one more level of confirmation for each step of the dance, while Israelis seemed to gather the other's intentions and take more for granted. Perhaps it would go easier doing it the second time in just a few hours.

He had managed to burn a plane load of fuel in those few action-filled hours. Much of the fuel was burned chasing a band of Saudi F-15s that turned out to be on a mission to bomb the same reactor. He hoped he would hear the intelligence side of that story someday soon, for the flight of Saudi planes had shown up over the target only minutes before their planned arrival. They were also painted with false IAF markings in attempt to fool someone – he was not sure who. Then there was the air to ground action as his four Eagles cleared up the few still operating anti-aircraft missile batteries around the reactor complex. He had been hit in one of his wingtip spare fuel tanks and had to jettison them after the last strafing run, which was why Yossi was now desperately low on fuel and praying for the sight of an USAF fuel tanker somewhere near the eastern edge of Iraq on their flight home. His group was only three planes now, having sent Yair home because of a malfunction in the control tabs on one wing. Sometime after turning homeward himself, he had heard the welcome confirmation of Yair's arrival home with two F-16s sent home after hitting the first target.

Yossi and his team of Eagles had overtaken the F-16s that had bypassed the first target at Arak and gone straight ahead to the second and more important target: the once-secret nuclear fuel processing plant buried under a set of rocky hills near Qom. They encountered less operative air defenses there. Yossi wondered in hindsight if possibly there were less elaborate anti-aircraft defenses so as not to draw attention to the dusty hills of the secret base.

The bombing had been trickier, requiring high and slow passes and precision strikes with huge bunker-busting bombs drilled deep into the earth before exploding. Their goal was to collapse and seal all the known entrances to the complex. After taking care of the air defenses, Yossi's group had been assigned to hit the parts of the base above the surface in order to degrade the site's ability to rebuild and recover its functioning anytime soon. They had done a thorough job. Now the three of them were flying a few minutes ahead of the group of F-16s.

Except for their Saudi visitors, no other aircraft had appeared to challenge them, either over Iran or now again over Iraq. That was lucky, for they had next to no fuel and no more than a couple air to air missiles left.

Yossi leveled off at 5,000 meters and was intently watching the sky to the north of his course for the converging flight of K-135 tankers and their F-15 escort. His tactical radar showed them still a dozen kilometers away. However, a half a minute later, an American-marked F-15 appeared and guided him further right, and soon he saw the welcome contrail of the tanker above as it was dropping down to his level. He wagged his wings at his escort and edged towards the welcome fueling target cone. He planned to slide right in and clamp on with no formalities this time. There was only the need to agree on the speed and altitude – and the cheerful Americans were willing to adapt to anything his tired brain could order his mouth to ask. Sixty seconds later the life-giving fuel was flowing again. Soon he was full enough for the run homewards, with fuel to spare for any air to air combat that might come his way in between. His companions drank their fill, and all soared aloft to where the American combat patrol kept watch to do a little visiting and chill while they waited for the F-16 flights to arrive for their refueling stop.

Mt. Hermon 0730

Once Sam had the taller half of his group above the cliff, he checked out the upper part of the gully, studying the angles of fire, the availability of cover. He estimated the distances to the upper and lower bunkers on either side of them. Then he huddled with his fourteen soldiers in a well-protected part of the deep crevice not far above the cliff that had stopped them until Eli showed them how to climb a chimney.

Eli wondered what part Sam would give him in the assault plans. The very top of their rocky gully offered good cover from both bunkers. It ended somewhere about a hundred meters higher in elevation above the upper bunker that had opened fire on them when they attacked the lower one some hours earlier in the morning. Now their small force was spread along the rocky couloir that drained snow melt and rain from a moderate sized basin of the upper mountain. He could now clearly see their men posted in secure clefts in the rock below the waterfall/cliff, still firing the occasional shot at the upper and lower bunkers. No one had let the enemy know of their presence above the narrow cliff yet.

Sam scratched a crude diagram of the situation in gritty mud that had collected in the rocky basin that would be a pool of water in the rainy season, and where his men now crouched, except for two who kept watch above. "Here is our gully, here is the group and their firing positions below the waterfall, and here we are, with good cover for laying down some fire on the upper bunker from here, here, and here," he said. He turned to point out the landmarks above that offered safe places to shoot at the upper bunker without exposing the shooter to any fire from the lower bunker. "These upper two spots are above the bunker, and the lower one is about on the level and should offer a good, straight on shot for the grenade launcher if we can lob it high enough to hit at this range. We're safe from the lower bunker at each of those points." Heads turned to confirm the angles, and one of the men with a rocket propelled grenade launcher crept up to the edge of the gully to steal another look at the bunker that was now not far away and a little down slope. He confirmed that he thought he could hit the firing slit if he could make a couple tries at it.

"So, here's my plan: we put two guys – Schmulik and Amnon, here at the lower spot, one plastering them with rifle fire, the other hitting the front with the RPG launcher. One guy each at the upper two spots hitting the firing slits from their angle and watching for a sortie from the back door. Eli, I want you and your sniper rifle at the upper spot. Try for banked shots off the right wall of the firing slit that might ricochet inside, anything to keep those machine guns quiet. Shimon, I want you in the middle spot. You're our best man for covering fire. I'm going to tell the guys below the waterfall to open up when they hear us start and for them to lay down some fire on the lower bunker to make them keep their heads down. The rest of us are going to be waiting at the upper bit of cover near the top of the gully up there," he pointed upwards to where their gully widened to form the upper mouth that channeled the rains that had gouged their deep, secure gully.

"We'll circle around above and behind the upper bunker and try to find the back door and blow it. Questions?"

"You sure there's not another bunker above and behind this one?" one of the soldiers who had helped drag their two wounded companions back to the shelter of the first gully asked.

"Pretty sure, that's what I've been trying to discover for the past thirty minutes. Anyone else see anything beyond them?" The men looked at each other and shook their heads one by one.

"Anyone got any other ideas, let's hear them." Sam urged.

"What about the lower bunker?"

"We clean them out after we get these guys. We'll have them covered from above and below, and maybe one of the machine guns will survive our surprise party."

"How about our wounded and the 'short guys?'" asked one of the taller soldiers, who had been amused that his five-foot-five and under friends had been unable to follow them up the waterfall chimney.

"We move the wounded to the lower bunker once we have it secured and wait for the helicopters they promised."

"And if this doesn't work?" the tall soldier asked.

Sam shrugged and made an impatient, but worried gesture. "Then we wing it and wait for nightfall and hope they don't have night vision either."

They went over the plan several more times until each knew his part. Eli had only 30 accurate sniper rounds left, but he had collected a few handfuls of 7.62 shells from the machine gun that had been mounted on Woody. They would fit his rifle in a pinch, but not have the same deadly accuracy of the needle pointed magnum loads that were designed for his gun. After his first few deliberate shots, he figured he would switch to the more available machine gun shells and keep firing with them until they were either successful or driven back into hiding again. He too had used his rifle scope and scanned the mountainside above and beyond the next bunker, and had scrutinized every crevice and shadow for further fortifications.

Their group waited nervously, checking weapons, boots, packs and pockets while Sam leaned over the edge of the top of the waterfall they had all climbed up and relayed the plan to the men below. Two of their group crept to the top of the gully to relieve their two guards so that they could come down and listen to the plans. They had already been partially briefed by Sam. He reassured the group that there was no sign of any other bunkers or troops moving on the mountain above except for a distant group of bunkers on another ridge that was out of firing range. However, there was some dead ground behind the near shoulder of the mountain guarded by their problematic bunker. No one could guarantee there were no threats there. Sam had studied the aerial and satellite photos, and had scoped out the mountain on his helicopter flight with Barak the day before. He told them it was fairly unlikely there was another bunker.

Sam returned from his consultations with the lower group, checked in with each of his companions, reviewed a few hand signals, and they set off up the gully to their respective firing points. Eli was out of breath by the time they reached his assigned spot, but had time to sit and recover as Sam and his assault team climbed higher. Sam had chosen well. Eli had a clear view of the bunker below. Someone would have to lean out of the deep firing slits in order to fire at him, which was not likely given the covering fire Sam had planned for them below. He was out of sight of the lower bunker completely, and had a choice of firing positions and good cover to shoot from. He took off his pack and began to arrange his ammunition, sorting it into magnum and machine gun rounds in separate clips within easy reach. He chambered a high powered round and edged to where he could see his target below and studied it with his scope. He could see each of the three firing slits in great detail, including pock marks around them where the concrete walls had been hit by their bullets. There was a regular rash of nicks in the flaring, angled mouth of the slits that allowed the defenders to command a very large angle of fire. The walls of the bunker were nearly half a meter thick, Eli estimated, for he could see the inner edge of the far side of the nearest slit with his scope. The interior of the bunker was lost in darkness compared to the bright morning sunshine. He could shoot into the hidden interior of the bunker at that angle, and perhaps bank a shot or two off the inner edges of the nearest two firing slits, kicking up a spray of concrete chips and perhaps sending bullet fragments into the interior. His position also commanded the disturbed earth around the back of the bunker where the exit and entrance door must be. Sam had told him to keep one eye on that area between shots to make sure no one came out to challenge their raiding party. He drilled the sight into his mind to try to remember that. It would be hard not to become absorbed in his precision firing and the view in his scope. He knew he would have to force himself to draw away and look elsewhere between shots once the firing started.

Eli was scanning the rocky mountainside beyond the bunker with his scope, looking for any lurking snipers, scouts or signs of life when the whoosh and boom of the first rocket propelled grenade drew him back to his target. He waited for the second boom to start firing with the rest of the group. He heard the staccato bang-bang-bang of semi automatic fire erupting below him. One of the two machine guns started spitting fire out of the nearest slit. He took careful aim at the darkness inside the lower corner of the bunker's opening. He inhaled, let out half the breath and fired. He drew the bolt back and chambered another high powered shell and remembered to glance at the back of the bunker before settling his attention back into the ring of his scope for a second shot. The riflemen below him had probably fired half a clip by now as he chose a spot on the far side of the firing slit to blast his second shot. He squeezed it off just as the third RPG blew up in a direct hit on the second firing slit. Eli worked the third round into his chamber, forcing himself to check the back door area. He could see Sam and his group racing across the mountainside in a ragged line, converging on the bunker, and smoke blowing out of the second firing slit from the rocket propelled grenade. The machine gun at his target slit had abruptly stopped firing, but he wanted to make sure they were not about to start up again. He pinged a third round into the shadows of the firing slit again.

So far, there had been no sign of a sortie from the back of the bunker, so Eli switched clips to the machine gun rounds with their blunter tips and lesser volume of powder in the brass casings. He was curious how accurate they would be, and sighted in on the lower lip of the embrasure so that he might see where his shot hit. He could tell from the size of the pockmarks made by his earlier bullets that they were making a noticeably bigger mini crater than the lighter 5.6 mm rounds fired from the M-16s. He aimed at the midpoint and fired, chambered another round and studied the point of impact of his previous round. Not bad, he thought, within about six inches of where he would have hit with a magnum round. He was so absorbed in his next shot that he almost forgot to check the back of the bunker until he was already settled in for his next round. He swore at himself and raised up in time to see Sam's group swarming around the area behind the bunker taking cover. He thought for a moment that he had let them down by missing a sortie from within when the blast of a cluster of several grenades taped together boomed from behind the bunker. They were attempting to blow the door. He held his rifle at the ready, watching to see if anyone burst forth or tried to clamber out of the firing slits.

He watched Sam's group pour fire at the blown door, and saw the flash of a pair of grenades explode within. It was over in a few more seconds. Eli saw Sam give the all clear signal with his rifle held over his head and shaken in triumph, and saw him and a few of his partners standing on top of the bunker scanning the terrain beyond as a burst of machine gun fire from within opened up on its former companion bunker down the mountain. After a few minutes of sporadic firing, he saw a white shirt on a pole pushed timidly from behind its steel back door, now dented and perforated with holes from their newly captured heavy machine gun. The firing that had echoed and banged from their section of the mountain suddenly stopped. In the minutes of quiet, they could hear distant sounds of a fire fight somewhere lower down and around the western flank of the massive peak with its network of ridges.

Sam gave a sharp whistle, and Eli saw a handful of men from the lower "short people's" group emerge from the base of their gully and start to fan out across the rocky mountainside below to approach the lower bunker that had been their original target and the site of their casualties early that morning. Eli could see the lone body of one of their group still lying where he had fallen near the back door of the lower bunker. He was not sure which of their group he had been, for they had gone up the mountain with only two-thirds of their team from the assault on the lodge. The rest were assigned to guarding the lodge and other chores lower down the mountain. Eli had been glad to have been picked for the assault team going up the mountain that morning, and now he felt like the king of the world looking down on their morning's accomplishments.

He heard Sam whistle again, and turned to see him gesturing in his direction. He quickly realized that Sam wanted him and his companions who had provided covering fire from the upper gully to turn around and cover their companions who were cautiously approaching the half-open back door of the bunker. He turned and took up a solid firing position that overlooked the lower bunker and acquired it in his scope. He was amazed to see how the .50 caliber bullets had chewed holes in its thick steel. They had been facing a formidable weapon in the bunker they had just captured; just how powerful was neatly demonstrated in the battered door he watched in his sights.

Eli heard orders shouted in Arabic from his companions below. They were crouched in a rough semi-circle perhaps 25 meters away from the door of the bunker, taking whatever cover they could find. He saw the door open slowly and a skinny, scared-looking soldier, stripped to the waist step out with his hands in the air. Four more followed him, also shirtless. They stumbled awkwardly away from the door of the bunker until they were about halfway to the Israelis, and then turned and lay down facing away from them with their hands still well over their heads. Eli watched three of his companions take covering positions near the prone enemy, while the rest edged to the back door. One tossed in a "flash bang" stun grenade and the other two were at the door in seconds, rifles at the ready. Nothing stirred below, and the two soon entered, backed up by the third who had thrown the grenade. The three other soldiers covered the five prisoners. A minute or two later, one of the Israelis emerged from within, giving the all clear. A hearty cheer sounded from the bunker behind him, and Eli could see Sam lower his binoculars with a grin that was visible from nearly 100 meters away in spite of the bright sun being behind him. It had now risen a hands breadth above the eastern shoulder of the mountain beyond him.

Eli glanced at his watch, it was near eight in the morning. The sky was clear of the promised helicopters, or indeed, of any kind of aircraft. Far below him, still in the shade of lower ridges, he could see the base of the Mt. Hermon ski area still in shadows, and a spidery network of trails. Somewhere far below he heard the deep bass thump of heavy artillery. Above him, he could see the summit ridge of their section of the mountain perhaps a kilometer beyond, and a good four or five hundred meters of altitude yet to climb.

Sam had told them that once they gained the ridge, it was another kilometer or two to the summit where there was a cluster of huts and communications towers that marked their ultimate goal. From the top, they could command the network of ridges that radiated from its height. Two more commando teams were working their way up the west and northwest parts of the mountain, with their own bunkers to face.

Sam had said the main assault would go directly up from the base of the ski area in order to recapture a large Israeli-built command post near the top. Another group would work their way up a main ridge north of there that overlooked a village on the Lebanese sector of the mountain. Sam and his small group had climbed the broad south face of the mountain, much of the way in plain view of Migdal Shemesh and exposed to Syrian view, which was why they had clung to their deep gully for much of the way. Eli could see Sam talking on his radio, probably reporting his objectives taken and checking in on the progress of the other groups. Eli collected his pack, putting the loose rounds in their respective pockets, and waited for Sam's signal to move.

His watch had crept along to well after eight thirty and Eli had dug the last of his moshav-grown apples from the depths of his pack when he heard Sam calling his name. He had been deep in thought wondering about Natalie and what was going on back at the moshav. He looked up to notice that his two fellow riflemen had left their gully and were nearing the bunker, while Sam was waving to him to follow. He picked up his pack, unkinked from his long rest among the cold rocks, and walked in the welcome sunshine to join his group at their captured bunker. He had already watched their two wounded members being carried to the lower bunker, and their fallen companion gently covered outside the door.

There was the welcome sound of a primus stove boiling up a pot of water and the smell of coffee in the now door-less bunker he had helped capture. He stooped and entered the low door and its short entrance tunnel. It took a while for his eyes to get used to the dim light. Three bright slits sent shafts of light within, as well as the open door, but the interior was shadowy and lit only by some candles. Eli was curious to see whether any of his bullets had landed inside, but the interior of the bunker was a mess from the one RPG and several hand grenades that had blown up inside. Fortunately he was spared most of the gore, for Sam and his group had dragged what was left of the defenders' bodies outside already and covered them with a tarp. There was a stone bench and concrete table that had survived the blasts, and one of Sam's recon men had a billy can ready to boil, and some mess kit cups arrayed around it waiting. He grinned at Eli, teeth white in his blackened face. "Coffee?" he asked. "Their sugar supply survived the grenades." Eli dug his cup out of his pack and looked for a place to sit down that was not splattered with debris and possible body parts.

Sam came in again as Eli was about halfway done with a hot, strong, very sweet cup of coffee. His barista at the primus was feeling generous since the bunker was well stocked, with most of the supplies surviving in sturdy tins with mouse and varmint-proof tops. Apparently mice and marmot-like rodents had been a problem for the bunker's former inhabitants, his companions surmised from the arrangements in the pantry. The big brass primus had survived the assault, as well as a couple of five gallon cans of kerosene tucked in a secure niche. The ammunition for the big .50 caliber machine guns had been well protected too. He could see the menacing shape of the surviving gun guarding the lower of the three firing slits. The other heavy machine gun was a twisted lump of metal parts on the floor. Eli wandered over to see just how much of a view it had of their gully and route up the mountain. In studying the angles of fire available to the heavy gun, he wondered how they had all survived with only one dead, for it commanded the approaches to the lower bunker and the lower part of the gully where he had climbed earlier that morning. He remembered his scramble under its fire earlier that morning and shuddered. However cozy their kitchen pantry nook might be, the bunker was cool, damp, and creepy feeling, so Eli decided to take the rest of his coffee outside and sit in the warm sunshine. The rest of their group felt the same way. He joined Sam and his group as they studied the final climb above them. It looked like a steep, but straightforward scramble up the nearest rocky shoulder above them.

"Any more old Indian tricks for getting us to the ridge top?" Sam joshed him.

"Just plain hard work," Eli said, contemplating the possible routes.

"I'm thinking the left side of the near ridge, just in case there are any more surprises on the Syrian side," Sam said. Eli agreed it looked like the safest way up.

"How are you feeling? Ready for more climbing, or do you want to stay here?" Sam asked solicitously.

"I've had a good rest and a great cup of coffee. I'm go for the summit if you are," Eli said confidently. And truly, aside from a few aches and pains from hugging the cold rocks of the gully for too much of the morning, Eli felt ready to go. He would rather be moving than sitting around getting stiff and cold. He didn't like the idea of sitting around a dark bloody bunker for sure.

"OK, you're in the summit group, make sure you have at least three liters of water and some food, and some kind of warm jacket, we could be up there a while," Sam said. "By the way, we've made it highest on the mountain so far. The other two groups are having some bunker trouble of their own, and some nasty cross-fires for the northwestern team. We pulled the easiest sector it seems."

Eli ducked back inside the bunker to top up one of his water bottles from the still-working water barrel with its tap in the kitchen nook. The group's barista was tidying up and appeared to be settling in for a long stay, and he bid Eli a cheerful farewell. His feet had been hurting the last few miles up the mountain, and he was glad to stop and settle in with a few companions to guard their hard-won bunker. The four men left to occupy the captured fortification had set upon the task of cleaning up the bunker with whatever tools they could find. Eli, however, was glad to head back outside. The bunker gave him the creeps.

Sam began the upward trek with a pair of his recon men climbing ahead on point. Eli joined a wiry, short Yemenite sergeant from the "short people's group" who had climbed up to join them. The two of them fell into the back of the line of Sam's summit group, which he realized was down to twelve of them. Counting it up in his mind, he realized that there were five men in the lower bunker not counting their two wounded and one dead, and four taking up residence in the upper bunker. That left twelve men, counting Eli, of their original two dozen to take the summit ridge. There was no way of knowing how many Syrians were up there, but there was no doubt that they were well aware of the three Israeli assault teams by now. With this not-so-comforting realization, Eli settled into his high altitude trudge, one breath for every step, sometimes two breaths. All of them were feeling the 2,500 meters of altitude by now, even the short powerhouse of a sergeant who labored along behind him.

After perhaps a kilometer of hard, steep hiking, they reached the rock scrambling part where the ridge steepened. So far there had been no enemy in sight, so they were able to concentrate their attention on the hands and feet climbing up the loose and treacherous band of crumbling rock. The angle was perhaps 45 degrees on average. Most had to sling their rifles on one shoulder and use both hands to heave themselves upwards. Eli concentrated on his footwork, and on keeping his weight on his feet and his body well away from the rock. There was a natural tendency on the steep parts to hug the rock, but Eli remembered his rock climbing experiences from an earlier lifetime where he had learned that keeping his body closer to the vertical kept his weight directly over his feet and gave him better balance and traction. He tried to convey the tip to the Yemenite sergeant who was slipping a lot and hugging the rock closer with every slip to the point that his feet were sliding even on easy sections. However, Eli's Hebrew was not up to the task, or else the sergeant did not grasp the concept, and he continued to struggle mightily.

A few hundred more meters of this breathless and concentrated effort brought them to the point where the steep rock band ended and the ridge eased off in a long, broader and more gently rising shoulder that led to the distant summit. They could see the array of communications towers against the sky. Sam and his group had spread out in the lee of some good-sized boulders that sheltered them from any shots that might be fired from the direction of the summit, or the other ridges that intersected with it. Eli could see another ridge to the east of them, slightly lower, that also snaked its way to the summit towers. It was bare of any people or structures, although he could see a sort of a trail along its crest.

Sam was studying the cluster of towers at the summit with his binoculars when Eli and the much bruised sergeant puffed to a stop in the lee of his boulder. After catching his breath at least partway, Eli propped his rifle on a rock and began to study the summit complex along side of Sam. The towers sprang clearly into view in his high powered scope, extra sharp in the thinner mountain air, and Eli began to scan the ground at their bases. There were some sturdy, small metal huts and a lone stone building that appeared fairly old and broken down. There were no signs of life that Eli could see. He counted eight of the tall towers, scanning them from top to bottom for possible hidden snipers or observers, checking where their guy wires were attached, and looking carefully at their anchors. Nothing was moving but a moderate breeze from east that smelled of dry earth and a faint tinge of gun smoke.

"I don't see anybody, do you?" Sam said dubiously.

"Not a soul," Eli agreed.

"Seems too good to be true," Sam said.

"Must not be true then," Eli said.

"That's what I'm thinking. They know we're up here. There were radios in both bunkers."

"Got to be hiding somewhere," Eli said. "But where?"

"Damned if I know. Those shacks could hold maybe a dozen guys each, but they look like they've been there long enough to be legitimate equipment shelters."

Eli agreed with that assessment. "Whose territory are we looking at?" he asked.

"Israeli. We had this lower, western summit until the war broke out, but there is a second summit to the east held by Syria that is a few dozen meters higher."

"So there would have been only a week to dig something and hide it on this part of the mountain," Eli thought out loud.

"Right," Sam agreed. "I guess we move a little closer and take another look, but I'm starting to wish we had hauled that .50 cal up here."

Sam then turned his binoculars from the summit to study the adjacent ridge to the east that also connected with their summit. There was perhaps a kilometer of distance between the ridges at the point where Eli and Sam sat, and they could see that there was a series of stone cairns marking the international border, and perhaps some kind of a stone hut near the end of the ridge a little over two kilometers away. Anyone in that hut would have a pretty clear view of their progress as they approached the summit. There was no way of seeing if the stone hut was occupied, but it would be safest to assume that it was. That meant that they either needed to detour along the left, or northwestern side of their ridge to remain out of sight, or risk being seen.

They simultaneously turned their attention to the even lower ridge to their left that ended short of the summit. Sam explained that this ridge on the Israeli side was being climbed by the middle of the three taskforces that set out for the summit that morning. He conferred awhile on his radio while his group sprawled in the morning sunshine, staying hidden from any casual observers on the Syrian held ridges beyond them. They could hear the thump of big guns firing from the base of the ski area. Israeli gunners were lobbing shells at targets on the back side of the mountain, Sam told them. They could hear sporadic firing in the distance well below them. "It looks like we're the first to the summit ridges. They are sending another half company around to follow our route, but they are at least three or four hours away. We're on our own up here. No helicopters to spare yet." Sam told them.

The group discussed their options: stay put and wait for the 50 or so soldiers huffing their way up the mountain below them, press on and try to capture the first summit that was nearly two kilometers away along a broad, but fairly exposed ridge, or perhaps descend and help with the assault on the Israeli complex at the top of the chairlifts that were somewhat lower down and would involve moving farther along their ridge and then finding a safe path that angled down. Eli could tell that Sam was sorely tempted to try for the summit towers, but afraid of a massive ambush. The rest of the group was feeling similarly cautious. After some debate, they decided to send one of their strongest hikers back down their ridge to collect the .50 caliber machine gun and four of the men assigned to guard the two bunkers, for they would soon be relieved by the party headed up the mountain behind them.

Sam was never one to sit still. As they waited for their machine gun and companions to join them, he set off with three others to reconnoiter the ridge ahead, planning to hug the western side and search for a possible way down to help the central assault group. Then he planned to creep as close as possible to the still empty seeming summit tower complex. He left the radio in charge of the Yemenite sergeant with instructions for keeping in touch with the commanders and other assault groups.

Eli had nothing to do but bask in the sun and watch their cautious progress as Sam and his three companions scuttled from rock to rock, crevice to crevice along the shoulder of the ridge. He was comfortably sprawled in a depression of coarse sand, flat rocks and lichen. A few tiny white alpine flowers nodded in the moderate and warm summer breeze that swept the summit ridge. He could easily fall asleep again if it were not for the intermittent chatter of the sergeant nearby with the radio and his fascination with watching Sam's progress.

Sam and his men were good, for Eli occasionally lost sight of them and had to watch carefully to spot their swift, short bursts of movement as they grew smaller and smaller in the distance. From time to time he turned his rifle scope on the summit communications towers and weathered metal equipment shacks, but still saw no sign of movement. Whoever might be hiding up there was well hidden and well disciplined, he decided with a shudder, for several times Sam and his three companions surely presented an easy shot for any snipers lurking in the shadows. At nearly two kilometers distance and at least another hundred meters altitude gain, the summit towers were well out of range of his rifle. One of their waiting group was similarly watching the progress of the man sent to fetch the machine gun. "They're starting up now," he announced. It had taken them nearly an hour to trek from the upper bunker to their present perch with only their light packs. It would take at least as long for the men lugging the heavy machine gun, bipod and ammunition. There was no sign of the relief company yet.

Eli turned his attention back to where he had last seen Sam. It took him a few moments to find him again, and he soon saw him and his men duck down the top of a steep gully that cut between the rugged rock ribs of their ridge. He knew they were searching for a possible way down to relieve the central group. However, about fifteen minutes later, as Eli was fighting another nap attack, he spotted them scrambling up the far side of the top of the gully where they had disappeared earlier. He watched as they contoured along below the ridge line, scrambling up and over the top of several of the rocky buttresses until they disappeared down another promising hidden gully. This time he most certainly dozed off, for he awoke to the puffing of the four men returning with the machine gun and four heavy boxes of ammunition for it. Eli felt guilty for sleeping while they had worked so hard, but noticed several of his companions rousing to the sounds also. The sun was now nearing the midpoint of its journey across the sky, and the wind had picked up to a dry but stiff breeze blowing in his face when he lifted his head and rifle to scope out the summit again. Still nothing stirring. His mouth was dry, so he got out one of his remaining water bottles and joined the puffing packers in downing a long drink. They had brought up some flatbread baked in a pan by their enterprising coffee chef, and the group shared out the welcome treat.

Sam and his scouting group had reappeared in the meantime, much closer to the summit and still creeping carefully in short scurries between covering rocks. The rested part of the group watched their progress keenly, with the occasional check back down the mountain to see if their relief group was in sight. It took a tense half an hour before Sam and his three recon veterans were within perhaps 100 meters of the first of the communications towers. Eli was sharing his rifle scope, and the sergeant was sharing his binoculars now with the rest of the group, so he only saw bits of their final approach. He heard a murmur of wonder from the soldier who reluctantly handed his rifle and scope back. Eli quickly relocated Sam, now crouched at the base of the first tower. His three companions soon crept to the small shed near its base, and he watched them pry a corner of the corrugated metal siding back. With the tiny men there for scale, he could now see that the shed was about the size of a large chicken coop, shorter than the height of a man. He watched as the group scuttled furtively towards the next tower in the complex, and grudgingly handed the rifle and scope to the next man who was beginning to make impatient noises next to him.

When Eli got his scope back again, Sam and company had advanced to the third of the eight towers, with still no sign of life up there aside from their miniscule friends. There was another interruption in their vigil when someone announced that the advance team from the relief company had reached the lower bunker. The sergeant with the radio relayed both bits of news to the command group. Sam was advancing on the fifth tower by the time Eli got another look through his scope. The distant figures were almost invisible without benefit of the scope or the binoculars. Ten minutes later they reached the farthest tower, and Eli watched them trot along further to where they could apparently see down the far side of the ridge. The four men who had hauled the machine gun and ammunition had rested and eaten by now, and the whole group was waiting restlessly for a signal to advance.

Finally a bright flash came from a signal mirror. The sergeant translated the code as it came. "All come quick!" They needed no further urging. The sergeant relayed the message to the command group as he set out at a quick jog across the rocky ridge. Eli collected his pack and joined them, but soon found he could not keep up with their dog trot pace. There was no need to cling to the side of the ridge and they made rapid progress along the broad back of the gently climbing ridge top. The ridge fell away to the west in the series of rocky ribs and gullies that Sam had skirted on his careful approach. The eastern or Syrian side was more gentle for a short distance before also plunging steeply. The dozen soldiers jogged along in a rough skirmish line, several meters apart. As the ridge began to climb a little less gradually, Eli found himself chugging along in the rear of the group as it spread out according to speed. He was keeping pace with a large soldier who was lugging the heavy machine gun on one shoulder or another, switching the burden every few dozen meters. His heavy pack probably held a belt or two of ammunition as well. Eli's pack was feeling heavy too, but he was sure he was carrying far less than half the burden of the large soldier. Nearly twenty minutes of breathless dog trot brought them to the first of the towers. From here they could see Sam and his three companions fanned out behind assorted boulders and obviously Sam was watching something on the far side of the mountain. Eli sensed that he had just run headlong into another fire fight. The man with the machine gun sensed it too, and slowed his pace to try to recover his breath. However, Sam soon spotted the man with the machine gun, and he was signaling him to take a position to his right, so the man redoubled his efforts and pounded ahead of Eli.

His former running mate was already setting up the big machine gun and feeding it a belt from his pack by the time Eli huffed and wheezed up to their makeshift line. Sam came scuttling by to greet him and give the machine gunner instructions. Peering over the top of their jumble of boulders, Eli soon saw what Sam had been watching. A small column of jeeps, trucks and some sort of small, tracked armored car was creeping its way up a narrow rocky track on the far side of the mountain. They were just over a kilometer or so away. Sam was barking into his radio while his sergeant recovered his breath and took in the situation.

Sam was pleading, apparently unsuccessfully, for helicopter support. "We're going to have to hold them off until our relief group can get here or some helicopters can be spared," Sam said, waving a hand at the approaching column. Eli estimated there were at least 100 soldiers in the dozen vehicles crawling their way along the mountainside. He also heard that the rest of their relief group had only reached the upper bunker a few minutes ago and was pressing on for their ridge. That put them nearly an hour away.

He unslung his rifle and began to look for a suitable post where he could have a clear shot at where the column would begin coming within range. Sam patted him on the shoulder and indicated a spot farther down the slope that would give him an even better vantage point and more choice of cover. Eli followed Roee, who had been one of Sam's summit foursome, and the two of them slipped crabwise down the slope, remaining out of sight of the approaching Syrian column.

"We think our helicopter reconnaissance scared them off the summit yesterday, because Sam says there was at least a platoon or more up here then," Roee told Eli as they settled into their positions. Roee had a low powered optical sight on his long-barreled M-16 that made it accurate up to two or three hundred meters. Eli was still sighted in at five hundred meters, although he had been hitting targets beyond that range with some success since the first day of the war. He surveyed his quarry for vulnerable tires, drivers and exposed gunners. To his relief, the column was only lightly armored. All but one of the vehicles was vulnerable to well directed fire, especially once their .50 caliber came into range. The advancing column had mostly light machine guns mounted on the jeeps, and one recoilless rifle that could prove a problem if not hit early in the coming ambush.

Sam waited until the column was painfully close. The lead armored car was only a couple hundred meters away when suddenly the .50 caliber machine gun opened up on it, ripping gaping holes in its light armor plating and stopping it in its half tracks. Eli had been tracking the gunner on the recoilless rifle, and squeezed off his first shot at the same time that Roee began pumping rounds into the suddenly stopped column. The dozen ambushers had fired for nearly half a minute before the first of the surprised Syrians diving for the cover of nearby rocks managed to begin returning fire in any organized fashion. One of the light machine guns was now firing from behind the wreckage of one of the disabled jeeps, and a few rocket propelled grenades lobbed short and burst in front of Eli and Roee.

Once the surprise wore off and the survivors of the savage first barrage rallied and took cover, finding targets grew difficult for Eli, even with his high powered scope. A large group had reformed behind a big rock outcropping, and another group behind the wreckage of one of the heavy trucks. Soon there was increasingly accurate return fire forcing him and Roee to duck and change positions. Eli was able to catch one or two advancing figures in the confusion. He was aware that the Syrians were beginning to press forward and make progress in spite of their still accurate fire. The odds were now perhaps five or six to one instead of the beginning odds of eight or ten to one. Eli was feeling hard pressed to find the courage to seek a new spot and get into another firing position against the hail of bullets flying around overhead. Roee was moving and firing, but obviously risking a lot to return each shot.

"It's kill or be killed," Eli told himself, but it felt like "kill and be killed" in this firestorm. He had come so far, to the top of Israel's highest mountain. He was not going to give up now. He heard confused yelling and saw men running towards the far side of their thin line. He squeezed off a shot, missed, chambered a new round and aimed again. He caught a man in the side where he was unprotected by a flak vest. Sam's group had left their flak vests behind because of the need for speed in the long climb up the mountain. That meant that each of them was vulnerable to hits that normally would be absorbed by the ceramic and Kevlar layers. Eli had only his trusty helmet for protection from bullets, and it was far from perfect in that department. He saw two of Sam's men fall, but the attack was beaten back thanks to their heavy machine gun.

A bullet pinged his helmet with a glancing blow and Eli turned to face four men charging from the cover of a boulder. He barely had time to swing his rifle around and fire, sighting down the barrel as best he could in a split second, for the scope was useless at this range. He dropped his man and was fumbling with chambering another round when Roee hit the attacker in the chest and face with three well placed shots from his semiautomatic. Bolt action rifles are great for accuracy, but almost worthless in a close encounter, Eli discovered. By the time he had his round chambered and gun up, the other two had dropped behind fresh cover and were attempting to retreat.

The two failed sorties discouraged the Syrians for a while, but Eli knew it could not last. He heard someone with a shrill sharp voice, probably an officer, berating the men behind the not so distant rock outcrop into what would probably be another attack. He could also tell that the .50 caliber machine gun had been firing shorter and shorter bursts. They had only been able to pack in four boxes of ammunition, not enough for a prolonged fire fight. Eli sensed that the Syrians must know this too. However, for the moment, he and Roee had the advantage in their end of the line, for they had shifted positions and were watching, ready to fire at anyone showing himself. Tenuous as it was, this was better than hiding behind a rock while a stream of shells whizzed overhead.

Suddenly Eli saw a figure running near one of the disabled jeeps. He raised his rifle, but Roee barked out a warning not to shoot. He acknowledged the warning, but used his scope to catch a glimpse – it was Sam, and Ronny too, heading for an abandoned jeep with an intact machine gun mounted in the back! Eli tried to watch with one eye while keeping the other eye on where he had last seen Syrian soldiers in his area. He had already seen one scuttle back from one rock to another seeking better shelter. He realized that the machine gun, if it worked, would be able to sweep the area behind the house-sized rock outcrop that was sheltering the bulk of the regrouped Syrian soldiers. Eli prayed that the gun would work and that Sam would not be spotted. As if in answer to his silent prayer, the gun erupted in a stab of flame and Sam poured fire at the unseen group. Moments later, Eli had his sights full of men trying to run out from the side of the rocks opposite the deadly machine gun.

As he and Roee fired away at the fleeing men, one of the two survivors of the failed charged popped up from behind a close by rock and unleashed a spray of automatic fire at Roee and Eli. Fortunately for them, the full automatic setting emptied the man's clip in moments without hitting either of them. They saw him throw the rifle away, turn and run in absolute terror. Shocked and amused at the same time, they let him go. The running soldier fell sprawling perhaps 50 meters away, picked himself up and ran headlong straight down the shoulder of the mountain top. He was not the only one running at this point. Eli noticed that Ronny had taken control of the recoilless rifle and was now banging away at the group still sheltering behind the large truck near the end of the convoy.

However, there were at least a couple dozen Syrians who were holding their ground, and their fire soon drove Ronny away from the exposed recoilless rifle. Sam was forced to take his captured machine gun from its mountings and take cover with it behind the wreck of the jeep. The short fight was beginning to look like a stalemate – with victory to the group that ran out of ammunition last, or was reinforced first. Eli consulted his watch. The soonest they could expect their relief company was still nearly half an hour away. That was several lifetimes at least in this deadly game.

He was sweeping the rocky terrain with his scope looking for an exposed target when he heard a blast of noise erupt behind him. He whirled to see three menacing black helicopters pop up over the ridge behind him at perhaps twenty to thirty meters high and coming impossibly fast. He rolled over and prepared to take cover from the new threat when he saw a blue and white Star of David on the nearest one. He could see the pilot and copilot plainly as the chopper thundered directly overhead, blasting him with the wash of its rotors and blinding him with swirling rocky dust and sand. Eli heard rather than saw their savage attack. He heard Roee's hoarse whoop of exultation and joined him in a

Golan! Day Eight

heartfelt cheer, yelling he had no idea what, just yelling a roar of relief and triumph to be alive.

In a matter of a minute or two, the ridge was swept clear of resistance. Sam had remounted his machine gun and was coordinating his men to disarm and line up about two dozen survivors. Many more had fled down the gullies of the eastern side of the ridge, and the helicopters left these alone. Eli and Roee emerged from the shelter of their rocks to join him, and the pair who had worked the .50 caliber machine gun moved in closer to where the prisoners were assembling to provide a second source of cover.

Two of the helicopters settled to a noisy landing and two groups of ten commandos each ran from their open doors, ducking under the rotors and jogging over to help. They were in full combat gear with packs and flak jackets and pockets bulging with clips of ammunition.

Eli picked up his pack again and found it much lighter. Perhaps twenty shells jingled in the pockets. He had half a bottle of water left and no food. He looked at Roee and saw a red stain spreading slowly down his left sleeve. Roee seemed unaware of the blood as he too rummaged in his pack and was producing empty clips to reload. Eli called to him and pointed to his left bicep. Roee looked at his arm absently, continuing his hunt for clips.

One of the commandos saw and came over, motioned for Roee to sit down, took out a knife and neatly slit open the bloody shirt sleeve, exposing two seeping scars where bullets had grazed his bicep. The soldier from the helicopter team put down his pack and produced a first aid kit, expertly sprinkled the wounds with an antiseptic powder that also acted to stop bleeding and soon had it wrapped up in a neat bandage.

Eli sat down on the ground next to Roee, took off his helmet and gazed at the new bullet scar in it. He barely remembered the pings that had drawn his attention to the charging Syrians about thirty minutes earlier. Roee looked at Eli's scarred helmet and grinned. He took off his own and pointed to his own collection of near misses. The commando medic offered them each chocolate bars, which they accepted with a grateful tired smile each. The soldier left them sitting there on the rocky ground, the afternoon sun warming their backs, eating their candy bars in wonder.

Sam came by sometime after the chocolate bars were finished and the two men were just sitting there staring at the efficient sorting and separating of the prisoners. He sat down wearily beside them after giving each an affectionate pat on the shoulder. Sam's helmet looked worse than either of theirs; he had the battered and bullet scored helmet still on his head, which had somehow survived the hail of flying lead and shrapnel. Sam stared at the line of wrecked vehicles.

"If we hadn't shot the shit out of all those Jeeps we might have had something to drive," he said ruefully. Indeed, the Syrian rolling stock was pretty thoroughly destroyed. "We're supposed to regroup back at the communications towers," Sam said, getting wearily to his feet. The towers were less than half a kilometer from the site of their ambush, but it seemed like a long walk back. Four others from their group sported fresh bandages, and two were limping awkwardly, but miraculously no one was dead of the sixteen men who had dug in to stop the Syrian company sent to reoccupy the summit. Eli had seen two fall, but their wounds were not as bad as they had seemed at first.

Before they left the job to the twenty airlifted commandos, Sam still had a couple shots left on the pocket-sized Leica camera he had carried through the war. He posed their weary group by the blasted armored car that had been the first vehicle in the Syrian relief force and had one of the commandos snap the last two pictures. They all joined arms and squinted into the bright afternoon sun.

All had refused to be airlifted out, but the limping two regretted their decision volubly and with a certain amount of self-righteous kvetching several times over before their slow moving group reached the communications towers. While they trudged towards the towers, a huge Chinook helicopter landed near the far towers and disgorged a large group of communications technicians and their support team. They soon started up a pair of portable generators and were struggling to erect a large canvas tent in the steady breezes that blew across the summit ridges.

Every now and then Eli gazed about him, taking in the amazing vistas that opened up right, left and ahead. Far away he could see the bluish horizon that marked the Mediterranean Sea. Walking had revived Sam enough that he was talking again. He wandered from person to person in their small group telling each one how amazingly they had performed over the past few days, and he had much to tell. When he got to Eli he walked along wordlessly for a while. Finally he said, "I promised Natalie that I would bring you back in one piece. Just a little while ago I thought for sure I had failed and led you and everyone in this group into an impossible fight. But after all you and I had been through in the last week – starting from the night I borrowed Woody and everything that followed – I couldn't believe it was all going to end that close to finishing the job we set out to do. I heard this morning that the whole Syrian Third and Fourth Armies are talking about surrender near Carmiel. It just didn't seem right, or fair. I had one and a half clips left and one more hand grenade and there was no way to retreat without being cut to shreds. I was starting to wonder if there was any way to surrender. But then I remembered our kayak trip on the Kinneret. How I thought we were totally lost and was about to freak out, but you just started looking around to see if there were any clues. It was about then I noticed that one of the machine guns appeared to be loaded and unharmed – and the question suddenly became how in the world to get there? Ronny and I snaked our way on our bellies from rock to rock until we could make a dash for it. But, man, I was

hugging that earth and praying for one more chance. Looks like I got it."
Eli hugged him, with tears in his eyes, and they walked along together.

Everyone naturally headed for the tent, although it was flapping and swaying in the wind too much to be much of a useful shelter. Eli suggested to one of the officers that they should stack low walls of rocks around the tent to deflect the wind. They looked at him as if he were inventing a new form of work with his absurd idea, but then a couple decided that perhaps it was worth a try when the windward wall nearly collapsed from the freshening breeze and started collecting portable rocks. Eli, ever the helper when it came to see an idea carried out, picked up a couple rocks to show them where to start their deflector wall, and soon sat down to watch numbly. The communications and support teams were soon wrapped up in their respective tasks, and so after a short visit, Sam and his group wandered off to get out of the wind behind one of the metal sheds away from the noisy generators and flapping tent. Sam requisitioned two boxes of rations from the stack of supplies being put away.

In the warm afternoon sun, with the rising wind blocked by a container sized steel equipment shed, Sam and his group were alternately schmoozing and snoozing as they waited for word on whether there would be a helicopter free to airlift them back to their motley collection of vehicles parked near the lodge. Otherwise they would have to walk down the ski slopes that the assault helicopters had helped clear of Syrians. In the meantime, they devoured every scrap of food in the ration cases.

The middle assault team never made it to the summit, but settled for reoccupying the surrendered command post that the Syrians had captured in the first day of the war. The team that had tackled clearing the northwest ridge could be seen flopped in a tired heap farther along the mountain. They had taken some casualties along the way, being caught between two fires at one point as well. They had done the job themselves by the time the helicopters arrived according the stories exchanged at the communications camp.

While they loafed in the warm sun and talked of the past days, the first of their relief company arrived from the direction they had first come to the summit ridge. Had the helicopter strike team not arrived well before them, this group would have found a battered but victorious company of Syrian regulars here on the ridge. That thought sent chills down Eli's spine despite the bright mountain sunshine. The commander of the group trekked over to meet up with Sam and explain that they could have been here more than half an hour earlier, but had been told to regroup and pack for a longer stay once the helicopter commando team had secured the mountaintop. They would be digging in and manning a perimeter around the communications complex, and were expecting a Chinook later in the day with supplies and some heavier weapons for a week-long stay at least. The captain told Sam that his two casualties were being stretchered out to the base of the mountain, and a grave was being dug for their fallen companion. The remainder of his company was reinforcing the two captured bunkers and also settling in for a week or more of guard duty.

"So, is the war over?" Ronny asked the newly arrived captain.

"Not quite. There is still a big mess down south, but there is talk of an eight hour cease fire to allow anyone who wants to withdraw back to Egypt to take what they can carry and scurry back. There is a push headed up the Hula Valley to Kiryat Shemona to clear the rest of the Golan, and word is that the Jordanians are withdrawing. The Lebanese border is still pretty volatile, Jerusalem is quiet, and nobody is talking about Jericho or Jenin with any definitive news."

The two groups traded news and stories for a while until the second group got up and started going through the motions of setting up a perimeter and planning a camp. Sam's group stayed where they were. Half were sleeping. Eli wasn't sure why he was still awake, for the warm September sun felt good and his body was bone weary. But he and Sam were talking about their plans for "after" the war, a concept that they had not been able to think about in concrete or realistic terms for more than a week.

Their beloved country was bloodied and bruised, badly bombed and still without power. However, the army and some form of government were still intact and gaining in strength and organization daily. As evidence for that, they had the communications teams noisily at work not far away, and promise that more Chinook helicopters were expected with supplies that might afford them a free ride down the mountain they had climbed foot by foot.

As far as Eli knew, he still had a reasonably intact house – one of only three in the whole moshav that was fully habitable as of his last stop there. He might even still have a job of sorts. Although he had not been able to contact his communications clients for more than a week, he was fairly sure that two or three would weather the storm and keep his services. If Israel could get him back on the Internet within a month or two there was hope of saving part of his business. Perhaps there was some kind of satellite phone solution that could work as a stopgap. However, one of his clients was probably in a panic with a major trade show coming up in Las Vegas next week. They may have hired another firm to come in and finish executing the communications campaign he had mapped out for them. Somehow trade shows in Las Vegas seemed like a fairy tale from a faraway land and time right now.

Eli and Sam were trading impressions of Las Vegas when one of the communications team came jogging around the corner of their shelter and puffed, "there you are. The prime minister wants to talk to you," he said, pointing to Sam. Both of them looked at the man in disbelief, but he insisted that the acting prime minister was on the line from Jerusalem and wanted to talk with Captain Samuel Hirsch.

Negotiations for a ceasefire and withdrawal of the trapped Syrian armies were crawling to a standstill. No one wanted the bombing and shelling to begin again, especially the hungry, demoralized, soldiers of the Syrian Third and Fourth Armies and their mercenary companions who had stormed into Israel a week earlier. But the Israeli soldiers were equally exhausted, and their supply of ammunition of every shape and size was running low. They had little stomach for starting up the shooting again. They had fought hard all week, pushed to the edge of disaster and defeat at nearly every moment, but holding on tenaciously and bringing the huge, two-army juggernaut to a shuddering halt, leaving fifty bloody kilometers of destruction in its wake from the Syrian border.

When she could, Anna kept up with tidbits of the Jordanian withdrawal, which was being handled through the Central Command even though it overlapped into her Northern Command area. Two Syrian armies and a horde of irregulars, armed thugs and looters were enough for her hard-working team at the top of Mt. Meron. The Jordanian army had pulled out of Nazareth, Uhm Al Fahm and Jenin overnight and was streaming back across the Jordan River, taking with them a stream of refugees convinced that this time the Israelis would carry out the massacre they had been sure was going to happen in 1948, and in 1967. But there had been no massacres then, and there certainly would not be any now. They would have to wait for another lifetime, for all Israelis wanted was to get their Israel back, and to stop fighting. They had enough of war.

With much help from the Israeli communications specialists, the group of four captains who were all that was left of the command group of the Fourth Army were able to get in touch with the generals of the Third Army one mountain away. The Third Army general staff knew about the suicidal final charge of their counterparts, and knew that they had no future waiting for them back in Syria, so they kept talking but doing nothing to put any of the talk about a withdrawal into action. The Syrian high command back in Damascus was insisting that their armies "fight to the last man." Anna could tell from the snatches of negotiations that were translated for her, that the regime in Damascus was deathly afraid of a mob of 60,000 angry, discouraged and disappointed soldiers surging back across its borders. They really DID want their army to fight on to glorious annihilation.

However, the surviving officers of the Third and Fourth Armies were dealing with Krembo Kramer, and, despite the name, he was no Twinky. Among other hints, he casually let the generals who had taken up residence in bomb shelters under a rural Arab village know that the Israeli Air Force had a few bunker busting bombs left, and he knew their exact coordinates. They had until 4 p.m. to decide exactly how their men were going to start walking home the next morning. Anna now had access to the aerial high definition TV pictures of the key command points in the areas where the Syrian armies were holed up being fed to her by circling unmanned drones. She and Crembo would know if any of the command groups tried to slip away. Their massive volume radio and satellite phone transmissions made the Syrian leaders easy enough to follow in any case. Her greenest trainees could easily find and program in the coordinates for a GPS guided bomb for any of the well-known voice signatures.

The Syrian generals were insisting that their soldiers keep their light weapons. They would certainly need them when they got back home – or risk being bushwhacked by any of the militias who stayed behind. Krembo was calmly pointing out that Syrian internal security affairs were not his problem, but security for his troops during the withdrawal was. The Syrian negotiators were trying to exempt hand guns from the weapons ban when the four p.m. deadline arrived. Krembo gave the generals one last opportunity to reach an accord, and then gave the signal for the waiting F-16s being loaded at the nearby Ramat David airbase to negotiate the much-patched runways and lumber into the air with their 3,000 kilogram loads. Anna listened to Crembo wish the Fourth Army general staff a pleasant eternity, and watched two huge craters blasted half a mile below the circling reconnaissance drone. She put down her earphones with mixed feelings of "good riddance" and disgust, and went to work trying to get the next highest ranking officers of the Fourth Army on the radio.

Moshav Yiftach 1700

The sun was inching towards the western horizon and there was still no word of Eli. Natalie tried to find a clear, calm place deep inside to check her instincts to see if he was still alive, but it was impossible to concentrate. It wasn't just her full household, or the challenge of putting together dinner for her wounded guests, Tali and her kids. It was Natalie's night to cook, and she was concocting a vegetable stew with some left over odds and ends of beans for protein. There was no flour left for baking. A few of the households on the Moshav had sacks of wheat that they were grinding and passing around to the other working kitchens. Natalie had loaned her grinder to speed up the process, but had not seen a bag of freshly ground flour arrive that day. A hearty stew, some fresh fruit from the orchards, they would eat well. She wondered for the millionth time how Rivka was doing in urban Jerusalem with no garden beyond a few herbs in flowerpots.

Golan! Day Eight

But Eli was foremost on her mind. The radio told her that there was a ceasefire in the north and south ends of the country, that the Jordanian army had retreated, and that the Syrian armies were talking surrender. Indeed, the Moshav had been calm for the past two days, with hardly anything to disturb its rural quiet. Those who were not on guard, hospital or childcare duty were doing what they could to repair the roofs on some of the less damaged houses. They were scavenging the few unbroken windows and trying to make them habitable for winter. That might bring the number of usable homes on the 150 home Moshav to about ten or eleven. Another ten or so might be fixable before the winter rains set in, leaving one house for every five or six families. However, they were big houses, and there was plenty of space in the bomb shelters if need be. The shelters tended to stay well above freezing even in the coldest winters, just like her half-earth-sheltered house. Thinking about her house brought her mind instantly back to Eli, who had built it with the help of a crew of friends and a few hired men.

Where was he? And who was this crazy Sam person who kept showing up and dragging him off on wild and foolhardy missions? Was he some kind of intelligence operative? He seemed to know too much and have way too much responsibility and latitude for a mere lieutenant. She would probably never know. She liked Sam, for he was 100 percent likeable. She even trusted him, a little. But to head off into the middle of World War Three with a 58-year-old man armed with a single-shot bolt-action rifle? That was insane. Sure, there were plenty of older men fighting, but most of them stuck around with the moshav defense groups. Right now they were busy trying to build a makeshift water tank for the community, not off galloping around the Golan in a funky old truck that was only a few years younger than that crazy lieutenant.

Natalie realized that she was clanging and banging her cookware and making a vigorous din in her mounting frustration and anger at the absurdity of the situation. Eli was good at building, not fighting. He should be helping the old guys build a rock and clay reservoir, not tearing around with a bunch of IDF hotshots. She knew only that Sam had something to do with reconnaissance, and they had a reputation for taking outlandish risks and surviving by the skin of their teeth. Eli was not that tough. In fact, on Shabbat and at least one other afternoon a week, he needed a good nap. Where was he now? She wondered.

Tali's kids helped her set the table and carry the steaming pot of soup to the living room. It was *Hoshanah Rabbah*, the last day of *Sukkot*, and they had eaten their last meal in the sukkah last night, missing Eli at every minute. But, watching Tali's children setting the table, she was reminded that they had no idea where their father was, had not seen him since at least two weeks before the war, and had no word from him since. Tali was looking strained as the days of relative peace brought no news. In fact, Natalie had packed her off to bed for a long nap, for she had not been sleeping well at night. The commotion of the cooking, smell of hot food and the bustle of people crowding around their big dining room table brought Tali, sleepy eyed and weary from the bedroom. Natalie felt guilty for not protecting her rest better, for she knew her friend needed a long, long unbroken sleep.

Natalie found herself squeezed beside the Syrian major, who was now able to hobble short distances with the help of a walker. His extensive abdominal wounds and tightly wrapped bandages kept him stiff and awkward, but his military bearing was naturally erect and correct, she decided. They made small talk over the stew, and he lavished praise on her for her cooking and hospitality, and asked solicitously about Eli's welfare. Natalie was starting to be used to him. Since the talk of the Syrian surrender, which he had also heard on the radio and from reports from soldiers returning from the field, she was less worried about him trying a desperate escape attempt. In fact, he was now sitting there at as polite a distance from her right elbow as the crowded table would allow, telling her of his postwar plans. He had wanted for years to leave Syria and take his family to England, where he had spent six or seven years in college and military officers training courses. As much as he loved the Middle East, London was the most interesting and civilized city he had ever lived in, and he feared there would be years of turmoil and bloodshed in a defeated Syria.

Even without the war, his adopted homeland, for his great grandfather had come to Syria from Basri in Iraq, had been growing more and more dangerous and unstable. With the massive defeat of its proud armies, there would be no center left. Into that power vacuum would move hundreds of petty tyrants and strong men – like the feudal war lords. That was his prediction, and he had no stomach (almost literally, he laughed, patting his swath of bandages around his midsection) for subjecting his family to that kind of chaos and upheaval. If the British consulate in Israel could consider his application, perhaps he could collect his family somehow. With those thoughts he lapsed into a deep reverie. Natalie got up to help organize the dishes and leftovers that were being cleared from the table.

What would Israel be like after the war? She wondered. Certainly it would not be the bloody chaos of Syria. But there were definitely leaner times ahead. There were still only half a dozen vehicles moving on the whole moshav. She wondered what had happened to Woody? Was Eli driving it somewhere up north on some crazy mission even now? It was battered and bullet scarred already, and its missing windshield made the old brown truck look especially forlorn, but it was chugging along fine to listen to Eli talk. Perhaps the truck was his ticket to something safe – say shuttling supplies and men behind the front. She hoped as much, but with smooth talking, secret agent Sam in the picture, there was no telling.

The Jewish sages said somewhere in the *Talmud* that whenever a man and a woman met a new guest, the woman would leave the encounter knowing at least five times as much about the newcomer, even though they sat at the same table and heard the same words. However, there was something about Sam that defied her womanly intuition, *binah* it was called in Hebrew. Although everyone had varying degrees of *binah*, women had ten times as much on average. In fact, that concept was the source of one of those bits of *Talmud* often misused and misunderstood by liberal feminists – the saying that a woman's *Dat*, her rational and logical judgment, was light compared to a man's. Taken in context of the whole discussion in the *Talmud*, it meant that in relation to her "heavy" *binah*, a woman's *dat* was light compared to a man's. This was a fact of life that Eli accepted readily, although Natalie teasingly reminded him of it when they were weighing a family matter or decision together. There was a slippery, secret side to Sam that she could sense, but not quite put her finger on. Perhaps she should accuse him jokingly of being a secret agent the next time she saw him. She hoped it would be soon, and not for the purpose of telling her that Eli had died somewhere along the way. She shoved that dreadful thought away in a hurry.

The warm, dry east wind that had blown all day was beginning to shift around to the north and bring with it just a hint of moisture. Perhaps there would be dew tonight. That would be welcome in the parched and dusty landscape that still had pockets of smoke, and a layer of dusty haze that gave them deep sunsets and slow sunrises.

Hoshanah Rabbah morning the men carried the *Sefer Torah* scrolls from the basement bomb shelter and held services in the main sanctuary of the moshav's largest synagogue for the first time since the start of the war. The windows were all broken, and large parts of the roof were torn away and open to the sky. One of the walls was crumbling in places, and one balcony of the upstairs women's section had fallen down. But the ark where the scrolls were kept, and the raised bimah where the Torah was read, were intact, along with most of the benches and schtenders in the men's section. Someone had carefully swept up the broken glass and shoveled out debris so that services could be held. They would still keep the scrolls safely stored in the bomb shelter *Shul* until the synagogue could be repaired, which would probably take months or perhaps more than a year. But this morning, the precious scrolls were brought up into the morning light, and held on the bimah while the rest of the congregation completed their seven circuits, holding their *lulavs* and *etrogs* for the last time of the seven day *Sukkot* holiday. Normally it was a joyous occasion, with much singing and some dancing. The real dancing would happen in the evening when the simultaneous holidays of *Simchat Torah* and Shemini Atzeret (the eighth day celebration or meeting) happened.

In Chicago, where Natalie grew up, and in the rest of the Diaspora, these were separate holidays. On *Simchat Torah*, the congregation read the last chapter of the Torah scroll, danced with all the Torah scrolls with wild abandon for seven long sessions, singing and carrying children on their shoulders and dancing until their feet ached. Then they would appoint a *Chatan Torah*, and a *Chatan Bereshit* – the bridegroom of the Torah and the bridegroom of the Book of Genesis, *Bereshit* in Hebrew. The bridegroom of the Torah would be treated to the last honorary aliyah of the final passage of *Devarim*, the Book of Deuteronomy as it is known to non-Jews. He would be called up with much pomp and circumstance to recite the blessing over reading the Torah under a *tallit* held over the *bimah* by the taller members of the *Shul*. The Torah would be held aloft after the reading, and there would be perhaps another outbreak of dancing and singing. Then the *Chatan Bereshit* would be called for the reading of the first chapters of Genesis with the same elaborate ceremony. The next morning, they would do it all again. Only perhaps it would be a little shorter, for the men would be tired from the night before.

Natalie always found the ceremony a little odd, since the *Shul* would generally still be in great disarray from all the dancing. Most of the men would have discarded their suit jackets long ago, if they wore them. This moshav was decidedly casual, and so a simple white dress shirt and a clean pair of jeans or slacks was the norm. Some of the older men from Europe or the UK still wore suit jackets. All but two holdouts had long since discarded their ties in acknowledgment of Israel's much warmer climate. The chairs and benches would have all been pushed back to make room for the dancing, and the listeners would generally be perched on a makeshift collection of chairs haphazardly arranged for the Torah readings at the end of all the dancing. Often there would be beer and wine bottles scattered around, for the young men often found dancing with the Torah for a few hours very thirsty work. However, Moshav Yiftach was a fairly sober group compared to the Chicago *shul*s she had known as a young woman.

She had come late so as to hear the Torah readings, but to miss most of the dancing – she missed Eli. She was used to watching him, for he liked to dance. In recent years, he would have a grandchild or two to throw in the air, or carry on his shoulders. She liked to watch his outright enjoyment. But this year he was somewhere else. She did not know where he was, or when he would be home. Without Eli and her grandchildren there, she could only watch so many turns around the bimah. Besides, the men were not quite in a joyous mood this year. They were tired, and worried, and it showed.

In Israel, *Simchat Torah* began on the same night as Shemini Atzeret. Despite living in Israel for many years, Natalie was still not used to the merger of the two holidays. Shemini Atzeret was, technically, a separate holiday, and called for two festive meals. A festive meal – by Jewish tradition generally meant three things should be part of the meal: wine, bread and meat or fish. Natalie had saved one bottle of wine from Eli's once full wine rack that he had built into a niche in their living room wall. Two loaves of fresh baked bread miraculously appeared just in time for their evening meal from the neighbor she had loaned the grain mill, but there was not a scrap of meat left, for the Moshav shochet had been called away to serve the larger communities farther south in the Golan and had not returned in time to slaughter any chickens or cows in time for the final holiday.

Mt Hermon 1600

Eli, Roee and Ronny were dozing when they heard the whumpeta whumpeta whumpeta of a big Chinook cargo helicopter approaching. It landed not far from the towers and soon disgorged a pair of jeeps armed with recoilless rifles, an anti-aircraft gun, and another mound of equipment. Sam came sprinting from the communications shed to collect his pack and what was left of his recon team – those who had not been helicoptered off the mountain in the first chopper to see to their wounds. "C'mon, they can give us a lift as far as Tzfat before sundown," Sam shouted over the helicopter's idling engines. "I'll have to leave you there and go on to Mt. Meron, but I can tell you the rest on board – grab your stuff."

With that he gathered his pack, for his rifle had never left his shoulder, and trotted off to the big waiting chopper. Dazed and wondering, Eli and his companions threw whatever they had taken out of their packs back in, cinched them up and trotted off after him. There were half a dozen others being airlifted out, and they all jammed together on the fold down bench seats on either side of the dim interior of the big airlift helicopter. As soon as the last one was in, the engines revved to near maximum, the blades changed their pitch and the huge craft lifted off in a sudden, stomach-wrenching lurch. Sam had motioned Eli to squeeze in beside him near the front of the cargo bay, while Roee and Ronny strapped in next along the bench. Roee had refused the earlier airlift, saying that his bullet wounds were minor, but Eli could tell they were bothering him from the way he gingerly handled his pack instead of his usual vigor.

"I'm being sent on a PR trip to America" Sam yelled at Eli and the rest of his group within earshot as the helicopter settled into a fast, level flight.

"A what trip?" Ronny yelled.

"PR- public relations – *hasbera*!" Sam yelled back.

Eli and the others looked mystified. The prime minister himself had called Sam to send him on a public relations trip?

"I know, I hate to leave when there is still fighting – but the PM says that the next battle is in the media – and to rally the worldwide Jewish community to help," Sam yelled.

"Why you?" Roee wondered at the top of his lungs.

Sam gave one of those "who knows" sort of shrugs but yelled back – "Remember that AP guy?"

Eli remembered him well, for he had spent a long time in the cab of Woody keeping him out of trouble.

"We're all famous – sort of – especially Eli." Sam shouted.

"Famous for what?" Eli wondered. The Chinook was beginning its descent towards the mountain community of Tzfat and drowned out any chance of asking. Eli tried to think where there was room for a big helicopter to land among all its quaint stone houses and narrow streets, but then he remembered the military base in the adjacent community of Canaan. They must get helicopters all the time there.

Sure enough, he saw the jury rigged radio masts of the military base flash by the half open side doorway where the crew chief was clipped in with a harness as the big chopper tilted perilously and dropped on its final approach. Eli glanced at his watch. In about forty minutes it would be *Shemini Atzeret*, the eighth day after the week long *Sukkot* holiday. Although fighting the war released him from most obligations and restrictions of the holiday – Eli suddenly felt swept with a wave of longing to stay in Tzfat and spend the final 25 hours of the holidays that he had missed while chasing around the war zone. If Sam was leaving, then perhaps he was no longer needed either. The war was winding down, and Eli felt he had risked his neck enough. Luck could only last so long. He was thinking about which of his many friends to run to if released from his military group when the helicopter settled to the ground with a gentle bump and a crescendo of noise.

All of them, except for Sam and a couple others seated near the front cargo bay unbuckled their lap belts and prepared to file off. Eli stood up, but Sam pulled him down and motioned to him to lean close for some words. The rotors kept turning and the rest of the team filed out, ducking instinctively under the downwash of the huge blades.

"I just wanted to say thanks for everything," Sam yelled, "and to let you know that Woody is being put to work up on Mt Hermon for the rest of the day. Then one of our guys is going to drive it to Carmiel the morning after *Shemini Atzeret*. We need to use it for a couple of days to guard prisoners on the march home. The word is that they are surrendering, and the plan is to walk them back to Syria, those that can walk."

Eli absorbed the information as best he could. Sam and the IDF were welcome to Woody as long as the old truck could be of use. But he longed to go back home, with or without his faithful truck. "What about me?" he shouted.

Sam grinned, "You're a free man – and a hero according to the US newspapers. You should hear what that guy wrote about us and our kayak trip across the Kinneret. He made it sound like a great military exploit! I can't wait to see a newspaper for real. The PM just read me a few lines."

"Free?" Eli echoed.

"Yes – you have an honorable discharge from my recon platoon. Although I hear that they need drivers for the prisoner march."

"Thanks." Eli yelled back, and shook Sam's hand. The rotors were beginning to gather speed and the crew chief hanging out the side door was gesturing to him to leave. "Come see us when you get back," he yelled after shouldering his pack. Sam nodded and gave him a thumbs up.

Eli clumped across the metal grating of the floor and out the side door, for the tail ramp was already swinging closed, making the cargo hold darker and cutting off their view of the orange sky. He accepted the crew chief's strong arm lock that half lowered him down to the ground, bent slightly in the rotor blast and waved goodbye, but the crew chief had already swung inside again and Eli waved to an empty doorway.

Trotting half doubled over away from the propeller wash, he joined Roee and Ronny. They watched the big helicopter lift off and wheel off in the direction of Mt. Meron, only a few kilometers away and framed in a red and flaming orange sunset.

"Did Sam tell you anything else about his trip?" Roee wondered as the racket of the helicopter faded in the distance.

Eli shook his head. "But he told me I have an honorable discharge and can go home now," he said, almost guiltily, for his companions had been serving for more than a month. They faced probably at least another month or two of service before they could return to their civilian lives.

But, there was no sign of jealousy, just good will. Roee said, "He gave us all the day off. He said he was going soft in his old age and maybe there is something to all these blessed holidays."

"I know just the place then. You two follow me – we can just get there in time for *Yom Tov*," Eli said, and set off in the direction of town. Fortunately, it was all down hill from the military base, for his legs were complaining again.

Five hours later, Roee and Ronny agreed that it was "just the place" as they pushed away from the table littered with bottles, empty dishes and the leftovers of a delicious Sephardi-style holiday feast. Eli had been relieved to see that his friend's house was intact, aside from some cardboard in the windows shattered by the blast of falling missiles. For the past week rockets and mortar shells had fallen in the tightly packed old city neighborhood perched halfway up Tzfat's crowded hillsides. Very few had been killed, for nearly everyone had moved underground in bomb shelters for the vicious first few days of the war. In the relative quiet of the past few days, even though armies came and went in the main valley off in the distance, Tzfat had been calm, except for an occasional rocket fired by Hezbollah militias still active in nearby Lebanon. The streets were empty of working cars and trucks, for anything that ran had been conscripted for use by the army. The occasional pile of stone rubble knocked down from walls made for detours when walking. Power was still out and the black out was still nominally in effect, but small lights shown from synagogue doorways and the occasional house. The Breslovers, the town's largest Chassidic group, had rigged generators to power their large synagogue at one end of town and it blazed like a beacon in the night, defying the blackout rules – but no one seemed to think it mattered at this point.

Eli, Roee and Ronny barely had time to wash up and arrange their packs in a spacious screened balcony stacked with mattresses for the household's frequent visitors before running off to synagogue with their host. Fortunately for their gnawing appetites, the small neighborhood synagogue, lit with candles and a few oil lamps, made quick work of the seven *hakafot* – keeping the dancing lively but brief, no more than ten minutes for the first and last, and probably more like three minutes each for the intervening five bouts of dancing with the little synagogue's four Torah scrolls. Most of the congregation had young children, and so they were eager to get home and begin their holiday meal. There was plenty of time for more dancing later for those who wished to honor the Torah further. Tzfat's yeshivot and some of the bigger synagogues would be dancing until well past midnight, their host told them. Roee and Ronny, tired as they were after a long day on the mountain, picked up the dancing quickly – for there were no real steps, just energy required. And each of them got to carry a Torah scroll for one of the later *hakafot*, and that brought out their inner reserves of energy and joy. The full little synagogue danced with the joy of a hard fought war narrowly won, with relief to have the end in sight, and with confidence that whatever tomorrow brought, they had survived today.

Following the dancing and the Torah reading, they trooped back through the darkened streets, punctuated with various dancing groups of young men and the sounds of singing from other *shuls* that were still going strong. Eli's friend had nine children, stair-stepping in age from just married to just out of diapers. Ronny looked pleased to be able to carry the youngest one, sound asleep on his shoulder, back from the services. Their meal had been superb – with pair of chickens stretched to the maximum with rice and vegetables and spicing enough to make up for the lack of meat. There were tasty salads of couscous, hummus, tehinah, taboule, home-cured olives and pickled vegetables, and lots of fresh baked bread and pitas to turn the simple meal into a memorable feast. Somehow their host's wine and liquor supply seemed inexhaustible, and everyone ended the meal more than a little tipsy.

The other guests were a young couple and their baby whose tiny apartment had been hit by a rocket early in the war. There was a middle-aged divorcee whose grown children still lived in America. She was beloved by all the host's children. There was also a shy, elderly widower who warmed up as the evening went on rounding out their full table. All shared stories of their experiences over the past week.

The young couple had been living with friends and doubling up in another small apartment nearby, with much of their time spent in the building's bomb shelter with their neighbors. They had been invited out for every meal during the war. They were the source of many stories on how their fellow citizens were coping. Eli found himself telling his story in somewhat disjointed reverse order, starting with their helicopter flight down from Mt. Meron. The helicopter ride impressed the children very much and needed to be told with much detail, with sound effects supplied by Ronny to the delight of the younger ones. Roee supplied technical details about the Chinook for the sake of the older boys. Their desperate fight against the Syrian company to hold the top of the mountain was glossed over in favor of telling the story of scaring the Azerbaijani company out of the captured moshav by the ruse of a tractor turned into a tank. They left out the bloody details of how they captured the real tanks.

The younger children dropped off one by one in snuggled heaps around the corners of the living/dining room. The older ones ventured off to visit friends or go dance with the yeshiva boys or form up a pack with other seminary girls. As the house quieted down, Eli could tell more of this story to his friend and host. He found he had all kinds of stories to tell. It felt strange to recall being in the shouk in Syria, or driving a captured truck with prisoners, or rolling around the Golan in Woody and ferrying tank and artillery shells. It was getting quite late by the time he reached the trip across the Kinneret. His host, (and hostess at various points between taking care of the meal, children and guests), listened in amazement and appreciation, for they had been friends for more than twenty years.

"You've had quite a war! I'm afraid things have not been quite so interesting here in Tzfat, thank G-d," his friend said. "The closest I've come to the war is slamming the bomb shelter door and scrounging for more candles."

"You have another job to do that is more important," Eli replied, gesturing at the four or five sleeping heads poking out of blankets and jackets around the room. "These little people are our future – and you'll have your hands full raising them and rebuilding Israel. I can't tell you what a mess it is between here and the border. The whole Golan from Tiberius northwards is in a shambles. My house is in more or less one piece, or was when I left, and thank G-d yours is too. I'm thinking that people like you and me will have one or two families staying with them for a very long time until homes can be rebuilt. That young couple here tonight, what were their names? There are a lot of people like them to take care of."

His host, Aharon, agreed. He had hosted a full table throughout the war, and realized it would probably continue for at least a year to come. Even before the war, the "Great Recession" as it had been called, had put a strain on those like him who earned some kind of a living. He had been frequently called upon to help out neighbors in need. The war only made that worse in many ways, although he hoped that jobs would be created in the rebuilding process.

"But forget about war and recession. How about joining the dancing going on at the yeshiva down the street for a little while? I'm still awake, what about you?"

"I don't know what I'm running on, except for your fine whiskey and your wife's world-class cooking. I'm game for an hour if you are," Eli said, getting to his feet with a stretch. Roee and Ronny declined the invitation to join the party and headed off to sleep.

It was close to midnight by the time Eli and his friend Aharon emerged from the remains of their feast and headed for the sounds of singing and dancing coming from the small yeshiva at the top of the street. However, before they could go into the candle-lit doorway, they were swept away by a pair of dancing Torahs. One Torah scroll was held aloft by the *Rosh Yeshiva* and another by a massive bear of a man, both men were wrapped in prayer shawls and trailing a crew of dancing, clapping young men as they burst from the doorway. Eli and Aharon fell in with them, swept along with the dancing. They soon found they were headed for the larger yeshiva farther along the hillside. As they neared their destination, they spotted hundreds more dancing in a wide part of the intersection of three streets that formed a bit of a makeshift square. There were more than two dozen men with Torah scrolls from the yeshivas and nearby synagogues in the middle of the revolving crowd of dancers. The two scroll bearers they were following worked their way to the center of the mob, leaving Eli and Aharon orbiting farther out where the crowd was less tightly packed. There was light only from a few gas lanterns hung from nearby balconies, for the sliver of moon gave little glow, and there were few stars visible in the still smoky night sky.

Around and around they went, singing the familiar songs from Psalms to different repetitive melodies, some familiar, some local favorites that Eli was not familiar with.

Eli was tired. His legs felt the ache of climbing Mt. Hermon that morning, his shoulders still felt the hunch of hauling a pack, and his cheek still felt the bruise of the kickback of his rifle. Roee had promised to watch Eli's rifle, so he was free of the hard, heavy awkward bulk on his shoulder for the first time in days.

And yet, deep within, he felt relieved, elated, as if his soul was somehow driving his feet to keep moving with the tempo, to celebrate with Israel yet another miraculous deliverance. Had he really woken up at the edge of the woods next to his truck in a parking lot at the Nimrod lodge only that morning? It was a lifetime ago already. The entrenched enemy they had faced that morning had crumbled into the sands of time. There was only Torah and Israel, Israel and the Torah – these were eternal, all else was dust.

Eli was lost in these thoughts when a young man grabbed him and spun him with manic energy. He was almost annoyed at the interruption of his thoughts and about to protest when he recognized the grinning face beneath the flying *peyot* and white "Nah-nach" *kippah*. It was the young man with the motorcycle who had brought Rabbi Beniyahu to his sukkah earlier in the week. He was instantly delighted to see him, and together they whirled with new energy until the young man pulled him insistently towards the packed center of the swirling crowd. Eli was beginning to feel somewhat trampled and more than a little claustrophobic by the time they reached the center of human maelstrom. But there, dressed in his simple white garb and wrapped in an enormous *tallit* , and carrying a Torah scroll more than half his size, he saw Rabbi Beniyahu. The young man danced him over until the three of them formed a circle. With a look of great delight, Rabbi Beniyahu handed Eli the huge Torah scroll, which was as heavy as it looked. Clasping it and kissing it, Eli joined his free arm with Rabbi Beniyahu and spun around and around with him until both were quite dizzy.

After awhile someone else came and took the scroll from Eli, and he felt a wave of exhaustion as he handed over its weight. Rabbi Beniyahu noticed, and steered him towards the edge of the crowd and into a nearby doorway. Eli was happy to follow, and happier still as the noise receded towards the interior of the house. There were women crowded together and talking in the first room overlooking the square and children sleeping in the second one they passed. They climbed up a winding stairway to a quiet study at the back of the house that was empty.

"How are you, my friend?" Rabbi Beniyahu asked, "would you like a cup of tea?"

Eli flopped into a comfortable old arm chair by the desk that was overflowing with books and papers. He agreed that perhaps a cup of tea would be nice, but big glass of water would be even more welcome.

"I'm sure Rabbi Meir has water as well. I'll be right back," the elfish little rabbi said, and disappeared into the hallway.

Eli could hear the shouted singing, muted by the stone walls of the older, Arab-style house with its high ceilings and deep set windows. He relaxed in the deep chair and studied the room with interest. It was obviously the private study of a very learned Rabbi, for every inch was lined with books from floor to ceiling and along all four walls and an alcove. Shelves even ran over top of the recessed windows that must look out at the mountainside behind, or some kind of a courtyard. There was a small, battered aluminum step ladder that stood in the clutter. It must be used to reach the top shelves, but had a fur streimel perched where the paint bucket would normally stand. Their host must be one of the Chassidic rabbis of the city, Eli surmised, but he could not recall a Rabbi Meir Something.

Rabbi Beniyahu came back with a cup of tea and a large glass of cool water. Eli said the "*shehakol*" blessing over the water and drank half of it down in a few gulps, feeling slightly embarrassed as the Rabbi said "amen" to his hasty blessing. The Rabbi said the same blessing over his tea and took a grateful sip. "Much better," he said. "Dancing is thirsty work,"

After inquiring about Eli's home and family, Rabbi Beniyahu proceeded to ask him about each of the past few days since they had parted, listening with rapt attention to every detail. He had heard the general story about the brief siege of Ramat HaGolan, but wanted to hear Eli's description from the front lines. Then he asked all about the next days spent clearing a section of the Golan. He was delighted with the story of fooling the enemy with a tank made out of a tractor, and using the remains of the real one as towed artillery. Eli also told what he had heard about the green tear gas used by the other groups to clear the border villages. Rabbi Beniyahu took so much pleasure in that story too that Eli had to stop and ask why.

"It's hard to explain," the rabbi explained. "But I want to understand how the Ribono Shel HaOlam is manifesting His power and miracles in this time – whether openly or slightly veiled. And so I want to know how much physical effort is required of His people for their deliverance compared to what would be considered "normal" in wartime. So when I hear that much bloodshed and death was avoided by a simple deception that proved almost miraculously effective, I rejoice for the Jewish people and anticipate the coming of our *Moshiach* in a less dire manner than has been described in, say Isaiah. And when you tell me that your small group of sixteen men were able to defeat more than one hundred men, I rejoice. But when I hear that half your number were wounded, even slightly, then I worry that the path is longer and harder. In either case, we were delivered from the hand of our enemies, and the few have defeated the many."

"And I want to know also about Israel's leaders and spirit – men like your friend Sam, who will go far, I am sure. I was not surprised to hear he was chosen to go abroad. For the battle for the soul of Israel is fought in the hearts and minds of all Israel. People like Sam and his men – who are caught in the war between material and spirit, secular and what is holy; they are the ones who will determine the character of the Israel to emerge from these ashes. I see the makings of a scholar in him, should he choose to learn Torah some day, but I think his talents are drawing him more to the political arena. He could be a fine leader, not just on the battlefield. This trip to America will help lay the foundation for that, and, I hope, open his eyes to the miracle of Israel even more.

"I'm glad Sam has found you as a friend. He looks up to you, and I have seen him watching how you combine Torah and action. Torah and *derech eretz* is the highest possible path. Sorry, I didn't mean to embarrass you, but I saw Sam, Roee and Ronny enjoy the spiritual dimension of your sukkah, the rightness and righteousness of your home – which you built with your own hands. They have seen you pray, and followed you across a lake, up a mountain and around the bimah with a Torah. And they have learned something from that experience.

"You recall I met Roee's father and grandfather, fresh off the boat from Russia as they say. Such died-in-the-wool communists and atheists you never met. And yet, there they were, stepping from bondage to freedom because of what? Because of a 3,500 year old religious covenant between G-d and His chosen people. I hear they have softened their views somewhat in their later years, but not much.

"You remember the young people asking me so earnestly: is this the 'Big One?' And perhaps you remember my answer – watch Jerusalem. What happens to Jerusalem after this war determines how much longer the Jewish people will spend in exile from their Creator. It is one thing to have the land. It is another thing entirely, as you have come to know from living here, to understand whose land it is. This is the holy land that the Creator of Heaven and Earth gave specifically to the Jewish people. Our past generation of politicians wanted to explain it some other way – so they could give it away. I can only hope that Israel's new leaders will remember that there is only one Israel."

Rabbi Beniyahu yawned and looked incredibly weary, and Eli saw and felt the weight of the ages upon the old rabbi's shoulders, as well as his own weariness. "How long, how long?" the Rabbi whispered. "Not long, not so long now, that's what your testimony tells me. Go in peace my friend, and continue to be a model of Torah and moral action, and all will be well with Israel. I don't know if I will merit to see the complete redemption in my day, or you in yours – but your children and grandchildren have grandstand seats. They are invited guests of the Holy One Blessed be He. Now, let me walk you down to the street before you fall asleep in that armchair and the Rabbi sits on you when he comes to learn with me after the dancing."

With that, Rabbi Beniyahu guided a sleepy Eli by the elbow to the street door. They both paused to watch the dancing of a crowd that was now less than a quarter what it was when they had left. There were now only the five Torah scrolls of the neighboring yeshiva orbiting at the center. Eli decided that the big bear of a man he had seen dancing with the Torah scroll earlier that night must be Rabbi Meir, and that he must be older than he first looked. He directed his tired footsteps away from the sounds of singing through the now quiet streets to the home of his friend where the door would be open for him.

One Year Later, *erev Sukkot*

Somewhere over the Negev,

Colonel Yossi Green had waited for this moment for most of his adult life. He pulled back the stick of the first Israel-designed and built stealth fighter prototype and pushed the throttle of its super-quiet turbofan engine to just past the redline. The ultralight, carbon-nano fiber jet responded like a dream – no, better than a dream, the g-force acceleration crushing him into the seatback could not be felt while sleeping. It was dangerously fast and delightfully responsive. And, the best part, it would cost less than a tenth of the frightfully overpriced F-35.

Thinking of the F-35 joint strike fighter never failed to give him a sharp flashback to the day, one year ago next week, when a pair of those over-engineered, over-complicated, too-many-cooks-in-the-soup planes had chased him and his wingman down the Jordan Valley. He had flown for his life at palm tree height along the shore of the Dead Sea. The unseen hunter had come within a few seconds of nailing him over its salty wastes before Yossi turned into the familiar shelter of Wadi David. The narrow, twisting desert canyon had saved his life – just as it had sheltered Israel's young king centuries ago. One F-35 splattered itself on the waterfall at the mouth of the wadi, and the second had been picked off by a waiting IAF F-16. The pilot of the bird of prey who sprung the trap Yossi set (with himself as bait), went on to edge Yossi out as the top IAF air ace of the *Sukkot* War by two kills. The feeling of relief and exhaustion that had flooded through Yossi in the moment after he heard of his pursuer's demise easily erased any possible feeling of envy or competition. Yossi and his wingman, Uri, were proud to come in tied for second place. They had twenty two confirmed kills each, not counting helicopters. For some reason, fighter pilots were fixed-wing snobs. They counted only armed, fixed wing aircraft in their air ace archives.

Just like the Wadi David maneuver, it was teamwork that counted more than any individual honors in that hard-fought, desperate war. Teamwork had given Dudu Galili the honor of being the only pilot in the world to shoot down an F-35 as well as laying the groundwork for each of his twenty three other kills. In fact, if one forgot about pilots and counted coup by plane, each of the legendary twenty four – the three wings of fighters sold on the sly by the U.S. to Israel on the second day of the war, had an average of 16 kills. But they had been flown by up to six different pilots each in a tremendous team effort. Together, they had neutralized the EMP-surviving air forces of Egypt, Jordan and Syria, while holding off undeclared combatants from Saudi Arabia and possibly Bahrain. The tiny gulf state had at least one plane unaccounted for that could not be explained by EMP damage.

But all that was history now. The lively little plane soared at more than 200 meters per second. It had nowhere near the F-15's power, but it didn't need it. This was a considerably lighter and more nimble aircraft.

If the F-15 was an eagle, then this trim little composite bird was more like a swallow. It was designed to move through the air with a minimum of turbulence. It generated only a moderate amount of hot exhaust to attract heat-seeking missiles. Its cooler-running, fuel-sipping, next-generation turbofan engine gave it the power and range it needed without pushing up costs in fuel, space needed for that fuel, and any excess fat that went with a larger airframe. His prototype was about the weight of a luxury sedan without fuel, about the weight of a small truck with fuel and weapons. It was devilishly hard to spot on any radar system yet invented.

Even its weapons were light and quick. Solid fueled, simple rockets were combined with sophisticated guidance systems, both pilot-controlled and automated. These new arrows could practically circle and wait until the target presented itself. But today Yossi was flying free. The armament racks were still in final testing, lagging only a month behind the airframe, guidance and engine teams. It was teamwork in every aspect of the new plane. Israelis were the world's most difficult, individualistic and independent people, yet they worked together from school to military to the university to the workplace in some of the most efficient and creative teams to be found anywhere. If anything, the shock and horrors of the nine-day *Sukkot* War had reinforced those bonds and turbocharged the Israel military and business sector in a way that could never have happened in the intermittent war/peace/war days of the last century.

The fact was that he was flying the world's most advanced stealth aircraft. It was filled with novel gadgetry and features from its thin-profile tires and landing gear to its EMP-proof-brain. Its fiber-optic, massively parallel and redundant wiring system was painted into its nano-fiber skin. Israeli designers simply took what they needed from the state of the art in each area, and re-invented it as needed.

The whole project had a five-year jump start from the concept phase to the initial design phase in the persons of a pair of retired Israel Aircraft Industries pilot/engineers. One had been involved in the only other Israeli-built jet fighter project, the Kfir/Nesher fighter that evolved from the French Mirage III in the mid 1970s in the aftermath of the Yom Kippur war. The other, many years his junior, had always dreamed of a lighter, cheaper, yet far more flyable fighter that could be built almost entirely in Israel. They had presented the postwar prime minister with a complete set of plans, scale models, computer simulations and a fast-track schedule for creating a flying prototype in 9 months. It had taken ten.

And so, as he pulled back his exhilarating climb well short of the plane's theoretical ceiling – the cabin pressure system was only a rough working model of the real thing – Yossi felt proud as a new parent to be the first to fly it more than a few test loops around the air field. He was flying a miracle born in Israel.

A new generation of fighters was only the tip of the composite wedge the New Carbon Consortium had planned. Their goal was not to sell war planes to the world. Never again would Israel care to be bombed or shot at by its own technology. While the rest of the Middle East stumbled in near darkness brought about by its own jihad, Israel had shined with a new and even brighter light.

Yossi felt it in the streets of his home town of Netanya every day. New companies were springing up like mushrooms after a spring rain. Capital was still scarce – especially the kind of cash needed to revolutionize the aircraft industry. But the New Carbon Consortium had international financing, tapping the deep pockets of several Jewish billionaires and near-billionaires in Israel, Canada, Brazil, the UK and the US. They had both cash and vision. That too was a miracle.

Even the *schnorrers* were walking with a new sense of purpose. The middle-aged schlepper who raised funds for a yeshiva in Bene Brak who had somehow had Yossi's address on his list from a check his father must have written to the school forty years ago appeared at his door for his twice a year appeal not long ago, seeking donations for the upcoming holidays. He had stopped smoking, lost weight, and bought a new black hat and coat. He pumped Yossi with an energetic talk about restoring Jewish values, the value of a good Yeshiva education, of building thinking skills, morals, ethics, Jewish pride, stable families and love of Israel. It was a far cry from the mumbled, guilt-and cigarette-smoke-flavored spiel of former years. In fact, Yossi had given the man a check for the first time in at least twenty five years. That probably guaranteed him a twice-a-year visit for the rest of the century. Now that the rabbi had stopped smoking, he might actually live a good part of it.

That summer the first real ripple of tourists returned, reassured perhaps by the relatively peaceful months that had followed the upheavals of the past fall and early winter. It had taken some time as those who wanted to be part of Israel sorted themselves out from those who thought they deserved their own state whittled out of a chunk of the Jewish homeland. OK, Gaza was still a mess, but hardly anyone went there. There were no more rockets at least. Nobody in the Gaza strip could afford rocket fuel, and no one of the formerly oil rich states around the Middle East was lining up to send them any.

Egypt struggled to feed its eighty-some million poor. Jordan showed a few glimmers of longing for a real democracy and a place in the un-EMPed modern world, but the monarchy fought back the crowds so far. Syria was still reeling from the impact of defeat-induced anarchy. Lebanon nursed its wounds and turned insular. There was some possible progress there wherever local people had turned out the militias and tried to create pockets of peace.

Yossi had made a couple overseas trips for the new government. While he was feted and feasted in each Jewish community he visited abroad, each time he had been glad to get back to the half-desert country that spread out below him. He rolled over and gazed up/downwards in sheer joy, seeing the tracery of ancient watercourses in shades of tans, browns and sunlight below him / above his head. Then he flipped back over a few times just for fun. What a bird!

One Year Later at a Kosher Restaurant in Naples

Anna stepped outside holding her cell phone and waved to the large black Mercedes sedan that was paused at the foot of the narrow street. She hung up and waited for the general's car to negotiate its way up the crowded block. Two security men climbed out of the back seat and gave her a brief glance before going inside to check the restaurant. General Frank Taylor got out of the front seat and came over to greet her, awkwardly holding a large bouquet of flowers. His driver stepped out the other side of the car and took up a post where he could see the front of the small, family-run kosher restaurant and a large area of the shop-lined street.

"Hello, General T, these are for you," he said, handing over the flowers and stood beaming down at her from his six-foot-three height. Fortunately he had skipped wearing his full dress uniform, but he was impressive enough with his four stars and ex-marine build.

"They're lovely, thank you," Anna said. They both stood by the car until Frank's two security men came out and gave him the all clear with a nod towards the door.

"Where's your shadow?" Frank asked, as he sat down at their private table upstairs.

"Oh, he's shopping for books at the Hebrew bookseller across the street. This area was all Jewish before the war. The proprietor's third son served in Lebanon and lives in Tel Aviv these days. I also went to school with one of his nieces."

Frank shrugged and looked around, "playing Jewish geography never fails to amaze me. How's the food here? Any chance of some kreplach?"

Anna smiled. "This is Naples, Frank. They know how to cook real food - not the Eastern European ghetto food you get in New York with your son-in-law. How's the grandbaby?"

"The grandbaby started second grade last week. Want to see the latest pictures?" he said, drawing out his cell phone and punching up a folder.

Anna admired the shots of a nicely dressed little girl in a variety of very American looking suburban settings and said some appropriately complimentary remarks before handing back the phone.

"So what's this about you getting married in October? How did you find time to fall in love and rebuild the IDF's information systems?

Anna blushed for the first time. "It's a long story, we'd better order that bottle wine I promised you and see about some salads and antipasto."

"You pick for us. My Italian stinks," Frank said, leaning back in his chair with a pleasant smile.

Anna stepped over to the stairwell and signaled to someone downstairs. In a few minutes an older, disgruntled, disheveled-looking man came halfway up the stairs. Anna had a brief but emphatic conversation with him in Hebrew and he cast a disapproving glance at Frank and disappeared.

"Ok," Anna said, playing with the stems of the bouquet lying on the table, "So you heard that the lucky man is Kobi's little brother?"

Frank settled himself to hear the story with an attitude that conveyed that he expected the full details.

"Actually, he's not so little. He's taller than Kobi – but not a corn-fed giant like yourself. While Kobi and I were living underground like moles for weeks, Ari was fighting house to house, village to village on the Lebanese border. So when I saw him a few months after the war, he looked older than either of us. In fact, he looked about a million years older…. The things he saw, the things he had to live with, the split second decisions he had to make every day to stay alive. His unit suffered 45% casualties in nine days, and that's counting only the dead and those so seriously wounded they were not able to sit and hold a rifle.

"One night over coffee at a hilltop café in Haifa he just started talking and talking, and I listened, and could picture everything just as he described it. It was like I had been there too, instead of staring at a bunch of monitors with disappointing numbers and blobs of data. When I was running up and down village streets and kicking down doors it was all drill – paintballs and laser tag, you know? But Ari was telling me about the real thing.

"When Ari talked about it, I could see it all through his eyes. The frustration of fighting all day to beat one dug-in group of Hezbollah and uproot them from a village only to find yourself facing, at the end of the day, an even larger and meaner bunch of militia who have been loafing around all afternoon watching the fight waiting to shoot whoever won. Or the pain of knowing that the RPG launcher in the bushes is probably held by a scared 14-year-old kid, those are the kind of things he talked about.

Frank looked as if he understood. Their waiter arrived upstairs with a bottle of wine, a basket of warm breads and two enormous salads.

"When did you start keeping kosher?" Frank asked between enthusiastic mouthfuls of crusty buttered bread and pesto when Anna came back to the table after washing her hands at a little sink at the top of the stairs.

"About six months ago. Ari and his sisters always kept kosher. Kobi was the only one to fall off the *derech* as they say. And you know what? I actually like it. I'm thinking about what I eat these days instead of stuffing myself with whatever is lying around that looks good."

They both dug in. Anna got back to talking about Ari after the salad bowls had gone about halfway down and they had made some serious progress on the bread basket. "I guess we complement each other, you know. He's hands on and concrete. I'm intellectual and abstract, and so he kind of grounds me and I open him up in a way that he seems to need."

"So how will it be having a lieutenant general on the general staff married to a sergeant and foot soldier?"

"As I said, we balance each other in a lot of ways. You can have all the generals you want but nothing gets done on the ground until some guy like Ari kicks some tails and gets his group in there to do the job… so who's the boss at home? That depends on what kind of job needs doing. The garden and the kitchen are all his. I'll do all the spreadsheets and flow charts," she grinned. "And if it needs changing, we've agreed to flip a coin."

"This is good wine, what is it?" Frank said, peering at the label.

"It's an Israeli cabernet from Dolev," she answered.

"Where's that?"

"Just the other side of Ramallah from Jerusalem. It's over the old 'Green Line' as they used to say before the war. They now opened the back roads into Ramallah and the main road the rest of the way to Highway 60 since the war. So the area has really become accessible. People can now build a house there without the whole UN having a cow.

"You don't miss our UN buddies?" Frank smirked.

"It's a whole lot more peaceful without all the damned peacekeepers!"

Frank raised his glass. "To the peace makers!" he said, patting the semiautomatic under his jacket. "But seriously, how many Arabs have moved back from Jordan since the war?"

"Nearly half of the ones who left during the war, and probably half again as many sneaking in and claiming citizenship."

"And yet terrorism is lower than before the war?"

"Carjacking is up, but we think that's more crime than terror. I can't remember the last bombing or shooting that wasn't family honor, crime or drugs.

"Amazing, but that's enough chit chat. Tell me about the Blackhawks-how in the hell did you get thirty of them flying in less than a week after an EMP?

"Well, first we had to figure out one. The rest were just hard work." Anna picked up a cigar-shaped bread roll and began to illustrate her narrative as if the dark rye roll was the body of a sleek Blackhawk.

"They took one bird and tore out every wire, gauge and electrical component. They completely stripped it down to practically just the motor, airframe and rotors. And then they started to work – a bunch of teams – each working one system at a time. One group took the engine – ignition and starting. Another took throttle control and fuel flow. Another took pitch and rotors – another took rudders and ailerons – another had the firing systems. Figuring out how to coordinate more than one system into the collective and the flight stick was tough. All they asked of the bird was to start, go forward, go up, go down, go right and left, and shoot. They didn't bother hooking up the windshield wipers. It was still the dry season, and if you flew through a cloud, well, tough until you could see again. No radar, no navigation beyond a simple compass taped to the panel, no altimeter even. It was visual flight rules only. No fuel gauge even, we just filled them up each time they landed and flew a lot of short missions. And you know, we didn't lose a single bird to running out of fuel. In the first Lebanon War, running out of fuel was the number two reason for crashes. No lights except for red flashlights taped to places where they needed to see. There was nothing but the most basic controls and something to shoot. They even flew at night whenever there was enough moonlight to see the enemy."

"Damn, so that's how you did it! We had a couple air bases full of Marine Corps mechanics and Sikorsky engineers trying to put an EMP'd bird back together without a war going on over their heads and they couldn't get one to fly in less than six weeks. And what flew out of there wasn't worth a damn in a real-time scenario. Something was always going down and messing up. So what weapons systems did they have working?"

"Forget the fancy automation and targeting. We had a guy hanging out each window with a 50 cal. Gatling on a makeshift swivel, and two guys more behind them using a shoulder-fired Stinger-type missile to take out the tanks. And in case they had their hands full, a couple of the hawks had a fixed 20mm cannon firing through a hole by the pilot's feet that he could shoot straight ahead with a button on his joystick."

Frank laughed a long time at the memory of all the elaborate firing systems devised by his hangers full of engineers. "We should have had more pilots and fewer PhDs.," he snorted.

The Golan, One Year Later, *erev Sukkot*

David and Sasha took much longer to find what they were looking for than they expected. So it was well past midday by the time they saw the charred hulk they had been seeking. Although the searing image of Yankel's burning tank was still etched deeply in their minds, finding it a year later proved difficult. For one thing, the world looked much different from the repaired windshield of their friend's wood burning pickup truck than from the hatchway of a Merkava tank. Easy terrain for a sixty-ton tank was bruising in a pickup truck, forcing so many detours that they skipped trying to follow their overland route where they had stalked and burned the Syrian supply column, and settled for trying to find it by landmarks on the road. The sides of the roadway were still littered with the burnt remains of the dozens of trucks they had destroyed a year ago – stripped now of everything of value and left to rust in the elements.

Yankel had led that predatory, but desperate charge along the southern flank of the traffic jam of troop transports, supply and fuel trucks exposed to their sudden attack from the rear. Military and civilian analysts were later to call their bold stroke one of the critical turning points of the northern front. Deprived in a matter of thirty minutes of more than half of their forward supplies, the Syrian advance had stalled many miles ahead at the tip of its armored thrust into the heart of Israel. Major Engel and Master Sergeant Sasha Petrenko wore silent medals of valor from a grateful nation on their dress uniforms, but it did nothing to bring back their beloved Captain Yankel Klein.

David and his family had gravitated to Moshav Yiftach for the *Sukkot* holiday. It had been the first refuge he found with his fleeing tank group – and a place where he had found warmth, help and hope. He, his wife, Anat, and their children were camped out in a pair of tents in the lee of a broken down house that had once been the home of one of Eli's neighbors. The neighbor's house still stood in ruins, and its owners had moved to Haifa for the winter, hoping to be able to build again next summer. David and his family would be having their holiday dinner with Eli and his family that night, along with his driver, Sasha, and Sam and his family.

Sasha, the wiry tank driver who had survived the hellish week at the controls of David's *Gimmel* One, had returned home to Tel Aviv to find himself a widower and with only two of five children. A sudden rocket had caught his wife and three older children outside the shelter one sunny afternoon late in the war. His young daughters cried and fussed whenever he left their sight, so he had been forced to leave the army to care for them. Sasha's own parents were too old and infirm to be of much help, and his wife's parents had left the country like many thousands of others. David knew the statistics by rote, having discussed them endlessly in his many talks since the war. Nearly 100,000 Israelis had fled the country in the first months after the war, but about 40,000 had come back from abroad, in addition to 20,000 new *olim* from the US, UK and Canada alone. Something about the war had woken up something inside – much the way the miracles of the 1967 war had awakened many Jewish hearts in its time.

David's wife had moved to the bed of the pickup to ride with the children as the two men grew tenser and less talkative the longer they searched and the more devastation they viewed. The littered landscape seemed frozen in time on a day that was very much still alive for them and more real than the September sunshine pouring in through Woody's replacement windshield. She hugged Avi, the oldest of their three sons, for he was looking solemn while the younger two were enjoying the ride in the fresh country air and sunshine. They were entertaining Sasha's surviving two young daughters. A random missile had caught their mother and older siblings on an errand outside their bomb shelter on an otherwise quiet day near the end of the Nine Day War. That's what they were calling it these days, although as the holiday of *Sukkot* drew near, the name the *Sukkot* War was regaining currency.

David stopped the truck a short distance away, almost exactly where he had stopped that early evening just under a year ago. He recalled the blast of fire and shock wave from the impact that had stopped Yankel's tank and nearly thrown him from his turret. Sasha was lost in his own memories of the moment. Both sat mutely, tears streaming quietly down their cheeks as they stared at the burnt shell that had once been a Merkava III – Yankel's *Alef* One.

However, the children were restless and were soon piling out of the back of the pickup and demanding their attention. So David and Sasha got stiffly and numbly from the cab, collected the wreath the children had made from flowers from Eli and Natalie's garden, and gathered up the modest metal plaque that one of Yankel's friends in the armored corps workshops had made. They ventured closer to the blasted remains of *Alef* One. From the back, the tank was mostly intact, with the crew door still swinging solidly on its hinges and open just as David had left it after pulling the loader out of its flaming interior. The hatch where Yankel had died was open to the sky. The interior of the tank had been burned and the hulk had long since been stripped of anything of value, chains, spare treads, mounting brackets and even some bolts that were easily reachable. They walked slowly around to the front, where a moderate sized hole gaped where the fatal shell had entered. It didn't look as big as they had imagined from that flaming wreck. Each could still feel the blistering heat of the fire, despite the warm sun that beamed benignly down upon the otherwise pastoral scene.

The small children were soon bored of peering at the tank, for they had seen hundreds of the real thing, and were looking for wildflowers to add to their wreath. Anat drifted back from supervising their search and put an arm around David. Avi, usually an awkward 15-year-old, had caught the solemn mood and put a caring arm around Sasha's shoulder. The two were almost exactly the same height. Earlier that morning Avi had given a short *hespid* over the graves of Yankel and his gunner, Schmulik. Each of them had been important figures in his young life. He remembered their moving heaven, earth and the entire IDF tank corps training schedule to make his bar mitzvah two years before. As he spoke, David had been reminded of Rabbi Beniyahu's graveside remarks the day they buried Yankel. It did seem fitting that this unconventional, hard-driving warrior had come to rest in a cemetery named for Yiftach, the illegitimate son who had been chosen to lead Israel in its time of troubles so many centuries before.

Although he remembered it like yesterday, there had been so many changes in the year since Yankel died that David felt like a lifetime or two had passed. The sun was well past noon and the day was growing hot as the breeze threatened to drop. David picked one of the flowers the children had dropped and placed it tenderly on the deck of the tank. He called to his youngest, who had wandered off with Sasha's two little girls and walked over to Woody and leaned on the battered brown door. Anat came over and leaned next to him and they watched the children dawdle their way back to the truck. He was glad that they had all come, and he was looking forward to spending the holiday with Eli and Natalie and their daughter's family. It would be a busy week. And this *Sukkot*, David had brought his own *lulav* and *etrog*.

One Year Later in a Dry Pasture in Syria

Amil did not come back from the war as Amil the rich man. He was still the goat boy, and he preferred it that way, he decided after a few weeks in town and a second trip into Israel. He and his uncle had ridden their six-donkey team straight into the Syrian retreat and had all their animals confiscated by a footsore regiment of disgruntled survivors. Instead of riches, they had come back six donkeys, two pistols, a watch and two bedrolls poorer. It took his uncle another two months to figure out that the television set he brought home simply would not work, and neither would the small microwave that he had traded a set of real silverware for. None of the electrical prizes they had carefully loaded into their captive Fiat worked. They had been a complete waste of space.

The old green Fiat Uno was another story, however. With a new battery and a set of starter relays and some really expensive parts from Nabi the mechanic, it ran pretty well. But Uncle Kassim never let him drive it, even though Amil's donkeys had towed it home from Israel. And the day Amil drove it anyway, to go see a certain young lady in the next village, Uncle

Kassim had gotten so angry over a little scratch in the already dented door that Amil simply moved out.

Now all he had to show for his wartime efforts was a really comfortable sleeping mat and a sleeping bag that was perfect for three seasons of the year. Nothing kept him quite warm enough when the winter rains came, but there was nothing new in that. He still had his goats. People still wanted goat milk and cheese, and there was always a market for their meat.

It had taken a while for his small herd to resume milking. All but one of his does either had mastitis or were so far along toward drying up when he returned from the war that it took half the winter to get all of them sorted out again. All except one, the little speckled brown and white who had always been his best milker. Somehow she had returned to production again almost without a hitch. And she had grown even more affectionate and less obnoxious if that were possible for a five year old nanny with a very opinionated personality. Go figure. He chucked a rock at a noisy blackbird who had scolded his flock enough.

Moshav Yiftach One Year Later – *erev Sukkot*

Eli decided to not to replace the two sukkah panels with the machine gun bullet holes. Sam agreed. It brought back sharp memories for both of them. And, for another thing, building materials were far too expensive one year after the *Sukkot* War, or Nine Day War – the two names were used interchangeably. The two bullet-scarred panels served as both a reminder of the war and a sign of just how lucky each of them and their families had been. At this time last year, midway through a sunny afternoon in the Golan, each of them had been fighting for his life against complete annihilation. A day later, on the evening of the holiday that both of their families were now busy preparing for, they had met in this sukkah. Sam discovered that Eli had a working, albeit wood-burning, pickup truck and had borrowed it for his command group. Over the next week, the war and circumstances had thrown them together in all kinds of strange ways, until they parted suddenly at the end. They parted in a helicopter paused near Tzfat to drop off Eli and the rest of Sam's rag-tag group while Sam was spirited off to various command posts and then flown to the United States for a post-war speaking blitz.

Sam was telling Eli all about his trip, for they had barely seen each other in the intervening year. As a corporate communications expert, Eli could sympathize with the grueling speaking schedule and endless fundraisers the Israeli government and the Jewish Agency had subjected the charismatic young hero to while milking every last dollar out of the trip. It made an IPO road trip seem like a picnic. Sam had stayed in the US and Canada so long that the government was eventually forced to send his wife and three young children along in spite of the high cost of trans-oceanic airfare – or face the outright revolt of their best drawing card.

Thanks to crossing paths with one of the few US reporters to brave the war zone, Sam Hirsh had emerged a kind of popular hero. Eli was a hero too, but mostly as a character in Sam's engaging and anecdote-filled war stories. The press loved Sam. And today, their faces both appeared on the cover of a number of newspapers and magazines spread out on the table before them. Most editors had used the iconic group picture snapped near the top of Mt. Hermon. That eloquent picture showed an exhausted, bloodied, yet elated group of sixteen soldiers posed for a brief moment in the harsh afternoon sun that cast the bullet-riddled wreck of an armored car and fresh chaos of the battlefield in stark relief. It had become a kind of visual shorthand for the *Sukkot* War in the same way that the exhausted but wondering paratroopers at the Western Wall had become the symbol of 1967. Eli was the second from the right, with his helmet on crooked and a slightly bewildered look. Roee next to him sported a fresh bandage on his arm and his shirt sleeve in shreds. Ronny was at the other end of the lineup, not far from Sam. Captain Sam Hirsh had his arm around the machine gunner, who cradled the big gun that probably saved their lives long enough for the helicopter assault group to make it the critical ten minutes to the mountaintop from their strafing runs at the war's bloodiest battle some miles away.

The press also loved the human chain unloading big artillery shells from a large wooden tour boat floating on a misty Lake Kinneret in the minutes before dawn on the second day of the war. Eli was one of the two chest deep men at the far end of the line stretching away from Sam's camera. The image caught him and his companion – whose name he never knew until well after the war, a school teacher from Tiberias it turned out – reaching up to accept a shell gingerly lowered from the stern by a pair of husky young men. Sam paused at that one as they flipped through the complete album of his sixty-odd pictures of the Nine Day War. He had only two rolls of film for the small range-finder camera that he tucked into his kit bag at the start of his call up a few weeks before the war. Fortunately for history, he had snapped only a few general shots of people on his base before the EMP hit and made his one of the few working cameras in northern Israel.

"You know, it finally hit me why people really resonate with this picture here in Israel," he said, smoothing out the plastic page encasing the enlarged photo that had been flashed around the world for the past year in digital form.

"Why?"

"It struck me a couple weeks ago as I was watching a program on TV that flipped through about a two minute history of modern Israel – and I saw one of the famous pictures of the Altalena – you know, the arms smuggling boat brought in by the Irgun in the final months before the War of Independence?"

"Yeah, the one that David Ben Gurion and the Palmach refused to let unload, and they had a faceoff on the beach with the Irgun? My heart always bleeds thinking about what Israel could have done with that one boat load of arms," Eli said ruefully.

"Exactly," Sam said, warming to his point. "So, look at this picture and what do you see? You see a critical boatload of arms and ammunition being unloaded – by everybody. Look at the people! You have these yeshiva types here in their black and whites, you have some Nah-nachs in their whites, you have some old guys and *chiloni* types in their shorts and shirt-tails out. You have a couple of grizzled looking kibbutzniks, and some tall, funny-looking old geezer with a grey beard reaching for a shell with a school teacher..."

"Wait a minute...." Eli protested. "I resemble that remark."

"And it's like a *tikkun* for the Altalena – everyone working together to save Israel instead of everyone working against each other because of ideology or turf..."

Eli studied the picture awhile. "You're right, there's a good op-ed in that Mr. IDF."

The press also loved Major David Engel, a tall, handsome, modest, soft-spoken but very articulate reserve tank commander who had been a partner in one of the greatest feats of survival and triumph in modern warfare. Overrun and hopelessly outgunned in the first hours of the war, Major Engel and two of his group of four tanks had escaped with the dashing tank ace Yankel Klein – who led the only one of eight merkava tanks to survive the first hours of the onslaught. Yankel had died a hero's death while he and David pursued and destroyed a massive Syrian supply column.

Most analysts credit their action with being the turning point in the northern land war – for without munitions, food, and fuel, the massive Syrian invasion had ground to a halt fifty kilometers from the border it had smashed a week earlier, and only twenty kilometers from the Mediterranean coast and from cutting Israel in two. Sam's little camera had caught the last known image of Yankel, pouring over a map with David, with Col. Eschol, now Lt. General Eschol, half seen. The picture was taken by candlelight in the very sukkah where the two men now sat.

What's more, after being promoted to major, David Engel had led the recovery of a quarter of the Golan Heights with a minimum of bloodshed. Critics still took issue with his use of colored tear gas to fool the Syrians into abandoning their positions and fleeing – but the majority of the world saw it as a stroke of genius and luck at a time when Israel desperately need both.

There were now about twenty habitable homes in Moshav Yiftach, and half a dozen trailers scrounged together. There were two new families, and three more talking seriously about making the move in the coming months. One of the families having long distance discussions with the moshav was Eli's oldest daughter and her husband, who would bring three wonderful and welcome young grandchildren in the bargain.

At the end of the Nine Day War there had been only three houses left standing, with eight others intact enough to be patched up by the time the rainy season came in earnest. Families doubled and tripled up in those eleven homes the first winter. About a third of the moshav's families moved out that winter, seeking shelter with relatives around the country. Others had lived mostly underground in their bomb shelters.

Tali and her kids moved in with Eli and Natalie, while their father was only home one week out of each month from his still-top-secret IDF job. However, that he had spent the whole war driving an ammunition truck around the Negev was not a secret. Whatever high tech system he had been working on when the war broke out had been put out of action by the EMP blasts. This time, he swore that the top secret systems, whatever they might be, were now EMP-hardened. From the tidbits that Eli had gleaned over the winter, it had something to do with remote sensing and monitoring – but whether it was keeping track of terrorist tunnels or enemy nuclear arsenals, Eli still had no clue.

This year, Tali and Yisrael were preparing their own sukkah next to the partially earth-sheltered house that Eli and others on the moshav had helped build for them. At this point it was only one bedroom and a kitchen/eating area. Next year, perhaps, they would add another wing with two more bedrooms and a combined living and dining room. It would be half the size of their previous house. It would make use of some of the remains of walls, floors and fixtures that had survived the shelling. With the high prices and rationing of concrete, two rooms were all they could build this year. Out-of-sight energy costs convinced them to build a smaller house and wait for solar panels to become available again. This winter they were heating with a woodstove made out of a 55 gallon gas drum. It was not very efficient, but it kept them very warm. Right now there was a nine-month waiting list for even the most elementary solar panel for a hot water system, and photovoltaic cells were almost unobtainable. They counted themselves lucky to have a home again, no matter how small. This winter, about a half of the displaced families had drifted back to the moshav. Various other families, as well as elderly parents, or sons and daughters were still scattered around the country.

Not only had Eli and Natalie been lucky, their daughter, Rivka, had also been fortunate. Her Jerusalem apartment had not been damaged in any of the shelling or street fighting that had broken out in the capital. She was here visiting with her husband and three small children while some friends borrowed their Jerusalem apartment for the week. Until the last minute they had hoped that their older daughter and grandchildren from Chicago would be able to come for a long overdue visit, but there was a waiting list for the few seats available to Israel now that El Al was the only airline to serve Tel Aviv. All other carriers found it too risky, or refused to fly to Israel if it meant losing all their Arab customers. They might have to wait until they made aliyah, at which time they were guaranteed a free flight.

It could be worse though. Syria still had no recognized government, and everyone refused to fly to Damascus except for mercenaries paid by any one of a dozen factions. Most of them arrived overland from Iraq, which was almost equally lawless, but at least had a parliament that met every few months to appoint a new prime minister.

Lebanon, on the other hand, was showing signs of stabilizing somewhat now that there were fewer foreign-funded militias there for the purpose of attacking the Zionist enemy. There were deep religious schisms to be sure, but without the wholesale introduction of armed and lawless bands with Syrian or Iranian backing, home-grown forces were able to carve out small but somewhat stable niches.

The Hashemite monarchy had survived in Jordan, but was hanging on by brute force while faced with hundreds of thousands of Palestinians who were demanding jobs and equal rights. Tens of thousands had leaked back across the border into Israel despite tight controls. Those who could make it back and had any kind of construction or skilled labor experience found themselves quickly employed in the cash economy that thrived wherever there was money to rebuild.

Egypt was on its third government since the war, and appeared hopelessly mired in economic doldrums with a rising population and disappearing economy.

Compared to its neighbors, Israel was showing signs of economic life once again. Losing its entire antiquated power grid at one blow had forced Israel to rebuild with the new energy realities in mind. However, there was an outright schizophrenia between short-term projects built to get city power turned back on quickly, no matter how wasteful; and longer term projects built with the view of ending Israel's reliance on fossil fuels.

The war did succeed in getting more than two thirds of the private cars off the heavily damaged road system – meaning that traffic jams now happened only in Tel Aviv, Haifa and Jerusalem on a scale several magnitudes less than the prewar era. With gasoline at the equivalent of $12 a gallon, few could afford the luxury of running a car these days, while the bus system had been heavily subsidized and rebuilt quickly. The electric car and recharging scheme started by a high tech billionaire and private consortium a few years before the war was just beginning to regain its momentum now that the power grid had sufficiently recovered to make enough electricity available for recharging. If Israel could get its power generation costs down quickly enough, it could soon have the largest all-electric fleet of cars in the world in terms of percentage of the market. In terms of sheer numbers, Hong Kong was the leading edge of the plug-and-drive revolution.

Talk of gas prices soon brought Woody back into Eli and Sam's conversation, carried out in snatches as they wired a new set of white, small, decorative LED lights to the sukkah. The lights were a present mailed from the US nearly six months ago that had gotten there just in time for the holiday.

Earlier that morning, their friends David and Sasha had packed their two families into the back of the old truck and driven out to the burnt hulk of a tank with a small metal sign painstakingly painted and crafted by the sole surviving member of that lost group – a loader who still carried scars over much of his body from the fiery inferno. It was Yankel's tank, of course. The two families had erected the sign, paid their respects, and shared their memories of the desperate fight as best they could. It was something the children may never understand; at least, their parents hoped they would never have to understand such things.

Sam and Eli tested their lights one last time, and flopped down in a pair of comfortable old camp chairs to share a glass of homemade beer. The brew was little dusky perhaps, but quite drinkable. It was the product of one of the moshavnik's attempts to create a home business. As a friend and encouraging voice among the many nay-sayers, Eli was privileged to help dispose of the experimental batches, and he had laid in a good supply for the holiday.

"Hey, this cheese is great. Did someone here in Yiftach make it?" Sam asked, spreading another cracker with a generous glob of soft, aromatic white cheese.

"No, actually you know the cheese maker pretty well. You helped carry him back from Syria with me."

"Captain Tzippori? But he's running a little startup in Tzfat flying anti-drone drones," Sam protested, looking at the cheese with a certain wonder and doubt.

"That came later," Eli explained. "First he joined his uncle's dairy and goat cheese operation. Remember how he swore he'd love goats forever after that little brown critter kept him alive? So while he was hobbling around during all those months of convalescence as they tried all those skin and bone grafts to save what was left of his leg – well, he helped his uncle. It helped him keep his sanity and his body got stronger much faster with all that hard work."

"I remember though that the doctors at the osteopathic rehab clinic were always complaining about the smell. Natalie and I used to drive him to Hadassah Hospital in Jerusalem once a month in Woody, just to keep in touch and as a good excuse to go see our daughter. We used to fill up the back with cheese on the way there, and as many trampers as we could squeeze in.

"The last couple times he was telling me about his anti-drone flying. It seems he got really depressed over the winter. You know those long rainy days and how grey and gloomy it can get for a few weeks on end. Finally his nephew challenged him to an air-to-air duel on one of those flight simulator games. Well, he held out for a couple weeks saying no…but finally he got badgered into playing the kid. You know how eleven year olds can be. Of course he lost. Big time. He lost over and over to this obnoxious little kid and half of his nephew's friends. Think about it, one of the ten hottest F-16 pilots in Israel before the war, and he's getting his tail kicked by half the dweebs in Tzfat. That hurt."

Sam allowed as how he knew how it must feel, because his little cousins could kick his butt in "Heavy Metal Recon" every time he got pestered into playing. "Shooting everything that moves with a mouse and a keyboard is NOTHING like the real thing," he declared. "I don't care how good the graphics are."

Eli heartily agreed. "Yeah, Chaim said the exact same thing. Only he added he'd like to see those little snots take him out while hanging upside down or pulling a couple high-G loops.

"But he got the hang of it eventually, and started showing those punks who could really fly. And along the way he met some of the gamers who had gone on to fly recon drones before the war. From gaming and talking to his fellow pilots who came to see him, he started to realize that there really were not very good countermeasures against drones. You know, the big, high-flying, nearly silent, impossible to spot on radar birds that everyone was building because no one could afford a fighter or bomber any more – except for those carbon fiber deals, but even those cost millions."

Sam knew the rest of the story. He had heard how Chaim Tzippori and a crew of out-of-work pilots, gamers and drone jockeys had started building prototypes of hunter-killer-drones that could fly for more than a day on "combat patrol" looking for incoming drones. Once they spotted them – and that was still tricky, they shifted from fuel sipping patrol mode into a super-charged killer that could make short work of any drone currently on the market.

"You know, it is such an Israeli thing to do," Eli remarked.

"What? Dream up a startup and build it in your uncle's hay shed?"

"That too, but I meant to create an entire industry out of a little technology, and then ten years later come along with a killer app that makes the first industry obsolete."

They chuckled at the irony, and enjoyed the last of their beers. Eli and Sam's pre-holiday work was done, except for a final mop up of the much-used shower, the only working indoor one for seven households. There were solar camp showers rigged up next door at Tali's with a scrap of tarp for a privacy screen. It would be time to make a last check of the Shabbat settings on Eli's one-of-a-kind electrical and water systems in a couple hours.

Roee was due to join their Sukkah reunion any time now. Ronny was busy elsewhere with his new girlfriend and sent his regrets. Eli hoped, but also doubted, that Roee would make the long hitchhike up to the Golan in time. Although there was plenty of pre-holiday traffic, all of the cars, trucks and buses were jammed full.

The women, however, were quite busy and the activity spilled out of Eli and Natalie's kitchen onto the back porch and into the dining room, which were serving a staging area for a battalion's worth of salads and side dishes preparing to advance on the sukkah when the time came for eating. Eli tuned into the talk floating out the open window and grinned. Natalie was telling Sam's wife, Irit, about the shock she received a few days after the war ended.

Eli had been pressed into service driving Woody with Roee and Ronny riding shotgun – or rather machine gun – to slowly cruise the flanks of an endless column of disarmed prisoners walking back to Syria. Because of the incredible numbers involved, the slow march home had taken a week for the defeated and discouraged soldiers to cover fifty kilometers.

Eli's guard duties had lasted for nearly the full week after the final shooting day of the war. A formal peace treaty had never been signed really. Half of the Syrian Army had surrendered, the Jordanian army had withdrawn, the Lebanese guerillas were finally driven back, and the Egyptian swarms pushed back to their side of the border. No treaty memorialized the occasion – so the war had simply ground to a halt out of sheer exhaustion on all sides.

Eli had no way of contacting Natalie, for phones were still not working, and messages haphazard, although he had sent word with quite a few acquaintances. She was reaching the peak of her description of her agitation, worry and beginnings of despair, with a few humorous flings at Eli's nonchalance about sending news whenever he was off on a trip generally. On a quiet sunny morning, three days after the shooting ended, an IDF APC had clanked up their street and come to a halt outside. Natalie described her heart dying silently within as she saw a pair of officers climb out and approach the house while a couple soldiers began to tug a heavy canvas bag from the back. She was nearly on her knees when the first officer asked politely if she was Mrs. Kaplan. "I couldn't get the words out of my mouth. All I could do was stand there and nod and stare numbly at that big heavy bag. I knew it was Eli's remains. The officers barely spoke a word of English, and they said they had something of Eli's for me, but I thought they meant they had something OF Eli for me."

Eli could see part of Irit's face, listening intently, knife and cucumber poised in mid-slice. Even though she knew perfectly well that Eli was outside with her husband, she knew the feeling well. She had experienced a hundred such shocks and frights during Sam's long military service, which was still dragging on despite the relative peace. "It turns out it was that damned kayak of his – he and Sam had left it in care of someone over in Tiberius and they were returning it!" There was a peal of laughter and the slicing of the cucumber resumed. Sam, who had paused to listen as well, chuckled too, remembering his uneasy voyage across the dark lake with the older stranger he had just met.

As a prank the night before, one or more people in the community had inflated the venerable yellow kayak, painted "INS KINNERET" on the bows, and hung it like an oversized decoration on the wall of Eli's sukkah. Eli and Sam could just see the tip of one end through the open window.

"I tell the 'reading the water' story with nearly every talk – especially the line about whether it's written in Hebrew or English. That always gets laughs in the US," Sam said. "I'm going to have to add the INS KINNERET postscript to the story now. Maybe I can get the Israeli Navy to make it official. They've already commissioned one of our makeshift gunboats as the flagship of a new Kinneret squadron."

"Don't you dare," Eli growled. "What? I want to have to ask the Navy for permission every time I take my boat to the lake with the grandkids? Natalie keeps threatening to have it bronzed and put on a pedestal somewhere for the pigeons..."

"OK, OK, just a thought...." Sam soothed. "But for my part, I was sure we were completely lost and were going to find ourselves in spitting range of a Jordanian patrol when the sun came up." He raised his beer and finished it.

Eli grinned and said, "the time I thought we were really up a creek without a paddle was when we came down the stairs into that madhouse of a bomb shelter on the mountain behind Tiberias. I still don't know how you got to the head of the line so fast without being punched, stabbed or shot."

"Old Israeli trick" Sam smirked solemnly, "kind of like catching and cleaning up three kids in time for *Shul*. Where did those little hooligans go?"

Glossary

Word or phrase	Definition or explanation
Akshav	Right now – immediately.
Alef, bet, Gimmel, daled	The first four letters of the Hebrew alphabet.
Aliyah	Literally "to go up." Aliyah is the act of moving (going up) to Israel. Also, an *aliyah* is the act of being called to the Torah in *shul*.
Amidah	Also known as the *Shemoneh Esrei* – the eighteen (actually 19 due to one added centuries later) blessings said silently while standing. It is an integral part of all three daily prayer services.
APC	Armored personnel carrier
Balagan	A great Israeli word meaning a total mess or screw up.
Baruch HaShem!	Literally "Blessed is the name" – said usually as meaning "Thank G-d!"
Beit Knesset	Synagogue
Bircat HaMazon	Prayer of thanks recited or sung after a meal where bread was eaten.
Bracha	Blessing.
B'seder	OK – in order.
Cast Lead	Code name for January 2009 operation to clear terrorists out of Hamas-occupied Gaza strip.
Challah	Braided loaf of bread
Daven davened, davening	To pray, prayed, praying.
Derech eretz	Good or righteous conduct
Druze	Religious community/sect found primarily in Syria, Jordan, Lebanon and Israel
Dud shemesh	Israeli name for a solar hot water heater and tank.
Elo-kim	A name for G-d.
Fedayeen	Arab partisans.
Golani Brigade	One of the major infantry units of the IDF, assigned mostly to the Northern Command.
Haftorah	Weekly reading of an appropriate portion from *Naviim* or *Ketuvim* after the *Shabbat* Torah reading.
Hallel	Psalms of thanks that are part of most Jewish holiday services.
Hesder yeshiva	Israeli program that allows religious young men to learn Torah in Yeshiva and serve in the IDF for only 18 months in their 5 year program.
Hezbollah	Islamic terrorist organization and political party active in Lebanon.
Hoshanah Rabbah	The seventh day of *Sukkot*.
IDF	Israeli Defense Forces.
Ivrit	Hebrew.

Kaddish	Special prayer said only with a *minyan* of men, said by mourners in memory of the departed well as after Torah study by a group and between major sections of the daily prayer services.
Kavanah	Concentration, focused attention.
Keffiyah	Traditional Arab headgear
Kesher	A connection or link.
Kibbutz	Collective community where land and most businesses are owned or run communally, though families live in private homes owned by the community.
Kiddush	A special blessing over wine said on *Shabbat* and holidays.
Kippah	Yarmulke, skullcap worn by observant Jewish men.
Knesset	Parliament of Israel
Kol ha kavod!	Literally, "All the honors," used colloquially like "good for you!" or "congratulations."
Lulav, etrog, four species	During the holiday of *Sukkot*, Jews recite a blessing over the four species (*arbeh minim*): a palm branch, 2 branches of the willow shrub, three of myrtle which are bound together in a *lulav*; and the etrog – a yellow citrus fruit similar to a lemon.
Medrash	Or *Midrash* – stories and apocrypha handed down by Jewish traditional oral history.
Merkava	Main battle tank developed and built in Israel first used in the 1980s. There are four generations from Merkava I to Merkava IV (MK-IV).
Mikveh	A ritual bath.
Miluim	Compulsory reserve duty required of most able-bodied Israeli men until age 50 – 55 who have been trained in the Israel Defense Forces (IDF).
Mincha	The afternoon prayer service.
Minyan	A "quorum" of 10 Jewish men needed for communal prayers.
Mishnah	Books of the Oral Law redacted in the early third century of the common era by Rabbi Yehudah HaNasi.
Mitzvah, mitzvot	Divine commandment(s).
Moshav	Cooperative community where land and services are controlled collectively, but homes owned privately. Plural *moshavim*. Moshavnik – a resident of the moshav.
Moshiach	The Jewish Messiah.
Mussaf	Additional prayer service added on *Shabbat* and holidays.
Nahal	Stream or small river valley.
Niggun, niggunim (pl)	Melody or song with no words.
Oleh, olim (pl)	One who immigrates to Israel – makes aliyah.

Golan! Glossary

Palmach	Israeli military group begun before statehood, one of the forerunners of the IDF.
Peace Now	Far-leftist peace group and political party in Israel.
Peyot	Sidelocks. Hair left uncut in front of the ears of many orthodox Jews–mostly Hassidim.
Pluga	Company.
Rachamim	Mercy or compassion.
Ramat Kal	Commander in chief, top general
Ribbono Shel-Olam	Literally "master of all the world," G-d.
Rosh yeshiva	Dean or head of a yeshiva.
RPG	Rocket propelled grenade
Ruach ha kodesh	Spirit of prophesy, divine inspiration.
SAM	Acronym for: Surface to Air Missile
Sava	Grandfather
Sephardi	Jew who follows the customs and traditions of Spain, North Africa and the Near East.
Shabbat	The Jewish Sabbath, which begins at sundown on Friday and ends shortly after nightfall on Saturday.
Shacharit	The morning prayer service.
Shehakol	General blessing said over foods not covered by a special blessing, literally "and everything."
Shemayim	Heavens.
Shemeni Atzertet	Literally, the eighth day of the meeting or assembly. A one-day holiday that acts as an eighth day of Sukkot.
Shul	Synagogue.
Shylah	A question about Jewish law.
Siddur	Prayer book.
Simchat Torah	Jewish celebration when all congregations finish reading the Torah and start over again from the beginning.
Sukkot	Seven day Jewish festival celebrated beginning on the 15th of the month of Tishrei (five days after Yom Kippur) Sukkot is the plural of sukkah, a booth or hut and recalls the temporary dwellings of the Jewish people during their 40 years of wandering in the desert after the Exodus from Egypt. Throughout the holiday all meals are eaten in the sukkah. The first and last day of the holiday are Yom Tovim.
Tallit or tallis	Prayer shawl with ritual fringes (tzitzit) tied at each of its 4 corners. Tallit katan – small version worn daily by observant Jewish men.
Talmid	Student.
Talmud	Also known as the Gemara or Shas, is the major written compendium of discussions of the Oral Torah which was codified in its current form about 500 C.E.
Tanach	Sometimes spelled Tanakh – acronym for Torah (the 5 books of Moses), Naviim (Prophets) and Ketuvim

	(writings – like Psalms) that are accepted as being written with Divine inspiration.
Tefillin	Small, black leather boxes containing parchment inscribed with verses from Torah, tied black leather straps, and worn by observant Jews during weekday morning prayers.
Tehillim	Psalms.
Wadi	A ravine, gully or dry valley.
Yeshiva	Religious high school or college for men.
Yiftach or Yivtah	Military leader and later Judge of the Jewish people in the Book of Judges, chapters 11 and 12. The fictitious moshav in this book is named for him. There is a real kibbutz named Kibbutz Yiftah near Kiryat Shemona, which has nothing to do with the one made up for this book.
Yishuv, yishuvim	Semi-cooperative Jewish community where services are shared but land and housing are private.
Yom Tov	Jewish holiday
Zeidie(s)	Grandfather(s)